"Take your

For a brief secon, ...ret glimmered in his expression. But he released her and stepped back. "I'm sorry. I don't usually manhandle women."

She wanted to believe him, but she'd suffered her share of men who did. So she refused to let him off the hook.

His loud exhale punctuated the air. "Please sit down. I'll behave."

He looked so contrite that a tingle of something like respect danced through her. But she refrained from commenting as another image taunted her. One of Ray's hands on her, tenderly stroking her, making her feel safe. No, not safe. Alive.

Fool.

Ray McCullen was anything but safe.

And judging from his brusque attitude, he was going to hate her when he learned the reason for her visit.

ROPING
RAY McCULLEN

BY
RITA HERRON

MILLS
BOON

First Published in Great Britain 2016
By Mills & Boon, an imprint of HarperCollins*Publishers*
1 London Bridge Street, London, SE1 9GF

© 2016 by Rita B. Herron

ISBN: 978-0-263-91904-2

46-0516

Our policy is to use papers that are natural, renewable and recyclable products and made from wood grown in sustainable forests. The logging and manufacturing processes conform to the legal environmental regulations of the country of origin.

Printed and bound in Spain
by CPI, Barcelona

USA TODAY bestselling author **Rita Herron** wrote her first book when she was twelve but didn't think real people grew up to be writers. Now she writes so she doesn't have to get a real job. A former nursery school teacher and workshop leader, she traded storytelling to kids for writing romance, and now she writes romantic comedies and romantic suspense. Rita lives in Georgia with her family. She loves to hear from readers, so please visit her website, www.ritaherron.com.

To Sue, who just had her own cowboy adventure!

Prologue

Ray McCullen hated all the secrets and lies.

He despised his father, Joe McCullen, even more for making him keep them.

In spite of the fact that his brothers, Maddox and Brett, thought he didn't care about them or the family, he had kept his mouth shut to protect them.

God knows the truth about their father had eaten him up inside.

Only now, here he was back at home on the Horseshoe Creek ranch waiting on his father to die, grief gnawing at him. Joe McCullen wasn't the perfect man Maddox and Brett thought he was, but Ray still loved him.

Dammit.

He didn't want to, but the love was just as strong as the hate.

Maddox stood ramrod straight in the hallway outside their father's room, his expression unreadable while Brett visited their dad.

Ray moved from one foot to the other, sweating. He and Brett had both been summoned to the ranch at their father's request—he wanted to talk to each of them before he passed.

Suddenly the door swung open. Brett stalked into the hallway, rubbing at his eyes, then his boots pounded as he jogged down the steps. Maddox arched a brow at him indicating it was Ray's turn, and Ray gritted his teeth and stepped into the room.

The air smelled like sweat and sickness, yet the sight of the familiar oak furniture his father had made by hand tugged at this emotions. His mother had died when he was just a kid, but he could still see her in that bed when he'd been scared at night and his daddy wasn't home, and he'd sneak in and crawl up beside her.

His father's cough jerked him back to reality.

Ray braced himself for a lecture on how disappointed his father was in him—Maddox was the perfect son who'd stayed and run the ranch, and Brett was the big rodeo star who'd accumulated fame and money—while he was the bad seed. The rebel.

The surly one who'd fought with their father, left home and never came back.

"Ray?"

The weak sound of his father's voice forced his feet into motion, and he crossed the room to his father's bedside. God, he didn't want to do this.

"Ray?"

"Yes, Dad, I'm here."

Another cough, pained and wheezy. Then his father held out a shaky hand. Ray's own shook as he touched his father's cold fingers.

He tried to speak, but seeing his father, a big brawny man, so thin and pale was choking him up. Joe McCullen had always been larger than life. And he'd been Ray's hero.

Until that day...

"Thank you for coming, son," his father said in a raw whisper.

"I'm sorry it's like this," he said, and meant it.

His father nodded, but a tear slid down his cheek.

"I'm sorry for a lot of things, Ray. For hurting you and your mama."

Ray clenched his jaw to keep his anger at bay.

"I know I put a heavy burden on you a long time ago, and it drove a wedge between the two of us." He hesitated, his breathing labored. "I want you to know that your mama forgave me before we lost her. I...loved her so much, Ray. I hated what I did to her and you."

Grief and pain collected in Ray's soul, burning his chest. "It was a long time ago." Although the hurt still lingered.

"I wish I'd been a better man."

Ray wished he had, too.

"When you find someone special, Ray, love her and don't ever let her go."

Yeah. As if he would ever tie himself down or fall in love. His heart couldn't handle loving someone else to only lose them.

His father coughed, and Ray swallowed hard, the weak sound a reminder that this might be the last time he saw his dad. He wanted to tell him that nothing mattered, that he wasn't ready to let him go yet, that they still had time.

But he'd been called home because they didn't have time.

"The will..." his father murmured. "I tried to do right here, tried to take care of everyone."

Ray tensed. "What do you mean—*everyone*?"

Joe squeezed his hand so tightly, Ray winced. But when he tried to pull away, his father had a lock on his fingers. "Ray, the ranch goes to you boys, but I need you to explain to Maddox and Brett. I owe..."

His voice cracked, his words fading off and he wheezed, gasping for air. A second later, his body convulsed and his eyes widened as if he knew this was his last breath.

"Owe what?" Ray asked. Did he tell Maddox and Brett about his other woman?

"Dad, talk to me," Ray said, panicked.

But his father's eyes rolled back in his head and he convulsed again, his fingers going limp.

Ray jerked his hand free, then rushed toward the door shouting for help. Maddox barreled inside the room and hurried to the bed.

Grief seized Ray as his father's body grew still.

He bolted and ran down the steps, anguish clawing at him.

Damn his father. He'd done it to him again.

Left him holding the secret that could destroy his family forever.

Chapter One

Two weeks later

Scarlet Lovett parked in front of the sign for Horseshoe Creek, a mixture of grief and envy coiling inside her.

This was Joe McCullen's land. His pride and joy. The place where he'd raised his family.

His *real* family. The one with his three beloved sons. Maddox. Brett. Ray.

Maddox was the oldest, the responsible one who was most like Joe in his devotion to Horseshoe Creek. He was also the sheriff of Pistol Whip, Wyoming.

Brett was the handsome, charming bull rider who was most like Joe in his flirtatious smile, his love for women and chasing dreams.

Ray was the youngest, the angry one who looked most like Joe, but he resented his father because he'd walked in on Joe with Barbara and knew about his indiscretion.

Scarlet watched a palomino at the top of a hill in the pasture as it stood alone, seemingly looking down at three horses galloping along together. Just like that lone horse, she had stood on the periphery of the funeral a few days ago, her heart aching, her anguish nearly overwhelming her.

Yet she'd felt like an outsider. She hadn't spoken to

the brothers. Had sensed they wouldn't want her to share their grief.

She wasn't part of that family. No, she'd lived with Barbara and Bobby, the *other* family Joe had kept secret.

The one the McCullen boys knew nothing about.

Well…except for Ray. And he didn't know about her or Bobby…just Barbara.

Still, Joe had been the closest thing she'd ever had to a father.

She swiped at a tear, her hands trembling as she unfolded the letter he'd left for her before he'd passed.

My dearest Scarlet,

I was blessed to have sons, but I never had a daughter—until I met you.

My sweet girl, the moment I saw you in that orphanage and looked into those big, sad, blue eyes, you stole my heart. I admired your strength, your spunk and your determination to make it in this world, no matter what hard knocks life doled out for you.

You taught me how to be a better man, that family is not all about blood.

I'm sorry I didn't have the courage to tell my sons about you and Barbara and Bobby when I was alive. In my own way, I thought I was protecting them, and protecting the three of you by keeping the two parts of my life separate.

Truthfully, Barbara and I…we were over a long time ago. She knew that and so did I. But I'm trying to do right by all of you now.

If you're reading this, you must have received the envelope I left for you. I have willed you a sum of money to help you make a fresh start, and a piece of ranch land with a small cabin on it for your own home.

Bobby will also receive a share, although you know that he resents me, and he's had his troubles, so I have placed stipulations on his inheritance.

But you…my dear, I know you will use your inheritance to further our work at The Family Farm and help the children, and that you will treasure everything Horseshoe Creek has to offer.

Ranching and living off the land has always been in the McCullen blood, and in our hearts.

Know that you are in my heart, as well.

Love always,

Joe

Scarlet folded the letter again and slipped it inside the envelope, then shifted her Wrangler into Drive and wove down the path to the farmhouse Joe called home.

She wiped at a tear as she parked, and for a moment, she sat and admired the sprawling house with the big porch. It looked so homey and inviting that she could easily picture Joe here with his sons, enjoying family time riding on the land, big dinners over a table piled with homemade food and fishing in Horseshoe Creek.

But she had a bad feeling those sons wouldn't welcome her.

Her stomach twisted at the idea of rejection, and she considered turning around and fleeing. Never contacting the McCullens and claiming what Joe had left her. Disappearing from Pistol Whip and starting over somewhere else.

Barbara and Bobby didn't care about her. No one did.

Except Joe. He'd seen something in her that had inspired her to be a better person.

He'd made her feel loved, as if she was important, when she'd never felt loved or part of a family before.

She looked down at Joe's handwriting again and remembered his words, and opened the door of her vehicle.

Joe had loved her and wanted her to have a piece of his land to remember him by.

She wanted it, too.

Like Joe said, she'd had hard knocks. She was a survivor and a fighter. But she also deserved love and a home.

She took a deep breath, strode up the porch steps to the front door, raised her fist and knocked.

RAY STARED AT the suitcase he'd brought with him when he'd come home, glad he hadn't unpacked.

The itch to leave Horseshoe Creek burned in his belly. The burden of his father's secret was just too damn much.

But the lawyer handling their father's will had been out of town, so they still hadn't dealt with that. And it *would* be something to deal with.

Maddox had also shocked him by asking him and Brett to stand up for him at Maddox's wedding to Rose.

Dammit, seeing his oldest brother happy and in love had done something to him. Not that the brothers had repaired their relationship completely, but two weeks back together on the ranch had mellowed their fighting.

While Maddox and Rose were on their honeymoon, Ray had agreed to oversee the daily running of the ranch. He'd forgotten how much he liked riding and driving cattle.

Brett was busy drawing up plans for the house he and Willow were building for them and their son. They had married in a private ceremony, then moved in to one of the cabins on the property until their dream house was ready. Meanwhile, watching Brett with his little boy, Sam, had stirred up feelings Ray didn't even know he had.

Like envy.

He shifted, uncomfortable with his thoughts. It wasn't

as if he wanted to get married or have a family. Not after the way his own had gotten screwed up.

He liked being alone. Liked hanging out in bars, meeting women who demanded nothing from him but a good night of sex. Liked owning his own private investigations business. He could take whatever case he wanted, travel to another state without answering to anyone and come home when he damn well pleased.

It'll all be over soon, he reminded himself. Maddox and Rose would be back in a couple of days.

And so would Darren Bush, the lawyer handling the will.

Of course, if his father had made provisions for *that* woman in his will as he'd implied in his private conversation with Ray, the storm would hit.

Maddox and Brett would both be pissed as hell.

Maybe they could pay off the woman and she'd be out of their lives forever.

Then Ray could go back to his own life. Sink himself into a case and forget about family and being the outcast.

The front doorbell dinged, and Ray waited for Mama Mary, the family housekeeper and the woman who'd raised him and his brothers after their mother died, to answer it. But it dinged again, and he remembered she'd made a trip into town for groceries, so he jogged down the stairs.

When he opened the door, he was surprised to see a woman standing on the porch. Instinctively heat stirred in his belly. He didn't know they made women like her in Pistol Whip.

She reminded him so much of those porcelain dolls his mother liked to collect that, for a moment, he couldn't breathe.

She was petite with long, wavy blond hair, huge oval-shaped baby blue eyes and milky white skin. A faint sprinkle of freckles dotted her dainty nose, making her look young and sweet. But that body told a different story. Her curves had been designed for a man's hands.

The wind kicked up, swirling her hair around her heart-shaped face, and she shivered and hunched inside her coat.

"Mr. McCullen?"

He nodded. "Yeah. I'm one of them. Who are you looking for? Maddox? He lives here."

She shrugged. "Actually I'd like to talk to Ray."

Her whisper-soft voice sent his heart into fast motion. "That's me." Did she need a PI?

She shivered again, then glanced in the entryway. "May I come in?"

He realized she was cold and that he'd been staring, and he stepped aside and waved her in. *Good grief.* Women didn't normally cause him to stutter or act like a fool.

But the combination of her beauty and vulnerable expression mesmerized him.

A wary look crossed her face, but she squared her small shoulders and followed him inside to the den. A fire roared in the ancient brick fireplace, the rustic furnishings the same as they had been when Ray lived here years ago.

The manners Mama Mary had instilled in him surfaced. "Would you like some coffee?"

"That would be nice." She clutched a patchwork home-made shoulder bag to her and sank onto the leather sofa in front of the fire.

He walked over to the sideboard in the adjoining dining area where Mama Mary always kept a carafe of hot coffee, then poured two cups.

"Cream or sugar?" he asked.

"Black," she said, surprising him. Half the women he met wanted that froufrou fancy flavored coffee and creamer.

He handed her the cup and noticed her hand trembling. She wasn't simply cold. Something was wrong.

"Now, you wanna tell me what this is about? Did my receptionist at McCullen Investigations tell you where I was?"

Again, she looked confused. "No, I didn't realize you were a PI."

Ray claimed the wing chair facing her and sipped his coffee. So, she wasn't here for a case. "I don't understand. If you don't need my services, then what?"

She fidgeted. "I don't know how to tell you this, except just to be up front."

That sounded serious.

"My name is Scarlet Lovett. I knew your father, Ray. In fact, I knew him pretty well."

Anger instantly shot through Ray. He'd been thinking how attractive she was, but he'd never considered that she might have been involved with his old man.

Well, *hell*, even from the grave, Joe McCullen kept surprising him. And disappointing…

He hardened his look. "*Damn*, I knew he had other women, but he was robbing the cradle with you."

Those big eyes widened. "Oh, *no*, it wasn't like that."

"He was a two-timing, cheating liar." Ray stood and paced to the fireplace as an image of his father in bed with Scarlet flashed behind his eyes. "How long was it going on?" And what did she want?

"Listen to me," Scarlet said, her voice rising in pitch. "Your father and I were not involved in that way. He was nothing but honorable and kind to me."

Yeah, I bet he was. He turned to her, not bothering to hide his disdain. "So what do you want?"

She set her coffee down and folded her arms. "He told me you were stubborn and resented him, but he didn't say you were a jerk."

Ray angled his head toward her. "You're calling me names. Lady, you don't even know me."

"And you don't know me." Scarlet lifted her chin in defiance. "But if you'd be quiet and listen, I'd like to explain."

Ray's gaze locked with hers, rage and grief and other emotions he couldn't define rolling through him.

The same emotions were mirrored in her own eyes.

Needing something stronger than coffee, he set the mug down, then strode to the bar and poured himself a finger full of scotch.

"I'll have one of those, too," she said.

He bit back a retort and poured her a shot, then carried the glasses back to the fireplace. He handed her the tumbler, then sank into the wing chair and tossed his back in one gulp. "All right. You want me to listen. Say what you have to say, then get the hell out."

SCARLET SHUDDERED AT Ray's harsh tone. She'd seen pictures of him and his brothers, and knew Ray was the formidable one.

He was also the most handsome. Sure Brett was the charmer and Maddox was tough, but something about that dark, mysterious, haunted look in Ray's eyes had drawn her.

Maybe because she understood how anger changed a person. She'd dealt with her own share over the years in the children's home.

But Ray had been lucky enough to have a father who'd wanted him. Even if Joe McCullen hadn't been perfect.

"So, spill it," Ray said. "Why are you here?"

"This was a mistake." She stood, fingers closing over the edge of her bag. "I'll leave."

She started past him, but Ray shot up and grabbed her arm. "No way you're leaving until you tell me what the *hell* is going on."

Her gaze met his, tension vibrating between them. She gave a pointed look at her arm where his fingers held her.

"Take your hands off me."

For a brief second, something akin to regret glimmered in his expression. But he released her and stepped back. "I'm sorry. I don't usually manhandle women."

She wanted to believe him, but she'd met too many men who did. So she refused to let him off the hook.

His loud exhale punctuated the air. "Please sit down. I'll behave."

He looked so contrite that a tingle of something like respect danced through her. But she refrained from commenting as another image taunted her. One of Ray's hands on her, tenderly stroking her, making her feel safe. No, not safe. Alive.

Fool.

Ray McCullen was anything but safe.

And judging from his brusque attitude, he was going to hate her when he learned the reason for her visit.

Chapter Two

Ray struggled to wrangle his temper as Scarlet took a seat again.

When he looked at her, he couldn't help but think about those damn dolls his mother had loved so much.

Just like them, she was almost too beautiful to be real.

Like them, she looked fragile, like a piece of china that could break if you held it too hard.

Yet she'd stood up to him and had a stubborn set to her chin that made him suspect there was more to her than surface beauty.

He could easily see why his father might have been attracted to her. But *God*...she was so young...

"I realize what I'm going to tell you may come as a shock," she said softly, "but it's what Joe wanted."

"How do you know what my father wanted?"

Her eyes flickered with uneasiness at his tone. "I told you that I knew him pretty well."

"So you said. But *how* did you know him? Was he your sugar daddy?"

Scarlet sucked in a harsh breath. "No. It wasn't like that, Ray. I met him at The Family Farm outside Laramie."

"The Family Farm?"

Scarlet nodded. "It's a home for children without parents, an orphanage. Your father volunteered there. I was ten at the time we met, but he took me under his wing."

For a moment, Ray couldn't respond. "I find it hard to imagine my father volunteering with children," he finally said. "He was a rancher. He worked the land."

Scarlet shrugged. "He told me once that he had to find a way to atone for his sins. That he hadn't always been the father he wanted to be, and he hoped giving back to some children without families would help make up for it."

Ray's dark gaze met hers, probing, skeptical. "He told you about Horseshoe Creek? About us?"

"Yes," Scarlet said softly. "He loved you and Maddox and Brett. He was proud of all of you."

Ray chuckled, but the sound was filled with sarcasm. "He was proud of Maddox. And maybe Brett because of the bull riding. But he didn't give a damn about me."

"That's not true," Scarlet said. "He loved you and hated what he did to you. That you knew his flaws."

"That I did." Ray made no attempt to hide his animosity. "He cheated on my mother with some woman named Barbara. But my mother loved him anyway."

Scarlet looked away for a second, which made him even more uneasy.

Her fingers tightened around the strap of that worn-out shoulder bag. "I'm sorry, Ray, I didn't come here to dredge up bad memories."

"My father just died, Scarlet. Coming home already did that." He exhaled. "So why did you come here? To tell me Dad did volunteer work?"

"Not just that, but to tell you what he did for me. I was alone and no one wanted to adopt me. But he gave me a home and a family."

A bead of perspiration trickled down Ray's neck. "What are you talking about?"

"He took me home to live with Barbara and Bobby. Their last name is Lowman."

"You lived with my father's mistress?"

She nodded. "For a while. With her and her son." She hesitated. "Their son."

Her words echoed in Ray's mind as if he'd fallen into a wind tunnel. "*Their* son?"

Scarlet nodded. "I'm sorry. I...thought he was going to tell you about Bobby before he passed."

A deep sense of betrayal cut through Ray, and he balled his hands into fists. He wanted to punch something.

He had known about the affair, but not that his father had another son.

SCARLET'S HEART SQUEEZED at the pain and shock on Ray's face. She didn't want to hurt this family, only to honor Joe's last wishes.

Ray raked a hand through his thick, dark hair, then walked over to the bar and poured himself another shot. He kept his back to her as he stared into the fire, his shoulders rigid.

She glanced around the living room, absorbing its warmth, giving Ray time to process what she'd told him.

She tried to put herself in his place, to understand how he must feel. Her grief over Joe's death was almost unbearable, and she wasn't even Joe's biological family.

She'd always looked up to Joe for the time he'd donated to the children's home, and had secretly hoped to meet his sons one day, sons that he took pride in and had talked about when Bobby wasn't around.

Joe and Bobby had a tumultuous relationship. Barbara and Joe had kept an on-again-off-again relationship over the years, but Joe had never married Barbara. He'd also been in and out of Bobby's life, partly by choice, partly due to Barbara's moody behavior.

But Joe had admitted to Scarlet once that he'd always loved his wife. No one could ever replace her.

In some ways, Bobby had a right to resent Ray, Maddox and Brett. Although Joe had financially supported him and Barbara, he'd never taken them to his ranch. Even after he lost his wife, he hadn't shared Bobby with his other three sons.

"So I have a half brother?" Finally Ray turned toward her, a harshness in his eyes. "How old is he?"

"Twenty-six," Scarlet said.

"Just a little younger than me," Ray muttered. "Damn my daddy. Even in death, he found a way to screw us."

"I'm sorry, Ray." Scarlet fidgeted. "I know this is a shock. Maybe I shouldn't have come, but—"

"But you did come," Ray snapped. "Because you and Bobby want something? What? Part of Daddy's money? The ranch?"

Scarlet flinched at his accusatory tone. Although she reminded herself that she'd just dropped a bombshell on Ray at a time when he was grieving. Lashing out was a natural reaction.

But Joe McCullen's words in that heartfelt letter echoed in her head. She had loved Joe, and even though he'd made mistakes in his life, he'd cared about her.

Ray must have read her silence as a yes. "That's it, isn't it? You want part of Horseshoe Creek?"

"Ray, please," Scarlet said, her voice quivering. "It's not like that."

Ray's jaw tightened. "Then how is it? You simply came to tell me you're sorry my father is gone? That he has another son, but that he doesn't want part of Dad's legacy?"

Actually Bobby *would* want part of it. And Joe had made

arrangements for him, only there were stipulations attached to it. She didn't know what those stipulations entailed, but whatever they were, Bobby would balk.

"I won't lie to you, Ray. I am here because your father left me something." She pulled the letter from her bag. "I had no idea he'd included me or Bobby in his will, but he did. A lawyer named Bush contacted me about the reading."

"Just as I thought," Ray said, animosity dripping from every word.

Self-preservation kicked in. "Listen, Ray, I didn't ask for this. And I don't think Bobby even knows yet. He and Joe didn't get along, and Bobby's had problems in the past, so I don't know what to expect from him now." She shoved the letter toward Ray. "Just read this letter your father wrote me."

Ray's dark gaze latched with hers, tension stretching between them, filled with distrust.

Her hand trembled as she waited for Ray to take the letter. When he snatched it, she finally released the breath she'd been holding, sank back in the chair and struggled to calm her nerves.

But the sight of Ray's big, tough masculine profile haloed by the orange-and-yellow firelight aroused feminine desires that she'd never felt. Desires that she had no right to feel for the man in front of her.

Desires that couldn't lead to anything.

But something about his strong jaw, that heavy five o'clock shadow and the intensity in his eyes reminded her of Joe. Joe, the man who'd been like a father to her.

Joe who'd sent her here to meet his sons.

She clutched her drink glass again and sipped it. The warm scotch slid down her throat, warming her. Yet the alcohol also reminded her of Joe.

Why had he put her in this awkward position?

He had to have known that Ray and his brothers wouldn't welcome her or want to share any part of their family ranch. That they would be angry, and that the truth would turn their world upside down.

RAY LEANED AGAINST the hearth as he studied the paper Scarlet had handed him. It appeared to be a handwritten letter to her.

In his father's handwriting.

My dearest Scarlet,
I was blessed to have sons. But I never had a daughter—until I met you.

That first line knocked the breath from his lungs. But he forced himself to read further.

By the time he finished, his gut was churning. These were his father's words. His father's sentiments.

Betrayal splintered through him.

Scarlet wasn't lying. His father had loved her, had lead a life that he'd kept from his sons.

What were Maddox and Brett going to say? They didn't even know about Barbara…

"I realize this is a shock to you," Scarlet said softly. "It was to me, too."

Still suspicious though, Ray narrowed his eyes, determined to see the truth beneath the pretty exterior. She was dressed in jeans and a denim shirt, boots, her long blond hair natural, and she wore little makeup or jewelry.

Not his idea of what a gold digger would look like.

But who was to say she hadn't conned his father into writing this when he was ill or on medication?

He'd worked as a PI long enough to know that con artists came in all shapes and sizes, that sometimes the most charming, alluring face hid a devious side beneath.

Scarlet had grown up in an orphanage. Wasn't it common for children who grew up without parents or in troubled homes to have mental problems? Maybe she wanted a family so badly that she'd latched on to his father and had taken advantage of him in a weak moment and convinced him to take her in.

He cleared his throat. He needed more information before he showed this to his brothers. "Where did you get this letter?"

"It came registered yesterday." She gestured toward the envelope. "You can see the return address on the envelope."

Ray hadn't paid attention to it, but he flipped the envelope over and noted the name of a law office. Bush Law, Darren Bush, attorney-at-law.

Darren Bush was his father's lawyer. So she hadn't lied about that.

"You realize I'll need to make sure this is legitimate."

Scarlet bit down on her lower lip. "Yes, but…I'd like the letter back. It's the last thing Joe ever wrote to me."

He clenched his jaw. "He wrote you other letters?"

Scarlet shrugged. "Not letters, but he gave me cards for encouragement when I lived at The Family Farm. And then on birthdays."

Resentment bubbled inside Ray. Why had his father treated her so special when he'd ignored him?

Because you knew what he did to your mother. And his anger and bitterness had driven a wedge between the two of them.

But *dammit*, his father could have tried.

"I'm sorry I upset you," Scarlet said. "I almost didn't come. But—"

"But you did," Ray said again.

"Yes," she said in a voice that cracked with emotion. "I don't want the money per se, but I admired Joe and having a piece of the ranch that he cherished means I'll always have a part of him. I know you and your brothers feel the same way."

Except they were Joe McCullen's blood. And she was… not family at all.

Although according to that letter, his father had loved her like a daughter.

Ray wished to hell he knew exactly how much money and land his father was talking about. And what about this half brother?

The letter mentioned that he had problems. Would he make trouble for the McCullens?

Chapter Three

Scarlet sensed it was time to leave. She hadn't expected the visit to go well, but she'd hoped…

What? That the McCullen men would welcome her into their family as Joe had?

They didn't even know her. Besides, according to Joe, the three brothers had their own differences to work out. Throwing a surprise half brother in the mix that they were unaware of and adding her—who was not even blood kin—had to rock their foundations.

They might even find some loophole to prevent her from receiving what Joe had intended her to have.

A pang hit her. If that happened, she'd live with it. Lord knows, she'd handled rejection before.

Truthfully, she wasn't even sure Barbara had ever wanted her.

At first she'd welcomed her as the daughter she'd never had, but later, Scarlet suspected Barbara had only tolerated her because she thought it might help her win Joe back.

And Bobby… He'd hated her from the beginning.

She stood, Ray's tormented expression tearing at her heart. "I really am sorry about just showing up. I wish Joe had told you about us."

"He was a coward," Ray said.

She bit her tongue to keep from agreeing. Even thinking that made her feel disloyal for all Joe had done for her. But she'd been hurt that her own mother had abandoned her when she was little, and she didn't understand why Joe had allowed his deception to continue for so long.

He had put Ray in a bad spot and left him harboring a secret that must have hurt him terribly.

"He said he wanted to protect your brothers," Scarlet said. "He hated disappointing you all."

"Don't defend him, Scarlet."

"I'm not defending him," Scarlet said. "But everyone makes mistakes, Ray."

Ray's frown deepened, making his eyes look haunted. "I'll call the lawyer and talk to him about this, but for now, I think you'd better go."

So much for making friends with Ray.

No wonder he and Joe had butted heads. They were both stubborn and hardheaded.

He gestured at the door, and she walked toward the entranceway. This old farmhouse had been in the family forever, Joe had said. It was homey and warm. The pictures of the landscape and horses on the walls showcased life on the ranch.

A family portrait of Joe, his wife and the three boys when they were little hung in the hallway like a shrine to the McCullens.

As a little girl, she'd been so alone when her mother had abandoned her. She'd lived on the streets for a few days with a homeless woman. She'd slept in alleys and deserted barns and eaten garbage.

Then she'd gotten sick and the old woman had pushed her into a nearby church with a note saying she had no home and needed help.

She'd developed rheumatic fever, and her heart had been weakened from her illness, making matters worse. No one had wanted to adopt a sick child, so she'd ended up at the children's home.

Ray opened the door and a gust of cold air blasted her, sending a shiver through her. She clutched her shawl around her shoulders and held her head up high.

She'd been called names, ostracized from social situations and left out of sports because she'd been small, sickly and poor.

She wasn't sickly anymore, and she didn't intimidate easily. Joe had taught her to respect herself and fight for what she wanted out of life.

She wanted a family of her own someday.

She'd hoped to be part of this one. But that didn't look as if it would happen.

So she hugged her shawl around her and ran to her Wrangler. Even if the McCullen men didn't want her in their lives, their father would forever live in her heart.

RAY IGNORED THE guilt stabbing at him for his rude behavior with Scarlet.

When people died, especially people who owned land or money, predators crawled out of the woodwork wanting a piece of the pie.

He had to investigate Scarlet and her claims. But if she was telling the truth about there being a half brother, then he and Maddox and Brett would have to deal with the fallout.

And there would be fallout. Especially if their father had left him part of Horseshoe Creek.

He watched the woman disappear down the drive, his throat thickening with mixed emotions. If his father had volunteered at this children's home and cared for her, it meant that he hadn't been the cold bastard Ray believed him to be.

Yet…how could he have lived such different lives? Two families…

After his mother's death, Ray had wondered if his father would marry that other woman. Barbara.

When he'd remained single, Ray had wondered why.

He still wondered.

He scanned the long driveway. Would Barbara show up next?

Wind swirled leaves inside the front door, and he realized Scarlet was long gone, so he shut the door. What the hell was he going to do now?

The furnace rumbled, the sound of wood popping in the fireplace, and he strode back to the living room and studied the family picture on the mantel.

The smiling faces mocked him. They looked like the perfect family.

But the picture was a lie.

Joe had another side to him. He'd slept with this woman Barbara and had a son with her.

And Scarlet…she was the wild card. The stranger he'd given a home to make amends for the mess he'd made.

Ray rolled his hands into fists. He had to find out the truth before the reading of the will.

Dammit, Dad, I'm still covering for you, aren't I?

Yeah, he was. But he hated to destroy his brothers' worlds if he could protect them. After all, Maddox and Brett had both just married.

Brett had been the womanizer, but he'd sowed his oats, and he wouldn't be a cheater like his old man.

One reason Ray had never gotten serious with a woman. If his old man hadn't been able to handle commitment, how could he?

He pulled his phone from his jacket, punched in Bush's number and left a voice mail.

"This is Ray McCullen. A woman named Scarlet Lovett paid me a visit and claims my father left her some money and land. She also claims my father had another son who is a beneficiary. My brothers don't know anything about this yet, and I want to be prepared, so I need to talk you to *before* the reading of the will. Call me as soon as you get this message."

An image of abandoned children living in a group home taunted him and made his gut squeeze with guilt. If Scarlet's story was true, he'd be a bastard to contest his father's wishes.

He grabbed his Stetson and headed outside. He'd drop by that group home and find out for himself.

SCARLET HELD HERSELF together until she reached the edge of the McCullen ranch, but she was trembling so hard by then she had to pull over. She parked beside a sawtooth oak and studied the sign for Horseshoe Creek, then gazed at the beautiful rolling pastures and the rocky terrain in the distance.

Joe had regaled her with stories about raising cattle and working with his sons on the ranch, and about cattle drives and branding in the spring. He'd had big dreams of expanding the horse side of the operation, but when Ray and Brett left Pistol Whip, he and Maddox couldn't handle expansion without them.

The sun was setting, painting the ridges of the mountains beyond a golden hue and the sky a radiant red and orange. Cattle grazed in the pasture to the east, and horses galloped near a stable to the west.

She understood why Joe had loved this land.

And why his sons would want to hold on to it.

Tears trickled down her cheeks. Ray and his brothers were still mourning their father.

So was she. But just like the rest of her life, she had to do it alone. She'd kept her distance at the funeral for fear someone would ask about her relationship with Joe. Plus, she'd respected him too much to intrude on his sons' day.

Maybe she should just disappear from the McCullens' lives now. Forget the will reading. Not ask for anything.

She had her memories of Joe. That was all she needed.

She started her engine and headed back toward her rental house.

She had survived being abandoned as a child, and now she'd earned her degree in social work and was helping other children like herself. She had a fulfilling job and she was giving back.

Even if she was alone at night, it didn't matter. There were children who depended on her. She wouldn't let them down just like Joe hadn't let her down.

Her stomach twisted. Which meant she couldn't run from the McCullens.

She needed the money Joe had left her to help The Family Farm.

RAY STUDIED THE sign for the children's home—The Family Farm. The house was set back on several acres with room for livestock and stables, but he didn't see any cattle or horses.

He maneuvered the drive and parked in front of the rustic wooden structure that reminded him more of a fishing lodge than a home for children.

Someone had probably designed it that way. *Smart.*

A big front porch overlooked the property, the two-story house more welcoming than he'd expected. A van was parked to the side with an emblem of a circle of children holding hands and the name painted on the side. Two other vehicles were parked in the graveled lot. Probably employees.

He climbed out and walked up the steps, then knocked. A pudgy middle-aged woman with a short brown bob answered the door. "Yes?"

"My name is Ray."

"Faye Gideon," the woman said with a warm smile. "What can I do for you?"

"May I come in and talk to you?"

A slightly wary expression flickered in her eyes, and she wiped her hands on a kitchen towel. "It's dinnertime for the kids. What's this about?"

He didn't want to divulge that he was a private investigator yet. "I recently met a woman named Scarlet Lovett. She said she grew up here."

Faye's eyes widened, but a smile flitted across her face. "Yes, Scarlet. She did live here. Now she's a social worker and helps place kids in forever homes when she can." She opened the door and stepped onto the porch. "What did you say your name was?"

"Ray McCullen."

She pressed her hands to her cheeks. "Oh, my goodness, I thought you looked familiar. You're one of Joe's boys, aren't you?"

Ray swallowed. "Yes, ma'am. You knew my father?"

"Of course!" Faye grinned. "He volunteered here. That's how he connected with Scarlet. But if you've met her, you probably know all of this."

So Scarlet's story was true.

"I'm so sorry about your daddy," Faye said. "We all loved him. He was so wonderful with the children. We used to be in this old house nearer to town, but it was small and run-down, and Joe helped us build this place. Now we have twelve rooms, a big kitchen and land for the children to run and play."

Ray couldn't believe what she was saying. This wasn't the man he remembered from his high school years at home.

"We're all sad that he passed and will miss him," Faye said. "Do you want to meet the children? They'll be thrilled to visit with one of Joe's sons. He talked about the three of you all the time."

Emotions welled in Ray's throat. Why hadn't his father told him about this place? About what he was doing?

Because you left and never came back. You refused to talk to him.

And now it was too late.

SCARLET PARKED AT her rental house outside Pistol Whip, still shaken over the conversation with Ray McCullen. But there was nothing she could do tonight except give him time to process the bombshell she'd dropped on him.

Heart heavy, she let herself inside the tiny house. Although it was small, she had filled it with homey furniture, handmade quilts and crafts from Vintage Treasures, and she'd hung photographs of the farmland where the orphanage was housed on the walls.

She loved the beautiful landscapes and had been excited about Joe's plans to add a stable and horses so the children could learn to ride. He'd also intended to add farm animals and assign the children chores to teach them responsibility. Working together would make them feel like a real family. God knows, most of them were plagued with self-doubt, insecurities and emotional issues.

She lit a fire in her fireplace, brewed a cup of tea, then grabbed her files and spread them on the kitchen table. She was most worried about one of the preteen boys, Trenton Akers. He was angry and lashing out at everyone, which made it more difficult to find him a forever home.

But there was a four-year-old, Corey Case, who a couple from Cheyenne were interested in. She opened the file on the couple to study their background check, but a noise outside startled her.

She went to the back door and peeked through the window in the laundry room. Wind hurled leaves across the backyard that jutted up to the woods. Night was setting in, the gray skies gloomy with shadows.

Suddenly she heard the doorknob jiggle, and she crept to the back door. A second later, the door burst open and Bobby appeared. He'd always been a foot taller than her, but he'd gained at least twenty pounds, making him twice her size.

Her lungs squeezed for air at the fury radiating from him. Beard stubble covered his face, and he reeked of alcohol and cigarettes. "Hello, sis. We have to talk."

Scarlet inhaled sharply. "Bobby, you're drunk. Come back when you're sober."

He gripped her arm, then dragged her toward the living room and shoved her against the wall. "No, Scarlet. We're going to talk now."

Fear crawled through her. She'd borne the brunt of Bobby's temper before, and barely survived it.

No telling what he'd do now that Joe wasn't around to protect her.

Chapter Four

Ray reluctantly stepped inside The Family Farm house.

Part of him wanted to deny everything Faye was telling him, go home and forget about Scarlet Lovett.

But he couldn't forget about her. Not if his father had included her and this other son in his will.

Bobby Lowman—his half brother.

*Good God…*he still couldn't believe it. His father had another son. One he and Maddox and Brett had known nothing about.

Maddox and Brett were going to have a fit.

As he scanned the interior of the farmhouse, he couldn't deny his father's influence. It reminded him of the house on Horseshoe Creek. Wood floors, sturdy oak furniture, a giant family table in the dining room, a kitchen adjoining it that held another big round wooden table and a butcher-block counter.

Landscape paintings and farm and ranch tools decorated the walls in the hall and the dining room where several kids of varying ages sat eating what smelled like home-made chicken potpie.

A brick fireplace in the dining room and another one in the living room added to the homey feel.

Laughter, chatter and teasing rumbled from the table.

"I told you it was dinnertime," Faye said. "The kids

take turns helping prepare the meal and cleaning up. Their rooms are down the hall. We have a maximum of four children to a room, and in some cases only two. Boys and girls are housed on opposite sides of the main living area."

She escorted him past the dining room to a large room equipped with several smaller tables and a computer area. "The children attend public school, and after school gather here to do their homework. We have volunteers who tutor those who need it."

Ray nodded, trying to imagine his father in this place. "My father tutored kids?"

"No, he said schooling wasn't his forte."

You could say that again.

"But he helped in other ways. He organized games for the kids, like horseshoes, roping contests and, twice a month, he brought a couple of horses over to teach the children grooming skills and how to ride."

She gestured at a back window that offered a view of the pastureland. "He planned to build a stable so we could house a few horses on-site. When the older boys discovered his son was a bull rider, they begged him to bring him here to meet them."

Ray shifted. "That would have required him to tell us about this place."

Faye's eyes flickered with compassion. "I never quite understood that, but I figured it wasn't my place to question your daddy, not when he was doing so much for us."

Hurt swelled inside Ray. Nice that he'd been a hero for these strangers when he'd lied to his own sons.

A little boy with brown hair and big clunky glasses ran in. "Miss Faye, we're done. Barry wants to know if we can go out and play horseshoes."

Faye ruffled the little boy's hair. "I'll be right there, Corey. You guys help Miss Lois clean up now."

Corey bobbed his head up and down, then ran back to the dining room. Ray heard him shouting that they could play once they cleaned up.

Faye squeezed Ray's arm. "You're welcome to stay and play a game with the children. They'd like it, especially since you're Joe's son."

Ray chewed the inside of his cheek. The air was suddenly choking him. "I'm sorry, I can't today. I have to go."

Faye nodded as if she understood, but her smile was sad. "I don't know what we're going to do now without Joe."

Ray didn't, either. But it wasn't his problem.

Was it?

Hell, if his father had made provisions for Scarlet and his illegitimate son Bobby, he'd probably made arrangements to take care of this place, too.

Another thing to discuss with the lawyer and his brothers.

He ignored the chatter and laughter in the dining room as he walked past it to the front door. When he made it outside, he inhaled the crisp cool air, but his stomach was churning.

He checked his phone, hoping Bush would return his call, but there were no messages. He had to find out if Bobby planned to attend the meeting and stake his claim.

Ray gritted his teeth. He'd kept the truth from his brothers long enough. They deserved a heads-up before their world fell apart.

He would tell them as soon as Maddox returned.

SCARLET TRIED TO gauge the distance between the couch and the bedroom where she kept the pistol Joe had given her.

He'd insisted she take self-defense classes and he'd taught her to shoot so she could protect herself. Unarmed, she was no match for a two-hundred-and-forty-pound angry, drunk man.

Knowing Bobby's triggers, that he liked to bully women and that he had no tolerance for people who crossed him, she forced her tone to remain calm. "What do you want, Bobby?"

"I want what's mine." He glared at her, then folded his arms and planted himself in front of her, legs apart on either side of hers, trapping her.

"I understand that and you deserve it."

Distrust radiated from his every pore. "You went to the old man's funeral?"

A pang of grief swelled inside Scarlet. "Yes, but I just watched from the sidelines." She lifted her chin. "I didn't see you there."

"Barbara talked me out of it." He gave a sarcastic chuckle. "I belonged there more than you did. You weren't family."

Scarlet bit her tongue but his hate-filled words hit home, resurrecting old hurts. "I figured it wasn't the time to introduce myself to the McCullen brothers."

It hadn't gone very well today, either.

Bobby removed a pack of matches from his pocket, and she barely resisted a flinch. Bobby had always liked setting things on fire.

He struck a match, lit it and held it in front of her, the orange glow flickering and throwing off heat as he moved it nearer to her face. "I should have been a McCullen," he said, a feral gleam to his eyes. "I should have had everything they did. That big damn ranch house and horses and land and...the privileges that came with it." The match was burning down, and he dropped it in a coffee cup on her table, then lit another and waved it in front of her eyes.

With one beefy hand, he shoved her into a chair. "Then he brought *you* home and treated you like you were his own kid."

Scarlet struggled to keep her breathing steady when she wanted to make a run for it. If she could reach her car, she could escape. And do what?

Call the police. She didn't want to, but she would if necessary to protect herself. "He felt sorry for me, that was all."

His intense look made her pulse hammer. "He gave you more love than he did me."

"That's because you wouldn't let him love you," Scarlet said. "You were always angry, acting out."

"I had a right to be mad. He cheated me out of his name and that ranch." The flame flickered low, nearly burning out, and he suddenly dropped the match into her lap. Scarlet shrieked as heat seared her thigh through her skirt, and she raked the match to the floor, then stomped it out with her boot.

Bobby's maniacal laughter echoed through the room. He grabbed her arm and hauled her to a standing position.

Scarlet sensed the situation was spiraling out of control. She had been a punching bag before and swore she would never be one again.

"Maybe he did when he was alive," Scarlet said as she yanked her arm away. "But he didn't forget you, Bobby. He left you something in his will."

Bobby's eyes widened in disbelief. "What are you talking about?"

"Didn't you receive a notice from his lawyer?" Not that she wanted to tell Bobby about it, but she had to do something to defuse the situation.

His bloodshot eyes pierced her. "His lawyer?"

"Yes," Scarlet said, desperate. "I received a notice to attend the reading." She extricated herself from Bobby's grip. "Let me get it and show it to you. He took care of you in his will, too. Maybe Barbara got the notice."

Bobby cursed, but he allowed her to pass. She heard

him in the kitchen digging through her refrigerator, and she rushed to her nightstand. She yanked out her pistol, reminding herself that she couldn't allow him to turn it around and use it on her.

She loaded it, then held it down by her side as she slowly walked back to the den.

Bobby popped the top on a beer as he stepped into the doorway, and she raised the gun and pointed it at him. "I want you to leave."

"You bitch." He started toward her, one fist knotted as if he planned to slug her, but she lifted the gun toward his chest.

Bobby froze, his jaw twitching. "You were lying about the lawyer and the will."

"No, I wasn't. Ask Barbara. We're all supposed to attend the reading."

Bobby hesitated, still contemplating what she'd said as if he thought she was trying to trick him. "What is this lawyer's name?"

"Darren Bush." Scarlet took a step toward him, her hand steady. "I don't want to use this, Bobby, but I will if I have to. Now, I don't have anything you want here. No money. Nothing of Joe's. And if you want to collect on whatever inheritance he left you, then you need to leave me alone or I'll either shoot you or have you arrested."

Pure rage flashed in his eyes, but he lifted the beer as if to toast her. "Shoot me and you'll go to jail."

"Make one more move, Bobby, and with your record, all I'll have to do is claim self-defense."

Bobby stared at her for a long tension-filled minute, his fury a palpable force. Then he downed the beer, crushed the can in his hand and threw the can at the fireplace. His boots pounded the floor as he strode to the door.

Her hand was shaking as he paused and turned back to face her. "You're going to be sorry for pulling a gun on me."

His evil laugh rent the air as he opened the door and stormed outside. As soon as the door slammed shut, her adrenaline waned, and she stumbled back to the couch.

Bobby didn't make empty threats.

He would be back for revenge. It was just a matter of time.

RAY PLANTED HIMSELF on a barstool at The Silver Bullet and ordered a beer. Tonight the place was packed, the country music was rocking, the dance floor was crowded and the women were on the prowl.

He tipped his hat at a brunette who'd been eyeing him ever since he walked in, then dropped his gaze to his beer. He had too many problems to even think about crawling into bed with a woman tonight.

Besides, another woman's face haunted him.

Scarlet Lovett's. He couldn't shake their conversation. Worse, he couldn't erase the image of her porcelain face with those damn blue eyes that reminded him of his mother's dolls.

Had his father seen that similarity? Was that the reason he'd been drawn to help Scarlet?

A brawny man with a beard and cowboy hat straddled the stool beside him, then angled himself toward Ray.

"You're one of Joe's sons, aren't you?"

Ray swallowed hard. He'd forgotten what it was like to live in a small town where everyone knew everyone else. And Joe McCullen had been well-known around the ranching community.

"Yeah, I'm Ray."

"Arlis Bennett," the man said. "I'm out at the Circle T."

Ray rubbed his chin. The owner of that ranch, Boyle

Gates, had been arrested for his involvement in a cattle-rustling ring.

"I'm planning to expand," Bennett said. "If you and your brothers decide to sell, give me a call." He removed a business card from his pocket and laid it on the bar.

Ray slid it back toward him. "We're not interested in selling. My brother Maddox plans to keep it a working ranch. And my brother Brett is staying to help."

Bennett tossed back his shot of whiskey with a nod. "Well, I just thought you guys might want to move on. That it might be too hard for you to stick around without your father."

Ray shifted, uncomfortable. "It is difficult, but the McCullens have put too much blood, sweat and tears into Horseshoe Creek to ever sell."

"Then I guess we'll be neighbors." Bennett stood and extended his hand. "Nice to meet you, Ray. Again, I'm sorry about your daddy."

Ray nodded and shook the man's hand. But something about the dark gleam in Bennett's eyes reminded Ray of a predator. Not that he should be surprised that someone wanted to buy the ranch.

There might be more offers down the road.

A buxom blonde brushed up against his arm, her eyes glittering with invitation. "Hey, cowboy. Are you lonesome tonight?"

Hell, yeah he was, but an image of Scarlet taunted him. He saw her beneath him in bed, naked and clutching him, that porcelain skin glowing with passion.

"Sorry, honey, I've got to go." He threw some cash on the counter to pay for the beer, then strode toward the door, disgusted with himself for being attracted to the damn woman. She was going to wreck his family.

A gust of wind blasted him as he walked to his Range

Rover, and he jumped inside, started the engine and drove to the ranch.

Just as he approached, he spotted smoke billowing in a cloud from the pastureland on the east side.

He cursed. Hopefully it was nothing but a little brush fire, but he accelerated, taking the curve too fast, tires screeching as he neared Horseshoe Creek.

The miles seemed to take forever, his heart racing with each one. Instead of the smoke dying down, it grew thicker, rolling across the sky, orange-and-red flames shooting upward.

He grabbed his phone and punched 911, praying the fire department could get there fast.

The winds picked up and the fire was spreading, eating up valuable pastureland and heading toward the new stables Brett had just had built.

Chapter Five

Ray jolted to a stop several hundred feet from the flames.

The fire department should be on the way, but he couldn't wait. He had to do something. He quickly scanned the blaze. One of the five barns Brett had had built was on fire, but the others were still safe, although if they didn't do something fast, it would spread.

The sound of horses whinnying and pounding their hoofs against the buildings echoed above the roar of the blaze.

He punched Brett's number, running toward the burning building to make sure it was empty as the phone rang. Three rings and his brother's voice mail kicked in. "Brett, it's Ray. There's a fire at the stables. I've called the fire department, but I need you to get over here now."

He jammed his phone into his coat pocket and checked the doorway to the first barn. Flames shot through the interior and seeped through the openings. He darted around back to the rear door and felt it. Warm, but not too hot.

He eased it open and glanced inside, heat instantly flushing his skin with perspiration. The right side of the barn was completely engulfed in flames, patches spreading through the interior, eating the floor and hay in the stalls.

No sign of horses inside, though. *Thank God.*

Still, if they didn't contain the blaze, the animals could be in danger.

He ran back outside, gulping in fresh air as he hurried to the second barn. Smoke thickened the air, the wind blowing fiery sparks into the grass by the second barn and quickly catching.

Dammit. Where was that fire engine?

Knowing he couldn't wait, he dashed inside the barn. Three horses stamped and kicked, pawing at the stalls to escape. Smoke seeped through the open doorway, making it hard to breathe.

He jogged to the first stall, unlatched the gate and yelled at the horse to get out. "Go on, buddy! It's all right."

The black gelding sprinted through the barn and outside. A siren wailed, and he ran to the next stall. The big animal was pawing and kicking wildly, obviously panicked.

"Shh, buddy, I'm going to set you free." He opened the gate, then jumped aside as the horse charged past him.

One more to go.

The siren grew louder, then the fire truck careened down the driveway and roared to a stop. Ray had reached the third stall, but the terrified horse stomped his feet. "Come on, boy, we have to get out of here."

The horse raised its front legs as he entered, whinnying and backing against the wall. Suddenly wood cracked and popped, and flames rippled along the floor in the front.

Then the scent of gasoline hit him.

Dammit to hell, had someone intentionally set the fire?

The horse jumped, his legs clawing at the air, his fear palpable.

"It's okay, boy," Ray said, forcing a calm to his voice to soothe the terrified animal. "I'm here. We have to go now."

The horse whinnied again, and Ray pulled a rope from the hook and inched his way closer, speaking softly until the horse dropped to all fours and let him approach.

He gently stroked the horse's mane, comforting him as

he lifted the rope and slipped it around his neck. He slowly led him from the stall and out the back door.

Rescue workers jumped into motion shouting orders and dragging out the hoses. Brett's truck barreled up and screeched to a stop.

Ray patted the horse's back and eased the rope from his neck. "Go, boy, get out of here!" He slapped the animal, sending him into a gallop across the pasture.

Ray swiped sweat and soot from his face as he hurried toward the firemen and his brother.

SCARLET WAS STILL shaking over the encounter with Bobby an hour later. She massaged her wrist where he'd grabbed her, knowing she'd have a bruise on it tomorrow. And not for the first time.

Bobby had resented her from the moment Joe McCullen had brought her home to live with Barbara.

She hadn't understood his reaction at the time. She'd been bounced from foster home to foster home and then she'd finally moved into the group facility, so being brought into a real family had thrilled her.

Until Bobby's resentment had festered and he'd started making her life miserable.

First it had just been ugly comments, the surly attitude at meals and school. Then the more sinister threats he'd whispered when he'd sneak up behind her in her room.

She shivered and pulled on flannel pj's as she recalled the time she'd crawled into bed and discovered a rattle-snake under the covers. Another time she'd found her bed full of spiders.

A month later, he'd tricked her into going with him in the car one night, then he'd left her stranded in the woods alone, with no way to get home.

Worse, there was the time he'd nearly drowned her in the pond.

Each time he'd threatened to kill her if she told anyone.

And Barbara…she'd doted on Bobby. Had felt sorry for him because he'd been deprived of the McCullen name and the opportunities that had accompanied it.

Although Joe had supported Bobby and tried to bond with him, it hadn't been enough for Barbara or her son.

She'd believed everything Bobby said and justified his bad behavior with a joke about boys being boys. She'd acted as if Bobby's violent outbursts were normal teenage behavior. And she'd blamed Joe for not being around all the time.

Barbara's own resentment over the fact that Joe would never marry her had blinded her to her precious son's sadistic side.

Just as she had every night since the snake incident, Scarlet turned down the covers and examined the bed to make sure no creepy crawler was waiting for her.

She breathed out a sigh of relief that the bed was clean. But Bobby's cold look haunted her as she closed her eyes. He wouldn't be satisfied until he learned what Joe had left him.

Even then, would it be enough?

And what would happen when he finally came face-to-face with his half brothers?

RAY RAN TOWARD the third barn to check for more horses with Brett on his heels. The first barn was completely ablaze, as flames climbed the front of the second.

Wind hurled smoke and embers through the air, wood popping and crackling. The firefighters were blasting both buildings with water, working frantically to contain the blaze.

"What the hell happened?" Brett yelled as he yanked open the barn door. "How did this start?"

Sweat poured down Ray's face. "I don't know. The first barn was on fire when I arrived. I ran to the second one to save the horses."

Together they raced inside to free the terrified animals trapped in the stalls. The horses stamped and whinnied, pawing and kicking at the wooden slats. A black quarter horse protested, but Brett had a magic touch with animals and soothed him as he led him into the fresh air.

Ray eased a rope around a palomino that was balking and slowly coaxed him through the door and outside, then away from the fire.

"Go on, boy," Ray yelled as he removed the rope and patted the palomino's side. The horse broke into a run, meeting up with the other animals as they galloped across the land.

Sweat trickled down Ray's neck as he and Brett rushed inside to free the last two horses.

When they'd rescued them, he and Brett stood and watched the firefighters finish extinguishing the blaze.

"I can't believe this," Brett said, coughing at the smoke. "We just got these buildings finished and settled the horses in last week."

"The insurance was taken care of, right?"

"Yeah," Brett said with a scowl. "But this will cost us time. I was hoping to start lessons in the spring."

And time meant money. Not that Brett didn't have some from his rodeo winnings, but he had invested a good bit into building a home for him and Willow and their son.

"At least we didn't lose any horses," Brett said. "I couldn't stand to see them get hurt or suffer."

That would have been a huge financial loss, too.

Ray gritted his teeth. "I smelled gasoline, Brett."

Brett's gaze turned steely. "You mean, someone intentionally set the fire?"

"We'll have to let the arson investigator determine that, but it looks that way."

Brett reached for his phone. "We should call Maddox."

Ray shook his head. "Wait. He'll be back day after tomorrow. We can handle this until then."

Brett winced as the roof to the first barn collapsed. "You're right. He should enjoy his honeymoon."

"You said you smelled gas?" the fireman said to Ray. "I called our arson investigator. As soon as the embers cool enough for him to dig around, we'll do a thorough search."

The blaze was beginning to die down, although the first building was a total loss. The front of the second building suffered damage, but hopefully the interior and stalls had been saved.

"I should have had an automatic sprinkler system installed," Brett said glumly.

Ray detected an underlying note of blame in his brother's voice. "You couldn't have known this would happen."

The smoke thickened as the wind picked up. "Yeah, but it did."

"We'll discuss installing them in the future."

Brett gave him an odd look. "I didn't think you were going to hang around."

Ray hadn't planned to. But they still had the reading of the will and the bombshell about their father's mistress and his son to contend with.

"I'll be here for a while, at least until things get settled." Which would probably be longer than he'd first thought.

Another siren wailed, and an official fire department-issued SUV barreled down the road. A sheriff's car followed. Deputy Whitefeather had probably been notified by his 911 call.

Both vehicles careened to a stop, the deputy climbing out followed by a tall, broad-shouldered man in a uniform.

Introductions were quickly made. The arson investigator's name was Lieutenant Garret Hawk.

"What happened?" Lieutenant Hawk asked.

"When I got home, I saw smoke and found the barn on fire," Ray explained. "I called for help, then ran in to rescue the horses. That's when I smelled gasoline."

Lieutenant Hawk acknowledged the other firefighters with a flick of his hand. "It looks like you lost one barn and part of another."

Ray nodded. "Thanks to your men and their quick response, or it could have been so much worse."

"You think someone set the fire?" Deputy Whitefeather asked.

"Our builders certainly didn't have gasoline out here," Brett said. "But I don't know who would sabotage us this way."

Ray bit the inside of his cheek. The first person that came to mind was their half brother. If Bobby was ticked off and thought he'd been left out of the inheritance, maybe he wanted revenge.

Then again, if Bobby expected to inherit a share of the ranch, why would he want to damage any part of it? Destroying buildings would only lower the value of the property. And if he was caught, he'd face charges and go to jail.

Lieutenant Hawk moved closer to the edge of the burning embers. Ashes, soot, burned wood and leather covered the ground. He knelt and used a stick to push aside some debris. A cigarette butt lay in the pile.

"Any of you smoke?"

"Not me or Brett," Ray said.

"How about ranch hands?" Lieutenant Hawk asked.

Ray and Brett and both shrugged. "It's possible," Ray said. "But they know better than to smoke around the hay."

Deputy Whitefeather walked around the edge of the embers then went inside the second barn.

"Did your father have any enemies?" Lieutenant Hawk asked.

Brett shook his head, but Ray didn't know how to respond. He wasn't ready to divulge the truth about his father's indiscretion to a stranger, especially when Maddox and Brett were still in the dark.

He would investigate the half brother himself. If he'd tried to hurt them by setting this fire, Ray would make sure he never saw a dime of the McCullen money or any piece of the land.

Chapter Six

Scarlet jerked awake to the sound of the wind whistling through the small house. Startled, she sat up and scanned her bedroom.

Outside a tree branch banged at the window, and she shivered, still shaken by Bobby's visit. Cool air brushed her skin, causing goose bumps to skate up her arms.

Wondering why the room felt so drafty, she tiptoed to the hall, but she froze at the sight of the open doorway leading to the back deck.

She had locked that door before she'd gone to bed.

Scarlet eased back into the bedroom and retrieved her gun from her nightstand. She checked the safety, then gripped it with clammy palms as she inched to the doorway.

She paused, cocked her head to the side and listened for sounds of an intruder. The wind ruffled the papers from the file on her desk in the corner, scattering them across the floor.

She scanned the small kitchen, but everything looked in place. Everything except the open doorway.

Her house only had the one bedroom and bath, and that bath opened both to the hallway and her bedroom. No one was inside.

The only hiding place would be the coat closet. Nerves on edge, she braced herself with the gun and inched to the closet. Her hand shook as she closed her fingers around the doorknob and twisted it. Holding her breath, she pulled it open, the gun aimed.

Relief flooded her. It was empty.

A noise sounded behind her and she spun around, gun still braced, but the sound was coming from outside.

She hurried to the door and searched the woods behind the house. Dogs barked, and a figure darted through the trees, but it was so dark it was impossible to see who it was.

Had that person been inside?

Shaken, she slammed the door, then knelt to examine the lock, but the lock was intact, not broken.

She locked it again and made a mental note to buy dead bolts, even a second lock for the top of the door.

Still, tension rippled through her. Why had someone broken into her house?

Her confrontation with Bobby taunted her, and she gritted her teeth. Tormenting her with scare tactics fit his sick, twisted style.

How many times when she was a teenager had he hidden in the closet or under the bed to frighten her? Once he'd even snuck into the back of the car and hidden. When she'd gotten in to drive to the store, he'd jumped up and acted as if he was going to choke her.

Shivering at the memory, she clenched the gun to her side, went to the kitchen and made a cup of hot tea. She couldn't go back to sleep now, not with her heart still racing.

But as she passed through the room, she stooped to pick up the papers scattered on the floor.

It was a work file, one that had landed on her desk just last week. She'd been called to a domestic violence scene and had been forced to pull the two-year-old little girl, Sandy, from her home. The mother was deceased, and the father, Lloyd Pullman, had been entertaining a girlfriend.

Both had been drunk and an argument had escalated into a physical altercation.

The neighbors had called to report the screams coming from next door. When she'd arrived after the police, the baby was soiled and crying, the woman bruised with a black eye. The father was in a drunken rage and in cuffs.

When she'd taken custody of the baby, he'd threatened to kill her.

She stacked the papers back in the folder with a frown. Was he out of jail now? If so, had he broken in to frighten her into giving him back his child?

THE NIGHT DRAGGED on as the firefighters finished work and watched to make sure the wind didn't reignite the fire. They had started searching the debris for evidence of foul play and had found a gasoline can a few feet from the barn, tossed into a ravine.

"He probably wore gloves, but we'll still check for prints," Lieutenant Hawk said. "Hopefully we can pull some DNA from that cigarette butt."

Ray made a mental note to find out if Bobby Lowman smoked.

"Can you think of anyone who'd want to do this?" Deputy Whitefeather asked Ray and Brett.

Brett raked a hand through his hair. "Not really. Although we might have ticked off the competition. Jebediah Holcutt started up an equine business last year. Breeds quarter horses and trains them." Brett blew out an exasperated breath. "But this is big ranch country. It can easily support two ranches offering lessons and training."

Ray considered the possibility. "True, but you're a celebrity, Brett. Given the choice between lessons from you or Jebediah, who are people going to choose?"

Brett shrugged. His brother might be a celebrity, but he

was humble. He'd even talked about setting up a camp for kids with problems, a therapeutic horse camp. His wife, Willow, had actually suggested the idea because her son, Brett's little boy, had suffered trauma from being kidnapped and had blossomed under Brett's care and tutelage in the saddle.

"I can check him out for you," Deputy Whitefeather offered.

Ray and Brett exchanged a questioning look, but Brett gave a clipped nod. "Okay. Maybe we can figure this out before Maddox gets back."

"Anyone else I should look into?" the deputy asked.

"Not that I know of," Brett said. "But I haven't been in town that long. If Holcutt didn't do this, we'll talk to Maddox when he returns. He would know best if Dad had any enemies."

Ray remained silent, still contemplating Scarlet Lovett's story about their half brother. He would check out Bobby Lowman.

"What about ranch hands?" Deputy Whitefeather asked. "Anyone have a beef with your father?"

"I doubt it," Brett said. "Dad was always good to his employees."

The deputy glanced at Ray, but Ray shrugged. "Like Brett said, we haven't been back in town long."

"What about that ex-con your father just hired?" the deputy asked. "The one that was in jail for the cattle-rustling operation?"

"Gus wouldn't do this," Brett said emphatically. "If anything, he owes the McCullens for clearing his name and getting him released so he could be with his family."

"All right," Deputy Whitefeather said. "Let me know when you talk to Maddox or if you think of anyone."

A bead of sweat rolled down Ray's forehead and he removed his handkerchief from his pocket to wipe it away. But his fingers connected with the card Arlis Bennett had given him.

"Come to think of it, I ran into a man named Arlis Bennett earlier. He took over Boyle Gates's ranch and said if we were interested in selling to let him know."

Brett frowned. "Gates was the man who set up Gus Garcia."

"Maddox arrested him for his involvement in that cattle-rustling ring," Deputy Whitefeather added. "Bennett is Gates's cousin."

Ray's pulse hammered. Gates probably wanted revenge. What if he put Bennett up to sabotaging operations at Horseshoe Creek? Maybe he even thought he could force them to sell?

SCARLET CONSIDERED CALLING the sheriff, but she had no real proof that anyone had broken in. Nothing had been moved or destroyed. The wind could have blown the file off the table instead of someone looking at it.

But she was certain she'd locked that door.

Unable to sleep, she finished her tea, then reviewed files, working on paperwork until dawn. She checked the locks again before she showered, then dressed and decided to visit The Family Farm. She'd check on Faye and the kids before heading to her office to meet with the couple adopting Corey. Connecting that little boy with a forever home was a reminder of the importance of her job.

She pulled from her drive, mindful of the speed limit since children lived in the neighborhood. Down the block, she spotted a black sedan. When she reached the street where it was parked, it pulled out behind her.

She frowned as the car rode her tail.

Irritated, she accelerated, then maneuvered a turn, hoping it would go the other direction. But it turned, as well. Hands sweating, she made a couple of more turns in an effort to lose the vehicle, but her paranoia increased as it stayed behind her.

She inhaled to calm herself. Bobby didn't drive a black sedan. What about Lloyd Pullman? She had no idea what kind of vehicle he owned.

Her shoulders knotted with tension. She turned into the gas station, then chastised herself for being paranoid when the car finally sped by.

She sat massaging her temple for a few seconds, gathering her composure, then steered her Jeep back onto the road. Still, she checked behind her and down the street as she made the short drive to The Family Farm.

As she parked, she continued to have the eerie sense someone was watching her.

Damn Bobby for making her paranoid.

She steeled herself, determined not to allow Bobby or Lloyd Pullman to terrorize her.

The scent of coffee and maple syrup greeted her as she entered the group home, and she found Faye and Millie, the cook, in the dining room with the children who'd gathered for breakfast.

Faye looked up and smiled, and Scarlet spoke to the children, pausing to chat with each one for a few minutes.

"I dreamed about riding a pony last night," Corey told her.

She ruffled his hair. "Well, maybe that dream will come true." The couple adopting him owned a small farm.

Danny, a fourteen-year-old who'd been bounced from foster home to foster home before becoming part of the family here, scowled into his plate.

"Hey, Danny," Scarlet said softly. "I heard you aced your algebra test yesterday."

He shrugged and dug his spoon into his cereal. "Waste of time."

She ignored his sour attitude. Danny acted tough, but it was an act to cover up the fact that he was hurting.

Faye motioned for her to join her in the kitchen. Scarlet followed and poured herself a cup of coffee.

"Joe McCullen's son, Ray, stopped by here yesterday," Faye said.

Scarlet's pulse jumped. "I'm sure he wanted to know all about me. If I was legitimate."

Faye wiped her hands on her apron. "He did ask about you, and about Joe. I told him how much Joe loved this place and how he helped build the farm."

Scarlet gazed out the window at the pastures. Thankfully, the house and land were paid off, but there was very little money to build the stables and add horses like Joe had planned. No money for the garden plot and farm equipment he'd suggested so the kids could grow their own vegetables.

All the more reason she'd stand up for herself if the McCullen brothers challenged the will. She could use whatever amount Joe had left her to help around here.

"Scarlet, is something wrong?" Faye asked.

"What do you mean?"

"I never quite understood why Joe didn't tell his family about this place. Or about you."

"I didn't understand it, either," Scarlet said. "But I'm sure he had his reasons."

Still, he'd hurt Ray and Bobby.

Faye nodded, although she looked curious. But she didn't push the subject.

"I have to go, Faye. I'm supposed to meet the Fullers about Corey in an hour."

Faye's expression brightened. "Good. That boy needs a real home."

So did all the kids. But it didn't always happen.

Scarlet squeezed Faye's hand. "I know what you mean. But this is a real home, too, Faye. Thanks to you and Millie and Lois, these children have love and family."

Faye blushed, and Scarlet gave her a hug, then slipped back through the house and outside to her car. For a brief second, down the street, she thought she spotted the same car that she'd feared was following her earlier. But it disappeared around the corner. The kids were laughing and talking as they walked to the school bus stop.

She climbed in her car, chastising herself for being so nervous, then headed to her office. But on the way, she couldn't shake the sense that she was being followed again. She punched the number for the sheriff's office in Laramie.

"This is Scarlet Lovett," she said. "Is Lloyd Pullman still in custody?"

"As a matter of fact, he made bail yesterday," the deputy told her.

Scarlet inhaled sharply as his threat echoed in her head. Had Pullman broken into her house the night before? Had he been parked down the street from her and followed her this morning?

"Do you know what kind of car he drives?" Scarlet asked.

"No, why?"

The temptation to tell him her concerns nagged at her, but she didn't want him to think she was irrational. "No reason. I was just curious."

"Listen, Scarlet, if he bothers you, let me know. Or better yet, call the sheriff in Pistol Whip. He can make it to your house faster than I can."

"Thanks. I will."

She hung up, keeping her eyes alert for the sedan again. Although traffic in Pistol Whip was minimal, early morning commuters were making their way to work. She pressed the brakes to turn into her office, but her Wrangler didn't slow.

Tires squealed, and she swerved then pumped the brakes, but the vehicle sped down the small hill, gaining momentum. A pedestrian crossing the street caught her eye, and she pounded the horn, terrified she was going to hit the woman. The woman screamed and darted to the sidewalk, just as Scarlet jerked the steering wheel to the right.

The Wrangler careened forward, tires bumping over the sidewalk. She was losing control and struggled to keep from crashing into the hair salon, but as she veered to the right to avoid it, she flew toward her own office building.

Seconds later, she screamed, glass pelting her from the windshield as the Wrangler rammed into the brick wall.

Chapter Seven

Glass shattered and pelted Scarlet, and her head snapped back as the air bag deployed.

Her lungs felt as if they exploded as the impact threw her forward.

She blinked, slightly dizzy from the force of the crash. What had just happened?

Her brakes…they hadn't worked…

Suddenly a shout erupted outside the vehicle. "Scarlet!"

Someone jerked at the driver's door. Reality fought through the shock immobilizing her, and she pushed at the air bag, searching for her seat belt. Her fingers found the hook, but when she tried to unfasten it, it was stuck. For a moment, panic seized her. She couldn't breathe. Her head hurt. Her legs felt numb.

Dear God…she couldn't move them.

Then the door swung open, and she heard the voice again. "Scarlet, are you all right?"

Her assistant, Hugh Weatherman. He must have had a pocketknife, because a second later, he ripped away the air bag and freed her. She was trembling all over as he cut away the seat belt.

"I called 911 when I heard the crash," Hugh said. "Are you hurt?"

It took another minute for Scarlet to pull herself from

the shock. "I don't know." She tried to move her legs, but her right one was stuck.

"Stay still," Hugh said. "The medics are on the way."

She nodded, numb and terrified.

Hugh pulled out a handkerchief and wiped at her cheek. "You're bleeding. Are you in pain?"

She shook her head. "No, but I can't move my legs."

"The front end is crunched," Hugh said. "You're probably just trapped by the metal."

A tremor rippled through her, and she fought back a cry of panic.

"Just hang in there, Scarlet, we'll get you out."

A siren wailed, lights flashing, and Scarlet laid her head back against the seat and tried to stay calm. A minute later, tires screeched as an ambulance and fire truck roared to stops.

Hugh yelled and waved them over, and a female medic greeted her. "You all right, ma'am?"

She nodded. "I think so. But my legs are trapped."

A fireman appeared behind her to assess the situation, and Scarlet braced herself as they began the process of sawing away the metal to free her.

RAY LET HIMSELF sleep for a couple of hours, but then hurriedly showered, dressed and headed to the deputy sheriff's office. Brett had already called the insurance company to handle the claim. He also insisted that they'd rebuild immediately.

But they had to find out who set the fire and prevent more sabotage.

Ray wanted answers and he wanted them before Maddox returned.

He entered the sheriff's office and found Deputy Whitefeather on the phone.

"Yes. I'll be right there." He hung up and grabbed his jacket. "Sorry, McCullen, there's been an accident. I need to go."

Dammit, Ray wanted to ask for his help looking into Bobby Lowman. "What happened?"

"Lady named Scarlet Lovett crashed her Jeep into the side of the building where she works. They're cutting her out of it."

Ray's heart hammered. "Is she all right?"

"I don't know. The ambulance is there now." He strode to the door, his keys jangling in his hand.

"I'll follow you," Ray said.

The deputy's brows furrowed. "Why? Do you know her?"

Ray gave a clipped nod. "Not well, but we've met."

"Suit yourself." Deputy Whitefeather hurried outside, and Ray jogged to his SUV and followed him.

More gray skies hid the sun, making the air feel chillier than it was. Wind beat at the trees, whipping tumbleweed across the side of the road as they turned onto a side street.

A stand-alone brick building bearing a sign for Social Services stood between the library and an empty warehouse.

The deputy veered into the parking lot, and Ray followed, his breath tightening at the sight of the Wrangler crunched into the brick structure. Just as he parked, the rescue workers pulled away a chunk of metal.

He parked and climbed out, tensing at the sight of the medics working to extract Scarlet.

In spite of the chill, sweat rolled down the back of his neck. Had she been hurt?

The deputy greeted one of the rescue workers and gestured toward the Wrangler. "What happened?"

"She said the brakes failed," the worker said. "She tried to stop but couldn't."

Ray's instincts jumped to life. The fact that Scarlet had just visited him and told him about her relationship to Joe and the will, then the ranch had been sabotaged and now she'd had an accident, all struck him as odd.

And too coincidental.

Had her car crash really been an accident?

A female medic was leaning over Scarlet checking her blood pressure. From his vantage point, he couldn't see if she was seriously injured.

He made his way to the stretcher just as the medics started to load her into the ambulance. "Scarlet?"

She groaned, and Ray's chest tightened. Blood dotted her arms and her cheeks looked pale, also speckled with blood. The medics had secured her neck and body on the board with straps, so she couldn't turn her head.

He stepped up beside her so she could see his face, but the deputy edged his way beside him and spoke first. "What happened?" Deputy Whitefeather asked.

"I don't know," she said in a raspy whisper. "I was on my way to the office when the brakes failed."

Ray gritted his teeth as the medic frowned at him. "We need to get her to the hospital," the female said. "She needs tests to make sure she didn't sustain internal injuries."

"Ray?" Scarlet said in a low voice.

He squeezed her hand, feeling the tremor running through her. He couldn't blame her for being shaken. She could have been killed. "I'll meet you at the hospital, Scarlet."

The deputy gave him a questioning look, but Ray ignored it. The medics loaded her in the back of the ambulance, then the driver circled to the front, hopped in and they sped off.

"How do you know her?" Deputy Whitefeather asked.

"She was close to my father," Ray said, giving away as little information as possible. He went to examine the Wrangler while the rescue workers stowed their equipment.

When Ray had first left the ranch, he'd worked at a garage. He wanted a look at those brake lines.

The deputy stepped up beside him. "What's going on, McCullen?"

"I don't know," Ray said as he examined the car. "It looks as if her brake lines were cut."

A frown marred the tall Native American's face. "First a fire is set at your ranch, now someone cut this woman's brakes." He lifted his hat and scratched his head. "What aren't you telling me? Do you think these incidences are connected?"

Maybe. Although if Jebediah Holcutt or Arlis Bennett had set the fire at the ranch, they wouldn't have any reason to hurt Scarlet.

But Bobby Lowman had motive to do both. Still, Ray couldn't divulge family secrets to this stranger, not before he had a chance to talk to Maddox and Brett.

"I don't know. It'd be best to talk to Scarlet and see who might want to hurt her."

SCARLET WAS SO relieved that she could move her legs and that she had no serious injuries that she wanted to shout. How could she have helped the kids at the orphanage if she'd been paralyzed or injured and needed a long recovery time?

But as the staff finished running tests and cleaned the small cuts and abrasions she'd received from the shattered glass, she replayed the morning in her head.

Her car had worked fine on the way to the orphanage, but she'd thought someone was following her. She also thought she'd seen the same car near The Family Farm. Had the driver cut her brakes while she was inside with the children?

The doctor shined a light in her eyes. "Did you hit your head?"

She blinked and followed the light as he moved it from side to side. "No. The air bag and seat belt saved me."

"Good thing. Although we probably should keep you overnight for observation."

"That's not necessary," Scarlet said. "I'm a little sore, but I'm okay."

He studied her for another moment. "All right. But if you feel dizzy or nauseous, come back. You may have a slight concussion."

Scarlet quickly agreed. Hospitals reminded her of being sick when she was young. Of needles and white coats and sterile odors and…being scared and alone.

She wanted to go home.

The doctor paused at the doorway. "Deputy White-feather is outside waiting to talk to you."

She nodded, smoothing out her tangled hair as a nurse escorted the deputy into the room. To her surprise, Ray McCullen followed him inside.

"The doctor said you don't have any serious injuries?" Ray asked.

"Yes. I guess I was lucky." Especially considering the way her car was crunched. "My ribs are bruised and I'm banged up, but I'm fine."

Ray's look darkened. "I wouldn't exactly say you were lucky."

"He's right," Deputy Whitefeather said. "Ray examined your car and so did a mechanic. Your brake lines were cut."

Scarlet's breath rushed out. "You mean someone intentionally wanted them to fail?"

"Yes," Ray said through clenched teeth.

Scarlet's heart hammered with fear. "I...I can't believe this."

"Miss Lovett," Deputy Whitefeather said. "Can you think of anyone who would want to hurt you?"

Scarlet glanced at Ray, her stomach churning. Bobby was at the top of the list. "I've made a few enemies with my job," Scarlet said, hesitant to point the finger at anyone.

"Someone specific come to mind?"

She ran a finger over the bandage on her arm. "A man named Lloyd Pullman was arrested for abuse. I removed his daughter from his custody. He was irate and threatened me."

Deputy Whitefeather tugged a small notebook from his pocket and clicked his pen, then jotted down the information. "Where is he?"

"I don't know." Scarlet wet her lips. Her mouth was so dry she felt as if she couldn't swallow. "Apparently Pullman made bail yesterday."

"I'll issue a BOLO for him and bring him in for questioning."

The deputy stepped from the room with his phone, and Ray moved closer. He paused at the edge of the bed then lifted a finger to trace the bandage on her forehead. "Does it hurt?" Ray asked.

She shrugged, her skin tingling at the concern in his voice. "Not much. I'm tough, Ray. I'll be all right."

"That's not the point," he said in a gruff tone. "The point is that someone tried to kill you."

His words sucked the air from her lungs again. Pullman had reason to hurt her. And Bobby despised her.

But Ray had reason to dislike her, too. If she was gone, she couldn't demand the McCullens make good on Joe's will.

Although she couldn't imagine Ray hurting a woman.

He lifted her arm and rubbed a finger over the bruise on her wrist. "You didn't get this from the accident, did you?"

Shame washed over her. On a conscious level, she knew that when a man abused a woman, it was not the woman's fault. But she also understood the vulnerability the victim felt.

She had decided long ago not to be a victim.

Bobby had caught her off guard last night. She wouldn't let it happen again.

RAY SILENTLY WILLED his temper in check. The moment he'd seen that bruise on Scarlet's wrist he'd known it wasn't caused by the accident. Hell, he could easily see a man's thumbprint where he'd gripped her.

"How did this happen? Was it Bobby?"

She bit her lip and nodded. "He came by last night. He was…upset."

"That doesn't mean he has the right to hurt you."

"I know that." Scarlet stiffened, then slid her legs over the side of the bed. "I handled the situation, Ray."

"How did you handle it?" he asked. "Did you call the deputy?"

Her hair fell over the side of her face like a curtain of gold as she shook her head. "I stopped him," she said. "Trust me, Ray. I'm not the kind of girl who allows a guy to beat up on her. I learned that lesson a long time ago."

Her words both infuriated him and stirred admiration for her. She might look like one of those porcelain dolls his mother had collected, but she was tough as nails and had spunk.

Her legs buckled as she attempted to stand, though, and she muttered a sound of frustration as she reached for the bed to steady herself. "I don't have time for this. I had a meeting today."

Ray placed his hands on top of hers, lowering his tone to a soothing pitch. "Don't worry about your appointments. Your assistant, Hugh, said he would reschedule."

She gave him a determined look. "That meeting is important, Ray. A family wants to adopt one of the little boys at The Family Farm. Corey is counting on me."

"I'm sure it'll work out," Ray said. "Now, I'm going to drive you home so you can rest."

Her gaze met his, a myriad of emotions glittering in her eyes. She didn't like being vulnerable or in debt to anyone, he could see that.

But she was in danger, and quite possibly from her own adopted brother who was irate because of their father.

He made a split-second decision. Deputy Whitefeather would investigate Pullman.

Ray would personally look into Bobby. Hell, he'd planned to anyway.

And if he'd tried to kill Scarlet, blood kin or not, the bastard would regret it.

Chapter Eight

Scarlet winced as she climbed in the passenger seat of Ray's Range Rover. "I could have called someone else, Ray. You don't have to drive me home."

Ray's jaw tightened. "It's not a problem, Scarlet. We need to talk anyway."

Talk? Had he told his brothers about her and Bobby? Had he already found a loophole to exclude them from their inheritance?

She rubbed her forehead and waited, not sure she wanted the answer. She'd fight for her share for the children at the home.

But she was tired right now, her head ached and she needed to pull herself together.

"Where is your place?" Ray asked.

She gave him directions, anxious as he made the turn onto the street where she lived. The houses were small but well kept. The children's toys in the yards indicated it was a family neighborhood. That was one reason she'd chosen it. She liked the homey feel.

"The one at the end," Scarlet said.

Ray pulled into the drive, but made no comment. He seemed to be assessing the place, though, as they walked up the path to the house.

"Can I come in?" he asked when she unlocked the door.

She supposed she might as well get it over with. "Sure." She went inside and dropped her purse on the table by the door, then walked to the kitchen.

"Coffee?"

"Don't go to any trouble for me."

"I'm not, I need a cup," Scarlet said. "It's been a long morning."

She made quick work of brewing a pot while he simply stood and watched her, his silence as unnerving as the dark intensity in his brown eyes.

When she handed him a mug, their fingers brushed and a tingle traveled up her spine. Her gaze flew to his, and something sparked in his eyes as if he'd felt it, too.

Dear heavens, was she so shaken and lonely that she was imagining a connection between the two of them? An attraction?

Ray probably saw her as an enemy or a problem he needed to get rid of.

Ray cleared his throat. "What exactly happened today?"

Scarlet carried her coffee to the den, turned on the gas logs and sank onto the couch. Ray followed, but stood by the fireplace, his posture rigid.

"I went to The Family Farm to check on things. Then I was on my way to the office to meet with this couple about an adoption."

"Anything unusual about that? Any problems with the adoption?"

She frowned as she replayed the morning in her head. "Not with the adoption. Corey's parents died in a car accident and he has no family. So there was no one contesting the adoption, if that's what you mean."

Ray gave a small nod. "Your car was running okay on the way there?"

A shaky sigh escaped her. "Yes. Although...I thought

someone was following me when I first left home." She picked at a thread on the afghan. "It was a black sedan. I noticed it down the street when I left and it pulled out behind me."

Ray's brows arched. "Did you see the driver?"

"No." She dragged the afghan onto her lap. "Although my nerves were on edge because last night I woke up and the door to the outside was open. I locked it before I went to bed, so I was afraid someone was inside."

Ray's expression hardened. "Did you report the break-in?"

She shook her head. "I searched the house, but there was nobody inside. Nothing was disturbed or taken. I figured the police would just think I left the door unlocked, and that the wind blew it open."

Ray made a low sound in his throat. "So you had a break-in, then you thought someone was following you this morning?"

"Yes. The sedan stayed behind me for a while. I turned into a gas station to see if it followed, then the car went on."

"You know anyone who drives a car like that?"

She sipped her coffee. "No, not that I can think of."

"What about Pullman?"

"I don't know what he drives."

"But he's dangerous?"

She nodded and sipped her coffee. "He was furious that I put his daughter into foster care. But I had no choice."

"You said he threatened you?"

"He did," Scarlet said. "I told him the court would require him to attend counseling if he wanted to be reunited with her. His wife's parents are supposed to be flying in soon and are asking for custody."

Ray glanced into the fire, then back at her and her arm

where the bruise had turned a dark purple. "When did you see Bobby?"

"He came by last night." Scarlet relayed their conversation in her head. "I told him about our talk. He was furious that Joe included me in the will."

"Then he grabbed you?"

"Yes," she said, determined not to reveal how much Bobby frightened her. "But I informed him that Joe also included him, and that appeased him slightly."

"So he left peacefully?"

"Not exactly. I pulled my gun on him and ordered him to leave. Bobby doesn't like to be shown up, especially by a woman."

"So he could have come back and broken in to scare you? And he could have followed you and cut your brake lines?"

"I guess it's possible."

Ray cleared his throat then sat down beside her. When his hand touched her arm again, that same ripple of awareness shot through her.

"My brother Brett started building stables for the horses where he plans to expand the ranch operations."

She frowned, confused.

"Someone set fire to them last night, Scarlet."

Scarlet's pulse clamored as the implications of his statement set in. Bobby had been upset with her and left in a rage. And he hated the McCullens.

Had he set fire to the barns to get back at Ray and his brothers?

RAY STUDIED SCARLET, disturbed by the feelings she aroused. He should have been suspicious of her. But his father had included her in his will and had cared for her.

He was beginning to understand the reason. She helped needy children and fought for what was right.

He didn't think she was capable of hurting anyone or causing damage to someone's property, especially with a fire. He saw no signs of ashtrays or cigarettes in her house either, and didn't peg her as a smoker.

Bobby, on the other hand, might not feel he was receiving enough compensation for being Joe's son.

He hated to admit it, but Bobby had reason to hate him and his brothers.

Scarlet hugged the blanket to her with a sigh.

Ray fought the urge to pull her in his arms. "I can see the wheels turning in your head, Scarlet. What are you thinking?"

Scarlet traced a finger around the rim of her coffee mug. "I don't know what to think," she said, her voice soft. Pained. "I hate to think that Lloyd Pullman would try to kill me. And I hate even more to think that Bobby set that fire at the ranch. But I know Bobby." She rubbed her wrist in a self-conscious gesture.

Ray arched a brow. "You think he's capable?"

Scarlet leaned her head back against the sofa, making Ray feel guilty. She probably had a killer of a headache and needed to lie down. "I'm sorry, if you need to rest, I'll go."

She shook her head. "No, we might as well talk about the situation. If Bobby is responsible for that fire or my accident, it's best we face it."

Her directness made his respect for her grow. Dammit, he didn't want to like her, but he did. No wonder his father had...helped her.

"Bobby smokes, and he likes fire. He used to burn trash in the backyard all the time. A couple of times when we were teenagers some of my things went missing. I saw him set them on fire outside in a garbage can."

Ray hissed between his teeth. "Go on."

"I was ten when Joe first introduced me to Barbara.

Bobby was fourteen. He had just hit puberty and was brooding and sullen."

Ray had been angry himself at that age. Angry because his father had cheated on his mother. And because his mother was gone. Killed by a drunk driver. But he hadn't set fire to things.

"Were my father and Barbara still involved then?"

Her eyes flickered with uncertainty. "Are you sure you want to hear this?"

"My mother was dead by then, Scarlet. I'm surprised he didn't marry Barbara after that."

"I think the guilt ate at him," Scarlet said. "Joe once told me your mother was the only woman he ever loved."

Emotions crowded Ray's chest, but he cleared his throat, determined not to let them show. Anger had been his best friend for so long that he didn't know what he'd do without it. It kept him strong.

"Then why did he keep seeing Barbara?"

Scarlet shrugged. "Barbara was in love with Joe," Scarlet said. "She could be charming and hard to resist. I think she met Joe in a weak moment, maybe when he and your mother were having some trouble, and he slept with her. When she gave birth to Bobby, he felt tied to her."

"But he kept coming back," Ray said, his voice hard.

"I can't explain, Ray. I don't understand myself. There was something there. Joe cared about Barbara. After all, she had his child. And he couldn't just desert her."

But he couldn't bring her into his family, either. He'd kept them separate, a secret from Maddox and Brett.

God, Ray dreaded telling them. Had hoped he'd at least understand the problem more when he did.

"Did Barbara pressure Dad to marry her?"

Scarlet massaged her temple. "Maybe before I came

along. As I grew older, I realized that she took me in to please Joe. That she thought he might marry her if she did."

"But then he didn't marry her," Ray said. "Did she resent you for that?"

Scarlet closed her eyes on a sigh. "Some, I think. Honestly, I'd been shuffled through so many foster homes before I wound up in the group home that I was simply glad to have a home without an abusive man in it."

Ray gripped his coffee cup so hard he thought he might break it. He didn't know if he wanted to hear the rest of her story, at least not that part.

"But then Bobby turned out to be just as bad."

He sat up straighter. "What do you mean?"

"He used to taunt me when no one was around. Play mean tricks on me. Put snakes in my bed. Lock me in the closet." She hesitated. "His animosity escalated when he started drinking, and he got rough."

He sucked in a breath. "How rough?"

"He knocked me around a few times, but usually the bruises weren't visible."

"What about Barbara? Didn't she do anything?"

Scarlet made a sarcastic sound in her throat. "She didn't know. As far as she was concerned, Bobby hung the moon. He was like a chameleon—he could put on an act when she was around that made him look like a saint."

Ray gripped his hands by his sides. Damn, he was beginning to detest his half brother.

"Did my father spend time with Bobby?"

"He tried," Scarlet said. "But Bobby was difficult. He was always getting in trouble, and he was belligerent with Joe."

So he and Bobby had both given his father hell.

"Did he get in trouble with the law?"

Scarlet nodded. "I think Joe paid someone to seal his juvenile record."

"What was he arrested for?"

"Vandalism, carrying a weapon to school, breaking and entering, DUI."

"Good grief," Ray muttered.

She fiddled with her hair. "I think he pulled a knife on a guy in a bar one night, too."

Ray contemplated all she'd said. "You said Bobby smokes and that he likes to burn things?"

She touched her leg and absentmindedly rubbed the top of her thigh, drawing his attention there. And making him wonder what had happened.

"Yes."

Had he burned her with a cigarette?

His mind took a leap. "Scarlet?"

Scarlet looked up at him, her face pale. "The vandalism charge—he and some of his buddies set fire to an old warehouse just to watch it burn."

Chapter Nine

If Ray had any doubt about the validity of Scarlet's story and the fact that Joe had cared for her, the photograph in the frame on the mantel alleviated it. In the picture, Joe stood beside a knobby-kneed teenage girl with pigtails and freckles. She sat in the saddle of a beautiful palomino, her eyes lit with joy while his father looked…softer than he'd ever seen him.

Another photograph showed his father, Scarlet and a brunette woman he assumed to be Barbara around a table holding a birthday cake with Scarlet's name on it. Scarlet looked to be about sixteen and was blowing out the candles, while the skinny, tall boy next to her glared at her. The boy had to be Bobby.

Ray tried to see a resemblance between Joe and Bobby, but didn't.

"I think it's time I met Bobby." Ray stood and glanced around the small living room. "Do you feel safe here?"

Scarlet pushed a strand of that silky hair from her forehead. "Yes. I have my gun." She reached for her purse and retrieved her cell phone. "I'm going to call about getting new locks installed, too."

"Good idea. Where does Bobby live?"

Scarlet winced as she shifted on the sofa. "I don't know.

I haven't seen him in months. He just showed up out of the blue."

"Would Barbara know?"

Scarlet nodded. "Probably. But if you're going to talk to her, let's go together. She can be a charmer, but I can usually tell when she's lying."

Ray considered her suggestion. "Confronting Barbara might be dangerous, especially if she's aware her son is causing trouble."

"If she knows, she'll protect him," Scarlet said. "That's why I want to go. I need to see her reaction when she hears about my accident and the fire."

Ray's phone buzzed, and he checked the number. Brett. "It's my brother. Let me take this."

He punched Connect then walked over to the window and studied the woods behind Scarlet's house.

"I've talked with the insurance company and the arson investigator is taking care of his end of the deal," Brett said. "The deputy said Jebediah Holcutt has been out of town for two weeks on a buying trip. So he's not our guy." Brett sighed. "I also asked the foreman to have the ranch hands meet me in the dining hall."

"What time?"

"Half an hour."

"I'll meet you there."

"You sure?"

"Yeah. Someone attacks Horseshoe Creek, the McCullen men have to stick together."

Brett agreed, and Ray hung up and turned back to Scarlet. "Get those locks changed while I meet with my brother and the ranch hands. Then I'll come back and we'll pay Barbara a visit."

It was high time he met his father's mistress. He wanted

to know if she had her own agenda before he dropped the bombshell about her and Bobby in his brothers' laps.

SCARLET CALLED A locksmith as soon as Ray left, then the mechanic who'd helped The Family Farm find an inexpensive van to transport the children to activities. He also fixed up used cars and sold them, and agreed to drop off a rental car for her.

Then she phoned Faye to explain what had happened while she waited for the locksmith to arrive.

"Are you sure you're okay?" Faye asked.

"Yes, I'm fine. Just let the kids know I'll be back as soon as possible."

Faye agreed and she ended the call and phoned Hugh. He'd already left a message on her cell. "I'm really okay," she assured him. "Did you meet the Fullers?"

"Yes, and they finished the paperwork. I sent it on through, so hopefully things will progress quickly."

"You're a lifesaver, Hugh. I don't know what I'd do without you."

"Ahh, I feel the same way, Scarlet. You know I'd do anything for you."

Scarlet hesitated before responding. Lately she'd sensed Hugh had a crush on her and didn't want to lead him on. But she didn't feel that spark when she looked at him.

Not like she felt with Ray.

But she couldn't allow herself to be attracted to Joe's son. For heaven's sake, if she acted as if she wanted a romantic relationship with him, he'd probably think she was after a bigger share of Horseshoe Creek.

The doorbell dinged, and she stood, grateful for the intrusion. "Thanks, Hugh. I have to go. I called a locksmith. He's here now."

"Okay. Do you want me to come by and stay with you later? I can bring dinner."

"I appreciate it, Hugh, but I'm going to visit Barbara."

"All right. But call me if you need me."

She thanked him, disconnected and rushed to answer the door.

A chuffy balding man in a gray uniform bearing the logo of the security company stood on the stoop with a clipboard. "Miss Lovett?"

"Yes." She motioned for him to come in.

"What exactly do you want done here?"

"I need dead bolts on all the doors along with a top lock on the French doors off the patio."

"Are you interested in a security system?"

"I would like one, but this is a rental house." Maybe she would ask the owner to install one. Although he'd probably up the rent and she could barely cover her bills on her salary now.

She stepped into the kitchen while he retrieved tools and supplies from his work van. While he worked on the locks, she punched Barbara's number. She worked at a hair salon in Laramie named Sassy's, but she'd always hoped that Joe would marry her and she could quit.

Barbara finally answered on the fifth ring. "Hello."

"It's Scarlet, Barbara. I need to see you."

A long-winded, exasperated sigh. "What about?"

"Joe and his will."

Tension stretched between them for a full second before Barbara finally replied. "Fine. Meet me at the house in a couple of hours."

"I will." Scarlet said goodbye without mentioning that she would be bringing Joe's son with her.

She wanted to see Barbara's gut reaction when Ray showed up on her doorstep.

BRETT WAS ALREADY inside the dining hall when Ray arrived. He parked outside, noting two ranch hands smoking beside the back porch. His suspicious nature kicked in, but he reminded himself that it wasn't uncommon for cowboys in Wyoming to either smoke or chew tobacco.

They would have to wait until the lab analyzed DNA on the cigarette butt found at the fire to determine who had dropped it in the barn.

The low rumbling of voices echoed through the front door as he entered. The place smelled like barbecue and cherry pie. Judging from the empty plates in front of the workers at the long wooden table, dinner must have been pretty damn good.

Ray had yet to meet everyone, and heads turned as he walked past the table to join Brett.

Brett clanged a big metal spoon against one of the pots to get the men's attention.

"I appreciate you all showing up," Brett said.

Clyde Hammerstone, the head foreman waved his hand in the air. "We're missing five guys. They're moving the herd from the east pasture to the south today."

Brett nodded. "I'll talk to them when they get back. But I wanted to tell you all what happened last night."

"You had a fire, didn't you?" a young guy in a cowboy hat and red shirt asked. "I heard the siren and saw smoke."

Brett explained about losing the barn and the damage to the other one. "If we hadn't arrived when we did, we might have lost the horses."

Concerned murmurs rumbled through the room.

"What caused it?" another ranch hand asked.

"That's the problem," Brett said. "We found a cigarette butt in the barn and smelled gasoline."

The two men Ray had seen smoking stepped inside the side door, but hung back. One was big and hairy with a scar over his right eye. The other man was thinner and walked with a limp.

Clyde coughed, a shocked look in his eyes. "You think someone set that fire on purpose?"

The young man in the hat and red shirt shot up from his seat. "Is that why you called us together? You think one of us did it?"

Brett and Ray exchanged a worried look, and Ray stepped up to speak. "I'm Ray, the youngest of Joe's sons. We're not accusing you of anything. Our father hired people he could trust and handpicked each one of you."

"Damn right he did," Clyde stammered.

"We respected your daddy," an older man with a salt-and-pepper beard said. "I worked for him fifteen years. I'd never do anything to dishonor him."

Ray cleared his throat. "That's the reason we called you here. We want your help. If you've seen anyone or anything suspicious around the ranch lately, let us know."

"Could be a strange vehicle or someone sneaking around," Brett interjected. "Or maybe you know someone who wants to sabotage this horse operation."

Disgruntled looks and words echoed through the room, and the two men Ray had seen smoking outside, spoke in a hushed tone to each other.

"I'm offering a ten-thousand-dollar reward for information that leads to the culprit's arrest," Brett added.

The men shifted and muttered, charging the atmosphere with tension.

If someone on the ranch knew anything helpful, that reward might tip them into talking.

The men began to disperse, talking low among themselves, and the two smokers inched toward the back door.

Ray gestured toward them. "Brett, do you know who those guys are?"

Brett narrowed his eyes to study them. "No, why?"

"I saw them smoking outside."

"A lot of the guys smoke," Brett said.

"I know." Ray chewed the inside of his cheek. "But they looked nervous."

"I'll check the work files and see what I can find on them."

"Thanks." Ray added them to the possible list of suspects. But first he had to talk to his father's mistress.

SCARLET HAD BEEN anxious about meeting the McCullen brothers, but being with Ray the first time he met Barbara compounded her nerves.

"Did you have the locks installed?" Ray asked as he opened the passenger door to his Range Rover for her.

"Yes. Hopefully the house is more secure now."

He closed the door and went around to the driver's side while she fastened her seat belt.

"I called Barbara at work and we're meeting at her house," she said. "But I didn't mention that you'd be with me."

"Good."

"Did you find out who set the fire?"

"Not yet." Ray started the engine and pulled from her driveway. She gave him Barbara's address and he entered it in his GPS, then drove toward Laramie. "Brett called the ranch hands together and offered a reward for anyone with information."

"Money usually talks," Scarlet said under her breath.

"We'll see."

Scarlet tried to ease the tension. "I was surprised to hear that he was giving up the rodeo."

Ray shrugged. "Me, too. But I think he'd had enough of the publicity. Besides, he always had a thing for Willow

James, and when he learned they had a child, he wanted to be with them." He cast her a questioning look. "Did my father talk about Willow and Sam? Did he know Sam was Brett's?"

Scarlet shifted, uncomfortable with the question. Joe had shared some of his feelings about the distance between his sons, but those had been private, heartfelt confessions. "He didn't say anything specific about the little boy. But he definitely missed you and Brett and wanted you to come home."

Ray fell silent and clenched his jaw as he drove, and Scarlet decided not to push the subject. They all had emotional baggage and were grieving. Only time and forgiveness would heal the wounds.

The rest of the ride passed in silence.

Scarlet hadn't visited Barbara in months and was surprised to see that she'd let the yard get overgrown. The shutters on the house needed painting and the bushes trimming.

Ray parked and turned to her. "Barbara probably hated us, didn't she? She blamed us for keeping our father from her."

"Ray, I can't begin to explain their complicated relationship."

"Was she prone to violence like her son? Did she ever hit you?"

Scarlet's face flushed with heat. She was torn between reality and gratitude for what Barbara had given her. Yet at the same time, Barbara's dysfunctional relationship with Bobby and with Joe had been difficult, especially since she was caught in the middle.

And according to Bobby, an outsider.

"Scarlet?"

"No, she never hit me. She was actually nice to me at

first. But as Bobby became more troubled, she had to give allegiance to her *real* child." She clutched the door handle. "I became part of the problem, another person who agitated Bobby and took time from Joe that he should have given her son." She sighed and opened the car door. "When I turned eighteen, I moved out on my own."

Ray's eyes darkened with questions. "How did you manage? Did my father help you?"

Was that derision in his voice?

"No, Ray. He offered, but I worked after school and summers waitressing and saved enough money to rent a room in an older house. I landed a scholarship and eventually earned my degree in social work."

Ray cleared his throat. "I'm sure Dad was proud of you."

"He was proud of you and your brothers, too, Ray." Scarlet touched his hand, aware again that her body tingled at the touch.

A sea of emotions clouded Ray's eyes, but the front door opened and Barbara appeared. Scarlet dropped Ray's hand, and she and Ray walked up the sidewalk together.

"Hello, Barbara," Scarlet said. "This is Ray McCullen. He wanted to meet you."

"Oh, my goodness," Barbara said with a slightly false ring to her voice. "This is a surprise. Scarlet should have told me you were coming."

"I know it's sudden, but I figured it was time we met." Ray shook her hand.

"Yes, I suppose so," she said as she released his hand. Then Barbara pulled Scarlet to her for a hug.

Scarlet stiffened, unaccustomed to her affection.

The moment didn't last long, either. Barbara whispered in her ear so only she could hear, "You're more devious than I gave you credit for, Scarlet. Now that Joe is dead, you're cozying up to his son to see what else you can weasel out of the McCullens."

Pain knifed through Scarlet at Barbara's accusation. Did Barbara really think she would sleep with Ray for money?

Chapter Ten

Ray didn't know what to expect from Barbara, but at least she hadn't shut the door in his face. Scarlet's earlier comment about Barbara's fake charm made him instantly wary.

Judging from Scarlet's pained expression, the woman must have said something hurtful when they'd hugged.

Scarlet straightened and pulled away from Barbara, her look chilly. "Ray and I just met," she said flatly.

Barbara invited them in and offered coffee, but they both declined. While he and Scarlet followed the woman to her den, he studied her, searching for whatever had drawn his father to her.

Barbara was probably in her late forties, attractive with wavy brown hair. Her voice dripped with honey, as if she was from the Deep South.

Her house was modest with simple furnishings, although she definitely liked frills and had decorated with yellow, orange and bright green, versus the earthy tones of the ranch. Of course, his father had lived with three sons, so the feminine touch had been missing in their home for years.

This house was in a neighborhood as well, no sprawling ranch with stables or barns or livestock, although he had noticed a gardening shed in the back. Had Barbara been content here or had she wanted a big place like Horseshoe Creek?

"I wondered when we would meet," Barbara said. "I expected that your father would introduce us at some point, but I guess he never felt comfortable doing that." Resentment laced her voice. "You're the youngest, right?"

Ray nodded.

"You knew about me?"

"Yes. When I was young, I saw the two of you together."

Barbara tapped a cigarette from a pack on the table and rolled it between her fingers. Ray remembered the cigarette butt they'd found at the fire. Was this one the same brand?

"I never meant to hurt your family and neither did your father. But he was going through a tough time back then and...well, I'm not going to make excuses. It...we just happened. I fell in love with Joe."

She held the cigarette up and looked at it for a moment, then tossed it on the table. "I'm trying to quit."

"How's that working?" Scarlet asked.

"Easier to give up than it was to give up Joe."

Ray waited, hoping she'd elaborate. But as he scanned the room, he saw a photograph of his father with Barbara, Bobby and Scarlet on the mantel, and betrayal burned his gut. It was sobering to see the truth—that his father had two different families and that he loved both of them.

But in loving them, he'd hurt everyone involved.

"Joe loved your mother, Ray," Barbara said, drawing him back to the conversation. "Funny, but I even admired him for that loyalty. I guess that's why I hung in there. I kept thinking that one day he'd love me enough to bring me home to Horseshoe Creek. That he'd be that loyal to me."

"If he'd been that loyal, he wouldn't have cheated," Ray said.

Barbara's look softened. "It's more complicated than that, Ray."

"I thought you weren't going to make excuses." He couldn't help the bitterness in his voice.

And despite Barbara's declaration of love, his father hadn't brought her back to the ranch or made her his wife. She must have resented that.

Barbara toyed with her bangs, pushing them aside. "I'm not. Joe knew he'd disappointed you when you found out about the affair. He never forgave himself for that."

Yet he hadn't totally given up Barbara, either.

"His guilt is the reason he couldn't bear to bring me and my son to the ranch."

That made sense. "That's one reason I'm here. About your son."

She angled her head, her eyes probing him. "You know about Bobby?"

Ray nodded. "Yes, Scarlet told me."

Disapproval glinted in her eyes as she looked at Scarlet. "I suppose you explained how you came to live with me."

"Yes," Scarlet said. "I told him about Joe volunteering at the children's home."

"He was devoted to that place," Barbara said, a note of fondness in her voice. "Apparently, when he was growing up, his best friend was in foster care. When he learned about the home near Pistol Whip, he dropped by to see what it was like. Then he decided to help make it a better place." She twined her hands together. "He got attached to Scarlet and brought her home."

"But your son wasn't too happy about that, was he?" Ray asked.

Barbara's smile faded. "He was an adolescent. Bobby needed more of Joe, not to share him…"

The sentence trailed off, and Ray filled in the blanks. He didn't want to share him with someone who wasn't even a McCullen.

Ray cleared his throat. "I'd like to meet Bobby."

"Really?"

"Yes, I figured we should introduce ourselves before the reading of the will."

She narrowed her eyes. "What's really going on, Ray? Scarlet? I know you're not here to suggest we all get together and be one happy family."

No, that wasn't in the plans, Ray thought. But if he explained about the fire, she'd know he suspected her son of arson and she'd warn him.

Then Bobby might run.

THE FRONT DOOR swung open, and Bobby loped in. Scarlet tensed, and Barbara jumped up to greet him.

"Son, I wasn't expecting you this early," Barbara said, her voice shaky. "Dinner won't be ready for a while."

Bobby's gaze raked over Scarlet then Ray, a sardonic look in his eyes. "I didn't know you'd invited *her*." He gestured toward Ray. "And you included one of my brothers. Now that's the real shocker."

Scarlet rubbed the tender spot on her thigh where he'd burned her with the cigarette. "Hello, Bobby."

Ray stood and extended his hand. "This is obviously awkward for both of us, Bobby, but I figured it's time we met."

"Yeah, about damn time." Bobby stared at Ray's proffered hand, but didn't accept the invitation to shake. "Now what is it you really want?"

Bobby strode toward the bar table by the fireplace and poured himself a drink. He didn't bother to offer Ray one, but leaned against the bar, animosity radiating from him. "You wanted to meet the illegitimate black sheep of the family?"

"I wanted to meet you, yes. I didn't know about you until Scarlet told me."

"Yeah, you can always depend on Scarlet to insert herself in the middle of family business."

His resentment rang through loud and clear, but Ray refused to indulge Bobby's self-pity. They were not going to make friends here, so he chose to be direct. "Where were you last night, Bobby?"

A muscle ticked in Bobby's jaw. "Why do you wanna know?"

"Did you go to Horseshoe Creek after you left my house, Bobby?" Scarlet asked.

Bobby tossed back his drink, but before he could speak, Barbara cleared her throat. "Bobby was with me."

Bobby jerked his head toward Barbara, then a grin curved his mouth. "That's right." He crossed the room and slung his arm around his mother's shoulders. "Mom and I had dinner and watched a movie, didn't we?"

"Yes," Barbara said with a tight smile. "I cooked Bobby's favorite chicken-fried steak."

Scarlet doubted that. Bobby had never stayed home with his mother when she lived with them. He was always out on the prowl.

Bobby rubbed his belly. "Dad always loved Mom's home cooking. She makes the best huckleberry pie in Wyoming."

Scarlet wanted to slap her brother for being so rude. He was intentionally trying to hurt Ray.

"Now, Ray," Bobby said as he took a menacing step toward Ray. "I have stuff to do. You got something you came here to say, say it."

Ray gestured toward the door. "Why don't we talk outside for a minute?"

Barbara looked panicked, so Scarlet tried to play mediator. "It's okay, Barbara. Ray just wants to discuss Joe's will."

Barbara's eyes flickered with surprise. "I see. He came here to try to buy us out of our share."

So she *had* received notification from the lawyer.

"That's not true," Ray said.

Barbara fidgeted. "Whether you and your brothers like it or not, Bobby was Joe's son," she said. "He lost out all his life. He deserves what Joe left him and you aren't going to deprive him of one damn cent."

"THAT'S NOT MY INTENTION," Ray said, although Bobby and Barbara were definitely a complication in his life.

Bobby squeezed his mother's arm. "Let me handle this, Mom."

Ray stepped outside with Bobby, braced for a confrontation. Storm clouds rolled in, darkening the sky, matching his mood.

Any man who hit or threatened a woman was a bully and a coward. McCullen men had been taught to respect and protect women, as well as those smaller and weaker than them, especially from people like this scumbag.

He's your half brother. Joe's other son, his flesh and blood.

It didn't matter.

Or did it? Could Bobby be redeemed?

"Scarlet told me that the three of you are named in the will," Ray began.

"Mom was right. You came to pay me off so I won't show up and burst your family's happy little bubble."

Ray ground his teeth. "My family doesn't live in a bubble. We've had our share of problems, but we don't take our frustrations out on women."

Bobby's nostrils flared. "You don't know what it's like to be the kid your daddy hid."

"Is that the reason you set fire to our barns?"

Bobby's lip curled into a sneer. "I don't know what you're talking about."

"That's right. You were here last night with your mother, weren't you?"

"You're damn right. Besides," Bobby said in a sinister voice, "if I'm named in the will, why would I go making trouble before the reading? I'm not stupid. I want to know if my father finally did right by me."

He had a point. Unless Bobby had some idea what had been left to him and he was ticked off about not getting more.

Ray squared his shoulders. "You'd better be telling the truth, because if I find out you set that fire, you're going to jail. And you'll never see a penny of that inheritance."

Bobby jerked him by the collar. "Listen to me, McCullen, your daddy screwed me over as a kid. He'd better not screw me over now that he's dead. And if you try to stop me from getting what's mine, you'll be sorry."

Ray met his gaze with a warning one, then he gripped Bobby's hand and peeled his fingers away. "Touch me again and *you'll* be sorry." He gestured toward the house where he could see Scarlet through the window. "About Scarlet—"

"My relationship with her is none of your business."

Ray gave him a menacing look. "I'm making it my business. Touch Scarlet again, and I'll kill you."

"WELL, I TAKE it that didn't go too well," Scarlet said as they drove away.

Ray clenched the steering wheel. "Bobby is a coward and a bully. If he hurts you or threatens you again, let me know."

Scarlet's heart fluttered. "Ray, you don't have to go to war for me. I can handle Bobby."

He gave her a dark look, emotions glittering in his eyes. "He may be blood related to our family, but he's not a

McCullen. My daddy taught us never to hurt a woman or child."

"Joe tried to teach him that, too," Scarlet said. "And Bobby pretended like he followed the rules. Until Joe wasn't around."

"Like I said, he's a coward."

Her cell phone buzzed as he drove toward her house, and she checked the caller ID. It was a text from Hugh asking her to dinner. She'd turned him down so many times she thought he'd get the message. She quickly texted back that she was busy.

"Who is that?" Ray asked.

Scarlet shrugged. "My coworker."

"Is there a problem?"

"No."

Silence fell thick for a minute. "You know we didn't talk about old boyfriends," Ray said quietly. "Is there someone in your past who would have cut your brake lines to get back at you for some reason? Someone other than Bobby?"

Scarlet's face flushed. "There aren't any old boyfriends, Ray."

Another heartbeat of silence, and she shifted, wishing she'd worded her answer differently. She didn't want Ray to see her as a total misfit. "Bobby hates me more than anyone. Although Lloyd Pullman has his reasons, too."

"The deputy has a BOLO out for him," Ray said. "Hopefully he'll pick him up, and if he cut those lines, he'll go to prison. Then you won't have to worry about him anymore."

No, but she'd still worry about his little girl until the child's grandparents were granted custody. Children needed parents, even if they weren't available all the time. They needed to feel loved.

Ray made a sound in his throat. "You know as much as I dislike Bobby, his argument made sense. Why would he sabotage us or the ranch before he learns what he inherited? Not only would he be hurting himself, but he's risking jail when he stands to have a piece of Horseshoe Creek."

Scarlet contemplated what he'd said. "That's true. Although sometimes when Bobby's drinking, he simply reacts instead of behaving rationally."

"I can see that," Ray agreed.

"How about other enemies Joe might have made? He was well-known in the ranching community."

"True. And Maddox just arrested a cattle-rustling ring. We're looking into some men associated with that."

They reached her house, and he turned down the drive. Her head was throbbing now, the day's events wearing on her. An image of her Wrangler diving into that brick building flashed back, and she shivered and reached for the door.

Ray caught her arm before she got out. "Are you sure you're all right?"

"Yes. I'm just tired and I have a headache."

Ray gently lifted her chin with his thumb and forced her to look into his eyes. Her heart fluttered again at the tender concern in his expression. "Call me if you need anything."

His gruff voice made tears burn her eyes. For a moment, heat flared between them, and she felt suddenly drawn to Ray. He was more like Joe than he realized. Of course, Joe had been a father figure.

Ray was no father figure; at least not to her. He was… sexy. Strong. Protective. A tough cowboy who made her think of kisses on a long hot Wyoming night. Of touches that weren't fatherly or brotherly, but titillating.

Her gaze zeroed in on his mouth, and she had the insane desire to kiss him.

He leaned forward, and she did the same, her body aching to be held, her lips craving the feel of his. His lingered near hers, his gaze darkening, as if he was torn.

His heavy sigh echoed in the air—a sigh filled with need, desire, hunger…doubt.

She should pull away. Stop this insanity before it got started.

But their lips touched, and Scarlet closed her eyes and lost herself in the moment.

HUNGER BOLTED THROUGH Ray as Scarlet's lips touched his. God help him, he couldn't resist.

He cupped her face in his hands and deepened the kiss, savoring the sweet taste of her desire. She lifted one hand to his shoulder, and he thought she was going to push him away. She *should* push him away, *dammit*.

But she stroked his arm instead as if she craved his warmth and strength, igniting his own need to protect and comfort her. She had been through hell today. She could have died in that accident.

And she was still in danger.

That realization brought reality crashing back. He had no business touching her. Kissing her. Wanting her.

His own father had considered her a daughter. Which made them what—almost half brother and half sister?

But they weren't related, and he hadn't grown up in the same house with her as an adopted sibling. She was nothing but a stranger.

Albeit a desirable, sexy one that was getting under his skin.

That realization made him pull away.

Passion lingered in Scarlet's gaze, her lips were swollen from his kiss, her face flushed with passion. He dropped his hands to his sides and balled them into fists to keep from pulling her toward him again.

He couldn't get involved with her. Maddox and Brett didn't know about Barbara, much less her or Bobby.

No telling how they would react. It would be even worse if he slept with Scarlet.

Slept with her? Yeah, that was where this was going. He had to put a stop to it before he crossed the line.

Chapter Eleven

Scarlet's body tingled with need as Ray pulled away from her. Why had he stopped?

That kiss was...tender and erotic, and she wanted it to go on forever.

"I'm sorry, Scarlet." Self-deprecation tinged his voice. "I shouldn't have done that."

Confusion washed over Scarlet, along with the feeling that she had done something wrong. Barbara's crude accusation about cozying up with Ray to get something from him taunted her. "No, I'm sorry, Ray. I...didn't mean to come on to you."

Ray's look darkened. "You didn't. It was me. I...it's just been a tense day."

"Yes, it has been." Although kissing him had soothed her anxiety and made her body hum with a different kind of tension. One that could bring them both pleasure.

"This thing between us is just..."

"Natural," Scarlet said softly. At least it was for her. And she was not the kind of girl who slept around. She could think of maybe one other man who'd made her feel hot from just a look.

And that had ended disastrously.

So would this if she allowed it to continue.

He removed his black Stetson and scraped his hand through his hair. "I was going to say it's complicated."

Silence stretched between them thick and unsettling. "I know. I…"

"Feel like we're almost family?" Ray asked.

Scarlet frowned. "No. You and I aren't related, Ray."

"Yeah, but my father thought of you as the daughter he never had."

Scarlet didn't know how to respond to that. "I understand that bothers you, but Joe had a big heart. The fact that Joe took me in and cared for me doesn't diminish the love he had for you and your brothers."

Ray released a weary breath. "Maybe not. But he should have had the guts to come clean before he died."

She supposed she couldn't blame him for being bitter. Joe had put them all in an uncomfortable spot. The man had a heart of gold, but dealing with confrontation was his weakness.

"You're right. I…wish Joe had told you about me and Barbara and Bobby."

Pain flashed in Ray's eyes. "So do I. I don't know how my brothers are going to react, but I owe them the truth."

She wet her lips with her tongue, but she could still taste Ray's heady flavor. She wanted more.

Of course, Ray might have a girlfriend. He was virile, sexy, a single bachelor. For all she knew he might even be engaged or have a child somewhere.

Ray's phone buzzed and he checked the caller ID. "It's Deputy Whitefeather. I'd better answer this."

Scarlet tugged her jacket around her and lifted a hand to wave goodbye, then hurried to her front door. If she didn't let Ray go now, she might invite him inside.

With her body still aching for him, that would not be a

good idea. She didn't want him to think she was trying to seduce him because she had her own agenda.

RAY WATCHED SCARLET go inside her house with mixed emotions. Hunger still heated his blood.

But he had done the right thing by calling a halt to that kiss.

"Ray," Deputy Whitefeather said. "I haven't been able to locate Pullman. He's not at his apartment or job."

"Where does he work?"

"A fertilizer plant. His boss said he's going to can him if he doesn't come in tomorrow."

Another thing the man would be ticked off about. Abusers generally laid the blame for their faults on everyone else.

He glanced back at Scarlet's, wondering if he should stay and watch her house in case Bobby or Pullman showed up.

"I called his cell and left a message for him to check in with me. I told him if he didn't, I'd issue a warrant for his arrest."

"Did you find out anything from Scarlet's car?"

"Not yet. I dusted the brake lines and car for prints, but didn't find anything useful. Whoever cut those lines must have worn gloves."

Smug bastard probably thought he'd get away with it. But Ray would find out who'd tried to kill Scarlet.

"I met Bobby Lowman, Scarlet's adopted brother." Even though he'd only just learned about Bobby, a smidgen of guilt nagged at Ray for implicating his own half brother in a crime. "It's possible he had something to do with her crash. They've had differences over the years. And he has a rap sheet."

"I'll do a background check on him," Deputy Whitefeather offered.

Ray thanked him, but kept silent about his relationship

to Bobby. Although Bobby had made a valid point about motive, Ray still wasn't ready to dismiss him as a suspect in the fire.

"Since you mentioned Arlis Bennett offered to buy Horseshoe Creek, I thought I'd have a talk with Bennett myself."

"I'll meet you at his place," Ray said.

"I don't know if that's such a good idea, Ray."

"I don't care." Ray started the engine and headed toward the Circle T, Boyle Gates's spread. "If he wants my daddy's land and is trying to push us into selling, I have a right to confront him face-to-face."

"All right, Ray, but let me do the talking," Whitefeather said. "I don't want this to turn into something bad. Maddox wouldn't like it if I had to arrest his brother."

Ray grimaced. Except Bobby was their brother, too, and if he had sabotaged them or tried to kill Scarlet, they would arrest him anyway.

Scarlet swallowed a painkiller for her headache and had just laid down hoping for a nap when her doorbell dinged. Almost asleep, she silently willed whomever it was to go away.

Although Ray might have returned…

Her heartbeat picked up at the thought. Foolish of her. She and Ray and his brothers and Bobby had a messy situation to contend with.

She traced a finger over the porcelain doll Joe had given her and grief nearly overwhelmed her. It was painful enough to lose her surrogate father. She didn't need to fall in love with his son.

Keeping her heart intact was something she had to do in order to survive. And Scarlet was a survivor.

The doorbell dinged again, and she threw aside the blue-

and-green Handmade by Willow quilt she'd bought at Vintage Treasures, and rubbed her eyes as she padded to the living room.

"Scarlet, it's me, Hugh. Let me in."

She groaned. More than anything she wanted to be alone right now, but she knew Hugh well enough to realize that if he was worried, he wouldn't leave without seeing for himself that she was all right.

They had met at the orphanage when they were kids, and he'd glued himself to her side. He was upset when she moved in with Barbara and Joe, but they'd stayed friends. Later when she went to college, she had encouraged him to get a degree and he'd surprised her by following in her footsteps.

When he'd landed the job at Social Services, they had reconnected.

But he wanted more. He'd hinted at it several times.

Unfortunately he wasn't her type.

No. Big, tough, dark-eyed, Stetson-wearing cowboys were her type. Men like Ray.

Lord help me.

"Scarlet?"

"I'm coming," she called as she unlatched the door. When she pushed it open, he stood on the other side, his reddish-brown hair in a mass of messy curls where he'd rammed his hands through it. One of his nervous habits that he hadn't been able to break.

"I'm so glad to see you," he said as he elbowed his way inside. "I've been worried sick about you."

Scarlet closed the door and followed him to her den. The room was chilly, so she lit a fire, grabbed the afghan off the sofa and wrapped it around her as she sank onto the couch. It might be rude, but she didn't intend to offer him a drink or even coffee because that would only prolong the visit.

"I told you on the phone that I was all right," Scarlet said. "Thank you for talking to the Fullers."

"No problem. It's all set with the judge for the final hearing."

Relief surged through Scarlet. "Then little Corey will finally have his family and can begin healing."

Hugh studied her, his hazel eyes more astute than she'd like at the moment. He could always tell when she was upset or worried.

"The crash wasn't accidental, was it?"

She shook her head. "No. My brake lines were cut. The deputy sheriff is investigating."

Shock widened Hugh's eyes. "It was that Lloyd Pullman, wasn't it? He's a violent man."

Scarlet shrugged, reluctant to point fingers at anyone. What if she named Pullman or Bobby and they hadn't cut her brakes? "I don't know yet, Hugh."

"Didn't Pullman threaten you when you removed his daughter from his home?"

"Yes, and he's out on bail," Scarlet said. "So be careful, Hugh. If he shows up at the office or anywhere else, do not engage with him."

"I won't, and neither should you." He studied the pictures on the mantel. When he turned to her, questions flared in his eyes. "Who was that man you were with earlier?"

Scarlet's pulse hammered. "How do you know I was with someone?"

Hugh's gaze darted sideways as if he was nervous. Another one of his tells. "He showed up at your office after the accident. And he brought you home, didn't he?"

An uneasy feeling rippled through Scarlet. "You were watching?"

"No. I mean I drove over and happened to see you get out of the car."

Had Hugh seen her kiss Ray? She wrapped the afghan tighter around her. She didn't know how to begin to explain her relationship with Ray. Especially since that kiss. "That was Ray McCullen, Joe McCullen's youngest son."

His brows climbed his forehead. "I wasn't aware you knew the brothers."

"I don't. Not really." Although she had kissed Ray and wanted to kiss him again. But his brothers would probably hate her when they discovered who she was. And there might be a court battle... "But I had to meet them because of Joe's will."

"He included you?"

"Yes. And Bobby."

Hugh grunted. "Let me guess. The McCullens didn't know about you or Bobby and they aren't too happy about his will."

Scarlet couldn't deny the obvious. "No, they didn't know about us. Ray does now, though."

"Do you think he'd hurt you?"

Scarlet bit back a laugh. Ray McCullen might be dangerous to her heart, but he was like Joe through and through. The one thing she was sure of was that he respected women.

Still, he and his brothers might try to exclude her from Joe's inheritance.

"No, Hugh, Ray won't hurt me. I think it was probably Pullman or Bobby who cut the brake lines. But I'm fine now, and the deputy is investigating." She stood. "I have a headache and would like to rest."

Hugh touched her shoulder. "Let me stay, Scarlet. I can watch out, make sure no one bothers you."

She couldn't sleep with Hugh in her house. He was making her more and more uncomfortable. "Thank you. I appreciate the offer. But the most important thing you can do to help me is to man the office and make sure things are running smoothly there. I don't want anything to ruin Corey's placement."

"Of course I'll do that. But…"

The concern in his eyes hadn't faltered. "But what? Is there something you're not telling me?"

He shifted and jammed his hands in his pockets with a sigh. "I'm sorry, Scarlet. I wanted to take care of this for you, but I decided you ought to see it."

Scarlet's shoulders knotted with tension. "See what?"

Hugh pulled an envelope from his jacket and handed it to her. Scarlet noted her name on the outside spelled with letters cut from a magazine.

"You opened it?"

"It wasn't sealed, and when I saw those cutout letters, I got worried. So I looked inside. It's not pretty, Scarlet. It's downright scary."

Scarlet took a deep breath and opened the envelope, then gasped. There was a picture of her taken from a distance as she exited her office.

Then another photo—except in this one her face had been crossed out with a black marker and the edges had been seared.

Chapter Twelve

Ray studied Arlis Bennett as he and Deputy Whitefeather seated themselves in the man's office. Bennett was Boyle Gates's cousin and seemed to have moved right into the Circle T, apparently hoping to keep Gates's operation running smoothly in his absence.

"You come to check up on me?" Bennett asked the deputy.

Ray scanned the room, noting the dark furnishings, photographs of Gates holding an award he'd won for his beef, then the ashtray on Bennett's desk. Was he a smoker?

"I thought we should talk." Deputy Whitefeather maintained a neutral expression, which Ray was beginning to realize was normal for the Native American. His wide jaw and high cheekbones framed dark, intense eyes that seemed to view everyone in the world with suspicion.

Bennett steepled his big beefy hands on top of the massive desk. "Do I need my lawyer?"

"I don't know, do you?" Deputy Whitefeather asked.

Ray liked the way the deputy operated. He was so still and calm that it was unnerving.

Bennett shifted. "No. My cousin asked me to move in and take care of things while he's away."

"You mean while he's incarcerated," the deputy pointed out.

Bennett's jaw twitched. "Yes. But if you've looked

into my background, and I'm sure you have, you know I'm clean."

"Boyle appeared to be clean, too," Ray pointed out, "but he took advantage of his ranch hands, my father and other ranchers in the area."

Bennett's ruddy face formed a scowl. "As I said, I'm here to clean up the business. You decide to take me up on my offer?"

Ray squared his shoulders. "No, my brothers and I aren't interested in selling any part of Horseshoe Creek. That land stands for family." He'd fight for the McCullen legacy if he had to.

Bennett drummed his fingers on the desk. "Let me know if you change your mind."

"We won't," Ray said firmly. "Although I believe someone might be trying to sabotage our plans to expand."

Bennett's bushy eyebrows drew together. "What are you talking about?"

"Someone set fire to the new barns we were building," Ray said.

Bennett made a low sound in his throat. "*Good God*, you think I'm responsible?"

Ray met the man's stare head-on. "I don't know. Are you?"

Bennett stood, jowls shaking as he clenched his jaw. "That's ridiculous. Just because my cousin crossed you, you have no right to accuse me of arson. Besides," he said, his voice rising with irritation, "maybe you set the fire so you could frame me and destroy the Circle T. If you run us out of business, Horseshoe Creek will prosper even more."

Ray shot up, furious. "That is ridiculous."

The deputy laid a hand on Ray's shoulder to keep him from attacking the man. "Bennett, where were you last night?"

Bennett glared at both of them, then flattened his palms on the desk and leaned forward, cheeks bulging. "I had dinner at the Cattleman's Club. You can ask the other twenty-five people there."

Ray gritted his teeth. He was making an enemy of Bennett, and for business's sake that wasn't a good idea. But he had to know the truth.

"You could have hired someone to set the fire," Ray said.

Bennett cursed and swung a thumb toward the door. "I'm through with your accusations and insults. Get out, McCullen."

"I would like to speak to your hands," Deputy Whitefeather said.

Bennett went very still, his calm demeanor returning, although his voice held barely controlled rage. "Then get a damn warrant."

"I don't need a warrant to have a conversation with them," Deputy Whitefeather said in a tone that brooked no argument.

A vein throbbed in Bennett's forehead. "Then I'll call my attorney."

Whitefeather shrugged. "Fine, if you have something to hide, go ahead."

Bennett picked up the phone on his desk. "I don't have anything to hide, but I don't intend to be railroaded for something I didn't do or let you ruin my reputation." He glared at McCullen. "You're going to regret this, McCullen."

"That sounds like a threat," Ray said.

"Take it however you want to take it. But when the other ranchers around here find out you're pointing fingers at the locals, no one is going to be your friend."

Ray understood the threat now. Bennett would blackball the McCullens in the ranching community, and that wouldn't be good.

Two could play that game. "You think they trust you after what your cousin did?" Ray asked.

Bennett's face heated. He knew Ray was right.

But had he or one of his people set that fire?

"Print me a list of your employees and call them together," Deputy Whitefeather said. "If you have nothing to hide, I'll be out of your hair in an hour or two."

Bennett muttered another curse, called his foreman, clicked a few keys and hit Print, then handed the deputy a list.

"I'm going with you to talk to my men," Bennett said.

Whitefeather stood. "Then let's get to it."

Ray wanted to accompany them, but his phone was buzzing. Brett. He snatched it up. "Yeah?"

"Gus Garcia wants to meet with us. He might have a lead on the arsonist."

SCARLET STARED AT the picture, fear mingling with shock. She flipped the envelope over and searched for an address or postal address. Except for her name, though, the envelope was blank.

"Where did you get this?" she asked Hugh.

"It was on the floor when I returned from lunch today. Someone slipped it under the door."

"Did you see anyone hanging around the office who could have left it?"

Hugh jammed his hands in his pockets. "No. The Fullers were the only ones who stopped by today."

"How about a strange car? Maybe in the parking lot or down the street."

"I didn't see anything," Hugh said, his voice slightly defensive. "If I had, I'd tell you, Scarlet."

"I know you would, Hugh. I'm just trying to figure out who left this. It might be the same person who cut my brake lines."

"Are you going to give it to the sheriff?"

Scarlet laid the envelope on the table by the sofa. "He's out of town, but I'll show it to Deputy Whitefeather. Maybe he can lift some prints from the envelope or picture."

Although she doubted he left prints. Whoever had sent this was clever and had probably worn gloves.

Hugh reached for her hand and pulled it into his. "I know this is scary, Scarlet. I'll be happy to stay here with you. You shouldn't be alone tonight."

Uncomfortable with the possessive look in his eyes, Scarlet squeezed his hand, then pulled away. "Thank you, Hugh, but I'm exhausted and really want to rest."

He gestured toward the sofa. "I'll stay out here."

"Hugh," Scarlet said, her voice firm as she led him to the door. "It's been a really difficult day, and I need to be alone. I'll see you at the office tomorrow."

He stood in the doorway for a few more seconds, lingering, obviously hoping she'd change her mind, but the longer he stalled, the more irritated she became.

"There is something you can do for me," she said, anxious to smooth over the tension. "Please open up the office in the morning. I'll be in after I drop this envelope at the sheriff's office."

He finally agreed and left. Scarlet locked the door, then watched him drive away, but just as she was about to head back to bed, lights flickered along the street.

She couldn't make out the type of car, but it slowed as it passed her yard, and suddenly the window slid down, giving her a view of the man's face.

Pullman.

"WHAT DO YOU think about Bennett?" Ray asked as Deputy Whitefeather walked him to his vehicle.

"I don't like him, but we need proof that he's done something illegal," Whitefeather said. "He could easily have paid someone to set the fire. I'll look into his financials."

"Does he have a record?"

"Nothing that I've found. But I'll keep digging." He gestured toward the man who was standing on his front porch watching them. "He's definitely suspicious, though."

"Let me know what happens with his hands. Brett called. I'm meeting him to talk to one of our men who might have information about the fire."

They shook hands and agreed to stay in touch. Ray jumped in his Range Rover and drove back toward Horseshoe Creek. The dark clouds thickened, casting a grayness to the land as night set in.

He wondered what Scarlet was doing, if she was resting. If she was safe.

Dammit, he shouldn't care so much.

He veered down the drive to the ranch, scanning the pastures and stables in search of trouble. The memory of those flames shooting in the sky haunted him.

The scent of smoke still lingered in the air as he drove past the burn site. Crime scene tape roped off the area, a reminder of the violence against them. Brett had moved the animals to another stable nearer to the main house.

They couldn't chance one of their horses being injured or…worse.

Sweat broke out on his brow at the very thought. Cruelty to animals ranked almost as high as cruelty to women and kids.

Brett had suggested they meet at Brett's cabin to keep other hands from suspecting that Garcia might be ratting one of them out.

Brett's wife, Willow, was outside playing horseshoes with Sam, the son she and Brett had had together. She looked up and waved, and he got out of his SUV, strode over and ruffled Sam's hair.

"Looks like your daddy's teaching you to be a pro," he said.

Sam grinned and tossed the horseshoe. "He gave me a riding lesson this morning."

"You'll be in the rodeo before you know it."

Willow shook her finger at him. "Don't start that, Ray."

He chuckled, enjoying the light moment, and glad Brett had finally come home.

Maybe it was time he returned for good, too.

He froze, wondering where that thought had come from. He was a rambling man. His detective work took him wherever the case led.

No ties. No one to question him.

Or to love him.

Although love had never been high on his priority list.

Brett appeared on the porch and waved him in. "See you in a bit, Sam. Keep practicing and we'll have a Mc-Cullen tournament."

Sam high-fived him, then Ray climbed the porch. Garcia was already inside with a cup of coffee when Ray entered.

"You remember Ray, Gus?"

"Yes, sir." Gus stood, wiped his hands on his jeans and shook Ray's hand. Brett had told him about Gates setting Garcia up for cattle rustling, and that the leader of the gang had threatened to hurt Garcia's family if he ratted out the real rustlers. Thankfully, Brett had convinced Garcia to talk and he'd given Garcia's family protection. Once the arrests were made, Maddox had offered Gus a job on the ranch.

"You have information about the fire?" Brett said.

Gus rubbed his jaw with work-roughened hands. "I don't

like to speak bad about the men. Most of them work hard and are like me, they need the jobs."

"I understand that you've had it tough, Gus," Ray said. "And trust me, no one will know that you talked to us. But our horses could have been killed in that fire."

"*Sí*, I understand." Gus spread his hands on the table and looked down at them. "I'm sorry, but I don't know who set the fire."

"Then why did you want to see us?" Ray asked.

"There is someone who has a grudge against your family."

Brett patted his back. "Who are you talking about?"

Gus sipped his coffee as they seated themselves around the table. Ray tapped his foot on the floor as they waited on Gus to talk.

He drummed his fingers on his leg. "One of the new hands, Marvin Hardwick, he used to work for Boyle Gates."

Ray and Brett straightened. "Hardwick, he's one of the guys I pointed out to you when we met at the dining hall, isn't he, Brett? He was smoking outside."

"Yeah, the other guy was Stan Romley. I looked at their employment files but they seemed clean."

Of course they could have faked information, Ray thought.

"You're sure Hardwick worked with Gates?" Brett asked.

"Yes, sir." Gus lifted his head, the mole at the corner of his mouth twitching as his lips thinned. "He worked for Gates when they framed me for the cattle rustling."

"Did he help set you up?" Brett asked.

Gus shrugged. "I don't know, and it don't matter now. But I heard him talking about those barns. He said he rode out there to check on the progress."

The chair legs rattled as Brett pushed back from the table. "I'm going to get him and make him talk."

Ray's phone buzzed. He checked the number. Scarlet.

He started to ignore it. He and Brett had work to do here. They finally had a lead. Although someone had tried to kill Scarlet earlier, so he couldn't ignore the call.

He excused himself and punched Connect. "Scarlet, I—"

"Ray, it's that man Pullman. He's outside my house."

Ray's heart stuttered with panic. "Keep the doors locked. I'll be right there."

Chapter Thirteen

Rain began to splatter the windshield, and the wind picked up, shaking the trees with its force as Ray drove toward Scarlet's. Another car zoomed up on his tail, and Ray cursed as the headlights blinded him.

He tapped his brakes to signal to the driver to get off his tail, but the car sped up instead. Clenching the steering wheel in a white-knuckled grip, Ray pressed the accelerator, maneuvering the Range Rover around a curve.

The car accelerated as well, riding him so close that Ray thought he was going to ram into him. Furious, he spotted a dirt road to the side and steered his vehicle onto it, his tires churning over gravel and rock as he tried to slow.

But he hit a slick patch and skidded, a boulder coming toward him. Determined not to collide with it, he swung the steering wheel to the right and barely missed it, then skidded another few feet until he lurched to a stop only inches away from a thicket of trees.

Breathing hard, he checked his rearview mirror, searching for the car, then cursed again when he spotted it barreling toward him.

Ray's instincts surged to life. He needed his gun.

He reached for the dash to unlock it, but suddenly the car slammed into his rear, jarring him. Cursing again, he scrambled to reach the gun, but before he could unlock the dash, a hulking man yanked open his door and jerked him from the SUV. Ray raised his fist to punch the man and tried to get a look at his face, but it was so damn dark and rainy all he could see was a shadow.

The man dodged the blow, then shoved Ray to the ground on his knees. He heaved a breath, spun around and rammed the man in the belly with his head, hoping to knock him backward. This SOB wasn't going to get the best of him.

Ray knew how to fight.

But just as he tackled him, something slammed into his lower back. Metal. A tire iron?

Pain screamed through his kidneys, and he dug his hands into the muddy ground to steady himself. Before he could recover, another blow came, this one higher. The blow knocked the wind from his lungs and sent him sprawling on the ground.

He spit out dirt and mud, swaying as he pushed himself up to fight. He grabbed the man's ankle, hoping to slam his fists into his knee and bring him down, but another blow from the tire iron to his kidneys sent him writhing in pain again.

Taking advantage of the moment, the bastard kicked the hell out of him. His boots pounded into Ray's back, then his knees. Ray struggled to breathe through the pain and get up, but the man had the strength of three men and knew where to hit.

Ray rolled to the side to dodge another blow, but the tire iron connected with the side of his head. Shock from the blow disoriented him.

He inhaled and grabbed at the man's legs to pull him down, but the tire iron caught him on the side of the head again and Ray collapsed.

He fought to stay conscious but he lost the battle, and the damn world went black.

SCARLET WATCHED THROUGH the window as Pullman slowed his truck and parked on the street. He had chosen a strategic spot giving him a view of her house.

Was he going to break in, or did he just want to frighten her?

Rain drizzled down, and he rolled the window up slightly, leaving it open just enough so she could see his menacing face in the shadows of the streetlight.

The tip of his cigarette glowed bright orange in the dark, smoke curling out the window and disappearing into the fog.

She inhaled sharply, determined not to succumb to panic. Ray was on his way. She was safe in the house.

Still…she rushed to her nightstand and retrieved her gun, then returned to the window.

In spite of her resolve to be strong, fear nearly choked her. He was gone. Not inside the truck.

Was he going to break into the house?

Heart pounding, she pushed back the curtain and scanned the street. He wasn't in front of the truck. Or at the rear.

She searched around the car, then her yard, but she didn't spot him anywhere. Sweating now, she inched to the door and peeked through the peephole.

Nothing.

A noise echoed from the back, and she startled, tightening her fingers around the gun handle. Forcing herself to be very still so she could hear, she listened for sounds of an intruder. The rain was coming down steadily now, the wind rattling the house.

Suddenly something banged the window in the back. A tree limb? Or was it Pullman?

A bead of perspiration trickled down the back of her neck as she inched through the living room and peered into the hallway leading to the laundry room and back door.

The wind whistled through the eaves of the house. Then another noise. Someone jiggling the door knob?

Terrified and praying Ray showed up soon, she gripped the gun at the ready. If Pullman tried to hurt her, she would shoot him.

A thumping started at the back door, and she held the gun in front of her, aiming it at eye level. If he was inside, she wanted him to realize she was armed.

Glass shattered, and her panic mushroomed.

"I have a gun," she called out. "And I'm not afraid to use it."

Suddenly the lights flickered off, pitching her into the dark. The scent of her own fear pervaded the air, and she fought a scream as a noise erupted behind her.

Back in the living room? How…

She couldn't wait on Ray. She snatched her phone from her pocket to call 911. A knock at the front door made her jump again.

It was loud, pounding.

Her hand trembled as she inched back to the front room. The knock sounded again, louder this time.

Then she looked through the peephole and Pullman was standing on the porch, his beady eyes glaring at her through the tiny hole.

RAY SLOWLY ROUSED back to consciousness. His back throbbed and his eyes were blurry, but he blinked, the world finally sliding into focus.

Damn. Some bastard had not only run him off the road, but he'd gotten the best of him and beaten him to a pulp.

That rarely happened.

He wouldn't get away with it.

He wiped blood from his right eye that was already swollen half-shut and peered around his surroundings to make sure his attacker was gone. His Range Rover was still sitting there, but the sedan was gone.

Relieved, he pushed himself up from the dirt, wincing as pain knifed through his lower back. Hell, he'd probably be sore for days.

Mentally retracing the past hour as he stumbled back to his vehicle, he scrambled to recall details of the man's face. But it had been dark and that first blow to his kidneys had sent his world into a blur. He thought the car was black, but it could have been dark green. He hadn't seen the license plate.

Hand shaking, he wrenched the car door open and fell into the driver's side. He fumbled for the keys, then realized they weren't in the ignition and spit out an obscenity. Had his attacker taken them so he couldn't follow?

More blood trickled down the side of his face and he swiped at it with the back of his hand, then searched the seat and floor, but the keys weren't there.

Frustration screamed through him, and he turned to scan the dirt by the car. It was so dark the ground and grass blended together, so he grabbed the flashlight he kept in the backseat and used it to light a path.

Pain throbbed through his body as he searched the bushes and trees. But either the man had taken the keys with him or thrown them into the woods.

It would take all night to find them.

Time he didn't have. Scarlet had called because Pullman was outside her house. She sounded terrified. He'd been on his way to her.

He bellowed in anger. He didn't have time to search the damn woods. He needed to get to Scarlet.

He hurriedly limped back to his SUV. Seconds later, he hot-wired the vehicle, then sped onto the road, slinging gravel in his haste to turn onto the highway.

He quickly glanced left and right, looking for that car again, but the road seemed deserted. Scarlet's terrified voice echoed in his ears, and he punched the accelerator.

If Pullman had hurt her, he'd never forgive himself.

Lights nearly blinded him as a car raced toward him. He tensed, bracing himself in case his attacker had returned, but the car flew past and disappeared the other direction.

Ray reached inside his pocket and grabbed a handkerchief, then wiped at the blood on his face as he maneuvered the curves and turns until he reached Scarlet's neighborhood.

The houses were spread apart, a few lights glowing from inside, cars parked in the driveways. He spotted a pickup parked in front of Scarlet's, and slowed before he reached it, scouting out her yard in search of the man.

Not wanting to alert Pullman of his arrival, he parked two houses away. Unsure if the man was armed, he jimmied open the locked dash and grabbed his weapon. Gripping his gun, he opened his door and slid from the seat, scanning Scarlet's front yard, then the side of the house for Pullman. Woods backed up to her property, which made it a great place to hide.

Anxiety knotted his shoulders as he inched behind some bushes and crept toward Scarlet's. He spotted a shadow to the side of the house and paused, studying the movement. It went from the side to the back, then disappeared.

Gritting his teeth, he crept closer, then inched his way into Scarlet's yard, staying close to the house and bushes so

Pullman wouldn't see him coming. By the time he reached the corner, Pullman had disappeared, though.

He circled the back, searching the shadows and trees, but didn't see the man anywhere. Dammit, was he hiding back there?

He walked to the opposite side of the house, but didn't spot him, then eased his way to the front again.

Pullman stood on the front porch knocking.

What was the bastard doing? Then the truth hit him—he'd been toying with Scarlet. The sick creep wanted to terrorize her.

Keeping his gun at the ready, he inched up the front to the porch. The stairs creaked as he climbed them, and Pullman swung around.

He slowly raised his hands. "Hold on, man. Don't shoot."

Ray kept his weapon trained on the man. "You found out she survived the car crash and came here to finish her off, didn't you, you bastard?"

Pullman actually looked surprised. "What are you talking about? I came here to apologize."

"That's a lie and we both know it. You tried to kill her."

"If I'd tried to kill her, she'd be dead," Pullman said through gritted teeth.

Ray didn't know whether to believe him or not. "I think you did. And now you're trying to intimidate her."

"She took my daughter from me." Pullman's lips curved into a sneer. "I'll do whatever I have to in order to get her back."

Ray removed his phone from his pocket to call the deputy. "Then go through the courts. And if I find evidence to prove you cut her brake lines you're going to jail for attempted murder." Ray snagged the man by the shirt. "I can have the deputy pick you up or you can get off her property now."

"Who the hell are you to tell me what to do?" Pullman snarled.

Ray gave him a lethal stare. "Someone you don't want to mess with. Now, Miss Lovett is filing a restraining order against you. If you bother her again, I'll give you a taste of your own medicine, then lock you up. And trust me, then you will never see your child again."

SCARLET HEARD VOICES echoing outside the door and looked through the peephole again. For the past half hour, Pullman had tormented her by circling her house, knocking on the windows and then running to the next one.

He wanted her to know that he could get to her.

He already was, just with his mind games.

Her breath gushed out in relief as Ray escorted the big man to his truck. Pullman slid in the seat, then gave her a sinister leer. In spite of what Ray had said, he wasn't finished with her.

Ray shoved the door shut, then Pullman took off, tires squealing as he screeched away. Scarlet hated that she was shaking and that he'd gotten to her.

But he had.

Ray strode back to the porch, his face illuminated by the streetlight. *Dear God.* His eye was bruised and swollen, his cheek purple and blood had dried on his forehead and below his eye.

She swung the door open, her heart racing. "Ray, my God, what happened to you?"

"I had an accident." He must have seen the fear in her eyes because he pulled her into his arms. She collapsed against him, so grateful to see him that she could barely breathe.

"He didn't hurt you, did he?"

"No, come on in." Forgetting her fear over Pullman, she

led him through the door and ushered him to the kitchen where she could examine his injuries. He was limping slightly and winced when he sat down. She wet a wash-cloth in the sink, brought it to him and tilted his chin up so she could clean his wounds.

"That looks like it hurts." She gently dotted away the blood with the wet cloth. "You need a doctor, Ray. Where else are you hurt?"

He caught her hand in his and stilled her movements. "I'm just banged up, don't worry about me."

"But you're all bloody and you have a black eye." She narrowed her eyes remembering her own accident. "Tell me what happened. Did someone cut your brake lines, too?"

He shook his head, then allowed her to continue clean-ing his forehead and eye. "Some man tried to run me off the road. I veered onto a side road and managed to stop, but he followed me and beat the hell out of me." Self-derision laced his voice. "I can't believe he got the better of me."

Scarlet gently stroked his hair from his forehead. It was sweaty and sticky with blood. But at least the cut above his eye wasn't too deep.

Still, she didn't know who was shaking more, her or him. "I don't think you'll need stitches. Show me where else you're hurt."

Ray shook his head. "I told you I'm fine. I'm just sorry I was late getting here. Did Pullman try to break in?"

A shudder coursed up Scarlet's spine as she remembered his taunting. "Not exactly."

Ray took her hands in his, the worry in his eyes touch-ing a tender chord inside her.

"What does that mean?"

Scarlet sighed and averted her eyes. More than any-thing she wanted Ray to wrap his arms around her again. To hold her.

Kiss her.

Stay with her tonight and keep her safe.

"Scarlet?"

"He just taunted me, Ray. He ran from window to window, banging and making noises, tapping at the windows, acting like he was going to come in."

"Sick bastard," Ray muttered. "He claims he didn't cut your brake lines, but we'll find a way to nail him. And you're going to take out a restraining order against him."

Scarlet nodded. "What about you? Did you recognize the man who attacked you?"

Ray shook his head. "No. But I'll file a police report."

Scarlet's gaze met his, the tension between them thick with worry and fear and…something else. A sexual tension she hadn't felt in a very long time.

She needed to step away. Remember all the reasons she shouldn't get involved with Ray. His brothers didn't even know about her. They had his father's will to work out.

"You should have called the deputy," Scarlet whispered.

Ray's breathing grew heavy, his gaze steeped in desire. Then he reached up and tucked a strand of hair behind her ear.

"I was too worried about you. Too afraid Pullman had broken in."

His voice triggered a warm tingling to start deep in her womb. She wet her suddenly dry lips, aching to touch him more intimately.

Ray murmured a sound of need. "Dammit, Scarlet, what are we doing here?"

"I don't know," she whispered. But she was helpless to stop the ache in her body and in her heart.

Ray must have sensed her need because he traced a finger over her lips with one finger, then drew her to him and closed his mouth over hers.

RAY'S BODY HEATED with need as Scarlet parted her lips for him. Images of his crash, of her accident, of that maniac Pullman getting to her flashed in his head, and he deepened the kiss, desperate to feel her against him.

He needed to know she was safe.

Her lips felt soft, tender. Her body quivered against his. He stroked her back and plunged his tongue into her mouth. She sighed into him, a breathy sound filled with desire, and he lifted her hair from her neck, then trailed kisses along the smooth column of her throat.

She tilted her head back, and he tasted the sweetness of her skin, making him want more. She tossed his Stetson to the sofa, then dug her hands into his hair, and he groaned, then they walked backward to her bedroom.

Raw need consumed him, and he pressed her against the wall, then eased open the top buttons of her blouse, dropping kisses along the sensitive skin of her throat as he pushed the fabric aside. She rubbed his calf with her foot, moving her body against his in invitation.

His sex thickened, hardening at the contact, and he made quick work of the rest of the buttons, exposing a dark blue lacy bra that barely covered her breasts.

He sucked in a breath. His body ached for her like he hadn't ached for anyone in a long time.

Bruises marred her torso, from the air bag, he assumed. But a couple of other scars caught his eye. Two small round ones that looked like cigarette burns. Then a crisscross one that had probably been made by a knife.

She must have realized he was looking at them, because she covered herself with her hands. "Ray?"

"Shh, it's okay. How did you get them?"

She tried to pull away, but he pressed his body into hers. "Tell me. Was it a foster parent? Bobby?"

"Both," she said in a pained whisper.

Dammit to hell. Pure rage engulfed him, but he held himself in check. Scarlet had obviously seen her share of angry men who took their anger out on women.

He would not be one of them.

Instead, his gaze met hers, and he tried to tell her with his eyes that she could trust him. She must have read the silent promise because she lifted her head and kissed him again, this time her kiss filled with a greedy kind of hunger that invited him to love her.

He wanted her. The sex would be epic.

But if he made love to her, would he be able to walk away from her later?

Chapter Fourteen

Chapter Fourteen

Fueled by passion, Ray kissed her deeply, then trailed his tongue down her breasts to those scars and gently kissed each one of them. Scarlet moaned and tunneled her fingers in his hair again, as he stroked her nipples through the thin lacy barrier.

She whispered his name, and he quickly unfastened her bra, his breathing husky at the sight of her breasts spilling into his hands. Her skin was soft, her breasts full and round, her nipples perfect rosebuds.

They stiffened at his touch, making his mouth water, and he lowered his head and drew one turgid pebble into his mouth. Scarlet whispered his name on a moan, letting him know she liked it, and he suckled her until her body quivered.

She reached for the buttons on his shirt and unfastened them, then slid her hands inside, raking her nails over his chest. He inhaled at her touch, his body humming to life with erotic sensations.

Then her finger slid over his bruised ribs and he winced. "I'm sorry, Ray."

"You can make it better," he said in a gruff voice.

His shirt fell to the floor and he walked her backward to the bed, but as they started to lie down, she shifted to move something.

A doll.

Ray froze, his heart thumping. That doll…the blond hair, big baby blue eyes…

For a moment, he felt as if he'd been sucker punched. "Where did you get that doll?"

Scarlet's eyes were glazed with passion, but his question dampened the mood. "Your father gave it to me."

Ray had no idea why that bothered him, but it did. "My mother collected those dolls," he said with a pang to his chest.

"I know," Scarlet said softly. "Joe told me about her, that she loved the dolls. That's the reason he wanted me to have one."

An image of his mother with those dolls haunted him. For some reason, it seemed wrong that his father would give away one of the few things they had left of hers. Not that he wanted the dolls, but…they had been special.

It felt like another betrayal, just as he'd felt betrayed when he'd seen his father with Barbara as a child.

Scarlet gently touched his arm. "Ray?"

He flinched slightly. Then his phone buzzed, and he yanked it from his pocket and checked the caller ID. Brett.

Damn.

Scarlet was half naked. His body shouted for him to take her to bed and finish what they'd started.

But that doll and his brother's call reminded him what was at stake. He'd felt betrayed by his father—how would his brothers feel if they discovered they had another brother, and that he had slept with the girl Joe had considered his daughter?

The girl he'd kept secret. The one who was going to inherit part of their family legacy.

"I…" Ray grabbed his shirt and backed away. He hated

himself for leaving Scarlet when she looked so beautiful. And so damn vulnerable.

His phone buzzed again, and he gestured toward it as he inched to the doorway. "I'm sorry, Scarlet. I have to take this."

She looked hurt, but she reached for her robe on the side chair. Ray left the room, feeling like a bastard.

SCARLET YANKED ON her robe and belted it, a flush creeping up her neck. She felt naked and lonely and...hurt.

What had she done wrong? Ray hadn't seemed repulsed by her scars. But the sight of that doll triggered a different reaction.

She closed her eyes, battling tears. She refused to cry over his rejection. But how dare he get her all heated up and needy, then leave her wanting more.

She tiptoed to the doorway and saw him pacing by the fireplace, his phone pressed to his ear. Maybe the phone call had been really important.

God knows they'd both almost been killed today. And the danger wasn't over. Someone was sabotaging the ranch, and Pullman wanted revenge against her.

All the more reason she needed Ray.

Needed him? The thought sent fear streaking through her. She had never needed a man before. And she couldn't allow herself to need Ray.

But this was a different kind of feeling, she silently reminded herself. She craved comfort, a pair of strong arms to lean on, a night of lovemaking to relieve the sexual tension brewing between them. Being with Ray would have reminded her they were both still alive.

Except...for that doll... The truth dawned, making her chest squeeze. It reminded him of the mother he'd lost as a child, and the fact that his father had betrayed her with Barbara.

That Joe had a second family. One who stood to throw a monkey wrench into their family business by taking part of it.

She wasn't part of the family.

That was the reason he didn't want her to have the doll. She was not a McCullen and no matter how much Joe loved her, she never would be.

A desolate feeling overcame her.

If Ray didn't want her to have that doll, he certainly wouldn't want her to have a piece of his father's ranch.

"WHAT HAPPENED TO YOU, Ray? You ran off like something was wrong."

Ray chewed the inside of his cheek. He hated lying to his brothers and had to tell them about Bobby and Scarlet soon.

But not tonight.

"I'm sorry. I had some business to attend to, then a man came out of nowhere, ran me off the road and attacked me."

"What?" Brett's voice rose an octave. "Are you all right?"

"Yeah, just bruised." His ego had taken a beating, too.

"Do you know who it was?"

"No, a big guy, two hundred pounds, scruffy. But it was dark and he came at me so fast that I didn't get a good look at his face."

"You talk to Deputy Whitefeather about it?"

"Not yet. But I will." Scarlet had to talk to him about getting that restraining order, too.

"Why did you call, Brett?"

A heartbeat of silence passed, and Ray regretted his defensive tone. They were brothers. Brett didn't have to have a reason.

"I found Hardwick, but I haven't talked to him yet.

I'm outside The Silver Bullet where I spotted his truck. I thought we might confront him together."

Ray glanced at the bedroom. In light of the night's events, he hated to leave Scarlet alone. What if Pullman returned?

Yet…if he stayed he'd be tempted to go back inside, apologize for being a jerk and ask her to give him another chance to love her.

He'd call the deputy to come over. Whitefeather could get the restraining order underway.

"I'll meet you at the bar in ten minutes."

Brett agreed, and Ray fought guilt over keeping silent about Scarlet. But he would tell Brett soon. He'd have to.

Tucking his shirt back in his jeans, he fastened his belt, retrieved his gun and Stetson and went to the bedroom and knocked. Regret needled him as Scarlet opened the door.

Pain glinted in her eyes, but she quickly lifted her head and masked it.

"That was my brother. We may have a lead on the arsonist. I'm going to meet Brett to question the man."

"Fine."

Her curt tone told him all he needed to know. She was ticked off.

"I'll call Deputy Whitefeather and tell him about the attack on me, and about Pullman. I'll ask him to come by and get the ball rolling on the restraining order."

She gave a quick nod. "Thanks, Ray."

He hesitated, tempted to pull her against him again and assure her everything was all right. But he couldn't promise that it would be, not until he talked to his brothers.

And not until he found out the truth about the fire at the ranch.

"Scarlet, I—"

"Just go, Ray," Scarlet said. "You were right to put a halt to things."

Her look dared him to argue. He couldn't. He agreed with her.

But that didn't mean he liked it. Hell, he still wanted her with a vengeance.

SCARLET PROMISED RAY she'd keep the doors locked until the deputy arrived.

But she was seething inside. She might understand Ray's hesitation over sleeping with her. And she should be grateful he'd left. But her body still tingled with need.

She wasn't the kind of girl who slept around. In fact, she'd actually climbed into bed with only two men in her life. Well, not men. Boys.

Once at seventeen when she'd first entered college, and she was young and foolish and thought she was in love. But she was inexperienced and happily-ever-after to her meant exclusivity and marriage. To him it had meant sex with no hassles.

The second time, she was twenty-one and had dated a prosecutor, but he'd decided to join a law firm that focused on defending hardened criminals. He'd wanted the money—and she hadn't been able to stomach the people he represented. Not after the violence and abuse she'd seen in her own life and through her work.

She made a cup of tea to settle her nerves, then heard the rumble of an engine and hurried to the window to make sure Pullman hadn't returned.

The deputy's car rolled to a stop and turned in the drive. Relieved, she set her tea on the coffee table, then unlocked the door.

Deputy Whitefeather looked solemn as he strode up the

steps. "Miss Lovett, Ray McCullen called and said you had trouble."

"Yes." She gestured for him to come in. "I need a restraining order against Lloyd Pullman."

"Tell me what happened."

She offered him some coffee, but he declined. So she led him to the den, explained the circumstances with Pullman's daughter and described the way the man had tormented her earlier.

The twisted man didn't realize that by threatening her he'd hurt his chances of regaining his child.

RAY SPOTTED BRETT'S truck when he pulled into the packed parking lot of The Silver Bullet.

Brett met him in the parking lot as he climbed from his SUV.

His brother caught his arm and frowned. "Hell, man, you *did* take a beating."

Ray had forgotten about his black eye and the bruises. "Don't remind me." He should have been faster to his gun.

"You been inside?" Ray asked.

Brett shook his head. "Figured I might need backup."

Ray nodded, and they walked into the bar together. Cigarette smoke clogged the air, and the room smelled of beer and whiskey. Country music was piped through the speakers, some sad song about a man losing a woman, which made him think of Scarlet.

Except Scarlet was not his woman and never would be.

Laughter and conversation echoed from the bar and a dart game was underway in the back corner. Two biker-looking dudes occupied the pool table.

Ray swept his gaze through the crowded room, and Brett nudged his elbow, then gestured toward a young man in his twenties with a goatee, cowboy hat and boots. The watch on his left arm looked expensive, and so did the signet ring he wore on his right hand.

Cowboys didn't usually make that kind of money. Maybe he'd earned his by working for the enemy.

Brett started toward the bar and Ray followed. He strode to the opposite side of the man while Brett moved in on the other. The man had just tossed back a shot and ordered another.

Brett indicated that he and Ray wanted a shot, and the bartender set three on the bar.

Hardwick went to pick up his glass, and Brett laid a hand on his shoulder. "We need to talk, man."

Ray set a hand on the other. "Yeah, Hardwick."

Panic flashed in Hardwick's eyes, the kind born of guilt. He slid off the barstool and sprinted through the crowd, pushing people in his haste to escape.

"Dammit," Brett muttered.

Ray cursed, too, then took off running.

Chapter Fifteen

"I can't believe he's running!" Brett said under his breath as Ray and his brother chased after Hardwick.

It certainly made the man look guilty.

Ray shouldered his way through the crowded bar, keeping his eyes on Hardwick as the ranch hand pushed his way to the front door. Brett darted the opposite direction hoping to cut Hardwick off before he reached the exit.

A brunette in a low-cut blouse touched his arm. "Buy you a drink, cowboy?"

Ray shook his head and forged on, catching glimpses of two other women attempting to snag Brett's attention. Although Brett had been a flirt and had had women galore when he was on the circuit, he barely noticed these ladies. He was completely devoted to Willow.

Ray spotted Hardwick elbow a couple aside in his haste to escape, then he darted out the door. Ray rushed by the bar and made it to the exit before Brett, but Brett caught up quickly as they ran outside.

Ray paused to scan the parking lot, the music still blaring behind them, this time the song about a man and his dog.

"There, he's getting in his truck." Brett gestured at a black pickup and a custom tag that read "BIGMAN". Hardwick wrenched the door open and jumped in.

"Stop, Hardwick!" Ray shouted as he jogged through the parking lot.

By the time he reached Hardwick's truck, Hardwick was screeching from the parking lot.

Ray grabbed his keys from his pocket and motioned to Brett. "Come on, we'll take my Range Rover."

The two of them jogged to his SUV and got in. He fired up the engine and roared from the parking lot in chase. Tires squealed as Hardwick sped up and veered onto a side road.

A little sedan pulled out in front of Ray. He cursed and slowed, irritated that another car was coming toward him, and he couldn't pass it.

"Up there!" Brett pointed to the truck.

"I see it." Finally the oncoming car zoomed by, then another. Ray sped up and zoomed around the sedan. Accelerating, he rode the edge of the road until he made the turn.

Hardwick raced around a curve ahead. Ray punched the gas and the Range Rover lurched forward, eating the distance between them.

Hardwick took a turn too fast and an oncoming gas truck appeared out of nowhere. Hardwick swerved to avoid it, but lost control and his truck left the road, flying toward a ravine.

Hardwick swung the truck to the right to avoid careening over the edge and diving into the hollow, but the truck spun out, then flipped to its side and skidded into an embankment. Glass shattered and metal crunched, sparks flying as it finally crashed to a stop.

"I'll call it in," Brett said as he reached for his phone.

Ray slowed the Range Rover and pulled onto the shoulder of the road, then jumped out and sprinted toward the vehicle.

It was upside down, the passenger side crunched against

the embankment. He dropped down to his knees to look inside. The air bag had deployed and Hardwick was strapped in, upside down, and blood dripped down his face.

His eyes were closed and he wasn't moving.

"The ambulance is on its way," Brett said as he ran up. "How is he?"

"Hard to tell," Ray said. "He's unconscious."

Ray reached through the broken glass and felt for a pulse. "He's alive, but pulse is weak."

A siren wailed in the distance, indicating help was on its way. Hardwick groaned and tried to open his eyes.

If he died, they'd never get any answers. "Why did you run, Hardwick?"

Another moan, and the man turned his head toward Ray.

"Did you set the fire at the barns on the ranch?" Brett asked.

Hardwick moved his head as if to shake it no, but it was difficult to tell. A siren wailed and the ambulance careened down the road toward them.

"Tell us," Brett said. "Did you set the fire?"

"No," Hardwick mumbled.

"You were working for Bennett?"

Hardwick coughed up blood, then faded into unconsciousness again. The ambulance roared to a stop, a fire engine on its tail.

Ray and Brett stepped aside as the rescue workers hurried toward them.

He didn't know if Hardwick would make it or not. But if he regained consciousness, they'd force him to talk.

SCARLET RUBBED HER ARMS, wondering where Ray was.

"I'll make sure the restraining order is in place and that Pullman knows about it," Deputy Whitefeather said. "Ray said he asked him about cutting the brake lines but he denied it."

"I wouldn't expect him to confess."

"If he did it, Scarlet, we'll find some way to get him."

"Thanks," Scarlet said. "I didn't want it to come to this."

Deputy Whitefeather gave her a sympathetic look. "It's not your fault. From what you've told me about the man, it sounds as if he has a pattern of abuse. He needs serious counseling and anger management classes."

"He also needs to stop drinking," Scarlet said. "I told him all this, but it only made him more furious."

"Sometimes it takes the court and a little jail time to knock some sense into people."

Even then it might not work. "The sad thing is that his child suffers. That little girl needs a father."

"Every kid does," the deputy said in a gravelly voice.

Scarlet didn't know the deputy very well, but she sensed they might be kindred spirits.

"Your father wasn't around?"

He shook his head, his long ponytail sliding over one shoulder. "No, I grew up on the reservation with my mother. I didn't even know my father's name until recently."

"I'm sorry," Scarlet said softly. "It sounds like you and I have some things in common."

The deputy's eyes darkened and, for a moment, she thought she detected some strong emotions pass through them. Pain. Anger.

He was a handsome man. Big-boned, tall, tan skin, high cheekbones, eyes dark brown and soulful. Sexy.

But he didn't stir the same kind of need inside her that Ray McCullen did.

He heaved a breath and stood. "You know the McCullen brothers?"

Scarlet twisted her hands together, not sure how to answer that question. "I just met Ray. But I knew their father, Joe."

Deputy Whitefeather's brows rose in question. "You knew Joe McCullen?"

"Yes." Scarlet thought of Joe and had to smile. "I lived in the children's home outside Laramie. Joe volunteered there. He also donated money to build a new house. We named it The Family Farm."

"Really? That was nice of him."

"He had a soft spot for kids without families." Scarlet debated how much to tell him, but chose her words carefully. "He brought horses over twice a month and gave us riding lessons. I guess you could say he became a father figure to everyone there."

The deputy's jaw twitched. "I never knew the man myself, but I heard good things about him. Maddox took his death hard."

"I guess he was closest to Joe," Scarlet said.

"Yeah, I guess so." He narrowed his eyes at her. "You must have been upset, too."

Scarlet's chest ached with grief. "Yes, I loved him. He actually helped place me in another home when I was around ten. He…was always there for me." It made her sad to think she'd never see him again.

With all the trouble that had happened this week, he would have been the first person she would have called.

Now she'd called on his son Ray…

But that had to end. When his brothers discovered the truth about Barbara and Bobby and her, the McCullens probably wouldn't want them in their lives.

The deputy's dark gaze met hers, and once again, Scarlet had the uncanny sense that he wanted to say more. Turmoil colored his expression, one she didn't quite understand.

"Here's my card, Scarlet. Don't hesitate to call if you need anything."

"Thanks, Deputy Whitefeather. By the way, did Ray tell you that someone ran him off the road and beat him up?"

"Yes." His demeanor changed, suspicions flaring in his eyes. "It does seem like someone's out to get the McCullens."

He couldn't possibly think she'd hurt Ray or the McCullens. But Bobby might… "I hope you find whoever did it. It could be the same person who set that fire."

The deputy squeezed her arm. "Don't worry, Scarlet, we'll get to the bottom of this. Just keep your doors locked and call me if Pullman shows up again."

She locked the door when he left and prayed no one else came to her house tonight. Not Pullman or Bobby.

Or Ray.

If he returned, she wouldn't be able to resist asking him to stay.

It took forever for the firefighters to extract Hardwick from his truck, board him and transport him to the hospital.

The medics said he had a concussion, cuts and abrasions, and they were worried about internal bleeding.

Ray drove Brett to retrieve his truck at The Silver Bullet, then they met at the hospital. If Hardwick regained consciousness, they wanted to be there to question him.

Ray went straight to the coffee machine while Brett called Willow to check on her and Sam.

Ray brought his brother a cup of coffee and sipped his own. It was weak but warmed his throat, and after being up most of the night he needed the jolt of caffeine.

Brett removed his Stetson and raked his hand through his hair. "Thanks, man."

"Look, Brett, we may be here for hours. Why don't you

go on home to Willow and Sam?" A twinge of jealousy niggled at Ray. Brett and Maddox both had families now, women who loved and cared about them.

Nobody gave a damn about him.

He'd always liked it that way. But Scarlet's face flashed in his mind—an image of her nearly naked, her cheeks flushed with passion—and he had an urge to go back to her tonight.

Brett glanced up at him, a sheepish look on his face. "I do miss them, but I don't want to let you or Maddox down, Ray. Finding out who set fire to those barns is important. They might try again."

Ray's gut tightened, feeling more connected to his brothers than he had in years. "You're right. If they attack the ranch, they attack us. All the more reason you should go home to your wife and son," he continued. "They need you. And someone should be on the ranch in case something else happens."

"I left Clyde in charge."

"I know he cares about Horseshoe Creek," Ray said. "But not like we do."

A grin tugged at Brett's face. "That mean you're not going to sell out and leave?"

"I'm not selling," Ray said emphatically. Although he didn't know if he'd stick around. Coming back home to Pistol Whip had triggered the sense of betrayal he'd felt at his father's affair.

It had also stirred good memories of carousing with his brothers when he was small. Of riding across the ranch, working with his hands and living off the land.

Not that he'd give up his PI business. He liked his work. But he could do that here...

He gritted his teeth. Was he really thinking about moving back?

"Seriously, Brett, go home. I'll call you if Hardwick wakes up and I talk to him."

Brett looked reluctant, but finally agreed. "Thanks, man."

Ray nodded, grateful Brett would be at the ranch tonight in case more trouble arose. If Bennett had hired Hardwick or someone else to set the fire, he could have others working for him.

Just as Brett left, his phone buzzed. Deputy Whitefeather. "Yeah?"

"I talked to Scarlet. She's safe now. I'll take care of the restraining order."

"Thanks. Any word on the DNA from that cigarette?"

"Not yet. I'll call the lab and ask them to hurry it up."

"Thanks. I'm at the hospital. We got a lead from one of our hands about a worker named Hardwick. Brett and I tracked him to The Silver Bullet but he ran. We chased him in our car, but he crashed. He's in the ER now."

"You want me to meet you there?"

"No, just find out what you can on Hardwick. If we can trace financials between Bennett and him, or if Hardwick has a record, we could use it to force him to talk."

"I'm on it, but so far on paper Bennett looks legit."

"Keep at it."

"I will." The deputy hesitated. "Call me if you remember anything else about the man who attacked you."

Ray agreed, and the deputy ended the call. Ray sipped his coffee and paced while he waited on the doctor to let him speak to Hardwick.

A half hour later, the nurse finally relayed the news that Hardwick was going to make it, and that he was awake.

Ray followed her to the ER cube, his body tense as he approached the man. Hardwick was battered and bruised, a bandage around his head, one arm in a sling. His eyes looked bleary as he followed Ray's approach.

"Looks like you're going to make it, Hardwick. I talked to the deputy. He'll transport you to jail as soon as you're released."

Hardwick's eyes widened in fear. "What the hell for? I haven't done anything."

"It was your cigarette butt in the barn, wasn't it? Did Bennett pay you to set the barn on fire?"

Hardwick coughed, his voice weak. "No, just to report back what you were doing."

Ray heaved a breath. So he admitted being at the barn. "I don't believe you," Ray said. "I think he wanted you to sabotage our place and that he has more plans, maybe something bigger."

Hardwick broke into another coughing fit, the machine beeping that his blood pressure was dropping.

The nurse rushed in with a scowl. "You'll have to go, sir."

Ray leaned closer to Hardwick. "If you didn't do it, give me a name."

Hardwick coughed again, struggling with each breath, and the nurse grabbed Ray's arm. "I said you need to leave."

Ray held firm and growled in Hardwick's ear. "Tell me, dammit."

"Romley," Hardwick choked out. "Talk to him."

Ray nodded, yanked away from the nurse and strode to the door. Romley was the hand he'd seen smoking with Hardwick.

He hurried to his Range Rover, then started the engine and drove back toward Horseshoe Creek.

His phone buzzed and he checked it. Brett. He punched Connect. "Yeah."

"Did Hardwick talk?"

"He said he didn't set the fire, but he was spying on our progress. He also told me to talk to Romley. I'm on my way back. I'll swing by his bunkhouse."

"All right. But listen, Ray. Maddox just called and said he and Rose will be home late tonight. He wants to talk to us first thing in the morning. Something about the will."

Ray's pulse jumped. "Did he say anything else?"

"No, but he insisted we both needed to be there." Brett hesitated. "I think something's wrong."

Dread balled in Ray's stomach. He felt as if a time bomb had started ticking inside his head.

Had Maddox discovered their father's dirty little secret?

Chapter Sixteen

Tension knotted every muscle in Ray's body as he drove back to Horseshoe Creek. Long ago, his father had built cabins on the property for the cook, the head horse trainer and groomer, and for the foreman and his family. He'd also built bunkhouses for ranch hands, especially those who took seasonal jobs.

Ten minutes later, he bypassed the cabin where Brett, Willow and Sam were living, noting the lights were off, so they must have turned in for the night. He scanned the ranch land as he drove, looking for trouble and praying he didn't find it.

That whoever had set that fire wouldn't return. But he couldn't count on that.

Brett had been working day and night overseeing the additions to the ranch, buying and bringing in more horses, and supervising the building of his home with Willow. The sprawling farmhouse was set on a hill by the creek surrounded by giant trees and pastureland with a view of the sunset that could be seen from the front porch. Brett had also built his own barn to keep horses for his family to ride for leisure.

Ray envisioned himself riding across the ranch with a woman and maybe a kid, and his mouth grew dry. Could he ever see himself settling down with a family?

Scarlet's face taunted him, and he nearly ran into a ditch. He blinked and yanked the Range Rover onto the road, then turned down the drive leading to the bunkhouses. The lights were off in most of them, as well. Ranch hands started at daylight and went to bed at dark.

Hardwick and Romley lived in the one on the end, and he slowed as he approached. His gaze swept the pasture behind and surrounding the bunkhouse, but didn't see movement.

Hoping to catch Romley off guard, Ray slowed his vehicle and parked at the first bunkhouse. He eased open the door and slid from the interior, tucking his gun inside his jacket as he walked. Gravel crunched beneath his boots, and the wind nearly ripped off his hat, but he jammed it firmly on his head and strode forward.

When he reached the bunkhouse, he realized there was only one truck parked by it. Was it Romley's?

He squared his shoulders, climbed the two steps to the stoop, then raised his fist and knocked. Once, twice. He paused to listen for sounds inside.

A light flicked on, and footsteps sounded inside. Ray braced himself for a confrontation as the door opened. A rail-thin young man in his early twenties stood on the other side, scratching his head, his hair sticking up. Not Romley.

"What's your name, man?" Ray asked.

"Curtis."

"Ray McCullen." Ray gestured inside. "I'm looking for Stan Romley."

"He's not here. Left out earlier."

"What do you mean, he left out?" Ray shouldered his way inside, flipped on an overhead light and surveyed the interior of the cabin. A main living area/kitchen and two rooms on each side, both rooms housed with bunks.

One bed was unmade. Curtis's. He'd obviously been sleeping. The rest of the beds were turned up, although a duffel bag, shoes and personal items filled one corner in the room opposite Curtis's.

Ray examined the clothes and bag. "Whose is this?"

"Hardwick's. It was just the three of us in here, but Romley came in about five o'clock, grabbed his stuff and rushed out."

Had Hardwick tipped him off that they were on to them?

"Did he mention where he was going?"

Curtis shook his head. "I asked him if he was coming back and he said no. I figured something must have happened and you all laid him off."

Ray silently cursed.

He checked the desk drawer in the corner, then Hardwick's duffel bag in search of a hint as to what the two men had planned.

That turned up nothing.

"Did he do something wrong?" Curtis asked.

Ray slanted the young man a curious look. "I think he and Hardwick set the fire that destroyed our new barns." He watched Curtis for a reaction. "Do you know anything about that?"

The young man took a step back, his lips thinning. "No. Hell, no."

"You help them?"

Curtis held up his hands in a defensive gesture. "Listen, Mr. McCullen, I just got this job last week. I only met Hardwick and Romley when I came on board."

"How about Arlis Bennett? Do you know him?"

"I've heard his name, everyone around Pistol Whip has," Curtis said.

"Have you ever worked for him?"

"No." Curtis's voice cracked. "I swear, Mr. McCullen, I wouldn't do anything against you and your brothers. I was hired on 'cause I'm a fan of Brett's, and I was hoping he could teach me some riding tricks."

Ray relaxed slightly. He could hear the hero worship in the young man's voice. And God knows, Brett had fans.

"Did you ever hear Hardwick or Romley talking about Bennett? Or about sabotaging our operation?"

"No," Curtis said. "But last night Hardwick said they needed to finish here and get out of town. I thought they had another job lined up."

They did, Ray thought with a grimace. A big paycheck, probably from Bennett.

SCARLET TOSSED AND turned all night. She kept listening for sounds of an intruder, afraid Bobby or Pullman would return.

Tomorrow at noon they would meet with the lawyer to hear the reading of the will.

As excited as she'd been over Joe's donation to The Family Farm, she was equally anxious about Ray's brothers' reactions.

She closed her eyes but shivered as she thought about Bobby—whatever stipulation Joe had put on his share, Bobby wouldn't like it.

Ray's sexy face materialized, replacing Bobby's antagonistic one, stirring feelings she couldn't allow herself to feel... Would she see him again after the reading?

A noise sounded outside, and she rolled over and listened. Wind, rain, the windowpanes rattling. The noises went on and on, keeping her nerves on edge.

Finally at dawn, she gave up on sleep, punched the pillow, got up and showered. A faint stream of sunlight wormed its way through the bleak-looking sky, the gray cast mirroring her mood.

She faced herself in the mirror and gave herself a pep

talk. Joe had included her because he knew she'd use her inheritance to help needy children. If the McCullens questioned her intentions, she'd find a way to convince them how much he'd cared about The Family Farm.

She dressed, taking more time with her makeup than usual to camouflage the bruises from her accident and the dark circles beneath her eyes due to lack of sleep.

Despite her nerves, she managed to eat some toast and sipped her coffee while she finished the paperwork for the Fullers' adoption. Then she drove to The Family Farm and spent the morning with the smaller children who didn't yet attend school.

As she left, Corey hugged her, and her heart warmed. One day she wanted a family of her own.

For now though these kids were her family just like Joe had been. It didn't matter if they were blood related. She loved them just the same.

And she would do everything she could to make sure they were taken care of.

RAY'S STOMACH WAS in knots as he entered his father's office. Mama Mary had set coffee in the office along with breakfast, but he couldn't eat until he talked to his brothers.

Maddox was waiting, a steaming mug in his hand, and Brett loped in a second later.

"I thought we'd better conference before the reading," Maddox said.

"Something wrong?" Brett asked as he poured his own coffee.

"I got a heads-up from Dad's lawyer that there were some complications to the will. He wouldn't elaborate, though."

Ray cleared his throat, irritated that Bush hadn't returned his call. He couldn't avoid the dreaded conversation any longer. "I planned to talk to you guys when you got back, Maddox."

Maddox arched his brows. "You know what this is about?"

Ray nodded. "You'd both better sit down."

Brett scowled. "What's going on?"

A muscle jumped in Maddox's jaw. "I don't like the sound of this."

He wasn't going to like anything about it, but Ray couldn't keep his father's secret any longer.

"There's something I need to say, and I want you both to just listen. It's about Dad."

Both his brothers looked confused.

"If you want to sell your share, just let us know," Maddox said.

"It's not that," Ray said. "It's the reason Dad and I didn't get along."

Brett ran a hand through his hair. "Ray, that's water under the bridge. We all had our differences."

"You don't understand," Ray said. "Just listen."

Brett started to smart off, but Maddox gestured to let Ray speak.

Ray took a deep breath and began. "Dad had an affair before Mom died. The woman's name was Barbara."

Brett looked shocked. Maddox did as well, although something else flared in his eyes. Recognition.

"You knew?" Ray asked him.

Maddox gave a short shake of his head. "No. At least not about the affair. I knew he dated a woman named Barbara later on, when we were teenagers."

"How did you know about it, Ray?" Brett asked.

The image of his father in bed with that woman taunted Brett. "I walked in on them one day. In bed. I was five."

"That's the reason you were always so mad at Dad," Maddox said matter-of-factly.

Ray nodded.

"Why didn't you ever tell us?" Brett asked.

"I didn't really understand what was going on, but I promised Dad I wouldn't tell. Later on, he claimed he broke it off with her, said he was sorry, that he loved Mom. He said he didn't want to hurt her so it would be our secret." He bit out the words. "I knew it was wrong, but I didn't want to hurt her."

Maddox crossed his arms. "So you didn't tell us, either."

"He didn't want you to know," Ray said, remembering the turmoil he'd felt. "You looked up to him. I didn't want to mess that up."

A tense silence ensued while his brothers processed the information. Maddox pinched the bridge of his nose, his face strained.

"I always thought Dad had a wandering eye," Brett admitted.

"He said Mom forgave him before she died," Ray said. "That's why he wanted to see me before he passed."

"I don't know what to say," Maddox muttered. "I'm sorry, Ray. You shouldn't have had to carry that burden all these years."

Another heartbeat passed. "There's more."

Brett pulled a hand down his chin. "What more can there be?"

"Dad and Barbara had a child. A boy named Bobby. He's about my age."

Maddox cursed and Brett dropped his head into his hands.

"That's what Bush was talking about, isn't it?" Maddox asked.

Ray nodded. "I'm afraid so."

Brett lifted his head, anger glittering in his eyes. "You knew about the kid, too?"

"Not until a couple of days ago," Ray said.

"Where is he?" Brett asked.

"He grew up living with Barbara not too far away."

Maddox cursed again. "This is unbelievable."

Brett jumped up and paced the room. "Dad should have told us."

"This guy Bobby? He wants part of Horseshoe Creek?" Maddox growled.

"I think so." Ray paused. "When I found out—"

Brett whirled on him. "How did you find out?"

"It's a long story," Ray began.

"Tell us everything," Maddox said in a tone that brooked no argument. "We have to know what we're up against before we walk into the lawyer's office today."

Maddox was right. Ray got more coffee and so did his brothers, and they gathered around the fireplace.

Both his brothers sat rigid as he explained about Scarlet's visit, The Family Farm and how she'd come to live with Barbara and Bobby.

"Apparently Bobby resented Scarlet. He hated us and her for the attention Dad gave us," Ray finished.

"So Bobby may want revenge against us." Brett paused, mind working. "Why didn't you tell me this before? He could have set the fire."

"I know that," Ray said. "I've been investigating him myself. Barbara claims he was with her that night."

"You met Barbara?" Maddox asked.

Ray nodded on a pained sigh. "I had to. I wanted to find out if either of them had anything to do with the fire."

"Let me guess—they alibied each other," Maddox said in a derisive tone. "Perfect cover."

"Hell, they could have been in on it together," Brett snapped.

"I'm aware of that." Ray braced his elbows on his knees.

"You're sure Dad included Barbara and this girl, Scarlet, in the will?" Maddox asked in an incredulous voice.

"Yeah. According to the letter Scarlet received. They'll probably be at the reading today. Although it doesn't make sense that they'd set the fire before finding out what Dad left them."

"What did he leave them?" Brett asked.

"I don't know. I called Bush and asked him to phone me back, but he never did."

"I can't believe Dad did this to us," Brett said bitterly. "What are we going to do?"

Maddox set his mug down with a thud. "I know one thing we're not going to do. Give in to them. They're not getting Horseshoe Creek. It belongs to us."

SCARLET SWALLOWED BACK nausea as she drove to the lawyer's office. Had Ray warned his brothers about her and Barbara and Bobby?

When she arrived, she spotted Ray's Range Rover along with the sheriff's SUV. Maddox had probably driven it to intentionally intimidate them.

She hoped Bobby behaved and Maddox didn't have to use his badge against him. Joe would have hated that.

Trembling with nerves, she parked, then closed her eyes for a moment, picturing Joe laughing with the kids at The Family Farm as he'd taught them how to mount a horse. The first time he'd helped her up, she'd fallen in love with the quiet-tempered palomino.

She'd wanted a horse of her own.

But that hadn't happened. He had given her a home, though. And for a little while, she'd thought Barbara loved her.

It didn't matter. She'd survived. She would get through today, take whatever Joe had offered and use it in his honor.

Her mouth was so dry, she dabbed lip-gloss on her lips, smoothed down the sweater she'd chosen to wear with her denim skirt and climbed out. Her boot heel caught on one of the stones in the parking lot, but she managed to stay on her feet until she reached the door of the office.

A bell tinkled when she entered, alerting the receptionist at the desk facing the doorway. The middle-aged woman rose and smiled at her.

"Miss Lovett?"

"Yes."

"Mr. Bush and the McCullens are waiting in Mr. Bush's office."

She gathered her courage and followed the woman into the office. The lawyer sat in a leather wing chair in the center while Maddox, Brett and Ray occupied chairs lined on one wall. A heavy-set woman with short curly hair sat by the men, her hands knotted around her purse. Scarlet recognized her from Joe's description—she was Mama Mary, the cook and housekeeper who'd been part of the family for years.

Three other chairs were situated on the opposite one.

If she hadn't been so anxious, she would have laughed. The lines had obviously been drawn.

The three McCullen men stood and faced her, all handsome as sin.

But the looks they were giving her were definitely wary. Not friendly. Antagonistic even.

Mama Mary's expression seemed more neutral, although she fidgeted as if she was nervous.

Ray's gaze met hers, and her stomach fluttered with that unrelenting need to be close to him.

"This is her?" Maddox asked.

Ray nodded, his expression unreadable. "Yes, Maddox, Brett, Mama Mary, this is Scarlet Lovett, the young lady Dad took under his wing at The Family Farm."

Tension stretched between them, riddled with unanswered questions and distrust.

Before she could speak, a noise reverberated from the outer room, then Bobby strode in, looking smug and raring for a fight. Barbara was right behind him, her hand on his arm, obviously terrified that Bobby was going to act out.

Judging from the fierce look in the McCullen men's eyes, they were prepared for battle, as well.

Chapter Seventeen

Ray struggled with mixed emotions as Scarlet slid into a seat. She looked small and uneasy, but she lifted her chin as if she didn't intend to let his brothers or the Lowmans intimidate her.

The lawyer cleared his throat. "Now that everyone is here, let's take a seat."

"Don't you think we should introduce ourselves?" Maddox asked.

Bush's face blanched. "I'm sorry, of course." Bush stood behind his desk. "I'm Darren Bush, Joe McCullen's attorney. While I've met you, Maddox, Brett, Ray and Mama Mary, I have not met Bobby and Barbara Lowman." He extended his hand in a friendly overture.

Bobby shook his hand but gave Ray and his brothers a cutting look. "You must be Barbara?" Bush asked.

She fluffed her dark bob with one hand, then shook Bush's proffered one. "Yes. It's nice to meet you, Mr. Bush."

She pivoted to face Maddox and Brett. "I understand that you may not feel this way, but I am glad to finally meet you boys. Your father adored all of you."

"He talked about us with you?" Maddox asked.

Barbara nodded. "Of course, I realize this is awkward and that finding out about me came as a shock to you, Maddox, and to you, Brett."

"Yes, it did," Brett said. "I still can't figure out the reason he never came clean."

Bobby stepped forward, his expression defensive. "You make it sound like it was my fault."

Brett squared his shoulders. "That's not what I meant."

Scarlet cleared her throat. "Joe kept his families separate because he didn't want to hurt anyone."

Maddox pivoted toward Scarlet. "You knew about us?"

"Yes. But not until a couple of years ago." Scarlet twined her fingers together. "After Joe got sick, he broke down and told me while we were riding one day. He said he wanted to make things right."

Ray turned to Bobby. "When did you learn about us?"

Bobby glared at his mother. "When I was a teenager. But not because Dad told me. I heard him and Mom arguing one night."

Ray jammed his hands in the pockets of his jeans. "Did you confront him?"

Bobby pulled at his chin. "Damn right I did. But he tried to justify keeping me away from you guys by saying he'd take care of me and Mom."

Bobby started to say something else, but Barbara caught his arm. "And he's going to, Bobby. I told you he loved you and he did." She motioned for him to sit down. "Maddox, Brett, Ray. I loved your father very much. He and I never meant to hurt you with our relationship. That's also the reason Bobby never tried to contact you. We both respected your father and his life with you."

Barbara sounded sincere, but Bobby's jaw twitched with resentment as if he didn't share that sentiment.

Scarlet's comment about Barbara echoed in Ray's head—in the beginning, Scarlet thought Barbara loved her. Later she realized the woman had only given her a home to appease their father.

Bush rapped his knuckles on the desk. "All right, now that we've made the introductions, let's sit down and get to it." He gave them all a stern look. "Let me remind you that this will was issued and signed by Joe McCullen, that the contents were his wishes. I spoke with him and witnessed the signing. Also, if there is any problem or if you want to contest any part of it, you must go through legal channels. I do not expect an altercation in here. I expect professional, mature conduct from everyone."

"Of course," Maddox said.

Bush glanced at each of them in turn, and they all agreed. Then everyone seated themselves, and Bush opened the document and began to read his father's last will and testament.

SCARLET SAT IN stunned silence in a corner all on her own while the lawyer read the will. Most of it was as she'd expected. Maddox, the oldest brother, was the executor.

He and Brett and Ray inherited the ranch along with Joe's assets, which included a hefty life insurance policy, their portion to be divided equally three ways. If one of them chose to sell his or her share of the ranch, they were required to sell to the other McCullens so the ranch would remain McCullen land.

He'd also made provisions for Mama Mary, ensuring her salary, a savings account and that she would remain part of the ranch family as long as she lived. Joe had also purchased an insurance policy in her name to take care of her if she became ill.

Mama Mary dabbed at her eyes as Ray squeezed her hand.

"Of course she'll stay," Maddox said.

Brett rose and hugged the woman. "You're our mama, you're family."

She hugged each of them, wiping at tears. Bush paused to allow her to regain control, then continued, "In addition, Joe had a secondary life insurance policy valued at two hundred and fifty thousand dollars, which is to be divided among Barbara and Bobby Lowman and Scarlet Lovett," Bush said.

Surprised looks floated around the room.

"Miss Lovett, Joe explained that you were the daughter to him that he never had. He admired your dedication and hard work with the children at The Family Farm, and for your personal use, he left you a sum total of fifty thousand dollars."

Scarlet inhaled, well aware that Bobby was seething as he sat ramrod straight beside Barbara. "In addition, he left you ten acres at the south end of Horseshoe Creek, land which already holds a cabin where you may live if you choose."

Maddox, Brett and Ray exchanged a look, but said nothing. After all, what was ten acres when they owned several hundred?

"In addition, he donated a hundred thousand dollars of his life insurance to The Family Farm. That money and its use are to be supervised and managed by you."

Scarlet smiled, grateful that Joe had been generous with The Family Farm. She intended to pay it forward just as Joe had done with her.

"I'd be honored," she said, then bit her tongue when the room fell into an awkward silence.

Mr. Bush shifted in his seat, obviously uncomfortable. "For the last section of the will, Barbara Lowman, Joe McCullen paid off the house you live in and left you a sum of fifty thousand dollars for your personal use."

Barbara's sharp intake reeked of disappointment.

"And last, Bobby Lowman, Joe McCullen named you

as his fourth son. You shall receive a lump sum of fifty thousand dollars along with a share of Horseshoe Creek, a section of seventy-five acres at the north end of the ranch that he recently purchased for you.

Bush addressed Bobby. "However, Joe placed stipulations on ownership of the property."

Bobby lurched up, eyes glinting. "What the hell?"

"What are the stipulations?" Barbara asked.

Bush directed his comments toward Bobby again. "Mr. McCullen stipulated that in order to receive your share of the life insurance policy and the property, you enter into a rehab program and receive counseling."

"What?" Bobby said in a seething tone.

"Sit down, son." Barbara took his arm to keep him from bolting—or attacking someone.

"There's one more stipulation," Bush continued. "While you do own the land he willed to you, if you choose to sell, you must sell to the McCullens. If you decide to keep the property and reside on it, you must work the land. Maddox will supervise and consult with you to help you set up a working operation so that you can make a profit and earn enough to live off."

RAY STARED AT the lawyer in shock. He felt the same unsettled surprise radiating from his brothers. Maddox looked as if he could shoot someone.

Bobby made a low menacing sound in his throat. "This is ridiculous," Bobby snapped.

"I'm sorry you feel that way," Bush said. "But these were Joe's wishes. If you want your inheritance, you are required by law to comply with the guidelines he established."

Barbara rubbed Bobby's back. "Come on, son. This is a lot to absorb. Let's get some lunch and talk."

Maddox stood and started to say something, but Barbara threw up a warning hand. "Not right now. We need some time."

The hurt lacing her voice tugged at Ray. As much as he resented what his father had done to them with his lies and betrayal, and as much as he wanted to protect Horseshoe Creek, he understood Bobby's anger and resentment. The last thing their half brother probably wanted was to be watched by one of Joe's sons and have to earn his approval.

How had their father expected Maddox or any of them to work together?

Bobby stalked from the room, Barbara behind him. The door slammed shut in their wake, leaving a mountain of tension lingering.

Scarlet glanced at Ray as if asking what she should do, but he had no answers. While he'd had a couple of days to accept her part in his father's life, Maddox and Brett had just learned about her and the Lowmans.

Disappointment flickered in Scarlet's eyes, then she rose, brushing at her skirt. "Thank you, Mr. Bush."

"If you'll leave your banking information with my secretary," Bush said, "I'll make sure the check is deposited directly into your account. As far as The Family Farm goes, the money for them will go into a business account to be used at your discretion for their needs."

"Of course," Scarlet said. "I work closely with the director. She and I are thrilled to honor Joe in this way."

Bush shook her hand. "Joe must have trusted you a great deal."

Scarlet glanced at Ray and his brothers, but the men remained silent.

"He knows how much the children and that place mean to me," Scarlet said. "It was my home for a lot of years. I intend to do right by those children, just like Joe did by me."

Bush nodded. "About the cabin and land—"

"We'll work that out later," Scarlet said. "I'm fine in my rental house for now."

Clutching her purse to her, she disappeared out the door.

Maddox folded his arms and began to grill the lawyer, but Ray ducked through the door after Scarlet.

He found her outside the office, her arms wrapped around her waist as she took deep breaths. She looked shaken and small and vulnerable.

Why had his father handled things this way? He'd left a damn mess.

He eased up behind her, struggling with what to say. "Scarlet, are you okay?"

She spun around, her lower lip quivering. "I'm fine, Ray. I loved Joe and miss him. And for the record, I never expected anything from him. You have to believe that."

He did believe her. "He wanted you to have it, though. He obviously loved you and that children's home."

Ray lifted his hand and stroked her cheek with the pad of his thumb. "Maddox and Brett just need time to process this."

Scarlet offered him a tentative smile. "I understand. I'm sorry."

Damn, she looked like an angel. "It's not your fault," Ray said. "My father made this mess." But they had to clean it up. And that wasn't going to be easy, not with Bobby's attitude.

"It is complicated," Scarlet said. "Joe wasn't perfect. He didn't tell you all the truth because he didn't want to disappoint you."

Ray's chest constricted. He'd done that a long time ago. But still, Joe was his father and he loved him.

"Do you plan to move into the cabin?" Ray asked.

"Yes, *do* you?" Maddox asked.

Scarlet's breath quickened at the sound of Maddox's

gruff tone. Ray dropped his hand from her cheek and turned to face his oldest brother. He'd never felt as if he could live up to Maddox.

"I don't know, but like I said, I'm in no hurry." Scarlet tilted her chin upward. "But I will use the funds he designated for The Family Farm for the good of the children. You're all invited to visit it and meet the children anytime you want. I think you'd be proud of what your father accomplished there."

"You certainly seem to know a lot about our father," Maddox said.

Scarlet flinched. "He was an important influence in my life for over ten years. I won't forget that."

"Why you?" Brett asked. "Why did he take you in?"

Scarlet's voice softened. "Joe saw how I grew up and knew he could let down his guard with me. You guys held him to a higher standard. He wanted to be your hero."

Maddox looked down at his boots, his face strained. Joe had been his hero. Until now.

Brett shifted and looked away, too, but he seemed to be contemplating her statement.

"Like I said, let me know if you want to come by The Family Farm." Scarlet clenched her purse with one hand, walked down the steps to her car and got inside. Ray wanted to follow her and make sure she was okay.

Hell, he wanted to hold her and kiss her and love her through the day and night.

But Maddox and Brett were waiting, and they had to talk.

"Was she sleeping with Dad?" Brett asked.

Ray's temper flared, and he spun around to face his brothers. "No. I investigated her when she first came to me. The director at the children's home assured me that she's legit. Joe thought of her as the daughter he never had."

Maddox scowled. "Maybe Dad wasn't sleeping with her, but you are, aren't you, Ray?" He glared at him. "You knew who she was, and that she and that woman and her son wanted part of Dad's ranch, but you jumped into bed with her anyway, didn't you?"

SCARLET MENTALLY SHOOK off her anxiety over the confrontation between Bobby and Ray and his brothers as she drove to The Family Farm. All in all, the meeting had gone better than she expected. At least Bobby hadn't started throwing punches.

But he was upset. There was no doubt about that.

Although Joe was right—Bobby needed rehab and counseling. If he committed to that, maybe he'd realize that Joe had given him an opportunity for a future. And perhaps one day a relationship with his half brothers.

She parked and rushed inside the children's home, then found Millie in the kitchen baking cinnamon rolls. The kids were in school now, the ones too young for school outside in the play yard.

Two volunteers watched the little ones while Faye was in the office on the computer.

She poked her head in. "Faye, I just came from the will reading."

"How did it go?" Faye asked.

"Good." Scarlet smiled. "He left a hundred thousand dollars to the home. I'm supposed to oversee how we use it. I plan to talk to a financial advisor about an investment plan so the money can keep working for us."

Faye blinked back tears. "That's wonderful, Scarlet. I knew Joe wouldn't let us down."

Maddox and Brett didn't exactly see his donation that way. And frankly, Ray hadn't exactly defended her in front of his family. If push came to shove, would he team up with them to contest her inheritance?

She pushed aside her worry and went to visit the children, then drove to her office for the afternoon.

Just as she was about to step inside, footsteps crunched behind her. She froze, but suddenly someone jerked her backward.

She tried to scream, but a cold, hard hand clamped down over her mouth, cutting her off. Then the man dragged her around the corner and pressed her face into the side of the building.

Chapter Eighteen

Ray clenched his jaw. "Why don't we discuss this at home?"

Maddox looked furious while Brett's expression was unreadable.

"He's right," Brett said.

"Fine." Maddox strode to his police vehicle and he and Brett followed him to the ranch in their own vehicles.

When they parked and went in, Mama Mary set her purse on the side table. "I'll get lunch."

"We'll eat later," Maddox said.

Mama Mary looked hurt. "I'm sorry, boys. I know today was difficult on you,"

"We'll work it out," Ray said, earning a contemptuous look from Maddox.

"Let's sit down in Dad's office," Brett suggested.

The four of them claimed seats around the coffee table in the sitting area.

Maddox took the lead and turned to Mama Mary. She wrung her hands together.

"You knew about Barbara and her son, didn't you?" Maddox asked.

Guilt streaked Mama Mary's face. "I knew about the woman, but not the boy. I…can't believe Mr. Joe left this world without explaining everything to you all."

"He was a coward," Ray said.

Maddox and Brett both nodded as if they agreed.

"Don't be too hard on your daddy," Mama Mary said. "He was just a man. None of you are perfect, either."

"I would never cheat on Rose," Maddox said.

Brett looked sheepish. "I know I was a player, but I'm committed to Willow now, and I would never hurt her by fooling around."

"It was a long time ago," Mama Mary said. "Besides, you don't know what caused him to stray. He and your mama…well, just like all couples, they had problems."

"What kind of problems?" Maddox asked.

"That's all I can say." Mama Mary tapped her foot up and down. "Just that there's always two sides to a story. Now your daddy is gone, try to remember the good times. How much he loved all of you. That he didn't tell you because he didn't want to upset you."

"Then why did he include his mistress and her son in his will?" Maddox asked.

Mama Mary gave Maddox a scolding look. "Because like it or not, they are family, Maddox. He had to do right by them, too. You best accept that fact."

Maddox's boots hit the floor and he paced to the window. "I may have to accept it, but I don't like it."

"I don't trust Barbara or Bobby," Brett added.

Ray cleared his throat. "We shouldn't trust him," Ray said. "He's been in trouble with the law before, and he can be violent. That's the reason Dad stipulated he needs to enter into rehab."

"How the hell am I supposed to help him set up his own spread?" Maddox said, his voice incredulous. "Didn't Dad realize what he was asking of both of us?"

"Yeah, even if we accept him," Brett said. "Bobby obviously resents us."

"And what about that girl Scarlet?" Maddox turned on

Ray again. "What if she's in cahoots with Bobby? Who knows that they won't come back and ask for more?"

"She's not like that," Ray said.

Maddox's brows rose. "Good God. You *are* involved with her, aren't you?"

Just like always, Maddox's disapproval rang through loud and clear.

"No," Ray said, although a voice inside his head shouted, *Liar.*

Ray's phone buzzed and he checked the screen. Deputy Whitefeather.

"I have to answer this." He pressed Connect. "This is Ray."

"Deputy Whitefeather. Listen, Ray, a man named Hugh Weatherman phoned the office. He says he works with Scarlet Lovett and that he spotted Pullman near her office."

"What about that restraining order?"

"Pullman's obviously not concerned about it. Anyway, this man, Hugh, claims Scarlet was supposed to be at the office a half hour ago, but he hasn't seen her. Said her car is outside, but she's not. I thought she might be with you."

"No. Are you at her office now?"

"No, I had a lead on Romley. I'm twenty minutes outside town."

Ray silently cursed. "I'm on my way. Keep us posted if you find Romley."

Whitefeather agreed, and Ray yanked his keys from his pocket.

"What's going on?" Maddox asked as he ended the call and headed to the door.

"Scarlet had to remove a child from her home, and the father is out to get her. That was her coworker. He's worried. Scarlet never showed at her office."

Maddox adjusted his weapon. "Where's her office?"

"I can handle this, Maddox," Ray said.

Maddox caught his arm. "I'm the sheriff. It's my job, Ray."

"Please, Maddox. I'll call you if I need you. Just stay here and figure out what to do about Bobby."

Ray rushed to the door. Right now he needed a break from his big brother, needed to find Scarlet and make sure she was all right without Maddox breathing down his neck.

But if that bastard had her, he'd call Maddox. That is, if he didn't kill Pullman himself.

Scarlet twisted sideways to escape the man's grip, but he dragged her farther down the alley between the buildings. He pushed her into an overhang from the abandoned warehouse, then shoved her face-first against the wall, grinding her cheek into the brick.

"Who are you? What do you want?" she managed to choke out.

"Just shut up and listen, Scarlet."

Bobby. She should have known when she smelled whiskey on his breath. "This is crazy, Bobby. You should be happy. You just inherited some money and land."

"Happy?" Bobby hissed against her ear. "Dad left me nothing compared to what those McCullen boys got."

"He left you enough to start a new life." Scarlet closed her eyes, tired of Bobby's selfishness. "Maybe he would have given you more if you'd been responsible."

He yanked her arm behind her back, making pain shoot up her shoulder. "He was the one who treated me badly. He was always at that damn ranch with his *real* kids. He was ashamed of me."

"No, he wasn't, Bobby. And it's not too late to make him proud," Scarlet said. "Take the land and build your own spread."

He shoved his knee against the back of her legs and she cried out in pain. "You didn't have to do anything to get your share."

"Yes, I did. I have a job helping those needy children. That's the reason Joe left me money. So take what he left you and be grateful."

"Yeah, take the leftover scraps just like I've always done."

"It's better than nothing," Scarlet said. "And if you go to rehab—"

"I don't need a damn bunch of people picking at my mind," Bobby rasped.

"But if you do that and work with Maddox, you can have your own ranch."

"I should have a fourth of Horseshoe Creek," he hissed. "How could Dad expect me to work under Maddox Mc-Cullen?"

Her mind raced with a way to defuse the situation. "Because Maddox is experienced and can teach you about ranching."

Bobby jerked her around and shoved her hands above her head. "You're so damn naive," Bobby said bitterly. "The McCullens are probably plotting right now to get rid of me."

Scarlet struggled for a breath. Unfortunately he might be right. "Maybe you should talk to them instead of me."

"That's right, you're not family at all. But you still received the same amount of money as me. Even more if you count the money for that damned orphanage."

A sinister gleam glittered in Bobby's eyes, and she realized where he was headed with this talk.

"You want the money Joe designated for those children?"

Bobby nodded. "It should be mine. I was his son."

"Don't be greedy," Scarlet said in a throaty whisper. "You know how much helping those children meant to Joe."

"More than his own flesh and blood," he said.

"No, but they were important to him."

"Just like you were. How did you worm your way into his affection?"

This was going nowhere good. "Just let me go, Bobby, and sleep it off. Tomorrow you'll see that Joe gave you a future to look forward to."

"I won't let those McCullens cut me out of what I'm owed."

Scarlet's heart pounded. That sounded like a threat. "Don't do anything stupid."

"Why do you keep defending them? They might contest the will so you don't get that money, either."

"I'm not defending anyone," Scarlet said. "I'm trying to honor Joe's wishes."

"Here's what you're going to do," Bobby said in a hoarse tone next to her ear. "You're going to sign your money and land over to me. That's only fair, Scarlet, since I shared my daddy with you. After all, you're not a McCullen and you never will be."

RAY THREW HIS Range Rover into Park in front of Scarlet's office building, then hurried up to the front door. Hugh met him on the outside stoop.

"Deputy Whitefeather said that you called about Scarlet. Did she ever make it?"

"No. And I'm afraid that awful man Lloyd Pullman got her."

"I'll take a look around." Ray eased down the steps and scanned the parking lot, listening for sounds. Scarlet's voice. A cry for help.

Nothing.

The car Scarlet had been driving was parked in the small parking lot beside a sedan and a minivan that probably belonged to her coworker and the client. He didn't spot any other vehicles, which worried him more.

If Pullman was here, had he abducted her and driven off?

A vacant building sat beside the office. He inched to the corner of the building and peeked around, ears straining for any sign of Scarlet or Pullman. One step at a time, he crept down the alley, pausing to listen every few feet.

Suddenly he heard a voice. Low. Angry.

"You're going to do it, Scarlet."

Not Pullman. Bobby.

Remembering he could be violent, Ray slipped his gun from inside his jacket and held it at the ready. One step, two, three, he crept closer until he spotted an overhang from the warehouse and heard Scarlet's voice.

"Bobby, it doesn't have to be like this—"

"Shut up, Scarlet. You're going back to work and call that lawyer and make the arrangements."

Ray eased from the shadows of the awning, his gun raised. Fury heated his blood when he saw the way Bobby had trapped her against the wall. "Let her go, Bobby." He aimed his weapon at the man's head. *"Now."*

Bobby jerked his head up, rage flaming in his eyes, then yanked Scarlet in front of him. Bastard.

"Go ahead, shoot."

Ray's gaze met Scarlet's. Fear clouded her expression, but she lifted her chin in a show of courage.

"This is not what our father wanted," Ray said.

Bobby cursed again. "Our father was a two-timing jerk who led my mother on for years and treated us like a second-tier family."

"I don't know why he did what he did," Ray said. "But Scarlet had nothing to do with Dad's choices."

"Yes, she did," Bobby snapped. "He chose to take care of her like she was his blood, when he left me all the time to go back to you and your brothers."

"That must have sucked," Ray said. "But giving you part of Horseshoe Creek and forcing us to work together must have been his way of finally making things right."

Bobby tightened his grip on Scarlet. "How did he think we could work together when we don't even know each other? When he cheated me out of what was mine?"

"Bobby, just let me go and we'll work all this out," Scarlet said in a pleading tone.

"She's right," Ray said. "We'll sit down and talk."

A siren wailed. Deputy Whitefeather on his way.

Panic lit Bobby's eyes, and he shoved Scarlet to the ground. She hit the cement with a yelp, and Ray ran forward to help her up.

"Scarlet," Ray said.

"I'm fine." She brushed her hair from her face just as the deputy's car screeched to a halt.

"Tell Whitefeather I'm going after Bobby." Then Ray broke into a sprint.

SCARLET WAS TREMBLING as she walked toward the front of the building. Hugh rushed outside to greet her, and Deputy Whitefeather climbed from his police-issued SUV and strode toward her. "Miss Lovett?"

"I'm okay," Scarlet said as he met up with her.

"Did Pullman hurt you?" Hugh asked.

She shook her head. "It wasn't Pullman. Bobby cornered me."

"Bobby?" the deputy asked.

"He's sort of my adopted brother," she said. "Ray can explain. He went after him."

"Do you need an ambulance?" Deputy Whitefeather asked.

"No." She massaged her wrist where Bobby had twisted it.

Ray raced around the corner then, his breathing choppy. "Damn. He got away. He was parked on the other side of the warehouse."

"I'll issue a BOLO on him," Deputy Whitefeather said.

"I'm not sure that's necessary," Scarlet said. "He just needs time to cool down."

"Scarlet, you can't let him get away with this," Ray said.

"I agree," Hugh interjected. "He's no better than Pullman."

They were right. She should follow through. But doing so would only fuel his animosity.

Then he might try to hurt Ray.

Chapter Nineteen

Bobby wouldn't get away with bullying Scarlet. Ray didn't care if they were blood related or not.

A real man didn't exert force on a woman for any reason. Period.

"Issue the APB, pick him up and bring him in," Ray said. "I'll update Maddox."

The deputy gave a clipped nod, then angled his head toward Scarlet. "Let me know if you hear from him or Pullman again."

Scarlet agreed, and the deputy left. Hugh moved closer. "You want me to drive you home, Scarlet? I'll be glad to stay with you."

"No, thanks, Hugh. But I think I'll get some files and work at home this evening."

Ray didn't miss the disappointment in the man's eyes when Scarlet pulled away from him.

Not that it should bother him if Hugh was interested or if she reciprocated his affection. He and Scarlet were just… what? Friends? Acquaintances? Two people who shared a love for his father?

Scarlet ducked inside the office, and Hugh trailed her as if he needed to be close to her. Ray followed them both, his eyes glued to Scarlet as she quickly gathered her files.

Bobby was still on the loose and Pullman was a wild card. He didn't intend to leave her alone and let either one of them get to her.

SCARLET STRUGGLED TO hold herself together as she gathered her files. Thankfully nothing was pressing at the moment.

Besides, she needed some time to figure out what to do about Bobby. Her experience as a social worker warned her that she needed to press charges, that allowing Bobby to get away with accosting her was abuse.

But he was Joe's son and Barbara would hate her if she pressed charges. They were the only two family members Scarlet had left.

If only Bobby would do as Joe requested and enter into rehab, he might finally let go of his anger and move on with his life. He and the McCullens might even learn to accept each other one day and be the family Joe had wanted.

You made a mess, Joe.

She could almost hear him whispering back that he knew it. But that he was hoping she could bridge the gap and pull his two families together.

A sarcastic laugh bubbled in her throat. *Too much to ask.*

"Ready?" Ray's deep voice reverberated with concern, causing a pang in her chest. She was more accustomed to rejection than having someone treat her with tenderness.

"Yes, just a minute." She locked her file drawer, then turned to Hugh. "Let me know if anything important comes up."

Hugh nodded, although he looked sullen as if he was pouting over the fact that she'd turned down his offer to stay with her. Knowing he'd had a hard life himself, and that he'd been a good friend, Scarlet leaned over and gave him a quick hug.

Hugh had been rejected so many times in his life that

she needed to be gentle. One day he'd find someone special that he belonged with.

She looked up at Ray, and her heart stuttered. Ray was the strong, rugged masculine type that made her hungry for sex. The protective type who made her feel safe.

The intensely caring type that made her dream about love.

But he would be leaving Pistol Whip soon.

Or would he? He'd inherited a third of Horseshoe Creek. Was there a chance that he'd stay and run it with his brothers?

A chance that he might learn to love her?

RAY CLENCHED HIS hands by his side, jealousy rearing its ugly head again. That smile was the only encouragement a man like Hugh needed to think he might win Scarlet's heart.

Ray had no idea why that irked him so much, but it did. Scarlet deserved someone strong and loving, someone who wanted a family, someone who understood her commitment to the kids at The Family Farm and the pain she'd suffered.

Hugh might fit that bill, though.

Still, he wasn't the man for Scarlet because…

Because why? He wanted her for himself?

That thought bounced around in his head as he followed her back to her house. He checked over his shoulder as he drove, well aware that either Pullman or Bobby might show up again.

Not that he didn't have his own enemies. He still had no idea who'd caused his crash and beaten the hell out of him. Or who'd set the fire at the horse barn. Arlis Bennett? Hardwick or Romley?

Bobby?

Bobby hadn't beaten him up, but he could have paid someone to do it. Maybe one of his hoodlum buddies?

He phoned Maddox to fill him in before he arrived at Scarlet's.

"Bobby attacked Scarlet?" Maddox said, his voice irritated.

"Yes. Whitefeather issued an APB for him."

Maddox muttered a sound of frustration. "This is a cluster."

Ray felt sorry for his older brother. At least he'd grown up with no illusions about their father being the perfect hero. Maddox had.

"I'll dig up everything I can on Bobby," Maddox said.

Ray relayed the charges on Bobby's rap sheet. "That's one reason Dad placed those stipulations on his share."

Worse, their father had tied them to Bobby Lowman and Barbara for the rest of their lives.

Scarlet might be the only gem in this tangled mess.

"Brett explained about the barn fire and Romley," Maddox said. "I'm going to question Hardwick at the hospital. Maybe he knows more than he admitted to you."

Ray sighed. "Whitefeather was researching Bennett's financials for a connection between him and Romley but hasn't found one."

"I talked to him," Maddox said. "The DNA on that cigarette butt was inconclusive."

Before they hung up, they agreed to keep each other posted. Scarlet parked, and he rolled in beside her and cut the engine. It took her a minute to gather her briefcase, then she locked the car and walked up the steps to the front door.

She glanced over her shoulder at him as he climbed from his Range Rover, and his heart lurched. She looked so fragile and beautiful, a tempting combination.

He hurried up the steps behind her. She dropped her briefcase on the table by the door, then flipped on a light. The tentative smile she offered him flooded his body with heat.

Her face looked pale though, and she gave a little shiver as if she was remembering her altercation with Bobby.

"I'm going to shower," she said, her voice cracking as she passed the kitchen and living room and crossed the hallway to her bedroom.

A second later, Scarlet's scream sent him running.

SCARLET STARED IN horror at her bed. At the doll...

"What's wrong?" Ray rushed in, weapon drawn, and pulled her behind him. "Is someone here?"

"No... I don't know." Scarlet pointed to the porcelain doll Joe had given her. It was so beautiful and reminded her of the day he'd told her he considered her his daughter.

Now that porcelain face was completely shattered.

An image of that burned photo flashed behind her eyes. Had the same person who'd left it smashed the doll's face?

Ray glanced at the doll, then quickly checked the closet and bathroom to make sure no one was inside. "It's clear," he said as he returned.

"But someone was here," Scarlet said, agitated. "Someone who knew what that doll meant to me." Someone who wanted to hurt her.

She retrieved the envelope with the photo in it and showed it to Ray. His gaze met hers, hot with anger. "Where did you get this?"

"Hugh said he found it at the office. Someone slid it under the door. I meant to give it to the deputy but forgot."

"I'll have Maddox send it and the doll to the lab. Bobby isn't going to get away with terrorizing you like this."

Scarlet wanted to cry out at the injustice of the situation, but she was trembling instead, and tears trickled down her cheeks.

"I never meant to ruin his life," she said, talking out loud. "But he resented me from the beginning."

Ray muttered a curse, his boots clicking on the wood floor as he strode over to her. "You didn't do anything wrong," he said in a gruff voice. "And you certainly didn't ruin his life. He's doing that himself."

Pain wrenched Scarlet's heart. "All I ever wanted was a family," she said. "To be wanted like the other kids."

But Bobby hadn't wanted her. And neither had Barbara. And now Bobby was determined to destroy her.

To avoid interfering with fingerprints, Ray used the afghan to move the doll to the dresser. Then he gently laid his gun on the end table.

"I can't believe he hates me so much," she said.

Ray stroked her back in small circles. "I'm sorry for how you grew up, Scarlet, but my father obviously loved you or he wouldn't have given you that doll. And he wouldn't have left you that cabin and a piece of his land. That meant more to him than the money because it was part of the McCullen legacy."

She'd thought the same thing. But...today had just been too much. Bobby wouldn't stop until he ran her out of town.

"I understand that your father made mistakes and you're all disappointed with him," Scarlet said, sensitive to their side. "But he was a good man deep down, Ray. No matter what happens, I'm glad he was in my life."

Emotions darkened Ray's expression, and he pulled her up against him. "Nothing is going to happen to you, Scarlet." He tilted his head to the side, his eyes heated, stormy.

And so sexy that Scarlet lost herself in the brown depths.

"I promise I'll protect you," he murmured. "Bobby won't hurt you as long as I'm around."

Her heart fluttered, the fear that had gripped her in its clutches slowly dissipating as his warm, strong arms surrounded her. Her body tingled with desire as he cradled her next to his chest.

Then he fused his mouth with hers. He tasted like honey and sex and the forbidden, everything she'd ever wanted in a man but had tried to resist.

She couldn't resist any longer.

Scarlet lifted one hand and slipped his Stetson off and dropped it into the chair by the bed, then tunneled her fingers through his thick dark hair. He deepened the kiss, probing her lips apart with his tongue, and she willingly gave in to him, tearing at his shirt to get closer to his hard, male body and the strength beneath.

RAY FORGOT ALL the reasons he shouldn't kiss Scarlet as her tongue danced with his. His body was on fire from wanting her. That hungry craving inside him couldn't be satisfied until he tasted and touched every inch of her.

She tore at his shirt, and he tugged at hers, his pulse pounding at the sight of the lacy bra barely covering her generous breasts. Her breath rushed out in a tortured sigh as if she needed him as much as he needed her, and he lowered her to the bed, crawled on top of her and kissed her again, telling her with his mouth that he intended to love her.

Chapter Twenty

Scarlet's body tingled with every touch of Ray's hands. He deepened the kiss, his body brushing hers in a sensual invitation.

She answered by rubbing her foot up and down his calf and meeting his tongue thrust with her own.

Except she wanted more. Wanted his clothes off so she could feel her foot against his bare leg. Her breasts against the hard planes of his chest. His skin against her own.

He trailed kisses along her neck and throat, causing her to shiver with longing, and she ran her fingers over his bare shoulders, savoring the way his muscles bunched and flexed against her hands.

Heat spiraled through her as he teased the sensitive area behind her ear, and his hands slid down to rub her breasts through her lacy bra. Her nipples stiffened, aching and begging for more, and he stripped her bra and closed his lips over one turgid tip.

She sighed in pleasure and ran her fingers over his bare skin urging him closer. He loved one breast then the other, suckling her until she felt the tugging sensations of an orgasm deep in her womb.

Desperate for more, she pulled at his jeans and, seconds later, they both stripped and lay naked in each other's arms. She had never seen such a handsome, virile man. His muscular physique robbed her breath and made her feel things she'd never felt before—the kind of aching hunger that needed sating and could only be satisfied by him.

Her breasts brushed his chest, titillating her even more, and he skimmed his fingers down her back to her waist, then lower to her hips. She undulated, desperate to be more intimate, and he kissed her again, deeply and more passionately than she'd ever been kissed.

He stroked her backside, then trailed more hot, hungry kisses down her throat and torso, pausing to love each inch of her as he stirred her desires. Another kiss in her navel, then his lips skated downward until she felt him drop tender love licks along her inner thighs.

She groaned his name and parted her legs, her body humming to life as he teased her sweet spot with his fingers and then his mouth.

Hot pleasure washed over her, and she quivered as he loved her, a dozen mindless sensations shooting through her as her passion exploded into sweet release.

THE SOUND OF Scarlet's erotic whisper of pleasure sparked Ray's hunger. She tasted like sweetness and woman, a heady taste that whetted his appetite for more.

His sex hardened, throbbing for release, and he rose above her and cupped her face in one hand while he braced his weight on the other. Her eyes were glazed with passion, her lips plump and swollen from his kisses, a sight that he imprinted in his brain forever.

An urgency throbbed within him as she kissed him again and slipped one hand down to cup his erection. He couldn't resist. He thrust himself at her center, and she guided him toward her. But when the tip of his hard body touched her intimately, he suddenly remembered protection.

"Condom." She nodded and he lifted away from her and

grabbed a foil packet from his jeans. He tore it open with his teeth, then she took it from him and helped him roll it on.

Her fingers against his bare skin was so titillating he thought he might explode in her hands. But he sucked in a breath, wanting to be inside her when he climaxed.

She stroked his back, then trailed her hands down his hips and over his butt and urged him between her thighs. He teased her center with his thick length, stroking her until she whispered for him to enter her.

Need and passion mingled with emotions that he'd never felt before. He was touched and honored to be in Scarlet's bed.

But he didn't have time to contemplate those feelings as she raked her nails over his back and guided him inside her. He filled her, then paused, allowing her a moment to adjust to his size. She was so tight that he didn't want to hurt her.

She moaned his name, and he fused his mouth with hers and kissed her again, this time thrusting his sex deeper, then withdrawing. Over and over he teased her until she clutched his hips.

"I need you," she whispered against his neck.

"I need you, too," he said, surprising himself when he realized that he meant it on more than one level.

She undulated her hips against him and wrapped her legs around him, and once again he forgot to think as he lost himself in the rhythm.

His lungs strained for air as he intensified his movements, driving deeper and deeper inside her until she cried out his name and another orgasm claimed her. Her body tightened around his, stroking his length until his own release teetered on the surface. Another kiss, then another moan and her pleasure triggered his own, and he spilled his seed inside her.

He pumped and thrust harder and faster, his heart racing as the two of them clung to each other.

SCARLET CLUNG TO Ray as the aftermath of their lovemaking lingered. She felt languid and happy and hungry, as if she already wanted more.

The thought terrified her. She hadn't had many relationships at all with men, had kept them at bay, unable to trust in their motives or affections. But with Ray, rational thought went by the wayside.

His heavy breathing bathed her neck as he moaned against her. She smiled and kissed his neck, sensations still rippling through her. He lifted himself from her and disappeared into the bathroom, and she suddenly felt bereft.

Was he going to leave now?

But he crawled back in bed with her and pulled her into his arms. She snuggled up next to him, easing her head into the crook of his shoulder as if that was where she belonged.

Ray twirled a strand of her hair between his fingers and toyed with it, and she rubbed his chest with her fingers, tangling them in the fine dark mat of hair on his chest. The moment was sweet and tender and made her feel closer to him than she'd ever felt with anyone.

They lay there holding and touching and caressing each other for what seemed like forever. At least she *wanted* it to last forever.

The wind whistled outside, banging a tree branch against the window, but instead of startling her, she closed her eyes, cocooned in the warmth of Ray's arms. Nothing could hurt her or frighten her as long as they were entwined.

But sometime later, Ray's phone buzzed from his jeans' pocket. She bit her lip, hoping he wouldn't answer it and break the intimate spell around them. It buzzed again though, and Ray hissed.

"I guess I'd better get that. It might be about Bobby or Pullman."

Hearing both men's names sent a shiver up her spine. Ray must have felt it because he hugged her again, then planted a kiss on her lips. "Don't move."

His words warmed her with the promise that he planned to return to her bed. He stood, and she had no shame about looking at his handsome muscular physique. He glanced down and noticed her attention to his sex, which was jutting out, ready and engorged, and he grinned.

"I said, don't move."

She laughed softly and hugged the pillow to her as he snatched his phone.

Just as he answered it, the doorbell dinged. Ray frowned at her in question, and she shrugged, then slipped from bed, grabbed her robe and tugged it on.

She pushed her tangled hair from her face, tightening the belt of her robe as she walked into the living room. She peeked through the front sheers and saw Hugh's car.

Relieved it wasn't Bobby or Pullman, but irritated at the interruption, she opened the door. "Hugh, what are you doing here?"

Hugh elbowed his way inside. "I knew you were upset about Bobby's attack and wanted to check on you."

Hadn't he seen Ray's car in the drive?

"I told you I'm fine."

Hugh's jaw twitched. He looked more agitated than usual. "Did something happen after I left, Hugh?"

"No, I just thought you might need me. Was your house okay when you got home?"

Scarlet's pulse jumped as she remembered the broken doll. "Why would you ask that?"

He shrugged, his thin lips forming a pout. "I just wondered. Didn't you get a locksmith to change your locks?"

"How did you know that?"

Hugh fidgeted. "You told me, don't you remember?"

Scarlet searched her memory. The past few days had been hectic and unsettling as she'd dealt with Ray, the McCullens, Pullman, Bobby and Barbara.

"I did have new locks," Scarlet said. "But as you see, I'm fine." In fact, she wanted him to leave so she could go back to Ray.

Speaking of Ray, he strode in, his jeans slung low on his hips as he buttoned his shirt.

Hugh made a disgusted sound in his throat. "So, this is how it is?"

Scarlet tensed at the edge to his tone.

Ray dragged on his jacket, then jammed his gun inside the interior pocket. "Hugh?"

"I was worried about Scarlet," Hugh said.

Ray glanced at Scarlet. "I have to go. Deputy Whitefeather has a lead on Bobby. Maddox is going to meet us at the location."

"I'll go with you," Scarlet said.

"No, it might be dangerous." Ray gestured toward Hugh.

"I'll stay with her while you're gone," Hugh offered eagerly.

Scarlet's temper reared its head. "I don't need a babysitter."

"No, you need a bodyguard," Ray said.

Scarlet caught Ray's arm. "Please, Ray, I'll go with you."

Ray's gaze met hers, the memory of their lovemaking still vivid in her mind. She wanted to go back to bed with him, not entertain Hugh.

Ray traced his finger down her cheek in a tender gesture. "I'll be back when we have Bobby in custody. Meanwhile lock the door."

Scarlet bit her tongue to keep from begging him to stay as he left her alone with her coworker.

RAY MADE IT to The Silver Bullet before Deputy Whitefeather. In fact, Whitefeather phoned and said the sheriff in Laramie had Pullman in custody. Apparently he'd caught Pullman attempting to steal a car. The man had been so loaded he'd admitted that he was going to hijack the vehicle, then steal his daughter and leave town.

Scarlet would be relieved to know he was in jail. This time he faced felony charges and wouldn't be released in a day or two, either.

The parking lot of the Silver Bullet was nearly full, country music blaring from the speakers as he stepped from his vehicle. He scouted out the exterior but didn't see Lowman, so he checked the alley to make sure he wasn't hiding out.

Hopefully Bobby had no idea the bartender had phoned Whitefeather. But Whitefeather had been smart enough to figure that if Bobby liked booze, he might show up at the closest bar in town tonight to drown his sorrows, so he'd alerted his friend.

Ray's senses were honed as he entered the bar, scanning the crowd for Bobby. Johnny Cash's voice boomed over the speaker, a line dance was in motion on the dance floor and the pool tables and dartboard corner were packed.

Ray eased his way through the crowd, avoiding eye contact with a redhead who gave him a flirtatious smile. He inched up to the bar and motioned to the bartender.

"You called the deputy about Bobby Lowman?"

The young man nodded and gestured to the back corner where a young man in a black leather jacket stood near the rear exit. Lowman slipped some cash from his wallet, and shoved it into the man's hands.

Then Lowman reached out his hand and the man laid a

.38 special in his palm. Ray tensed, dropping back behind a group of cowboys so Bobby wouldn't see him.

Ray kept his cool and waited, then watched Lowman slip out the back exit. Determined not to let Bobby escape, especially now that he was armed, Ray wove through the crowd and eased out the back.

Gravel crunched as his boots hit the parking lot, the wind carrying the scent of garbage, stale booze and cigarette smoke. Three cowboys were huddled around a truck bed smoking, a woman and man were necking under the awning of the neighboring building and a truck engine fired up.

Expecting it to be Bobby, Ray left his cover and dashed to the right to see the license, but a bullet zinged by his head.

Ray ducked behind the corner and pivoted to see the shooter's location just as another bullet pierced his hat.

Chapter Twenty-One

Scarlet folded her arms, anxious to get rid of Hugh. "I thought you were working this afternoon, Hugh. I need you to make sure everything at the office is going smoothly."

"Don't worry, everything is in good shape at work. But you seemed so upset earlier, I had to see you." Hugh reached out and rubbed her arm.

Uncomfortable with the way he was looking at her, she stepped into the kitchen. "How about some coffee or tea?"

"Coffee would be great."

She nodded, pulled a filter from the cabinet, measured the coffee and poured the water in. Seconds later, the deep, rich scent of hickory filled the air, soothing her nerves. Ray was going to find Bobby and things would be all right.

"I had a meeting with a couple who are interested in adopting Rachelle."

Hope budded in Scarlet's chest. Rachelle reminded her of herself at that age. Small, slightly sickly, shy. Lonely. She was ten and had asthma but she was a sweet little girl who needed a loving home. "That's great. What did you think of the couple?"

"They're nice, stable and say they want an older child. The father is a pharmacist, the wife is a tutor at a child learning center."

"That sounds promising." Scarlet poured them both coffee and handed Hugh a mug.

"What's going on with you and that McCullen man?" Hugh asked.

Scarlet blew on her coffee. "It's complicated, Hugh."

"He's Joe's son. We both know Joe cheated on his wife. You think his son will be any better?"

Scarlet inhaled sharply. She hadn't realized Hugh harbored animosity toward Joe. "Where is this coming from, Hugh? Joe helped you at the orphanage just like he did me."

"He took you away from me," Hugh said in a low voice.

Scarlet stared at him in shock. "That's not true, Hugh. He gave me a home, that's all."

"But you left The Family Farm and I was alone."

She wanted to argue that there had been ten other kids in the home at the time. But she knew exactly what he meant. Even in a crowded room, you could feel very much alone.

"I'm sorry, Hugh, I never realized you felt that way."

Pain flashed in his eyes. "I thought we were a team," he said. "That we were inseparable."

"Hugh, we were kids. The past ten years we've both grown up. We have a good partnership at the social services agency."

Hugh moved toward her and set his coffee on the counter. "But we can be so much more, Scarlet."

Scarlet placed her coffee beside his. She had to be gentle. "Hugh, I like you as a friend and coworker, but that's all there can be between us."

A frown pulled at Hugh's thin face. "Because you're in love with Ray McCullen?"

Yes. But Scarlet had no idea where things stood with Ray, or where they were going.

"This is not about Ray," Scarlet said.

"You need me," Hugh said. "You and I are alike."

"Hugh—"

"Please, Scarlet. I can keep you safe from whoever sent that picture and from the person who smashed your doll."

Scarlet went very still. "How did you know about the doll?"

Hugh's eyes widened. "You told me."

"No, I didn't," Scarlet said. "I just found it when I got home earlier."

Hugh's eye twitched. "Well…you did mention it. You must have forgotten."

"No, Hugh, I didn't." The hair on the back of her neck prickled. Hugh had given her that envelope with the burned picture inside.

And the doll—he knew Joe had given it to her. Was Hugh trying to frighten her into his arms?

RAY DODGED ANOTHER bullet, crouching low and straining to catch a glimpse of Bobby. "Give it up, man," Ray shouted.

Footsteps pounded and he glanced around the corner and saw Bobby heading toward a pickup. More footsteps sounded, and Maddox barreled into the alley, pausing, his weapon drawn.

Ray pointed to the rear parking lot. "He has a truck in the back."

"Stay behind me." Maddox held his gun at the ready and led the way down the alley. Another bullet pinged off the brick wall as they crept to the end. Bobby made a run for his truck, putting him out in the open.

Maddox stepped from the corner of the building and aimed his gun. "Stop, Lowman, or I'll shoot."

Bobby dove for the truck though, forcing Maddox to act. He fired a shot, the bullet pinging the ground at Bobby's feet. That made the man freeze and throw up his hands in surrender.

"Don't move," Maddox ordered as he inched forward. Ray provided backup, his own gun aimed at Bobby.

"You're really going to take your own brother to jail?" Bobby's angry words were slurred as he turned to face them.

"You shot at us," Ray said.

Maddox kept his gun aimed at Bobby's chest to make sure the man didn't try to shoot again or run.

Rage oozed from Bobby's pores, mingling with the stench of alcohol.

Eyes focused on Bobby, Maddox lifted Bobby's .38 from his hand and tucked it in the waistband of his jeans.

"I wasn't trying to kill nobody," Bobby muttered. "I just wanted you to leave me alone."

"Just like you didn't try to hurt Scarlet," Ray said, not bothering to hide his disdain.

Maddox unhooked the handcuffs from his belt, jerked Bobby's hands behind him, spun him around and snapped the handcuffs around his wrists. "A few nights in jail might be good for you."

"I don't belong in jail," Bobby wailed. "I should have been a McCullen."

"You jerk," Maddox growled. "Our father gave you a chance when he willed that land to you. But you aren't going to get it this way."

Bobby jerked against the cuffs. "That bitch Scarlet doesn't have to do anything, he just gave it to her and she's not even family."

Ray barely contained his animosity toward Bobby as he jammed his gun in his jacket. "Scarlet has nothing to do with this. This is about you. If you want to be part of the McCullens, then start acting like one."

"But—"

"He's right," Maddox said as he gave Bobby a shove.

"McCullen men don't go around beating up and harassing women. And they sure as hell don't go on drunk tears and shoot at the law. Hell, Bobby, you could have killed Ray or some innocent bystander."

Bobby protested, but Maddox pushed him through the alley between the buildings. When they reached the front parking lot, a few patrons were leaving The Silver Bullet and paused to watch, looking guarded as Maddox opened the back door to his police SUV and pushed Bobby inside.

Ray's phone buzzed and he checked it, worried about Scarlet. But Brett's number appeared. He punched Connect.

"Yeah?"

"Ray, there's another fire!"

Ray clenched the phone in a white-knuckled grip. "Where?"

"The house. I called the fire department."

"Maddox is here with me. We'll be right there."

Maddox froze, brows furrowed. "What the hell's wrong?"

"The house is on fire." Ray snatched his keys from his pocket and jogged toward his Range Rover.

Maddox's eyes glittered with panic. "God, Rose is home." He wrenched open his car door. "Follow me." Maddox jumped in the vehicle, flipped on the siren and sped from the parking lot.

Ray followed, praying no one was hurt.

SCARLET DIDN'T LIKE the dark road her thoughts had taken. She and Hugh had known each other for years. They'd been friends. Coworkers.

He also suffered from depression and took medication for bipolar disorder to control his erratic mood swings.

How could she have missed the signs that he was more troubled lately? That he might have developed an unhealthy attachment to her?

She massaged her temple, feigning a headache. "Hugh, I appreciate you coming, but I'm really tired and need a nap."

"Let me hold you while you rest." Hugh reached for her hand. Her skin crawled, but she forced herself not to react.

"That's sweet, Hugh, but I need to be alone." She took his hand and led him toward the door. "Keep me updated on that couple who want to adopt Rachelle."

He stood at the door, his hand gripping hers a little too tightly. "Please let me stay, Scarlet. We've been good friends forever. We can be more."

"I'm sorry, Hugh," Scarlet said. "There's too much going on in my life for me to have a relationship with anyone."

His mouth settled into a thin line. "What about Ray McCullen?"

She swallowed hard. "Ray and I met to discuss his father's will. Joe left money for The Family Farm, and I wanted to make sure the McCullens didn't contest it."

"Really? Is that all there is to it?" he asked, his voice laced with suspicion. "Because it looked like more."

She wanted more. But what did Ray want?

"Yes," she said, careful not to antagonize Hugh. "Now, please, let me lie down. I'll call you later."

He reluctantly stepped outside, and she peered through the window to make sure that he drove away.

Then she reached for the phone to call Ray. Hugh's fingerprints would definitely be on the envelope he'd given her with that burned photo inside. But what about the doll?

If his fingerprints were on it, she'd know that he was the one who'd smashed it.

RAY'S PHONE BUZZED just as he veered onto the drive leading to the ranch house. Fear seized him at the sight of the smoke curling upward in the distance.

Maddox bounced over the dirt road, gravel flying, his siren roaring.

The phone buzzed again and he snatched it up. When he saw Scarlet's name, panic bubbled inside, and he connected the call. "Scarlet?"

"Yes, did you get Bobby?"

"Yeah, he's in handcuffs in Maddox's car, but there's a fire at the ranch. We're on our way there now."

"Oh, my God," Scarlet gasped.

Ray spun down the drive, the smoke thickening as he drew closer. Flames shot into the sky, lighting it with orange and red. He had to go. "Are you okay?"

"Yes. How did the fire start?"

"I don't know. I'll call you back when I find out more." Satisfied she was safe with Pullman and Bobby in custody, he hung up, then swung to a stop behind Maddox in the drive.

"Rose!" Maddox threw the car door open and jumped out, sprinting toward the house. Ray followed suit, grief pummeling him at the sight of their homestead in flames. The left side where the master bedroom was located was engulfed, and the flames were spreading to the living area.

The firefighters were already working to roll out the hoses and douse the flames.

"Rose!" Maddox shouted over the roar.

Ray scanned the front yard and spotted Brett talking to one of the firefighters.

"Rose!" Maddox yelled again.

Rose emerged from the side of an ambulance, a blanket wrapped around her, and ran toward Maddox. He hauled her into his arms, his shoulders shaking with emotions as they hugged.

Relief flooded Ray when he saw Mama Mary standing by the ambulance, and he jogged over to her.

She threw her arms around him, her big body trembling. "Lordy, Mr. Ray, I can't believe this. We can't lose your daddy's house!"

"Don't worry about the house, Mama Mary." Ray tightened his grip on her. He couldn't have stood to lose her. "I'm just glad you're okay."

Tears streamed down her face, and she hugged him and kissed his cheek. Finally she pulled back, drying her eyes and swiping her hair into its bun.

Ray cleared his throat, his own eyes stinging. "What happened? How did the fire start?"

"I don't know," Mama Mary said. "Miss Rose was at work. She said she and Mr. Maddox were going out for dinner tonight, so I went to my church supper. When I got here, Miss Rose was pulling up. Smoke was pouring from the house so we ran inside to see if it was the stove, but the smoke was so thick we couldn't see anything, and flames were in the bedroom." She heaved for a breath. "Rose called 911, then she grabbed the fire extinguisher, and I tried beating it out with a blanket, but it was spreading too fast."

Ray took a deep breath and squeezed her arm. "I'm just glad you weren't hurt."

Maddox and Rose joined them, Maddox's face etched with love for his new wife.

"I'm so sorry, Ray," Rose said. "Mama Mary and I tried to put it out."

"Don't worry about it," Ray said. "We're just grateful the two of you are safe."

"You don't know what started the fire?" Ray asked.

Rose shook her head. "No, but I…thought I smelled gas."

"Like the stove was left on?" Maddox asked.

"I didn't leave the stove on," Mama Mary's voice quivered. "At least I don't think I did."

"No, not the stove," Rose said. "Like gasoline."

Ray and Maddox exchanged looks. "The same person who set the barn fire probably started this one."

Maddox hauled Rose close for a kiss. "Let me look around. See if we find anything suspicious."

He glanced at Bobby. Bobby was staring at the fire as if he was mesmerized.

But Bobby had been at the bar when the fire started. If he hadn't set it, who had?

SCARLET PUNCHED THE accelerator, anxious to reach Horse-shoe Creek. Had Bobby set fire to the ranch house to hurt Ray and his brothers?

The wind picked up outside, shaking tree limbs and tossing tumbleweed across the road as she veered down the drive. She thought she spotted a vehicle behind some bushes, but sped on, worried for the McCullens.

Smoke billowed in the darkening sky, flames lighting the darkness as she approached. Ray's Range Rover and Maddox's police car were parked in the drive, the fire engine close to the house.

Bobby was inside the back of the police SUV, staring at the blaze, a sinister smile on his face.

Scarlet shivered, threw the car into Park and reached for the door.

Another car barreled down the drive and screeched to a stop behind her. She glanced in her rearview mirror and saw Barbara slide from her BMW and walk toward Maddox's vehicle.

Scarlet stepped from her car and faced Barbara. "What are you doing here?"

"I came to talk to the McCullens about how they're treating my son."

"Barbara, for God's sake, now isn't the time. Their house

is on fire." She grabbed Barbara's arm, but the woman shoved her away.

"Stay out of this, Scarlet." Barbara stopped beside her son, then jerked the door open.

Maddox and Ray strode toward her.

"What the hell are you doing?" Maddox shouted.

"Scarlet?" Ray said.

Before she could respond, Barbara pulled a gun from her purse and aimed it at her.

Barbara turned a sinister look at Ray and Maddox. "Let my son go or she's dead."

Chapter Twenty-Two

Ray's gut pinched at the sight of Barbara aiming that gun at Scarlet.

"What are you doing, Barbara?" Scarlet said.

"My son was neglected, and now you McCullens are ganging up on him," Barbara shouted over the roar of the blaze.

Ray held up a hand to calm Barbara. "He attacked Scarlet, Barbara. He also opened fire at me. He's a grown man. He has to answer for that."

She kept the gun trained on them, yanked open the back door and motioned for Bobby to get out. He slid from the vehicle, a smile on his face. "Hey, Mom."

Barbara frowned. "I'll deal with you later, son."

She swung the gun toward Maddox. "Give me the handcuff keys."

"What are you going to do, Barbara? Run?" Maddox asked. "Then you and Bobby will never get what Dad left you."

Hatred glistened in Barbara's eyes. "My son should have had equal shares with you. And your father should have married me."

"Barbara, Joe only wanted Bobby to get help," Scarlet said.

Ray's lungs squeezed for air as she turned the gun on

Scarlet again. "And you…you played on Joe's sympathy and robbed my son of time with his father." She angled her head toward him and Maddox. "You are such fools, just like Joe. You fell for Scarlet's sweet little act. But she's the one who got my Bobby into trouble when they were young."

Scarlet gasped. "Barbara, that's not true."

"Of course it is. You talked Bobby into breaking into that rich lady's house and stealing her jewelry." She addressed Maddox. "You're the sheriff. I'm sure you investigated her, didn't you? That's what you do. Find out everyone's background so you can protect the McCullens."

Ray's head jerked toward Maddox, and guilt flashed in his oldest brother's eyes. "Maddox?"

"She was arrested when she was a juvenile."

Scarlet paled and bit down on her lip. "That was a mistake. Bobby lied and implicated me in a break-in, but I was cleared."

Ray didn't know what to believe. He couldn't imagine the sweet, giving woman he knew doing anything illegal, although she had had a troubled childhood.

Barbara waved the gun toward Maddox. "Now, you're going to do the right thing. You're going to unlock those handcuffs and let us drive away. Then you're going to drop the charges against Bobby and give us what's owed us with no strings attached."

Maddox inched forward. "You're not helping your son by doing this, Barbara. He'll just keep on drinking and hurting other people. Dad didn't want that."

Barbara released a sardonic laugh. "Funny how he couldn't get past Bobby drinking, but he sure as hell covered up for your mother."

Ray's heart hammered and Maddox went still. Brett had joined them, his look confused. "What does that mean?" Ray asked.

"Your daddy lied to you about me. I was the good one. Your mama was the one who couldn't hold her liquor."

"Shut up, Barbara." Mama Mary eased up beside Maddox and folded her arms beneath her ample bosom, facing Barbara like a mama bear protecting her cubs. "Just because he wouldn't marry you doesn't mean you need to hurt these boys."

"They should know the truth," Barbara said. "Maybe they wouldn't be so damn judgmental then."

"What's she talking about, Mama Mary?" Maddox asked.

"Your perfect mother," Barbara said. "She didn't die because a drunk driver hit her. She was the drunk driver. She rammed her own car into a tree and killed herself."

Shock slammed into Ray. Judging from Maddox's curse and Brett's sharp hiss, they were equally stunned.

Behind them, the firefighters were still working to save the McCullen home.

"We're going to walk away and you're going to drop those charges." Barbara snatched the handcuff key from Maddox, then tossed it to Bobby. He quickly unlocked the cuffs, then flung them to the ground.

Barbara backed toward her car, motioning for Bobby to get in. Bobby had to pass Scarlet to reach the passenger side. He paused to tweak her hair and give her a gloating look. "Finally you'll get what you deserve. Nothing."

Maddox seemed to have recovered from the shock of Barbara's statement more quickly than Ray. "Did you set this fire, Barbara?"

"Setting fires is not my style, so don't try to pin that on me or my son." She jumped in the car, keeping the gun aimed at them until she revved up the engine. Then she slammed the door and sped away.

Ray took one look at Maddox who already had his keys

out. "Stay here and take care of the women," Maddox told Brett. "I'm going after them. They're not going to get away."

Scarlet reached for Ray's arm. "Ray—"

"I'm going with him," Ray said, his emotions all over the place.

Was Scarlet the sweet, innocent woman he'd thought, or had she deceived his father and now him to get her share of the ranch?

SCARLET'S CHEST ACHED as Ray and Maddox followed Barbara and Bobby.

She'd seen the doubt in Ray's eyes. He believed what Barbara said about her leading Bobby into trouble.

Disappointment mixed with anger. All her life she'd fought to be somebody, to fit into a family, to overcome being tossed aside as a child. But Joe had been the only one who'd seen the good in her and loved her.

She'd hoped with Ray…

Brett was watching her as Rose and Mama Mary approached. Needing to leave before she burst into tears, she climbed in her car, but her hands were shaking so badly she dropped the keys on the floor.

The scent of smoke and burned ashes and…betrayal made her head swim. She'd known Barbara resented her and that Bobby was jealous of the attention Joe had given her, but she'd never thought Barbara would lie to punish her. But she had.

Ray's reaction cut to the bone, too.

The flames were dying under the deluge of water the firefighters were dumping on it, but the house was a wreck and would need major renovations.

She found her keys, jammed them in the ignition and started the engine.

Her gaze met Brett's through the front window of her car as she backed up, and everything became clear to her.

She didn't belong here.

She never would.

MADDOX PHONED DEPUTY WHITEFEATHER for backup as he started the SUV, and gave him the license plate for Barbara's car.

"Do you think she was telling the truth about Mom?" Ray asked Maddox as he barreled down the drive to chase Barbara.

A muscle jumped in Maddox's jaw. "I don't know."

"Did Dad ever mention Mom drinking?"

Maddox shook his head, although his silence troubled Ray. He strained to remember his mother as a child, but all he recalled was how beautiful she was. That she made sugar cookies with him and sang to him at night.

"Maddox?"

Maddox released a weary sigh and accelerated, gaining speed on Barbara. "He never talked about it, but now that I think about it, I saw him helping her to bed a few times. I…didn't realize what was happening. But the next day I found an empty vodka bottle by the sofa. Dad saw me with it, and later I heard him and Mom arguing."

So it could be true. Ray felt as if he'd been sucker punched. "Maybe she was drinking because she knew Dad was cheating."

"Maybe," Maddox muttered although he didn't sound convinced. "I don't think we can believe anything Barbara says, though."

Maddox maneuvered a curve, then they spotted Barbara veer down a side road. The SUV bounced over ruts as Maddox flew up on her tail.

"About Scarlet?" Maddox said.

Ray's insides churned. "Yeah, you said she had a record."

"I'm sorry. You like her, don't you?"

He wasn't sure *like* was the word. He wanted her. He had come to admire her.

He might even…love her.

But had their relationship been based on lies?

"I've got a call in to Judge Winters," Maddox said. "He'll tell me what really went on."

Ray gave a clipped nod, too torn to respond.

Seconds later, they closed in on Barbara. She raced down the road, then disappeared around a curve. Maddox spun around the curve, her lights fading as she increased speed.

Tires squealed as Maddox accelerated, taking the curve on two wheels. Ahead, he spotted the lights of Barbara's car, then Maddox closed in. Seconds later, she lost control and slammed into a tree.

Maddox jolted to a stop a foot behind her and jumped out, weapon drawn. "Stay in the car," he ordered Ray.

"Hell, no, brother." Ray pulled his own gun from inside his jacket. "I've got your back."

Bobby eased from the car, staggering slightly, and Barbara crawled out, then spun around, weapon aimed. But Maddox was too fast. He jumped her, and they fought for the gun.

Bobby started toward Maddox to help his mother, but Ray tackled him, then shoved his gun in the bastard's face.

"It's over, Bobby. Time to face the music."

Bobby's sinister eyes pierced him. "You'd better not hurt my mother."

A gunshot sounded, and they both froze and glanced sideways.

"Mom!" Bobby shouted.

Ray saw the gun hit the ground, then Maddox pinned Barbara against the side of the car.

"Give it up, Barbara," Maddox growled. "I don't want to hurt you or Bobby, but I'm not going to let you escape, either."

"You owe me, Maddox," Barbara cried. "And Joe owes our son."

"He'll get what he deserves." Maddox tossed a pair of cuffs toward Ray, and he rolled Bobby over and snapped them on while Maddox cuffed Barbara.

"This isn't fair," Barbara whined. "I deserved his love. She was a drunk."

Maddox said nothing. He shoved her in the back of his squad car, and Ray did the same with Bobby, although Bobby was cursing a blue streak. When they slammed the door, Ray wiped sweat from his forehead.

But Barbara's accusation against their mother taunted him. Mama Mary had commented that their parents had problems. If what Barbara said was true, their father could have turned to Barbara because of their mother's drinking, not the other way around.

If so, he'd been too hard on their father. But their dad should have explained the situation to them when they got older. They would have understood.

Or would they? Ray had already built up such a wall and harbored so much anger that he hadn't given his father a chance.

SCARLET LET HERSELF into her house, chastising herself for getting involved with Ray. She shouldn't have slept with him.

And she certainly shouldn't have fallen in love with him.

Love? Do I love Ray?

Yes. How could she not? He was all the things she'd ever wanted in a man. Strong, handsome, noble…

But he didn't trust her. That doubt in his eyes tore her insides out.

And Ray's brothers…they would never accept her.

So how could she possibly make a home on the piece of land Joe had left her? She would always remind Ray and his brothers of their father's indiscretion. And of his lies.

Why had she ever imagined that she'd fit into their lives? Or that Ray could love her?

Tears blurred her eyes, but she swiped at them and she made a decision. She took out a pen and pad and began to write.

Dear Ray,
I'm sorry for the trouble my presence in your father's life caused you and your brothers. And I'm sorry that Joe never told you about me or Bobby and Barbara.

I loved your father and I appreciate all that he did for me, more than you'll ever know. But I realize now that I can't make a home on the land that he gave me.

You may not approve, but I do plan to keep the money he designated for The Family Farm.

You and your brothers can reclaim the land Joe left me as part of Horseshoe Creek. It belongs to your family, not to me.

She started to write Love, Scarlet, but thought better of it and simply signed her name.

A noise echoed from the back, and Scarlet froze. She strained to hear, then recognized the sound. The wind beating a branch against the glass pane.

Relieved, she stood and walked to the bedroom. Tomorrow she'd search for a place to move, someplace that wasn't so close to Pistol Whip and Ray.

Another noise startled her. *The branch again?* Irritated

at herself for being so jumpy, she decided to check it out. But just as she entered her bedroom and reached out to flip on the light, a shadow moved in her bathroom.

Scarlet turned to run, but footsteps pounded, then a man grabbed her from behind.

Chapter Twenty-Three

Deputy Whitefeather met Ray and Maddox at the sheriff's office. Barbara and Bobby continued to deny that they'd set fire to the McCullen house. Both had also denied sending Scarlet the burned photo and smashing her doll.

Then Barbara had evoked her rights to an attorney for her and her son.

"Let's let them sit in jail overnight," Maddox said. "Maybe when Barbara realizes how much trouble she and Bobby are in, she'll confess."

Ray knew he should relax about Scarlet. Barbara, Bobby and Pullman were all in custody.

But a sick feeling knotted his stomach.

He had hurt Scarlet.

"Brett texted that the fire is out," Maddox said. "The arson investigator is there. I want to talk to him."

Deputy Whitefeather nodded. "Go ahead. I'll stay here and hold down the fort."

Ray wanted to get Bobby alone and pound a confession out of him, but Maddox insisted on sticking to the law.

The urge to see Scarlet nagged at Ray.

But he owed his brothers his support. He also wanted to find out who set fire to the house as much as Maddox. Rose or Mama Mary could have been inside and died. And what if Brett's son had been injured?

Ray followed Maddox out the door before he went back in and beat Bobby to a bloody pulp.

Maddox was quiet as they drove to the ranch. "If Bobby and Barbara didn't set fire to the barn and house, who did?"

"Romley is still missing," Ray reminded him.

"True. Hardwick insisted that he was only supposed to report our progress to Bennett, that he wasn't the arsonist. I'm going to find that son of a bitch Romley and get to the truth."

Ray nodded, although his mind wandered back to Scarlet. She'd rushed to the house when she thought they were in trouble, not because she wanted anything from them.

Because she cared.

But when Maddox mentioned her past, a sliver of doubt had crept in.

Not because of Scarlet, but because he had trouble trusting. Seeing his father with another woman had tainted his idea of relationships.

Dammit, he could trust Scarlet. She was the sweetest, most selfless person he'd ever known.

Brett, his family and Rose met them at Maddox's vehicle when they arrived. Rose threw her arms around his brother, obviously grateful to see he'd returned safely.

Maddox pulled away and kissed her. "I'm going to talk to the arson investigator."

Seeing both his brothers happy with their own families triggered a deep-seated loneliness in him.

Making a snap decision, he told Maddox he was going to check on Scarlet. Maddox's dark gaze met his. Brett raised his brows in question.

"You don't want to hear back from that judge first?" Maddox asked.

"I don't need to. I know Scarlet. She deserves everything Dad left her. If you guys don't agree, then I'll buy her share from you."

He didn't bother to wait on a response. He didn't care what they said and he didn't need their approval.

He jumped in his Range Rover and headed toward Scarlet's.

FEAR RIPPED THROUGH Scarlet as the man pushed her onto the bed. The scent of cologne and chewing gum hit her.

Hugh.

She squirmed and pushed at his hands, and he finally released her. But his heavy breathing rattled in the dark room as he towered over her.

God help me. It had never occurred to her that Hugh could be dangerous. "Why are you doing this? I thought we were friends."

"Because you know," he said, his voice accusatory.

"Know what?" she said, playing dumb.

She was on her own now. Joe was gone and so was Ray. She had to stall. Pray she could keep him calm and talk him out of doing anything irrational.

"That I burned that photo. That I smashed that damn doll." He paced in front her, swinging his hands. "But I did it because I love you."

"You scared me half to death out of love?" Scarlet said.

He stared at her, eyes wild. "I've always loved you. Ever since we were kids."

She struggled to recall what had happened to his parents. If she was correct, his father had stalked his mother after their divorce. He'd probably justified his obsessive behavior, claiming it was love.

"I wanted to protect you, to be the one to comfort you when Joe died." His voice rose to an unnatural level. "You were supposed to turn to me, not that blasted McCullen."

Scarlet bit her tongue to keep from defending Ray. Doing that would only agitate Hugh more.

"I'm sorry if I didn't pay you enough attention," Scarlet said, grappling for reason. "I've just had so much on my mind. Joe's passing, and then Pullman and his daughter, and little Corey."

"Who was there to help you through all that?" Hugh pounded his fist on his chest. "I was, Scarlet. I've always been there for you."

Yes he had. But she didn't feel the same attraction to him that she did toward Ray.

A loud knock echoed from the front, and she clenched the quilt as Hugh swung around. "Who the hell is that?"

"I don't know," Scarlet said.

"Probably that SOB McCullen." Hugh strode into the living room and Scarlet raced after him.

"Hugh, I'll get it."

But Hugh blocked her from the door, pulled a gun from his jacket and ordered her to be quiet.

"Scarlet, I know you're in there," Ray called. "Let me in."

Hugh pointed the gun at her. "Get rid of him," he ordered.

A tremor rippled through her, and she nodded.

She'd do anything to protect Ray.

Inhaling a calming breath, she inched her way to the door, but left the chain attached as she turned the bottom lock.

Ray's dark eyes met hers through the crack. "Scarlet," he said softly. "Please let me in."

She shook her head. "Not tonight, Ray, I'm tired."

"We have to talk about earlier… I'm sorry."

She had to get rid of him, fast. "There's nothing else to

say." She grabbed the letter she'd written to him earlier and shoved it through the opening.

His fingers closed around it, his eyes questioning. "What is this?"

"It's goodbye, Ray."

Trembling, she slammed the door shut. She leaned against it breathing heavily as she looked into Hugh's troubled eyes.

A slow smile curved his mouth, and he feathered her hair from her cheek. "See, now, everything will be all right. You and I will be together just like it should have been all along."

RAY SKIMMED THE letter Scarlet had written. She was leaving town because he and his brothers had given her hell.

That wasn't what his father wanted.

It wasn't what he wanted, either.

He leaned against the door, debating on how to change her mind, but footsteps and voices echoed from inside.

Voices—not just Scarlet's.

A man. Had Pullman gotten out of jail?

He leaned against the door, straining to hear. They were arguing.

Scarlet had seemed nervous.

A yelp sounded inside, then something slammed against the wall and his instincts surged to life. Not bothering to question what he was doing, he jiggled the doorknob. Scarlet hadn't locked it, and it opened just enough for him to see her coworker.

He clutched Scarlet's arm trying to pull her toward the bedroom, but she was resisting.

Pure rage flooded Ray, and he rammed his shoulder against the door and knocked it open. Scarlet gasped and Hugh looked startled, then Ray caught the shiny glint of metal. Hugh had a gun.

"What's going on here?" Ray asked, debating on how best to approach the man.

"I thought you left," Hugh said. "Scarlet and I want to be alone, don't we?"

He tightened his grip on Scarlet's arm and she nodded, but she was trembling.

"If you want me to leave, you're going to have to put that gun down," Ray said.

Hugh gaped at the pistol as if he'd forgotten he was holding it. "I would never hurt Scarlet. I love her."

"If you love me, Hugh, then let me go," Scarlet said in a low voice.

Indecision played in Hugh's eyes. "You and I have been through so much, Scarlet. We belong together."

The man sounded delusional. Ray wanted to reach for his gun, but he couldn't take the chance. Instead he raised his hands in surrender.

"Seriously, man, I get what you're saying. Just put the gun on the counter, then I'll walk out."

"Please, listen to him, Hugh. I don't want you to get hurt."

Hugh narrowed his eyes at Ray as if he sensed a trap. "Leave first, then I'll put down the gun."

Ray shook his head. "Not going to happen."

Hugh raised the gun again. "You can't have her. She's mine."

Scarlet stepped in front of Ray, putting herself in between the men.

"Scarlet, move," Ray growled.

But she lifted that chin again. She was stubborn. "Shoot Ray and you have to shoot me," she said softly.

Hugh looked panicked. "Get out of the way, Scarlet."

Ray reached for her arm to pull her behind him, but she jerked away and turned to face Hugh, blocking him.

"Hugh, you and I both grew up with violence around us. You hated the way your father treated your mother." Her voice was gentle. "You're not going to turn into him. I won't let you."

Ray had no idea what that meant, and he didn't want to.

Scarlet held out her hand, palm up. "Now, please. Give me the gun and we'll work this out."

Fear throbbed through Ray. But a second later, Hugh handed her the gun. He broke down and began to cry, and she pulled him into her arms.

"I'm going to call his therapist," she said. "He must be off his meds."

Ray kept his eyes on Hugh. If he made one move, he'd shoot the sick jerk. "The only way he doesn't get locked up tonight is if he admits himself for treatment."

Hugh dropped his head into his hands and rocked himself back and forth. He seemed to disappear inside himself.

Scarlet patted his back in a comforting gesture and made a phone call. Ten minutes later, he drove Scarlet and Hugh to meet the man's therapist at the psychiatric ward where they admitted him.

When Scarlet was satisfied Hugh was settled, Ray drove Scarlet home. She looked wrung out, as if she needed someone to lift the weight of the world from her slender shoulders.

He wanted to be that someone.

"He's bipolar. I should have seen the signs that he was off his meds," she said as he walked her to the door.

Ray rubbed her arms up and down to soothe her. "Scarlet, it's not your job to save the world. You've had your hands full with your work and Pullman, and Bobby and Barbara." His brothers had also given her a hard time.

But that would stop. He'd made a stand tonight, and he

hoped they accepted his decision. That is, if Scarlet would have him.

Had he and his family hurt her too much for her to love him?

SCARLET'S NERVES WERE on the brink of shattering.

Ray stood at the door, lingering, making it even more difficult for her to say goodbye.

"Thanks for helping me tonight," Scarlet finally said. "I know you need to go back to Horseshoe Creek. Did Bobby or Barbara admit to setting the fire?"

"No, and that's the damnedest thing," Ray said. "Bobby confessed that he hired that thug to beat me up, but he wouldn't cop to the fires. If he and Barbara aren't responsible for them, that means our ranch and my family may still be in danger."

The thought of anyone attacking Ray terrified Scarlet. "Then you should go home."

As much as she wanted Ray right now, his brothers needed him more. They'd just buried their father and someone was trying to destroy their ranch, their home and their livelihood.

Her keys jangled in her hands as she unlocked the door and stepped inside.

But Ray stepped in behind her. "What about you, Scarlet?"

She turned to look at him. He was so close he was touching her, his gaze boring into hers, probing.

"What do you need?" he asked in a raw whisper.

She needed him. But how could she ask him for love, when she and her adopted family had torn the McCullens apart?

Chapter Twenty-Four

Ray shuffled from foot to foot, his stomach churning. No woman had ever tied him in knots like this.

He couldn't even think straight.

Was she giving him the brush-off? Did she want him to leave her alone?

He couldn't blame her if she did. Except for his father, all the men in her life had disappointed her. His brothers hadn't exactly welcomed her into their lives. Bobby had resented her and tormented her. Even Hugh, her friend, had frightened her with his sick games.

And he…he hadn't jumped to her defense the way he should have back at the ranch.

He cleared his throat twice to make his voice work. "Scarlet—"

"Ray, go home where you belong. Make up with your brothers and put your family back together the way your father wanted."

He remembered the letter she'd written him, relinquishing her piece of land. "My father wanted you to have part of Horseshoe Creek, too."

Scarlet's face twisted in pain. "You have no idea how much that means to me, Ray. I loved your father, mistakes and all." Her lower lip quivered. "But there's no way I can live on any part of the ranch and be your neighbor when you and your brothers don't want me there."

Ray's heart gave an odd pang. His father had made mistakes, but loving and caring for Scarlet hadn't been one of them. She might not have been born a McCullen, but she had earned her way into his father's heart.

And into his.

"You're right," he said, his voice firm. "I don't want you to be my neighbor."

Sadness tinged her beautiful eyes, but she nodded. "I understand."

"No, you don't." For the first time in his life, he let the bitterness toward his father go and allowed the love that he'd found fill his heart.

Scarlet blinked back tears. "Yes, I do, Ray."

"No, you don't." He pulled her up against him. "I don't want you to be my neighbor because I want you to be my wife."

A heartbeat of silence passed, then Scarlet's soft gasp. "What?"

"I love you," Ray said, as he gazed into her beautiful eyes. "I love you and I want to marry you and for us to build a home together on Horseshoe Creek. And I want to volunteer at The Family Farm and continue what my father started there."

For a moment, she simply stared at him, her mind processing what he'd said. He loved her. He wanted to help her at the children's home.

He wanted to marry her…

As his words sank in, her frown faded into a smile, and she clasped her hands around his neck. She would really be a McCullen and have the family she'd always dreamed of. "I love you, too, Ray."

He tilted his head, his lips a fraction of an inch away from hers. "Then you'll be my wife?"

Tears blurred her eyes.

"Scarlet?"

"Yes, I'll marry you, Ray. I love you with all my heart." She stood on tiptoe and kissed him with all the passion in her soul.

Ray twirled her around, then carried her straight to bed. Frantic to touch each other, they tore at each other's clothes, lips melding, bodies gliding, passion bursting between them as they made love.

For tonight, nothing mattered except that together they had found each other.

Maybe his father had known all along that Scarlet was meant to be in the family. Maybe even that she was meant to be with him.

Epilogue

Two weeks later

Deputy Roan Whitefeather couldn't believe he'd been invited to the McCullen ranch for Ray McCullen's wedding to Scarlet Lovett. Guitar music strummed as Scarlet stepped under the gazebo by the creek to join with Ray.

Roan didn't belong here.

But he knew more about this family than they knew about themselves.

Knew Joe had more secrets that would rattle the brothers even more than finding out about Barbara and Bobby Lowman.

Maddox, Brett and Ray had already started rebuilding the main farmhouse where Maddox and Rose would live. Brett and Willow's house was almost finished and ready to move in.

Ray had drawn up plans for himself and his new wife, and they were temporarily living in the cabin Joe McCullen had left Scarlet.

Hugh was in treatment at the psychiatric ward. Evidence had proven that he had given Scarlet the burned photo and that he'd smashed the doll.

The brothers were still grieving, but seemed to have mended fences among themselves. They had found a website on Barbara's computer where she'd researched how to cut brake lines, and used it to push Barbara for a confession. She claimed she'd only wanted to scare Scarlet. She and Bobby had pled out on lesser charges but would serve some time, and Bobby had agreed to rehab. One day they might win their way back into the McCullens' favor, but that would take time.

Whitefeather stood at the edge of the ceremony, studying the crowd, searching for anyone suspicious that might want to hurt the McCullens.

Maddox, Brett and Ray were determined to find out who'd set the fires. So far, the arson investigator hadn't found DNA to tie it to Romley or anyone else.

At this point, Romley was still missing, and they suspected he was connected to Arlis Bennett, but they needed proof.

He would find it, though. Just like he would find out the truth about how Joe had died.

The brothers hadn't questioned that their father's illness had killed him.

But *he* had.

And he wouldn't stop until he learned if Joe McCullen had really died of natural causes.

Or if he'd been murdered.

* * * * *

There were things that needed to be said.

She gathered her courage. "I'm not sure there's much to be gained from going over old ground, but—" she took a breath "—but if I hurt you, I'm sorry."

He stared at the coffee in his cup. "If you hurt me?" he repeated softly. "If?"

He wasn't going to let this be easy. She understood. She deserved this. "When," she corrected. "When I hurt you."

He looked up. "I guess I'd really just like to know what happened."

"You left," she said.

"I enlisted. We had discussed it. You said you would wait."

She had intended to. And she had wanted to. Then things had happened. But nothing she could tell Bray about. Nothing she could ever tell anyone about.

URGENT PURSUIT

BY
BEVERLY LONG

First Published in Great Britain 2016
By Mills & Boon, an imprint of HarperCollins*Publishers*
1 London Bridge Street, London, SE1 9GF

© 2016 by Beverly R. Long

ISBN: 978-0-263-91904-2

46-0516

Our policy is to use papers that are natural, renewable and recyclable products and made from wood grown in sustainable forests. The logging and manufacturing processes conform to the legal environmental regulations of the country of origin.

Printed and bound in Spain
by CPI, Barcelona

Beverly Long enjoys the opportunity to write her own stories. She has both a bachelor's and a master's degree in business and more than twenty years of experience as a human resources director. She considers her books to be a great success if they compel the reader to stay up way past their bedtime. Beverly loves to hear from readers. Visit www.beverlylong.com, or like her at Facebook.com/beverlylong.romance.

To mothers and daughters and the love they share.

Chapter One

Bray got off the plane in St. Louis, Missouri, and shuffled alongside all the other passengers through the terminal. He'd slept the entire flight, but since it was just over two hours from New York to St. Louis, it was not nearly enough time to make up for the past three months, when any rest in excess of four hours a night was considered a luxury.

And when you made your living working as a drug enforcement agent, *luxury* wasn't part of your everyday vocabulary. But now he had five whole days of downtime, a well-earned vacation as his boss had coined it, to catch up on his sleep.

For months, he'd been planning to travel to Missouri in November for Thanksgiving. Had expected turkey would be served at Chase's upscale, albeit rather sterile, apartment in St. Louis. Had not imagined Chase would move the event to the family home in Ravesville—or that he'd add something else to the holiday weekend.

He'd been casual, too casual Bray now realized, when he'd asked Bray how he might feel about extending his stay through Sunday. Bray had assumed he was looking for help to get the house ready for sale.

He'd almost fallen off his chair when Chase had announced that he was getting married on the Saturday after Thanksgiving, and would Bray serve as a groomsman? Bray had laughed and said, "Hell, yes." Then Chase, apparently oblivious that at Bray's advanced age of thirty-seven it was good to have some time to adjust to shocks, had kept going. He wanted to buy the family home, to settle in Ravesville with his new wife, Raney.

"Of course," Bray had said. Then added, "Is there anything else?"

All Chase had said was to expect a call from Cal.

He'd had to wait forty-three hours for his youngest brother to call. And when Cal announced that Bray needed to make sure he could get time off for two trips west because he was engaged and would be married at Christmas, Bray hadn't minced words. "I'll come but I'm sure as hell not drinking the water. The Hollister boys are falling fast, and I'm going to save myself."

He was happy for his brothers. But he knew that marriage wasn't for everyone. He'd come close once, but it had been a long time ago. He'd gone to war, and Summer Wright had married somebody else.

Chase had shared that she was divorced with a couple of kids. Still living in Ravesville. Didn't matter. He and Summer were old news.

He stepped up to the car-rental counter and took the keys for the Chevy Impala. In New York, he had a sweet little BMW convertible but he rarely drove it. Paid a hundred bucks a month to park it down the street from his Brooklyn condo. He mostly worked out of an old, beat-up Honda that was owned by the agency. There was nothing on it to steal, and it already had so many dents that the joke was he could run down some scumbag drug dealer and not even have to file a report.

He found his car in the lot and was on the road in less than a minute. Ravesville was ninety miles southwest of St. Louis in the middle of nowhere. He glanced at his watch. With luck, he'd be there for dinner.

There was a lot of traffic for a Tuesday, but finally, when he was twenty minutes out, he called Chase's cell phone.

"Red or white?" he asked when Chase answered.

"We've got plenty of both. Don't worry about bringing any wine. Meet us at the church on the corner of Main and Portland. You're just in time for rehearsal."

"I could slow way down," Bray said.

"Get your sorry self here. My bride wants to meet you."

At the edge of Ravesville, he saw the gas station where he'd worked his junior and senior years. Like most places, the gas had been self-serve. Bray had worked the inside counter, taking money, selling hot dogs and learning to hate the smell of fountain pop.

Frank Baleeze, who had owned the place, had been his dad's best friend. Once Bray turned sixteen, he'd offered him a job.

It was probably Frank's fault that Bray had become a marine. The man had talked about his years in the corps with such pride. Bray had wanted to be part of something like that.

When Bray had come home for his mother's funeral eight years earlier, Frank had already sold the station and retired to Florida. Even so, Bray stopped in at the old place for gas.

They no longer sold hot dogs, and all the soda was in cans. Their main business was lottery tickets.

It was just more proof that the old saying about not being able to go home again was indeed fact.

The church was close, and Bray found a place to park.

For as long as he could remember, his mother had been a regular attendee at the Lutheran church. He and his brothers had been baptized and confirmed here. His parents had both had their funerals here.

When Bray entered, he saw Chase first, standing next to a very pretty woman with short white-blond hair. Then there was Cal, with his arm slung around a stunningly beautiful woman with dark hair.

Next came hugs and introductions. Once he'd met Raney and Nalana, he was convinced that his brothers might have fallen, but they'd landed in cotton. The women were gorgeous *and* nice.

"Reverend Brown would like us to do a walk-through," Raney said, pointing to the minister at the front of the church.

Clara Brown had performed both his father's and his mother's funerals. She was close to sixty and had a soft voice, but when she spoke, people listened. She'd known his mother better, and the eulogy that she'd delivered had been heartfelt and poignant, a fitting send-off for a good woman.

Bray waved to her. There was a middle-aged woman he didn't know sitting at the piano. He gave her a quick nod and belatedly added a small smile. His partner on the job would have been proud. The guy, who'd recently met his one true love after a nine-month spree of online dating, was always telling him he needed to do that more. "You're scary tough," Mason would say. "Unapproachable. That turns people away, especially the babes. Try smiling."

Every once in a while, he remembered.

"Nice to see you again, Bray," Reverend Brown said. She stepped off the altar and walked toward them. "Just so you know," she said, looking at Raney, "my ceremonies start and end on time. My assistant will be stationed with you and your attendants in the back of the church. I'm counting on the three of you," she said, switching her gaze to the three Hollister men, "to figure out how to get yourselves out of the back room, through the side door and standing at the altar once the second song starts. Can you manage that?"

"I'll keep him from running out the back door," Bray said.

"No worries there," Chase said, winking at Raney.

"I hope not," Reverend Brown said, a smile in her voice. "It's unfortunate that the maid of honor and other bridesmaid couldn't be here for rehearsal, but I'm counting on the rest of you to fill them in." Bray remembered that Chase had said that Raney wanted her two friends to be able to spend Thanksgiving with their families, so the women wouldn't arrive until late Friday night.

No big deal. How tough could it be to walk down the aisle?

Tough enough that ten minutes later, Reverend Brown was making Raney do it a second *this-time-slower* time when Bray heard the sound of squealing tires and a slamming car door. Seconds later, someone pounding down the church steps to get to the basement. Then shouting. A man, loud. A woman, softer, muffled.

And the hair on the back of his neck stood up.

Raney stopped midaisle, turned and started for the back of the church. Chase caught up with her in just a few steps. Four feet later, Bray clamped a hand on his brother's neck and gently grabbed Raney's arm. "This is your practice," he said. "I've got this."

Both Raney and Chase hesitated, and then Chase gave a quick nod. "Be careful," he said.

When Bray got to the top of the basement stairs, the yelling was still going on. He went fast but quietly down the thirteen steps. Rounded the corner, saw the back of a man and realized that he'd grabbed the person in front of him and was starting to shake them.

"Hey," Bray yelled. And that caused just enough delay that he was able to get across the room, land a hand on the man's shoulder and whip him around.

The man hadn't touched him, but he'd felt as if he'd taken one in the stomach.

He hadn't seen Summer Wright for fifteen years, and there she was. As beautiful as ever with her red hair. Her face was pale, and the fingers she had pressed up to her lips were shaking.

"What the hell?" The man was snarling and pushing at Bray.

Two quick moves and Bray had the man on his knees with his left arm wrenched high behind his back. "Shut up," Bray said calmly.

"Are you okay?" he asked Summer.

She nodded.

So maybe he wouldn't break this man's neck. "What's going on here?" Bray asked.

The man tried to twist away. "I'm having a damn conversation with my wife," he said.

"Ex-wife," Summer said. She swallowed hard and looked at Bray. "You can let him go," she said softly.

So this sorry excuse for a man was Gary Blake. "I don't think so."

She licked her lips. "He'll just make trouble for you if you don't."

Many years ago, Blake had been an officer on the local police force. Based on the uniform, he still was. He leaned close to Blake's ear. "I'm going to let you up," Bray whispered. "But if you make one move in her direction, I'm going to take you down, and I'm going to make it hurt."

When Gary Blake was back on his feet, he whirled toward Bray. "Who the hell are you?" he demanded.

"Bray Hollister."

He could tell the minute the name registered. Blake stood perfectly still, as if debating what to do next. Finally, he turned back toward Summer. "We're not done," he said. Then he walked out of the room.

Bray heard his feet on the stairs, heard the front door, heard a vehicle start. He heard all that while he watched the woman he'd once loved lower herself into a chair, as if her knees were about to give out.

"I figured you'd be home for the wedding," she said.

He didn't answer because he heard more noise on the stairs. Then Chase, Raney, Cal and Nalana were in the basement. Reverend Brown and the piano player were behind them.

"Everything under control?" Chase asked, looking at Bray.

Bray shrugged. Hell, no. He wasn't in control. This woman had broken his heart. She'd chosen someone else. And he'd let that simmer in his gut for years until he'd finally believed he was over her.

And the past five minutes had proved that he'd been lying to himself for years. "Great. Just great."

Raney crossed the room and wrapped an arm around Summer. "Don't worry about these," Raney said. "We'll finish them up."

He'd been so focused on Summer that he'd missed the twenty or so square glass vases that were on the kitchen counter behind her.

Summer shook her head. "Absolutely not," she said, her voice sounding shaky. She cleared her throat. "I've only got a few to wash, and then I'll load them in my van," she added, more confidently.

Raney looked as if she might want to argue, but instead, she gave a quick nod. She looked up at Bray. "I understand you already know Summer."

There wasn't a sound in the room.

"She and her sister, Trish, are handling the flowers and the food for the reception that we're having at the Wright Here, Wright Now Café," Chase finally jumped in. "The church is letting us borrow the vases."

Nobody seemed inclined to want to discuss Gary Blake and what had just happened. Was it because of the potential of Reverend Brown and the other woman hearing the conversation?

Reverend Brown, astute as ever, turned to leave. "Julie and I'll be upstairs. Nice to see you again, Summer."

No one spoke until the door at the top of the stairs opened and closed again.

Then Nalana stepped forward, walking toward the sink where the remaining vases were submerged in soapy water.

Summer held up a hand. "No. Please. I'm almost finished, and I'm sure you all have lots of catching up to do."

The message was clear. *You have to catch up with Bray since he hasn't been around for forever.*

Summer focused on Raney and Chase. "I won't let him ruin any part of your wedding. I promise."

Raney shook her head. "You are not responsible for his poor behavior."

Summer sighed. "I'm just terribly sorry this happened. It's…embarrassing."

"It's not you who should be embarrassed," Chase said. "I think I might have to go drop-kick Blake into the next county."

"Oh, please. I've got a bigger foot and a stronger kick. Let me," Cal said.

That got a small smile from Summer. Bray was happy to see that and happier still to see the easy camaraderie between Chase and Cal. It hadn't always been that way, and he wasn't sure why. But he liked this.

"I'll help Summer finish up here," Bray said.

His brothers exchanged a quick glance. "Well, okay, then," Chase said. He and Cal, each with an arm slung around his woman, went back upstairs, leaving him alone with Summer, who was back on her feet.

"This isn't necessary," she said.

He deliberately rolled up his shirtsleeves, then walked over to the sink and plunged his hands into the lukewarm water. "I'll wash. You dry."

She pressed her lips together. Finally, she let out a loud sigh and grabbed the dull white dish towel.

They didn't talk for the five minutes it took to finish washing the vases. Nor for the seven minutes it took to pack all twenty in two big cardboard boxes. Finally, Bray said, "Now what?"

"Now I load them in my van," she said.

He hoisted a box up. "Lead the way."

She started to lift the other.

"Leave it," he said. "It's too heavy. I'll get it on the second trip."

She led him up the back stairs of the church and outside. There sat an old red van that had seen better days. There were several scratches and a couple of small dents, one that looked pretty new. "What happened here?" he asked, thinking it could have been made by a man's boot. Did Blake take his anger out on objects, too?

She smiled. "Errant football. I said it was a wild throw. Keagan said I should have jumped higher."

"Keagan?"

"My son."

Ahhhh, yes. The child that she'd had with Gary Blake within the first year of their marriage. Bray set the box down, perhaps harder than necessary, but he didn't hear anything break.

He went back inside for the other box. She was standing next to the open van door and stepped aside so that he could shove the box in. Which he did—a little more gently.

"You have a daughter, too, right?" he asked.

Summer's face softened. "Adalyn. We call her Adie. She's five."

"How do they feel about the divorce?" he asked.

There was enough light from the streetlight that he could see her pretty green eyes cloud over. "Probably like any kid feels about a divorce. Sad. Confused. Relieved," she added, her voice quiet.

That pulled at his gut. Was it even possible that Blake had used his fists on them, too? "Did your ex ever—"

She walked to the side of the van, opened the driver's-side door and got in. She started the engine. Finally, she turned her head sideways and made eye contact. "Never. He knew I'd kill him if he did that."

Chapter Two

She had been having a pretty good day until her ex-husband had decided to show up at the church. The restaurant had been pleasantly busy, and when she'd left at two to attend Adie's Thanksgiving Day party at her kindergarten, the sun had been shining and she'd been excited about Chase and Raney's upcoming wedding. She and Trish were determined that the reception was going to be phenomenal. For what Chase was paying them, he deserved something special.

After the party, she'd driven Adie home and waited another half hour for Keagan to get home from school. It was his first year at Ravesville High, and he detested it when she picked him up in the van. "I'm not a little kid," he'd say.

He wasn't. But neither was a fourteen-year-old boy an adult. She was full-time busy trying to balance her natural tendency to keep him close and protected with the reality that she needed to let go, let him have more independence, let him make more decisions, even let him make a few mistakes.

When she'd been that age, she'd been an adult. Out of necessity. What was it Trish used to say? *We were pushed out of the nest early, and we had to either fly or crash.*

They'd flapped their wings hard and managed to stay in the air, taking turns buying groceries, cooking dinner, doing laundry.

They'd had each other, and together, they'd managed to mostly hide a big secret.

She didn't want anything like that for Keagan. Generally, all she really hoped for was for him to pick up his clothes off the floor and shower regularly.

Today, once he'd got home, they'd had a brief conversation, which mainly consisted of her brightly telling him about her day and asking about his and getting a few grunts in response. Then she'd left him in charge of Adie. In the past, she'd have had her mom come over to watch the kids. They loved having Grandma at the house. But in the past year or so, if she was going to be gone for only an hour or so at a time, Keagan watched Adie so that he could earn some babysitting money to buy a new bike.

She was proud of him for realizing that he needed to work for the money, that she simply wouldn't be able to hand over a couple hundred dollars. The restaurant was doing well, and she and Trish were able to take small salaries, but by the time she paid rent and all the other assorted bills of raising children, there was little left.

She couldn't count on Gary. He was now over six months behind in child support. And he had become more and more volatile over the past months. She still had sore ribs that substantiated that today's incident had not been an isolated event.

But never before had it been a public event, and she was mortified. Bad enough that Chase and Cal Hollister and their wonderful fiancées should witness it, but having Bray be the one to break it up had been almost more than she could be expected to bear.

He looked fabulous. He had his thick brown hair pulled

back into a little ponytail at the nape of his neck, and the short beard he wore, which was so popular now, made him look super sexy and…well, even a little dangerous.

And when he'd had Gary on his knees, practically begging for relief, it had been easy to see that it wasn't false advertising. He'd always been a tough guy. Probably why the Marines had been a natural fit. And now that he was a DEA agent, his natural persona had been fine-tuned and he was sleek and dangerous.

Gary wasn't that tough, but he did play dirty, and she'd tried to warn Bray. Bray would find his car towed for parking too close to a fire hydrant or get a ticket for going thirty-four in a thirty-mile-an-hour zone. Or worse. He'd come out after an evening meal and find his windshield cracked or his tires flat. That was what had happened to the one man Summer had dated postdivorce. Needless to say, the poor guy hadn't bothered to call again.

And she was powerless to do anything about Gary. Because he knew the secret. He was part of the secret.

At the intersection, she stopped at the four-way sign. To the left was the Wright Here, Wright Now Café. At night, it was under Trish's careful watch, allowing Summer to be home with the kids. If she went to the café tonight, her twin would instantly sense that something was wrong, and she'd force Summer to blurt out the truth.

No, she'd leave the vases in the van tonight and unload them tomorrow. She wasn't ready to deal with her reaction to Bray, let alone talk about it to someone else. Plus, she'd probably left Keagan and Adie alone together for long enough. She turned right and drove the mile to her house. It wasn't until she was pulling into the one-car attached garage that she noticed the car behind her.

For a quick minute, she thought it might be Gary, back for round two. But it wasn't.

She got out and faced Bray Hollister, who was acting as if he had every right to follow her home and park in her driveway. "What are you doing here?" she said, almost wincing when she heard how bitchy she sounded.

It was just that seeing him again after so many years was too much. She hadn't had time to prepare, time to put up her defenses. She'd been ready for him to be at the wedding reception, and she'd already planned on how she would handle the encounter. She'd be polite, a little distant, too busy to chat for long.

Now she felt naked and raw from her encounter with Gary, and she wasn't sure she had the emotional maturity to go up against the only man she'd ever really loved.

"I wanted to make sure you got home okay."

"Oh." She felt so very small. And mean. "Thank you."

They stared at each other. She could hear Mitzi barking and glanced over Bray's shoulder. Across the street, she could see the small white dog through the window. She was on the back of the couch, her nose pressed to the glass.

Bray turned his head to look.

"That's Trudy Hudder's house," Summer said.

"Junior English?" Bray asked.

She nodded. Mrs. Hudder had introduced literature to every student in Ravesville for forty years before retiring a few years earlier.

Adie liked to play with the dog. Would listen to hear Mitzi outside and then sneak out for a quick couple of dog kisses.

Summer whipped around to make sure her children were not at the door or with their own noses pressed up against the window. The blinds were down, thank goodness. Sometimes Keagan forgot to do that when it got dark. She turned back to Bray.

"It's been a long time," he said. "I thought we might get a drink or something."

"I can't. My children are home alone."

"You have a coffeepot?"

Bray had always loved coffee, from the time he'd been a teenager. Her, too. They'd been the only sixteen-year-olds who ordered coffee with their pizza. She should lie. Tell him she gave it up years ago. When she married someone else.

"I do," she said.

"Works for me." He took a couple of steps toward her, closing the ten-foot gap.

This was such a bad idea. She'd avoided having a conversation with this man for fifteen years. Had been hoping to avoid it for another fifteen. She held up her hand.

He stopped.

Bray would not force his way in. That had never been his way. He had always been a gentleman.

She could give him ten minutes. She owed him much more. She motioned with her hand for him to follow her.

They went into the house through the garage. When they stepped into the kitchen, she could hear the television blaring in the family room. There were dirty dishes on the counter that hadn't been there when she'd left less than two hours ago. There was also a big splotch of milk on the floor, as if Adie might have been trying to pour a glass and the jug had been too heavy.

She just couldn't worry about it now.

"I'm home," she yelled.

"Mama," Adie said. Feet came thundering around the corner.

Summer leaned down and scooped up her little girl. "Hey, slow down," she said, holding her tight.

Adie squirmed in her arms. She pointed to Bray. "Who's that?"

"This is Mr. Hollister," Summer said.

Bray waved. "Hi, Adie. How about you just call me Bray. That's a lot easier to say."

"Bray," Adie repeated. "Like *neigh*," she said, making the sound of a horse.

Bray smiled. "Exactly."

Adie turned back to her. "You're late," she said. "We're hungry."

"I know, sweetheart. I'll start dinner in just a few minutes," she said. She let Adie slide down her body. Once the little girl's feet hit the ground, she was off.

"Mom's home and there's a man with her." Adie's voice floated back to them.

The volume on the television went down. In came Keagan, his thin shoulders slouched forward, his too-long hair in his eyes.

She reached out a hand to ruffle his hair. He jerked away. He was staring at Bray.

"Thanks for watching Adie," Summer said. "This is Bray Hollister. We...we were in school together."

Bray stepped forward, extended his hand. It took Keagan a second, but he stuck his arm out.

"Nice to meet you, Keagan. I understand you like football."

Keagan didn't answer. He turned to his mother. "I thought you were going to the church for vases."

"I...did. Remember, it's Chase Hollister who is getting married. Well, Bray is Chase's older brother. He's home for the wedding."

"Dad stopped by," Keagan said.

"When?" she asked quickly.

"Right after you left."

Thank goodness. She'd hoped he hadn't come by after the incident at the church. "I saw him. He stopped by the church."

"He seemed upset about something."

He had seemed more volatile than usual. A simple conversation about switching the weekend the kids would be at his house had gone south so fast that she still wasn't sure what had set him off. He hadn't looked good, either. There had been dark circles under his pale blue eyes, as if he hadn't slept well for some time.

Maybe trouble at work. Gossip had been swirling recently about a fight between Gary and a newly hired officer named Daniel Stone. Nobody seemed to have the details, and neither Gary nor Daniel was talking about it. Probably at the direction of Chief Poole. He was probably embarrassed that his small department was a topic of conversation.

But she'd officially given up making excuses for Gary's behavior when she'd signed the divorce paperwork. Never ran him down in front of the kids, but didn't try to build him up to be father of the year, either. "You don't need to worry about your dad," she said. "Did you do your homework?"

He gave her the *you're so stupid* look. "We don't have school until next Monday."

That was right. Tomorrow was the day before Thanksgiving, and the kids were getting a nice long holiday. "Well, you can watch a little more television. Just keep the volume down," she suggested.

Keagan looked between her and Bray. "What are you going to be doing?"

The bad mother in her so wanted to tell him that it was none of his business. Since starting high school three months earlier, Keagan had got progressively more distant, rarely volunteering any conversation and definitely not interested in anything Summer was doing.

But she was the adult. Supposedly smarter, more mature. "I'm going to have a little conversation with Mr. Hollister and then I'm going to fix dinner. I'll call you when it's ready," she said.

He took the hint and shuffled out of the kitchen. The small space got quiet again. She got busy making a small pot of coffee. Out of the corner of her eye, she saw Bray grab a paper towel off the roll and wipe up the spilled milk on the floor. He found the garbage under her sink.

"Thanks," she said. She scooted around the dirty dishes on the counter. She still missed having a dishwasher, but the house had been perfect in so many other ways for the three of them that she hadn't quibbled over small things. It was in a safe neighborhood and she could afford it. Those were the important things.

When the coffee was done, she poured cups for both her and Bray and carried them over to the kitchen table, where Bray had taken a seat. "Cream or sugar?" she asked.

"Black. Like always," he said.

Some things never changed, but some things had changed so much there was no going back. She took a sip too soon and burned her tongue. Still, for lack of anything better to do, she took another one. Finally, she set her cup down. "So, how was your flight?" she asked.

He took a sip of his own coffee. "It's been a long time, Summer. You really want to talk about my travel?"

Hell, no. But everything else was fraught with danger. One wrong step and it could blow up. But yet there were things that needed to be said. She gathered her courage. "I'm not sure there's much to be gained from going over old ground, but…" She took a breath. "But if I hurt you, I'm sorry."

He stared at the coffee in his cup. "If you hurt me?" he repeated softly. "If?"

He wasn't going to let this be easy. She understood. She deserved this. "When," she corrected. "When I hurt you."

He looked up. "I guess I'd really just like to know what happened."

"You left," she said.

"I enlisted. We had discussed it. You said you would wait."

She had intended to. And she had wanted to. Then things had happened. But nothing she could tell Bray about. Nothing she could ever tell anyone about. "I met someone," she said. It was the story she'd stuck to for fifteen years.

"Gary Blake."

She nodded.

"He's a real prize," Bray said, his tone bitter.

Gary hadn't always been this way. In the beginning, he'd been…fine. Attentive. Hardworking. And she'd thought it would be enough. "Bray, did you ever marry?" she asked tentatively.

"Nope."

The silence in the room stretched out. Finally, Bray shifted in his chair. "At the church, you said that Gary had never beaten your kids. There was something you didn't say."

"What's that?"

"That he'd never beaten you."

She was so weary. So damn tired of protecting everybody else's interests. "He didn't. And I would not have thought him capable of it. But about two months ago, we got into an argument because he was supposed to pay some fees for Keagan's sports. But he was really late and the coach had told me that he was going to have to suspend

Keagan. Gary got really mad and pushed me down. And…
and then he kicked me. My back got pretty bruised up."

She saw a wave of emotion cross his handsome face.
"Kicked you like a stray dog," he said, his tone bitingly
sharp.

She put her hand out. Touched him. His skin was so
warm. "It's over," she said.

"Did you report it to the police?"

"He is the police."

"He's got to have a boss."

She shrugged. "I made a decision. I did what was best
for me and my family."

"By what happened today, I don't think he's turned
over a new leaf. The next time he might really hurt you.
What are you going to tell your children when you've got
a broken jaw and a busted eye socket?"

The image made her sick. "That's not going to happen," she said.

"Maybe somebody needs to make sure of that," he said.

She stood up. "Don't you even think about getting involved, Bray Hollister. You can't waltz back in here and…
and mess things up."

"Mess things up? Honey, I thought that was your department."

She would not cry. She would not. "My children are
hungry," she said, her voice flat. "If you'll excuse me, I'm
going to fix them dinner." She walked over to the door
that led to the garage, opened it and reached to turn on
the garage light.

She heard a sharp bark and saw that Mitzi was outside,
peeing in the front yard. Trudy, already in her nightgown,
stood on the front porch, staring across the street. Great.

Bray followed her out of the house. She stood to the
side and let him walk past.

Trudy waved. "Nice to see you again, Brayden. I wondered if you'd be back for the wedding."

"Wouldn't miss it," Bray said. "Nice to see you again, Mrs. Hudder."

She wondered how he could sound so polite. Her voice would have come out strangled. She felt as if her throat were closing up.

Without a backward glance, Bray got in his car and started it. He backed out of the driveway and sedately drove off.

Fifteen years ago, there'd been screaming tires and a racing engine.

She closed the garage door, went back inside her house and then very carefully let herself slide down the back of the door until she was sitting on the floor.

Then she started to cry.

BRAY TEXTED CAL, telling him that he wouldn't be there for dinner. It was the chicken's way out, he knew, but he simply wasn't up to the questions that either would be asked or, if everyone decided to give him a pass, would be hanging in the air, hovering, threatening to smother them all.

So, what was it like, seeing Summer after all these years?

Jarring. Exhilarating. Disappointing. Painful. His emotions were all over the place.

She was still beautiful. He'd always loved her red hair. In high school, she'd worn it longer, but now it just touched her shoulders. Her skin was still lovely, freckle-free unlike most redheads. There were a few lines by her pale green eyes that hadn't been there fifteen years ago, but still, she looked more like twenty-seven than thirty-seven.

Her children were the undisputable proof that the years had truly gone by. Adie was a doll, with her strawberry blonde hair and her big blue eyes. And Keagan, well, he supposed he'd be a good-looking kid if he bothered to get rid of the disdain that poured off his skinny adolescent frame.

Bray appreciated that the kid had hoofed it into the kitchen quickly upon hearing that his mother had brought home a man. That told him something. It didn't happen often. Not that that mattered. Summer hadn't said it, but the message had been clear. *We're done. Been done for a long time.*

When he'd first heard that Chase and Raney intended to get married in Ravesville, he'd fleetingly wondered if he might run into Summer while he was home. He hadn't dwelled on the possibility, had merely considered it, decided that it would be no big deal and moved on.

All that proved was that at age thirty-seven, he was living in denial, maybe not all that different from a kid hooked on meth who said he could stop anytime he wanted.

He drove through Ravesville, making a full stop at the end of every block. The same irritating four-way stop signs had been there when he'd been seventeen. Then, he'd done a casual rolling stop, too cool in his old Cutlass convertible to be bothered by rules. And more often than not, Summer had been at his side, her pretty red hair blowing in the wind.

He turned right at the edge of town. Just like old times. On most warm nights, of which there were a lot in Missouri, he and Summer had gone to Rock Pond, the local swimming hole.

They never did a whole lot of swimming there. Instead, he'd pull the old sheet out of his trunk, spread it on the ground, and in the dark of night, he'd make love to Summer.

And afterward, she would cling to him, her sweet

young body so firm, yet so soft, and tell him that she loved him and that she would always be his.

As he drove onto the property, he could see that they were still actively working parts of the old quarry, still blasting away. He went around the bend in the narrow road, got close to the section that had been filled with water for many years and killed his lights. It was not a warm night. Not much chance of encountering naked teens doing grown-up things. With little care for the cold, he got out of the car, boosted himself up onto the hood and leaned back against the windshield. He put his hands behind his head and stared up at the sky.

He'd been a half a world away, trying not to get blown up, and the memories of this place, his time with Summer here, had kept him sane.

Everything happened for a reason. That was the mantra that his mother had lived by. Even when her husband had died too young, leaving her with three adolescent boys to raise, she'd said those words. Even when she married Brick Doogan, who hadn't an ounce of the character that his dad had.

He'd survived four years in the military when others hadn't. He'd clawed his way back after learning that the girl he'd left behind had married someone else, and he eventually got a college degree on Uncle Sam's dime and a job in New York. Others had come back too screwed up to do the same. He managed to keep a whole lot of drugs off the streets and a bunch of unknown kids alive without getting a knife in his gut when others bought it. He'd built a very satisfactory life and pushed the old memories to the back of the virtual closet, where they belonged.

But now they were clawing to get out, ripping apart his gut, making him want to howl at the quarter moon.

He slid off the hood, got in and turned his car around.

When he got to the end of the long lane, he turned right instead of left. He still wasn't quite ready to go home. He drove through town. At the edge, he turned around. Drove down the main street again. Killing time.

Not true. He was looking for Gary Blake. He might as well admit the truth.

Somebody needed to teach him a lesson, and right now, it would feel damn good to put his fist through something. It might as well be Blake's face.

He pulled over and used his smartphone to find Blake's address. He recognized the street. As he drove the six blocks, he knew he was probably about to do something really stupid.

But sometimes a man just had to do what he needed to do.

Chapter Three

Wednesday, 10:00 a.m.

Bray was nursing his third cup of coffee when he heard the sound of a car pulling into the Hollister driveway. Chase and Cal were at the sink, washing and drying, because Raney and Nalana had cooked breakfast. He, as the honored guest, was getting to sit.

Which was helpful since he was fighting a headache that was likely a combination of jet lag, long-term fatigue and one too many beers. He'd come home around midnight. The house had been dark, but it had been easy enough to find his way upstairs, avoiding the step that squeaked and finally getting into the brand-new bed that was the centerpiece of his newly decorated bedroom.

Raney and Chase were making a home of the old place. It was unexpected, sort of like the new camaraderie between Chase and Cal. He was going to ask about that. Sometime. Just not now, when the brain cells weren't yet all firing.

He heard the sound of a door opening and shutting. "Expecting someone?" he asked.

Chase looked at Raney and she shook her head. Cal walked down the hallway to look out the front door.

"It's Poole," he said.

"Who's Poole?" Bray asked.

Cal walked back into the kitchen, exchanged a quick look with Chase and said, "The police chief. Anything we need to know about last night?"

Bray shook his head. "Why look at me?"

Nalana smiled. "Because the rest of us were in bed by nine o'clock."

Bray returned the smile. "That's because my brothers are both lucky sons of…guns." He pushed back his chair. "I might as well get this."

He waited for the knock. Counted to five, then opened the door. On the other side was a man, probably midsixties, his belly hanging over his belt, looking as if a fast walk, let alone a real chase after an enemy, would take him down.

"Bray Hollister?" the man asked.

"Yes."

"I'm police chief Poole. I'd like to ask you a few questions."

He heard a rustle in the kitchen and knew that if he gave any indication that he was uncomfortable with the request, his brothers were going to figure out a way to get Poole off their porch.

"Sure," he said. "Come on in."

He led the chief into the living room and motioned for him to have a seat. The man sat in the armchair, making the cushions sink. Bray sat on the couch and relaxed back against a pillow.

"I understand you arrived in town yesterday."

"That's correct."

"From New York." The man practically wrinkled his nose.

Bray nodded. He was tempted to make a joke that living in the city wasn't a crime the last time he'd checked.

But he kept his mouth shut. Poole was uncomfortable, and that was making Bray doubly so.

"And you drove straight to Ravesville from the St. Louis airport?"

"Yes."

"And what did you do once you got to town?"

"I went to the church on the corner of Main and Portland. My brother is getting married there this weekend."

"And you had some conversation with Gary Blake?"

"Conversation? Is that what he called it?" Bray asked. He was disgusted. The guy tried to rough up his ex-wife and then whined to his boss because Bray had got the better of him.

"I didn't speak with Gary. Julie Wentworth is my sister-in-law. She plays the piano every Sunday and for almost every wedding in town."

Piano player Julie and Reverend Brown had not witnessed his physical interaction with Blake. They would only be able to report on what they'd overheard.

Not true. They would be able to support that Summer had been upset—to the point that her voice had been shaking.

"I understand you and Summer Wright were an item in high school. That was before my time in Ravesville. Is that correct?"

An item? "We dated," he said. If Poole wanted to know more than that, he was going to have to ask somebody else.

"Uh-huh. So, after you left the church, where did you go?" Poole asked.

Bray made sure his face showed no reaction. But his brain, which might have been idle in the kitchen, was now working itself back to fighting weight. "I went to Summer's house."

"Why?"

"She had some vases in the back of her van. They were heavy. I thought she might need some help carrying them."

"How long were you there?"

Bray sat up, feeling as if his pancakes were going to be on the chief's shoes. "Did something happen to Summer? To one of the kids?"

He was going to kill Gary Blake.

The chief shook his head. "I drove by the Wright Here, Wright Now Café on my way here. I verified that Summer was working her shift, as usual. Therefore, I assume her children are fine."

Verified. The man had made sure Summer was working. So whatever was wrong, Summer and her family were involved in some way.

"If there's nothing else," Bray said, standing up. He had things to do.

Poole didn't take the hint. "What time did you leave Summer's house and where did you go?"

Bray had a fairly good idea the man already knew what time he'd left. Perhaps he'd talked to Mrs. Hudder. He decided to cut to the chase. "I left around seven. Drove around town for a while." No need to tell him that he'd driven to Blake's house, that he'd pounded on the door, wanting the son of a bitch to have the guts to show his face. "I was hungry, so I went to the One Toe In Bar and Grill for a cheeseburger and some beers."

"What time did you leave the bar?"

"Close to midnight. Why?"

"Anybody there going to be able to verify that?"

He'd sat alone in a back booth, but he'd had the same waitress for most of the evening. He assumed she'd be able to. "I think so."

"You better hope so, Mr. Hollister."

Bray shrugged. "Look, I've been a good sport and answered all your questions. Now why don't you tell me why the hell you're asking them?" Maybe Gary Blake's pride had been more damaged than he'd thought and the man had gone to his boss to complain about his interaction with Bray. If he had, that was pretty damn stupid. Nothing like hanging out your own dirty laundry.

Chief Poole hefted himself out of the chair. He pulled up his pants and they immediately sagged below his belly again. "Gary Blake was scheduled to start work at seven this morning. When he didn't show, Officer Stone drove to his house."

"And?" Bray prompted when the police chief stopped.

"And Gary wasn't there."

"Big deal," Bray said. "Maybe he got his days mixed up and he thought he had a vacation day. He's out shopping for a turkey right now."

"There were signs of a very fast exit from the house. A small amount of blood at the scene."

He could see Summer's eyes, hear the sincerity in her voice. *He knew I'd kill him if he did that.* "So, he cut himself shaving and went to the emergency room."

"Maybe," Chief Poole said. "But, you know, police officers make a lot of enemies."

Bray wanted to see Blake's house. Cops in small towns weren't well trained in investigating crime scenes—they simply didn't see enough of them.

But as much as he wanted to view the scene, he wanted to see Summer more. He had to know what she'd done. Had his questions about Blake spurred on memories that she'd been unable to deal with?

"How long are you expecting to be in town, Mr. Hollister?"

"Through Sunday."

"And you're staying here at this house?"

Bray nodded.

"Good," the chief said. "I want to know where I can find you if I have more questions."

Bray didn't answer. He simply watched the man walk to the front door and let himself out. He counted to three before his brothers got to the living room.

They each had the same worried look in their eyes. Probably right now were thinking of good defense attorneys.

"Listen," he said, "I didn't do anything to Gary Blake."

"Blood at the scene," Chase said.

"Small amount. I heard the man," Bray said, irritated. He'd been back in town for less than a day, and Gary Blake, who had caused him so much heartache years ago when he'd married Bray's girl, was still causing trouble. "There's probably a list of people a page long that want to get Blake for one reason or another."

"Summer," Cal said.

Bray didn't say anything.

"You don't think she did something, do you?" Chase asked.

Bray had no idea what Summer was capable of. "I don't know," he said. "But I think I better ask her."

SUMMER HAD REALLY never thought much about Charlie Poole. He'd been Gary's boss for about five years. He was polite to her when he came into the restaurant, ordered two eggs and bacon with a side of biscuits and gravy every day of his life, and tipped poorly.

She'd never had cause to worry about him until now, when he'd come in and asked if he could speak to her privately.

"We don't have much private space," she said.

He said nothing. She put down her coffeepot, led him back to the kitchen, smiled at Milo, the grill cook, to let him know that everything was okay and took a spot in the corner, where she could keep an eye on the dining room through the small window in the swinging door.

She felt sick when the chief told her why he was there. Gary. Missing. Blood at the scene. An open gallon of milk on the table. A half-eaten bowl of cereal. The back door unlocked and not closed tight.

What the hell? Her first thoughts were of her children. What would she tell them?

But before she could get her head around it, Chief Poole started asking questions.

"I understand you were at the church yesterday," he said. "That you and Gary were in the basement."

Julie had probably mentioned it to her brother-in-law. She was a lovely piano player but a terrible gossip.

"Yes."

"I didn't think you two had much to do with each other anymore."

"We share children," she said. "This coming weekend was Gary's weekend to have them, but he needed to switch."

"Why?"

She'd wondered the same thing. Normally, it wouldn't have been a big deal to switch. But because she would be busy catering the wedding, she'd pushed back a little. That had seemed to set him off. "I don't know."

"So after you left the church, you went straight home?"

"Yes." It dawned on her that the chief hadn't asked any questions about what had happened at the church between her and Gary. Was it because Julie had given him enough that he'd realized that his second-in-command might have been in the wrong and he didn't want any additional documentation of the fact?

And speaking of documentation, the chief wasn't making any notes. He had yet to pull his notebook from his pocket. In his left breast pocket, he had the same kind of notebook that Gary never went anywhere without. Once, early on in the marriage, she hadn't realized that he hadn't removed it from his pocket and she'd put it in the washing machine. That had caused a crisis that involved attempting to dry out thirty or so small pages because he'd needed those quick notations to fill out the endless reports that he'd hated.

Maybe the chief had a really good memory. Or maybe he realized that she didn't have anything to gain by harming Gary.

"And did you have any visitors last night?" he asked.

She wasn't trained in police work, but thought she might be a better interrogator than the chief. He clearly already knew that she had indeed had a visitor. Perhaps he'd already spoken to Mrs. Hudder. Or to Bray.

He'd been upset when he'd left her house. She'd known that he was having difficulty dealing with what she'd told him. Had he taken out his anger on Gary?

Had Bray become sucked into the tangled relationship that she had with her ex? It was a horrifying thought. When would her bad decisions stop hurting Bray Hollister?

She was confident that he would tell the truth, that he would not run from it. He'd always had more character than her. "Bray Hollister stopped by. He didn't stay long. Then I fixed my children dinner, watched some television and went to bed by ten."

"Can anyone verify that you were home all evening?" he asked.

Had she been wrong about his intent? Was she really a…suspect? She pressed her hand to her empty stomach.

Hell, yes, there were times I wanted him gone, she wanted to say. But admitting that she'd spent valuable time she didn't have as a single parent imagining how nice it would be if he would simply disappear wasn't going to help her.

"No," she said. "But I was." She looked through the small window in the door and saw that four new customers had come in while she'd been talking with the chief. They were looking around, staring wistfully at the coffeepot, probably wondering where the heck she was. "I really need to get back to the dining room," she said. As Milo flipped his pancakes, he was slapping the flat end of his stainless-steel spatula on the hot grill, letting her know that he was watching and ready to assist if she needed it.

"Just a couple more questions," Chief Poole said, holding up his hand. "Has Gary ever done this before, just disappear unexpectedly?"

Once or twice toward the end of their marriage, he'd been gone for a few days. *Getting his head together.* That was what he always told her. She suspected that involved a stack of chips and a deck of cards, but by then, she hadn't really cared enough to probe.

"Sometimes to fish or to gamble." It dawned on her that the chief probably knew Gary as well as she did. That made this an even more awkward conversation.

The chief nodded. "I probably should check to see if his rods are still there."

She didn't say anything, hoping he'd get the hint and leave.

"Do you know anybody who had a particular beef with Gary?"

She sighed. "He's been a cop in the same community

for more than fifteen years. I imagine there are any number of people who aren't fond of him. The speed trap out by the high school is particularly irritating and probably hasn't endeared him to many."

"Anybody with a complaint more serious than a moving violation?"

"You'd know better about that than me," she said.

"I may want to talk to your children."

"Not without me, and not until I've talked to them first," she said, her voice stern. She didn't care if he was the police chief.

"I'll be in touch," he said. He took a step. Stopped. "I'd appreciate it if you'd keep this conversation between us," he said. "You know how gossip spreads in Ravesville."

She did. And it would make people uneasy if they thought that something had happened to one of their police officers.

She nodded, and Chief Poole pushed open the swinging door, walked the length of the café and left through the front entrance. Thirty seconds later, Summer followed him out of the kitchen, smiling, greeting customers, putting on the show of her life. But her head was whirling. So much so that she delivered eggs instead of French toast to one of her favorite customers. Apologizing profusely, she ran back to the kitchen to get the order replaced.

"What's going on?" Milo asked.

"I'll tell you later," Summer promised.

She took another quick minute to pull her cell phone from her pocket. She pressed the button for Gary's number. It went straight to voice mail. She waited for the beep. "Gary, it's Summer. Listen, please call me. It's important." She pressed End.

Maybe she should call Trish, too. She knew Gary pretty well. Maybe she would have some ideas.

No. It wasn't the type of news a person delivered over the phone.

Was the chief serious that he intended to talk to her kids? Would he wait and give Gary time to show himself?

For the first time in a very long time, she wished she could suddenly make Gary appear. What the hell was he up to now? Was it possible that he was really in trouble? Did this have anything to do with the absolutely horrible mood he'd been in?

She had lots of questions and no answers. She went back to the dining area and cleared two dirty tables.

She heard the soft tinkle of a bell and looked to the front door. Bray Hollister, his expression giving nothing away, walked in and took a seat at the counter. He wore blue jeans, a blue-and-gray flannel shirt, a dark gray insulated vest and cowboy boots. Every woman's eyes in the place followed him, whether they were twenty years old or sixty. He positively oozed sex appeal.

She contemplated going back to the kitchen for the rest of her life. "Morning," she said, mindful that just three stools away were other customers. "Coffee?" she asked, holding up the pot.

Bray nodded.

She poured the cup and slid it in his direction. He took a sip. "Busy day?" he asked.

"Busy enough," she said.

"Had a visit from the chief yet?" His voice was pitched low.

"Yeah. You?"

He nodded. "Are you doing okay?" he asked.

No. She was a mess. "I think so."

"Got anything you need to tell me?" he asked.

"I was about to ask you the same thing."

He shook his head. "I didn't touch your ex."

She believed him. Relief flooded her system. "I didn't, either."

He studied her. Then nodded. "Okay, then. What now?"

"Now I figure out what the hell happened to Gary before it bleeds over and affects me or our children."

Chapter Four

Wednesday, 11:00 a.m.

"But before I do that," she said, "I have to talk to my kids. Chief Poole said he might need to question them."

Bray picked up a sugar packet. Set it down. "He's doing his job. A man is missing. A cop. He needs to turn over every rock that he can."

"But they're my rocks. My baby rocks," she said.

She would be the kind of mother who would protect her children with her last breath. "They might know something and not even realize it. You might, too," he said, his tone suggestive. "Tell me about your ex."

"I've got customers to wait on," she said, clearly not interested in his suggestion. He understood. He really didn't want to talk about the son of a bitch, either. There weren't many that could make the claim, but Gary Blake had bested Bray, in all the ways it counted. Reason enough to hate him.

If Blake was screwing around somewhere, oblivious to the concern he'd left behind, dismissive of the blow his children would bear when they heard he was missing, well, Bray was going to hand him his lunch, and the guy would need a blender and a straw to eat it. "What time does Trish come in to relieve you?"

"Normally at two and works until nine. But it's Thanksgiving eve, so we're not open tonight. The café will close at two today and reopen at six on Friday morning. And with any luck, Gary will come in for his coffee to go at eight thirty, just like every other day."

"You're still going to talk to your kids today?"

She nodded. "I have to pick them up at Trish's. She's babysitting. I know I need to do this but I'm not sure what to tell them."

"The truth. But maybe not the whole truth."

She let out a huff. "That's my specialty," she said in a disgusted tone. Then she walked away.

What the hell did she mean by that? Bray contemplated that question for the next three hours as he sat on the stool. Summer stopped filling his coffee cup and generally ignored him until he flagged her down and ordered a grilled ham-and-cheese sandwich for lunch. She hadn't said a word when she'd slid the plate in his direction, but it didn't escape his notice that she'd remembered to add a side of mayonnaise so that he could dip his French fries.

Finally, ten minutes after she'd put the closed sign in the window, all the other customers were gone except him. "I'm going with you when you talk to your children," he said.

"They don't know you."

"I'm not going for them. I'm going for you."

That shut her up. She got out the vacuum and plugged it in. He grabbed it out of her hand. "Let me help," he said. "You can get out of here faster."

It had been driving him crazy for the past three hours watching her literally fly around the room. Taking orders, clearing tables, making pot after pot of coffee, taking cash at the register up front. He'd wanted to jump in and help but had known that would spread like wildfire through the small town. The fact that he'd been sitting at the counter for an extended period probably already had tongues wagging. He'd recognized a few people from his high school days. Had nodded at one or two, but nobody had approached to engage in conversation.

After the floor had been vacuumed and the counters wiped down, and she'd rolled a tray of clean silverware into white napkins, Summer excused herself to use the restroom. Seconds later, the cook pushed through the swinging door.

"Who are you?" he asked, his voice flat.

"Bray Hollister." He'd been gone a long time, but he was pretty good with faces. He didn't think he'd ever met this man. He was probably midfifties, slight build but wiry, with hair pulled back into a ponytail like Bray. However, his was much longer and almost black. His face had several scars, none of which he'd got from working behind a grill. "Who are you?" Bray asked.

"That's not important. What's important is that you understand that Summer and Trish Wright are special to me. If you mess with them, you mess with me. And that would be a mistake on your part."

Most people wouldn't even attempt to intimidate Bray. But this guy was a natural. Bray appreciated his intensity and willingness to take him on.

He was glad that this man was in Summer's corner. "I don't intend to mess with either of them. I'm an old friend." Bray heard the bathroom door open.

"I'll be watching you," Milo said.

"All finished?" Summer asked the cook.

"Thirty minutes. Then I'm out of here."

"Don't work too late," she said. "Uh, Milo, this is Bray Hollister. He used to live in Ravesville. Bray, Milo Hernandez. Best grill cook this side of the Mississippi."

If she noticed the stillness between the two men, she ignored it. "Milo, I have something to tell you."

The cook looked at Bray.

"He can stay," Summer said. "He knows."

And in a very controlled way, Summer told the man about her conversation with Chief Poole, the suspicions that foul play might be involved. His expression never changed.

"The chief asked me to keep this quiet, but I wanted you to know," she said. "You're like family."

"What can I do to help?" he asked.

She shook her head. "Keep your ears open. If you hear anything, call me right away." She gave the man a quick hug. Over her shoulder, he made eye contact with Bray.

"I've got this," Bray mouthed.

The man gave a sharp nod. "Call me if you need me, Summer." He went back into the kitchen.

"He's something," Bray said.

"He was a godsend," she said quietly. "He arrived in Ravesville just weeks after Rafe's death." She looked at him. "You may not know. Trish was married. To Rafe Roper. He wasn't from around here. But he worked construction, and when they built the new mall near Hamerton, he rented a house near here. Trish fell hard and fast, and they got married just months after he arrived in town. But sadly, just nine months later, he went on a float trip, you know the kind, with inner tubes and coolers of beer. Somehow he got separated from his buddies and drowned."

"Poor Trish." He had always really liked Summer's twin.

"It was horrible. The worst of it all was that his body was never recovered. Trish was devastated. She couldn't work. I couldn't expect her to. I thought we would lose the restaurant for sure. I couldn't keep it going on my own. And then Milo turned up."

"Out of the blue?"

"He'd been in prison. Not a lot of places will give an ex-con a job."

"But you did."

"From the very beginning it felt right. He saved us. Worked like a dog. And then when Trish finally was able to come back, he stayed."

"I think he's fond of the two of you."

"It's mutual. He didn't like Gary. I think it was the natural dislike between a cop and an ex-con."

Maybe. Or maybe Milo was just a good judge of character. But he didn't say that. There was nothing to be gained from running down Blake at this point.

Summer shut most of the lights off in the café, leaving on the one behind the counter. She locked the front door from the inside and then led Bray out through the kitchen. Milo had his back to them, cleaning the grill. Summer stopped. "Are you sure you won't come for Thanksgiving dinner?" she asked the man.

He half turned. "No, I've got some things to do," he said. "But it means a lot that you'd invite me," he added.

"If you change your mind, just show up. You know we'll have plenty of food," Summer said, opening the back door.

Her red van was parked in the alley next to a big garbage Dumpster. "My car is out front," he said. "Swing around and I'll follow you to Trish's."

"She's just a half mile west of town," Summer said.

Bray waited until Summer had unlocked her door and got in before jogging around the side of the building to his own car. As he turned the corner, his eye automatically scanned the area. The habit had saved his life more than once.

Today, he didn't see anything unusual. Nobody hanging by his car. Nobody across the street, watching the entrance of the café. Nobody…

Wait. The building across the street was a redbrick three-story. On the first floor was an office. Frank Oswald, attorney at law. The windows were dark. Evidently no pressing legal matters to attend to on the afternoon before Thanksgiving.

The second and third floors were apartments with four large arched windows spread across the face of the building. There it was. Second floor. Second window to the left. A shadow. A man had been standing at the window, watching the café. When Bray had rounded the corner, he'd moved fast, stepping aside, out of view.

Why?

He wanted to pound up the stairs and demand answers. But there was Summer's van. So he ignored his instinct and let the person believe his surveillance had gone undetected.

He got in his car, started it and pulled away from the curb. Summer drove three miles under the speed limit. He wasn't sure if that was normal or whether she was trying to delay the conversation with her children.

Three minutes later, a half mile out of the city limits, Summer put on her left turn signal. She pulled into a long lane that led up to a sprawling brick ranch with a side-load garage with the door up. There was no car.

There was probably an acre of yard and several different gardens that were bare now but would likely be lush with flowers in the spring and summer.

"Sure she's home?" he asked, once he joined Summer at her van.

"Yeah. Her car is in the shop. I'm going to take her to pick it up."

"Nice place."

"It's too big for Trish, but it's the house that she and Rafe bought together. I don't think she can let go of it yet."

A big German shepherd raced around the corner of the house. He stopped short with a low growl when he saw Bray.

The front door of the house opened and Trish stepped outside. Bray would have recognized her anywhere. She still wore her red hair to her waist, as both she and Summer had done in high school.

"Duke," she called. "Settle down. He's a friend." She came off the porch and hugged Bray.

The dog stopped growling, but he looked at Bray with serious black eyes. Bray was confident that if he made one wrong move toward Trish or Summer, the dog would rip him apart.

"It's good to see you," Trish said. "It's been too long."

"I know," he said simply. But because there was no need to dwell on the past, he didn't. "Nice dog," he said. "I hope," he added with a wink.

Trish smiled. "Don't worry about Duke. He was a stray, just showed up one day. But from the minute I took him in, he's been devoted to me. He was super easy to train. Summer's kids adore him."

"How were they?" Summer asked.

"Adie talked nonstop and I got a couple full sentences from Keagan, so I think, overall, it was a pretty great day."

"Good," Summer said.

Trish stared at her sister. "What's wrong? Did something happen at the café?"

Bray wasn't surprised. Trish and Summer had always been in tune with each other. There really was truth to the notion that twins were able to sense things about each other.

"Something weird is going on," Summer said.

Trish said nothing, but Bray could see by the set of her jaw that she was preparing herself for bad news. This was a woman who'd had a few blows already in her life.

"Chief Poole came to see me today. Gary didn't show up for work. And when Daniel Stone went to his house, there were signs that he abruptly left, and a small amount of blood was found at the scene."

"Oh my," Trish said. "Weird and very creepy." She looked over her shoulder as if to verify that the kids were still inside. "I guess it's good that he thought to tell you."

"He was questioning me. I'm a suspect," Summer said.

Trish sucked in a breath. "Of all the stupid, idiotic, senseless—"

"Stop," Summer said.

Bray wanted to smile. In addition to being able to practically read each other's minds, these two were fiercely protective of each other. He remembered getting his car egged by Trish when she'd seen him with another woman once, not realizing it was a friend of the family he'd picked up from the airport.

"Chief Poole said he might need to talk to the kids. I can't let them get surprised by this."

"Of course not." She turned and took a step toward the house. Then stopped. "What do you think happened to Gary?"

"I have no idea. He's been even more moody than normal lately. But this kind of stuff doesn't happen in Ravesville. I'm scared."

"Did you try his cell phone?"

"I did. Goes right to voice mail."

"He's done this before," Trish said.

"I told Chief Poole that. But this seems different." Summer squared her shoulders. "But I swear to you, if he's somewhere warmer, with a fishing line in the water, I'm going to strangle him with it."

Trish smiled. "I hope you didn't mention that to Chief Poole."

"No. But he probably knows enough about our situation that he wouldn't be surprised."

Trish opened her front door and motioned for Summer and Bray to enter first. She followed them in, with the dog close to her side.

"Hey, guys," Summer said. "Mom's here."

Again, Adie came running around the corner. Bray wondered if the little girl ever walked anywhere. She stopped fast, almost pitching forward, when she saw Bray. "You came back," she said.

He smiled at her. "I did. Remember my name?"

"Bray-Neigh," she said.

"Close enough," he said.

Summer stuck her head around the corner. "Keagan, can I see you for a minute?"

The kid ambled into the kitchen. He wore pajama pants and a faded green T-shirt. "Yeah," he said, ignoring Bray.

"Come here," Summer said to her children. She led them over to the kitchen table and she sat down. She pointed for them to take chairs. "I have something to tell you," she said. "I don't want you to be worried or scared. I *do* want you to understand what's happened."

"What, Mama?" Adie asked.

"This is about your dad. He was expected at work this morning and he didn't show up. Chief Poole is concerned about that."

"Maybe his alarm didn't go off," Keagan said.

"He's not at the house," Summer said. "Do either of you know anything about where your dad may have gone? Did he say anything to you yesterday?"

"He said, ''Bye, Adie,'" the little girl said.

Summer leaned forward and gave her little girl a hug. She looked over Adie's shoulder at her oldest child. "Keagan?"

"He was mad that you weren't there," Keagan said. "Nothing too odd about that."

Bray could tell that it pained Summer to hear her child so coldly remark upon the relationship she had with her ex.

"It's possible," she said, "that Chief Poole might want to talk to you about your dad. All you need to do is tell the truth. Whatever it is, just tell the truth."

"Did something bad happen to Dad?" Keagan asked.

"I don't know," Summer said honestly. "But what I do know is that a lot of good people are concerned about him and doing their very best to find him. I think they will. I do."

Keagan looked at Bray for the first time. "I think it's strange that something happens to my dad the same day you show up."

Bray didn't take offense. In fact, he gave the kid some credit. Hearing that his dad was MIA but still being able to piece together information told him the teen was probably a good thinker.

"Keagan," Summer said, censure in her tone.

Bray waved it away. "I'm a federal agent, Keagan. In New York City. I arrest drug dealers. I'm good at following clues. And I'm going to do everything I can to find your dad."

"Why? You don't even know him."

"You're right. But I've known your mom for a really long time and I'm doing it to help her."

"Whatever," Keagan said. He looked at his mother. "Now what?"

"Now we go on about our lives," she said. "We don't know that something bad has happened to your dad. Everything may be just fine and there's a good explanation for why we can't find him. I don't want you to worry. In fact," she said, looking at Trish, "we have to take Aunt Trish to pick up her car in Hamerton. After that, we can swing by the mall. We need to pick up a few things for Chase and Raney's wedding reception, and I thought we might have dinner at Capaghetti's."

"Spaghetti at Capaghetti's," Adie said in a singsong voice. "And garlic bread. Is Bray-Neigh coming, too?"

Summer looked at him. "Not today, sweetheart," Summer said. "Mr. Hollister is in town to see his family. I'm sure he's anxious to get back to them," she added, definitely letting him know that he wasn't welcome on their little excursion.

Summer's pushing him away was a familiar pain. Trish was frowning at her twin. He understood. It had been the same way fifteen years before, when he'd come back to Ravesville only to learn that Summer had married Gary Blake. When Summer had refused to give him any reasonable explanation, he'd gone to Trish.

"I don't get it," she'd said. "I love you, Bray. You know I do. But she's my sister."

He'd left quietly fifteen years ago. He could do it again. He stood up. "Nice to see you again, Trish," he said.

"You, too," she whispered.

He looked at Summer. "Be careful."

"Go get your things, kids" was all she said.

Chapter Five

Wednesday, 4:00 p.m.

Summer drove and Trish rode shotgun. Adie sat in the middle seat and Keagan climbed all the way to the back of the van.

"Bray looks good," Trish said.

Summer checked to make sure both her kids wore their earphones. Bray hadn't looked simply good. He'd looked wonderful. "Yeah."

"No ring," Trish said.

"Nope. He told me he'd never married."

Trish nodded. A few miles went by. "Lousy timing, this thing with Gary."

Summer gave her a sideways glance. "Something may have truly happened to Gary. I don't think we can fault his timing."

"Gary has become such a jerk these past several years that it's hard to care about him," Trish admitted. "Not when I see my sister making the same mistake for a second time."

She didn't have to ask what the mistake was. Trish had always thought she was a fool to marry Gary instead of Bray. It was hard to argue the point. "Trish, I know you mean well, but Bray and I are very different people than we were fifteen years ago. I have two children. An ex-husband. A business. Lots of baggage. He's a single city guy. We're in two different worlds."

"He still looks at you the same way."

Eight simple words. *He still looks at you the same way.* In so many ways, she wanted to be that young girl, the one who had sneaked out of the house so that they could drive out to the old quarry and make love. She'd loved lying close to Bray, feeling his warm skin next to hers, feeling him slip inside her and knowing that nothing could ever come between them.

Until something had. Something bad. "I suppose I should tell Mom about Gary," Summer said. "She might know more about his schedule than the rest of us. She talks to him more often."

"We can swing by her house when we're done at the mall," Trish said. "Are you going to tell her that Bray is back? I think she always liked him."

But she had liked her vodka more. And that had changed the course of all their lives. Her own. Summer's. Bray's. Even Gary's. But Trish didn't know that. It was the only secret that she'd ever kept from her twin.

"I don't see the point," Summer said and turned up the radio.

When they got to the car dealer, Trish went to the service door to pay for her vehicle. Then Summer followed her to the mall. The mall was never not busy, but this afternoon, maybe because people were home getting ready for Thanksgiving Day dinner, it was perhaps less busy. There were actually parking spots.

Inside the sprawling two-story building, Adie skipped along next to her, and Keagan hung back and walked next to Trish. They went to the party store first and bought the decorations they would need for the wedding. Silver and white bows for the tables. Pretty silk flowers in shades of violet and lilac and pale gray. Not necessarily traditional colors for a fall wedding, but when she and Trish had discussed it with Raney and Chase, Raney had seemed to have very definite ideas about the colors. It must have been some kind of inside joke because every time Raney had looked at Chase, as if to check his opinion, he'd simply rolled his eyes and said, "If you love those colors, I'm sure I will, too."

Now, as she and Trish debated over scented or non-scented votive candles, Adie shifted restlessly next to her, anxious to look at the paper-plates-and-napkins aisle. She would be six in three months and was already looking forward to her birthday. For the past two years, it had been all things princess related, and Summer didn't see that changing.

Keagan amused himself looking at the New Year's decorations that had already made their way to the shelves. She knew that he understood much better than his little sister the implications of an adult to suddenly be missing. Adults weren't supposed to do things like that. He was probably worried. She had deliberately not mentioned that there had been blood. That was more than they needed to know at this point, more than they should be expected to handle.

That was why she'd suggested the trip to the mall. Trish had already told her that she'd be happy to get the things they needed. Summer just thought the trip would be a good diversion. Maybe she'd even splurge a little and let them each buy something.

She let Adie lead her to the birthday-party aisle, and they spent the next fifteen minutes picking out the perfect plates and napkins. Then it was time to check out. When they left the store, she hung back, letting Keagan take the lead. He probably wouldn't verbalize what he wanted to do, but he might wander there.

Sure enough, he led them to the small arcade that was at the end of the mall. There were at least twenty kids inside, standing in front of machines. He looked over his shoulder at Summer.

"Thirty minutes," she said. She started to follow him inside, but Trish grabbed her arm. "He's not going to want his mother to be with him," Trish said.

"You're right," Summer admitted.

"Listen, I'll wait outside on this bench. If he tries to leave, I'll tackle him. If there's trouble inside, I'll start cracking heads."

Summer hugged her twin. "You always have my back," she said.

"I know," Trish said, her tone smug. "Going for aunt of the year. Vote early and often."

"I'm going to take Adie to get some shoes. She's growing out of the ones she has on."

"Okay. Leave the other bags here. Once we're done, I'll take Keagan home. How about I get Capaghetti's to go and we forget about Mom for the night. Keagan and I'll meet you at your house."

She would see her mother the next day at Thanksgiving dinner. By then, Gary might be back and they wouldn't even need to have the conversation. "That sounds perfect," she said. Summer grabbed Adie's hand and led her little girl through the busy mall.

When they got to the store, Adie insisted on tie shoes, stating that Velcro was for babies. She tried on at least ten pairs before they found one that fit and was the exact right shade of pink. Summer paid and she let Adie carry the bag. On the way out of the store, she glanced at her watch. Close to five. If she and Adie hurried, they would be home and have a salad made by the time Trish and Keagan arrived with the spaghetti.

They were thirty feet from the exit when she felt someone brush up against her left side. She turned to look, but at the same moment, she was pushed hard. She knocked into Adie and struggled to keep them both from going to the ground.

Furious, she swung around and saw a man, his face partially obscured by the hood of his gray sweatshirt. His arm was close to his body.

He had a gun. And it was pointed at Adie.

"If you scream, I'll shoot her," he said. He nodded his head at a side door. "Step through there. I just want to talk to you about your ex-husband."

Summer could see that none of the other busy shoppers were paying them any attention. Would he really shoot if she screamed? Could she take the chance?

No, she could not.

She gripped Adie's hand even tighter and walked through the door. There, another man stood, his face obscured by a ski mask.

Too late she saw that he had something in his hand.

Oh, Adie, she thought.

WHEN BRAY GOT HOME, Raney and Nalana were in the kitchen. Raney was making a green-bean casserole and Nalana was rolling out pie shells.

"What kind?" he asked, giving them each a quick hug.

"Pumpkin. Any word on the man who is missing?"

"Nope. Not sure if that's good or bad news. Where are my brothers?"

"Tearing out the bath," Raney said, pointing to the hallway that led to the downstairs bedroom and attached bath.

His parents' room. His mother and Brick's room. So many ghosts. "You trust them with a hammer?" he asked.

"More than we trust them with Thanksgiving dinner," Raney said. "Want a drink?"

"I'll get it." He grabbed three beers from the fridge, opened them and carried them to the bedroom. He arrived in time to see his brothers wrestle the double-sink vanity through the bathroom doorway.

"Hey," he said.

Cal spied the beers and smiled. "It's five o'clock somewhere."

"It's practically five o'clock here," Chase said, grabbing one for himself.

Bray looked at his watch. By now, Summer should have finished at the mall and be on her way to eat the spaghetti dinner that Adie had been so excited about.

What kind of Thanksgiving were those kids going to have if their dad didn't show up?

"How was Summer?" Chase asked.

"Holding up pretty well. Chief Poole had already been to see her." Bray took a deep pull on his beer. "What do you think of Gary Blake?" he asked, looking at Chase.

"When I first brought Raney to Ravesville, we had a little trouble. She was run off the road. Blake was the investigating officer. I thought he was a lazy cop. Then later, we learned that it might have been something very different."

"What do you mean?"

"He might have had a reason to brush it under the rug. The description of the car matched one driven by Sheila Stanton."

"The same Sheila Stanton that you dated?" Bray asked.

"The same. But we couldn't prove it. And then we learned that they'd had a thing. But they were quiet about it. It helped us understand why he wasn't interested in arresting her. When we were in St. Louis so that Raney could testify against Harry Malone at his murder trial, we heard that Sheila had left town rather unexpectedly."

"So he's nursing a broken heart?" Bray asked.

"Broken heart. Bruised pride. Something in between," Chase said. "Don't feel sorry for him. He's a small-town cop with a big ego that gets in the way of him doing the right thing. I don't think he's got a whole lot of friends here."

"So there are plenty of people who think he's a horse's ass. That's not generally enough to get you in trouble."

Chase set his beer down. "I'm not sure if I should say anything, but given what almost happened yesterday, I think you should know. More than a month ago, Raney happened to see a big bruise on Summer's back. When she asked Summer about it, she got the impression that Summer didn't want anybody to know about it. I don't know if it was Gary Blake."

"It was," Bray said. "Summer ended up on the wrong end of his boot."

Cal set his beer down. "She told you that?"

Bray nodded.

"And you're sure you didn't kill Gary Blake last night?" Cal asked.

Bray shook his head. "I thought about it. Went to his house and knocked on the door. Nobody answered. I guess that gave me enough time to channel my anger in a more manageable direction."

"You didn't tell Chief Poole that," Chase said. "If he finds out that you were at Blake's house, he's going to have more questions."

"I guess I'll deal with that at the time," Bray said. "There's no evidence connecting me to a crime. I didn't do anything." He finished his beer and walked over to look at the paint can that was sitting near the bathroom door. "'Snapdragon in Splendor.' What the hell kind of color is that?"

Chase shrugged. "Talk to Raney," he said. "I just put it on the walls."

Cal put down his empty bottle. "I've got to get going," he said. "I told Gordy Fitzler that Nalana and I'd be there by six."

"Old Man Fitzler?"

"Yeah. He's selling his house. Nalana and I looked at it the other day. We want it. His daughters are home for the holiday and he wants to make sure they're okay with the decision."

With his index finger, Bray pointed at his brothers. "You two? Both staying in Ravesville? Living down the road from each other?"

Cal smiled. "Makes it easy to borrow a cup of sugar."

Something had definitely happened here. He chose his words carefully. "I'm glad that the two of you feel comfortable borrowing sugar from each other. That's a nice change."

"The best," Chase said.

"It's important to know that there's always...sugar close by," Cal added.

Yes, it was. "But how does staying in Ravesville work with your jobs?" Bray asked Cal.

"Well, Nalana was evidently so highly valued that when she told her bosses that she intended to quit so that she could live with me in Ravesville, her bosses were quick to offer up an alternative that will allow her to remain with the FBI but work remotely, as long as she's willing to travel some."

"And for you?" Bray asked.

"I'm not interested in being in another country if Nalana is here. I'm setting up a little engineering shop in the outbuilding at my new house. I know a thing or two about ships and submarines and just maybe have an idea or two of how to make a better flyswatter."

"Sounds about perfect for a formal navy SEAL with a mechanical-engineering degree." Bray turned to Chase. "How about you? This remodeling can't keep you busy forever."

"Thank the good Lord for that," Chase said, draining his beer. "I'll stay on the job with the St. Louis police department for now. They're going to work with me and try to group my shifts together so that I work three on and four off one week and four on and three off the following week. That way I'll have seven days off in the middle of every two weeks to be here. I've still got my condo and can stay in St. Louis when I need to. And Raney, well, there is a lot to do on the house yet and she's really good at that. Plus, we're hoping to start a family quickly." He looked at his brothers. "I never saw myself as a dad, and suddenly, I can't see myself as anything else."

The three men looked at one another. They were brothers who had lost their own father too early. "You'll make a great one," Bray said.

He turned when he heard footsteps coming down the hall. Raney and Nalana entered.

"What's going on?" Raney asked, looking at Chase first, then Cal.

Chase smiled. "Bray was admiring your paint choices."

Raney sighed. "Sticks and stones," she said breezily as if discussions about paint colors were old stuff to her.

"We were talking about sugar—you know, how much you need for baking and...other stuff," Cal added.

Nalana wrinkled her nose. "You don't bake," she said.

Cal shrugged. "Yes, but I did say I'd cook the turkey tomorrow. I'm looking forward to dinner. It's got to be better here than on a mountain in Afghanistan. That's where I was last year at this time. Let me tell you, a turkey MRE leaves a lot to be desired."

"Hard to argue that," Bray said. Even though he was unsettled about how he'd left Summer, he was happy to be here with his brothers and the women who were important to them.

His phone rang. Speaking of Summer. "Hi," he said.

"Bray," she said, her voice thick with tears. "I need you."

"Honey," he said, already moving. "What's wrong?"

"They took Adie. She's gone."

Chapter Six

"Who took her?" he demanded, his heart starting to beat fast.

"I don't know. Two men."

"Where?"

"At the mall."

"Have you contacted the police?"

"I can't," she said. "They put a rag over my mouth and knocked me out with something. I don't think I was out for very long, but when I woke up, Adie and both the men were gone. They left a note."

"What did it say?"

"'Don't tell the police or anyone else. If you do, you'll never see your daughter again.' Oh, Bray, what am I going to do?"

"You did the right thing. You called me. Now where are you?"

"In my car. About five miles from the mall. I was shaking so much I couldn't drive. I pulled off. I'm at a gas station at the intersection of Highway 8 and Sycamore Road."

"Is anybody watching you? Were you followed?"

She didn't answer right away. "I don't think so," she said. "Nobody seems to be paying any attention to me."

"Okay. Stay there. Lock your doors. Don't get out of the car. I'll be there as soon as I can."

She didn't say anything.

"Summer," he said, his tone firm. "Promise me that you'll do what I asked."

"I promise," she said.

"Did you tell Trish?"

"Not yet," she wailed. "Oh, God, what am I going to tell Keagan?"

"We'll figure it out. I'm on my way." He disconnected the phone and turned to his family. "Summer's five-year-old daughter has been kidnapped."

Raney and Nalana both gasped. Chase and Cal gathered their women close.

"What's your plan?" Cal asked, his voice calm.

"She was warned not to call the police. So we won't. For the time being. But we need access to info that the police could normally provide. They took her from the mall in Hamerton. There's got to be video surveillance of the parking lot, the entrances and the interior hallways."

Nalana stepped forward. "On it. I work with a guy who can tap into any system known to man. He'll be able to get it."

Bray nodded.

"Do you think this has anything to do with Gary Blake's disappearance?" Chase asked.

"I don't know, but I think it's a hell of a coincidence, and I don't much believe in coincidence. Summer's son and sister could also be at risk."

"Raney and I'll take that one," Chase said. "We won't leave their side. You want us to tell Trish what's going on?"

"Yeah, but not Keagan." Summer would want to tell her baby rock.

Bray swung his gaze to Cal. "Can you follow me in your car? Once we get more details from Summer, I'm going to want you to go to the mall and look for physical evidence."

Cal fished his keys out of his pocket. "Let's roll."

Bray pulled his Glock 27 out of the holster on his belt. He had, of course, flown with his gun, but with a very limited amount of ammunition. He looked at his brothers. "Do you have some ammo that I can have?"

"Absolutely," Chase said. "It'll just take me a minute. It's upstairs."

While Chase was gone, Raney left the room and came back with two high-powered flashlights. "These might come in handy," she said.

They would. And when Chase came in moments later with enough ammo to defend a small city, he was struck by the knowledge of how important family was at a time like this. You could count on them.

He was almost out the door when Nalana came running toward him, carrying a soft blanket. "For Adie," she said, "when you find her."

BRAY DROVE VERY FAST, and his mind was going even faster. His car was too quiet and it allowed his mind to shift into dangerous territory. Blame. He should have gone with Summer to the mall, whether he was invited or not. He should have realized Blake's disappearance might mean something more, that Summer and her children were at risk.

But knowing that there was little to be gained by would-have, should-have games, he forced himself to focus on more productive thoughts.

Was it possible that Summer and Adie had simply been in the wrong place at the wrong time? That the kidnapping was random, not associated with them specifically?

That the kidnappers had chosen the mall as a likely place to be able to play grab-and-run with a child?

Possible but doubtful. Much more likely that Adie had been the target and the mall had presented the best opportunity. They hadn't hurt Summer. The thought that they could just as easily have put a knife in her back or a bullet in her head made him almost need to roll down his window and get sick.

When he reached the gas station, he saw Summer's car. She was sitting in the driver's seat, staring straight ahead. He drove around the perimeter of the gas station twice before pulling into a spot next to her.

He saw Cal pull into one of the bays and get gas. Unless someone knew them well, nobody would guess that they were together.

He opened his door and heard the *click* of Summer's passenger door unlocking. He opened the door and slid in.

She looked terrified. He wanted to take her into his arms and promise her that everything would be okay.

Instead, he reached over, laid a hand on her thigh. "We'll get her back," he said.

"What kind of monsters steal a child, Bray? What kind?" she asked, her voice breaking.

The worst kind. But there was nothing to be gained by saying that. She already knew that. "Tell me again what happened."

"Adie needed shoes. Trish said that she'd take Keagan home. We bought the shoes and we were walking toward an exit when a man bumped into me. He had a gun. Said he wanted to ask me something about Gary."

"What?" he said sharply. This was new information. He made an effort to gentle his voice. "Try to remember exactly what he said."

"I don't know exactly, but it was something like, 'I want to ask you a question about your ex-husband.'"

Well, that settled that. It was not a random kidnapping. They had known Summer. And this definitely had something to do with her ex.

"Then he said if I didn't do what he said, he'd…he'd shoot Adie."

"You did the right thing."

She shook her head. "My daughter is gone. How could I have done the right thing?"

She was playing the blame game, too. "You couldn't take the chance," he said. "Have you ever seen this man before?"

"No."

"Describe him."

"Late forties, early fifties. White. Very pale skin. Big nose. Brown hair combed to the side, I think. He wore a gray sweatshirt with the hood up. I couldn't see a lot of his face."

"That's okay," he said. She'd been terrified but she was remembering important details. He glanced in the side mirror. Cal was washing his windshield. Nobody else seemed to be paying any attention to them. "Anything else?"

"Taller than me. Probably close to six feet. His pants were dark. But his shoes were light. White athletic shoes."

"Anything about his voice? Accent? Odd cadence?"

She shook her head. "Not really. He sounded…sort of like you. Like he might have lived on the East Coast for a while."

"Did you see his gun? Can you describe it?"

"I saw it. I don't know anything about guns. It was black. Seemed big. He…he had on gloves. They were black, too. Under them, I could see the shape of a big ring on his left hand."

"Okay. What happened after he threatened Adie?"

"He pushed me through a set of double doors that led to a hallway and an exit."

He held up a hand, stopping her. "What part of the mall? Where are the doors located?"

"The southeast end, near Penney's. Just past the toy store. I remember because I was hoping Adie wouldn't ask to go inside. I was hurrying to get home."

"What happened when you went through the doors?"

"There was another man standing there. He had on a ski mask."

"Tell me about him."

She closed her eyes. "Dark clothes. I couldn't see his face or hair, but his eyes were blue. Light blue."

"Probably Caucasian," Bray said. "Height and weight?"

"Shorter than the other guy but still taller than me. So maybe five-nine, five-ten. Stocky. Or maybe just his coat made him look that way. It was a puffy one. Dark. Black or blue."

"Did he talk?"

"No. He's the one who covered my mouth with a rag."

"What else?" Bray prompted.

"When I woke up, Adie was gone. They left this." Holding an envelope by its edge, she handed it to him.

Don't call the police if you ever want to see your daughter again.

The note was on the back side of an envelope, handwritten, printed, all capital letters. Blue ink. "Recognize the writing?" Bray asked, knowing it was a long shot.

"No." She turned in her seat. "Bray, I don't know what

to do," she said. "Every minute that goes by, Adie could be in more danger. Hurting." Her pretty eyes filled with tears. "Should I go to the police?"

"I don't think so," he said. "I don't think you're being watched. Which makes me believe that they've got another way to know if you go to the police."

"But…" Her voice trailed off. "Are you suggesting that the police are involved?"

He shrugged. "I don't know who's involved. But this seems to have something to do with your husband, and he's a cop. Our job is to try to draw logical conclusions based on what we know."

"I can't be logical. I can't even think."

He studied her. "Listen, I have to ask. Do you think it's possible that your ex staged all of this—his disappearance, Adie's kidnapping. Could this be an end run to avoid a potential custody battle?"

"I've never threatened to take the kids away from Gary. Just the opposite. He's the one who cancels his weekends or brings them back early."

Bray pulled his phone from his pocket. He dialed Cal. When his brother answered, he succinctly gave him the location of the abduction and a description of both men. Cal promised to be in touch.

"Who was that?" Summer asked.

"Cal. He's been here the whole time. I want him to go to the mall, see if there's any physical evidence at the scene. Make a few discreet inquiries."

"I appreciate his help," she said.

"The whole family is in on it. Nalana is reaching out to an FBI contact to get the video footage of the mall, and Raney and Chase are going to tell Trish and stay with her and Keagan, just in case."

He could tell by the look on her face that she understood what he was saying. They all needed to be careful.

"I need to tell my mother," she said.

"We will. Is she still in Ravesville?"

"Yes. Still at the old house."

"Okay. Here's what we're going to do. You're going to drive back to the mall and park the van in the lot. Then we'll take my car."

"Why?"

"This red van sticks out like a sore thumb. If we plan on sneaking up on anything, I'd feel better in my bland rental." Plus, if they'd planted some kind of tracking device on the van, he didn't want to make it easy for them.

"It's just so crazy. If these men know Gary then they know that I'm a part owner of a small business. Everybody knows that's not terribly lucrative. I don't have money for a ransom."

"Is it possible that you have something else of value?"

She turned her head. "Like what?"

"I don't know. Something of your ex's."

"I can't imagine. He's been out of the house for over two years. His stuff is gone."

"Some information?"

"Gary and I don't chat a lot. If we talk, it's about the kids. Never his work." She glanced at her cell phone, which was sitting on the middle console. "I don't have a home phone. They need to call my cell." She paused. "They didn't ask me for my phone number."

"They could get it from your ex," he said.

She nodded. "Then why the hell don't they call?" she asked, her tone angry. "That's what kidnappers do, right? They call. They make a demand."

He'd been a beat cop before he'd gone to work at the DEA. Had never worked a kidnapping case, but he was pretty sure that Adie hadn't been snatched for a big ransom. There might not be a call. But he wasn't taking her hope away from her. "We'll be ready when it comes. I promise you," he said. He put his hand on the door. "Are you confident that you can drive?"

"Yes," she said. "I'll park in the lot by Penney's."

He got out and waited while she pulled out of the lot. Then he fell in behind her. She drove much faster than she had the day before, and in just minutes, they were back at the mall. She got out of her van, then stopped, reached back inside and pulled out a bag.

"Adie's shoes," she said, getting into his car. "I...I want her to have them right away when we find her."

Her voice had cracked at the end. And he knew that she was a hair away from unraveling. It made his own heart hurt. The men who'd done this were going to be very, very sorry. He was going to make sure of that.

When they pulled up in front of the two-story on Elmwood Street, Bray saw that her mother had painted the house at some point. It used to be white. Now it was yellow. The old garage that sat behind the house had been torn down and a new one put up. The door was up and he could see an older Ford parked inside. "That your mom's car?"

Summer nodded. "She's always leaving the door up. I've told her a hundred times to make sure she puts it down. She's always telling me to quit worrying, that nothing bad ever happens in Ravesville." Summer turned to him, her expression bleak. "I guess she can't say that anymore."

Something horrible had happened. To her granddaughter. Bray reached out his arm, put two fingers under Summer's chin. "We're going to get Adie back. You have to stay positive."

"Thank you," she whispered. "Thank you for being

here, for being somebody that I knew I could call, that I knew would help me. It's more than I deserve after... everything."

Now was not the time for questions, not the time to ask why she hadn't waited for him. "I'm not going anywhere," he said.

Chapter Seven

Wednesday, 6:00 p.m.

Summer didn't bother to knock. "Mom," she called out as she opened the door.

"In the kitchen."

They walked down the short hallway. Flora Wright was at her stove, stirring a pot of something. She turned, her spoon in the air.

The years had been kind to Flora Wright. Her brown hair was streaked with gray and there were lines on her face that hadn't been there fifteen years ago. But all in all, better than what he'd expected. Flora had been a hard drinker, and in a small town, the talk had been inevitable. Bray had heard it. His parents, too. His mom had been smart enough to tell him to make his own decisions about a person's worth and not let someone else do it for him.

He'd told Summer to ignore it and she'd done her best, but he'd always known that it was a source of embarrassment to her. Trish had simply been angry about it, and that had caused a lot of tension in the Wright house, with Summer smack-dab in the middle as peacemaker.

He was pretty confident Summer's mom had given up the bottle. Good for her. "Hi, Flora," he said.

"Bray." Her smile was genuine. "I heard you were back

for your brother's wedding." She turned to her daughter. "What's wrong?" she asked immediately.

"Someone took Adie," Summer said.

The spoon hit the tile floor with a clatter. "What?" Flora asked, putting her hand on the counter, as if to steady herself.

Summer told her mother about the mall and then about Gary, too. By the time she was finished, Flora was tight-lipped and pale.

"What do we do?" she asked.

"We wait," Summer said. "But in the meantime, Mom, can you think of anything about Gary that would help us understand why he might have suddenly disappeared?"

"He hasn't been happy since the divorce," Flora said.

There was a look exchanged between mom and daughter that he couldn't decipher. Had Flora been upset about the divorce? Any parent probably would be, especially because there were children involved. But it seemed like something more.

"It's been two years, Mom," Summer said. "Why now?"

"He's been out of town a lot these last couple months," Flora said.

How would she know? The question must have been in his eyes, because she shrugged and said, "He pays me to clean his house. It's hardly been dirty."

"You never mentioned that you were cleaning his house," Summer said, her voice tight.

"I clean houses, Summer. You know that."

"But... Never mind—it's not important," Summer said, waving a hand.

Bray was glad that she was staying focused, but certainly the relationship between Gary Blake and his ex-mother-in-law was interesting. "Do you have a key to his house?" Bray asked.

Flora nodded. "For the kitchen door. What are you going to do?"

"Search it. There's got to be a clue somewhere that can lead us to Adie."

Flora pulled a silver key off her key ring. "What should I do?"

"I'll call my brother Chase. He'll be in touch."

"HOW YOU HOLDING UP?" Bray asked when they were back in his car.

She was petrified. "Fine," she said.

He nodded. "Your mom looks good."

She understood the subtext. "She stopped drinking fifteen years ago."

"Must have been a big year."

She turned her head.

"That's the year you married Blake."

He was getting too close. She needed to change the subject. "Chief Poole may have somebody watching Gary's house."

"We won't get caught," he said confidently.

She needed to draw upon that confidence. Maybe it would leak over and she'd feel more in control. Adie had now been gone for an hour. And no word from anybody.

She gave him directions to Gary's house. It was at the edge of town, one block off the main street. He'd been renting it since the divorce. The owners were both in a nursing home and their son was grateful to have Gary in the house. He might not feel the same if it came to light that something bad had happened to Gary there. People were superstitious in small towns, and it might make it hard to ultimately sell the property.

It seemed impossible that it had just been this morning that Chief Poole had come to the café and told her that

Gary was missing. Once the chief had given her details, she'd understood the seriousness of the situation. But before that, when he'd simply said he was missing, her very first thought had been relief. The interaction with Gary at the church had been so charged with unexpected anger. She simply wasn't up to dealing with that again. Especially not with Bray in town.

"It's down this street," she said.

Bray didn't turn. Kept going straight. Turned at the next street instead. "How many houses in?" he asked.

"Five." They drove another hundred feet. "It's the two-story colonial. You can see the roofline from here."

Bray pulled the car over and killed his lights. "So his backyard butts up to this house's backyard?" he asked, pointing at a smaller brick Cape Cod.

"Yes."

"Okay. This is the way to go in. Maybe you should stay here," he said.

"No," she said simply. Not an option. She might not have a right to be in Gary's house, but she was the one with the key. She would not let Bray take this risk alone.

She grabbed a flashlight and opened her door, causing Bray to hurry to catch up with her. He carried a flashlight in one hand and his gun in the other. "Keep your light off for now," he whispered. "We'll only turn it on if we absolutely have to."

Her eyes adjusted to the dark, and she was able to see enough that she didn't trip and fall. Someone in the neighborhood had lit their fireplace. A comfortable smell, so at odds with the terror that was flowing through her veins.

As they walked through the neighbor's yard and into Gary's backyard, she prayed that a dog wouldn't suddenly alert the neighborhood to their presence. Or take a bite out of them. But the night stayed quiet. "This is it," she said.

Bray turned on his flashlight, keeping it mostly pointed at the ground. "Big house for a single guy," he said softly.

"Not a lot of rental property in Ravesville. I think he took what he could get. That door there leads to the kitchen. It's the one that wasn't closed tight."

"Chief Poole told you that?"

"Yes. Not you?"

Bray shook his head. "Probably didn't think I needed the details." He paused. "Maybe he thought I knew them," he added.

It was very dark in the backyard. Street side, it would be different because there were lights on the corners of each block. It had been a good idea to come this way.

The house was completely dark. They approached and Summer handed Bray the key. Then she held the flashlight while he unlocked the door. When he opened the door and used the tail of his shirt to wipe off any prints, the enormity of what they were doing settled down upon her.

They were disturbing what might be a crime scene. But she kept going, knowing she would do far worse to get Adie back.

She had, of course, been to Gary's house several times, dropping off and picking up the kids. She knew her way around the downstairs. The kitchen had a bath and laundry room off to one side. Then there was a family room and a formal dining room that had been empty of furniture since the day Gary moved in. The son had left everything except for the dining room set, because he needed one.

The milk and the cereal bowl that the chief had described were still on the table. She pointed to them. "This is Chief Poole's evidence of a quick departure."

Bray flicked his flashlight toward the floor, then the back door. "And that's the blood."

It looked like a smear of brown dirt on the back of the cream-colored wood.

"What are we looking for?" she asked.

"I don't know. Just keep your eyes open for anything that looks odd or interesting." As they walked from the kitchen to the family room, he pointed at the closed drapes and said, "We got lucky. Still, be careful with your flashlight and don't turn on any other lights."

After a quick search of the downstairs didn't net anything of value, they took the steps. She had never been in the upstairs. There were two bedrooms across from a bath. The first one was Adie's. There was a chest of drawers and a bed, with two dolls that she'd taken from home perched against the pillows.

Waiting. For Adie to come and play.

Summer covered her mouth. Where was her child?

She forced herself to move on. The next bedroom had to be where Keagan slept, but one wouldn't have been able to tell. There was nothing of the boy in the room.

The bath across the hall was clean. Her mother had probably seen to that. Her mother cleaned houses four days a week and generally told her, in excruciating detail, about each house. But she had never once mentioned that she was cleaning Gary's. She'd probably expected that Summer wouldn't be happy about it.

She didn't care. Her mother could have lunch with Gary every day for all it mattered to her.

At the end of the hall was the master suite, with a big bedroom and an attached bath. In the corner of the master was a big desk. If the kids' rooms had been sterile, this was the exact opposite. There were dirty clothes on the floor, piles of newspapers at the end of the bed, a pile of what might be clean yet unfolded laundry on the dresser and several take-out food bags crumpled up in the garbage can in the corner. There were two more on the floor nearby as if Gary had been eating in bed and tossed the bag but hadn't quite hit the mark. The room smelled of old greasy French fries and onions.

Something told her that Gary had instructed her mother to leave his room alone. She picked her way around the debris on the floor. He needed to be a little less protective of his man cave and a little more hygienic.

The only thing that seemed orderly in the whole room was the desk in the corner. It was clear with the exception of a spiral notebook and two pens, both from the Wright Here, Wright Now Café.

Bray followed her over. With the tips of his fingers, he picked up the notebook, ran his thumb along the edges to see the pages. Then again. They were all blank. He put the notebook down.

Then he knelt. His fingertips again protected by his shirttail, he opened the three drawers on the one side of the desk. Pens, paper clips and rubber bands in the top. A stack of unused file folders in the middle. And in the bottom, a plastic bin marked "Insurance." Bray opened it up and there was a stack of Explanation of Benefit forms.

"He covers the kids," Summer said.

Bray closed the bin and shoved it back in the drawer. "Nothing here," he said. "Does the desk seem unusually clean?" he asked.

"Given the rest of the room, yes. But Gary has always been tidy with paperwork."

"But no bank statements, no credit-card bills, no tax returns. Absolutely nothing financial."

She tried to remember where Gary had kept those things when they'd been married. They'd had a joint checking account where paychecks got automatically deposited. Statements had come to the house and been filed somewhere in the office that sat next to their family room. Bills had come in the mail. And he'd paid them. It had been his task, the way cooking dinner was her task.

"He was switching over, doing lots of things electronically. Everyone has been, right? It's easier. Better for the environment."

"Maybe he's green down to his shorts. Or maybe he didn't want to take the chance that his ex-mother-in-law would stick her nose where it didn't belong." Bray walked over toward the walk-in closet.

Summer followed. It was half-empty, reminding her that Gary had never been a clotheshorse. He'd worn a uniform every day, so there wasn't a big need to have a lot of clothes. There were some dress pants and maybe five shirts. Several extra uniforms.

Bray pushed clothing out of the way so that he could see the shelves behind them. A few books, a stack of car magazines. Bray systematically shook each one, to see if something would fall out.

They were just about to back out of the closet when Summer saw the lizard-print cowboy boots. She could never remember seeing Gary wear boots of any kind, let alone boots like this.

It was enough to make her reach for them. To make her pick one up. She dumped it on end. Nothing. Did the same with the other boot. Nothing there, either. Was just about to put them back when she decided to stick her hand inside.

And that was when she felt it. A key, taped to the inside top of the boot. She pulled, and key and tape came together.

"What's that to?" Bray asked.

She looked at it, saw the engraving. "It's from a bank in St. Louis. Maybe for a safe-deposit box." She looked up at Bray. "Gary and I never had a safe-deposit box at a bank in St. Louis. At least I don't think we did."

Bray looked at his watch. "I want to know what's in that box, but it's six thirty on the Wednesday before Thanksgiving. The banks are probably all closed."

Summer shook her head. "Not necessarily. Some of the banks have started offering extended banking hours," she said. "As late as eight or nine o'clock at night. The competition is fierce."

He took another look at the key, then pulled his smartphone from his pocket and punched buttons. In just minutes, he was dialing. "Can you tell me how late you're open?" he asked.

"Eight," he repeated, probably for her benefit. "Thank you," he said and hung up.

"This is terrific," she said. "Let's go."

"We're an hour and a half from the city. In good traffic. Plus, we have a key, but if your name's not on the list, you won't be able to get into it."

He was right. She needed to think. There was really only one option. "You can pretend you're Gary."

"They aren't going to take my word for it. They'll ask for identification."

"I have his passport. I found it recently. We got it when we went to Mexico for a vacation. I think he forgot about it. I remember that his picture wasn't great—a little blurry. His hair was longer then, not the length of yours, but maybe, if someone doesn't look too close, you could pass for him."

He didn't look convinced. She knew it was a long shot, but what other leads did they have? "We have to try," she added.

"It's going to add another ten minutes to run by your

house to get his passport," he said, already moving toward the stairs.

"We have to make it," she said, running to catch up. "The banks will all be closed tomorrow."

BRAY PUSHED HIS rental to ninety and moved in and out of the traffic that was on Interstate 44. Thankfully, traffic was light on the highway. They didn't talk.

Summer stared straight ahead, glancing every few minutes at her phone perched on the console between them. Twenty minutes into the trip, a phone rang and she jumped.

It was his cell phone. Cal. He put it on speaker. "Yeah," he said.

"I checked the hallway at the mall and it was clean, except there was a receipt, folded and wrinkled, as if it might have come out of a pocket accidentally."

Like maybe when somebody pulled their gloves out of their pocket. "For?" Bray asked.

"A gas station in St. Louis. Purchase was made earlier this afternoon, for forty-two gallons."

"Forty-two," Bray repeated. "Are they driving a semi?"

"I checked the price. Matches up to regular unleaded. Not diesel."

"I guess we look for vehicles with a big tank," Bray said.

"We can maybe do better. Nalana is going to have her guy try to get into the security tapes from the gas station," Cal said.

"Did he get anything from the mall?"

"Yeah. We're sorting through it now."

"Okay. Call me when you've got something," Bray said. "We're on our way to St. Louis to look at a safe-deposit box."

"Good luck," Cal said and hung up.

"It's something," Summer said after a long pause.

"Bits and pieces. That's how most crimes are solved. Rarely is there a big reveal. It's more often a process of paying attention to everything and sorting through what is important and what isn't."

Again she was silent for a long moment. "What if that takes too long?" she asked finally.

He didn't have an answer for that. "After we go to the bank, I want you to eat something," he said, changing the subject.

She shrugged. "I'm not sure I can."

"You need to," he said. "You never ate lunch."

"I was already planning the trip to Capaghetti's."

Her day had turned out very differently than she'd planned. Wasn't that the way it always worked? The things you worried about rarely happened and then, out of nowhere, you'd be slapped upside the head with something out of left field. Car accidents. Brain tumors. Little kids with handguns. He glanced at his left shoulder. Only time he'd ever taken a bullet had been from a ten-year-old. He'd been busting the kid's father when the kid had crawled out from under the bed with a .38. He'd managed to stay standing long enough to keep the dad subdued and he'd got an attaboy from his boss for having the wherewithal not to return fire.

When life tossed you lemons, you tossed 'em right back. Only choice you had. You kept going.

"You have to eat," he said. "You need to stay strong."

"Stay? I'm not strong," she argued.

"Don't underestimate yourself. You're a single parent with two kids and you have your own business."

"Not strong in the ways that count," she said.

He waited for her to continue, but that appeared to be all she was willing to say. She was probably stronger than she thought. At least he hoped she was. She was going to need to be. He glanced at his watch. They were making good time. Even if they hit some traffic closer to the city, they should be okay.

He looked at Gary Blake's passport that Summer had tossed onto the dash. She'd been right. The quality of the picture wasn't great. Plus, the man's straight hair had been unkempt and shaggy around his face. When Bray had looked at it, he'd pulled the rubber band out of the short ponytail that he pulled his hair back into when he wasn't working.

"I suppose you can't do anything about your cheekbones," Summer said.

He'd got the clean lines of his face from his mother. Blake's face was rounder. "Nope."

"It'll be okay," she said, looking at the clock on the dash.

He hoped so. He reached for the passport again and opened it. This time, with one eye on the road and one on the page, he studied the signature. Tight, cramped script. Small loop in the *Y*. The *E* at the end of *Blake* was just a line. "Okay. I'll practice at the stoplights once we get to St. Louis."

"It's a crime to impersonate someone to gain access to their bank records?" Her tone had changed. A half hour ago she'd been full speed ahead, and now she sounded as if she were putting on the brakes.

"Yes," he said.

"Gary's the type that might not take it well."

"Even if I'm doing it for him. For his child."

"He hates you."

That surprised him. He knew why he hated Blake, but what kind of beef could he have with Bray? He'd won. He'd got the girl. "Why?"

"I don't know," she said quickly. "But you're taking a risk. Too big a risk." She paused. "It could be your career. It's too much to ask. I'll find another way."

"You're not asking," he said. "I'm volunteering. You're right. We need to know what's in that box. And we need to know it quickly. Focus on that. Nothing else."

He saw her swallow hard. But she didn't argue. Ten miles went by before she turned to him. "Why don't they call, Bray? Why the hell hasn't anyone called?"

"I don't know," he said. "But we won't stop until we find her. We won't."

The traffic got heavier as they got closer to St. Louis. He could see Summer looking at the clock on the dash every few minutes. He drove fast, speeding up to avoid red lights. He was not going to have this woman have to wait days to see what was in that damn box.

He saw the big bank at the corner and took the first parking spot he could find. He took one more glance at the signature and shoved the passport into his pocket.

He opened his car door. "Come on, honey. It's show-time."

Chapter Eight

Wednesday, 7:53 p.m.

The bank had big heavy doors, shiny marble-looking floors and a security guard standing near a flagpole. Summer forced herself to slow down to a walk and she pasted a smile on her face.

"Good evening," she said.

The man nodded.

There was a row of teller bays but only two were open. Young girls, no older than twenty-five, were manning them. It made sense. New hires would be working the night before Thanksgiving. Those with greater seniority were home defrosting the turkey and making pie.

She could only hope the staffing pattern continued through to the safe-deposit-box area.

Off to the left was customer service. It was dark.

Beyond that, there was a sign on the wall. Safe-Deposit Boxes.

There was a desk and one of those rope things that they used at concerts and similar events to keep the crowd back. But there was no crowd. Not even anyone at the desk.

As she and Bray walked toward the sign, one of the young women behind the teller counter started toward them.

"Can I help you?" she asked. Her name badge said Treena.

Bray nodded in her direction. "I'm Gary Blake and I need to take a look at something in my box."

"Oh, sure," she said. Treena seemed to be looking over their shoulders as if expecting reinforcements to appear. But then she gave a little shrug and sat at the desk.

She tapped on the keyboard of the desktop computer. The screen came alive. "You said your name was Blake," she said.

"Gary Blake," Bray said pleasantly.

She keyed it in. Then looked up. "Do you have your key?"

Bray held it up.

"I'll need to see a picture ID," she said.

"Of course." Bray pulled out the passport and handed it to her. She opened it, looked at the picture.

Looked up at Bray.

He didn't flinch.

Treena looked across the bank. At what, Summer had no idea. She could feel the breath in her lungs. Burning.

Treena looked at Bray one more time, then the passport picture.

"It's a terrible photo, isn't it?" Summer said, moving a step forward. "I kept telling my husband to get a haircut."

Treena turned to Summer. "Are you Mrs. Blake?"

"I am," Summer said. "But I'm not on the box," she said, as if she knew that to be true.

"That's right. But if you had some identification you could show me, that would be helpful."

Summer opened her purse. Her license, anything of importance, said Summer Wright. Opposite of helpful.

She unfolded her billfold and pulled out her library

card. It was more than five years old but had her picture and, more important, had her name as Summer Blake.

Treena looked at it and smiled. "Thank you." She used a swipe card that hung on a lanyard around her neck to open the glass door that led back to the safe-deposit boxes. "Follow me, Mr. Blake," she said.

Summer walked over to the waiting area and sank down in one of the leather chairs, just seconds before she was sure that her knees were going to give out. She looked at the clock on the wall. Seven fifty-seven.

Three minutes to spare.

She felt as if she might throw up, and she was grateful that she hadn't eaten for many hours.

It was five and a half minutes later that Bray came through the glass door followed by Treena. He was not carrying anything.

Summer could barely contain her disappointment.

"Thank you," Bray said from somewhere far away.

"You're welcome, Mr. Blake. You two have a nice Thanksgiving," she said.

Adie loved pumpkin pie with more whipped cream than pie. Oh, God. She felt dizzy.

"You, too," Bray said. He stood in front of Summer's chair, held out a hand. "Let's go, honey."

When she didn't move, he pulled her from the chair and put his arm under her elbow and steered her toward the door. "Hang on," he whispered, no hesitation in his stride.

Now what? It was all she could think. Now what would she do to find her baby?

She heard the security guard locking the door behind them. Forced one foot in front of the other.

With his hand still cupped around her elbow, he steered her back to the car. He opened the passenger side and gently pushed her in. Then he was around the car. Inside.

"Are you okay?" he asked.

She was never going to be okay again. "Yes," she lied. He'd told her that she was strong. She'd better start trying to prove him right.

He unzipped his jacket and pulled out a handful of 8.5-by-11 lined sheets of paper, folded over. Maybe eight or ten. She looked closer. They were likely from the spiral notebook on the top of Gary's desk.

"The only thing in the box was these," Bray said. "I didn't take time to look at them."

She made some sound at the back of her throat. Something short of a sob. She'd been so sure that there was nothing. She reached for the papers.

"Keep them in order," Bray said, "in case that means something, and only touch them by the edges."

The pages were mostly blank. Except that each one, in the middle of the page, had one line of numbers. She quickly flipped pages. There were eleven of them. "What is this?" she cried. "What the hell is this?"

"I don't know."

She pressed her hand against her forehead. The headache that had been lurking ever since that man had put something over her mouth threatened to take her under.

She shoved the papers back at Bray. They did her no good anyway. Did Adie no good.

"It's obviously in code," Bray said. "We have to figure it out."

"That could take days," she said.

He started the car.

"Where are we going?"

"Back to Ravesville. We need Cal and Nalana to help us. Maybe Chase, Raney and your sister, too. The more eyes the better."

"My mother is a wiz at crossword puzzles. I know it's not the same, but she's good at figuring things out."

"Her, too. I got a text from Chase earlier. He and Raney brought Trish, Keagan and your mom to his house." He slowed for a red light, but when there was no traffic coming, he didn't stop.

It was fifteen minutes before she voiced what she'd been thinking since Bray had first pulled the papers from inside his coat. "This cannot be good for Gary. He's into something bad, isn't he?"

"Looks like it," Bray said. "But until we figure out the code, we won't know. Maybe not even then. But that can't be our focus. Our focus is on finding Adie."

He understood. He really did. "Why didn't you marry, Bray? Why didn't you marry and have a houseful of children? You'd be such a good dad."

The car ate up another two miles before he answered. "It just never felt right," he said.

"It's not too late," she said.

His head turned sharply. "What do you mean?"

"It's not too late. You can still find someone wonderful to spend your life with, to have your children."

He sighed. "Yeah, I'll start working on that."

They didn't talk again until he pulled into the driveway of the old house. Lights were on, both upstairs and downstairs, making it look welcoming. Safe.

Adie should be the one who felt safe. That was her job as a mother, to make her daughter feel safe. To be safe.

And she had failed.

And her son, who made her feel inadequate on her best days, was in the house. She would see the disgust in his eyes.

Bray opened his door. Got out. Walked around the car and opened her door. She forced herself to move. To walk up the steps, across the front porch, toward the door that she'd walked through a hundred times during high school when she and Bray had been dating.

When things had been simple. And she'd thought her life was going to be very different.

Bray opened the door, motioned for her to go in.

She did and was almost knocked over by the body that burst out of the kitchen.

Young, sweaty male. Gangling arms that hugged her until she couldn't breathe.

Keagan.

She pulled back. Held his thin face. "Oh, Keagan," she said.

"I love you, Mom," he said, his eyes only full of love.

It was exactly what she needed to keep going.

THE FIRST THING Bray noticed was that there was an extra person in the room that he hadn't expected.

Milo Hernandez. When Summer saw him, she hugged him.

"I called and told him about Adie," Trish said. "I told him he didn't need to come."

By the look on the man's face, it would take a bulldozer to move him out of the house. And the look he was giving Bray said *go ahead and try*.

No way. This guy was solidly in Summer's and Trish's corners and that made him okay by him. And if Chase, a St. Louis police detective, was nervous about having an ex-con in the room, he wasn't showing it.

"Glad you're here," Bray said.

Milo gave him a short nod.

Then Bray focused on Nalana. She had her laptop open, waiting for them. There was a somewhat grainy picture of the two men entering the mall, two separate shots of them walking through the mall and then one final one of the man in the gray sweatshirt loitering near the spot where Summer had been attacked. The man who had been wearing the face mask had not yet pulled it on. He was midforties, and most interestingly, he had a port-wine stain on his cheek.

Nalana passed around her laptop. "Does anybody recognize either one of them?"

Summer studied the photos. She even let Keagan, who had literally begged to not have to leave the room, take a look. That was smart. It was possible that the boy had seen something that she hadn't.

But with the exception of Trish, who thought the man in the gray sweatshirt looked somewhat familiar but couldn't place him, nobody recognized either man.

"There are six separate driving entrances to this particular mall," Nalana added. "Cameras on all six. It took a while but we identified their car. A 2010 white Pontiac Grand Prix. We checked the plates. Unfortunately, they match up to a 2012 red Mustang that was totaled two months ago and currently residing in a junkyard."

"Did you talk to the junkyard?" Bray asked.

"Yeah. We tracked down the owner. Has no idea when the plates might have been lifted."

"Okay. What time did the Grand Prix arrive at the mall?" Bray asked.

Nalana gave Summer a quick glance. "About five minutes after Summer did."

He could see that the news hit Summer hard. That meant that she'd been followed from Ravesville, to the garage where Trish had picked up her car and then on to the mall.

"I guess I was pretty oblivious," said Summer, proving that he'd guessed her thoughts accurately.

"We both were," Trish said.

"You weren't any less observant than anybody else under the circumstances," Chase said. "When people have bad intent, it's hard to thwart their plans."

Summer looked up from the computer. "These are all shots of them entering the mall. What about when they left the mall?"

Nalana licked her lips. "It might be difficult for you…" Her voice trailed off.

"Show me," Summer said.

Nalana pressed a few keys. And there it was. The two men were walking in the parking lot. The man with the bulky jacket was carrying Adie. Her head was on his shoulder.

He could have been a dad carrying a sleeping child.

"Oh," Summer gasped. "They drugged her," she said.

Bray put a hand on her shoulder. "Probably. You recovered from that. She will, too."

"I'm going to kill them," she said, her back teeth jammed together.

"We will if we have to," Bray said easily. He pulled the computer screen away from her.

Milo looked satisfied with that answer.

"She's just a baby," Summer said. Then she looked up, saw her son, her mother, her sister. "No, she's not," she said more confidently. "She's a smart little girl. We've talked about what she should do if she was ever lost. She knows my cell-phone number, knows how to call me. She'll know that we're coming, that we'll find her."

Summer was being strong for her family. He wouldn't have expected anything else.

"What about video from the gas station?" Bray asked.

"My friend is working on that. It's a big chain. They have better web security than most. But he'll get it."

Bray pulled out the papers. Touching just the very edges, he spread them out on the table. "This is what was in…"

He looked at Keagan. He'd been referring to Gary Blake as "Blake" or "the ex," but he didn't want Keagan to perceive that he was disrespectful of his dad and slip back into attitude. "...Officer Blake's safe-deposit box in St. Louis." He looked at his brothers. "I suspect we all have had some experience in breaking codes. Probably you, too, Nalana."

"Limited," she said. "Most of it's done with computers now. I could probably ask for access to one, but I'm not sure that I can do it without somebody having to approve the request. It's out of my regular scope."

"I understand," Bray said. "I don't think that this is going to be that tough."

"We should start by identifying what's in common," Flora said.

Bray looked at Summer's mom, who was sitting on the edge of her chair, her eyes moving across the pages. She was right.

"Okay, what do we have?" he asked.

"Every page has just one line," Trish said, getting the dialogue going.

"Each line only has numbers, no letters," Cal added.

"Toward the end of each line," Summer said, "periods begin to be interspersed with the numbers. Every line has at least a couple periods. Some have more."

That was the easy stuff. It got harder from there. They studied the pages, sometimes walking around the table to get a better view.

"They range in length from thirty-nine digits to sixty-eight digits," added Chase.

More circling. No one said anything. Twenty minutes went by. Finally, Flora put a finger in the air. "Those six," she said, pointing, "have a common stretch of seventeen numbers."

Chapter Nine

Wednesday, 10:00 p.m.

That got everybody's attention. Flora pointed out the six and everyone studied them more carefully.

"We need a word with seventeen letters," Keagan said, his young voice high with emotion.

"Not necessarily," Bray said gently. "We can't assume that one number stands for one letter. For example, an *A* could be a 13. We'd be better off to think of groupings. What groupings or groups would Officer Blake have knowledge of?"

"How do we know this is Gary's list?" Flora asked. "Maybe it belongs to someone else and he was just keeping it for some reason."

"Maybe," Bray said. "We can't ignore possibilities, but I think it is more likely that if it was important enough for him to keep safe, then it's his list. Also, the paper matches the notebook on his desk. The notebook that was otherwise empty."

"Types of crimes," Raney said. "He's a cop. He would know people who committed the same type of crime."

"Good," Bray said. "What else?"

"Last names," Cal said. "Ravesville is a small town,

and lots of people are related to one another. There could easily be six people with the same last name."

"Keep going," Bray said.

"Customer preferences," Cal said carefully. "You could have six who bought the same thing."

The adults around the table looked at one another, easily catching on that if Blake had been selling something, it was likely illegal. The comment went over Keagan's head. He didn't point out the fact that his dad wasn't in sales. Bray could see that Summer's eyes had turned thoughtful, as if she were remembering things and trying to piece them together with what Cal had suggested.

"What's the easiest way to create a code if you want to turn letters into numbers?" Bray asked.

"Easiest?" Chase considered. "Easiest is an *A* is a 1, a *B* is a 2 and so on."

"You got any blank paper?" Bray asked.

Cal opened a kitchen drawer and pulled out a spiral notebook. Bray flipped it open. Bray took the seventeen common letters and applied that logic and got gibberish.

"Or, to mix it up a little, *A* is a 5, *B* is a 10, *C* is a 15 and so on. There could be a million combinations. We need a computer," Chase said.

"Three is his favorite number," Keagan said.

Bray tried assigning a 1 to an *A*, a 3 to a *B* and so on but got nothing. He wrote out the alphabet and next to the *A* put a 3. Then he put a 4 next to the *B* and so on. When he applied that logic, the room suddenly erupted with energy.

It was Ravesville. The seventeen digits stood for Ravesville.

Bray wanted to slap himself upside the head. He'd been too focused on the fact that it was one line and not in the traditional format of an address to give the idea due consideration.

From that point, it became easier. They hit a bump in the road and lost time when they realized that he'd used a different convention for the numbers versus letters. With numbers, he got tricky and used multiples of six. A six was really a 1, a twelve was really a 2 and so on. The periods in the line separated days, months and years.

392 Wolftail Road, Ravesville 3/3/2014 in code was 185412 25171482231114 201736 20324721241114147 18.18.120624.

"Ravesville. Hamerton. Port," Summer said, when they had finally deciphered all eleven. "All towns, relatively close. And the addresses, I don't know exactly where they are but I recognize some of the road names."

Everyone nodded. "You're right," Bray said. "I even recognize a few."

"And the dates. There's nothing older than two years ago," she added. She looked at Bray. "What the heck is this?"

Chase was busy mapping the locations on his iPad. "Some of these places don't look so great," he said. He showed them a picture of a run-down farmstead. Then a second one.

"Unfortunately, I think our only option is to go to these places and try to figure out what ties them together."

"Eleven places," Summer said. "While they are all in this general area, a couple of these points are probably at least one hundred miles apart. It's a big area to search. Especially in the dark."

It wasn't great circumstances, but he didn't see an alternative. "You want to wait until morning?" he asked.

"No," she said sharply. "Of course not."

"Relax," he said easily. "Me neither. But now I insist that you eat something. We can't be driving all over the countryside and have you pass out."

"Something quick," she said. She glanced at her watch.

He knew what it said. They'd worked as quickly as possible to break the code, but it was almost eleven o'clock.

"How about BLTs and fruit salad?" Raney said.

"That would be great," Summer said.

Raney and Nalana left the room. Trish gave her twin a hug, and she and Flora followed them.

"Keagan, you should probably try to get some sleep," Summer said. "We'll wake you if we hear anything."

"I shouldn't have told her that her dolls were stupid," Keagan said, his voice choked up.

Summer wrapped her arms around her son. "You are a really great older brother. Don't doubt that. How many times have you watched her for me lately? At least five times. I would never have allowed that if I didn't trust you a hundred percent. She adores you and she knows that you love her."

"Are we going to get her back?"

The question hung in the air. "Of course we are," Summer said, as if there could be no other conclusion. "I promise."

Bray was amazed. Summer was fearful down to the marrow of her bones, yet there was no way she was going to let her son know that. Now was the time for reassurance, for hope.

He was going to do everything in his power to make sure that this woman didn't have to go back on her promise. "Keagan, you can take my room upstairs. First door. Bathroom across the hall."

Once the boy was upstairs with the door closed, Summer put her head in her hands. "I hope I didn't just make a very bad mistake," she said softly.

Bray wrapped an arm around her, aware that his brothers and Milo were watching. "You did exactly right," he said. "Exactly right."

He looked at Chase. "You and Raney are okay with staying here with Trish, Keagan and Flora?"

"Absolutely," Chase said.

"I'll stay with them," Milo said. "Then you and Raney can search, too. I could probably get us some additional resources fairly quickly, too, if we need them."

Bray didn't even want to contemplate who those resources might be. But Milo standing guard made sense. Summer and Trish trusted him implicitly. They were good judges of character. But how would Chase feel about leaving Milo in the house without any Hollisters present?

"Do you have a gun?" Chase asked.

As an ex-con, he should not. Milo lifted up his loose shirt. He was carrying a 9 mm. "I'm a good shot and won't hesitate when it comes to protecting them."

"Good enough for me," Chase said. Bray let out his breath. Emergencies made strange bedfellows.

"Okay, we'll split into three groups. Chase and Raney, Cal and Nalana, and Summer with me. Chase and Cal, you can each take three. They're the ones farthest out, so you'll have the most travel time. Summer and I'll take the remaining five. We ought to be able to cover everything within a couple hours. And…and maybe we'll get lucky. We might only have to look at two or three."

"It's a plan," Cal said.

"Okay. Be careful," Bray added, knowing it was unnecessary. Cal was a former navy SEAL and Nalana was an FBI agent. Chase was an experienced detective and, well, quite frankly, he wasn't going to let anything happen to Raney. They could certainly handle themselves. But he also knew that good cops, the very best ones even, could let their emotions get in the way when the safety of a child was at stake.

And mothers? Well, it went without saying that Summer should not be looking for her own child. Objectivity had gone out the virtual window the minute that thug had pushed her at the mall.

But he also knew that he didn't have the heart to ask her to wait at home. It meant that he'd need to be super vigilant and smart enough to protect both of them.

It wouldn't help anyone if Adie was found safe and sound but lost her mother in the process. And the idea of that possibility hit him like a .38 in the gut.

"What's wrong?" Cal asked.

"Nothing," Bray said, waving his hand. He needed to get his head straight. Fast. "Can I use this?" he asked, picking up Chase's iPad.

"Sure," Chase said. He looked at Cal and inclined his head toward the kitchen. Both men walked out, leaving him alone with Summer.

"Your family is pretty great," she said.

"Your mom was the one who cracked the code open. Her recognizing that there were common stretches of numbers really helped."

"Sudoku and crosswords pay off," she said. She closed her eyes.

He started plugging in addresses.

"What are you doing?" Summer asked after a few minutes.

"A reverse lookup on the address." He kept going, finally pushing a list in Summer's direction. "Recognize any of these names?"

"This guy eats at the restaurant," she said.

Richard Bridge. He shuffled through the stack of pages

one more time, stopping at the eighth page. "His address is 4903 Brewster Road."

She shook her head. "Richard Bridge has to be at least eighty-five years old. He lives in the assisted-living facility on the edge of town. He might have lived on Brewster Road at one time." She studied the names again. "Why are there only seven names? There are eleven addresses."

"The other four don't come up with anything. Not sure what that means."

Raney poked her head into the dining room. "Food's ready," she said.

BRAY MOTIONED FOR her to precede him out of the room. Then he caught up and pulled her chair out for her. Did the same for her mother, who was moving toward the table. Would have probably assisted Trish but Cal beat him to it.

The Hollister men had old-fashioned manners. Polite. Protective. Brave. White knights in shining armor.

Bray with his too-long hair and dangerous eyes would laugh at the comparison.

While they were eating, Bray continued to study the iPad and make notes in the spiral notebook. Finally, he looked up. "This probably isn't quite right," he said, "and certainly not to scale, but I wanted to get a feel for the relationship of one location to the next."

There was a big X with eleven smaller Xs around it. "I assume the big X is Ravesville," she said.

He nodded.

She pointed at one of the closer ones. "How far is this from Ravesville?"

He bent his thumb at the first joint. "This represents thirty miles."

It was a crude map, but it did the trick. She pointed at the two Xs the farthest from the big X. "I underestimated.

It means that between these two points, there's almost two hundred miles."

"That's why we're dividing and conquering."

She sucked in a deep breath. His ability to systematically work the clues probably served him well as a DEA agent.

The BLT was delicious, but she could force herself to eat only half along with a couple of bites of fruit. Halfway through the quick meal, Nalana's cell phone beeped.

She picked it up. "We have something on the gas receipt." She went to get her computer that she'd left in the dining room. Within seconds, she was pulling up a video image of the white Grand Prix pulling into the station. The man in the gray sweatshirt got out of the passenger side and began to pump the gas. His hood was up. When he finished, he motioned for the driver of the car, who was not clearly visible, to move forward. Then a pale green Maxima pulled in and he put gas in that vehicle, too. Then he pulled cash from his pocket and walked into the convenience store, presumably to pay.

He'd pumped forty-two gallons because he'd filled two cars. Now the receipt made sense. But who was the guy in the green car? The angle of the camera was all wrong to see the drivers of the vehicles; it was positioned to see the pump and the person standing next to it. There was one other angle that picked up the license plate.

They already knew the license plate for the Grand Prix was not good. The green car didn't even have one.

"The party is getting bigger," Bray said, running his tongue over his teeth.

Nobody answered. The man in the green car was just one more person to worry about. She pushed her plate aside. Bray frowned at her, but he didn't ask her to eat more. Instead, he carried both their plates to the sink and pulled his car keys from his pocket. "We'll stay in touch," he told the group.

Trish stood up and hugged Bray first. "Take care of her," she said.

Then she hugged Summer. "You are stronger than you think."

It was similar to what Summer had told Trish when Rafe had unexpectedly died.

Sometimes life was just so damn hard.

They were back in the car before she spoke. "Chase and Raney are supposed to get married on Saturday."

"I don't think they're worried about that right now," he said.

"They should be," she said bitterly. "None of us should have to be worrying about something like this."

Bray shrugged. "No argument on that. But that's not going to be our focus. We've made a lot of progress in a few hours. Finding the safe-deposit key in those boots was very important."

"We don't know that for sure. These addresses may mean nothing."

He plugged the first address into his GPS. She looked at the estimated travel time. Thirty-nine minutes. It would be after midnight when they arrived.

Way past bedtime for a five-year-old. She prayed that Adie was somewhere where she could actually sleep.

Bray was looking at her, his eyes gentle with concern. "They mean something. Not sure what, but something. And I have to believe that's getting us one step closer to Adie."

She blinked back tears. "How can you be so sure? So positive?"

He reached for her hand and cradled it between his own. His skin was warm, a little rough. Wonderful. "I

know what you're doing," he said. "You're trying to prepare yourself for more disappointment. But it's okay to
be hopeful. It's okay to expect the best."

"Is that how you do your job every day, Bray? Is that
how you live in a world of drug dealers and all the bad
people associated with that business?"

"It doesn't hurt to be able to see the positive," he said.
Then he looked at their joined hands. "I wasn't able to always do that," he said.

"What do you mean?"

"When I came back from the Marines and you'd married Gary, I didn't think I'd ever be positive about anything again. I thought my life was over."

She could feel her throat threaten to close. "I'm sorry,
Bray. I really am."

He looked as if he wanted to ask for more of an explanation, but then he shook his head sharply. "We should
go."

He was giving her a pass. If she had any guts, she'd
tell him the truth.

"You're right," she said, buckling her seat belt. She
turned up the radio.

Chapter Ten

Wednesday, 11:30 p.m.

Now that they were back on the road, Summer was quiet. It gave him a moment to think.

The abductors had initially told Summer that they had a question about her ex-husband. But they hadn't asked her the question. They'd simply knocked her out and taken Adie.

What was the likelihood that the men didn't have something to do with Gary's disappearance?

Almost none.

And the only reason that they would need his child was if they meant to somehow use the child to force Blake to talk or to do something he wasn't inclined to do.

It was a powerful bargaining chip. And one that would force most men to act quickly.

Unless the guy was a real ass.

He wished he knew more about Blake and what made him tick. And how much he cared for his daughter.

But those weren't the kind of questions that he could ask Summer. She was smart. In a minute, she'd understand the path his brain was taking. He wasn't going to plant a seed that Blake might sacrifice his own child to save himself.

Fifteen minutes away from their destination, his GPS took them off the highway and onto a secondary paved road. But ten minutes later, after two more turns, pavement ended and it turned into rough gravel. He had to reduce his speed to forty-five, and even so, rocks were bouncing up and hitting the vehicle.

On both sides of the road were open fields. The fall harvest had happened at least a month ago and now it was just acres of chopped-off stalks and clods of dirt. It was a clear night, but there was only a quarter moon. Visibility was adequate for fifteen or twenty yards but faded fast.

At least it wasn't raining or snowing.

He almost smiled. He'd heard the story about how Cal had found Nalana in a snowdrift during a freak early-winter storm. She'd had bad guys on her tail.

They'd survived that. He and Summer would survive this.

And they would rescue Adie. No other option was acceptable.

"You have arrived at your destination on the right."

The woman on his GPS sounded pretty confident, but Bray wasn't all that sure. There was a mailbox that somebody had knocked over, lying in the grass at the edge of the overgrown lane. He pulled off to the side of the road and killed his lights.

"We walk in from here," he said.

"I wish I'd worn jeans," Summer said.

She had on a red sweater, a black-and-white skirt that was just short enough to be interesting and black tights. Her shoes were black flats. She had on a blue-jean jacket with a scarf around her neck. It was what she'd worn to the mall. He probably should have told her to change into jeans, but he hadn't been thinking about clothing.

"I hope there aren't any snakes," she added.

He really hoped he found a couple of the two-legged variety.

He handed her a flashlight and grabbed the other one for himself. He carried it in his left hand. Using his right hand, he opened the middle console and removed his gun. He tucked a couple of extra clips into his vest pocket. They jostled against the lock-picking set that Chase had tossed him just before they'd left the house.

They quietly shut their car doors and started up the lane. It had deep ruts and Bray could see faint vehicle tracks. It was impossible to know how recently they'd been made. "Keep your light down," he said. "Don't wave it around."

The lane was a good quarter mile in length. And there was no pot of gold at the end of it. Nope. Just a dilapidated old two-story white farmhouse with a crumbling foundation on the north side that gave it an overall slightly lopsided look. Behind it were two outbuildings. One was a midsize barn, missing most of one side. The second was much smaller, maybe the size of a two-car garage. It was in better shape.

There wasn't a light on in the entire property and it had a deserted feel. But that did not mean that Adie couldn't be somewhere. People had been known to take children and stash them in isolated places.

This place meant something to Gary Blake. Meant enough that he'd rented a safe-deposit box to preserve the record.

"Are we going inside?" Summer whispered.

"Yes," he said. "Doing okay?"

He heard her breathing and saw her square her shoulders. "Don't worry about me," she said.

Yeah, like that was going to happen. "Let's go. Stay behind me."

He waited until she nodded. Then he started forward.

There was no sidewalk, so he went through the yard. There were dry weeds up to his knees and patches of black dirt. No grass. He stopped twice to listen. Didn't hear anything.

He motioned for Summer to stand on one side of the door and he took the other. Then he reached for the door-knob.

Locked.

That didn't necessarily mean that nobody was inside. Even if the house was abandoned, any number of people in the backwoods of Missouri might be attracted to it. And most of them up to no good. None of them would welcome a visit.

He rapped loudly on the door.

Waited.

A second time.

He pulled out his tools and within minutes had the door open. He kicked it with the toe of his boot. Then he stepped forward, gun drawn.

It was pitch-black.

He listened. Waited for a sound that would tell him that somebody lurked in the dark corners.

But it was quiet. He used his flashlight. The house was empty, with the exception of two folding chairs that were in what was once probably the living room.

He turned and motioned for Summer to come in.

There was threadbare carpeting and an overwhelmingly bad smell of cat urine. There were no draperies, just old white ill-fitting shades on all the windows. He flipped his flashlight up. There were electrical connections for ceiling lights but no bulbs.

"I'm going upstairs," he whispered.

It looked about the same as the downstairs. The three bedrooms were empty, and when he poked his head in the bathroom, he saw that there was no water in the toilet. He tried the faucet. Nothing.

He went back downstairs and almost had a heart attack when he didn't see Summer. Then he heard her in the back of the house. She was standing in the kitchen. Most of the cupboard doors had been removed. The shelves were bare. There was an old stove but no other appliances.

He saw a door that likely led to the basement. He motioned to Summer that he was going to look.

It was a stone basement that smelled damp. There was a furnace and water heater, both of which looked as if they hadn't worked in several years.

There was no five-year-old child.

He went back upstairs. "There's nobody here," he said in a normal tone.

"Now," Summer said.

"What do you mean?"

"The folding chairs aren't dusty. Somebody has sat in them recently."

She'd have made a hell of a cop. "I know. But it might have been last week," he added. They didn't want to add two plus two and come up with five. There was no reason to think that this house had anything to do with Adie's disappearance.

Other than the fact that it was on a list that had been in Blake's safe-deposit box.

"I'm fairly confident that whoever lived here had a cat," she said drily.

"That smell does linger. Maybe that's why the owners left—they couldn't stand it any longer." He moved to the door. "I'm going to check the other two buildings."

"I don't think she's here," she replied.

"I don't, either," he said. "But we need to look, just in case."

Adie wasn't in either of the other buildings. They were both empty, although there was a pile of leaves in one corner of the smaller building that made it look as if someone might have left the door open and the wind had blown them in.

He crumpled one of the leaves in his hand. It was still moist. From this fall for sure. So at one point in the recent past, the open door had been closed. By somebody.

Probably the person who had dusted off the folding chairs with their back end.

He had a pretty good idea of what the place was.

And there were two options. Blake had been a cop. He might have been investigating something that led him to this address.

Although this was clearly out of the jurisdiction of the Ravesville Police Department.

They walked back through the door and he pulled it shut behind them. "Summer, what's the drug situation around here? Did your ex ever get involved in any investigations?"

"Rural Missouri probably isn't all that different from other rural areas. Of course there are drugs. Just like there are drugs in cities. You know about that."

"I do. But the distribution method is different in the city versus a more rural area. Isolation offers opportunity that a city of eight million doesn't have. Plus, in the city, we quite frankly have more resources than the rural area."

"Nobody has been making meth in that house. Unless meth smells like cat urine."

He shook his head. "Not making it here. But maybe it's a drop-off point. No need to have a recliner—a folding chair will do. Customers are in and out. Nobody lingers. I'd really like to know if your ex had a legitimate reason to know about this place."

She blinked several times. He could tell she was thinking. Processing. Finally, she shook her head. "Lately, Gary has been so volatile. The least little thing set him off. And I know that can be a sign of drug use. But I don't think he was. I really don't. Why does it have to be drugs? Why couldn't it be something else?"

"It could be, and I'll admit to having a predisposition to thinking drugs first. But I've got to tell you, it feels right.'"

"We just don't know what side Gary was on," she said.

Speaking of sides, he recalled that his brothers had told him that Gary had been involved with Sheila Stanton, who had recently left town unexpectedly. "Do you know anything about his relationship with Sheila Stanton?"

"He *had* a relationship with Sheila?"

He hated to be the one to tell her this. "According to Chase and Raney. They thought that might have clouded his judgment."

"Maybe. The Stantons were old money in Ravesville. But I never thought a whole lot of her. She treated people like dirt. I remember when Chase dated her," she said. "He was maybe a year or two out of high school. I was always surprised when I saw them together."

"Raney is ten times the woman," Bray said.

"For sure. When we first met, Chase was pretending that they were already married. We later learned that he was protecting her because she was a witness at an upcoming trial. It's nice to know that they're going to make their cover story a reality."

"And assuming that Sheila didn't leave town unexpectedly because she was torn up over Chase, we should probably figure out where she went. Do you have any-body that you can ask?"

"One of my good customers did her hair. She might know."

"When we get to the car, call her," he said.

"She'll be sleeping."

She was right. It wasn't the kind of question that you got somebody out of bed for. Certainly not under usual circumstances, and they didn't want anybody thinking there was anything unusual going on. "Okay. We'll wait a bit for that. Let's go to the next place on the list."

She turned to look at him. "Bray, I don't know what I'd be doing without you. I know I didn't have the right to ask you to help. But I knew that if anyone could find Adie, you could. Thank you for not sending me away."

She had tears in her eyes. And that was his undoing. He pulled her into his arms. And under a quarter moon, he kissed the woman who still held his heart in her hands. It was sweet and familiar, yet sharp and edgy and very dif-ferent, too. She tasted of bacon and tomatoes, and it was easy to sink into her soft lips.

And he didn't stop until her body stiffened in response to the faraway sound of a barking dog. She pulled back. Her breath was coming fast. Her lips, wet from his, were trembling.

There were a thousand things he could say. A thousand questions he could ask. But now wasn't the time. "I would never send you away, Summer. Know that in your heart. Now let's get out of here."

SHE USED TO dream about kissing Bray Hollister again. When she was married, for sure. She'd hidden that from Gary, but in the end, he'd still known.

Even after the divorce, while the dreams had been less

frequent, they'd been no less intense, no less of a painful reminder of all that she'd given up.

But now that it had actually happened, she realized that her dreams had paled in comparison. He'd left her as a boy and now he was a man. Big and strong and so very confident.

And he'd made her shake with need.

Somehow she'd managed to get herself back in the car, and now, as she hugged her door, she told herself that he was just a kind man comforting an old friend.

But as hard as she tried, she wasn't buying it.

He'd kissed her as if he'd been saving up for years. And she'd felt the energy all the way to her toes.

"How far is the next house?" she asked. Her daughter was missing. She was a horrible person to be thinking of anything else.

"Eighteen miles," he said.

His cell phone buzzed and he answered it. "Hey, Cal." Then he listened. Summer wished she could hear what Cal was saying. Whatever it was, Bray didn't look surprised. "Okay, go on to the next one," he said. He listened for another minute. Glanced at her. Gave her a soft smile. "She's fine," he said. "Strong." Then he hung up.

"You're giving me too much credit," she said.

He shook his head. "Cal just talked to Chase. They've each finished one search. Cal's property didn't even have a house, just an outbuilding. Nothing there. Chase found a rural farmhouse with no outbuildings. House still had some furniture but it was clear that nobody had been there for some time."

"So, in general, they found exactly what we did," she said.

He nodded. "Three down. Eight more to go."

She looked at the clock on the dashboard. "We're running out of time."

"We don't know that. They haven't called your cell phone yet."

"Maybe they're watching my house. Maybe they're wondering where I am. If I've gone to the police."

"They might be. But I don't think that can be helped. But that reminds me," he said. "Across the street from the café, there's a three-story building. Who lives on the second floor?"

"Why?"

"Today when we were leaving the restaurant, I saw somebody in the window, watching the café. When I came around the corner, he pulled back fast."

"He? That's odd. A single woman rents that space but she's always traveling. I've spoken to the owner of the building and she said that she's probably only seen her three or four times in the last year, but she doesn't care because the rent is always paid on time. Maybe she's letting someone stay there."

"Someone who didn't want to be seen."

"Or maybe someone who didn't want to seem nosy."

"Maybe. But it seemed to me that he was watching the café. And he didn't want me to know that."

Chapter Eleven

Thursday, 12:30 a.m.

Her head was spinning. In addition to the mysterious list and the news about Sheila Stanton and Gary, now a suspicious watcher merited consideration. Was that somehow also related to Gary and this mess? It was really just too much to process.

And it had been seven and a half hours since they'd taken Adie. A lifetime to a child. A horribly long time to be frightened or hurt.

She felt the BLT in her stomach rumble. She pressed her hands to her midsection.

"What's wrong?" Bray asked.

The man saw everything. Thought of everything. He'd been that way when he was young, too. That was why when he'd come home from the Marines, she'd barely given him any explanation. She'd known that he'd see through her lies if given half a chance.

"Nothing different," she said, hoping he'd let it go.

He gave her a long look but didn't press it. He punched the address for the next location into the GPS and they took off. "Has Gary dated anyone else besides Sheila since your divorce?"

It was a logical question. He was methodically thinking

of all possible leads. Still, it was awkward talking about Gary to Bray. "A couple of times that the kids were there, Maggie Reynolds joined them for dinner. She worked at the library. I think Keagan understood that his dad was dating but Adie didn't get it. I don't think it worked out because they haven't mentioned seeing Maggie for at least six months. Plus, I've seen Maggie with Porter Gates several times. He owns the gas station at the edge of town. The one you used to work at."

"I know Porter. We both started at the station on the same day. Odd to think that could be me."

"What?" she asked.

"When I got back to Ravesville, if things had been different, maybe I'd have gotten my old job back at the station. In time, maybe I'd have decided to buy it."

She couldn't see Bray doing that. She'd always known that he was destined for bigger and better things than Ravesville. And even at eighteen, she'd worried that she was holding him back because she'd known that she couldn't leave her mom. Maybe it was another reason why she'd ultimately agreed to The Plan. That was what she'd coined what Gary, her mother and she had come up with that long-ago night. The Plan.

It made it seem less half-baked, less crazy. Less wrong.

They rode in silence for another five minutes. Then Bray turned to look at her. "If it's not a jilted lover from Gary's past who might want to do him harm, is there anybody that you might have been seeing who would still consider him competition?"

She could feel heat in her face and was grateful that the car was dark with the exception of the dimly lit dashboard. Could she be as blunt with him as she'd been with Trish? Why not? "I'm divorced with two kids, a mortgage and a business loan. I'm not a great catch."

"You're kidding, right?" he said, his tone incredulous.

She felt very warm. There wasn't a woman alive who wouldn't want Bray Hollister to say something like that to them. But they were no longer seventeen-year-old kids flirting in a parked car. "I dated one person after the divorce," she said, carefully ignoring his remarks. "When Gary found out, he didn't react well. There were words. Anyway, my date ended up paying for dinner and for two tires that had been slashed. Of course, we couldn't prove it was Gary, but I think he quickly figured I wasn't worth the trouble."

"I guess I hope your ex is still okay, but I've got to tell you, he's tough to like."

"I know. More so the last couple years. In fact, now that you mention it, he's been having trouble with another officer on the Ravesville police force."

"What kind of trouble?"

"I don't know. We were divorced by the time Daniel Stone started, but I heard a few things at the restaurant that he wasn't getting along with Gary. I think the chief had to get involved on a couple of occasions."

"So that might be someone else to look at," Bray said.

"Our list is growing," she said. "We should be eliminating possibilities, not adding."

"Better this than not having anything to go on," Bray said.

True. At least she was doing something. Otherwise, she'd simply be staring at a silent phone.

Their GPS led them to a graveyard. "Are you sure this is it?" Summer asked. She did not like graveyards. Once every year, she made herself visit the one where her father had been buried for the past seventeen years but she always disliked it. She rolled down her window so that she could better see the address that had been painted on the gate.

Don't walk across my grave.

She swore she could hear the warning in the soft night wind. It was a small graveyard, like one you'd see in most any rural community. Maybe a couple hundred graves, a few with big headstones, many with much smaller and modest markings. There was a rusty iron fence around the perimeter with a big gate, wide enough for a hearse.

Bray pointed at the address. "Matches what we have," he said.

"I was afraid of that." She opened her door, her flashlight gripped tightly in her hand. Bray joined her. The gate was not locked, swinging open easily when Bray flipped the wide latch.

"I saw a movie once," she whispered. "A man had kidnapped a child and he buried her alive in an old grave. There was a pipe sticking up from the ground. That was how she got her air. It was horrible."

"It was a movie," he said gently. "But we'll keep our eyes open."

There were three large trees in the cemetery but they had lost all their leaves. Now they looked like hulking giants with thousands of gnarled and knotted arms. There was one tall light, in the very middle, which meant that very little light reached the far edges.

"You start at that side. I'll take this one," Bray said. "Be careful and don't trip."

She saw that there were many headstones that were flat into the ground. She glanced at the dates. Many dated back to the late nineteenth century. There was one, a woman who'd been born in 1889 and died in 1918, a short twenty-nine years later. *Alice Whay, wife of Jonas and mother of Thadias.* She found herself saying a silent prayer. *Please, Alice. I'm so sorry you were taken too soon from your own child, but please, please, if Adie is here, watch over her. Please do not let her be alone.*

And because her emotions were a damn roller coaster, the next minute she was kicking at some dirt, mad as hell that it was highly likely that drug dealers had seen fit to denigrate this space by using it as a distribution point.

She saw Bray stop near a freshly dug grave and her heart plummeted. She could not move. "Bray?" she said, her voice carrying in the night.

He waved. "It's okay," he said. "It's a new grave but not that new. The gravestone says the man died in September."

She sucked in a deep breath and kept walking. They met in the middle. "I'm going to check that shed." Bray spoke softly.

The white shed with peeling paint was at the rear of the graveyard. It was not any bigger than most people's family rooms. It had two small windows and it was dark inside. She followed him.

There was a padlock on the door. "What are you going to do?" she asked.

"I'm not leaving here until I know she's not in there," Bray said simply. He took his flashlight and knocked out one of the windows.

Then he stuck his upper body inside, along with his flashlight. After a long moment, he pulled back. "It's storage. Lawn mower and shovels and rope. Things like that. She's not inside."

They went back to the car. "How many times?" she asked.

"How many times what?"

"How many dates are next to this address?"

Bray picked up the list. "Four."

"I hate them for that," she said simply.

"Me, too," he said and reached to plug in the next address.

Twenty-five minutes later, they arrived in the neighboring community of Port. It was even smaller than Ravesville, with a population of 753. Or so the sign at the edge of town said.

The GPS led them to a four-story building at the intersection of Main Street and Lincoln, the only cross street in the two-block business district. Roosevelt Elementary. "I didn't think it could get worse than a graveyard," she said. "Schools should be sacred."

"If it makes you feel any better, it looks as if this one has been closed for a couple years."

"Not much better," she said. "But I think you're right. This school district was consolidated into Ravesville about two or three years ago. That's happening all over the country. There are probably empty schools in lots of small towns."

"In big towns, too. But in my world, most of the drugs are distributed at functioning schools, mostly by the low-level echelon. The truth is, we could bust somebody every day. Multiple people every day. Sometimes we have to just let it happen because we're ultimately trying to get the small creep to lead us to a bigger creep."

"That must drive you crazy," she said.

"Yep," he said.

She could tell he didn't want to talk about it. He was the type who wouldn't want to turn his back on any wrong-doing.

"How many dates for this one?" she asked.

He looked. "Three. But the last one was just three weeks ago. I think that was the most recent one of all."

There were several open spots in front of the school

and she expected him to pull into one of them. She was surprised when he didn't.

"Listen," he said, "I'm going around the block a couple times." He turned on Lincoln Avenue. It had simple single-family homes on both sides with detached garages. Middle class. Maybe not even that. He made a couple more turns and was back on Main Street. All the businesses on the street were closed. There was a community center for seniors, an alterations shop, a thrift store and a cash store. There was a small grassy area between the cash store and the school.

It was depressing.

The small community was asleep. Bray parked. He didn't get out of the car.

"What's wrong?" she said.

"I don't know. Something just doesn't feel right. See that gas station?" he said, pointing up the street.

"Yeah."

"It's got an open sign blinking in the window but everything else is dark."

"So, some clerk forgot to shut it off when he or she left for the night."

"Maybe," he said. He still didn't move.

Tingling started at the base of her spine and moved upward. "Bray, do you think she's here? Is that it?"

He turned to her. "I'm sorry. It's not that. It's different. Let's go check it out. Just stay close, okay."

"How are we going to get in?"

"Well, it would have been easy if they hadn't boarded up those windows."

It was one of those buildings where the first-floor windows were level with the ground.

"Let's go around back and I'll boost you up. If you stand on my shoulders, you should be able to reach the windows on the second level. If you can get in, then you can come open the door for me. I'd rather not have to break it if I don't have to."

"What if there is an alarm?"

"Then we're going to run like hell," he said. "This is an unincorporated village. They don't have their own police. Probably state cops would need to respond."

He opened his door. There was enough street light that they didn't need their flashlights. They hurried around the school, staying close to the building. "Let's go," Bray said, bending down. "Get on my shoulders."

She froze. It was exactly what he'd told her in the car but she hadn't really processed it. He wanted her to sit on his shoulders. Then he was going to stand, and then so was she. Simple enough. She'd have the sides of the building to balance against. She wouldn't fall.

But she was going to have to wrap her legs around him and plaster herself up against the back of his neck.

Now the tingling was in other parts besides her spine.

"Uh… I've got a skirt on."

"I'm not going to be looking up it," he said, his tone gently exasperated. "And…it's not as if I haven't seen it before."

If that was supposed to make her feel better, it was having the opposite effect. It had been more than fifteen years since she and Bray had been lovers, but her body remembered.

"Come on," he said, looking up at her. He patted his shoulders. "I won't drop you."

She could do this. She could. She hiked her skirt up and put her left leg over his left shoulder. Did the same with her right leg. Her thighs were wrapped around his neck. She scooted up so that her bottom wasn't hanging in the air.

Yup. The tingling parts liked it.

He put his strong hands around her calves. She could feel the heat through her thick tights. He stood up. "Careful," he whispered.

The time for that was long past.

"Okay, now you stand up," he said.

She pulled her left leg up, got her foot situated on his shoulder. Did the same with her right foot. Thankful for her flat shoes and strong thigh muscles, she started to rise. When she was fully upright, she could easily see in the window. It was dark inside. She turned on her flashlight. "I can see some—"

"You two just step away from the building. Keep your hands where I can see them. I've got a gun and I know how to use it."

Chapter Twelve

Thursday, 2:00 a.m.

Gun! She teetered on his shoulders. Bray's hands tightened on her calves. "We'll be happy to do that," he said, his voice calm. "I don't want to drop her. I'm going to turn around and squat down so that she can jump off. Okay?"

He clearly didn't want to make any unexpected moves. She wanted to twist around, to see who was behind them, but she followed Bray's lead. It couldn't be a cop. No police officer would say that he had a gun and knew how to use it.

"Okay, but don't try anything funny."

It was another line from a bad movie. Bray did exactly what he'd told the man he was going to do. He turned, carefully squatted so that she could dismount and then promptly pushed her behind him.

But not before she had seen that the older man, in a red-and-black plaid jacket and a black stocking cap, did indeed have a gun. A rifle. Pointed at them.

"I told Mary that you'd be back. Your kind always are." The man's voice was scratchy, as if he had a cold.

"Sir, I'd appreciate it if you'd lower your gun," Bray said, his voice still calm.

It dawned on her that this was unlikely the first time that he'd faced a gun.

But those other times he hadn't had her to worry about. She suspected her presence there was weighing heavily on Bray. He was that kind of guy. She stood very still, not wanting to distract him.

"You going to leave some more of your poison? You going to ruin another young man's life? Ruin his family?"

The man's voice had cracked at the end and she had a pretty good idea of what they were facing. Either this man's son or grandson or someone special to him had been harmed, maybe killed, by drugs that had been delivered here. She felt ill with the thought that Gary might have had something to do with it.

"My name is Brayden Hollister," Bray said. "I am a federal agent with the Drug Enforcement Agency. I know about the trouble here, sir. I've come to help."

There was a long pause. She couldn't stand it. She looked around Bray. The man was staring at them, his mouth open. He still had not lowered his gun.

"I'd be happy to show you some identification if you'll put your gun down," Bray said.

The man shook his head. "We can't get no police to pay attention. Why the hell is a federal agent suddenly taking notice?"

"The activity here, sir, is part of a larger operation. The wrongdoing will not go unpunished. How about if I reach into my pocket and pull out my identification? I'll toss it over to you."

The man must have nodded. She wondered briefly if Bray was going to go for his gun but he didn't. He did exactly what he'd said. He reached into his pocket and pulled his billfold out. Then he tossed it toward the man.

She peeked again. The man picked it up and flipped it

open. He studied the badge or whatever it was that Bray carried with him.

The man's shoulders started to shake and his gun wobbled dangerously.

"Put your gun down," Bray ordered, his voice sharp.

"Who's she?" the man asked.

"None of your concern," Bray answered. "I'm going to ask you one more time—put your gun down."

The man knelt down and laid his rifle on the ground. Bray moved fast, grabbing it and handing it to her. Then he pulled his own gun, looking around. "Is there anyone with you?" he asked.

The man shook his head. "My brother and I've been taking turns for two weeks, watching the building. He owns the gas station up the road. It was my night."

"What happened here?" she asked.

"My Bobby had been turning his life around. Making something of himself. Providing for his wife and his child. And then his wife asked for a divorce. Sent him back into a bad time. If I'd have known that he was doing drugs again, I'd have tried to stop him."

There was more to the story. She could feel it. Had the drugs killed him? "Where is Bobby now?" she asked.

"Flat on his back at the rehabilitation hospital. He isn't ever going to walk again. He took those damn drugs and thought he could go a hundred miles an hour on the highway."

She didn't ask for the details. She'd heard enough. "I'm sorry," she said. "For your son. For your family."

The man said nothing.

"Do you know who sold your son the drugs?" Bray asked.

The man shook his head. "I don't want to know them. I just want them to pay."

"What's your name, sir?" Bray asked.

"Walt Meeker."

"And is Mary your wife?"

"Yes."

"Okay, Walt. You go home and tell Mary that the people who sold those drugs to your son are going to be punished. I'm going to give you back your gun, but I need you to promise to put it away and let law enforcement do their jobs."

Bray nodded at Summer and she stepped forward to hand Walt his gun. He took it without a word. He stared at them for a long minute. Then he turned and slowly started walking down the street. A block away, he got into a pickup truck. They heard it start, and when he pulled out, he turned off before he passed them.

Summer let out the breath she'd been holding. "That was brilliant. To admit to being a DEA agent. It was the one thing you could have told him that would have made him put his gun down."

"Let's get out of here," Bray said, clearly uncomfortable with the praise.

"What about looking inside?"

"There's no need. Adie isn't here. Walt and his brother have been watching this building for days. They'd have seen activity."

He was right. She walked back toward the car. "I can't help feeling bad that we lied to him. He thinks there is going to be some justice for his injured son."

"I didn't lie," Bray said. "Right now, we have to focus on finding Adie. But once we do that, I can focus on helping Walt even the score."

They got in the car. "Do you think he would have shot us?" she asked.

Bray didn't answer for a long minute. When he did

speak, his voice was hoarse with emotion. "I was a marine. Then a beat cop and now a federal agent. I have faced my share of danger. And I have never been as scared as I just was when I thought that old man might accidentally get a shot off and I'd have lost you. Again."

His words burned her. "Oh, Brayden," she said.

She was suddenly across the console and in his arms. Their kiss was hot and greedy and full of all the emotion of potential loss and exhilarating gain.

He put his hand under her shirt, cupped her breast, stroked the tip of her nipple. His tongue was in her mouth. Blinding need streaked through her.

She wanted. She desperately wanted.

And then she heard a phone ring. Thought it was hers at first. She pulled back, yanking her shirt down. Heat rose to the top of her head.

Bray was answering his phone. "Yeah, Cal," he said.

The guilt swamped her. Her daughter was missing. Missing. And she'd been sprawled over Bray like a teenager in heat.

He ended the call. But he didn't look at her. He just stared out the windshield.

"What did he say?" she asked.

"No luck. He and Nalana are on their way to look at the last address on their list."

"Six down, five to go," she said. She was not going to talk about the kiss.

"About what just happened," he said, his voice sounding strained.

"No," she said. "We are not going to talk about it. We are not going to think about it. And we sure as hell aren't going to do it again."

He drummed his fingers on the steering wheel. Emotion poured off of him, almost in visible waves. He turned to her. "Fine. But when this is over, we damn sure are going to talk about it. I let you push me away fifteen years ago, Summer. I slunk away like a whipped dog. And that was the biggest mistake I ever made. I should have fought for you. I'm not going to make that same mistake again, even if it means that I have to fight *with* you."

She wasn't sure what to think about that. But whatever the reprieve, she was grateful for it. Adie. She needed to think about Adie. "Now what?" she said.

"We go to the next address." He punched it into his GPS and stared at the screen. "We know this place," he said.

She looked. It was just outside of Ravesville. On the same road as Rock Pond. Based on the GPS, very close to Rock Pond.

She did not want to go there. Not with Bray. Not when her nerves were stretched to the point of breaking. But if Adie might be there, then nothing would keep her away.

"Let's go," she said.

It was a fifteen-minute drive. Bray turned down the road that led to the quarry and ultimately to Rock Pond.

"It's been years since I've been here," she admitted. After she'd married Gary, she'd come often, making up stories about going to the library or the grocery store so that she could come sit by the pond. Here was the one place that she had always felt closer to Bray. After Keagan had been born, she'd brought him with her, as if there were some way that she could introduce her young son to Bray. *Be happy for me*, she'd often thought. Always followed by *I'm so very sorry*.

She hadn't realized at the time that Gary knew, that he had seen her car there. She'd discovered that in one of their very ugly arguments that had happened shortly after she'd told him that she was leaving.

And after her divorce, when she was officially free of scrutiny, she hadn't been able to come anymore. It didn't feel right. She'd made a mess of things and she couldn't forgive herself, let alone seek forgiveness from Bray in a place that had been so special.

This was the first place they'd made love. They'd both been seventeen. It should have been awkward and hurried and uncomfortable. It had been sweet and slow and amazing.

"I was here on Tuesday night," he said.

She didn't know what to say to that. She settled on "Why?"

"Because after I left your house, I was really angry. I needed to calm down, to go someplace where I could think. There are good memories here."

She couldn't tell him how those memories had sustained her in the first few years of her marriage. "I didn't handle that conversation in my kitchen well. I always thought when the time came to have that discussion, I'd do a better job. That I would be able to be dispassionate."

"Dispassionate?" he repeated.

"Unemotional. Detached."

"I know what it means. I'm just surprised. That's the one thing you and I never had." He shook his head. "Dispassion."

He was right. Theirs had been an intensely passionate relationship. But they'd been so young. Really, just kids. What did they know about the real world, about all the things that would bury passion and make it easy to settle for safety?

"Looking for Adie out here in the dark will be like looking for a needle in a haystack," she said.

"I think it's not a likely hiding place," he said. "The only structure is the administrative offices for the quarry, but unless the kidnapper owns the quarry, I doubt that's the place."

"It's probably a really good spot to hand off drugs," she said. "Young people still come here. They drive around the pond, sometimes stopping. It would be as simple as one driver rolling down his window with the stuff and the driver in the other car handing over cash. How many dates on the sheet?"

He looked. "Five. The last one in May of this year."

"Maybe they avoid this spot during the summer months. Too much traffic, too many people hiding in the bushes."

"Getting poison oak on their…assets," he said, humor in his tone.

Who could forget that? "It was dark when I put the blanket down. We'd have been fine if we hadn't gone down to the pond afterward and wrapped ourselves up in that damn blanket." As it was, she'd been cradled in his lap, mostly protected. His bare back had taken the brunt of it.

"I itched for a damn week," he said. "But I couldn't exactly explain that to my mother, could I?"

Kids. They'd just been kids.

It wasn't supposed to last.

But it had hurt so much when it hadn't. "We should check the next place," she said.

He looked as if he wanted to say something else, but he nodded and started to enter the next address in his GPS. He stopped.

"What?" she said.

"I think it might be time to talk to the police."

"I thought you said that we were doing everything they could be doing?"

"Not for that reason. I want to talk to Daniel Stone. He's the cop who discovered that your ex was missing.

Plus, there's known friction between him and your ex. I want to know more about that."

"He'll be in bed."

"I don't think so. Somebody has to work the night shift. I don't think Chief Poole is doing it."

"Are you crazy? I can't go to the police. They told me not to."

"We're not going to talk to him about Adie."

"But they won't know that. If someone is watching the police, all they'll see is me meeting with Stone. That will be enough for them to think the worst."

"That's why we need to think of another way," Bray said.

"I'm not at my creative best," Summer responded, sarcasm heavy in her tone.

"I've got an idea," he said. "You know my stepbrother, Lloyd Doogan?"

Summer nodded. "It's always hard for me to remember that he's actually related to you. I mean, I realize he's not blood, but your mother was married to his father. Earlier this fall, he showed up at a birthday party that was being hosted at the café for Gordy Fitzler. He was really drunk and I think Chase and Raney had to deal with him."

"I heard about that. Based on what Chase has told me, he seems to think Lloyd is trustworthy and not out to harm the Hollister family in any way."

"I'm not sure I see how Lloyd can help us. He's…he's slow," Summer said, as kindly as possible.

"I know. I don't know what the official diagnosis is, but I remember that he wasn't able to finish high school. His father used to say some cruel things about him. Mom used to say that Lloyd's drinking was his way of coping with a world that he didn't always understand. All I know is that I suspect it's not all that unusual for the Ravesville police to have to respond to some incident that Lloyd Doogan is involved in. If somebody is watching the police, they're not going to think anything of it. But when Daniel Stone responds, you and I are going to be there."

"It might work," she said.

"It better," he replied and pushed down on the accelerator. "Do you know Lloyd's address and phone?"

"No. I probably could figure out where he lives. Like I said before, there isn't that much rental property in Ravesville."

Bray tossed his cell phone at Summer. "That's okay. Text Chase and get the information from him."

She did, and within minutes, there was a return text. "He thinks Lloyd may have a phone but he doesn't have the number. He does have the address. It's just a few blocks away from the café."

"Let's hope he's home," Bray said.

"Do you think we should look at any more of these addresses?" Summer asked.

"Let's talk to Officer Stone first."

"I hope Lloyd Doogan is willing to assist," Summer said.

"Me, too," Bray said, gripping the steering wheel tighter. "If he's not, I'm not sure what we're going to do."

Chapter Thirteen

Thursday, 2:45 a.m.

Lloyd lived in a one-room apartment on the lower level of a three-story building. There was no doorbell, so Bray knocked. When there was no answer, he knocked a second time, harder.

A minute later, the door opened. Lloyd looked rumpled and disoriented but Bray didn't smell any alcohol. He was pretty confident that they'd simply awakened him.

"Hi, Lloyd," Summer said. "It's Summer Wright."

"Hello." He didn't ask why they were at his door. Maybe people showed up at his apartment at all hours of the day.

"Lloyd, I'm Bray Hollister. Do you remember me?"

Lloyd stared at Bray for a long minute. "Yes," he said finally.

Bray glanced over his shoulder at the dark street, making sure they were still alone. "May we come in?"

Lloyd stepped back and they entered. The inside of the small apartment was dimly lit and smelled musty. There was a couch and one chair. There were three drying racks and all of them had wet clothes hanging over them. He suspected that Lloyd simply washed his clothes in the sink and that the expense of a Laundromat was money he didn't have.

Summer and Bray took the couch. Lloyd stood by the chair for a minute, then finally sat down.

Summer looked at Bray and he nodded. On the way here, they'd discussed the approach. Neither was sure what Lloyd would easily understand or be able to figure out. "I need your help," she said. "I need to talk to Officer Stone but I don't want anybody to know that I'm doing that. I want Officer Stone to come here so that I can talk to him."

Lloyd said nothing.

Bray leaned forward. "Lloyd, can you call the police department and tell them that you need an officer to come to your house?"

"I don't like the police," Lloyd said.

Of course he didn't. "They won't be upset once they know why you called them," he said. He hoped he was right. "All we need you to do is to call them and tell them that somebody broke into your apartment and you need the police to investigate."

Lloyd stared at them. "Did you break in?" he asked.

"No. No, we didn't, Lloyd," Bray said, trying hard to hang on to his patience. He was tired and frustrated, and he had no idea if this was worth their time. "But you're going to pretend that we did. And then when the police arrive, we will tell them the truth."

"Tomorrow is Thanksgiving," Lloyd said.

Summer nodded. "It is."

"Raney and Chase invited me to dinner," Lloyd said.

"That's nice," Bray said. "Summer and I'll be there, too."

"We're family," Lloyd said.

"Yes, we are," Bray said easily. "Do you have a phone, Lloyd?"

"In the kitchen." Lloyd got up and led them through the narrow doorway into a dark room. He turned on the light. The space was small but probably adequate for a single man. There was a stove, refrigerator and double sink. There was a small table with two chairs.

Lloyd had had frozen pizza for dinner. The box was still on the counter and his dirty plate was in the sink.

Most important, there was a green phone hanging on the wall. A good old-fashioned landline.

"Here's what you need to say," Bray said. "'My name is Lloyd Doogan and I live at 349 Plover Street in Ravesville and somebody broke into my apartment.'" Bray paused. "Can you repeat that for me, Lloyd?"

"My name is Lloyd Doogan. Somebody broke into my apartment. My address is 349 Plover Street in Ravesville."

"Close enough," Bray said. This might actually work. "The person who answers the phone might ask if the people who broke in are still there and you need to say no. Okay?"

Lloyd nodded.

Bray lifted the telephone receiver. He punched in 911 and handed the phone to Lloyd. He stood very close to Lloyd, attempting to hear the other end of the conversation so that he could prompt Lloyd appropriately.

Lloyd didn't need any prompting. He said his spiel just like he'd practiced.

"That was perfect, Lloyd," Bray said. "Thank you very much."

Lloyd didn't respond. He simply led them back to the living room, where he took the chair and they took their spots on the couch. They didn't talk. After a minute, Bray got up and brought both of the kitchen chairs into the living room.

Was it possible that they were putting their trust in the wrong man? What if this Daniel Stone was behind Gary's disappearance? It was no secret that they didn't get along.

Was the relationship much worse than anyone else had suspected?

If he was behind Gary's disappearance, then it was a foregone conclusion that he had something to do with Adie's kidnapping.

Bray knew they were running out of time. Adie had been missing for ten-plus hours. And still no call. They had to take the risk of confronting Daniel Stone.

They heard a car pull up and then the slam of the door. Stone had arrived without lights or a siren. Probably didn't think Lloyd Doogan rated either.

There was a sharp knock at the door. Bray motioned for Lloyd to answer it.

"Lloyd?" Officer Stone had transferred from somewhere in the Deep South, and his accent hadn't faded in the time that he'd been in Ravesville. "You called 911 about a break-in?"

Lloyd nodded and stepped back. Officer Stone walked in. With his foot, Bray closed the door behind him. The officer swung around and started to reach for his gun.

Bray put his hands up. "I'm Bray Hollister. I think you know Summer Wright. We needed the opportunity to talk to you without anybody seeing us."

"Anyone else here?" Officer Stone asked.

"Nope."

"What's Lloyd got to do with this?"

"We asked him to make the call," Bray said. "My mother was married to his father."

"I guess I had heard that. You know, making a fake 911 call is a crime," Officer Stone said.

"I know. I'm a DEA agent in New York City. I'm hoping that you won't hold it against him once you hear our story. Can we sit?"

Officer Stone took one of the kitchen chairs, and Bray

took the other. Summer sank down onto the couch and Lloyd took his chair. Bray looked at Summer, silently asking if she wanted to take the lead.

She drew in a deep breath. "I believe you know that, at one time, I was married to Gary Blake."

Daniel Stone nodded.

"We were divorced about two years ago. We have two children."

Another nod.

"This morning I learned that when Gary didn't show up for work as expected, you went to his house. There were signs of a fast departure and a small amount of blood at the scene."

Daniel didn't nod but he didn't look surprised. He wasn't giving anything away.

"I was questioned by Chief Poole but I did not have anything to do with it."

"I'm not sure where this is going," Officer Stone said.

"I want to know if you had something to do with it."

He let out something between a sigh and a laugh. "Summer, I can appreciate your concern for your ex-husband. But you need to leave the investigating to the police. If he's really missing, we'll find him."

If he's really missing.

He said it easily. Certainly not like a man who knew for sure what had happened to Gary. Summer glanced at Bray. He gave her a gentle nod.

"At five o'clock this afternoon, two men approached me at the Hamerton Mall. They said they wanted to ask me a question about my ex-husband. I was with my five-year-old daughter, Adie. They knocked me out with something and they took her."

The officer sat up straighter in his chair. "What's the demand?"

"There isn't one," Bray said.

Daniel Stone said nothing, but the look he gave Summer was sympathetic. "Where's your son?"

"With Trish."

"Are they alone?" Stone asked.

"Milo, our cook, is with them," Summer said.

"Good," Stone said.

Another cop in the Milo Hernandez Fan Club. Bray was going to figure that out at some point, just not right now.

"Why didn't you report this earlier? Get the FBI involved?"

"The kidnappers told me not to go to the police. And quite frankly, with Gary being a cop, I wasn't exactly sure who I could trust."

Officer Stone did not attempt to defend the police department. That was interesting.

"But they haven't made any contact with me. I had to take a chance on you."

"You did the right thing," Officer Stone said.

Bray stood up. "We need to know everything you know about Gary Blake. We understand the two of you aren't especially close coworkers and we'd like to understand that better. Anything that could help us identify who might want to harm him or his family."

Officer Stone looked from Summer to Bray. "There's information I can't share with you. But suffice it to say that it wasn't happenstance when I joined the Ravesville Police Department."

"I remember when you came," Summer said. "It was after Mary Michael's resignation."

"That was arranged," Officer Stone said.

Which meant that somebody had pulled some strings

to plant this man in the Ravesville Police Department. That was a significant investment.

"What do you know about my ex-husband?" Summer said. "About his disappearance?"

"From what I can tell, I think your husband was a decent cop at one time. Maybe never a good one but generally on the right side of the law. Then something changed about two years ago."

She'd divorced Gary about two years ago.

Bray could see the distress in her eyes. "Don't take this one on, Summer," he said.

"Probably good advice," Officer Stone said. "I think Gary made some bad decisions. Some recently and perhaps one or two a very long time ago," he added.

"What do you mean?" Summer asked.

"What do you know about a man named Brian Laffley?"

Chapter Fourteen

Thursday, 3:30 a.m.

Summer could feel the blood in her veins freeze. She'd never met Brian Laffley, but he'd changed her life. "Nothing," she said.

"Name doesn't mean anything to you?" Officer Stone pushed.

She shook her head. She hadn't talked about the man for fifteen years. She wasn't going to start now. "What bad choices did Gary make?" she asked, deliberately trying to get Daniel Stone off the topic of Laffley.

"Cards. Slots. Video poker. And I understand he's especially bad at the horse races."

Gambling. Financial trouble. That was consistent with some of the arguments she'd had with Gary. Money had become such a touchy issue with him. It was also consistent with Bray's comments when they'd been at Gary's house that it was odd that there weren't financial records around. He was taking steps to ensure that his secret stayed just that.

"And he's also turned a blind eye toward some drug trafficking that happens in and near Ravesville."

She felt sick. Even though they hadn't been married, she wished Gary had come to her. She would have tried to help him, tried to find another way to get himself out of the hole he'd dug.

"He's not dealing himself?" Bray asked.

"I'm not actually sure about that." Officer Stone rubbed the back of his neck. "Let me see your badge," he said.

That seemed to come out of nowhere. But Bray didn't hesitate. For the second time that night, he pulled out his wallet. He handed it to Officer Stone.

The man examined it. He drew in a deep breath. "In the spirit of collaboration, I'm going to share something with you. Don't put too much faith in Chief Poole's…ability to find your ex-husband."

"Ability?" Bray questioned.

"Ability. Interest. Commitment. Choose your own noun."

He was saying something without really saying it. And now Adie, sweet little Adie, with her thousand-watt smile and her bear hugs, could pay the price. "My daughter is missing, Officer Stone," Summer said. "I don't have time for innuendo."

"Chief Poole doesn't have your daughter," he said. "There's been someone sitting on him since we realized Gary was missing. I can't say anything else."

"Oh," she said, unable to keep her exclamation inside. This was getting so terribly complicated.

Bray got up, came around behind the couch and put a steadying hand on her shoulder. "Take a breath," he whispered.

She sucked in much-needed air.

"What do you know about his relationship with Sheila Stanton?" Bray asked.

"Not a lot of people know about that," Officer Stone said. "They were very discreet. This is probably not what I should tell the ex-wife, but I think he took the breakup with her hard."

SHEILA STANTON'S NAME had come up one too many times. "We plan on talking to her," Bray said.

"Good luck. I don't think you'll find her terribly trustworthy," Officer Stone said.

"She's a bad person," Lloyd chimed in.

He wasn't inclined to debate that, thought Bray. But how could he fault her for lying when he was fairly confident that Summer had just done the same thing when she'd said she didn't recognize the name Brian Laffley? The cop might have bought it, but Bray knew Summer much better, knew how she cocked her head to the right, just the slightest bit, when she was lying.

He didn't know Brian Laffley. He was sure about that. The name meant nothing to him. But it had meant something to Summer and to Gary Blake.

He liked Daniel Stone. And he'd had to talk to him for only about thirty seconds before realizing there was more to the man than being a small-town cop. When he'd admitted that he'd come to Ravesville for a reason, Bray hadn't been the least bit surprised.

He saw Summer stifle a yawn. She'd probably been up since four or five this morning, because the café opened at six. "Maybe you should make a pot of coffee," he suggested.

She nodded and got up. When she went into the kitchen, Lloyd followed her.

Bray waited until they were out of earshot. "Who is Brian Laffley?"

"*Was*, not *is*. Brian Laffley—that's not his real name, by the way—was a federal agent working undercover in this area for several months. There was reason to believe that a large and rather sophisticated counterfeit money operation originated near Ravesville. He disappeared one night. His body was never found. Of course a full investigation ensued but with no luck. That is, until about two years ago. A builder was excavating a site and a body was found. It was taken to the county morgue. Preliminary efforts to determine identity commenced, but when the coroner went back to finish the job the next day, the remains were gone."

Bray rubbed his temple. "I'm not sure I get where this is going."

"They said it was a mistake on the part of the funeral home. They had retrieved the body and already cremated it."

"Unbelievable," Bray said. "Honest mistake?"

Daniel Stone shrugged. "Funeral home said they got a call to pick up a John Doe. The people who worked at the morgue were intensely interviewed and none of them admitted making the call. We were playing catch-up the whole way because all of this happened before those of us in the know about Brian became aware that a body had even surfaced. We didn't know until the work that the coroner had done bubbled up through the system and then we were confident we had a match. It was Brian Laffley, and somebody went to great lengths to make sure that his body was destroyed."

"Cause of death identified?"

"Gunshot wound."

Was it possible that Brian Laffley had something to do with Blake's and Adie's disappearances? He'd told Summer earlier that it would be bits and pieces of information that would ultimately lead them to Adie. They just needed to figure out how all the bits and pieces fit together. It was getting more difficult by the minute.

But he appreciated that Stone had shared the information with him. He decided it was a good time to ask another question. "Earlier today, when Summer and I were leaving the café, there was someone across the street, on the second floor, watching the building."

"How do you know that?" Officer Stone asked, his tone decidedly more guarded.

"I saw his shadow."

"Really?"

Bray nodded.

"Well, Mr. Hollister, that tells me that you're pretty good. But don't worry about it. It has nothing to do with Adie's disappearance."

"If somebody is watching Summer's business, I want to know about it."

Officer Stone studied him for a long minute. "I know the person. He's not watching Summer. There's nothing to be worried about." A cupboard door shut in the kitchen. "Now, that's all I'm going to say," Officer Stone added. "And we never had this conversation."

Maybe the man had been watching Milo Hernandez, the ex-con. But if it wasn't Summer, Bray guessed he was good with it for now.

Summer and Lloyd came back, each carrying two cups. Lloyd gave one to Officer Stone and Summer gave him one. He took a sip. It was good.

Bray felt his cell phone buzz and he took it out of his pocket. It was Cal. "Yeah," he answered.

"Chase just finished up with his second place. He said it was a deserted gas station that hadn't pumped any gas since it was $1.67 a gallon. No sign of Blake or Adie but somebody had been there recently. There was a cigarette butt near the front door. We're at our third place right now. It's another deserted farmhouse. There was a fire. Either when people were living here or after they were gone. Can't really tell. No sign of recent activity."

That meant that a total of eight addresses out of the eleven had been searched and were big fat zeros.

"Thanks, Cal. Go home. We'll be in touch."

When Bray hung up the phone, he turned to Summer and shook his head. "Sorry," he said.

She nodded. "I think we need to tell Officer Stone about what we found. In the box," she said, somewhat cryptically, probably in the event that he didn't agree.

But he did. He pulled out the papers that he'd put into a large plastic bag at Chase's house. He opened the bag and carefully pulled out the top sheet. "Take a look at this," he said.

Officer Stone frowned. "What is that?"

"It's a list of addresses. We had to break the code. We found it in Gary Blake's safe-deposit box," Bray said.

"I didn't know he had a safe-deposit box," Officer Stone said.

"Me either," Summer admitted. "We found the key at his house."

"You searched his house?"

She looked him in the eye. "My mother cleans his house. She has a key and can come and go. She'd forgotten a mop there. I was trying to find it for her."

Officer Stone smiled. "Of course. I was there about noon," he admitted. "I didn't see the key."

"Did you check his boots?" Summer asked.

"I did. Shook them good."

"Did you put your hand inside?"

Stone smiled. "No, I did not." He looked at the papers. "All those have just one line?" Officer Stone asked.

Bray nodded.

"Can I see what you translated them into?"

Bray handed him the one-page document that he'd created with the eleven addresses. He watched the man scan the list. He didn't seem particularly interested in any of the addresses except one. "It sounds like you've got somebody checking these. Has anybody looked at this one?"

Bray shook his head. "Recognize it?"

"No. That's why I'm interested in it. The rest of these are all familiar."

That told Bray that he'd been right when he'd assumed the deserted sites were known drop-off points. But in rural areas, where a handful of officers were responsible for hundreds of miles, it wasn't generally a cost-effective means of waging the battle on drugs to stand guard over a particular location over a prolonged period of time.

If Officer Stone was interested in one particular address, then so was Bray. Especially because it was one of the addresses where there had been no result to the reverse-lookup inquiry. "We'll check it out next."

"I can do it," Officer Stone said.

Bray shook his head. "No police. We took a chance on coming to you and telling you the truth. Please don't make us regret that."

He could tell that irritated Officer Stone. That was tough.

"But," Officer Stone said, "I can help you. Let me."

Bray shook his head. "We can't take the chance. Right now, we're doing everything that the police could be doing."

"Maybe," Officer Stone said. "But you really should contact the FBI. They have the experience to deal with this kind of thing."

They might have plenty of experience handling a traditional kidnapping where a ransom demand had been made. This was different.

"We're going to figure this out," Bray said. "I appreciate you letting me know that this address might bear looking into. If you hear anything, please call my cell." Bray rattled off the number. Officer Stone entered it into his phone. In turn, he gave Bray his direct number.

Bray turned in Lloyd's direction. "I assume that Lloyd isn't in any trouble for the 911 call."

Officer Stone waved a hand. "No trouble. It was pretty smart," he added. "I'll report back in that Lloyd was confused and close out the call. You two need to be careful. I know you're used to dealing with scum like this," he said, looking at Bray, "but don't underestimate them." He turned to look at Summer. "I hope you get your little girl back safe and sound. I've seen her when you've had her at the café. She's a little doll."

"Thank you," Summer whispered.

Officer Stone gave Bray another long look before shaking his head and leaving quietly.

Bray turned to shake Lloyd's hand. "Thank you."

Lloyd smiled. "I'll see you at dinner later. It's Thanksgiving."

Chapter Fifteen

Thursday, 4:30 a.m.

There was no name on the mailbox. Bray hadn't expected one, but he also hadn't expected that it would be a forty-minute drive on the back roads of Missouri only to find a gated estate, tucked into the hills.

It had been a scary last ten minutes. When he'd thought they might be getting close, he'd cut his lights. There was no need to advertise their arrival.

When he'd seen the ten-foot gate, he hadn't even slowed down as they'd driven by. There were no doubt cameras on the entrance, perhaps triggered by light or motion, and he wasn't giving anybody a good look.

Now, parked a half mile down the road, they sat.

"How do we get in?" Summer asked, her voice soft, as if someone might hear them.

"I don't know," he admitted. "This guy doesn't want unexpected company."

"It's certainly big enough to hide a man and a small child," she said.

"Yeah. But somehow it doesn't feel right. I mean, whoever owns this has big money. And based on what we know so far, it's a safe bet that they got it via illegal drugs. But it's clearly somebody's home. Do you bring that kind of stuff into your home? On Thanksgiving? When your family is coming?"

"We don't know that any of that is happening. Maybe he doesn't believe in Thanksgiving. Maybe he has no family."

"You could be right," he said. "The hell of it is, I'm not sure we can do much about it. If we try to approach, we're going to get intercepted, maybe shot. We can't take the chance. I won't let you take the chance."

"I have to," she said.

He was afraid that she was just about to make a break for it. He reached over, put his hand on her arm. "No."

"She's my child," she said simply.

"I know that, damn it. And I would move heaven and earth to get her back for you. But we can't just approach the gate and start asking questions."

"When we needed to talk to Daniel Stone, you said we needed to find another way. We need to do the same thing now. Find. Another. Way." Her words were sharp. Insistent.

And he didn't want to tell her no.

But he was going to have to.

"Summer," he said, "we have to be—" He stopped. There was a flicker of light in the distance. He rolled down his window. There was a new noise in the predawn air. An engine.

A vehicle was approaching, and by the sounds of it, perhaps a truck. He listened for another thirty seconds. It was huffing and puffing up the hills, the engine whining. It was definitely a truck, and one badly in need of a tune-up.

Not likely owned by anyone who lived in this house.

But maybe by someone who did work at the house.

Which meant that the gate would open and they would drive through.

Which might give him and Summer a chance to run through the gate on foot without being seen. A very slim chance.

"Let's go," he said.

"What?"

"There's nothing out here on this road but this house. So I'm making the assumption that that truck is coming here. When the gate opens, we might have a chance to sneak in."

She moved fast. And within minutes, they had jogged down to the gate. The truck was closer now, maybe less than half a mile.

"Over here," he said, pulling her into the weeds across the road. They needed to avoid any spot that might get picked up by the truck's headlights. But they needed to be fairly close if they were going to run in behind the truck.

The lights came over the final hill, blinding them. But he could tell the truck was slowing. It turned into the driveway and stopped, the nose of the truck just feet away from the gate. The driver, a young man wearing a base-ball cap backward, leaned his head out the window and pressed the button on the call box. "Morgan's," he said. "I got a delivery."

Was it even possible that at this time of the morning a vendor was delivering something to this house? On Thanksgiving?

Motioning for Summer to stand still, Bray moved far enough that he could see the side of the truck. *Morgan's Delicious Deli, St. Louis, Missouri.*

It looked as if the people in the big house were entertaining for the holiday and they'd decided to order in.

"Proceed." That from the speaker, near the call box. A man's voice. Then the gate started to slide open.

The young driver rolled up his window.

Bray heard the grind of shifting gears.

The gate was halfway open.

Soon.

They were taking their first step forward when the entire area was flooded with light. Bray dived for the ground, taking Summer with him. He covered her body with his. They were in deep grass that was sharp and dry, and the ground had a pungent smell.

He heard the truck move. Lifted his head just inches. Saw the gate closing. Felt the despair flood his system.

Five seconds after it closed, the lights went off, once again plunging the area into darkness. He helped Summer sit, then stand. "Are you okay?" he asked.

She didn't answer. She simply stared at the gate that was barely visible now even though it was less than ten feet away.

"We couldn't try it," he said. "It was too risky."

"I know," she whispered.

Even though she had to feel as if she'd got kicked in the teeth, she wasn't taking it out on him. She was amazing.

"What do you know about Morgan's Delicious Deli in St. Louis?"

"Nothing. I've never heard of it."

"Let's get out of here," he said. "We can look it up in the car."

They hurried back to the car and he started the engine to get the heater going. It was only about forty degrees outside and neither one of them had a heavy coat. With his lights still off, he pulled the car back onto the road, putting distance between them and the property. After he'd gone two miles, he finally turned his lights on and picked up speed. Ten minutes later, they were back on the highway.

He pulled off to the side again and used his smartphone. "Morgan's Delicious Deli has a small restaurant and a catering business for private parties. Upscale events. That's how they advertise it on the website."

"So if it's legitimate, it's as simple as somebody in the house ordered some food. Maybe they're having a big breakfast and everybody gets up early."

"If it's not legitimate, then maybe somebody was in the back of that truck."

"Maybe Adie," Summer said, her voice faint.

"That's a long shot," he said.

"I know," she admitted. "But I'm getting desperate. It's going on twelve hours."

"I think it's time to wake up your friend and get Sheila's address. We cannot ignore the fact that she left Ravesville, the place that she and her family have lived in for generations, just weeks before a man she's supposedly having a fling with disappears."

"I know. That seems odd but not any odder than the idea of Gary and Sheila being together. She…" Her voice trailed off. "Look, I don't really know her all that well, and at the risk of sounding like a jealous ex-wife of the new mistress, it's just hard for me to see her with Gary. She thinks a lot of herself. Maybe that's because of her family money. Maybe it's because she's very pretty. Gary just wouldn't be…enough for her."

But he'd been enough for Summer. That made absolutely no sense. He waited to see if she'd offer something more, but she didn't seem inclined.

SHE PULLED OUT her cell phone and scanned the numbers. Jacqui was a good customer. Her shop was just down the street from the café. She was forty-seven, fresh off her third divorce, and every day she had a new story about being single again in what was, to her, the new world of online dating.

It rang. A second time.

It was just after five. What were the chances that Jacqui was awake? Three times. Four. It would kick into voice mail soon. What the hell was she going to say?

"Hello," Jacqui said. She sounded awake.

"Hi. It's Summer Wright."

"Oh my gosh," the woman squealed. "I am so glad that I'm not the only one up at the crack of dawn defrosting my turkey. Who knew the little guy was going to be hard for so long. Wish my ex had had that problem."

Summer forced herself to laugh. "Mine's taking up most of the sink," she lied. "Hey, I won't keep you because I'm sure you're busy, but I was wondering if you'd have an address for Sheila Stanton."

Jacqui paused. "I do. But I guess I never thought that you and Sheila were that close."

"We were moving some booths at the café and I found a pair of really nice sunglasses that had fallen behind one of them. I remember seeing Sheila wear them. I thought she might appreciate having them back."

"I have her phone for sure and her mom gave me the street address of her apartment. But I don't have the apartment number." Jacqui rattled off the information.

Summer scribbled it on a slip of paper she pulled from her purse. "Thanks, Jacqui."

"No problem. I hear that cute Bray Hollister that you used to date in high school is back in town. Maybe you need to arrange a little Thanksgiving celebratory drink at the quarry. Unless times changed between when you and I went to high school, I'm betting you spent a night or two on a blanket out there."

Summer felt the heat start low and rapidly spread until she felt as if her face were burning. "Got to go," she mumbled and hung up.

She looked at Bray. Jacqui had a loud voice, and she was confident that Bray had heard every word.

"I got Sheila's address," she said.

"Uh-huh," he said. He took the paper from her and entered the address into his GPS.

Was he going to let it go? Could she be so lucky?

He put the car in gear. "I'm adding this to the list."

"What list?"

"The list of things we're going to talk about."

Chapter Sixteen

Thursday, 5:30 a.m.

They were quiet until they pulled into Sheila's condominium complex in the central-west end of St. Louis. The building was brick, eight floors. Nice enough but certainly nothing special. Cars were jammed tight along the street parking. It took two passes around the block before a car pulled out and Bray could take the spot.

Fortunately, when they'd left the Big House, as Summer had decided to call it, they were a third of the way to St. Louis already. They'd been able to finish the drive in about an hour. Still, Summer could feel her agitation growing with every second. When they finally got to the door of the building and she saw that it was a locked entrance, she wanted to pull her hair out. There were buttons to push to ring the residents, but none of them were marked for Stanton. There were two that were not marked with names, just with the apartment number. "She's probably not even home," she said.

"Let's find out," Bray said, pushing the first unmarked one. They waited. There was no response. He went on to the next one. Within seconds of pushing the button, a woman answered.

"Yes."

It was Sheila. Summer gave Bray a quick nod.

"Sheila, it's Bray Hollister," he said.

There was a pause on the other end. "*Bray* Hollister?" came the response.

"Probably hoping for Chase," Bray whispered. He pushed the button. "Yes. May I come up?"

Sheila didn't respond, but they heard the sound of the door releasing and Bray grabbed the handle. They took the elevator up to the fifth floor and knocked on 5B. Bray stood square in front of the door so that Sheila would be able to see him through the peephole.

Sheila opened the door. She was wearing red silk two-piece pajamas. The shirt buttoned up the front and the pants were wide-legged. The first three buttons of the shirt were undone, making it fairly obvious that she wasn't wearing a bra. When she saw Summer standing behind Bray, her expression changed from interested to irritated.

"Thanks for seeing me," Bray said.

Sheila shrugged. "I was curious," she said. "And not willing to turn my back on an opportunity," she said suggestively. "But I'm not into sharing," she added, looking at Summer.

"Hi, Sheila," she said. "Would you have a minute that you could talk to Bray and me? It's about Gary."

Sheila's eyes didn't change, but her mouth did turn down at the corners. "It's pretty early to be visiting," she said.

True. But they hadn't awakened her. She'd been up. Her hair was brushed, falling perfectly straight, shorter in the back, longer in the front, angled toward her chin. Full makeup, including lipstick. She could not be human.

"Gary has been missing since yesterday morning," Summer said as they went inside and took a seat in Sheila's living room.

"I know."

Summer opened her mouth, then shut it. She was not exactly sure what to ask next. But luckily she didn't have to.

"My mother uses Chief Poole's wife's floral shop. She has a standing order. Fresh flowers in the foyer and all that."

She and Sheila had grown up in two very different types of houses. In the Wright house, they hadn't worried about having fresh flowers; they'd worried about having bread and were even more grateful when it was fresh.

"My mother ignores most of what the woman tells her but she did listen when it was about Gary. She was aware that we...had a brief entanglement."

It appeared that everyone had known about Gary and Sheila. It made her feel even more stupid that she'd missed it. She must have been the only one in Ravesville who hadn't known.

"What do you think about him being missing?" Bray asked.

"I don't think anything about it. Listen, I haven't seen Gary since I left Ravesville two weeks ago."

"And you haven't talked to him, either?" Bray pushed.

Sheila shook her head. She looked at Summer. "No offense," she said, "but what we had wasn't that much."

Summer couldn't care less what they'd had. But she wasn't walking away from Sheila if the woman had information that could be helpful. "This is important, Sheila. Do you have any idea where Gary might be?"

"Why is it so important?" Sheila challenged.

"My children are at risk," Summer said. "I can't say more than that, but I am absolutely confident that my children are at risk."

Sheila studied her. "Unfortunately, you may be right. I think your ex-husband has been hanging with people that you probably wouldn't want to have sitting at the counter of your little café. You and your sweet sister would probably find them objectionable."

"Why?" Summer pushed.

With one hand, Sheila pushed one side of her hair behind her ear. "Because even *I* find them objectionable," she said. "And my standards are questionable."

"What are they into?" Bray asked.

"I'm not really sure," Sheila said. She held up a hand. "Don't give me that look. I'm not stupid. I didn't want to know. I overheard a phone conversation, okay? And I could tell that the person on the other end wasn't happy about something. When Gary got off the phone, he was really agitated. He tried to laugh it off but I knew it was something."

"What did the other person say?" Bray asked.

"He said he wanted his money."

"When was this?"

"Maybe three or four weeks ago."

Was it possible that Gary had gambled away such a large amount that he was, as they say, borrowing from Peter to pay Paul? Had he borrowed from the wrong people and they weren't interested in an IOU?

"Did you tell Gary to break it off with them?" Summer asked. Had Gary got sideways with some bad people because he was trying to make his new girlfriend happy, trying to keep her from leaving?

"I did not," Sheila said. "Gary and I were…" Her voice trailed off. "Gary and I were never going to be a long-term thing. I knew that. I thought he did."

He probably hadn't. Gary was obtuse when it came to relationships. Their marriage had been over for years before she'd finally asked for a divorce, and still he'd been terribly surprised. But that wasn't the important thing right now. "Was it drugs?" Summer asked. "Was that what Gary was involved in?"

Sheila stood up. She was clearly done with them. "Drugs. Prostitution. Money laundering. Gambling. List all the vices you can think of. I'm not sure which one these people were involved in. All I can tell is that whatever it was, it's not good."

"Don't you think it's a strange coincidence that Gary goes missing shortly after you leave Ravesville?" Bray said.

"My mother said the same thing," Sheila said. "I think she was actually a little worried that I might have done something. You see, Gary didn't take the breakup well, thought he could convince me different if I'd just listen. He was becoming a bit of a stalker."

Had Gary been so intent upon changing Sheila's mind that he'd done something crazy? Done business with the wrong people?

"The thing between Gary and me was probably a mistake," Sheila said. "And I hope that nothing bad has happened to him. But it's not my fight."

Bray looked at Summer. The message was clear. They weren't getting anywhere.

"I'm sorry we bothered you," Summer said.

Sheila didn't answer.

They were at the door, almost through it before she spoke.

"If it helps, Gary was talking like he was going to have a pile of money really soon. I think he thought it would make a difference to me."

Bingo.

"Would it have?" Bray asked, his tone sarcastic.

She shook her head. "Not enough money in this world."

HIS BRAIN WAS going down a path and it didn't look good for Blake. If Blake was dealing drugs, then he was collecting money that ultimately had to be paid to the higher-ups. Was it possible that he'd been stupid enough to gamble that money away and then try to tell the boss that he was a little short?

People ended up in the river wearing cement shoes when they pulled that kind of stunt. Or with a bullet in their head.

And that could explain Blake's absence, but it didn't explain why the kidnappers needed Adie.

The only explanation was that they were trying to convince Blake to talk. About what?

Damn. He felt as if he were trying to fit a square peg into a round hole. Bray resisted the urge to slam his car door. He knew that Summer had to be as frustrated, and he was the one who needed to stay positive.

He was pretty confident that Sheila Stanton wasn't lying. She probably was the type to take a hands-off approach toward anything that had the potential to affect her negatively. When she'd figured out that Gary was hanging with a bad crowd, she'd cut bait quickly.

She hadn't, quite frankly, cared enough about Gary to try to pull him back, to protect him.

"Now what?" Summer asked.

Bray looked at the clock. It was going on six. Starting to get light. Twenty-four hours ago, Summer had been unlocking the front door of the café, never dreaming how bad her day was going to become. She had to be exhausted. She had a pinched look around her pretty mouth and there were dark circles under her eyes. "You need to get some rest," he said.

"I can't rest." She stared out the side window, still looking at Sheila Stanton's building. "Besides, you have to be just as tired as I am."

"There are times on the job that I don't get much sleep. I'm more used to this."

She shrugged. "I just need some coffee. Maybe some toast."

It was Thanksgiving, but someplace had to be open for breakfast. It wasn't sleep, but caffeine and food would be better than nothing. He started the car and pulled away from the curb.

"We need to go back to the Big House," she said. "We have to find a way to get in and search that property. We can't leave it undone."

It was possible that they'd see a way inside that hadn't been clear in the dark. And he had to admit that his gut was also telling him that that location was important. It was a fortress in the middle of nowhere. Why?

To keep people out or to keep them inside?

For the first time since this whole thing had started, he drove aimlessly, his mind working on the possibilities. Up one street, down another. There were cars parked on both sides of the street but very little traffic.

What was the best way to get in?

Maybe it was time to ask the police for help. Regardless of the instructions they'd received, maybe it was time to bring in other resources.

They could get a search warrant. Might be a little more difficult today, given that it was Thanksgiving, but a child was missing. People would move quickly.

And Adie might pay the price for that.

Nervous kidnappers were a scary thing. He turned the corner.

And almost ran into what might be a solution.

Chapter Seventeen

Thursday, 6:00 a.m.

The delivery truck for Morgan's Delicious Deli was parked at the end of the alley, its back end jutting out far enough that it caused Bray to swerve to avoid hitting it.

The driver, the one who had pushed the button on the gate, was wheeling an empty cart toward the building to the immediate left.

Morgan's Delicious Deli had its lights on and was open for business. Bray took the first available parking spot. "Let's hope they have coffee."

Summer turned to him, her eyes excited for the first time in hours. "Are we going to ask them about the Big House? Ask them what they saw there?"

"I don't know," Bray said. "Let's play it by ear."

Even though he wanted to storm the place and demand answers, Bray strolled in, holding the door open for Summer. There were only two other customers, a man and a woman, in the small eating area. The place had a clean tile floor, three wooden booths along the front window and four other small tables. Along one wall was a counter with stools for additional seating. The wall was a mass of electrical outlets. Customers could bring any one of their many gadgets and be assured of a place to plug it in.

There was a big refrigerator with glass doors where customers could help themselves to a selection of water and juices and prepackaged salads. The room smelled of raisin toast.

A woman, probably late thirties, wearing a white chef's coat, was behind the counter. "Number six," she said, pushing a tray of food forward. The man at the table got up and fetched the food, grabbing a bottle of ketchup off the counter before he headed back to his table. Bray paid him no attention.

The cooking area and food-prep areas were protected by a chest-high counter, but the truck driver had entered by a back door and was now in the kitchen, opening refrigerator doors and pulling out silver trays topped with plastic wrap.

The woman turned her attention to Bray and Summer. "Good morning," she said.

"Morning," Bray said. "Boy, were we happy to see that you were open, with it being Thanksgiving and all."

She smiled. "Three hundred sixty-five days a year," she said. "Leap year can't come too soon," she joked. "What can I get you?"

"Coffee and whole wheat toast," Summer said.

"Same," Bray added, pulling out some cash. "I never thought about getting the whole Thanksgiving feast catered," he said easily. That was a lie. That was exactly what he and Chase had usually done when they'd shared Thanksgiving dinner.

The woman handed him a brochure with a plump roasted turkey on the front. "Maybe for next year. We'll take care of everything," she said. She gave Bray his change, poured two cups of coffee into thick paper cups and handed one to each of them. "I'll get your toast," she said.

Bray and Summer took the table closest to the counter.

Bray sat so that he faced the kitchen. The woman had put four slices of bread into a big white toaster and stood in front of it. She was talking to the man. Her voice was low. She didn't look happy.

He watched her pick up a list and it appeared she was checking off items. Then she looked in the refrigerator that the man had been pulling trays from and pulled one more. The man put all three of them on his cart and wheeled it toward the back door.

"Are you sure you have everything this time?" the woman asked, her voice louder.

The man nodded, looking contrite. "I'm sorry about that, Greta. I didn't realize that there was cold food in addition to the hot items."

"It's fine." The woman's voice softened. "I just wish it wasn't a hundred miles there and back. But it's worth doing the return trip. We don't have many like the Pataneros account."

Return trip. One hundred miles there and back.

Bray looked at Summer. She nodded, telling him she understood. The driver was headed back for another delivery to the Big House. He heard a *pop* and the woman turned to butter their toast. She looked over her shoulder at the driver, who now had the back door open. "You want some breakfast before you go back out?"

The man considered. "Maybe a cup of coffee and one of your cinnamon rolls. I'll eat on the road. Let me get these in the truck and I'll be back for it."

The woman finished buttering Bray's and Summer's toast and put two slices each on two small plates. "Number seven," she said.

Lucky seven, thought Bray. "Can we have those to go?" he said.

"Sure." She opened a foam container, dumped all four pieces into it and slid it across the counter.

Summer waited until they were outside before she whispered, "What's going on?"

"Keep walking toward the car," he said under his breath. Once they were inside, he took a sip of his coffee and watched the truck driver exit from the back of the truck. "Get ready," he said. "We're going to have to move fast."

"Move where?" she demanded.

"That driver is going back to that house and we're going with him."

"With?"

"Yes. In the back of the truck." He winked at her. "Any questions?"

She seemed to consider. "Yeah. Can I bring my coffee?"

THE MINUTE THE man was back inside the deli, they were moving. Walking fast, not running. At the truck, Bray turned the handle and it swung open. It was dark and cold inside. It was a big step up and she hiked up her skirt to take it. Bray followed her in and pulled the door closed.

"What if he comes back?" she said, wrapping her arms around herself. "What if he forgot something else?"

"We have to hope that doesn't happen. Let's get as far back as possible. If he has to shove something else in, hopefully he'll open the door quick, get it settled, and he won't see us."

"What if he does?" she asked.

"Then I'm going to distract him long enough for you to get out and head for the car. Then I'll catch up."

"What are we going to do when we get through the

gate? When he opens the door there, we'll be in an even worse position if he sees us."

"Don't worry," Bray said. "I'll figure something out."

Don't worry. That was all she'd been doing since she'd been bumped at the mall. "I wish we could see what was going on," she said, her voice low.

"I know. Here—eat your toast."

"You brought it?"

"Of course. It's a forty-five-minute ride. You need something to do," he said confidently. He pulled his keys from his pocket and turned on the mini flashlight. "These don't look too bad," he said, nodding his head at the two trays of fresh fruit kebabs. "Kind of fancy," he said. He looked at the third tray. "Salmon and capers. Whatever happened to oatmeal for breakfast?"

She laughed, just couldn't help it. And it felt so good. They were stowed away in the back of a truck, about to be discovered at any minute, and he wanted to talk food.

She stopped laughing abruptly when they heard the driver's door open. Felt the driver sink into his seat. Heard the engine turn over.

Felt the truck start to move.

She sat down quickly to avoid falling down and realized that it was going to be difficult to keep from crashing into things. Bray followed her to the floor.

Before she realized what he was doing, he sat behind her with his legs extended and pulled her tight into his body.

She started to resist.

"Let me keep you safe," he said.

Bray Hollister always did have a way with words. She settled back into his chest, loving the feel of his strong arms wrapped around her, his chin resting on her head.

Stowed away in the back of a strange truck, no doubt about to be discovered, she felt safe.

Amazing.

She ate her toast and drank her coffee, and then she closed her eyes.

And didn't open them again until Bray was gently shaking her. He leaned close to her ear. "Wake up, honey. We have to be very close," he said, "and the truck is slowing down."

"Did you sleep?" she asked, stretching her neck.

He shook his head.

Of course not. He'd been watching over her. "Tell me what we need to do," she said.

"We're going to have to get out while the truck is still moving," he said. "It's the only way. Based on what I could see last night, once the truck gets through the gate, there's a long drive that curves at least once before it reaches the house. It's uphill and there's a sharp curve, so he's going to have to slow way down. That's when we make our move."

She nodded. She was going to jump from a moving truck. Well, okay.

Her fear had to pale in comparison to what poor little Adie had endured. Still on her bottom, she scooted closer to the door.

The truck stopped. She heard the driver announce himself. Then the muffled crackle of someone on the other end, granting them admission. She couldn't hear the gate—it moved too smoothly. But the truck was inching forward, picking up speed, then slowing.

Bray held out his hand, helped her stand. Then he kissed her hard.

"Big jump," he said and unlatched the door. "Bend your knees when you land. Nothing to it."

Chapter Eighteen

Thursday, 7:30 a.m.

She didn't have to jump because Bray, with a hand on each of her hips, literally tossed her out of the back of the truck. He hadn't warned her because he hadn't wanted to scare her. But he'd also intended that she end up as close as possible to the tree line at the side of the road.

She was still in the air when he jumped, knowing that it wasn't going to be possible to shut the door that had swung wide open. Which meant that when the driver got to the house and went to unload his truck, he was going to find the door open.

Hopefully the guy would simply thank his lucky stars that nothing had fallen out, causing him to make yet another trip back to this location.

He saw Summer hit the ground. She bent her knees too much and pitched forward, onto all fours. He hit the ground a step behind her, scooped her up with his hands again on her hips and literally pushed her into the trees.

He grabbed her hard to stop their forward momentum. Her face was white and she was breathing hard. Her palms were scratched and one finger had a small cut, likely from landing hard on a rock.

"Are you okay?" he asked, checking her for other injuries.

"Did he see us?" she asked, ignoring his question.

"I don't think so," he said. "He'd have stopped the truck pretty fast. Let's just hope that if there are cameras on the road, nobody is watching the screens." He grabbed her hand. "Let's go. We need to work our way up to the house."

The fall foliage was still damp, likely from rains earlier in the week. It didn't snap or crackle, but it was hard to see the dips and holes, and several times he had to pull on Summer's hand to keep her from falling.

It was crazy of him to bring her here. He should have demanded that she stay behind.

She'd have hated him for that. He was too damn much of a coward to risk that. But now he was risking her life.

He could see the house now. It was huge. No other word for it. A sprawling two-story with a main house and wings off to both the east and the west. Red brick. White pillars. Circular drive.

Pretty fancy for rural Missouri.

The Morgan's Delicious Deli truck was parked in front. The engine had been turned off. The back door was open but the driver was still sitting in the cab of the truck.

Bray was close enough now that he could see the driver had his cell phone in his hand and was texting someone. Hopefully it wasn't 911.

"Now what?" Summer asked.

Getting inside the gate had been a huge accomplishment but would be for naught unless they got inside the house. "I've got an idea," Bray said, "but you're going to have to stay here, out of sight."

"I don't like the sounds of this," she said.

The driver opened his door.

Damn. "I don't have time to explain," Bray said. "You have to stay hidden. I texted Cal while you were sleeping in the truck. He and Nalana are driving here right now, in two separate vehicles so that they can leave one for us. He knows we're going to try to get inside." Bray looked at his watch. "He's expecting another text in twenty-five minutes, at eight o'clock. If that doesn't happen, he's going to know something is wrong and he'll get help."

The driver was walking to the back of his truck. He was going to see the open door any second.

"But—"

He kissed her. "Don't show yourself, no matter what happens. Promise me."

She nodded.

He took a step.

"Bray," she said, her voice a whisper.

"Yes."

"I need you to know. I never stopped loving you."

Bray felt his heart lurch in his chest. He'd been waiting years to hear something like this.

Out of the corner of his eye, he saw the driver stare at the open door, his hands on his hips. Then the man stepped into the back of the truck.

It was now or never.

"Same for me, Summer," he said. "Exactly the same."

WHEN THE DRIVER got out of the truck with a tray in his hands, Bray was standing on the sidewalk. "Hey, thanks for coming back," he said, using his East Coast accent to the max. "My sister really appreciates it."

The driver nodded. "No problem. Our mistake," he said.

"Let me help you with those trays," Bray said, holding out his hands. They weren't shaking, which was a damn miracle since Summer had picked about the worst possible time to drop her bombshell. *I never stopped loving you.*

"I can get them," the driver said.

"I insist," Bray said. *Get your head in the game, Hollister.*

"Well, thanks," the driver said, handing off the tray he held and turning to step back inside the truck for another.

Bray slowly let out his breath. Working undercover for so many years had taught him that sometimes you had no choice but to simply act as if you belonged there.

It was going to get tricky fast if somebody opened the front door. But it stayed shut, and soon the driver was back with a second tray. Bray motioned for him to proceed.

"Same place as before?" the driver asked.

"Yes," said Bray.

The driver didn't head for the front door. Instead, he walked toward the wing that extended eastward. He opened a big wooden door that led into a breezeway of sorts that connected the wing to the main house. Bray thought it looked like the lobby of an expensive hotel. The floor was marble, the walls were covered in textured wallpaper, and there was a piece of art perched on an easel that probably cost what he made in a year.

At one end of the elaborate space, there was a door. The driver opened it and they were in a big kitchen that had enough stainless steel to make a restaurateur green with envy. There were two side-by-side refrigerators with glass fronts. The driver opened one of the doors and slid his tray inside. Once he was done, Bray stepped forward and bent his knees so that he could put the tray he was holding onto the shelf directly below. He was just straightening up when he heard a noise at the door. He turned and saw a woman, thin, all in black, probably midthirties, in the doorway. Her dark hair was in a ponytail. She was looking at the driver.

"I told Tom that if you hurried you'd make it back in time. He got upset for nothing. I'm sorry about that. It's just that breakfast on Thanksgiving Day has always been his deal."

"Totally understand," the driver said. "I'm just really sorry, Mrs. Pataneros, that we didn't get it right the first time."

Bray said nothing. The woman hadn't even looked at him.

"No harm done. Everyone is just starting to gather anyway. I put the egg casseroles in the oven on low just like you said."

"Great. I've got one more fruit tray and that will do it," the driver said. He started walking out.

Bray followed him. The woman gave him a half smile, like one that people gave to strangers when they weren't sure what to say to them. He did the same in response and kept walking. Ten steps into the breezeway, he glanced over his shoulder to verify that the woman hadn't followed him. The driver was almost at the door.

He took a sharp right and headed up the wide, shiny wooden stairs to the second level.

SUMMER WAS COLD and the only thing she could do about it was wrap her arms around herself. She had on her jean jacket, and while it had been plenty warm the night before, it hadn't been sufficient for an hour ride in a refrigerated truck, nor for standing in wet grass, when the morning temperature was midthirties at best.

She should have been, at the very least, warm from embarrassment. She'd told Bray that she'd never stopped loving him. Why the hell had she done that? Not that it wasn't true, but why admit it now? To him?

Because she couldn't bear the thought of him never knowing it. And she was confident that there was danger inside this house. When Bray had walked up to the truck, as though he had every right to, her heart had almost stopped.

He was taking a great risk. For her. For her child.

Was it any wonder that she'd never stopped loving him? But was it too late?

It didn't matter how much she loved Bray if Adie didn't come home safe. She would never be able to forgive herself or forget the horrible situation that had brought them back together.

She saw the driver come back outside. But no Bray. What the hell was he doing in there?

The driver carried in another tray. He didn't seem concerned that he'd lost Bray somewhere.

Now he was back, hands empty. Shutting the door of the truck, checking to make sure it was latched tight. Then he was in his vehicle. He started the engine and came around the circle driveway, headed straight toward her.

She kept perfectly still, knowing that it would be movement that attracted the man's gaze. Time seemed to crawl by, but it was only seconds before he was past her, on his way back to St. Louis and his own Thanksgiving dinner.

She looked at her watch. Bray had been inside for eleven minutes. What the hell was she going to do if he didn't come out? He would expect her to work her way toward the gate, to get to the vehicle, to get away. Could she leave him? How could she not if it meant that she would still be free to look for Adie?

The toast in her stomach rumbled and her legs felt weak. She contemplated sitting down.

Instead, she drew in a deep breath. Then another. Bray would come back. He would not leave her. Not willingly.

BRAY WAS IN the upstairs hallway when he had to quickly duck into an empty bathroom. Voices, louder now, coming closer. A man and a woman, talking about Black Friday shopping. Her excited, him resigned.

Now they were past.

He counted to five, then poked his head out. The wide hallway had thick beige carpet and was in the shape of an L, with doors on both sides. The couple had come from the section that he couldn't get a visual on. He moved forward, intent upon starting at the back and working his way forward.

He did not encounter any more people, but it was obvious that three of the four very large guest suites were occupied. When he was done, he was comfortable that neither Adie nor Summer's ex was in that section of the house. At one point, he looked out of one bedroom window, trying to see Summer. But even knowing where she was, he couldn't spot her.

If somebody in the house had discovered her and they touched one hair on her head, he was going to kill them all.

He moved fast, knowing that he needed to cross into the main house and search it and the other wing before he could go. The second floor of the main house was rectangular in shape, with two bedroom suites on each side and the whole rear of the house dedicated to a media room and a well-stocked library.

Only one of the four bedroom suites was in use. He suspected the owner of the house liked his privacy and made sure his guests were comfortable in the more distant wings.

He could hear voices, one talking over the other. The family had gathered below, anxious for their breakfast egg dishes and smoked salmon. Silverware clanked against plates. Someone laughed too loud. His stomach growled in response to the smell of cinnamon drifting up the open staircase.

He moved toward the remaining wing. It was set up exactly like the other. It did not take long to search all the rooms, although he had a bit of a start when he opened one door and a young male, naked to the waist, was stretched across the bed. He was sound asleep and there was an odor in the room that was part sweaty teen and part marijuana smoke.

Maybe he'd stumble down by the time they pulled the turkey out of the oven later today.

Bray finished his search. He knew there was no need to search the first floor. With this many people in the house, nobody would be brave enough to keep two kidnapping victims that close. But he found himself hesitating as he contemplated the best way to exit the house. There was no basement, not unusual even for expensive houses in these parts.

He'd seen Mrs. Pataneros, but he really wanted a look at her husband, wanted to see the man who saw fit to put this kind of opulence in the middle of nowhere. Wanted to be able to describe him to Summer, just to make sure it didn't mesh with anybody that she knew.

He went back to the main section and slowly descended the stairs, thankful that it was quality workmanship and there wasn't a single squeak. He eased around a corner. The dining room was huge, probably eighteen by thirty, and there was a long table that took up a fair portion of the room. He counted. Seven on one side, six on the other, one at each end. If Sleeping Beauty upstairs had made it to the table, there would have been sixteen.

They were all listening to a young girl of maybe ten years old talk about her horseback-riding lessons. He could see the man at the head of the table and assumed it was Mr. Pataneros. He was very tall and very thin and did not fit Summer's description of the kidnappers or the video from the mall. He swallowed his disappointment and was about to turn away to make his final escape when the man to Mr. Pataneros's right turned his head.

Bray saw the port-wine stain on his face. He barely had that processed when the man across the table lifted his hand to reach for the fruit kebabs and Bray caught the sparkle of a gold ring with black filigree and a big red stone.

A ring big enough that it could be seen under a pair of thin cotton gloves.

The man with the ring reached over and rubbed the girl's head. "So proud of you, Victoria," he said. "You did all that yesterday and still managed to get to breakfast on time. More than I can say for your brother," he added, frowning at the empty chair.

"Let it go," said a woman with hair the exact same shade as Victoria's. "He got home safe last night. That's what matters."

Bray wanted to bust in, shove the kebab down the man's slimy throat and demand answers, but he didn't. Years of training kicked in. He would not risk Adie's safety for the short-lived pleasure of inflicting some pain on these two.

Very quietly he walked from the main house into the east wing, where he had entered just thirty-six minutes ago. He opened the door, walked out, but before he disappeared into the tree line, he did one more thing.

Then he moved fast, working his way back to the spot where he'd left Summer.

Only she wasn't there.

Chapter Nineteen

Thursday, 8:10 a.m.

Summer heard the men's voices before she saw them. They were walking up the paved driveway, conversing in Spanish. Both were dressed for outside work in blue jeans, flannel shirts and insulated vests.

Both carried shovels.

And her heart started to race. It was Thanksgiving Day. What would someone need a shovel for?

To dig a grave.

She put her hand over her mouth, afraid that she might not be able to keep her anguish silent.

She had to follow them. She had to know.

They did not head for the house. Instead, they turned down the road that led to the right. She waited until they got a hundred yards away before she started to follow them.

It meant she had to cross the road. That couldn't be helped. She was going to have to take the chance that if no one had seen them jump out of the back of the truck, then nobody would see her now.

Stepping carefully so as not to make a sound, she kept them in sight. Every ten steps or so, she would pause and listen. At one point, she realized that the sounds had changed.

And so had the smell of the air.

Horses.

Another fifty feet and she saw the circular riding corral and the long white stable. The men had entered, leaving the big doors at one end open.

She felt relief course through her body. They weren't burying bodies. They were mucking out horse stalls.

She felt her cell phone buzz in her skirt pocket. It was a text from Bray. Where are you?

She texted back. Approximately 1300 feet east of where you left me. She'd been counting steps and she was walking toward the morning sun.

Stay there, came the reply.

Within minutes, he was there. Holding her close. He was shaking.

"You scared me," he whispered in her ear, "when I couldn't find you."

"I saw two men walking. With shovels."

She saw the understanding in his eyes. He knew what she'd been thinking.

"We have to get out of here," he said.

"Did you find anything?" she asked.

He nodded. "I think so."

Now it was her turn to shake. "What?"

"I'll tell you everything. But first, we have to go. I'm going to text Cal and let him know that we'll be on the road in three minutes."

She had a thousand questions but she kept them to herself as she hurried behind him. When they got to the edge of the property, Bray motioned for her to stay in the trees. Then he ran across the road, entered the guard shack, and suddenly the gate was sliding open like magic.

He motioned for her and she ran for all she was worth. They were still running two hundred yards later when they saw Cal's SUV over the hill. Bray reached under the front right wheel well and came out with keys.

Then they were inside and moving fast. Bray pressed on the accelerator, navigating the rural road with confidence.

She looked over her shoulder. No one was chasing them. Yet.

Bray was watching the rearview mirror. She knew he was likely worried that somehow the gate opening had tripped some kind of alarm in the house.

"Tell me everything," she said.

He tossed her his phone. "First, there are pictures of the license plates for all the cars that were parked at Pataneros's house. Forward them to Chase. He'll be able to run the plates and get us a name and address of the owner."

She did so and set his phone back onto the middle console.

He took his eyes off the curvy road just long enough to make eye contact. He explained about the people in the suites and the young male who had been asleep and smelled of marijuana. "Port-wine-stain guy is there," he added.

She grabbed his arm, so fast and so hard that the vehicle swerved to the side. "We have to go back. Now."

Bray shook his head. "I searched the whole house. I don't think Adie and your ex are there, so it would do us no good to go back."

But that man, that awful man, had to know where Adie was. Summer wanted to shake the truth out of him. No. She wanted to beat it out of him. She wanted to hurt him. Badly.

The intensity of the hate that she felt almost overwhelmed her. It threatened to take her under, to keep her from being able to think, to plan.

She stared into Bray's eyes. *Help me* was her silent plea.

"This was a big break, Summer," Bray said. "I think I might have seen the other man, as well. He was dark-haired, light-skinned, and wearing a big gold ring with lots of black filigree and a big red stone. I'd be willing to bet that's the ring you saw under his black gloves."

Gold ring. Lots of black filigree. Big red stone.

She let those words roll around.

"What?" Bray demanded, still watching her eyes.

"I've seen a ring like that before."

"On who?" Bray said quickly. "Do you have a name?"

"I do, but it doesn't make sense. Well, maybe it does."

"Tell me."

"Several years ago, I went to an office Christmas party with Gary. Chief Poole hosted it at a restaurant in Hamerton. It was a fancy place. We got dressed up."

"Someone there wore a ring like this?" Bray said.

She nodded. "Yes. Chief Poole. He told me it was his college ring."

BRAY CONSIDERED THAT. "From the beginning, we thought that whoever had committed the crime had some way of knowing if you followed directions and contacted police. You would have either gone to Poole or perhaps to the FBI, who would have notified Poole out of professional courtesy, and either way, he'd have been in the loop."

"But he was the one who told us that Gary was missing. He questioned us."

"Yeah. And his investigation was perfunctory at best. I gave him a pass, figured he was a small-town cop and didn't have any experience with this kind of situation. I think he questioned both of us because it would have seemed really odd if he didn't. After all, Reverend Brown and Poole's sister-in-law Julie had overheard our exchange in the church basement. But when he talked to me, he didn't even take notes."

"With me either. Let's assume he had to do something," Summer said, "once Officer Stone had stopped by Gary's house and seen the mess and reported it. He couldn't ignore it because he knows how information flows in a small town."

"I agree. I suspect Poole wouldn't have done anything about Gary's absence. But since someone else had noticed, he had to play the part of the concerned employer who just happens to be local law enforcement."

"But Officer Stone said they had people on Chief Poole, watching him. He was confident that he hadn't kidnapped Adie."

She looked so hopeful that he hated to break the news to her. "Unfortunately, Summer, I think it's possible that Poole is involved in this up to his neck. He may not be the one who kidnapped Adie or your ex, but I think he probably knows something about it. This has to be big. Very big. Kidnapping is a federal offense. If he's in any way an accessory to a kidnapping charge, he knows he's going to do some serious prison time. Cops don't do well in prison. I suspect he'd rather die."

"What do we do?" she said, her voice ragged.

"Tell me about Poole. What do you know about him?"

She ran her fingers through her hair. "Not much. I know he came to Ravesville about four or five years ago. Gary was mad that he didn't get a promotion to chief at the time, but the mayor and Gary weren't close and he ultimately had responsibility for the decision. It was tense between Gary and Chief Poole for a while, but then that changed and they seemed to be getting along better."

"Sheila said he was married."

"Yes. Like Sheila says, his wife owns a flower shop in Hamerton, so I didn't see her very much."

Flower shop. Independent business. Deliveries coming and going at all times of the day, nobody paying attention. "So they're probably closed today."

"Sure." She turned to look at him. "Oh my gosh, Bray. You think they're at the flower shop?"

"I don't know. But we're not that far away and we should check it. What's the name of the flower shop?" Bray asked. He was driving very fast.

"I don't know. I was never there. But I know it's on the main street that runs through town. There can't be more than one."

"Let's hope not," he said, his tone curt.

"What?" she said, looking frightened. "Bray, there's something you're not telling me. I know it. You have to tell me all of it. I can't bear not to know."

"Honey," he said. He wanted to stop the damn car and pull her into his arms, but there was no time. "I've told you everything."

But he hadn't. He hadn't told her about the young girl relating the story about riding her horse or about how her father had sat there, making a big show out of listening to his daughter's tale, all the time knowing that he'd taken someone else's daughter. It was driving him crazy that he didn't know if the man was able to eat his eggs without fear of heartburn because he hadn't harmed Adie or because it was over.

There was no way he was going to tell her that it was possible that they were too late.

When they got to Hamerton, it didn't take them long to find the flower shop. Poole's Pansies and More was in the middle of the block. There was a big closed sign in the front window.

He drove past, made a right and took another sharp right into the alley that ran behind all the businesses that lined the main drag. There was one parking space by the back door. It was empty. She expected him to pull in, but he didn't. He continued on, three more businesses, finally pulling in between the red pickup truck and the black Toyota that were parked at the Laundromat.

They walked back to the flower shop. "I don't see any security cameras," Summer said.

"Maybe we'll get lucky," Bray said.

SHE HAD FORGOTTEN that he was carrying lock picks. Was it really just a little over eight hours since she'd seen him pick the lock on that very first ramshackle house? It seemed like a lifetime ago. But again his skills were handy. The door opened within seconds.

And then the alarm started ringing. It was loud and it hurt her ears. "We're going to have to hurry," Bray yelled.

How could she even think? There were small tables with plants and candles and inexpensive gifts. A big refrigerator was against the wall, and in it were several vases of fresh flowers. On the bottom shelf was a bucket of carnations.

It looked like every other small flower shop she'd ever been in. There was no sign of Gary or Adie. "Is there a basement?" she asked.

Bray shook his head. He was standing in the middle of the room, simply looking around.

"What are you looking at?" she demanded. Her hopes had been raised and, again, stomped on.

"For anything that doesn't look quite right," he said.

She closed her eyes, took a deep breath, opened them again. Surveyed the room.

Flowers in the cooler. Check. Plants near the sunny window. Check. Bulbs in bins by the door. Check. She walked toward the back room where there were two worktables that were probably three feet wide by six feet long. On one, more than twenty pots with brightly colored poinsettias sat ready. After Thanksgiving was over, those would probably be moved to the front. Check.

On the other table were... She stepped closer. Grave-site markers, some round wreaths and some in the shape of a cross, all decorated with silk flowers. She stared at the one at the end closest to her. She'd seen one just like it last night, when they'd been wandering around the graveyard. That made sense. Funeral flowers and burial-plot decorations were probably big business for flower shops. She was just about to turn away when she saw the two pots, half filled with dirt, at the far end of the table.

That didn't make sense. You wouldn't pot plants in dirt in the same area that you were arranging silk flowers. She got close and tried to lift the pot. It was too heavy. She could dump it, maybe, but then there would be dirt everywhere. But she didn't want to walk away from it. She took off her jacket, rolled up her sleeve and plunged her hand into the dirt all the way up to her elbow.

And she felt something besides dirt. She got a grip and pulled her arm out.

In her hand was an envelope full of cash. Stuffed full of hundreds and fifties. Thousands and thousands of dollars.

"Bray," she screamed.

He came fast. Saw the cash, the messed-up dirt, and didn't even bother to roll up his own sleeve before he stuck his arm into the remaining pot. He pulled out a matching envelope.

They'd been inside for almost two minutes. Time was running out.

"Now what?" she said.

In response, Bray walked up to the counter and pulled a blank sheet of paper out of the printer. He picked up a black Sharpie, too. He wrote his cell-phone number in big letters, folded the paper and put it back into the second pot. Then he patted the dirt down in both pots.

"I don't know why I was worried about security cameras," she said, shaking her head. "I didn't realize we were going to leave a card."

He smiled. "It's time for them to come to us. Let's go," he added, putting both envelopes of cash in his coat pocket. He opened the back door and out they went. They hurried down the alley and got into their vehicle.

They were out of the alley, back on the main drag, before they saw a police car round the corner.

Chapter Twenty

It was a Hamerton police car with one officer. Bray didn't speed up or slow down. The cop's eyes were totally focused on the flower shop. He was probably wondering how long it would take him to figure out how to shut off the alarm.

He figured Poole and his wife wouldn't be far behind. If the alarm system worked like most, they would have got a call from the alarm company. That would have spurred action. The alarm company, upon learning this was likely a real event, would have dispatched local police, and Poole and his wife would have jumped into the car. But they lived in Ravesville, which was a twenty-minute drive.

Bray intended to be long gone before they arrived.

Poole and his wife would notice right away that the money was gone. It was doubtful that they'd tell the Hamerton police. Hard to explain that kind of cash hidden under some dirt.

But once they got the Hamerton cop out the door, Poole would no doubt use the police resources at his disposal to try to find out whom the cell number belonged to. But he wouldn't be successful. One of the benefits of being an undercover DEA agent was that his cell-phone number was registered to a fictional Frank White in Boise, Idaho.

Then Poole would have no choice but to call the number.

This was about to get very interesting. And while he might enjoy screwing with Poole for a while, the stakes were too high. Adie had been gone for sixteen hours.

Summer could not be expected to take much more.

So he was going to squeeze Poole hard and fast.

"What is Poole doing with this kind of money?" Summer asked, sounding a little dazed. "And is this the same money that Gary thought was about to fall into his lap?"

"I don't know. But I'm starting to think that there's more to the relationship between Poole and your ex than anybody knows. It's not your typical boss-employee thing."

"I don't see Gary as a drug dealer," Summer said.

He bit back a sharp reply. How could she still believe in the man?

She held up a hand. "I know what you're thinking," she said. "That I have blinders on when it comes to Gary. I don't. I know that he's not perfect. But I just don't see him as a drug dealer."

Bray knew way better than most that drug dealers came in all sizes, shapes and colors. Bank executives with penthouse apartments in Manhattan, housewives in Brooklyn, gang leaders in the Bronx. All kinds of people, some you might automatically suspect and some you'd never dream of, were making a ton of money. As a result, the money that moved through legitimate commerce as a result of illegal drugs activity was staggering.

And made it a damn difficult war to fight.

"It's possible that he was investigating something,"

Bray said, hardly believing that he was offering up a solution that would exonerate Summer's ex.

She didn't respond for several minutes, but he could tell she was thinking. They were back on the highway, headed toward Ravesville. His phone should be ringing any minute.

Summer shifted in her seat. "Maybe Gary was blackmailing Poole."

Now, that was interesting. "Why would you think that?" Bray asked, careful to keep his tone neutral.

"It…it seems like something he might do."

"Because…?"

"Because he's done it before."

THE MINUTE THE words were out of her mouth, she wanted to take them back. But in her heart, she knew it was time. Past time. Bray needed to know the truth.

The car was slowing fast and Bray made a quick turn onto a side road. He drove until he had crested the first hill so that he was no longer visible from the highway. He pulled off to the side of the road and put the vehicle in Park. Then he turned toward her. "That's quite a bombshell," he said. "I think I need to hear more."

She could put him off. She could tell him that she just couldn't do this right now because of her concern for Adie. And he'd back off. Because he was that kind of guy.

A good guy.

Whom she'd let believe a lie for fifteen years.

She drew in a breath. "When you enlisted in the Marines, I intended to wait. I meant what I'd told you."

He said nothing, but she could tell by the set of his jaw that he was prepared to hear something difficult.

"My mom always drank too much. I knew that when

I was a ten-year-old. But after my dad died, it got worse. You were gone then, so you didn't see it," she said.

He nodded. "I always felt bad that I wasn't able to get home for his funeral."

"I understood. Anyway, after that, she was really bad for a few months. Then she seemed to want to change. Over the next year, she tried a few different programs. Unfortunately, she failed all of them. Trish was basically done with her but I still had hope. And then something terrible happened."

She had never told anyone about this. And now she was about to tell the person it had hurt the most.

Well, not the most, perhaps. That would have been the dead man. And his family.

"What?" he asked softly.

"She was driving home from the bar. It was late. She hit a pedestrian and killed him."

"Who?" Bray asked.

"His name was Brian Laffley."

"Stone asked you about him," Bray said, his voice hard. "You said you didn't know the name."

"I lied. I've been lying for a long time." She swallowed hard.

"What happened?"

"Gary was the cop on duty. I knew him, of course. He'd moved to town just a year or so earlier. In a small town, everybody knows the police. Especially when they're young and sort of handsome. Lots of my friends had a crush on him. And, well, he'd asked me out a few times."

Now she could see the anger in Bray's eyes. She knew what he was thinking. He'd been off fighting a war and she'd been messing around with the new guy in town.

"I didn't go," she said. "I always said no. But unfortunately, I think maybe that made me more interesting. Maybe more of a challenge."

"You've always been a beautiful woman," Bray said. "He'd have been a fool not to have been interested."

He wasn't going to be giving her compliments when he'd heard it all.

"Gary brought my mother home that night. Trish was on a date but I was home. Mom was a wreck, just sobbing. It was her third DUI and she'd killed someone. She was going to prison."

"He brought her home?"

Summer nodded. "Yeah. Not exactly proper police procedure. But then again, nothing was proper about that night." She stared at her shoes. "Gary said that he could make it all go away. That he would get rid of the body. That Mom wouldn't be arrested, wouldn't be charged with any crime."

She looked up, into Bray's eyes. He was so smart. He knew what was coming. "If?" he prompted.

"If I married him."

BRAY GRIPPED THE steering wheel, trying to come to terms with what Summer had said and then tying it together with what Officer Stone had said. It was a bad horror movie with images coming at him from all directions.

Summer thought her mother had killed someone. And she'd allowed it to be covered up. That meant she had been willing to be an accomplice to a homicide. That was one blinking light at the edge of his vision.

But her mother hadn't hit Laffley and killed him. Officer Stone had said that it was a gunshot.

It all came back to Gary Blake.

Had he killed Brian Laffley? Had Summer been married to a killer? When he'd said that he could make it go away, did that include getting rid of Laffley's body? But had he screwed that up, too?

When he somehow became aware that Laffley's body had resurfaced, did he orchestrate the mix-up at the funeral home?

The only thing he knew for sure was that he'd used Laffley's death to entrap Summer into marriage. And Summer had let him.

And hadn't trusted Bray enough to tell him the truth when he'd come home just months later.

For years, he'd believed she simply didn't love him enough.

He wanted to punch something.

"Bray," she said.

He cut her off. "No. Don't say anything else. Not just yet." He felt as if he couldn't get enough air. He opened his door. Fumbled his way out of his seat belt and out of the car.

Stood perfectly still in the chilly, quiet morning air and drew in a breath, then a second one. He felt the cold air burn his lungs, clear his head. He got back into the car. Turned to her.

"You need to know something," he said. And then he told her about his conversation with Officer Stone.

She listened, not saying a word. When he was done, she shook her head. "That's not possible. My mother saw the man. Saw him crumpled up next to her car."

"She was drunk. She probably didn't inspect the body. I suspect that she probably passed out and your ex found her. Then he either drove her car to where Laffley's body was or he moved Laffley's body to where your mother was. Somehow, he connected the two events."

Her eyes widened as what he'd said sank in. "You think he shot Laffley?"

"I have no idea. Maybe he did. Maybe he was involved in something bad and discovered that Laffley was a federal agent and decided that he needed to disappear. Or maybe he was a cop on duty and discovered a dead man? Then when he saw your mom, it was simply fortuitous. Either way he did something really wrong. He either murdered a man or concealed the murder of a man."

She started to cry. And she couldn't catch her breath. She wrapped her arms around her stomach and her body shook with loud, racking sobs.

Was she crying for the son of a bitch? Was she worried that he was going to go to jail? It was more than he should be expected to take. Before coming back to Ravesville, he'd have sworn that Summer Wright could never do anything to hurt him again, that she'd broken him once but now he was immune.

He'd been wrong.

But still, he hated to hear her cry. Through all this, she'd been steady, but this was the thing that had pushed her over the edge.

Was it even possible that she still felt something for her ex? He opened his car door because he felt sick.

"Oh, Bray," she said, sniffing. "I don't—" she swallowed "—blame you for leaving. I am...so sorry." She hiccuped. "I hurt you so badly. For nothing. I'm so sorry."

She wasn't crying for her ex. She was crying for him.

"Aw, honey. I'm not leaving. Ever." He closed his door, pulled her into his arms and held her. He patted her back until she was spent and her head drooped on his shoulder.

Finally, she lifted it. Her eyes and nose were red and she looked very weary. "What do we do now?"

"We put this aside," he said. "Laffley is dead. Has been for a long time. We focus on finding Adie."

He picked up the two envelopes of money and started

counting. He was almost done when his cell phone rang. He looked at it, recognized the number. "It's Chase. After we find Adie, we'll sort the rest out," he said, finishing his earlier thought. He swiped his phone and clicked the button so that it was on speaker. "Yeah," he said.

"I've got the information you wanted on the license plates," Chase said. "The BMW is from Chicago. I did a little quick research. The man is Pataneros's brother. The other two, the Lexus and the Camaro, have the same address. Same last name. Pitard."

That made sense. The young man who had smelled like pot probably drove the Camaro and his parents drove the Lexus.

"I couldn't find any connection between them and Pataneros," Chase said.

"I think I might know the connection. It's to Chief Poole. I suspect they might have been college buddies," Bray said, glancing at Summer. "What's their address?"

"8713 Bluehound Road."

Bluehound Road. Bray reached for the list of properties they'd searched. "One of the abandoned properties was on Bluehound," he said to Chase.

"I know. At 5211 Bluehound. The two places are a couple miles apart. I'm guessing several tax brackets, as well, based on the vehicles and that they're friends with Pataneros."

"I think you're probably right," Bray said. Something didn't make sense but he couldn't put his finger on it.

"You want Cal or me to check it out?" Chase asked.

"No." If Poole was working with Pataneros, they needed to make sure that they had Pataneros and his friends wrapped up tight before word got to them that Poole had been taken down. They might blow away in the wind. And Adie might never be found. "I've got Cal watching Pataneros's place, seeing if anybody moves. I'm on my way. Join me there. It's time to figure out what these guys know."

"We'll need to be careful," Chase said.

Bray understood. If things went south fast and Pataneros and the other two were killed, the trail to Adie would disappear.

"We will be," Bray said. "I'll be there as fast as I can, maybe twenty minutes."

Bray turned to update Summer, but before he could, his phone rang again. "It's Poole," he said.

Chapter Twenty-One

Thursday, 9:25 a.m.

"You left a number, so I'm calling," Poole said.

"I appreciate that," Bray said. When he'd talked to Poole yesterday, he'd poured the East Coast on thick. Now he wiped it from his delivery, staying Midwest all the way. He wanted to make sure that Poole didn't know whom he was talking to. "I thought you might want to talk about the money."

"I don't like talking about money with strangers," Poole said.

Bingo. "You can call me John."

"John what?"

"Just John," Bray said.

"You're messing with the wrong people," Poole said.

"Messing with some rich people, you mean," Bray countered.

"What do you want?"

"I want in on some of the action. This is a lot of money, but I've been watching you. You cover a lot of geography. I don't think that's fair."

There was a pause on the other end of the line. "I'm not sure I know what you're talking about," Poole said.

Bray picked up the sheet of paper with the addresses.

"Really. Well, maybe this will jump-start your memory." He rattled off the address of the cemetery.

Now there was an even more pronounced pause. Bray resisted the urge to fill the silence. He could see that Summer was moving in her seat and she was clenching and unclenching her hands.

"Well, then," Poole said, "I'll ask one more time. What is it that you want?"

"I want a meeting with your boss."

"Why?"

"Because I want to discuss business with him. Quit asking stupid questions," Bray said.

"Well, you know, it's Thanksgiving."

Bray started to whistle. Off-key. Stopped after a few bars. "If you want me to blow the lid off your little organization, keep talking crap."

"I'll give my boss a call," Poole said.

"You do that. But don't make me wait too long," Bray said. He hung up.

"Oh my God," Summer said. "What are you doing?"

"I'm getting your daughter back," he said, starting the car.

"How?"

"I know all kinds of people like Chief Poole. To generate this kind of cash, he's got to have a big-time operation going. He is not going to let some punk weasel his way in. He's going to want to deal with me quickly and efficiently, but first he needs to figure out if I'm working alone or if I've shared any of what I know with someone else. You can automatically assume that he thinks he's three times as smart as me. He's going to try to find a way to get his money back and shut me up. For good."

"I wish we knew how Gary fits into this," Summer

said. "Whether he was part of it or simply trying to cash in and they decided he was a bug that needed stepping on."

"We'll know soon enough," Bray said. He, quite frankly, didn't give a damn about Gary Blake. Through his duplicity, he'd changed a lot of lives, Bray's included.

"About what I told you," Summer said.

"Not the right time," Bray said.

"But—"

Bray's phone rang. Bray let it ring three times before he answered. "Yeah."

"He's agreed to a short meeting."

"Fine. There's a park in Ravesville. I'm sure you know it," Bray said.

"No. We'll meet you at 1403 Hazel Road."

Bray quickly glanced at the list of addresses on his sheet. It didn't match any of them. "Where is that?"

"Get a map," Poole said, his tone sharp. "And be there in an hour." He hung up.

Bray punched the address into his GPS. It was northeast of Ravesville, about fifteen miles. From where they were right now, it was a thirty-minute drive.

He dialed Daniel Stone. When the officer answered, Bray didn't waste any time. "By now, if you really have people sitting on Poole, you know that he's moving. He went to his wife's flower shop in Hamerton. Now he's headed for 1403 Hazel Road. He thinks he's meeting me. He's anxious to do that because I removed about $200,000 from a couple flowerpots. I'm not sure what you all have been waiting for, but I think it's time."

Officer Stone laughed. "We've been waiting because we couldn't find the damn money. Thank you. Where are you?"

"I'll let you know." Bray hung up. It was time to join Chase and Cal.

Chapter Twenty-Two

Thursday, 9:43 a.m.

Adie had been gone for more than sixteen hours. Summer desperately needed to hear her child's voice, feel her small arms around her neck, smell her little-girl smell that was some unique combination of shampoo, peanut butter and strawberry lip gloss.

Now that it seemed as if they might be close, she was more frightened than ever. What if they were too late? What if Adie was…?

She couldn't bear to think the word.

Bray had turned the car around and was headed back to the main road. When he got to the stop sign and started to turn right, she put her hand on the wheel. "Stop," she said.

He didn't shake her off even though she could tell that he was impatient to move forward. "What?" he asked, his tone calm.

"When you searched Pataneros's house, you said that it was clear that everyone had spent the night."

He nodded.

"Have you ever met a friend for an early-morning breakfast?"

Now he was looking at her as if she'd lost her mind. "I have."

"So did you go over the night before?"

Bray shook his head.

"It doesn't make sense that Pitard and his whole family spend the night at Pataneros's house when their own house is less than ten minutes away. Why wouldn't they simply just get up early and drive over?"

"Maybe they did something together last night. You know, they started celebrating early."

"You said the one kid who was sleeping reeked of pot. I don't think they were doing that as a family activity."

Now Bray started strumming his thumb against the steering wheel. "The wife said that Thanksgiving Day breakfast was always a big deal to Pataneros. I suspect the good wife is oblivious to how her husband makes all his money. But she would think something was very odd if suddenly he didn't want to have the Thanksgiving Day event, especially since the food was already ordered. And he probably always has his brother and his best friend and their families join him. Tradition. That's what Thanksgiving Day is. You eat the same food with the same people, year after year."

"But this year they had a problem," Summer said.

"Yeah. Your ex. If they took him, they would need a place to stash him."

"If you lived nearby, you might take your family to your neighbor's house the night before if there was something going on at your own house that you didn't want your wife or kids to see," Summer said.

"Exactly." Bray picked up his cell phone.

"What are you doing?" she asked.

"I'm going to get a visual of Pitard's house." He punched some keys. In just seconds, he was handing her the screen. The image was amazingly clear. Pitard's house was not as lavish as Pataneros's house but it was still probably over a million dollars, in a part of the country where somebody could get a real nice place for $200,000. It was a two-story colonial, white with black shutters. There was an attached three-car garage with all three doors down. There was an in-ground swimming pool and a couple of acres of yard, surrounded by trees on three sides.

"Very isolated," she said.

"Yeah, no neighbors around to hear much of anything."

She pointed at the screen. "Those are basement windows," she said.

"I think so," he agreed.

She felt sick. "What should we do?"

Bray didn't answer. He simply cranked the wheel and took off fast toward Pitard's house.

"Do you think it's possible," she asked, now breathless that she'd put forth the possibility, "that Adie and Gary are there?"

Bray pushed the accelerator to the floor and the car was flying down the road. "We'll know in ten minutes," he said.

THE MORE HE thought about it, the more certain Bray became that Summer was onto something. Thank goodness she'd put it together. There'd been something nagging at him that told him that something wasn't right with what Chase was telling him about the addresses, but quite frankly, he wasn't really trusting his instincts right now.

Summer had not loved Gary Blake. She had married him to keep her mother out of jail.

Yet she'd had two children with him. That stung. "Can I ask you something?" he said. He should be concentrating on driving, but he couldn't wait another minute.

"Of course," she said.

"I get that you married your ex because you were try-

ing to help your mom. But you had Keagan and then Adie.
I'm not sure I get that."

"And I stayed married to him for a long time."

Her tone said it all. She understood what he was asking.

"Once I had made the decision to marry Gary, I was
determined to make the best of it. He told me over and
over again how much he loved me, and I thought if I tried
hard enough, I could love him, too. I got pregnant with
Keagan almost immediately, and having him…well, that
strengthened my resolve to make my marriage work. Gary
was good with his son."

She stopped. Bray remained silent.

"After a few years, I knew that I was never going to
love Gary. Not like he wanted to be loved or professed to
love me. I…I had been in love. I knew what it felt like.
And that wasn't what I felt for Gary."

Bray felt as if he had an elephant sitting on his chest.
He gripped the steering wheel hard, letting his emotion
have some small physical outlet.

"When I tried to talk to Gary about it, he always told
me that he was patient, that he could wait for me to really
love him. And for years we drifted along like that, but I
had pretty much made the decision that I was going to have
to leave. Then when Keagan was eight, Gary arranged for
us to go on a honeymoon. We'd never taken one and he
booked a week at an all-inclusive resort in Mexico. I almost
told him no, but he was so excited about it, said that he
thought it might make a difference between the two of us."

"Did it?" Bray asked.

"Well, it did, but not in the way you might think. I was
taking birth control pills to prevent the possibility of another pregnancy and I thought I'd packed my pills but they
weren't in my suitcase when I arrived. Gary saw that I

was upset and immediately went to the small store at the resort and bought other protection."

She turned to look out the window. "I got pregnant with Adie on that trip. And so help me God, I didn't want to be pregnant. I didn't want another baby." She paused. "Maybe I'm being punished for that now."

"No," Bray said. "That's not how it works."

"After I had Adie, I stayed with Gary for another year or so but I just couldn't do it. I told him I wanted a divorce, and the kids and I moved into an apartment that Trish helped us get."

"How did he react?"

"He was angry and he let it slip that he'd thought another child would make the difference. That's when I realized that he'd deliberately taken my birth control out of my suitcase. For all I know, he poked holes in the condoms, too. But I couldn't be mad about having Adie. She was a delight from the day she was born. I will never regret having either her or Keagan. It wasn't a marriage of love, but something wonderful, two somethings, came out of it. I can't regret that."

"What I witnessed in the church wasn't a happily divorced couple," Bray said.

"I know. For the first two years after our divorce, Gary was very cold to me. He took the kids on his weekends and he paid child support, but there was very little interaction between the two of us. Then it got really weird. He stopped paying child support. When I told him he needed to, he warned me that if I pushed it, he was going to tell the truth about what my mother had done."

"He would have implicated himself," Bray said.

"I know. I told him that. He said that he'd deny it. He said that he'd hidden the body but would make sure it was found and that my mother's DNA was all over it. I didn't know if he was telling the truth and my mother never had any memory of what really happened that night. So I stopped asking for support. Gary started to see the kids less and less, but when he had them, he was good with them. I never worried about that."

Bray looked at the GPS. They were within a mile now of Pitard's house. He slowed down. He didn't want to have to deal with Gary Blake right now. But he really, really wanted to bring Summer's little girl home. And he probably wasn't going to be able to do one without the other.

If they were in the house, he was going to do everything he needed to do to get them out of there.

But he wasn't going to do it without Summer knowing the truth.

He pulled the car off to the side of the road. "Summer, there's something I need you to know."

She swallowed hard. He could see the delicate muscles of her throat working. "I don't expect you to ever be able to forgive me," she said.

He reached for her hand. It was cold. "I fell a little bit in love with you when you were sixteen and you dipped your French fries in mayonnaise on our first date and gave the waitress at that seedy little bar and grill a five-dollar tip because the table next to us stiffed her. I thought, this girl is different. And then when you were seventeen and used your prom-dress money to pay for a lawyer for your mom because she'd gotten a DUI, I knew I had something special. And when we made love for the first time at Rock Pond, I knew that I wanted to make love to you until I was ninety."

"Oh," she said, her eyes filling with tears.

"When I enlisted, I knew it probably wasn't fair to expect you to wait. But I wanted you to. Desperately. And when I came home and realized my life was never going to be what I had hoped and dreamed about all those long nights in a faraway desert, I was angry."

He stroked his thumb over the light blue veins in her small hand. "But I never, ever stopped loving you. I'm not angry anymore. You did exactly what I would have expected you to do. You took care of your mom the way you'd been taking care of her since you were a kid. You tried to make the best of a bad situation. You've been doing that since you were a kid, too. You said you don't expect forgiveness. There's nothing to forgive, Summer. There's only love. I love you."

And then she was in his arms. And he was kissing her. Her lips, salty from her tears, had never been sweeter. "I love you, too," she said, her mouth close to his ear. "I always have. I always will."

"Then let's go get your daughter," he said, praying harder than he'd ever prayed before that Adie was safe.

WHAT THEY HADN'T been able to tell from the online picture was that the house was not visible from the road. There was a narrow blacktop lane, a mailbox with the address stenciled on in gold letters, with an attached black plastic sleeve designed to hold a newspaper. Somebody had delivered the *St. Louis Post-Dispatch* that morning but nobody had picked it up yet. There was no security gate or visible security cameras. Pitard had kids. That would have likely been a big hassle with a family that was always coming and going.

"We walk in," he said.

He parked the car off to the side of the road, near where the yard ended and the trees started. Then they walked up the hill, staying very close to the tree line. When they crested the hill, they could see the house.

It looked very much the same as the online photo except that, today, there was a light green Maxima in the driveway.

Exactly like the light green Maxima that had got gas courtesy of the men who had abducted Adie.

He held up a hand, stopping Summer. Then he pulled out his cell phone and pushed the button that he'd entered into his phone while they'd been eating BLTs in the kitchen.

"Dawson Roy," the man answered.

Chase's partner with the St. Louis police department. Chase had made contact with him at Bray's request, put him on notice that they might need some police assistance quickly.

"Dawson, this is Bray Hollister. I'm at 8713 Bluehound Road in Ravesville. I need immediate backup."

"My pleasure, Bray," Dawson said. "My friends in the state police are ready to rock and roll."

Bray hung up. "I think it's always a good idea to have a backup plan."

"Thank you," she whispered.

The man inside would most certainly be armed. Bray had his own gun in his hand. But Summer was not armed. Vulnerable.

"You won't consider staying here," he said, as they stopped forty feet from the house.

"No," she said. "Adie has only seen you twice. She'll be frightened. She needs to know I'm here."

"Just be careful," he said. "Whoever is here is probably going to shoot first and ask questions later." Damn, this sucked. They'd just found each other after all these years and now there was danger that could rip them apart.

He just couldn't let that happen.

"We're going to try to enter through the garage and

get inside the house that way. People forget to lock their interior door all the time," he said.

But that was going to be harder than he'd hoped when he tried the side door of the garage and found it locked. "We're going in through there," he said, pointing at the window next to the door. He was ready to break it with his flashlight when he realized that there was just a little gap between the window and the frame. It was one of those types that cranked out, and when somebody had closed it, they hadn't latched it from the inside. If he could get his fingers inside and pull it open, it might just work.

"Let me," Summer said, seeing what he'd seen. "My fingers are smaller." They were, and it took her just seconds to open the window.

He listened for an alarm but didn't hear anything. "Let me go first," he said. He got in and turned to help her. Once she was inside, he pointed at the two empty spaces in the cold garage. "I bet a Lexus and a Camaro go there." There was a workbench with some tools. He picked up a heavy wrench and handed it to Summer. "You played softball in high school. I know you've got a hell of a swing." Then he saw the roll of duct tape and put it in his coat pocket.

There was the door that led to the house. "If they're here, I'm betting they're in the basement," he said.

She pulled at his sleeve. "Please try not to shoot anyone. I don't want Adie to see that."

She was killing him here. "I'll do my best." He opened the door, edged around the first corner. Motioned for Summer to follow. It was the kitchen. A sterile-looking room, done in black and white with all stainless-steel appliances. There wasn't even a dirty dish on the counter. It didn't look as if anyone even lived in the house. From there, they searched the rest of the first floor. There was a formal living room, a dining room, a bathroom and a more casual family room. In this room, there was an open staircase that led to the basement.

He listened. And thought maybe he could hear a television. Yep. Somebody was watching the Thanksgiving Day parade.

He took the first four steps. It was a finished basement, probably where the kids hung out.

But not today.

Two more steps. He could see the flat-screen television now. It was on the far wall.

Two more steps. He could see almost the whole room. There were couches and chairs and…there he was. The guy watching the parade. He had a bag of chips on his lap, a beer in his hand and a Glock 27 on the table next to him.

Bray took the remaining four steps, walked up behind the guy and put his gun to his temple. "Happy Thanksgiving," Bray said. "Don't move."

The guy's leg twitched but that was it. Bray motioned for Summer to get the duct tape from his pocket.

He handed her the gun. "Pull the trigger if he moves," he said, loud enough for the man to hear. He got in front of the man, tossed the chips aside and set the bottle of beer on the table. Then he quickly tied the man's wrists together, then his ankles. He took his gun back from Summer.

"Know him?" Bray asked.

Summer shook her head. She was staring at the two doors. One right next to the other. Both shut.

Bray took one last look at the guy. He was probably somewhere near the bottom of the pecking order. Low enough that he got to do guard duty on Thanksgiving Day. Bray took the heel of his palm and knocked it against the man's forehead. His head snapped back. "You better hope that that little girl is okay," he said.

Then he opened the first door. Gary Blake's arms were stretched over his head, his wrists tied to the bed. He wore his pants and a white T-shirt. His eyes were closed. The man's face was barely recognizable. He'd been beaten badly and there was lots of blood on his shirt. Bray heard Summer gasp.

Gary opened the one eye that he could. Saw Summer. "Adie," he croaked.

"We'll get you help," Bray said. "Hang on."

Summer was already moving toward the other door. She opened it before he could get to her. He heard another gasp.

Chapter Twenty-Three

Thursday, 10:05 a.m.

Summer saw her little angel sitting on the bed, propped up against a pillow, a book in her lap. She was wearing the same clothes that she'd had on at the mall.

"Mama," she said. "I missed you."

Summer stumbled into the room and wrapped her arms around her child. She pulled her tight.

"Daddy's hurt," Adie said.

"I know, honey," Summer said. "We're going to help him. Don't you worry about anything."

In the background, she could hear Bray talking. He was on his phone.

"Are you hurt? Did they hurt you?" she forced herself to ask. She ran her hands down her little girl's arms, her legs. Cupped her sweet face in her hands.

"No. But I'm hungry," Adie said. "They said I couldn't see Daddy again until breakfast. Is it time for breakfast?" she asked, looking up at the ground-level window and seeing the light.

"It is, yes. And I'm going to make you the best breakfast ever," Summer said, sniffing her tears back. "You can wear your new shoes." She would not cry and scare her child any more than the poor little girl had been scared. "And you can see your dad in just a little while."

Bray stepped forward. "Let's get the two of you out of here. I just talked to Dawson again. There's an ambulance on the way."

"I need to talk to Gary," Summer said. "Can you stay here with Adie?" Thus far the little girl did not seem overly traumatized by what had happened to her father and to herself, but Summer definitely didn't want her seeing Gary in that condition.

"Make it fast," Bray said. "Nalana is on her way to get you and Adie out of here." He turned toward Adie. "Can you show me the pictures in your book, Adie?"

Summer slipped out of the room. Bray had cut the rope that had tied Gary to the bed and Gary was awkwardly rubbing his shoulders. "I'm sorry this happened to you," she said.

"How's Adie?" he asked quickly.

"I think she's okay."

Gary closed his one eye and sighed. He looked like a small, deflated man.

"They said they were going to kill both of us when they got back if I didn't tell them what they wanted to know."

"Why the hell wouldn't you just tell them, Gary? How could you put your daughter through this?"

Again, he opened the one eye. "You must really think I'm a son of a bitch," he said, his tone raspy. "I would have done anything I could have to save Adie, to protect her."

"Then I don't understand."

"I couldn't tell them what they wanted to know because I didn't know the damn answer."

"I don't understand."

"It's complicated."

"I think I deserve to know," she said.

He sighed. "You know some of it. It started with Brian Laffley."

"I know my mother didn't kill him."

"How…how long have you known that?"

"For about an hour," she said.

He shook his head. "Well, then, I wish I'd had the opportunity to tell you myself. You know, a man has a lot of time to think when he's waiting for somebody to come back and kill him, and I'd made the decision that if Adie and I did manage to escape, I was going to tell you the truth."

Oddly enough, she believed him. "Did you kill Laffley?"

"Of course not," he said. "For God's sake, Summer, what I did was wrong. I should never have pretended that your mother hit him. I should never have coerced you into marrying me. But I'm not a killer."

"What happened?"

"I knew Laffley. He'd been in town for a few weeks, living at that run-down hotel at the edge of Ravesville. I thought he was a bum. I'd encountered him a couple times and he always smelled like alcohol. I was working nights then. I took a stroll through the park and found him. He'd been shot. I was just about to call it in when I got a radio call about a vehicle parked on the street. Based on the description, I knew it was your mom's car. I put two and two together and I guess I came up with five."

"Why?" she asked. "I just want to know why."

"Hell, Summer, I don't know. I'd been asking you out for months and you would never say yes. You were the prettiest, nicest girl in Ravesville and I…I was just Gary Blake. I wanted what I couldn't have and I found a way."

"Brian Laffley's body surfaced about two years ago and then disappeared from the morgue. Did you do that, too?"

He shook his head. "I knew the body had been found. And I knew the coroner was looking at it. I didn't realize it was missing until I heard that everybody at the funeral home was getting questioned. I was dating Maggie Reynolds."

"How...? Never mind." She had forgotten that Maggie had taken a job as a secretary at the funeral home after she left the library.

"You know, she was the one who took the call from the coroner's office. The instructions were to pick up the body and dispose of it immediately. But everybody at the coroner's office was denying that they made the call. Maggie was really upset about it. Besides the guy who found the body, there were only two people who knew about it. Me and Chief Poole. I didn't make the call. It had to be him. The only reason the chief would have had to get rid of Laffley's body was if he was responsible for killing the man. I think he panicked."

"But Laffley died years before Chief Poole came to town."

"I know. I would never have connected it if he hadn't made the call. Poole was a grunt on the St. Louis police force at the time of Laffley's death. But I think even then he had business dealings in Ravesville. Bad business. Probably something that involved Pitard and Pataneros, who were living here. Not sure what it was, but something bad enough that he got crosswise with a federal agent."

"You never told Poole what you knew?" Summer asked.

"Nope. But things were starting to make sense. You see, I'd stumbled across a pretty big drug drop and had arrested a guy. But then suddenly, the evidence was missing and there was no case. I pretended that I didn't care. Sometimes," he said, looking a little ashamed, "it helps to have a reputation as a lazy cop."

He sat up on the bed, holding his ribs. "I put a tracking

device on Poole's car. Everywhere he went, I knew about it. It didn't take me long to figure out his favorite places or the schedule for deliveries. I'd be waiting there before he showed up. Poole wasn't at the bottom of the food chain, handing off drugs to the end user. He was higher up, a firmly entrenched middleman."

"You should have reported him," she said.

He grimaced. "I intended to. But... I wanted him to sweat first. He never should have had that job. It should have been mine. I started sending him anonymous letters, letting him know that someone knew."

She could hear the sounds of approaching sirens. Bray had no doubt let them know that he had the bad guy subdued and there was no need to come quietly. In just minutes, Gary would be taken away.

"The people who did this to you. Were they acting on Poole's orders?"

"No. Poole worked for them, not the other way around."

"That makes no sense."

Gary moved and grimaced. "Damn. I think they broke a couple of my ribs."

She did not have it in her to feel sorry about that.

"I think Poole figured it out," Gary said. "He told his friends who were also his bosses that I knew and that I was going to go to the authorities. He also told them that I'd stolen a whole lot of money from him, money that Poole owed to them. That's what they wanted from me. Money. And I kept telling them that Poole had it, that he was the one who was trying to screw us all. But they just kept talking with their fists. I got to the point where I started to not care if they killed me." He looked up. "But when they showed up with Adie and said that they would kill us both if I didn't tell them where the money was, I...I couldn't believe it. I love that little girl. You know I do."

She heard the sound of a door opening, footsteps up above, then on the stairs. "I know you do, Gary. And for what it's worth, I'm glad you're okay. But if you ever, ever do anything like this again, that puts my children in danger, I'm going to kill you myself."

Then she walked out of the room, ready for the rest of her life.

Epilogue

Thursday, 6:00 p.m.

The Hollister house hadn't had this much activity for some time. His mother would have been delighted to see her old dining room table laden with food and the chairs full of family. Chase stood, ready to carve the turkey. Raney sat next to him. Then Cal, Nalana, Lloyd Doogan and Flora Wright. Bray took the far end and to his left was Summer, Adie, Keagan, Trish and Milo.

Family. Friends. Joy.

Not for everyone. And rightly so. The Pataneros brothers were in custody, along with Pitard and the man at his house. Poole, too. It would take a while to sort out, but Bray was confident that for the foreseeable future, their holiday meals were going to be served in a prison cafeteria.

Summer's ex was in the hospital and then would face his own set of legal challenges for what he'd done to Laffley's body. Suffice it to say, he'd never work as a cop again.

Bray reached for Summer's hand. This afternoon, he'd asked her to marry him, and without one moment of hesitation, she'd said yes. They'd talked to the kids together and Adie had been delighted that Bray-Neigh was sticking around, and Keagan, well, he'd mumbled "Congratulations" and offered Bray a seat on the couch so he could watch some football.

He rubbed his thumb across Summer's palm. "I love you," he whispered.

"I've loved you forever," she whispered back, her pretty eyes shining.

And he knew that to be true.

* * * * *

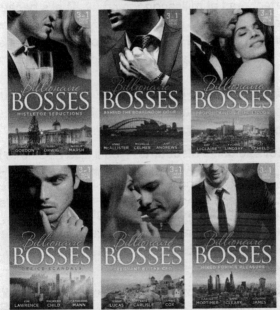

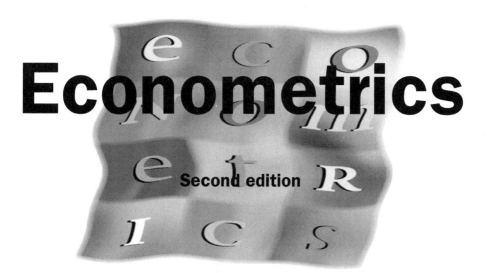

Econometrics

Second edition

The Late Jon Stewart

University of Manchester

and

Preparation for publication and additional material for second edition

Len Gill

University of Manchester

FINANCIAL TIMES

Prentice Hall

An imprint of **Pearson Education**

Harlow, England · London · New York · Reading, Massachusetts · San Francisco
Toronto · Don Mills, Ontario · Sydney · Tokyo · Singapore · Hong Kong · Seoul
Taipei · Cape Town · Madrid · Mexico City · Amsterdam · Munich · Paris · Milan

First published 1991
Second edition published 1998 by
Prentice Hall Europe
Pearson Education Limited
Edinburgh Gate
Harlow
Essex CM20 2JE
England

and Associated Companies throughout the world

Visit us on the World Wide Web at:
http://www.pearsoneduc.com

Typeset in Times 10/12pt
by the Alden Group, Oxford

Printed and bound in Great Britain by Biddles Ltd, *www.biddles.co.uk*

Library of Congress Cataloging-in-Publication Data

Available from the publisher

British Library Cataloguing-in-Publication Data

A catalogue record for this book is available from
the British Library

ISBN 0-13-589474-3

10 9 8 7 6 5 4 3 2

04 03 02 01 00

Contents

Preface to first edition

When I set out to write this book, my objective was to provide an up-to-date treatment of core econometric theory, at a technical level which corresponds to the main econometrics course unit in a typical undergraduate programme, and which would also serve for qualifying examinations at postgraduate level. Students taking such courses have varying patterns of prior training, but some exposure to basic statistics, some knowledge of economics and a passing acquaintance with matrix methods are fundamental requirements.

In compiling the material, I have discarded or compressed some of the less widely used topics that have traditionally been included in econometrics texts, and I have changed the emphasis at various points, in recognition of the tension that exists between theory and practice. To illustrate the problems that arise in practical application, a number of worked examples are included, all based on live data. Because no attempt is made to sanitise the worked examples, students begin to understand that conclusions based on simple models have to be treated with caution, and that the idealised representations suggested by econometric theory do not always provide a complete answer when trying to tease convincing explanations of economic behaviour from imperfect data.

The book is structured so that each chapter has a well-defined purpose. Chapter 1 provides an overview, intended to demarcate a common starting line. Chapter 2 reviews basic regression theory in some detail, covering both mathematical and statistical foundations, but leaving the student with a rather limited practical toolkit. To offset this, the final section in Chapter 2 provides initial estimates for some very simple models, using data sets that are listed fully at the end of Chapter 1. Chapter 3 continues with a more operationally oriented treatment of classical regression topics, again illustrated by worked examples. A key feature of this chapter is a full discussion of the logic of variable addition tests; this provides a firm basis for the subsequent introduction of a more elaborate set of test procedures that can be expressed in variable addition form.

Chapter 4 has a different emphasis in that it is primarily concerned with theoretical tools rather than practical application. It is here that the fundamentals of large sample theory, maximum likelihood and instrumental variable estimation are first introduced. At this stage, instrumental variable estimation is seen as a method for dealing with potentially endogenous regressors, without assuming full specification of some wider model.

Chapter 5 deals with disturbance problems, both from the traditional viewpoint of alternative patterns of disturbance behaviour and from the perspective of misspecification in the systematic part of a model. Tests for heteroscedasticity and serial correlation are again illustrated by worked examples.

Chapter 6 introduces lags and dynamic models, and concludes with a brief introduction to the 'new' econometrics of unit roots and cointegration. This material is linked into Chapter 7, which offers a more detailed discussion of ARIMA processes and the methods of univariate time series modelling.

Chapter 8 is concerned with simultaneous equation models. Although the basic ideas are developed in the context of models which are linear in endogenous variables, there is also explicit recognition of the fact that few models actually satisfy this constraint. Finally, Chapter 9 offers some extensions of earlier material, including an introduction to limited dependent variable models, a brief review of methodological issues, and some concluding remarks on practical application.

Given a desire to limit the overall size of the book, there will inevitably be favourite topics that I have omitted, but I feel that what is offered makes for a reasonably coherent one-year course. Almost all of the material has been tested in the classroom, and I have had useful comments from both students and their teachers. I have particular reason to be grateful to my colleagues Martyn Andrews, Robin Bladen-Hovell, Len Gill and Denise Osborn, and to two anonymous referees. Of course, none of these individuals bear responsibility for the use that I have made of their suggestions and help. Last, but not least, I owe thanks to my family; they always know when I am in writing mode, but usually have the good sense to stay out of the way.

Jon Stewart

Preface to second edition

My own intention in revising Jon Stewart's *Econometrics* for a second edition was to create a personal memorial to my colleague and friend Jon Stewart, who died in 1993. The object of the revision was to increase the emphasis in the text on unit roots and cointegration, in line with the popularity of these topics in the literature, but without compromising the spirit of the first edition. This involved a break up of the existing time series material and its reorganisation into three new chapters, Chapters 6, 7 and 9, along with a considerable amount of new material.

The subject of unit roots and cointegration is a difficult one and I have tried to make enough of the theory accessible without compromising the insights to be gained from that theory. I took a conscious decision to go beyond cointegration in single equations, resulting in a new chapter on vector autoregressive models and system-wide cointegration in these models. Inevitably this material is relatively difficult, and I have again tried to simplify the presentation to focus on the essential points. I regard the wide availability of software packages offering system cointegration computations as a partial justification for covering this material.

Other chapters have been revised to reflect the needs of this new material. For example, issues of serial correlation now appear first in Chapter 6. There is more material on multivariate regression models and seemingly unrelated regressions, as preparation for system cointegration, and this has been inserted at the beginning of Chapter 8. The discussion of identification in that chapter has also been extended a little.

In a revision such as this, one cannot change the intention of the original book too much, and in particular, one cannot dramatically increase the length of the text. As a result, some readers' favourite topics will still have been omitted in the revision; this seems inevitable.

In using the new edition as a course text, one could construct two styles of course for the original audience of advanced undergraduate or introductory postgraduate students. One is a relatively basic introduction, using selections of material that an instructor feels appropriate for the level of the students. This would use Chapters

1–3, Chapter 4 for large sample theory, Chapter 5 for some cross-sectional issues, Chapters 6 and 7 for dynamic models and inference, and Chapter 8 for multiple equation and simultaneous equations models. In this type of course, many theoretical details can be omitted, and practical work with the example data sets substituted. Another possibility is a course on topics in time series, stressing theoretical details or applications, according to the taste of the instructor and the amount of time available. This would use Chapters 6 and 7, part of Chapter 8, and Chapter 9. A more advanced version of such a course would pay more attention to the theoretical details than applications.

Another aspect of the revision is the updating of the data sets for the examples. In the process, several more data sets have been added, some derived from the UK *Office of National Statistics* data bank, whilst others are well known and popular in the literature. The data sets themselves are available on the internet from the site

http://les.man.ac.uk/~msrbslg/

Brief descriptions of the series and their sources are also available there. It is perhaps worth warning users of these data sets that it is not possible to guarantee that they will get the same numerical results as presented in the text. There are too many variable factors at work – different computers, software, methodologies, as well as inherent sensitivities in the data sets themselves. One should, however, get results that are 'near'!

Finally, I want to thank my colleagues Ericq Horler and Denise Osborn for valiantly wading through an assortment of drafts and providing suggestions for improvement: they are, of course, not responsible for defects of the text.

Len Gill

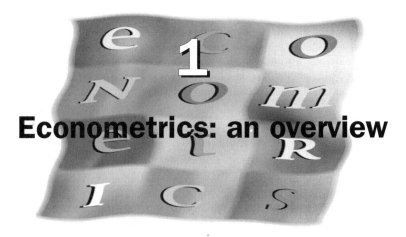

1
Econometrics: an overview

1.1 / Introduction

An exercise in the application of econometric methods involves the following elements:

(a) formulating an *economic model* appropriate to the questions to be answered;

(b) reviewing the available *statistical models* and the assumptions underlying these models, and selecting the form most suitable for the problem to hand;

(c) obtaining appropriate *data*, properly defined and matching the concepts of the economic model;

(d) finding suitable *computer software* to enable the calculations necessary for estimation and testing of the model to be carried out.

Econometric theory tends to focus on item (b), but successful application requires attention to all four aspects of the exercise. Of course, econometric methods are not developed in a vacuum. The needs of economic theory have always had a strong influence on the forms of model in which the econometrician is interested, the nature (and limitations) of data have had a powerful influence on the evolution of a methodology within which the formal procedures of econometrics can be employed, and the ability to use computers to implement the techniques developed by the econometric theorist has been of paramount importance in ensuring the wide-spread acceptance of econometrics as an indispensable part of the economist's toolkit.

The ultimate objective of the econometric exercise is a version of the chosen economic model in which unknown parameters have been replaced by estimates, and in which the underlying structure has been exhaustively tested against observed data. This is what is meant by an *econometric* model, as distinct from an economic model, which might be a purely theoretical construction.

The very general description given here is something of a simplification, because models are built for a purpose, and that purpose will itself have an impact on the

1

way in which the model is designed. It is not realistic to separate 'construction' and 'use' as totally distinct stages in the process, since the use of a model invariably suggests modifications that can be made and problems that require corrective action.

Suppose, for example, that we have constructed a model using macroeconomic time series data, by which we mean observations on a set of macroeconomic variables at regularly spaced points in time. Such a model might be used for counterfactual simulation of the recent past – asking what would have happened had the values of certain key variables been changed. Alternatively, the model might be used for forecasting or future simulation. Forecasting is usually taken to imply an attempt to specify a set of values that the forecaster believes is the most likely set of values to hold at some future date. Future simulation may represent a situation that the investigator does not expect to actually occur. Instead, it is a 'what if' exercise, looking at what would, or might, happen if certain key variables are changed from their 'most likely' values. Each of these exercises will reveal modifications that are needed, and it is very important to realise that econometric models are never fixed, unchanging entities, but, rather, the product of continuous experimentation and development.

Any econometric model or, for that matter, any economic model, will seek to explain the behaviour of at least one economic variable, usually by reference to the behaviour of other economic variables. Those variables that are 'explained' by the model are described as *endogenous* variables. Variables whose values are taken as given, rather than explained, are *exogenous* variables. Given the complexity and degree of interdependence in real economic systems, few variables are truly exogenous and it is important to understand the difference between what is taken to be the case for the purposes of constructing a model, and what is true in an absolute sense. Economics abounds with examples of partial analysis, in which attention is focused on one particular aspect of a system, assuming everything else to be unchanged. So there is nothing unusual in treating some variables as exogenous, despite knowing that many of the variables in question would be influenced by various kinds of feedback, were we to investigate a complete system.

1.2 / Types of model

Accepting that the distinction between endogenous and exogenous variables is made in the context of a particular model, we may now construct a simple taxonomy of model types. Consider two time periods, $t - 1$ and t, and let exogenous variables be represented by the letter X and endogenous variables be represented by the letter Y. From the econometrician's viewpoint, there are important differences between model types, depending on exactly how the exogenous variables are linked to the endogenous variables, and on whether there is also interaction between individual endogenous variables.

If there is only one endogenous variable, the model will consist of a single equation in that variable and this corresponds to a *single equation* model. In the simplest case, it is assumed that the behaviour of a single endogenous variable, Y, can be represented as a linear function of a single exogenous variable, X. As we shall see shortly, such relationships are seldom exact, but for the moment this problem is ignored. Hence the simplest form of model is

$$Y_t = \alpha + \beta X_t; \ t = 1, \dots, n. \tag{1.1}$$

In (1.1), the parameter β measures the effect on Y of a unit change in X. The parameter α can be interpreted as the value of Y when $X = 0$, though one has to be careful about taking this interpretation too literally in practice. Note that α is usually described as the *intercept*, and β as the *slope*.

Since the purpose of the model is to represent the generation of some particular set of observations on the endogenous variable, the statement of the model refers explicitly to individual observations, identified by the index $t = 1, \dots, n$. Often, these are observations through time, though they could equally well be based on a cross-section, for example of households or firms, at a single point in time.

Lags and dynamics

If the model is based on time series data, then (1.1) corresponds to a *static* model: Y in the current period depends on X in the current period, there are no linkages from one time period to the next, and there is no delay in the response of Y to a change in X.

If Y reacts to X with a delay, the model is said to involve *lags*. In the equation

$$Y_t = \alpha + \beta X_{t-1}; \ t = 1, \dots, n, \tag{1.2}$$

Y is determined by the value of X in the previous period, so Y reacts to changes in X only after a one-period delay. Since (1.2) is not static, it must be taken as an example of a *dynamic* model, although from the econometricians's point of view, there is not all that much difference between the properties of a model based on (1.1) and a model based on (1.2).

A more interesting dynamic formulation arises when there is a lagged *endogenous* variable on the right-hand side. A simple example is

$$Y_t = \alpha + \beta Y_{t-1}; \ t = 1, \dots, n. \tag{1.3}$$

Given a starting value for Y, for period $t = 0$, and values for α and β, equation (1.3) could generate a complete time path for the endogenous variable, that is, a complete set of values $Y_t; \ t = 1, \dots, n$. It is this type of process, feeding forward endogenous variable values from one period to the next, that corresponds most closely to what is usually meant by a study of economic dynamics. However, in the literature of econometrics, it is usual to take the term dynamic to mean 'not static', so the class of dynamic models must include any case in which either a lagged endogenous variable or a lagged exogenous variable is present.

Returning now to the static model, notice that equation (1.1) is a special case. A more general version is

$$Y_t = \beta_1 + \beta_2 X_{2t} + \dots + \beta_j X_{jt} + \dots + \beta_k X_{kt}; \ t = 1, \dots, n. \tag{1.4}$$

In equation (1.4), we have introduced k distinct exogenous variables, $X_1, X_2, \ldots, X_j, \ldots, X_k$, though one of these is a 'variable' that does not actually vary at all; there are considerable advantages in using β_1 to denote the intercept term, and treating β_1 as though it were associated with a variable X_1, which always takes the value $X_1 = 1$. Hence (1.4) involves $k - 1$ 'genuine' X variables, $X_2, \ldots, X_k$, and a further implicit 'variable', X_1, which is always equal to 1. For the genuine variables, a typical parameter β_j now measures the effect on Y of a unit change in X_j, *with all other exogenous variables held constant*.

The notation used in equation (1.4) suggests that there are no lags, but for the purposes of describing operations to be performed on the model, where what matters is simply the number of variables on the right-hand side, the examples

$$Y_t = \beta_1 + \beta_2 X_{2t} + \beta_3 X_{3t}; \ t = 1, \ldots, n \tag{1.5}$$

and

$$Y_t = \beta_1 + \beta_2 X_{2t} + \beta_3 Y_{t-1}; \ t = 1, \ldots, n \tag{1.6}$$

are essentially similar. However, the two cases will typically lead to models with different statistical properties, and for the purposes of statistical analysis, we may well end up by treating the two cases rather differently.

Multiple equation models and simultaneity

Equations (1.3) and (1.6) share the characteristic of having an endogenous variable on the right-hand side, though in both cases the endogenous variable is lagged. A further possibility is that the equation has one endogenous variable on the left (in common with all models considered so far), but also has another endogenous variable on the right. An example is

$$Y_{1t} = \beta_1 + \beta_2 X_{2t} + \beta_3 Y_{2t}; \ t = 1, \ldots, n, \tag{1.7}$$

where Y_1 and Y_2 are both endogenous and X_2 is exogenous. If Y_2 is endogenous, there should logically be a second equation which explains how Y_2 is generated. If the second equation is made explicit, we would have a *multiple equation* model. This seems fairly straightforward, but there are some complications. Suppose that the second equation is written as

$$Y_{2t} = \gamma_1 + \gamma_2 X_{3t} + \gamma_3 X_{4t}; \ t = 1, \ldots, n. \tag{1.8}$$

In this case the logic of the model is that Y_2 is determined in equation (1.8) from given values of two additional exogenous variables, X_3 and X_4. The value obtained for Y_2 is then fed into (1.7), in which Y_2 and X_2 are used to determine Y_1. Because there is a definite order in which the endogenous variable values are determined, (1.7) and (1.8) form what is known as a *recursive* model. An alternative possibility is that the second equation has Y_1 on the right-hand side, for example

$$Y_{2t} = \gamma_1 + \gamma_2 X_{3t} + \gamma_3 Y_{1t}; \ t = 1, \ldots, n. \tag{1.9}$$

It would now be quite wrong to suggest that (1.9) 'explains' the behaviour of Y_2 whilst (1.7) 'explains' the behaviour of Y_1; the mathematical logic would be that both equations together determine Y_1 and Y_2, for given values of X_2 and X_3. In this case there is no definite order in which Y_1 and Y_2 are calculated and (1.7) and (1.9) together form a *simultaneous equation* model. An alternative description is that there is *simultaneity* in the equation system.

It is sometimes convenient to describe the left-hand side variable in an equation as *dependent* and the right-hand side variables as *explanatory*. This is reasonable when all right-hand side variables are exogenous, since exogenous variables are supposed to explain the behaviour of endogenous variables. It is certainly not accurate to use this description in a simultaneous equation model, because variables on the right-hand side may be endogenous, which means that their behaviour is explained by the model. Such variables are definitely not 'explanatory'.

As we shall discover in due course, there are differences in estimation procedures appropriate to static and dynamic models, single and multiple equation models, and models involving simultaneity. Initially, we shall focus attention on single equation static models. This is not because the static case is particularly realistic; indeed, there are not very many examples that can be adequately represented within such a framework. The reason for choosing to start in this way is that many basic ideas can be developed in the context of the static single equation model, and such ideas do often carry over, albeit with some modification, to more complex cases.

Nonlinearity and choice of functional form

A final comment concerns linearity in the examples considered so far. In each case, the equation has been linear in parameters. To emphasise the point, note that

$$Y_t = \beta_1 + \beta_2 X_{2t} + \beta_3 X_{3t}; \ t = 1, \ldots, n$$

is linear in parameters, whereas

$$Y_t = \beta_1 + \beta_2 X_{2t} + \beta_2^2 X_{3t}; \ t = 1, \ldots, n$$

is not, since the parameter β_2 enters both as β_2 and as β_2^2. It is not necessary at this stage that equations be linear in the economic variables as originally observed. For example, the Cobb–Douglas production function is

$$Q_t = aL_t^b K_t^c,$$

where Q is output, L is labour services and K is capital services, with a, b and c as parameters. Taking (natural) logarithms on both sides of the equation, we obtain

$$\ln(Q_t) = \ln(aL_t^b K_t^c) = \ln(a) + \ln(L_t^b) + \ln(K_t^c)$$
$$= \ln(a) + b\ln(L_t) + c\ln(K_t). \tag{1.10}$$

If Y is set equal to $\ln(Q)$, $X_2 = \ln(L)$, $X_3 = \ln(K)$, $\beta_1 = \ln(a)$, $\beta_2 = b$ and $\beta_3 = c$, (1.10) can be written in the standard form for an equation that is linear in parameters:

$$Y_t = \beta_1 + \beta_2 X_{2t} + \beta_3 X_{3t}. \tag{1.11}$$

Although this *is not* linear in economic variables as originally observed, it *is* linear in parameters and in the new variables which are formed as simple transformations of the original variables.

It is worth noting that when the log-linear form is used, as in (1.10), the parameters of the standard form (1.11) are elasticities. In terms of partial derivatives

$$\beta_2 = b = \partial \ln(Q)/\partial \ln(L) = (\partial Q/\partial L) \cdot (L/Q).$$

This corresponds to the definition of the partial elasticity of Q with respect to L. The assumption that parameters are constant for $t = 1, \ldots, n$ implies that elasticities are constant in the log-linear form, whereas if we had used a linear production function

$$Q_t = \beta_1 + \beta_2 L_t + \beta_3 K_t,$$

then $\beta_2 = \partial Q/\partial L$, and it would be the slope or response coefficients that would be constant, not the elasticities.

The example above illustrates the importance of selecting and understanding the implications of the *functional form* for a model. In many cases, it is possible to transform a nonlinear relationship between economic variables into a model which is linear in parameters, though this cannot always be done. If there is a good reason for selecting a functional form that cannot be transformed in this way, then nonlinear estimation methods are used. A specification should not be forced into a particular form simply to avoid the use of nonlinear methods.

1.3 / Random disturbances

The model types discussed in the preceding section represent exact, deterministic relationships between economic variables. With the exception of technical identities, such as those based on a national accounting system, it is seldom if ever the case that observed relationships are of this kind. Thus, whilst it is true that gross domestic product (GDP) at market prices is the sum of consumers' expenditure, gross investment, government expenditure, exports and stockbuilding, less imports, it is not true that real consumers' expenditure is an exact function of real personal disposable income, or that household expenditure on a particular commodity is an exact function of disposable income and relative prices.

What is missing from the models of the preceding section is an explicit recognition of the inexact nature of the relationships that we wish to represent. This omission is corrected by adding a set of random *disturbances* to each equation. For example, the single equation static model becomes

$$Y_t = \beta_1 + \beta_2 X_{2t} + \ldots + \beta_j X_{jt} + \ldots + \beta_k X_{kt} + u_t; \quad t = 1, \ldots, n. \tag{1.12}$$

Here u_t is used to denote a typical disturbance term.

A disturbance is not simply an error. It is assumed that some effort has gone into specifying the relationship between Y and $X_1, X_2, \ldots, X_k$: in particular, it is assumed that both the list of variables and the functional form have been carefully selected, using economic theory and any previously accumulated empirical evidence to justify the choices made. If this is the case, disturbances represent an inherently unpredictable component of the behaviour of Y, over and above that part of Y that is explained by the behaviour of the X variables. Somewhat crudely, the main part of the model represents 'knowledge', whilst the disturbances represent 'ignorance'. It follows that the obvious way to represent the behaviour of disturbances is to use the concepts of probability and random variables.

Probability model for disturbances

The essence of a probability model is that one cannot predict the value that a random variable will take, even though it may be possible to make statements about the probability of a value falling within a given range. Since disturbances are assumed to be inherently unpredictable, they are treated as random variables. In fact, each disturbance is treated as a distinct random variable. It is vitally important to understand the implications of this idea.

Using the single equation model as an example, we have

$$Y_t = \beta_1 + \beta_2 X_{2t} + \ldots + \beta_j X_{jt} + \ldots + \beta_k X_{kt} + u_t; \ t = 1, \ldots, n.$$

The logic of the model is that observed Y_t values are not exactly equal to the values suggested by the underlying linear function of the X variables, because disturbances u_t typically take nonzero values. Only one realisation of each u_t is deemed to actually occur, though there is a probability distribution for each u_t that describes all the other possible values that *might* have occurred, together with the associated probabilities. It follows from this that only one value is observed for each Y_t, although, according to the model, there are many other values that might have occurred.

Assumptions concerning the random disturbances

To make progress, it is necessary to be rather more specific as to the properties of the disturbance distributions. In the simplest case, the following additional assumptions are made:

$$E(u_t) = 0; \ t = 1, \ldots, n \tag{1.13}$$

$$\text{var}(u_t) = \sigma^2; \ t = 1, \ldots, n \tag{1.14}$$

$$\text{cov}(u_t, u_s) = 0; \ s \neq t; \ s, t = 1, \ldots, n. \tag{1.15}$$

These state that each disturbance has a zero mean, that the variance of each distinct disturbance takes the same value σ^2, and that the covariance between all distinct pairs is zero. An alternative, slightly stronger, version of (1.15) is the assumption of independence between all distinct pairs u_s, u_t.

According to assumption (1.13), there is no *systematic* tendency for disturbances to be positive rather than negative, or vice versa, so there is no systematic tendency for observed Y_t values to be either greater or less than the values suggested by the underlying linear function of X variables. Assuming that the X variables are exogenous, and are treated as nonrandom fixed quantities, the *expected* value of Y_t is equal to the underlying linear function, that is,

$$E(Y_t) = \beta_1 + \beta_2 X_{2t} + \ldots + \beta_j X_{jt} + \ldots + \beta_k X_{kt}; \ t = 1, \ldots, n.$$

Observed Y_t values are greater or less than the corresponding expected values because the realisations of u_t; $t = 1, \ldots, n$ are greater or less than zero. The discrepancies between observed and expected Y values are explained in terms of random variation, and not in terms of any systematic effect.

Now consider the variance of each disturbance. Assumption (1.14) suggests that each disturbance has the same variance σ^2, which implies that the extent of random variation of Y_t around $E(Y_t)$ is the same for each observation. This can be interpreted as suggesting that each observation Y_t contains the same amount of information about the underlying linear relationship, being no more subject to uncertainty or 'noise' than other observations. Sometimes (1.14) is thought to be too restrictive and it may then be necessary to let the disturbance variance change between observations, giving the general specification

$$\text{var}(u_t) = \sigma_t^2; \ t = 1, \ldots, n.$$

This condition is known as *heteroscedasticity*. In fact, any disturbance 'problem', such as heteroscedasticity, can occur for one of two reasons. It may arise with a perfectly adequate specification of the main part of the model, because of some known characteristic of the model or data. It can also occur because the main part of the model is not correctly specified, and behaviour is attributed to disturbances that ought properly to be considered in the deterministic part of the model. The implications of the two sources of disturbance problem are rather different, as we shall discover in due course.

The third assumption made above is that there is no connection between the behaviour of individual disturbances, the sense being that if one did have values for some disturbances, there would be no advantage in terms of predicting the behaviour of other disturbances. Relaxation of this assumption would require some specific hypothesis as to how individual disturbances are related, and this class of alternatives corresponds to what is known as *serial correlation*. In such a case, at least one covariance between distinct disturbances would be nonzero:

$$\text{cov}(u_t, u_s) \neq 0; \text{ for at least one } s \neq t.$$

Again, this may arise with a correctly specified model, but it may also be taken as indicative of the fact that the model is not correctly specified. Econometric theory typically proceeds on the assumption that model specifications are correct, apart from the specific problem currently being considered. In practice, interpreting evidence concerning the breakdown of assumptions is not always as straightforward as the theory may suggest.

So far, it has been assumed that random disturbances are added to a single equation model in which all other terms on the right-hand side are nonrandom. But the addition of disturbances to some of the model types considered in section 1.2 leads to the conclusion that right-hand side variable observations cannot always be treated in this way.

A simple example is provided by equation (1.3). If random disturbances are added to this equation, we have

$$Y_t = \alpha + \beta Y_{t-1} + u_t; \; t = 1, \ldots, n. \tag{1.16}$$

In (1.16), the disturbances u_t; $t = 1, \ldots, n$ may or may not be 'well behaved', but the fact that Y_t depends partly on u_t means that Y_{t-1} is partly determined by u_{t-1}, at least for $t = 2, \ldots, n$. Given that Y_{t-1} has a random component, it is clearly not possible to treat observations on Y_{t-1} as nonrandom quantities.

There are several ways of classifying (1.16). It is certainly dynamic rather than static. In fact, it corresponds to a difference equation, to which random disturbances are added, the implication of which is that Y_{t-1} itself becomes random. An equation of this kind is known as a *stochastic* difference equation, where the word 'stochastic' has the same meaning as 'probabilistic' or 'random'. Remember that in this context, random means 'controlled by the rules of some probability distribution', which typically makes some ranges of value more likely than others.

Equation (1.16) is also a simple example of a stochastic *process*, where the word 'process' carries the connotation of progression through time, or at least implies some definite sequencing of observations. An important characteristic of such a process is that a change in any disturbance, say u_1, may influence not only Y_1, but also all subsequent values Y_2, Y_3, and so on. Hence, in the time series context, a change in any disturbance can in principle change the entire future time path of the dependent variable.

Finally, we have used (1.16) as an example of a single equation model in which at least one right-hand variable is random, or stochastic. Although, initially, we examine the theory of single equation models from the perspective of nonrandom right-hand side variables, it is as well to be aware from the outset that not all models satisfy this particular assumption.

1.4 / The single equation model in matrix form

It is already apparent that a fairly cumbersome system of notation is needed to write down the different forms of model that we wish to use, in a way which is sufficiently general to allow for different numbers of observations and different numbers of variables. Such problems can only increase as we move from static to dynamic models, and from single to multiple equation models. A much more concise system of notation is possible if similar elements are collected together into row vectors, column vectors and matrices.

Matrix methods are used in a number of different ways. Initially, all that we want is a statement language, to enable models to be written in a concise but general form. The statement language can also be used to give formulae for manipulating models in a way which is not dependent on the particular number of variables present in a specific application. But it rapidly becomes apparent that matrix algebra is a powerful tool for derivation and proof, and an investment of time in mastering the basics of the algebra will pay handsome dividends. Appendix A provides a summary of matrix methods at a level sufficient for this text. The purpose of this section is to show how the single equation model is written using matrix and vector notation.

In ordinary (scalar) form, the single equation model is

$$Y_t = \beta_1 + \beta_2 X_{2t} + \ldots + \beta_j X_{jt} + \ldots + \beta_k X_{kt} + u_t; \; t = 1, \ldots, n. \tag{1.17}$$

In matrix form, the model becomes

$$y = X\beta + u, \tag{1.18}$$

where y represents an $(n \times 1)$ vector of observations on the dependent variable, X is an $(n \times k)$ matrix, each column of which contains observations on one of the right-hand side variables, β is a $(k \times 1)$ vector of unknown parameters, and u is an $(n \times 1)$ vector of disturbances. To incorporate an intercept term, the first column of X is set so that each element is equal to 1.

The individual columns of the matrix X can be represented as a set of $(n \times 1)$ vectors

$$X = [x_1 \ldots x_j \ldots x_k].$$

Here x_j is used to denote a typical column. A typical row of X is written as x'_t. If there is potential confusion between the transpose of a column and the notation used for a row, the row is written as x'_t and the transposed column as $(x_j)'$. A typical element of the matrix X (variable j, observation t) is written as X_{jt}. This is the reverse of the usual matrix convention, since here X_{jt} is *column j* and *row t*. The logic is that the partition by variables is the primary partition, with the second subscript acting to identify an individual element in a given column:

$(x_j)_t$ refers to element t of vector x_j

$= $ variable j, observation t

$= $ column j, row t of X

$= X_{jt}$.

If it is necessary to write (1.18) as a set of individual rows, this would be

$$y_t = x'_t \beta + u_t; \; t = 1, \ldots, n. \tag{1.19}$$

Note that element t of the vector y is identical to observation t on variable Y, which was written earlier as Y_t. Hence Y_t and y_t have exactly the same meaning.

To ensure that the reader has fully understood the conventions of the matrix form, y, X, β and u are written out in full below:

$$y = \begin{bmatrix} y_1 \\ y_2 \\ \vdots \\ y_t \\ \vdots \\ y_n \end{bmatrix}, \quad X = \begin{bmatrix} X_{11} & X_{21} & \cdots & X_{j1} & \cdots & X_{k1} \\ X_{12} & X_{22} & \cdots & X_{j2} & \cdots & X_{k2} \\ \vdots & \vdots & & \vdots & & \vdots \\ X_{1t} & X_{2t} & \cdots & X_{jt} & \cdots & X_{kt} \\ \vdots & \vdots & & \vdots & & \vdots \\ X_{1n} & X_{2n} & \cdots & X_{jn} & \cdots & X_{kn} \end{bmatrix}, \quad \beta = \begin{bmatrix} \beta_1 \\ \beta_2 \\ \vdots \\ \beta_j \\ \vdots \\ \beta_k \end{bmatrix}, \quad u = \begin{bmatrix} u_1 \\ u_2 \\ \vdots \\ u_t \\ \vdots \\ u_n \end{bmatrix}.$$

In the statement $y = X\beta + u$, the term $X\beta$ represents a matrix multiplication: the $(n \times k)$ matrix X is multiplied by the $(k \times 1)$ vector β, to give the $(n \times 1)$ product $X\beta$. Element t of the vector $X\beta$ is

$$(X\beta)_t = x_t'\beta = \sum_j X_{jt}\beta_j$$

$$= \beta_1 X_{1t} + \beta_2 X_{2t} + \ldots + \beta_j X_{jt} + \ldots + \beta_k X_{kt}$$

$$= \beta_1 + \beta_2 X_{2t} + \ldots + \beta_j X_{jt} + \ldots + \beta_k X_{kt}; \text{ if } X_{1t} = 1.$$

Turning now to the disturbance properties, assumptions (1.13)–(1.15) can be rewritten in a form suitable for use with the matrix representation (1.18). The assumption of zero mean disturbances is written as

$$E(u) = 0 \tag{1.20}$$

where 0 is a zero vector. The constant variance and zero covariance assumptions are written together as

$$\text{var}(u) = \sigma^2 I \tag{1.21}$$

where I is an $(n \times n)$ identity matrix. Notice that the expectation of a vector is also a vector, whereas the variance of a vector is defined to be a matrix, known as the variance covariance matrix, which has variances on the main diagonal and covariances in the off-diagonal positions. Hence (1.21) states that $\text{var}(u_t) = \sigma^2(1) = \sigma^2$; $t = 1, \ldots, n$ and that $\text{cov}(u_t, u_s) = \sigma^2(0) = 0$; $s \neq t$. Given that $E(u) = 0$, (1.21) can also be written as

$$\text{var}(u) = E[u - E(u)][u - E(u)]' = Euu' = \sigma^2 I.$$

If heteroscedasticity is present, $\text{var}(u)$ becomes a diagonal matrix with nonidentical elements down the main diagonal. If serial correlation is present, $\text{var}(u)$ is no longer diagonal. Both cases are covered by the alternative specification

$$\text{var}(u) = \Sigma$$

where Σ is at least positive semidefinite and is usually positive definite.

For some purposes, most notably for inference in small samples, disturbances are assumed to be normally distributed. The correct form for this assumption is that u has a *multivariate* normal distribution. This can be written as $u \sim N(\ )$, and taken together with (1.20) and (1.21), the full specification is

$$u \sim N(0, \sigma^2 I). \tag{1.22}$$

Although we frequently use symbols that could refer to scalar or matrix quantities, the context should always make clear what is intended. Where possible, lower case letters are used for vectors and upper case letters for matrices. Where scalar and vector quantities with the same symbol coexist, the scalar quantity will have a subscript. If a vector is obtained as a partition of a matrix, the vector will have a subscript, but a scalar element will then have two subscripts. A matrix element also has two subscripts. Symbols such as 0 may have different dimensions in different cases, but again the context should make the meaning clear.

1.5 / Estimators and their properties

It was argued in Section 1.3 that an important implication of the probability model for disturbances is that Y_t represents either a random variable or a realisation of a random variable, depending on the context. When we are examining the theoretical implications of the single equation model, Y_t represents a random variable. When Y_t appears in a formula giving instructions for a calculation to be performed on given data, it is taken to represent a single observed value, which means that it is interpreted as a realisation.

Clearly, nothing is changed by writing the model in matrix form as

$$y = X\beta + u.$$

For the purposes of examining the implications of the model, y is interpreted as a vector of random variables (a random vector). It follows that any function of y must also define a random variable or a random vector, depending on whether the function is scalar or vector valued. From now on, it is convenient to use the term 'random variable' to cover both single random variables and random vectors, it being understood that a random variable may be scalar or vector valued.

At some stage, the unknown parameters of a model have to be replaced by estimates, and any method of estimation will surely make use of the available data, including the observations on the dependent variable. The logic of the model suggests that whilst only one realisation of the vector y occurs in practice, other realisations might have occurred, and each of these would give different estimates of the parameters. It follows that any method of estimation defined by an expression involving y can be interpreted as the definition of a new random variable. A random variable used to estimate unknown parameters is known as an *estimator*. A particular realisation, for a given set of data, is an *estimate*. From what we have said, it is clear that the estimation exercise will have to be given a probabilistic interpretation.

Properties of estimators

Since the implied probability distributions for estimators are typically continuous, it is extremely unlikely that an estimate is exactly equal to the unknown true value. On the other hand, there is a definite probability associated with the event that the estimate lies within some chosen region around the true value. To render such probability statements operational, it is necessary to derive the exact form of the estimator distribution, though this may sometimes prove to be difficult, in which case one would look for a suitable approximation. At the very least, we should attempt to find some information concerning the distribution, such as the expectation and variance, assuming of course that these moments exist.

If estimation is to be given a probabilistic interpretation, the choice between different methods of estimation will be based on statistical criteria. At this stage, it is convenient to move away from the specific context of econometric modelling, to consider any method of estimation based on an underlying probability distribution. Initially, suppose that we have a scalar estimator, $\hat{\theta}$, used to estimate a single unknown parameter, θ. If it is possible to find the expectation and variance of $\hat{\theta}$, the following properties will help in deciding whether or not $\hat{\theta}$ is a 'good' estimator to use:

1. Unbiasedness: if $E(\hat{\theta}) = \theta$, the estimator $\hat{\theta}$ is said to be unbiased. The expectation over all possible realisations is equal to the true parameter and there is no *systematic* tendency to either underestimate or overestimate the true value.

2. Minimum variance: if $\text{var}(\hat{\theta})$ is at least as small as the variance of any other estimator in some clearly defined class of possibilities, $\hat{\theta}$ is said to be the *minimum variance* estimator in that class. Two equivalent descriptions are that $\hat{\theta}$ is *best*, or that $\hat{\theta}$ is *most efficient* in that class. The class in question is often that of unbiased estimators, or that of linear unbiased estimators. By selecting a minimum variance estimator, we reduce the uncertainty associated with estimation to the minimum possible level for estimators of the chosen class.

Asymptotic properties and large sample approximations

A further set of properties are those which hold in the limit as the number of observations is increased. These are described as large sample asymptotic properties, and they include consistency and asymptotic efficiency, which are roughly the equivalent of unbiasedness and minimum variance in a finite sample. Such properties are used when it is impossible, or at least difficult, to establish finite sample results. The estimator $\hat{\theta}$ is said to be consistent if

$$\lim_{n \to \infty} \Pr[|\hat{\theta} - \theta| > \delta] = 0; \text{ for any } \delta > 0. \tag{1.23}$$

This condition states that as the sample size increases, the *probability* of $\hat{\theta}$ being different from θ will tend to zero, which implies that the probability distribution of $\hat{\theta}$ will eventually collapse onto the single value θ. An alternative statement of

(1.23) is

$$\text{plim}(\hat{\theta}) = \theta$$

where plim( ) indicates the probability limit.

The concept of asymptotic efficiency is a little more difficult, since it depends on the existence of a limiting distribution for a suitably scaled function of the estimator. We therefore need to look first at the concept of a limiting distribution. At this stage, the discussion is somewhat informal; a more detailed treatment of large sample theory is given in Chapter 4.

If a random variable is to have a limiting distribution, it must depend in some way on the sample size. If this is true and the actual distribution in a finite sample converges to some limiting form as the sample size is increased without limit, then the random variable has a limiting distribution.

Now suppose that $\hat{\theta}$ is a consistent estimator for some parameter θ. The condition for consistency means that $\hat{\theta}$ cannot have a limiting distribution with a nonzero variance, as this would contradict the idea that the distribution of $\hat{\theta}$ eventually collapses onto a single point. It is therefore necessary to find a scaled function of the estimator that has a limiting distribution with a variance that is both finite and nonzero. For example, we may find that as $n \to \infty$, $\sqrt{n}(\hat{\theta} - \theta)$ has a limiting distribution with variance q, where $0 < q < \infty$. Often the limiting distribution is normal, though it need not be so. If the limiting distribution of $\sqrt{n}(\hat{\theta} - \theta)$ is normal, then $\hat{\theta}$ is said to be *asymptotically normal*, though it is more accurate to state that in a large finite sample, $\hat{\theta}$ is *approximately* normal, with mean θ and variance q/n.

It is now possible to define the concept of asymptotic variance. Some authors use this term to describe the variance of the limiting distribution of the scaled function of the estimator, which corresponds to the value q in the example above. For our purposes, it is convenient to take the asymptotic variance to mean the variance of the approximation used in a large finite sample, which corresponds to q/n in the example given. This is consistent with what is usually meant by an asymptotic standard error, which is the square root of an asymptotic variance, using our definition, with any unknown parameters replaced by (consistent) estimates.

As a final step, we return to the idea of an asymptotically efficient estimator. Suppose that there are two estimators, $\hat{\theta}$ and $\tilde{\theta}$, and that $\sqrt{n}(\hat{\theta} - \theta)$ and $\sqrt{n}(\tilde{\theta} - \theta)$ both have definite limiting distributions. If the variance of the limiting distribution of $\sqrt{n}(\hat{\theta} - \theta)$ is at least as small as that of $\sqrt{n}(\tilde{\theta} - \theta)$, then $\hat{\theta}$ is asymptotically more efficient than $\tilde{\theta}$. Sometimes, an estimator is said to be asymptotically efficient, without qualification. This usually means that the estimator has the minimum asymptotic variance amongst all estimators of a certain type, and often refers to the class of all consistent estimators, or to the class of all consistent asymptotically normal estimators.

Vector estimators

If $\hat{\theta}$ is a vector estimator, $E(\hat{\theta})$ and $\text{plim}(\hat{\theta})$ are vectors and $\text{var}(\hat{\theta})$ is a matrix. Properties involving $E(\hat{\theta})$ and $\text{plim}(\hat{\theta})$ translate directly into equivalent vector expressions.

Properties requiring comparison of variances are interpreted in the following way. Let $\text{var}(\hat{\theta})$ and $\text{var}(\tilde{\theta})$ signify variance covariance matrices for two estimators. $\hat{\theta}$ is said to be more efficient than $\tilde{\theta}$ if $\text{var}(\tilde{\theta}) - \text{var}(\hat{\theta})$ is positive semidefinite (psd). The statement

$$\text{var}(\tilde{\theta}) \geq \text{var}(\hat{\theta})$$

is understood to imply exactly this form of (matrix) inequality. Similarly, if $\sqrt{n}(\hat{\theta} - \theta)$ has a limiting distribution with a variance covariance matrix Q, the asymptotic variance of $\hat{\theta}$ is defined as the matrix $n^{-1}Q$, and this may be written as $\text{avar}(\hat{\theta})$. If two estimators have (different) asymptotic variances defined in this way, and

$$\text{avar}(\tilde{\theta}) - \text{avar}(\hat{\theta}) \text{ is psd,}$$

then $\hat{\theta}$ is asymptotically more efficient than $\tilde{\theta}$.

The fact that estimators have probability distributions means that apparent relationships between economic variables can, within the logic of our models, be due entirely to a statistical accident. For example, in the single equation model, a parameter β_j could be zero, implying no relationship between Y and X_j, given the other variables in the model. But an estimate of β_j could be, indeed is almost certain to be, different from zero. The purpose of statistical testing is to decide whether a nonzero estimate of β_j arises purely because of random variation, or whether some real effect exists. Similar problems arise throughout the process of constructing an econometric model, because we have only a limited sample of observations on which to base our decisions. At each stage, it will be necessary to devise appropriate test procedures, which attempt to minimise the probability of drawing the wrong conclusion from the available evidence.

1.6 / On the use of live data

In this chapter, I have attempted an overview of some of the issues that arise in formulating a certain type of statistical model, which can then be used as the basis for examining relationships between economic variables. Many of the details require further clarification, and we still have to make a start on finding operational procedures for estimating unknown parameters, and for testing the validity of the estimates obtained.

All of this involves a considerable amount of groundwork, and one can easily lose sight of the fact that the ultimate objective is to use the statistical model, together with observed measurements from a chosen economic system, to attempt to find something of value to say about the way in which real economies behave.

Given the complexity of economic processes, we have to recognise some limitation on our ability to analyse live data fully, until such time as we have a comprehensive selection of econometric methods at our disposal. This tension between theory and application arises because theoretical development is sequential, with all the early discussion conducted under strong assumptions. Unfortunately, real economies do not reveal correspondingly simple behaviour patterns, so virtually any data set we choose will involve complexities that we are not fully prepared for. It is certainly possible to use live data to illustrate the mechanics of estimation and testing, but it is highly unlikely that simple examples will actually satisfy all the underlying statistical assumptions.

To cope with the problem of sequencing, we must accept that the statistical procedures used in numerical examples will only be valid if the current set of assumptions is satisfied. After the exercise has been carried out, it will usually be possible to conduct a post-mortem, and, in the early stages, this will almost always reveal some violation of assumptions. Good econometric practice would then require either a revision of the proposed model or the use of different procedures, appropriate to a weaker set of conditions on the statistical model. But at that point in the discussion, we will often be prevented from following either strategy, because techniques for dealing with more elaborate models or alternative conditions for estimation will simply not be available. For this reason, all conclusions concerning the problem to hand must be tentative, and may be revised by looking at the same data again at a later stage.

In order to have some data available before starting on a discussion of estimation and testing, we conclude this chapter with a brief description of four data sets, all but one of which relate to the UK economy. Given that the underlying economic theory is also simplified, it is clearly possible to construct similar exercises for other countries, though a full analysis of any data set is likely to involve some country specific features.

When selecting initial examples, one does have to be careful, because certain types of data are just not amenable to simplified analysis. Small samples of cross-section data may be suitable, and some mileage can be obtained from annual time series. Quarterly data are not appropriate for introductory examples, because the relatively high frequency of observation implies that there is almost always a need for dynamic adjustment mechanisms, and this is a complication that we wish to avoid in the early stages.

The four data sets are used to consider (i) the relationship between aggregate consumers' expenditure and aggregate disposable income; (ii) the relationship between money, activity and interest rates; (iii) the relationship between the price of output and the cost of inputs at the macro level; and (iv) the relationship between a country's growth rate of per capita GDP, its GDP per capita and stock of human capital. Data sets 1, 2 and 3 are based on annual time series, and data set 4 is derived from a cross-section.

Data set 1: UK consumption and income

Data set 1 provides annual observations on real consumers' expenditure (RCONS) and real personal disposable income (RPDI) for the United Kingdom, 1963–94. For future reference, the table also gives the implicit deflator for consumers' expenditure (PCONS) and a real liquid assets series (RLIQA). By inspecting the series

Data set 1 Consumers' expenditure and income, UK, 1963–94

Year	RCONS	PCONS	RPDI	RLIQA
1963	170.874	0.119	185.426	143.6387
1964	176.044	0.123	193.247	148.0732
1965	178.493	0.129	196.998	150.9225
1966	181.550	0.134	201.207	151.8134
1967	185.985	0.138	204.171	159.1884
1968	191.209	0.144	207.772	162.2431
1969	192.366	0.152	209.684	160.8553
1970	197.873	0.161	217.675	164.7640
1971	204.139	0.175	220.344	167.3029
1972	216.752	0.186	238.744	171.1452
1973	228.615	0.202	254.329	180.9307
1974	225.317	0.236	252.360	175.1271
1975	224.580	0.292	253.814	162.4075
1976	225.666	0.338	253.012	154.3047
1977	224.892	0.388	247.695	151.5747
1978	236.909	0.424	265.925	157.5943
1979	247.212	0.482	281.084	162.6909
1980	247.185	0.561	285.411	162.5811
1981	247.402	0.624	283.176	164.4888
1982	249.852	0.678	281.722	170.4307
1983	261.200	0.711	289.204	179.2827
1984	266.486	0.746	299.756	192.3458
1985	276.742	0.786	309.821	201.4593
1986	295.622	0.817	323.622	212.2632
1987	311.234	0.852	334.702	222.1150
1988	334.591	0.895	354.627	239.9989
1989	345.406	0.948	371.676	252.3291
1990	347.527	1.000	378.325	265.7550
1991	339.915	1.074	377.969	270.8771
1992	339.537	1.124	386.804	279.9093
1993	348.447	1.163	393.125	287.4050
1994	358.230	1.193	396.181	291.4049

Key:
RCONS Real consumers' expenditure (£ billion, 1990 prices).
PCONS Implicit deflator, consumers' expenditure (1990 = 1.0).
RPDI Real personal disposable income (£ billion, 1990 prices).
RLIQA Real liquid asset holdings of personal sector (£ billion, 1990 prices).

Source: Derived from ONS database.

PCONS, and noting that this takes the value 1.0 in 1990, we can deduce that the real variables are measured in terms of 1990 prices.

In principle, one should be able to consult any source which quotes UK data for recent years to find exactly the numbers shown here. However, this overlooks the fact that data for given years occur in different 'vintages', and may be subject to revision long after the original publication date. The simplest way to obtain common macroeconomic time series is to download observations from an on-line database, since this avoids the need to retype data for subsequent computation. But an on-line data source will be constantly updated, and this means that even with precise definitions it can be difficult to reproduce a given data set exactly. To overcome this problem, one must either refer to a dated version of a published source, or list the actual observations used.

The observations in data set 1 are consistent in principle with the annual UK ONS publication *Economic Trends, Annual Supplement*. The series RCONS and RPDI were obtained from the original data simply by conversion from £million to £billion, and the implicit deflator PCONS by converting the original series from $1990 = 100$ to $1990 = 1.0$. The remaining series, RLIQA, was constructed in a rather more round-about way: the details are found in Appendix B.

The purpose of introducing data set 1 is to enable us to consider the estimation of a consumption function. The simplest specification is a two-variable linear relationship, which can be written as

$$C_t = \alpha + \beta D_t + u_t; \ t = 1, \ldots, n, \tag{1.24}$$

or, using more general notation, as

$$C_t = \beta_1 + \beta_2 D_t + u_t; \ t = 1, \ldots, n, \tag{1.25}$$

where C is real consumers' expenditure and D is real personal disposable income. Alternatively, we could consider a formulation in which it is the elasticity of consumption with respect to income that is constant, rather than the marginal propensity to consume. This is achieved by specifying a relationship that is linear in logarithms, giving

$$\ln(C_t) = \beta_1 + \beta_2 \ln(D_t) + u_t; \ t = 1, \ldots, n. \tag{1.26}$$

Note that the symbolic names C and D coexist with the 'computer' names, which are RCONS and RPDI respectively.

In practice, it is unlikely that the simple specifications shown above will be adequate, and at the end of Chapter 2, we consider some possible modifications.

Data set 2: UK demand for money

Data set 2 provides annual observations on real total domestic expenditure (RTDE), nominal total domestic expenditure (QTDE), the interest rate on long-dated government stock (INTL) and a measure of the nominal narrow money stock, 'retail deposits and cash in M4' (M4), for the United Kingdom, 1963–94. Total domestic expenditure is defined as GDP at purchasers' values plus imports less exports.

Data set 2 will be used to explore a simple demand for money function of the form

$$\ln(M_t/P_t) = \beta_1 + \beta_2 \ln(A_t) + \beta_3 \ln(r_t) + u_t; \ t = 1, \ldots, n \tag{1.27}$$

Data set 2 Money, activity and interest rates, UK, 1963–94

Year	RTDE	QTDE	INTL	M4
1963	288.856	30.814	1.0530	2.228
1964	307.559	34.037	1.0580	2.428
1965	312.417	36.256	1.0643	2.612
1966	317.366	38.395	1.0691	2.670
1967	329.964	40.985	1.0680	2.790
1968	341.032	44.390	1.0754	2.829
1969	341.179	46.853	1.0905	2.968
1970	349.045	51.270	1.0921	3.279
1971	357.267	57.323	1.0885	3.544
1972	372.979	64.466	1.0890	4.022
1973	402.565	76.242	1.1071	4.309
1974	393.599	88.949	1.1477	5.006
1975	386.710	108.923	1.1439	5.808
1976	397.225	129.328	1.1443	6.280
1977	396.143	146.204	1.1273	7.217
1978	411.909	167.515	1.1247	8.269
1979	426.915	197.906	1.1299	8.915
1980	414.792	227.537	1.1378	9.595
1981	408.223	249.322	1.1474	10.148
1982	417.916	274.649	1.1288	125.736
1983	438.768	302.895	1.1080	141.044
1984	450.949	326.498	1.1069	157.774
1985	464.316	354.291	1.1062	177.164
1986	487.330	388.179	1.0987	199.957
1987	513.083	428.721	1.0947	220.542
1988	553.461	488.953	1.0936	256.317
1989	569.719	537.279	1.0958	279.953
1990	566.238	566.238	1.1108	309.810
1991	548.532	581.897	1.0992	335.928
1992	549.543	605.295	1.0912	373.243
1993	561.346	638.400	1.0787	394.510
1994	580.092	675.164	1.0805	410.469

Key:
RTDE Real total domestic expenditure (£ billion, 1990 prices).
QTDE Nominal total domestic expenditure (£ billion, 1990 prices).
INTL Interest rate on long-dated UK Government securities, expressed as
  $(1 + \text{rate}/100)$.
M4 Nominal money stock M4 (£ billion).

Source: Derived from ONS database.

where M is nominal money, A is real activity, P is the price level and r the rate of interest. The logarithmic form is used to make the (partial) elasticity of money with respect to activity constant, rather than the slope of a linear relationship between money and activity. The partial relationship between money and the interest rate is also a constant elasticity form: this allows for some curvature in the graph of

(M/P) against r. Since r is measured as $(1 + rate/100)$, $\ln(r)$ is approximately equal to $rate/100$, and if r were used instead of $\ln(r)$, only the intercept would be expected to show any significant change.

One point that is well illustrated by this example is the problem of deciding how best to translate the conceptual measures of economic theory into hard and fast data definitions. There are several measures of money that one might use, each with different coverage, several different activity or income measures, and a variety of possible interest rates. We choose here to measure money as M4, real activity as RTDE, real purchases for domestic purposes, the price level as the implicit deflator (QTDE/RTDE), and interest as INTL, a long-rate government stock. These are not necessarily the most appropriate definitions, and they are chosen in part to give as long a run of annual observations as possible. It should also be noted that money series are notoriously subject to changes in coverage of the reporting institutions; no attempt has been made to allow for this in data set 2, and there may be some consequential effect on the results that we obtain.

Data set 3: UK costs and prices

Data set 3 provides annual observations on unit labour costs (ULC), unit import costs (UMC) and the implicit price of output, which is labelled as home unit costs (HUC). In this example, all three series represent derived data, expressed in index form, with 1990 values equal to 1.00. These data will be used to examine the proposition that the price of output, represented by HUC, can be explained simply in terms of labour costs and import costs. Once again, it is convenient to express this in logarithmic form, giving a model which we can write as

$$\ln(HUC_t) = \beta_1 + \beta_2 \ln(ULC_t) + \beta_3 \ln(UMC_t) + u_t; \ t = 1, \ldots, n. \tag{1.28}$$

As with the other proposed models, it remains to be seen how well this will stand up in practice.

Data set 4: Convergence of growth rates

Data set 4 is somewhat more extensive, and is thus not shown in tabular form. It is a selection of countries and variables from the *Barro–Lee* data set utilised in Barro and Sala-i-Martin (1995). It consists of data on the growth rates of GDP per capita over the periods 1975–80 (GRSH54) and 1980–85 (GRSH55) for a cross-section of countries, the average 1975–85 values of a number of other variables, and the 1975 values of some further variables. The objective is to see whether the *absolute convergence hypothesis* holds, that is, do countries with lower initial levels of GDP per capita (in logs, GDP575L) and human capital stocks subsequently experience higher growth rates of GDP per capita? In other words, 'poorer countries typically grow faster per capita and tend thereby to catch up the richer countries' (Barro and Sala-i-Martin, 1995: 420). Versions of this data set are publicly available, and thus the variable names given in the data set are employed here.

Data set 3 Costs and prices, UK, 1959–94

Year	ULC	UMC	HUC
1959	0.098 721	0.072 183	0.098
1960	0.101 470	0.078 407	0.100
1961	0.105 999	0.075 214	0.103
1962	0.110 464	0.075 602	0.107
1963	0.111 362	0.077 895	0.109
1964	0.114 780	0.083 758	0.112
1965	0.120 925	0.083 521	0.117
1966	0.126 897	0.085 145	0.122
1967	0.128 681	0.089 650	0.125
1968	0.131 673	0.102 431	0.129
1969	0.138 591	0.106 706	0.134
1970	0.152 226	0.116 783	0.144
1971	0.162 675	0.124 708	0.160
1972	0.181 177	0.138 771	0.176
1973	0.193 796	0.176 694	0.190
1974	0.232 684	0.254 605	0.222
1975	0.306 253	0.271 875	0.283
1976	0.336 194	0.333 334	0.324
1977	0.368 672	0.381 021	0.364
1978	0.410 219	0.397 487	0.409
1979	0.470 799	0.466 178	0.461
1980	0.570 234	0.503 303	0.546
1981	0.625 097	0.532 198	0.601
1982	0.654 369	0.589 330	0.643
1983	0.674 136	0.650 112	0.680
1984	0.709 043	0.765 420	0.716
1985	0.738 397	0.783 833	0.755
1986	0.765 878	0.770 585	0.774
1987	0.793 449	0.813 070	0.813
1988	0.841 700	0.865 339	0.862
1989	0.912 572	0.968 440	0.928
1990	1.000 000	1.000 000	1.000
1991	1.078 093	0.969 787	1.058
1992	1.123 311	1.037 615	1.107
1993	1.129 050	1.131 332	1.146
1994	1.119 709	1.177 660	1.166

Key:
ULC   Unit labour costs (1990 = 1.00).
UMC   Unit import costs (1990 = 1.00).
HUC   Implicit deflator for GDP at factor cost (1990 = 1.00).

Source: Derived from ONS database.

The objective with this data set is to see if there is a relationship of the form

$$AVGR_t = \beta_1 + \beta_2 GDP575L_t + \beta_3 SYRM75_t + u_t; \ t = 1,\ldots,102 \tag{1.29}$$

where $AVGR_t$, the simple average of GRSH54 and GRSH55, is the average growth rate of GDP per capita over the period 1975–85. In (1.29), β_2 represents the rate of convergence, that is, the responsiveness of the per capita growth rate to a proportional change in GDP575L. Thus one would expect $\beta_2 < 0$. The variable SYRM75 represents part of the country's stock of human capital in 1975, and thus $\beta_3 > 0$ would be expected. In practice, additional indicators of human capital are used as explanatory variables, as well as variables representing the characteristics of the country that are expected to influence the relationship, such as measures of political instability.

This is the only cross-section data set used in this book. The Barro–Lee data set in its most complete form contains data on 138 countries over six five-year periods. Cross-section data sets are often much larger than this, if they are constructed from annual governmental countrywide surveys, for example the Family Expenditure Survey in the UK or the Current Population Survey in the USA. Such surveys will typically contain observations on several hundred variables for each of several thousand households or individuals. Data sets of this sort have their own characteristic problems, often associated with their sheer size: it is impossible to discuss these issues in a book like this.

There are several other data sets used at specific points in the remaining chapters, and these are introduced and described as needed.

1.7 / Further reading

There are many books on econometrics covering some or all of the material of this chapter. The four mentioned here are broadly of a higher level than this text, and generally provide more extensive coverage of topics than is possible here. Goldberger (1991) is a textbook specifically oriented to the linear regression model. Gourieroux and Monfort (1995) is a two-volume monograph-cum-textbook which covers a huge range of topics in a high-level but readable manner. The style is firmly rooted in statistical theory, and quite mathematically advanced, although still very clear. Davidson and MacKinnon (1993) is another high-level source, very valuable for its overall perspective on a number of topics. Another well-established and more advanced textbook is Greene (1993), which is a good reference source, but its coverage lacks the intuition and overall perspective of Davidson and MacKinnon or Gourieroux and Monfort.

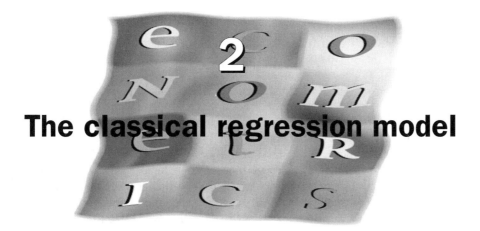

2

The classical regression model

2.1 / Introduction

The primary purpose of this chapter is to focus on what is known in statistics as the 'classical' regression model. This corresponds to our single equation model

$$Y_t = \beta_1 + \beta_2 X_{2t} + \ldots + \beta_j X_{jt} + \ldots + \beta_t X_{kt} + u_t; \ t = 1, \ldots, n \qquad (2.1)$$

with certain additional assumptions concerning the right-hand side variables and disturbances. The assumptions are that the right-hand side variables are nonrandom, and that the disturbances have zero mean, constant variance, either zero covariance or independence between distinct disturbances u_s, u_t and, for inference in small samples, that u_t has a normal distribution. Listed separately, we have

(a) 'fixed X': X_{jt} nonrandom; $j = 1, \ldots, k; \ t = 1, \ldots, n$;

(b) 'zero mean': $E(u_t) = 0; \ t = 1, \ldots, n$;

(c) 'constant variance': $\text{var}(u_t) = \sigma^2; \ t = 1, \ldots, n$;

(d) 'zero covariance': $\text{cov}(u_t, u_s) = 0; \ s \neq t; \ s, t = 1, \ldots, n$
    or 'independence': u_t, u_s independent; $s \neq t; \ s, t = 1, \ldots, n$;

(e) 'normality': $u_t \sim N(\ \ ); \ t = 1, \ldots, n$.

As written, assumption (e) states that each disturbance has a univariate normal distribution. What we actually require is that the joint distribution of all disturbances is multivariate normal. If independence is assumed, this distinction is not important, since independence and univariate normality together imply multivariate normality.

To ensure that the normality assumption is correctly stated, we can combine assumptions (b), (c), the independence version of (d), and (e), by writing $u_t \sim NID(0, \sigma^2)$. This indicates that the u_t are normal and independently distributed, with $E(u_t) = 0$ and $\text{var}(u_t) = \sigma^2$. Because univariate normality and independence are included, multivariate normality is implied.

23

A second variant, which is useful when we do not wish to assume normality, is $u_t \sim IID(0, \sigma^2)$; this means that the u_t are independent and identically distributed, and includes (b), (c), the independence version of (d), and the further assumption that all characteristics of the u_t distributions are identical, including all moments, and not just the mean and variance. For random variables which are $NID(0, \sigma^2)$, this last property holds anyway, since the common mean and variance imply that the individual distributions are identical.

One further point concerns the relationship between the two versions of assumption (d) above. Independence implies zero covariance, but zero covariance does not always imply independence. Independence is therefore a stronger assumption than zero covariance. However, when taken together with multivariate normality, zero covariance does imply independence. Finally, note that when two random variables have zero covariances, they are said to be *uncorrelated*.

The terminology used to describe regression models can seem a little confusing. Equation (2.1) is a single equation model with fixed (nonrandom) values for the X variables. The model expresses Y as a linear function of the X variables, but a random disturbance is added to this function, so observations on Y have a random component. This type of model may also be described as a *multiple* regression model, to distinguish from the 'two-variable' model of elementary statistics.

In regression theory, the right-hand side variables are described as *regressors*. Under the specific assumptions of classical regression, the regressors are nonrandom. This clearly rules out any case in which endogenous variables appear on the right-hand side, whether these are lagged or current values. The reason is that, either implicitly or explicitly, such values are determined by one or more relationships which have random components. Although regression techniques may still be applied to models with endogenous variables on the right-hand side, such models cannot fully satisfy the assumptions of classical regression. However, if we are operating under classical conditions, we cannot have endogenous variables on the right-hand side, so it is entirely reasonable in this context to refer to Y as the dependent variable and to the regressors as explanatory variables. The purpose of the classical model is to explain the behaviour of Y in terms of *given* values of the X variables.

In matrix form, equation (2.1) can be written as

$$y_t = x_t' \beta + u_t; \quad t = 1, \ldots, n \tag{2.2}$$

or as

$$y = X\beta + u. \tag{2.3}$$

In (2.2), a single observation on the dependent variable is written as y_t, rather than Y_t, to signify a single element from the vector y in (2.3). Also in (2.2), x_t' is a row vector containing observation t on each of the X variables: this corresponds to a single row of the matrix X in (2.3).

When the matrix form (2.3) is used, assumption (b) is written as $E(u) = 0$, where 0 is a zero vector. Assumption (c) and the zero covariance version of assumption (d) are written together as $\text{var}(u) = \sigma^2 I$, where I is an $(n \times n)$ identity matrix.

Assumption (e) is written as $u \sim N(\quad)$. Since u is a vector, it is understood that $u \sim N(\quad)$ denotes multivariate normality. Assumptions (b), (c), (d), and (e) together give $u \sim N(0, \sigma^2 I)$.

The assumptions of classical regression are restrictive, and it seems likely that properties derived from the classical regression model will sometimes have to be modified for practical application. It will also be necessary to find ways of testing assumptions, so that we know when modified procedures are required. But the first step is to understand basic regression methods, for only then can we appreciate the significance of possible modifications.

2.2 / The least squares principle

A model in the form of equation (2.1) embodies the assumption that there exists a set of 'true' parameters, $\beta_1, \ldots, \beta_k$, for which the linear form of model is acceptable, and that for *these* values, the disturbances u_t; $t = 1, \ldots, n$ have the properties specified. Neither the parameters nor the disturbances are observable, though parameters can be estimated and one can find calculated *residuals* which are the empirical counterparts of the unobservable disturbances.

There are many ways in which one could estimate model parameters; the least squares principle suggests selecting estimates in such a way as to minimise the sum of squares of *observed* model errors. From equation (2.1), the model is

$$Y_t = \beta_1 + \beta_2 X_{2t} + \ldots + \beta_j X_{jt} + \ldots + \beta_k X_{kt} + u_t; \; t = 1, \ldots, n$$

or, alternatively,

$$u_t = Y_t - \beta_1 - \beta_2 X_{2t} - \ldots - \beta_j X_{jt} - \ldots - \beta_k X_{kt}; \; t = 1, \ldots, n. \tag{2.4}$$

Now let $b_1, \ldots, b_k$ represent any set of estimates for the parameters $\beta_1, \ldots, \beta_k$ and let e_t; $t = 1, \ldots, n$ represent residuals (as opposed to 'true' disturbances). By analogy with (2.4), the residuals are

$$e_t = Y_t - b_1 - b_2 X_{2t} - \ldots - b_j X_{jt} - \ldots - b_k X_{kt}; \; t = 1, \ldots, n. \tag{2.5}$$

For any given set of parameter estimates, the residuals are the observed model errors.

The next step is to define the sum of squares function:

$$S = S(b_1, b_2, \ldots, b_k) = \sum e_t^2$$
$$= \sum (Y_t - b_1 - b_2 X_{2t} - \ldots - b_j X_{jt} - \ldots - b_k X_{kt})^2. \tag{2.6}$$

To minimise S with respect to $b_1, \ldots, b_k$, the expression in (2.6) is differentiated with respect to each b_j in turn, and the derivatives are set equal to zero. The resulting conditions are then used to solve for the least squares estimates. The second-order conditions confirm that a solution obtained in this way is indeed a minimum of the sum of squares function.

Least squares conditions: scalar form

Before carrying out the differentiation of S, note from (2.5) that

$$\partial e_t / \partial b_j = -X_{jt}; \ j = 1, \ldots, k; \ t = 1, \ldots, n.$$

One can then use the chain rule to split the differentiation of S into two stages, as follows:

$$\partial S / \partial b_j = \partial \left(\sum e_t^2 \right) / \partial \beta_j = \sum (\partial e_t^2 / \partial \beta_j)$$

$$= \sum (\partial e_t^2 / \partial e_t) \cdot (\partial e_t / \partial \beta_j)$$

$$= \sum (2 e_t)(-X_{jt})$$

$$= -2 \sum X_{jt} e_t; \ j = 1, \ldots, k. \tag{2.7}$$

Finally, setting $\partial S / \partial b_j = 0$, we obtain

$$\partial S / \partial b_j = 0 \ \Rightarrow \ -2 \sum X_{jt} e_t = 0$$

$$\Rightarrow \ \sum X_{jt} e_t = 0; \ j = 1, \ldots, k. \tag{2.8}$$

Equation (2.8) specifies k conditions that must be satisfied by least squares residuals: using (2.5) to substitute for e_t makes clear that these are also conditions on the least squares parameter estimates. For example, if $j = 1$, and $X_{1t} = 1$; $t = 1, \ldots, n$, then

$$\sum X_{1t} e_t = \sum e_t = \sum (Y_t - b_1 - b_2 X_{2t} - \ldots - b_k X_{kt}) = 0.$$

For $j = 2$,

$$\sum X_{2t} e_t = \sum X_{2t} (Y_t - b_1 - b_2 X_{2t} - \ldots - b_k X_{kt}) = 0.$$

Continuing in this way, and rearranging so that all terms in $b_1, \ldots, b_k$ appear on the left-hand side, we obtain a set of k linear equations in the k unknown values $b_1, \ldots, b_k$. For reference, the equations are

$$b_1 n \qquad + b_2 \sum X_{2t} \quad + \ldots + b_j \sum X_{jt} \quad + \ldots + b_k \sum X_{kt} \quad = \sum Y_t$$

$$b_1 \sum X_{2t} + b_2 \sum X_{2t}^2 \quad + \ldots + b_j \sum X_{2t} X_{jt} + \ldots + b_k \sum X_{2t} X_{kt} = \sum X_{2t} Y_t$$

$$\vdots$$

$$b_1 \sum X_{jt} + b_2 \sum X_{jt} X_{2t} + \ldots + b_j \sum X_{jt}^2 \quad + \ldots + b_k \sum X_{jt} X_{kt} = \sum X_{jt} Y_t$$

$$\vdots$$

$$b_1 \sum X_{kt} + b_2 \sum X_{kt} X_{2t} + \ldots + b_j \sum X_{kt} X_{jt} + \ldots + b_k \sum X_{kt}^2 \quad = \sum X_{kt} Y_t.$$

$$\tag{2.9}$$

Normal equations in matrix form

At this stage, the use of scalar algebra leaves us with a problem. It has been possible to obtain the so-called *normal equations* of least squares, but there is no simple way of writing down the solution for $b_1, \ldots, b_k$ without using matrix algebra. To proceed, we need to note that the sums of squares and products on the left of (2.9) have a definite pattern that can be represented by a $(k \times k)$ matrix of the form

$$X'X = \begin{bmatrix} n & \sum X_{2t} & \cdots & \sum X_{jt} & \cdots & \sum X_{kt} \\ \sum X_{2t} & \sum X_{2t}^2 & \cdots & \sum X_{2t}X_{jt} & \cdots & \sum X_{2t}X_{kt} \\ \vdots & \vdots & & \vdots & & \vdots \\ \sum X_{jt} & \sum X_{jt}X_{2t} & \cdots & \sum X_{jt}^2 & \cdots & \sum X_{jt}X_{kt} \\ \vdots & \vdots & & \vdots & & \vdots \\ \sum X_{kt} & \sum X_{kt}X_{2t} & \cdots & \sum X_{kt}X_{jt} & \cdots & \sum X_{kt}^2 \end{bmatrix}.$$

If it is not obvious that $X'X$ has this structure, the reader should refer to section 1.4, and write the product of X' and X in terms of the individual elements of the X matrix.

Next, consider the terms on the right of (2.9). In this case, the sums of products can be arranged in a $(k \times 1)$ vector of the form

$$X'y = \begin{bmatrix} \sum Y_t \\ \sum X_{2t}Y_t \\ \vdots \\ \sum X_{jt}Y_t \\ \vdots \\ \sum X_{kt}Y_t \end{bmatrix}.$$

Finally, the elements $b_1, \ldots, b_k$ can be arranged in the $(k \times 1)$ vector

$$b = \begin{bmatrix} b_1 \\ b_2 \\ \vdots \\ b_j \\ \vdots \\ b_k \end{bmatrix}.$$

It is then possible to write equations (2.9) in matrix form as

$$(X'X)b = X'y. \tag{2.10}$$

Again, this can be verified by writing $X'X$, b and $X'y$ in terms of individual elements, and using the rules of matrix multiplication to show that (2.10) does correspond exactly to the normal equations (2.9). Provided that $(X'X)$ can be inverted, the solution for b can now be written as

$$b = (X'X)^{-1}X'y. \tag{2.11}$$

It should be noted that, besides the normal equations and the explicit solution (2.11), there is an alternative form for the least squares conditions:

$$(X'X)b = X'y \Rightarrow X'(Xb - y) = 0$$
$$\Rightarrow X'(y - Xb) = 0$$
$$\Rightarrow X'e = 0. \tag{2.12}$$

Equation (2.12) is the matrix equivalent of (2.8), and it is often useful to characterise the least squares conditions in this way.

Least squares conditions from matrix differentiation

Instead of obtaining the normal equations by using scalar calculus, and then translating to matrix form, it is possible to obtain the normal equations directly, by using the matrix calculus operations described in Appendix A. In matrix form, the sum of squares function is

$$S = S(b) = e'e = (y - Xb)'(y - Xb)$$
$$= y'y - b'X'y - y'Xb + b'X'Xb$$
$$= y'y - 2b'X'y + b'X'Xb.$$

The last line above follows since $b'X'y$ is (1×1), and is therefore scalar and equal to its transpose $y'Xb$. The term $b'X'y$ is a linear form in b and $b'X'Xb$ is a quadratic form in b; the rules given in Appendix A show that

$$\partial S/\partial b = -2X'y + 2X'Xb$$
$$= -2X'(y - Xb) = -2X'e. \tag{2.13}$$

Setting $\partial S/\partial b = 0$ gives the condition

$$-2X'e = 0 \Rightarrow X'e = 0; \text{ as in (2.12)}$$
$$\Rightarrow X'(y - Xb) = 0$$
$$\Rightarrow (X'X)b = X'y; \text{ as in (2.10).}$$

To check the second-order conditions, (2.13) is differentiated again with respect to b, giving

$$\partial^2 S/\partial b \, \partial b' = 2(X'X).$$

A matrix of the form $X'X$ is at least positive semidefinite, and is positive definite if $X'X$ is nonsingular. The least squares solution is therefore a minimum of the sum of squares function.

Notation for least squares estimates and residuals

Initially, we used $b_1, \ldots, b_k$ to denote any set of estimates for the parameters $\beta_1, \ldots, \beta_k$ and e_t; $t = 1, \ldots, n$ to denote the corresponding residuals. From now on, we reserve the symbols $b_1, \ldots, b_k$ (and the vector b) to signify *least squares* estimators, or the corresponding estimates, and we use e_t; $t = 1, \ldots, n$ (and the vector e) to signify *least squares* residuals.

The fact that we have had to redefine symbols in this way illustrates a common difficulty of notation which arises whenever an estimator is derived by maximisation or minimisation of some criterion function. In (2.6), the sum of squares function was written as $S = S(b_1, \ldots, b_k)$ because it was important at that stage to distinguish between true values of parameters and the corresponding estimates. In future, we shall write the sum of squares function as

$$S = S(\beta_1, \beta_2, \ldots, \beta_k)$$
$$= \sum (Y_t - \beta_1 - \beta_2 X_{2t} - \ldots - \beta_j X_{jt} - \ldots - \beta_k X_{kt})^2$$

or as

$$S = S(\beta) = (y - X\beta)'(y - X\beta),$$

and it is to be understood that such a function is defined for any value of β, and not just for the single 'true' parameter vector that is assumed by the statistical model to exist somewhere in the parameter space. $S(b)$ would then represent the *minimum* value of $S(\beta)$, found by setting β equal to the least squares estimates. When we are not using a criterion function, β is still taken to represent the single 'true' vector.

Existence and uniqueness of least squares estimates

If $(X'X)$ can be inverted, the least squares solution is unique, and only one set of estimates is possible for a given set of data. The condition under which unique least squares estimates exist can be expressed in different ways, but essentially it is that no single X variable can be expressed as an exact linear function of other X variables. Equivalently, no single column of the matrix X must be an exact linear function of other columns of X. If this condition is satisfied, we may say that the columns of X are linearly independent, or that the matrix X has full column rank, or that $\text{rank}(X) = k$, or that $\text{rank}(X'X) = k$, or finally that $(X'X)$ is invertible or non-singular. Any one of these conditions is both necessary and sufficient for the existence of unique least squares estimates.

The two-variable regression model

The results obtained above can obviously be applied to the special case of the two-variable regression model

$$Y_t = \beta_1 + \beta_2 X_{2t} + u_t; \; t = 1, \ldots, n.$$

The description 'two-variable model' derives from the presence of the two genuine variables Y and X_2, but this is also the case in which there are two regressors ($k = 2$). The regressors are the genuine variable X_2 and the artificial variable X_1, which is implicitly present because there is an intercept term.

Although the two-variable model is usually too simple to be of much practical value, it can be useful as an expository tool, and for this purpose, it is sometimes convenient to write the model as

$$Y_t = \alpha + \beta X_t + u_t; \; t = 1, \ldots, n. \tag{2.14}$$

Applying (2.8) to the model written in this form, we obtain the conditions

$$\sum e_t = 0 \text{ and } \sum X_t e_t = 0.$$

Applying (2.9), we get the normal equations

$$an + b \sum X_t = \sum Y_t$$

$$a \sum X_t + b \sum X_t^2 = \sum X_t Y_t,$$

where a and b are the least squares estimates of α and β. An algebraic solution can be obtained by elimination of a, to give

$$b = \left[\sum X_t Y_t - \left(\sum X_t \right) \left(\sum Y_t \right) / n \right] / \left[\sum X_t^2 - \left(\sum X_t \right)^2 / n \right]. \tag{2.15}$$

The intercept is then calculated as

$$a = \left(\sum Y_t - b \sum X_t \right) / n = \bar{Y} - b \bar{X}, \tag{2.16}$$

where $\bar{Y}$ is the sample mean of the observations Y_t; $t = 1, \ldots, n$ and $\bar{X}$ is the sample mean for X_t; $t = 1, \ldots, n$. An alternative form for (2.15) is

$$b = \sum (X_t - \bar{X})(Y_t - \bar{Y}) / \sum (X_t - \bar{X})^2. \tag{2.17}$$

To show that (2.17) is indeed identical to (2.15), simply multiply out the brackets in the numerator and denominator of (2.17), noting that

$$\sum X_t \bar{Y} = \sum Y_t \bar{X} = \left(\sum X_t \right) \left(\sum Y_t \right) / n = n \bar{X} \bar{Y},$$

with similar results for $\sum X_t \bar{X}$. For a full discussion of the scalar algebra of the two-variable model, see Stewart (1984: ch. 2).

If the two-variable model is used to illustrate the solution by matrix inversion, equation (2.11) gives

$$\begin{bmatrix} a \\ b \end{bmatrix} = \begin{bmatrix} n & \sum X_t \\ \sum X_t & \sum X_t^2 \end{bmatrix}^{-1} \begin{bmatrix} \sum Y_t \\ \sum X_t Y_t \end{bmatrix}.$$

Direct inversion leads to (2.15) as an expression for b, but some manipulation is needed to show that the expression obtained for a is identical to (2.16).

Example 2.1

In the two-variable case, it is feasible to calculate least squares estimates by hand, though the usefulness of this is limited to ensuring that the algebra is understood. From data set 1 in section 1.6, we can obtain observations on real consumers' expenditure (RCONS) and real personal disposable income (RPDI), which can be used to estimate the parameters of the model

$$C_t = \alpha + \beta D_t + u_t; \ t = 1, \ldots, n$$

where $C = RCONS$ and $D = RPDI$. To apply the formulae given above, equate C with the dependent variable Y and D with the right-hand side variable X. Note carefully that for the purposes of this illustration, we use 28 observations, from 1963 to 1990, rather than all observations from 1963 to 1994.

Given some patience, and possibly at the third or fourth attempt, one can use a hand calculator (or spreadsheet) to obtain the following sums of squares and products:

$$n = 28; \qquad \sum_{t=1}^{28} X_t = 7395.529; \qquad \sum_{t=1}^{28} Y_t = 6691.723;$$

$$\sum_{t=1}^{28} X_t^2 = 2\,034\,944.03; \qquad \sum_{t=1}^{28} X_t Y_t = 1\,843\,038.735; \qquad \sum_{t=1}^{28} Y_t^2 = 1\,670\,034.37.$$

Application of (2.15) gives a numerator value of 75 580.47 and a denominator value of 81 592.27. Hence

$$b = 75\,580.47/81\,592.27 = 0.926\,319.$$

Application of (2.16) gives

$$a = [6691.723 - (0.926\,319)7395.529]/28 = -5.674\,85.$$

In general, methods used for hand calculation are susceptible to rounding error, and if the value of b is rounded before proceeding to calculate the value for a some slight inaccuracy will occur.

If the number of regressors is greater than two or at most three, hand calculation is extremely tedious, and given the widespread availability of suitable computer software, it seems pointless to elaborate on the details of this approach. Although we shall sometimes illustrate the calculation of quantities derived from the regression estimates, it is assumed in subsequent examples that the reader has access to either a statistical computer package, or preferably an econometric estimation package, of which there are now several excellent examples on the market. The calculation required for the initial exercises is *ordinary* least squares (OLS), though in a package designed for general statistics, this is likely to be described as a multiple regression. The computer output provides more than just parameter estimates (or regression coefficients). There will also be standard errors, t test statistics, R^2, and various statistics which are used to test the validity of the assumptions of the classical regression model.

Each of these measures will be explained in due course, and we shall not attempt any analysis of the estimated consumption function until this additional information is in place.

2.3 / Predicted values, residuals and the definition of R^2

The estimated counterpart of the model $y = X\beta + u$ is

$$y = Xb + e, \tag{2.18}$$

where least squares estimates are used in place of the unknown parameters, and least squares residuals are used in place of the unobservable disturbances. What the regression calculation does is to split the observations on the dependent variables into two components, the predicted values and the residuals. The predicted values, denoted as $\hat{y}$, are the values obtained by treating the estimated equation as an exact linear function of X. Hence

$$y = \hat{y} + e,$$

where

$$\hat{y} = Xb \tag{2.19}$$

and

$$e = y - \hat{y} = y - Xb. \tag{2.20}$$

In scalar form, the predicted values are written as

$$\hat{Y}_t = b_1 + b_2 X_{2t} + \ldots + b_j X_{jt} + \ldots + b_k X_{kt}; \; t = 1, \ldots, n \tag{2.21}$$

and the residuals are

$$e_t = Y_t - b_1 - b_2 X_{2t} - \ldots - b_j X_{jt} - \ldots - b_k X_{kt}; \; t = 1, \ldots, n. \tag{2.22}$$

Whereas $\hat{y}$ represents that part of the dependent variable observation vector that is explained by the behaviour of the variables in X, the residual vector e represents a component of y that cannot be explained in this way.

It is easy to overlook the fact that in deriving the formula for the least squares estimator, we have already obtained certain mathematical properties of the least squares method; in particular:

1. Parameter estimates are chosen so as to minimise the sum of squared residuals.
2. Least squares residuals must satisfy the conditions $X'e = 0$ (see equation (2.12)).

Equation (2.12) defines what are known as *orthogonality* conditions on the least squares residuals. The conditions are

$$X'e = 0 \; \Rightarrow \; (x_j)'e = 0; \; j = 1, \ldots, k$$
$$\Rightarrow \; \sum_t X_{jt} e_t = 0; \; j = 1, \ldots, k. \tag{2.23}$$

In scalar terms, orthogonality requires that a sum of products be zero. In vector notation, an inner product must be zero. The geometric interpretation of (2.23) is that each vector x_j represents a direction in n space, and the residual vector e must lie in a direction 'at right angles' to each of the x_j directions.

There are several algebraic identities that follow directly from (2.23). Since the residuals are orthogonal to the columns of X, and $\hat{y}$ is an exact linear function of X, it is not surprising to find that the residuals are also orthogonal to the predicted values. The proof of this is extremely simple. From (2.19), $\hat{y} = Xb$, and from (2.23), $X'e = 0$. Hence

$$\hat{y}'e = b'X'e = 0 \Rightarrow e'\hat{y} = 0$$

$$\Rightarrow \sum \hat{Y}_t e_t = 0. \tag{2.24}$$

Since $y = \hat{y} + e$, it now follows that

$$y'y = (\hat{y} + e)'(\hat{y} + e)$$
$$= \hat{y}'\hat{y} + e'e + \hat{y}'e + e'\hat{y}$$
$$= \hat{y}'\hat{y} + e'e; \text{ since } \hat{y}'e = e'\hat{y} = 0. \tag{2.25}$$

The partition of y into components $\hat{y}$ and e is an orthogonal partition; the inner product $\hat{y}'e$ is zero and the sum of squares of elements of y can be expressed as the sum of two component sums of squares. In scalar terms (2.25) is

$$\sum Y_t^2 = \sum \hat{Y}_t^2 + \sum e_t^2. \tag{2.26}$$

Sum of residuals from a regression with an intercept

If there is an intercept in the equation to be estimated, $X_{1t} = 1; t = 1, \dots, n$, and one of the conditions in (2.23) states that

$$\sum X_{1t} e_t = \sum e_t = 0. \tag{2.27}$$

From this, we can deduce that an estimated regression must pass through the sample mean values of the data:

$$Y_t = \hat{Y}_t + e_t; \ t = 1, \dots, n$$

and

$$\sum Y_t = \sum \hat{Y}_t + \sum e_t = \sum \hat{Y}_t; \text{ since } \sum e_t = 0.$$

Hence

$$\sum Y_t/n = \sum \hat{Y}_t/n$$
$$= \sum (b_1 + b_2 X_{2t} + \dots + b_j X_{jt} + \dots + b_k X_{kt})/n$$
$$\Rightarrow \bar{Y} = b_1 + b_2 \bar{X}_2 + \dots + b_j \bar{X}_j + \dots + b_k \bar{X}_k. \tag{2.28}$$

It is important to stress that it is only for models which include an intercept that we have shown that the sum of residuals is zero, and that the regression must pass through the point of sample means.

Total, explained and residual sums of squares

If there is an intercept in the model, there is never any difficulty associated with 'explaining' the sample mean $\bar{Y}$; the intercept estimate, b_1, is chosen so that $\bar{Y}$ is an exact function of $\bar{X}_2, \ldots, \bar{X}_k$. Any measure designed to show how well the behaviour of the dependent variable is explained by the behaviour of the regressors should therefore take the explanation of $\bar{Y}$ for granted, and should measure the extent to which *variation* in Y can be explained by *variation* in the variables $X_2, \ldots, X_k$.

The amount of the variation in the dependent variable observations can be measured by the sum of squares about the sample mean. This quantity is often described as the total sum of squares (TSS):

$$TSS = \sum (Y_t - \bar{Y})^2. \tag{2.29}$$

Provided that the model contains an intercept, the total sum of squares can be split into two components, the explained sum of squares (ESS) and the residual sum of squares (RSS). Equation (2.26) shows that we already have a partition of the 'gross' sum of squares, $\sum Y_t^2$, into the sum of two components:

$$\sum Y_t^2 = \sum \hat{Y}_t^2 + \sum e_t^2,$$

and one of these components is the residual sum of squares (RSS)

$$RSS = \sum e_t^2. \tag{2.30}$$

The extension to 'deviation' sums of squares is straightforward:

$$Y_t = \hat{Y}_t + e_t \Rightarrow (Y_t - \bar{Y}) = (\hat{Y}_t - \bar{Y}) + e_t$$

and

$$\sum (Y_t - \bar{Y})^2 = \sum (\hat{Y}_t - \bar{Y})^2 + \sum e_t^2 + 2\sum (\hat{Y}_t - \bar{Y})e_t.$$

From (2.24), $\sum \hat{Y}_t e_t = 0$, and from (2.27), $\sum \bar{Y}e_t = \bar{Y}\sum e_t = 0$. Hence

$$\sum (Y_t - \bar{Y})^2 = \sum (\hat{Y}_t - \bar{Y})^2 + \sum e_t^2. \tag{2.31}$$

If the explained sum of squares is defined in terms of the variation in predicted values, $\hat{Y}_t$, about the sample mean, $\bar{Y}$, then (2.31) can be written as

$$TSS = ESS + RSS, \tag{2.32}$$

where

$$ESS = \sum (\hat{Y}_t - \bar{Y})^2.$$

Since all the terms in (2.32) are sums of squares, they are all nonnegative. We can assume that TSS is nonzero, since there would be little point in trying to model a dependent variable which exhibits no variation. Then

$$RSS \geq 0 \Rightarrow RSS/TSS \geq 0,$$

$$ESS \geq 0 \Rightarrow TSS - RSS \geq 0$$

$$\Rightarrow RSS \leq TSS$$

$$\Rightarrow RSS/TSS \leq 1,$$

and

$$0 \leq (RSS/TSS) \leq 1. \tag{2.33}$$

Definition of R^2

The most commonly used measure of goodness of fit is the statistic known universally as 'R squared', defined as

$$R^2 = 1 - RSS/TSS$$

$$= 1 - \sum e_t^2 / \sum (Y_t - \bar{Y})^2. \tag{2.34}$$

Since (RSS/TSS) lies between 0 and 1, R^2 also lies between 0 and 1. In the case of a perfect fit to the observed data, all the residuals are equal to zero, RSS is equal to zero, and R^2 is equal to 1. If the estimated equation is so poor that none of the variation in the dependent variable is explained, $RSS = TSS$, and R^2 is equal to zero. It is important to remember that if there is no intercept in the model, the partition shown in (2.31) is not valid, and it is then theoretically possible to obtain a negative value for R^2. In this case, one might consider using the statistic

$$R_*^2 = 1 - \sum e_t^2 / \sum Y_t^2.$$

This is always bounded by 0 and 1, but R_*^2 cannot be compared directly with the conventional R^2, and problems arise when comparing the goodness of fit of two regressions, one involving an intercept, and one which does not.

Definition of $\bar{R}^2$

It is always possible to increase the value of R^2 by adding explanatory variables to a model. Indeed, if there are n explanatory variables and n observations, it is possible to obtain a perfect fit, that is, $R^2 = 1$. Since any set of linearly independent variables can be used to achieve this effect, it proves nothing about model adequacy to increase R^2 in this way, and many authors prefer to report an adjusted measure

$$\bar{R}^2 = 1 - [(1 - R^2)(n - 1)/(n - k)]. \tag{2.35}$$

In (2.35), there is a penalty weighting in the term $(n-1)/(n-k)$, to try to compensate for any increase in R^2 that could be achieved merely by adding arbitrary variables. This measure is usually referred to as 'R bar squared'.

Example 2.2

To illustrate some of the results of this section, we continue the calculation started in Example 2.1. The hand-calculated version of the two-variable consumption function gives predicted consumption values that can be written as

$$\hat{C}_t = -5.674\,85 + 0.926\,319D_t; \quad 1963\text{–}90.$$

If one had to work by hand, it would not be sensible to evaluate individual predicted values and residuals. Instead, one would exploit the algebra of this section to derive a 'short cut' formula. From equations (2.19) and (2.25), we have

$$e'e = y'y - \hat{y}'\hat{y} = y'y - b'X'Xb$$

$$= y'y - b'X'X(X'X)^{-1}X'y = y'y - b'X'y.$$

In the context of a two-variable regression, this gives

$$\sum e_t^2 = \sum Y_t^2 - a\sum Y_t - b\sum X_tY_t$$

which is algebraically equal to

$$\sum e_t^2 = \sum Y_t^2 - \left(\sum Y_t\right)^2 \Big/ n - b\left[\sum X_tY_t - \left(\sum X_t\right)\left(\sum Y_t\right)\Big/ n\right]$$

$$= \sum(Y_t - \bar{Y})^2 - b\sum(X_t - \bar{X})(Y_t - \bar{Y}).$$

Equating C with Y and D with X, we then have the following results:

$$TSS = \sum(Y_t - \bar{Y})^2 = \sum Y_t^2 - \left(\sum Y_t\right)^2 \Big/ n$$

$$= 1\,670\,034.37 - (6691.723)^2/28 = 70\,778.769,$$

$$RSS = \sum e_t^2 = \sum(Y_t - \bar{Y})^2 - b\sum(X_t - \bar{X})(Y_t - \bar{Y})$$

$$= 70\,778.769 - 0.926\,319(75\,580.47)$$

$$= 70\,778.769 - 70\,011.6198$$

$$= 767.1492.$$

Since all 'short cut' formulae tend to involve the subtraction of large numbers to give a relatively small answer, the effect of any initial rounding error is amplified when using a hand calculator. However, a good degree of accuracy is preserved when using a spreadsheet, as here.

With a little help from the computer solution, a more precise value can be obtained. Table 2.1 lists the predicted values and residuals, and from these values, we find that

Table 2.1 Predicted values and residuals in Example 2.2

Predicted values	Residuals
166.0888	4.785 229
173.3335	2.710 488
176.8081	1.684 866
180.7070	0.842 989
183.4526	2.532 380
186.7883	4.420 705
188.5594	3.806 583
195.9616	1.911 368
198.4340	5.705 023
215.4782	1.273 754
229.9149	-1.299 930
228.0910	-2.774 010
229.4379	-4.857 870
228.6950	-3.028 970
223.7697	1.122 273
240.6565	-3.747 520
254.6986	-7.486 590
258.7068	-11.521 800
256.6365	-9.234 450
255.2896	-5.437 580
262.2203	-1.020 300
271.9948	-5.508 820
281.3182	-4.576 220
294.1023	1.519 653
304.3660	6.868 038
322.8229	11.768 130
338.6157	6.790 321
344.7748	2.752 226

$RSS = \sum e_t^2 = 767.149\,199$. It is obvious from the algebra given above that $b \sum (X_t - \bar{X})(Y_t - \bar{Y})$ must be an alternative expression for the explained sum of squares in a two-variable model with an intercept term, so $ESS = 70\,011.6198$. Alternatively, ESS can be calculated directly from predicted values. This gives

$$ESS = \sum \left[\hat{Y}_t - \left(\sum Y_t / n \right) \right]^2 = \sum Y_t^2 - \left(\sum Y_t \right)^2 / n$$

$$= 1\,669\,267.217 - (6691.723)^2 / 28 = 70\,011.619\,78.$$

The calculations performed here confirm the identity $TSS = ESS + RSS$, and apart from a small rounding error in the listing of predicted values, we see that the sum of predicted values, $\sum \hat{Y}_t$, is equal to the sum of observed values, $\sum Y_t$, and that the sum of residuals, $\sum e_t$, is equal to zero. Note, however, that these identities hold only for models which include an intercept term.

The value of R^2 is $1 - RSS/TSS$, giving $R^2 = 0.989\,16$. This looks very good, but it is actually quite easy to obtain a high R^2 when Y represents an aggregate macro-economic time series variable measured as the level, rather than as the change or rate of change between one observation and the next. Finally, note that

$$\bar{R}^2 = 1 - [(1 - 0.989\,16)(27/26)] = 0.988\,74.$$

Predicted values and residuals: *P* and *M* matrices

To conclude this section, we present a rather more powerful approach to the analysis of predicted values and residuals. The payoff from the algebra below is not immediately apparent, but the approach developed here does have several useful applications. From (2.19), the predicted values are

$$\hat{y} = Xb = X(X'X)^{-1}X'y = Py \tag{2.36}$$

where $P = X(X'X)^{-1}X'$. The residuals are

$$e = y - Xb = y - X(X'X)^{-1}X'y = My \tag{2.37}$$

where $M = I - P = I - X(X'X)^{-1}X'$. The matrix P can be thought of as an operation which transforms observed values into predicted values, for a given regressor matrix X. The matrix M is an operation which transforms observed values into residuals, again for given X. Both P and M have the property that they are *symmetric idempotent*, that is,

$$P = P' = PP \Rightarrow P = P'P,$$

$$M = M' = MM \Rightarrow M = M'M.$$

Moreover, $PM = P'M = M'P = MP = 0$, so that $\hat{y}'e = y'P'My = 0$. This confirms the orthogonality property of the predicted values and residuals obtained by least squares regression.

It is important to realise that the approach developed above is quite general. At the moment, we are only concerned with a single regression of y on X, but in due course, we need to consider alternative regressions, and 'P' and 'M' type matrices will play an important part in the analysis. For example, we can split the regressor matrix X into two parts, X_1 and X_2, where X_1 has $(k - g)$ columns and X_2 has g columns. By analogy with the argument above, a regression of y on X_1 would produce predicted values $P_1 y$ and residuals $M_1 y$, where

$$P_1 = X_1(X_1'X_1)^{-1}X_1',$$

$$M_1 = I - P_1 = I - X_1(X_1'X_1)^{-1}X_1'.$$

Indeed, one could go further and consider regressions *between* variables in X. If each variable in X_2 were to be regressed on the variables in X_1, there would be g separate regressions, one for each column in X_2. Once this is understood, we can refer to the regression of one matrix on another, and we can still use 'P' and 'M' type matrices to represent the generation of predicted values and residuals. Hence $P_1 X_2$ would be the matrix of predicted values from the regression of X_2 on X_1, and $M_1 X_2$ would be the matrix of residuals. This idea is used, with modified notation, in section 3.2, and again in section 3.5. For the moment we note that regressions between variables in X are clearly possible, even though the application of such an idea is not yet obvious, and we also note that these are known as *auxiliary* regressions, to distinguish them from the main regression of interest, which is still that of y on X.

2.4 / Statistical properties of least squares estimators

The discussion so far has concentrated on the mathematical properties of least squares estimation. In this section, we turn to statistical interpretation.

The explicit form for the least squares solution vector, given in equation (2.11), shows that

$$b = (X'X)^{-1}X'y.$$

The matrix form of the single equation model is

$$y = X\beta + u.$$

Hence we have directly that b is a function of the random disturbances

$$b = (X'X)^{-1}X'y$$

$$= (X'X)^{-1}X'(X\beta + u)$$

$$= (X'X)^{-1}X'X\beta + (X'X)^{-1}X'u$$

$$= \beta + (X'X)^{-1}X'u. \tag{2.38}$$

The logic of the model is that different realisations of the vector u would give different realisations of y, though only one realisation of u is deemed actually to have occurred, so that only one y vector is actually observed. Equation (2.38) extends this logic to the vector b. One set of estimates is actually obtained, but (2.38) shows that different realisations of u would give different realisations of b. The nature of the random variation in b can be derived directly from the assumed form of random variation in u.

Equation (2.38) is a linear function of the random vector u, and if X is considered to be nonrandom, the weights in the function are also nonrandom. For this type of function, the following properties are easily derived. Let v be an $(n \times 1)$ random vector, A be a $(k \times n)$ nonrandom matrix and c be a $(k \times 1)$ nonrandom vector. Then $L = c + Av$ defines a $(k \times 1)$ random vector, which is a linear function of v, and

(a) $E(L) = c + AE(v)$

(b) $\text{var}(L) = A \cdot \text{var}(v) \cdot A'$

(c) $v \sim N(\ ) \Rightarrow L \sim N(\ )$.

Applying these rules to equation (2.38), we have

1. $E(b) = E[\beta + (X'X)^{-1}X'u]$

$\qquad = \beta + (X'X)^{-1}X'E(u)$

$\qquad = \beta; \text{ if } E(u) = 0$

$\qquad \Rightarrow b \text{ is an unbiased estimator of } \beta;$ \hfill (2.39)

2. $\text{var}(b) = \text{var}[\beta + (X'X)^{-1}X'u]$

$\qquad = (X'X)^{-1}X' \cdot \text{var}(u) \cdot X(X'X)^{-1}$

$\qquad = (X'X)^{-1}X'(\sigma^2 I)X(X'X)^{-1}; \text{ if } \text{var}(u) = \sigma^2 I$

$\qquad = \sigma^2(X'X)^{-1}X'X(X'X)^{-1}; \text{ since } \sigma^2 \text{ is scalar}$

$\qquad = \sigma^2(X'X)^{-1};$ \hfill (2.40)

3.   If u is multivariate normal, then b is also multivariate normal.

If properties (1), (2), and (3) are taken together we have

$$b \sim N[\beta, \sigma^2(X'X)^{-1}].$$ \hfill (2.41)

For future reference, it is important to link specific properties of b to specific assumptions. We have assumed that $y = X\beta + u$ represents a correctly specified model, that X is a nonrandom matrix and that $(X'X)$ is nonsingular, which requires the columns of X to be linearly independent. Then if $E(u) = 0$, b is unbiased; if $\text{var}(u) = \sigma^2 I$, $\text{var}(b) = \sigma^2(X'X)^{-1}$; and if u is normal, b is normal.

Gauss–Markov theorem

The least squares estimator b belong to the class of linear unbiased estimators of the parameter vector β. Linearity means that it is possible to write the estimator as Cy, where C is a $(k \times n)$ matrix of nonrandom elements. An arbitrary linear estimator, $\tilde{\beta}$, is unbiased if $E(u) = 0$ and $CX = I$, where I is a $(k \times k)$ identity matrix. To see this, write

$$\tilde{\beta} = Cy = C(X\beta + u),$$

$$E(\tilde{\beta}) = E(CX\beta + Cu)$$

$$\qquad = CX\beta + CE(u)$$

$$\qquad = \beta; \text{ if } CX = I \text{ and } E(u) = 0.$$

The variance of $\tilde{\beta}$ is given by

$$\text{var}(\tilde{\beta}) = \text{var}(CX\beta + Cu)$$

$$= \text{var}(Cu)$$

$$= C \cdot \text{var}(u) \cdot C'$$

$$= \sigma^2 CC'; \text{ if } \text{var}(u) = \sigma^2 I.$$

The Gauss–Markov theorem states that the least squares estimator b is best linear unbiased (BLU). To show this, we must establish that the difference between $\text{var}(\tilde{\beta})$ and $\text{var}(b)$ is positive semidefinite. Amongst other things, this means that $\text{var}(\tilde{\beta}_j) \geq \text{var}(b_j)$, for all $j = 1, \ldots, k$. By writing $C = (X'X)^{-1}X' + D$, an arbitrary estimator can be related to the least squares estimator, and

$$CX = I \Rightarrow (X'X)^{-1}X'X + DX = I$$

$$\Rightarrow I + DX = I$$

$$\Rightarrow DX = 0,$$

$$CC' = [(X'X)^{-1}X' + D][(X'X)^{-1}X' + D]'$$

$$= (X'X)^{-1}X'X(X'X)^{-1} + DD'; \text{ since } DX = 0 \text{ and } X'D' = 0$$

$$= (X'X)^{-1} + DD' \geq (X'X)^{-1}; \text{ since } DD' \text{ is psd.}$$

Hence

$$\text{var}(\tilde{\beta}) = \sigma^2 CC' = \sigma^2[(X'X)^{-1} + DD']$$

$$\geq \sigma^2(X'X)^{-1} = \text{var}(b). \tag{2.42}$$

Note that the proof above assumes that X is nonrandom, that $E(u) = 0$ and that $\text{var}(u) = \sigma^2 I$. Under these conditions, the least squares estimator is BLU. Note also the form of matrix inequality used above: the statement $A \geq B$ is shorthand for the statement that $A - B$ is positive semidefinite.

Residuals and the estimation of σ^2

In dealing with the regression model, it is easy to forget that $\beta_1, \ldots, \beta_k$ are not the only unknown parameters. We have assumed that $\text{var}(u) = \sigma^2 I$, but we have not assumed that σ^2 is known. The statistical theory relevant to the estimation of σ^2 is summarised below.

The parameter σ^2 is the common variance of each disturbance u_t; $t = 1, \ldots, n$, that is, of each element of the vector u. However, u is unobservable, and the closest proxy available is the residual vector $e = y - Xb$. A little algebra will show how e is related to u:

$$e = y - Xb$$

$$= y - X(X'X)^{-1}X'y$$

$$= My; \text{ where } M = I - X(X'X)^{-1}X' \text{ (see equation (2.37))}.$$

Moreover, M has the property $MX = 0$:

$$MX = [I - X(X'X)^{-1}X']X = X - X = 0.$$

Consequently,

$$e = My = M(X\beta + u) = Mu. \tag{2.43}$$

Recall, from section 2.3, that M is symmetric idempotent – that is, $M = M' = MM \Rightarrow M'M = M$. A quadratic form in a standard normal vector and a symmetric idempotent matrix has a χ^2 distribution, with degrees of freedom equal to the rank of the idempotent matrix. Specifically, if $u \sim N(0, \sigma^2 I)$, then $u/\sigma \sim N(0, I)$, and

$$e'e/\sigma^2 = u'M'Mu/\sigma^2 = u'Mu/\sigma^2 \sim \chi_r^2, \tag{2.44}$$

where $r = \text{rank}(M)$. It is an exercise in matrix algebra to show that a symmetric idempotent matrix has rank equal to trace, and that $\text{trace}(M) = n - k$.

We now have the result that the sum of squared residuals from the least squares fit has, when scaled by σ^2, a χ^2 distribution, with $(n - k)$ degrees of freedom. Amongst other things, this tells us that

$$E(e'e/\sigma^2) = n - k. \tag{2.45}$$

Equation (2.45) holds because a χ^2 distribution has expectation equal to degrees of freedom. By exchanging the nonrandom quantities σ^2 and $n - k$, we obtain

$$E[e'e/(n - k)] = E\left[\sum e_t^2/(n - k)\right] = \sigma^2.$$

This shows that an unbiased estimator of σ^2 can be obtained from the formula

$$\hat{\sigma}^2 = \sum e_t^2/(n - k). \tag{2.46}$$

Equation (2.46) can also be obtained directly, and does not in fact depend on the normality assumption that leads to (2.44).

Independence of b and e

Equations (2.38) and (2.43) show that b and e are both linear functions of the disturbance vector u. We already have rules that enable us to look at each linear function separately, and the usefulness of these rules is enhanced considerably if we also consider the covariance between two linear functions. If $L_1 = c_1 + A_1 v_1$ and

$L_2 = c_2 + A_2 v_2$ are linear functions of the random vectors v_1, v_2, then

$$\text{cov}(L_1, L_2) = A_1 \cdot \text{cov}(v_1, v_2) \cdot A_2'. \tag{2.47}$$

A special case arises when L_1 and L_2 are functions of the *same* random vector v, for then $\text{cov}(v, v) = \text{var}(v)$ and

$$\text{cov}(L_1, L_2) = A_1 \cdot \text{var}(v) \cdot A_2'. \tag{2.48}$$

Now consider the linear functions

$$b = \beta + (X'X)^{-1} X' u$$

$$e = Mu; \text{ where } M = I - X(X'X)^{-1} X'.$$

Since b and e are functions of the same random vector u, we have from (2.48),

$$
\begin{aligned}
\text{cov}(b, e) &= (X'X)^{-1} X' \cdot \text{var}(u) \cdot M' \\
&= (X'X)^{-1} X'(\sigma^2 I) M'; \text{ if } \text{var}(u) = \sigma^2 I \\
&= \sigma^2 (X'X)^{-1} X' M' \\
&= 0; \text{ since } MX = 0 \Rightarrow X'M' = 0. \tag{2.49}
\end{aligned}
$$

Recall that if two random variables have zero covariance, they are said to be uncorrelated. What we have shown is that each element in the least squares estimator vector b is uncorrelated with each element in the least squares residual vector e.

Under normality of the disturbance vector u, the result $\text{cov}(b, e) = 0$ is strengthened to *independence* between elements of the vectors b and e. Given normality, b has a multivariate normal distribution (equation 2.41) and $e'e/\sigma^2$ has a χ^2 distribution (equation 2.44). If b and e are independent, then b and $e'e/\sigma^2$ are independent, since $e'e/\sigma^2$ is a function of e in which e is the only source of random variation. Hence, under normality, we have distributions for both b and $e'e/\sigma^2$, and these distributions are independent.

Standard errors and the t distribution

Now consider how one can use the information that the least squares vector b has a normal distribution, whilst $e'e/\sigma^2$ has an independent χ^2 distribution with $(n - k)$ degrees of freedom. The fact that the vector b has a multivariate normal distribution implies that a single element, b_j, has a univariate normal distribution. Hence

$$b_j \sim N(\beta_j, \sigma^2 a_{jj}),$$

where $a_{jj} = [(X'X)^{-1}]_{jj}$, the jth diagonal element of $(X'X)^{-1}$. The standard normal variate corresponding to b_j is

$$z_j = (b_j - \beta_j)/\sigma\sqrt{a_{jj}}.$$

This cannot be used directly for inference, because σ^2 is unknown, and if σ^2 is replaced by $\hat{\sigma}^2$ the resulting statistic has a t distribution, not a standard normal distribution.

The relevant theory is that if z is a standard normal variable and w is a χ^2 variable with r degrees of freedom, and z and w are independent, then the ratio

$$t = z/\sqrt{(w/r)}$$

has a t distribution with r degrees of freedom. Applying this result to the standardised distribution of b_j and the χ^2 distribution of $e'e/\sigma^2 = (n-k)\hat{\sigma}^2/\sigma^2$, we obtain

$$t_j = [(b_j - \beta_j)/\sigma\sqrt{a_{jj}}]/\sqrt{[(n-k)\hat{\sigma}^2/\sigma^2(n-k)]}$$
$$= (b_j - \beta_j)\hat{\sigma}\sqrt{a_{jj}}; \text{ since } \sigma \text{ and } (n-k) \text{ both cancel.}$$

Hence

$$t_j = (b_j - \beta_j)/\hat{\sigma}\sqrt{a_{jj}} \sim t_{n-k}. \tag{2.50}$$

It is conventional to refer to the square root of the *estimated* variance of b_j as the standard error of b_j

$$se(b_j) = \hat{\sigma}\sqrt{a_{jj}}.$$

Contrast this with the square root of the *theoretical* variance of b_j, which is $\sigma\sqrt{a_{jj}}$. Equation (2.50) can now be rewritten as

$$t_j = (b_j - \beta_j)/se(b_j) \sim t_{n-k}. \tag{2.51}$$

Note that t_j is the standard normal variable z_j, with the unknown parameter σ^2 replaced by the estimated disturbance variance $\hat{\sigma}^2$.

Testing the null hypothesis $\beta_j = 0$

In writing down the model $y = X\beta + u$, it is assumed, at least implicitly, that none of the parameters $\beta_j; j = 1, \ldots, k$ is zero, for otherwise the corresponding variable, X_j, would have no effect on the dependent variable, and there would be no point in including X_j in the list of regressors. However, the least squares estimator b_j is a random variable, with a continuous probability distribution, so it is highly unlikely that b_j would be zero, even in those cases in which the true parameter is zero. It is clearly possible for the model builder to assume that X_j does influence the behaviour of the dependent variable, only to find that there is no evidence from the data to support this view. The evidence must consist of more than a simple inspection of the value of b_j; what is needed is a test which attempts to distinguish between a non-zero value of b_j that arises because β_j is nonzero, and a nonzero value of b_j that arises when β_j is zero.

From equation (2.51), we have that

$$t_j = (b_j - \beta_j)/se(b_j) \sim t_{n-k}.$$

If $\beta_j = 0$, this becomes

$$t_j = (b_j - 0)/se(b_j) = b_j/se(b_j) \sim t_{n-k}. \tag{2.52}$$

Whereas (2.51) always has a t distribution (at least under the classical regression assumptions), equation (2.52) defines a test statistic, which only has a t distribution if it is true that $\beta_j = 0$. The null hypothesis to be tested is written as $H_0: \beta_j = 0$, and we say that (2.52) has a t distribution 'under the null hypothesis'. Under the alternative hypothesis $H_1: \beta_j \neq 0$, (2.52) is not distributed as t_{n-k}. It is this fact that forms the basis of a test procedure.

If a variable t_j does have a t distribution, with a given number of degrees of freedom (df), then tables of the t distribution can be used to find critical values $t_{df}^{\alpha/2}$, such that

$$\Pr(-t_{df}^{\alpha/2} \le t_j \le t_{df}^{\alpha/2}) = 1 - \alpha$$

for

$$\Pr(t_j > t_{df}^{\alpha/2}) = \Pr(t_j < -t_{df}^{\alpha/2}) = \alpha/2.$$

In the present context, t_j is the test statistic defined in (2.52), $df = n - k$ and α is the *significance level* adopted for the test. This is the probability of finding a value of t_j which is greater than $t_{df}^{\alpha/2}$ or less than $-t_{df}^{\alpha/2}$, if it is true that $\beta_j = 0$. For example, if $\alpha = 0.05$ and $df = 20$, then from Table C.1 in Appendix C, the value of $t_{20}^{0.025}$ is found to be 2.09. By choosing α to be 0.05, we have ensured that there is a relatively small probability of finding a value of t_j in a region defined by the tails of the t distribution, if β_j is really zero. An observed value of t_j which is either less than -2.09 or greater than 2.09 is therefore taken as evidence that β_j is *not* zero, and $H_0: \beta_j = 0$ is rejected in favour of $H_1: \beta_j \neq 0$. If the value of the test statistic lies between -2.09 and 2.09, we are not able to reject the null hypothesis.

The procedure described above is a *two-tailed* test, since rejection of H_0 occurs in both 'tails' of the null distribution. If the objective is to show a positive relationship between Y and X_j, given the presence of other regressors, one could set up the null hypothesis on the boundary value $\beta_j = 0$, and specify the alternative $H_1: \beta_j > 0$. In this case, rejection at a 5% significance level would occur if the calculated value t_j is greater than the critical value $t_{n-k}^{0.05}$. For obvious reasons, such procedures are known as *one-tailed* tests.

As stated above, the significance level of a test is the probability of rejecting the null hypothesis when H_0 is actually true. It is always possible to reduce the probability of this particular type of error (known as *Type I* error), but only at the cost of increasing the probability of failing to reject a null hypothesis which is actually false (a *Type II* error). Whereas the Type I error probability can be chosen by the investigator, the Type II error probability depends on what the truth is – in this case the value of β_j – and also on the quality of the data. As we shall see in section 3.5, there are various forms of data deficiency, including insufficient observations, insufficient variation and high measured correlations between regressor variables, which can lead to high probabilities of Type II error in the t test. It is not always safe to interpret a failure to reject $H_0: \beta_j = 0$ as a clear signal that the variable X_j should be deleted from the list of regressors, and it is for this reason that we insist on the terminology 'failure to reject' rather than 'accept', when the value of a test statistic does not lead to rejection of the null hypothesis.

Example 2.3

If the calculations for the two-variable consumption function (Example 2.1) are carried out by matrix inversion, the (2×2) inverse matrix is

$$(X'X)^{-1} = \begin{bmatrix} 0.890\,728\,66 & -0.003\,237\,14 \\ -0.003\,237\,14 & 0.000\,012\,26 \end{bmatrix}.$$

The formula for the disturbance variance estimator is $\hat{\sigma}^2 = \sum e_t^2/(n-k)$. Using the results of Example 2.2, this gives

$$\sigma^2 = 767.1492/(28-2) = 29.5057.$$

The standard error of the intercept is therefore

$$se(a) = \sqrt{[29.5057(0.890\,73)]} = 5.126\,56,$$

while the standard error of the slope is

$$se(b) = \sqrt{[29.5057(0.000\,012\,26)]} = 0.019\,02.$$

The t test statistic for $H_0: \alpha = 0$ is $-5.674\,85/5.126\,56 = -1.107$, whilst that for $H_0: \beta = 0$ is $0.926\,319/0.019\,02 = 48.702$. Again, some slight rounding error occurs here, but this is irrelevant when considering the conclusions to the t tests. With 26 degrees of freedom, the critical value for a two-tailed test at a 5% significance level is 2.06, so both null hypotheses are easily rejected. Neither result is unexpected, and this is particularly true of the result concerning the slope; it would be very strange indeed if we were not able to find strong rejection of a null hypothesis which says that income has no effect on consumers' expenditure.

Large sample distribution of b

As well as the small sample properties obtained in this section, the least squares estimator also has large sample properties, which hold under assumptions considerably weaker than those of the classical regression model. Large sample theory is discussed in some detail in Chapter 4; here we want to say enough to indicate that least squares estimation can sometimes be used when the assumptions of the classical regression model are not strictly satisfied.

There are two cases that we can mention at this stage. If the regressors in X are non-random and the disturbances are $IID(0, \sigma^2)$, but we do *not* assume normality of the disturbance distributions, it can still be argued that b is normal, or more accurately that b is approximately normal, with the mean β and variance $\sigma^2(X'X)^{-1}$, provided that the sample is reasonably large. In order to establish this result, there are some conditions that must be satisfied, but for the moment we leave this to one side. The important point to make is that results and procedures derived from the normality assumption can often still be used as approximations, given certain technical considerations and a reasonably large sample.

A second case of interest is when X contains some columns that are random, but which are uncorrelated with the disturbances. An example is provided by the simple dynamic model:

$$Y_t = \beta_1 + \beta_2 X_{2t} + \beta_3 Y_{t-1} + u_t; \; u_t \sim IID(0, \sigma^2); \; t = 1, \ldots, n. \tag{2.53}$$

If (2.53) holds for periods $t = 1, \ldots, n$, there is implicitly a second equation which shows how Y_{t-1} is determined, at least for $t = 2, \ldots, n$:

$$Y_{t-1} = \beta_1 + \beta_2 X_{2,t-1} + \beta_3 Y_{t-2} + u_{t-1}; \; t = 2, \ldots, n.$$

Since Y_{t-1} depends partly on u_{t-1}, it is clear that Y_{t-1} is random for $t = 2, \ldots, n$. Consequently, (2.53) has at least one regressor which is random, and the 'fixed regressor' assumption cannot hold. It is shown in Chapter 7 that if there is no serial correlation and the underlying difference equation in Y is stable, one can often treat a model such as (2.53) in much the same way as a static model, although the justification is based on large sample properties, and inferences drawn from very small samples do have to be treated with some caution.

Although much of the analysis in the next chapter is still conducted under classical assumptions, we now know that some relaxation of these assumptions is possible, and that such relaxations do not necessarily invalidate all the results and procedures developed so far.

2.5 / Computer solutions and model evaluation

At this point, we have established a number of results that relate to the classical regression model, but the examples have only illustrated small parts of the calculations involved, and we have yet to show how one might evaluate an estimation exercise in a more complete and critical way.

Turning first to the model of aggregate consumer behaviour, we start by reconsidering the two-variable consumption function, using this to illustrate some practical aspects of a computer-based analysis. As before, the observations on consumers' expenditure (RCONS) and disposable income (RPDI) are taken from data set 1.

Because there are so many alternative programs that one might use, it is impossible to discuss the mechanics of any single package here. But, there is some basic information that any program will produce, and the printout shown in Table 2.2 illustrates the style of presentation of a typical core output.

The first thing to note is that although the basic data file contains observations on three variables for 1963–94, neither the full set of variables nor the full set of observations is used in the regression actually performed. The ability to select subsamples of observations is almost universal, and the sample used is indicated in the first line of the printout. Likewise, almost all packages admit variable names, and the next line shows that RCONS is the dependent variable in this regression. The output then indicates the regressors chosen, giving the name of the regressor, the coefficient or parameter estimate, the standard error and the 't value' for each variable. In terms

Table 2.2 Regression results: linear consumption function

Sample based on observations 1963–90
Dependent variable is RCONS

Variable	Coefficient	Standard error	t value
INTER	−5.674 850	5.126 559	−1.106 95
RPDI	0.926 319	0.019 016	48.711 54

Degrees of freedom 26 from 28 observations

Residual SS	767.1492
Total SS	70 778.77
Disturbance variance	29.505 74
R^2	0.989 161
DW statistic	0.4291

of the notation of this chapter, these correspond to b_j, se(b_j) and t_j, the last being the t test for $H_0: \beta_j = 0$.

In Table 2.2, the regressor labelled INTER corresponds to the 'variable' X_1, which allows for an intercept term. The program should give you some means of creating this regressor internally, rather than actually entering a column of ones as data. However, you do usually have to include such a variable explicitly in the list of regressors; otherwise, you will obtain a regression with no intercept, and this will force the estimated regression plane to pass through the point of origin against which your data are measured.

Underneath the information that relates to each regressor, the number of degrees of freedom is given, followed by the residual sum of squares, the total sum of squares, the disturbance variance estimate ($\hat{\sigma}^2$) and the value of R^2. In some cases, numbers may be given in a format such as 7.077 877E + 04, which means that the value 7.077 877 is to be multiplied by 10^4. This type of presentation is used where a fixed format would lose too much accuracy, or where the range of possible results is too wide to fit comfortably in the layout adopted by the programmer. The final piece of information, labelled the 'DW statistic', is discussed later in this section.

At this stage, there seems to be very little in the core of the typical output which really tests the adequacy of the proposed model. The t statistics indicate that the intercept is not significantly different from zero, although the slope is, and the value of R^2 is high. But these results are not unexpected, and they offer no real discrimination against possible alternative models. However, there is one thing that we have not done, which is to examine the behaviour of the residuals.

The least squares residuals are the empirical counterparts of the unobservable disturbances. If a graph of residuals against observation number shows any regular behaviour, such as a cyclical pattern, or a relatively long sequence of values moving in one direction, this may be taken as evidence that successive disturbances are not independent. Similarly, any tendency for the residuals to become

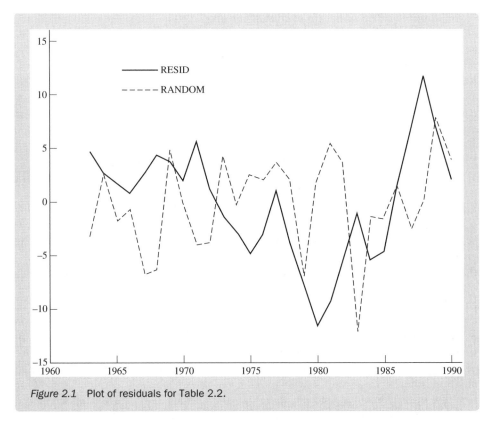

Figure 2.1 Plot of residuals for Table 2.2.

progressively more variable would tend to contradict the assumption of constant disturbance variance.

The graph of residuals from the linear consumption function is shown in Figure 2.1. To help with the interpretation, this is superimposed on the plot of a variable named RANDOM, which is computer generated, with zero mean, constant variance and zero covariance between successive observations. Although there are one or two large values in the residuals series (RESID), it is difficult to be sure of any systematic tendency for the residual variance to increase over time, and we reserve judgement on this for now. There is a more obvious tendency for successive residuals to follow each other, with too few sign changes relative to a purely random choice of positive and negative values. This indicates possible serial correlation of the residuals, but it remains to be seen what we should do as a result of this finding.

One possible way forward is to assume that the main part of the model is correct, but that we have badly behaved residuals because the underlying disturbances happen to exhibit serial correlation. This sees the presence or absence of serial correlation as a set of logical alternatives, without suggesting any reason for one variant rather than the other. Presumably, the correct response to this interpretation would be to look for an estimation method that can allow for more elaborate disturbance behaviour.

An alternative and rather more convincing argument is that if the main part of the model is correctly specified, the disturbances should represent totally unpredictable and unstructured information, and should therefore be 'well behaved'. Under this interpretation, the residuals may appear to exhibit serial correlation because the main part of the model is not correctly specified, and this is causing systematic influences to be assigned incorrectly to the disturbance term. In this case, the appropriate corrective action is to respecify the main part of the model, and then to make a second attempt at estimation, without changing the method used, to see whether the apparent disturbance problem has now disappeared.

In the light of this discussion, we now return to the interpretation of the Durbin–Watson (DW) statistic. This is designed to reveal the presence of a certain specific pattern of serial correlation, but as with the graph of residuals, it can also pick up the effects of any misspecification in the main part of the model. Values of the DW statistic fall between 0 and 4 and, in general, the closer the value is to 2, the more acceptable our estimated relationship will be. Full details of the formal test are given in section 7.5, but for now, we can take 'low' or 'high' values of DW to indicate that there is almost certainly something wrong with the estimated equation.

In our example, $DW = 0.43$, which is definitely on the low side. We therefore conclude that something is wrong, and that we need to try some modification of the model. Amongst the possibilities are changes in functional form, the introduction of new regressors, and the introduction of some dynamic element, using lags of either existing or additional variables. Variables that have been suggested as possible determinants of aggregate consumption include liquid asset holdings, the rate of inflation, interest rates, and labour market variables such as unemployment. More recently, in the United Kingdom, there has been evidence of a link from nonliquid wealth to consumption, but annual data are not sufficiently rich to support extensive experimentation with all these effects together. We therefore content ourselves with two simple modifications, which are also used to illustrate a further important feature of a typical computer package.

Suppose that instead of arguing that the marginal propensity to consume is constant over time, which is implicit in the linear specification, we assume that the elasticity of consumers' expenditure with respect to disposable income is constant. This modification is achieved by using the natural logarithms of RCONS and RPDI in place of the raw observations.

All computer packages designed for general statistics or econometrics offer the facility for creating transformations of the basic data though, again, the precise mechanisms for achieving this do vary. In our example, we need to use a (natural) log transformation to create variables which we name LNRCONS and LNRPDI.

The results from the modified estimation are given below. For this exercise, we have chosen a 'reporting' format, where the estimated equation is laid out with estimates replacing unknown parameters, standard errors in brackets underneath the corresponding parameter estimates, and associated statistics given below that. In practice, one should report much more than this basic information, but at this stage we could not easily interpret a more extensive set of output statistics. The results are

$$\ln(\hat{C}_t) = -0.105 + 1.001 \ln(D_t); \quad 1963-90$$
$$\qquad\qquad (0.107) \quad (0.019)$$

$$n = 28 \qquad df = 26 \qquad RSS = 1.1038 \times 10^{-2}$$

$$VAR = 4.245 \times 10^{-4} \quad R^2 = 0.990 \quad DW = 0.445.$$

(2.54)

In (2.54), RSS is used as an abbreviation for the residual sum of squares and VAR as an abbreviation for the disturbance variance estimate. Notice that the estimated equation is written with $\ln(\hat{C}_t)$ on the left-hand side; an alternative is to write $\ln(C_t)$ on the left, with an additional term on the right to represent a residual. In practice, this nicety is often ignored, and reported equations are frequently written as in (2.54), but with the actual dependent variable on the left, rather than the predicted values.

Direct comparison of (2.54) with the linear consumption function is complicated by the fact that the dependent variable has changed, and this means that statistics such as R^2, the residual sum of squares and the disturbance variance are not directly comparable between the two versions of the model. What we can see is that the value of DW is still low, and this suggests that changing the functional form has not removed the apparent serial correlation in the residuals. The next step is to try adding a new economic variable in order to see whether this can give a more obvious improvement in the results.

The new variable to be tried is the rate of inflation; for convenience, this is based on the consumer price deflator PCONS, which is given in data set 1, rather than a retail price index. Using P_t to denote an observation on the variable PCONS, the measure used is $\ln(P_t) - \ln(P_{t-1})$, which is a close approximation to the proportional rate of inflation $(P_t - P_{t-1})/P_{t-1}$. The transformations needed are the creation of $\ln(P_t)$, which we name as LNPCONS, and a differencing operation, to give a variable which we call DLPCONS. This last step could cause one problem, in that the value of DLPCONS in 1963 should be obtained by subtracting the value of LNPCONS in 1962 from the value of LNPCONS in 1963. But if the value of LNPCONS in 1962 is not available, the value of DLPCONS in 1963 cannot be obtained. Consequently we must start the estimation in 1964. In the preceding example, we started in 1963, but once DLPCONS is used, this is no longer possible. Most computer packages will warn you, or prevent you from using nonexistent observations, but this is something to bear in mind when using lag or difference transformations.

The third version of our consumption function is given below, with the symbol Δ used to represent the first difference operator:

$$\ln(\hat{C}_t) = -0.134 + 1.01 \ln(D_t) - 0.257 \Delta \ln(P_t); \quad 1964-90$$
$$\qquad\qquad (0.093) \quad (0.017) \qquad\quad (0.070)$$

$$n = 27 \qquad df = 24 \qquad RSS = 6.7901 \times 10^{-3}$$

$$VAR = 2.829 \times 10^{-4} \quad R^2 = 0.9935 \quad DW = 0.756.$$

(2.55)

The revised equation does have a more acceptable value of DW than before, and the

Table 2.3 UK demand for money

Sample based on observations 1963–90
Dependent variable is LN(M4/P)

Variable	Coefficient	Standard error	t value
INTER	−32.0590	3.783 800	−8.473
LNRTDE	6.3362	0.662 338	9.566
LNINTL	−21.2180	4.816 100	−4.406

Degrees of freedom 25, from 28 observations

Residual SS	8.085 7
Total SS	37.691 84
Disturbance variance	0.323 43
R^2	0.785 48
DW statistic	0.776 7

inflation variable does appear to have some effect, with a t statistic equal to -3.67. The lower tail 5% critical value for a two-tailed test with 23 degrees of freedom is -2.07, so if β_3 represents the parameter on the inflation variable, we can apparently reject $H_0: \beta_3 = 0$.

Although (2.55) represents some improvement, the value of DW is still too low, and it is not clear that all the underlying statistical assumptions are satisfied. It is therefore premature to conclude that we have an acceptable model of consumer behaviour, and we shall return to this example in due course.

We now present and briefly review initial results from the other data sets given in section 1.6. Equation (1.27) proposed the simple demand for money function:

$$\ln(M_t/P_t) = \beta_1 + \beta_2 \ln(A_t) + \beta_3 \ln(r_t) + u_t; \ t = 1, \ldots, n.$$

Using observations for the United Kingdom for 1963–90, taken from data set 2, the core printout is as shown in Table 2.3.

The coefficient on the activity variable cannot reasonably be interpreted as the elasticity between real money and activity, since the dependent variable only partially represents the real narrow money stock. It is clearly very significant, however. The interest rate effect is significantly different from zero, and has the expected sign. R^2 is markedly lower than that for the consumption function, but more than 70% of the variation in the dependent variable observations is explained by variation in activity and interest rates. However, the DW statistic is very low, and this means that one should be extremely cautious in interpreting the results obtained. At a later stage, we shall produce additional test statistics which show that the chosen version of the demand for money function is unstable, and that several of the underlying statistical assumptions are not satisfied.

Turning next to data set 3, we estimate the following relationship between the implicit price of output (HUC), unit labour costs (ULC) and unit import costs

(UMC):

$$\ln(\widehat{HUC_t}) = 0.0018 + 1.001\ln(ULC_t) - 0.014\ln(UMC_t); \quad 1960-90$$
$$\quad\quad (0.007) \quad (0.052) \quad\quad\quad (0.044)$$

$$n = 31 \quad\quad\quad df = 28 \quad\quad RSS = 1.2084 \times 10^{-2}$$
$$VAR = 4.316 \times 10^{-4} \quad R^2 = 0.9994 \quad DW = 0.834.$$

$$(2.56)$$

Here, almost all the work is done by unit labour costs, with unit import costs not significantly different from zero. R^2 is extremely high, but DW is again very low. Since this is becoming a regular feature of static models based on time series data, we have a second attempt at (2.56), this time adding a lagged value of $\ln(HUC)$ to see what difference this makes. The results are

$$\ln(\widehat{HUC_t}) = 0.0252 + 0.659\ln(ULC_t) - 0.062\ln(UMC_t)$$
$$\quad\quad (0.0035) \quad (0.034) \quad\quad\quad (0.018)$$
$$\quad\quad + 0.286\ln(HUC_{t-1}); \quad 1960-90$$
$$\quad\quad (0.023)$$

$$n = 31 \quad\quad\quad df = 27 \quad\quad RSS = 1.7803 \times 10^{-3}$$
$$VAR = 6.594 \times 10^{-5} \quad R^2 = 0.9999 \quad DW = 1.99.$$

$$(2.57)$$

Superficially, there is a considerable improvement here, in that unit import costs now have a t value of 3.44 with the DW statistic moving to 1.99. The coefficient on $\ln(ULC)$ has fallen sharply, but this now measures the short-run elasticity associated with ULC; the long-run elasticity is obtained by dividing the short-run estimate by 1 minus the coefficient on the lagged dependent variable, giving $0.659/(1-0.286) = 0.923$. This point is explained further in Chapter 6.

Again, looking forward somewhat, there are still some reasons for caution here. When formulating dynamic models for time series observations, one is not entirely free to choose the dynamic specification, without regard to the nature of the time series involved. It is also true that the Durbin–Watson statistic is not a reliable indicator when a lagged value of the dependent variable appears in the list of regressors, and this fact alone could account for some of the improvement observed in (2.57).

The last example uses cross-section data. Equation (1.29) suggests the estimation of a relationship between the average rate of growth of per capita GDP (AVGR), the initial level (i.e. in 1975) of the GDP per capita (GDP575L) and a human capital measure (SYRM75, the average years of secondary schooling in 1975 for the male population over 25) for the 102 countries of the Barro–Lee data set – data set 4 – for which all the selected variables are available. This gives

$$AVGR_t = 0.0333 - 0.0047\,GDP575L_t + 0.0138\,SYRM75_t;$$
$$\quad\quad (0.0259) \quad (0.0036) \quad\quad\quad (0.0037)$$

$$n = 102 \quad\quad\quad df = 99 \quad\quad RSS = 5.7007 \times 10^{-2}$$
$$VAR = 5.758 \times 10^{-4} \quad R^2 = 0.153\,35 \quad DW = 1.51.$$

$$(2.58)$$

The connection between the coefficient on GDP575L and the implied annual rate of convergence is

$$\text{annual convergence rate} = -\frac{1}{10}\ln[1 + (10)(-0.0047)] = 0.0048,$$

roughly 0.5% per year (Barro and Sala-i-Martin, 1995: 422, 432). The t value for this coefficient is only 1.31, which suggests that this convergence rate is not very precisely estimated. The coefficient on the human capital variable has the expected positive sign, and the t value of 4.86 suggests a relationship between per capita growth rates and human capital measures. The most obvious feature of these results is the very low value for R^2. It is not unusual to find low R^2 values for equations estimated from cross-section data on countries or individuals or households, because one expects a considerable amount of apparently random variation over and above that explained by any relationship that may exist. Even so, equation (2.58) is poor, and in this case, the only way of improving the result is to control properly for other variables.

This observation is particularly important in the current example, where the chief parameter of interest is β_2 in (1.29), since this determines the annual rate of convergence. To illustrate, three other human capital measures and four country characteristic variables are included in (1.29). The human capital measures are SYRF75 (the average years of secondary schooling in 1975 for the female population over 25), HYRM75 and HYRF75 (the average years of higher schooling in 1975 for the male and female populations over 25). The country characteristic variables are LNLIFEE03 (the log of LIFEE03, the average life expectancy at age 0 over 1970–74), GOVSH53 (the average ratio of real government consumption expenditure to real GDP over the same period), PNST45a (the average over 1975–85 of PINSTAB4 and PINSTAB5, which are measures of political instability over 1975–79 and 1980–84), and TOT45a (the average of TOT4 and TOT5, the average terms of trade shock over 1975–79 and 1980–84). The inclusion of all these variables produces the equation

$$AVGR_t = -\ 0.158\ -\ 0.0196 GDP575L_t + \ 0.020 SYRM75_t$$
$$\qquad\quad (0.073)\quad (0.0055)\qquad\qquad\quad (0.007)$$

$$\qquad -\ 0.011 SYRF75_t + \ 0.0219 HYRM75_t$$
$$\qquad\quad (0.007)\qquad\qquad (0.0304)$$

$$\qquad -\ 0.038 HYRF75_t + \ 0.079 LNLIFEE03_t \qquad\qquad\qquad (2.59)$$
$$\qquad\quad (0.040)\qquad\qquad (0.025)$$

$$\qquad -\ 0.028 GOVSH53_i - \ 0.053 PNST45a_t + \ 0.116 TOT45a_t$$
$$\qquad\quad (0.032)\qquad\qquad (0.015)\qquad\qquad\quad (0.066)$$

$$n\quad = 102 \qquad\qquad df = 92 \qquad RSS = 4.0349 \times 10^{-2}$$
$$VAR = 4.3858 \times 10^{-4} \quad R^2 = 0.4008 \quad DW = 1.38.$$

Here, the inclusion of additional variables has increased the R^2 value, but more importantly, has produced a significant value for the coefficient of GDP575L, and which implies an annual convergence rate of just over 2%. This value is broadly consistent with that found by other investigators using a variety of equations and estimation methods. Even though (2.59) is an improvement over (2.58), it is still not completely satisfactory, since a number of the additional variables included are not significant.

A final point concerns the interpretation of the Durbin–Watson statistic in the example given above. Although serial correlation is a phenomenon usually associated with time series data, it is possible for the DW statistic to detect misspecification in a cross-section regression if the observations are ordered in some way and the missing variable has a pattern which is associated with that ordering.

At this stage, we should perhaps take stock of what has been learned from the examples given. The set of techniques available is still limited, and the economic theory used is distinctly naïve, but it is already clear that one does need to be very careful when drawing conclusions from an exercise in applied econometrics. Where apparently acceptable results are found, it is often the case that a more extensive diagnosis is needed before one can have any real confidence in the inferences to be made. Where very poor results are found, we need to understand why this may be, before dismissing the underlying theory as unsupportable. By improving the set of techniques at our disposal, we can certainly improve our ability to discriminate between acceptable and unacceptable representations of economic behaviour, but there is always a need to push very hard at any set of results, in order to be sure that one really understands what has been revealed.

2.6 / Further reading

Goldberger (1991) and Greene (1993) give detailed coverage, whilst Davidson and MacKinnon (1993) and Gourieroux and Monfort (1995) are also helpful.

3

Classical regression: further topics

3.1 / Introduction

The statistical analysis conducted in the preceding chapter depends crucially on the assumption that the model specification is known to be correct, but most of the examples discussed in section 2.5 suggest that simple models frequently appear to be misspecified in some way. It is obvious that, in practice, one will usually have to conduct a sequence of experiments before an acceptable representation is found.

This raises a number of questions. If assumptions are violated, then all procedures which depend on those assumptions are suspect. To understand the implications of this, we need to look at the relationships that exist between various attempts at estimation. If these relationships are not understood, it is possible to incorrectly interpret results from preliminary experiments, which subsequently turn out to be based on erroneous assumptions.

In subsequent sections of this chapter, we expand considerably on the basic regression theory to introduce a number of topics that are very relevant to the process of constructing more realistic and acceptable models. In section 3.2, we look at the effect of adding regressors to an existing equation, and show how one might choose the two alternative specifications offered by such an experiment. In section 3.3, this analysis is extended to the case in which one has to decide whether or not to impose a more general set of linear restrictions on the parameters of a model. In section 3.4, we look at experiments involving the addition or deletion of observations, and consider how this can be used to give additional tests of model adequacy.

In all these procedures, it is assumed that the data are sufficiently informative to allow clear decisions to be made. However, this is not always the case, and the issue of data adequacy is discussed in some detail in section 3.5. Finally, in section 3.6, we look at the specific problems of using quarterly data, and show how one can incorporate the effects of a qualitative variable such as 'season' into a single equation model.

3.2 / Variable addition: some general results

In this section, we consider what happens when new regressors are added to an equation obtained from a regression of y on X. Two sets of results follow from this. On the one hand, we can extract certain properties of least squares regression which have application well beyond the confines of the classical model. This is so because many techniques of estimation and testing employ the regression calculation at various stages, and the *mathematical* properties of least squares therefore have application in cases in which the classical statistical properties no longer hold. The second set of results does depend on classical assumptions, but gives valuable insights into the wider problem of choice between competing models.

Consider two alternative models:

$$y = X\beta + u \tag{3.1}$$

and

$$y = X\beta + Z\gamma + u, \tag{3.2}$$

where X now has $(k - g)$ columns and Z has g columns; this preserves for (3.2) the convention of k variables on the right-hand side of the equation. Then suppose that least squares regressions are run on each of these models, giving estimated equations written as

$$y = Xb + e \tag{3.3}$$

and

$$y = X\hat{\beta} + Z\hat{\gamma} + \hat{u}. \tag{3.4}$$

It is implicit in the notation used here that a regression of y on X and Z does not produce either the same estimator for β or the same set of residuals as a regression of y on X alone, and this is confirmed by more explicit expressions obtained below. A useful starting point is the observation that a regression of y on X requires that $X'e = 0$, whilst a regression of y on X and Z requires that $X'\hat{u} = 0$ and $Z'\hat{u} = 0$. These statements of the least squares conditions are used repeatedly in the algebra which follows.

The regression of y on X

From previous results, we have directly that

$$b = (X'X)^{-1}X'y$$

and

$$e = y - Xb = My; \text{ where } M = I - X(X'X)^{-1}X'.$$

The regression of y on X and Z

If we wrote X and Z together as a single matrix, it would be easy to write down an expression for the combined estimator, containing both $\hat{\beta}$ and $\hat{\gamma}$. However, this would be uninformative: what we require are separate expressions for $\hat{\beta}$ and $\hat{\gamma}$. Amongst other things, this will enable us to compare b and $\hat{\beta}$ as alternative estimators for β, and also to find general expressions for subvectors taken from a complete vector of least squares estimators.

From equation (3.4), premultiplying by Z', we have

$$Z'y = Z'X\hat{\beta} + Z'Z\hat{\gamma} + Z'\hat{u}$$

$$= Z'X\hat{\beta} + Z'Z\hat{\gamma}; \text{ since } Z'\hat{u} = 0.$$

Provided that $Z'Z$ is nonsingular, this gives

$$\hat{\gamma} = (Z'Z)^{-1}Z'(y - X\hat{\beta}). \tag{3.5}$$

Equation (3.5) expresses $\hat{\gamma}$ in terms of the (unknown) solution for $\hat{\beta}$. A complete solution for $\hat{\gamma}$ can be obtained as follows.

Starting again from equation (3.4), premultiply by the matrix $M = I - X(X'X)^{-1}X'$. This gives

$$My = MX\hat{\beta} + MZ\hat{\gamma} + M\hat{u}.$$

However,

$$MX = [I - X(X'X)^{-1}X']X$$

$$= X - X = 0$$

and

$$M\hat{u} = [I - X(X'X)^{-1}X']\hat{u}$$

$$= \hat{u}; \text{ since } X'\hat{u} = 0.$$

Hence

$$My = MZ\hat{\gamma} + \hat{u}. \tag{3.6}$$

Now premultiply by Z', to obtain

$$Z'My = Z'MZ\hat{\gamma} + Z'\hat{u}$$

$$= Z'MZ\hat{\gamma}; \text{ since } Z'\hat{u} = 0.$$

Provided that $(Z'MZ)$ is nonsingular, it is possible to solve for $\hat{\gamma}$, to give

$$\hat{\gamma} = (Z'MZ)^{-1}Z'My. \tag{3.7}$$

Several comments are in order here. In the algebra above, we have assumed that both $Z'Z$ and $Z'MZ$ are nonsingular. Provided that the columns of X and Z together are linearly independent, so that the regression of y on X and Z is actually possible, the necessary inverse matrices do exist. Next, we have used algebraic equivalences that have a ready interpretation. For example, $MX = 0$ corresponds to the rather obvious statement that a regression of X on X would generate a perfect fit, and therefore zero residuals. The statement $M\hat{u} = \hat{u}$ indicates that it is not possible for X to explain anything about $\hat{u}$, since $\hat{u}$ is the component of y that cannot be explained in terms of X and Z. A regression of $\hat{u}$ on X therefore produces 'zero fit', and residuals $M\hat{u}$ which are equal to $\hat{u}$.

Equation (3.7) provides an expression for $\hat{\gamma}$, but we do not have a corresponding expression for $\hat{\beta}$. By reversing the roles of Z and X, and introducing the more explicit notation

$$M_X = I - X(X'X)^{-1}X'$$

$$M_Z = I - Z(Z'Z)^{-1}Z',$$

it follows directly that

$$\hat{\beta} = (X'M_ZX)^{-1}X'M_Zy, \tag{3.8}$$

whilst $\hat{\gamma}$ will now be written as

$$\hat{\gamma} = (Z'M_XZ)^{-1}Z'M_Xy. \tag{3.9}$$

It must also follow that $\hat{\beta}$ could be written as

$$\hat{\beta} = (X'X)^{-1}X'(y - Z\hat{\gamma}) \tag{3.10}$$

by comparison with equation (3.5).

Formulae linking the two regressions

So far, we have not made explicit the fact that b is generally different from $\hat{\beta}$ and e is generally different from $\hat{u}$. From equation (3.10)

$$\hat{\beta} = b - (X'X)^{-1}X'Z\hat{\gamma}$$

$$\Rightarrow b = \hat{\beta} + (X'X)^{-1}X'Z\hat{\gamma}. \tag{3.11}$$

From equation (3.6), modified to use the more explicit residual generator matrix M_X, we have

$$M_Xy = M_XZ\hat{\gamma} + \hat{u}.$$

But M_Xy defines the residuals from the regression of y on X. Hence

$$e = y - Xb = M_Xy = \hat{u} + M_XZ\hat{\gamma}. \tag{3.12}$$

Equation (3.11) shows that b will be the same as $\hat{\beta}$ if $\hat{\gamma}$ is zero: the two estimators will also be the same if $X'Z = 0$. Both these conditions are very unlikely in practice. So, in general, b is not the same as $\hat{\beta}$. Likewise, e is not generally the same as $\hat{u}$, though the two sets of residuals are the same if $\hat{\gamma} = 0$.

Residual sums of squares

Another key result is that which shows the linkage between the two possible values of the residual sum of squares (RSS). Equation (3.12) shows how e is related to $\hat{u}$, and on forming the sum of squares of elements of e, we obtain

$$e'e = \hat{u}'\hat{u} + \hat{\gamma}'Z'M'_X M_X Z\hat{\gamma} + 2\hat{\gamma}'Z'M'_X\hat{u}.$$

The least squares conditions $X'\hat{u} = 0$ and $Z'\hat{u} = 0$ imply that $\hat{\gamma}'Z'M'_X\hat{u} = \hat{\gamma}'Z'\hat{u} = 0$. The cross-product term is therefore zero, and, since $M'_X M_X = M_X$, we have

$$e'e = \hat{u}'\hat{u} + \hat{\gamma}'Z'M_X Z\hat{\gamma}. \tag{3.13}$$

Equation (3.13) is important because the second term on the right is used in testing the null hypothesis $\gamma = 0$, and it is often convenient to compute $\hat{\gamma}'Z'M_X Z\hat{\gamma}$ as the difference between two values of the residual sum of squares. It is also important to note that $\hat{\gamma}'Z'M_X Z\hat{\gamma}$ is the sum of squares of the elements of the vector $M_X Z\hat{\gamma}$, and is therefore nonnegative. This gives the result

$$e'e \geq \hat{u}'\hat{u}. \tag{3.14}$$

It is not surprising to find that, apart from the special case in which $\hat{\gamma} = 0$, the addition of regressors leads to a *decrease* in the residual sum of squares, whilst the deletion of regressors leads to an *increase* in the residual sum of squares. In a regression of y on X and Z, $\hat{\gamma}$ is by definition the value that minimises the sum of squared residuals. By omitting the regressors in Z, the estimate of γ is effectively set to zero, which is not generally the minimising value. Hence the residual sum of squares from a regression of y on X is greater than (or equal to) the residual sum of squares from a regression of y on X and Z. This also explains why the value of R^2 is either increased or unchanged as variables are added to a model. From equation (2.34) in section 2.3, $R^2 = 1 - RSS/TSS$: as regressors are added, RSS is decreased or unchanged whilst TSS is unchanged, so R^2 is either increased or unchanged.

Statistical results

There is an important point to make before considering a comparison of statistical properties between the regression of y on X and the regression of y on X and Z. Statistical analysis is always conditional on an assumption as to the nature of the 'true' model. In an absolute sense, the true model is a rather absurd notion, since all models represent some simplification of reality. In practice, we look for a model in which the assumptions made are not strongly contradicted by the data. For the purposes of econometric theory, the true model is effectively the basis of a conceptual experiment – we ask how estimators and test statistics would behave under certain specific assumptions embodied in the model currently designated as 'true'.

In this spirit, we shall first analyse the behaviour of the estimators b and $\hat{\beta}$ under the assumption that b is used when $\gamma = 0$ and the true model is

$$y = X\beta + u, \tag{3.15}$$

whereas $\hat{\beta}$ is used when $\gamma \neq 0$ and the true model is

$$y = X\beta + Z\gamma + u. \tag{3.16}$$

In both cases, the regressors are assumed to be nonrandom and, because we assume that the correct estimator is used, whichever model happens to be correct, we can treat u as a 'well-behaved' disturbance, with $u \sim N(0, \sigma^2 I)$.

From section 2.4, we know that if (3.15) is the true model, b is best linear unbiased, with

$$\text{var}(b) = \sigma^2 (X'X)^{-1}.$$

If (3.16) is true, then $\hat{\beta}$ and $\hat{\gamma}$ must be best linear unbiased, since they are the correct least squares estimators for this model. We do, however, need to find explicit expressions for the variances associated with $\hat{\beta}$ and $\hat{\gamma}$.

To find the properties of $\hat{\beta}$ when (3.16) is true, we start from equation (3.8), and substitute for y, using equation (3.16) to carry out the substitution. This gives

$$\hat{\beta} = (X'M_Z X)^{-1} X'M_Z y$$

$$= (X'M_Z X)^{-1} X'M_Z(X\beta + Z\gamma + u)$$

$$= \beta + (X'M_Z X)^{-1} X'M_Z Z\gamma + (X'M_Z X)^{-1} X'M_Z u$$

$$= \beta + (X'M_Z X)^{-1} X'M_Z u; \text{ since } M_Z Z = 0.$$

Then

$$E(\hat{\beta}) = \beta + (X'M_Z X)^{-1} X'M_Z E(u)$$

$$= \beta; \text{ if } E(u) = 0;$$

$$\text{var}(\hat{\beta}) = \text{var}[(X'M_Z X)^{-1} X'M_Z u]$$

$$= (X'M_Z X)^{-1} X'M_Z \cdot \text{var}(u) \cdot M'_Z X (X'M_Z X)^{-1}$$

$$= \sigma^2 (X'M_Z X)^{-1}; \text{ if } \text{var}(u) = \sigma^2 I. \tag{3.17}$$

As expected, $\hat{\beta}$ is unbiased, and equation (3.17) gives an explicit expression for $\text{var}(\hat{\beta})$. Since $X'X = X'M_Z X + X'P_Z X$, where $X'M_Z X$ is positive definite and $X'P_Z X$ is positive semidefinite (psd), we have

$$X'X - X'M_Z X = X'P_Z X \text{ is psd}$$

$$\Rightarrow (X'M_Z X)^{-1} - (X'X)^{-1} \text{ is psd}.$$

Hence

$$\text{var}(\hat{\beta}) = \sigma^2 (X'M_Z X)^{-1} \geq \sigma^2 (X'X)^{-1} = \text{var}(b). \tag{3.18}$$

As before, a matrix inequality of the form $A \geq B$ signifies that the difference $A - B$ is psd.

At the moment, this result is of limited relevance, since it says only that the estimator that you would use if (3.16) were true has a larger variance than the estimator that you would use if (3.15) were true. But as we shall see below, the result still holds when we recognise that only one of the estimators can be correct, and we can therefore say that, in general, as regressors are added to a model, the theoretical variance of the parameter estimators is increased, except in certain special and highly unlikely cases in which the variances are unchanged. Note that this result does *not* apply to standard errors of the parameter estimates, which involve the estimated disturbance variance, $\hat{\sigma}^2$, rather than the true disturbance variance, σ^2.

Omitted variables

We now consider what happens if b is used when (3.16) is the true model, and what happens if $\hat{\beta}$ is used when (3.15) is the true model. Looking first at the case in which regressors are omitted, we analyse the properties of b when

$$y = X\beta + Z\gamma + u.$$

The analysis is as follows:

$$b = (X'X)^{-1}X'y$$

$$= (X'X)^{-1}X'(X\beta + Z\gamma + u)$$

$$= \beta + (X'X)^{-1}X'Z\gamma + (X'X)^{-1}X'u;$$

$$E(b) = \beta + (X'X)^{-1}X'Z\gamma + (X'X)^{-1}X'E(u)$$

$$= \beta + (X'X)^{-1}X'Z\gamma; \text{ if } E(u) = 0;$$

$$\text{var}(b) = \text{var}[(X'X)^{-1}X'u]$$

$$= (X'X)^{-1}X' \cdot \text{var}(u) \cdot X(X'X)^{-1}$$

$$= \sigma^2(X'X)^{-1}; \text{ if } \text{var}(u) = \sigma^2 I.$$

The incorrect omission of the variables in Z produces a biased estimator of β, since $E(b) \neq \beta$, except in the special case $X'Z\gamma = 0$. If $\gamma = 0$, there is no bias because b is then the correct estimator to use, and if $X'Z = 0$, there is no bias because the exclusion of Z has no impact on the estimation of β. But these are special cases and, in general, b is biased when Z is excluded incorrectly.

Turning now to var(b), we see that even when b is biased, the variance of b is still correctly given by the formula

$$\text{var}(b) = \sigma^2(X'X)^{-1}.$$

This confirms at least one part of our earlier assertion that the theoretical variance is not affected by choosing the 'wrong' list of regressors.

One aspect of omitted variables analysis that is sometimes overlooked is that the disturbance variance estimator is also biased by the incorrect exclusion of regressor variables. If σ^2 is estimated from the regression of y on X, when (3.16) is the true model, the estimator used would be $e'e/[n - (k - g)]$, and this is biased upwards, the bias being given by the expression

$$E[e'e/(n-k+g)] - \sigma^2 = \gamma'Z'M_XZ\gamma/(n-k+g).$$

Incorrectly included variables

Now consider what happens if $\hat{\beta}$ is used when (3.15) is correct, that is, when γ is actually zero. One could take the expression for $\hat{\beta}$ given in (3.8) and use (3.15) to substitute for y, but this is not necessary. All that we need to do is to check the results already obtained when $\hat{\beta}$ is the correct estimator, to see whether the fact that $\gamma = 0$ makes any difference. From the arguments above equation (3.17), it is clear that the condition $\gamma = 0$ has no effect, and that when $\gamma = 0$, $\hat{\beta}$ is still unbiased, with

$$\mathrm{var}(\hat{\beta}) = \sigma^2(X'M_ZX)^{-1}.$$

Since we have now shown that the expressions for both $\mathrm{var}(\hat{\beta})$ and $\mathrm{var}(b)$ hold whichever model is true, we can apply the inequality $\mathrm{var}(\hat{\beta}) \geq \mathrm{var}(b)$ and state that the cost of incorrectly including the variables in Z is that this produces an estimator with unnecessarily high variance. If γ is zero, b is the best linear unbiased estimator, and although $\hat{\beta}$ is unbiased, it is inefficient, because there exists an unbiased estimator which has a smaller variance.

The analysis above gives results which are easily summarised. The incorrect omission of a set of regressors produces biased estimates of the parameters associated with the regressors that are included, whilst the incorrect inclusion of a set of regressors produces inefficient estimates, that is, estimates which do not have the minimum variance consistent with unbiased estimation.

Testing the null hypothesis $\gamma = 0$

In practice, we do not know whether γ is zero or not. We therefore need a test of the null hypothesis $\gamma = 0$ against the alternative $\gamma \neq 0$. Notice that the alternative implies that at least one element of γ is nonzero, not that all elements of γ are nonzero. To proceed, we argue first that $E(\hat{\gamma}) = \gamma$ and that $\mathrm{var}(\hat{\gamma}) = \sigma^2(Z'M_XZ)^{-1}$, by analogy with the results obtained above for $\hat{\beta}$. Then, if $u \sim N(0, \sigma^2 I)$, it follows that

$$\hat{\gamma} \sim N[\gamma, \sigma^2(Z'M_XZ)^{-1}]. \tag{3.19}$$

For a $(g \times 1)$ random vector v, distributed as $N(\mu, \Sigma)$, where Σ is nonsingular, the quadratic form $(v - \mu)'\Sigma^{-1}(v - \mu)$ has a χ^2 distribution with g degrees of freedom. Applying this to (3.19), we have

$$(\hat{\gamma} - \gamma)'[Z'M_XZ](\hat{\gamma} - \gamma)/\sigma^2 \sim \chi_g^2,$$

and, under H_0: $\gamma = 0$,

$$\hat{\gamma}'(Z'M_XZ)\hat{\gamma}/\sigma^2 \sim \chi_g^2. \tag{3.20}$$

Under classical assumptions, with fixed regressors and normal disturbances, we can use (3.20) to derive an exact small sample test for the null hypothesis $\gamma = 0$. Under rather weaker conditions, we can use (3.20) with any consistent estimator of σ^2 to give an approximate large sample test. Before showing how the small sample test is obtained, it is worth mentioning that many of the tests described in later chapters can be formulated as so-called *variable addition* tests, effectively using the same logic as that of the test of H_0: $\gamma = 0$. For the moment, we confine our attention to this specific case, but the ideas developed here will prove to be useful in other contexts.

The *F* test for H_0: $\gamma = 0$

As it stands, (3.20) is not a valid test statistic, because it involves the unknown parameter σ^2. For reasons which parallel those underlying the use of the t distribution in place of the normal distribution when σ^2 is unknown, so here the F distribution is used in place of a χ^2 distribution.

An F distribution is formed as the ratio of two independent chi-square variables, each divided by the associated degrees of freedom. From section 2.4, we know that under classical assumptions, including normality, least squares residuals are distributed independently of the parameter estimators. In the context of the regression of y on X and Z, this means that $\hat\gamma$ and $\hat u$ are independent, and that any function of $\hat\gamma$ is independent of any function of $\hat u$, provided that neither function involves other random variables. In particular,

$$\hat\gamma'(Z'M_X Z)\hat\gamma/\sigma^2 \quad \text{and} \quad \hat u'\hat u/\sigma^2$$

are independent. The first of these is distributed as χ^2_g under H_0: $\gamma = 0$, whilst the second has a χ^2 distribution with $(n-k)$ degrees of freedom. This last result also follows from the discussion in section 2.4, as a general property of least squares residuals, and it therefore applies to the residuals $\hat u$ from a regression of y on X and Z, even if it subsequently turns out that the true value of γ is zero. The ratio

$$F = [\hat\gamma'(Z'M_X Z)\hat\gamma/g\sigma^2]/[\hat u'\hat u/(n-k)\sigma^2]$$

therefore has an F distribution, with g and $(n-k)$ degrees of freedom, under the null hypothesis $\gamma = 0$. Since the unknown σ^2 cancels, we have the operational test statistic

$$F = [\hat\gamma'(Z'M_X Z)\hat\gamma/g]/[\hat u'\hat u/(n-k)] \sim F_{g,n-k}, \text{ under } H_0\text{: } \gamma = 0. \tag{3.21}$$

A calculated value of F which is greater than the critical value $F^{0.05}_{g,n-k}$ will lead to rejection of the null hypothesis $\gamma = 0$, in favour of the alternative $\gamma \neq 0$, at the 5% significance level.

Alternative expressions for the *F* test statistic

The test statistic given in (3.21) can be expressed in a number of different ways. Equation (3.13) shows that the quadratic form in the numerator can be calculated as the difference between the residual sum of squares from the regression of y on

X, and the residual sum of squares from the regression of y on X and Z. This gives an alternative and easily computed form of the F test:

$$F = [(e'e - \hat{u}'\hat{u})/g]/[\hat{u}'\hat{u}/(n-k)]. \tag{3.22}$$

If the computer program has a facility for calculating (3.21) directly, then an F test of the null hypothesis $\gamma = 0$ can be performed by simply running the regression of y on X and Z and calling the appropriate test routine. Otherwise, the test requires that *two* regressions be run, one of y on X, and the other of y on X and Z. Equation (3.22) can then be used to compute the test statistic from the reported values for the residual sums of squares corresponding to $e'e$ and $\hat{u}'\hat{u}$. Notice that the denominator in (3.22) is equivalent to the disturbance variance estimate, as obtained from the regression of y on X and Z.

There is considerable intuitive appeal in the idea that a test statistic can be based on a comparison of values of the criterion function used originally to define the estimators, under the null and alternative hypotheses respectively, and this is exactly what happens in (3.22). If the sum of squares function is written as

$$S(\beta, \gamma) = (y - X\beta - Z\gamma)'(y - X\beta - Z\gamma),$$

then $S(b, 0)$ represents the minimum value of the function under the set of restrictions which states that γ must be zero, and $S(\hat{\beta}, \hat{\gamma})$ is the minimum value without the restrictions $\gamma = 0$. Since $S(b, 0)$ and $S(\hat{\beta}, \hat{\gamma})$ are simply values of the residual sum of squares, under H_0 and H_1 respectively, (3.22) can be written as

$$F = [\{S(b, 0) - S(\hat{\beta}, \hat{\gamma})\}/g]/[S(\hat{\beta}, \hat{\gamma})/(n-k)]. \tag{3.23}$$

The version of the F test statistic presented in (3.23) still ties us down to a rather specific case, and a final version, which will be used in subsequent examples, is

$$F = [(S_R - S)/g]/[S/(n-k)]. \tag{3.24}$$

To apply (3.24) to the special case represented by (3.22), we simply set $S_R = e'e$ and $S = \hat{u}'\hat{u}$. In the next section, we shall discuss the application of (3.24) in a wider context, in which S_R represents the residual sum of squares from a regression in which *any* set of g independent linear restrictions is imposed on the parameters, whilst S is the residual sum of squares from a regression without those restrictions imposed. For the moment, we note (3.24) as a form of the F test which can be used to test the specific restrictions embodied in the null hypothesis $\gamma = 0$, but which can also be used, without further modification, to test other sets of linear restrictions.

Example 3.1

In section 2.5, we discussed the estimation of a consumption function which included real personal disposable income and an inflation variable in the list of regressors. Various reasons have been put forward as to why inflation might influence real consumers' expenditure, including the fact that inflation erodes the purchasing power of liquid asset holdings. This suggests that one might include real liquid asset holdings, either as an alternative to or together with the inflation variable. Unfortunately, given that we are still working with annual data, this creates a problem, since the relevant UK data series on liquid assets is available only from 1963 onwards. But subject to this limitation on the number of observations available, we can use the liquid assets variable to illustrate the application of the F test.

To see whether liquid assets and the inflation variable together add significantly to the explanation of consumer behaviour, we need a first (restricted) regression excluding DLPCONS and LNRLIQ. This is the same equation as (2.54) but estimated over the period 1964–90. Then, a second (unrestricted) regression including these variables is needed. The first regression gives $RSS = 1.061\,74 \times 10^{-2}$, whilst the second, with DLPCONS and LNRLIQ included, gives $RSS = 3.5516 \times 10^{-3}$. If the model corresponding to the second (unrestricted) regression is written as

$$\ln(C_t) = \beta_1 + \beta_2 \ln(D_t) + \beta_3 \Delta \ln(P_t) + \beta_4 \ln(L_t) + u_t; \; t = 1, \ldots, n,$$

where L is the symbolic representation of RLIQ, the null hypothesis to be tested is $\beta_3 = 0$ and $\beta_4 = 0$. This involves the addition of two variables to the restricted model or, equivalently, the imposition of two restrictions on the unrestricted model. Using the F test statistic as written in (3.22) or (3.24), we have

$$e'e = S_R = 1.061\,74 \times 10^{-2}, \quad \hat{u}'\hat{u} = S = 3.5516 \times 10^{-3},$$

$$k = 4, \quad n = 27, \quad g = 2,$$

where k is the number of regressors *after* the addition of DLPCONS and LNRLIQ, that is, in the unrestricted model. The F test statistic is

$$F = [(10.6174 - 3.5516)/2]/[3.5516/(27 - 4)] = 22.879.$$

The 5% critical value for the F distribution with 2 and 23 degrees of freedom is 3.40, so H_0 is rejected in favour of the alternative that one or both of β_3 and β_4 is different from zero.

By running the relevant regressions (all for 1964–90), one can also find that the liquid assets variable and inflation are both significant when included individually, but only liquid assets remains significant when both variables are included together.

Tests using nR^2

To conclude this section, we consider a further variant of the variable addition test, largely as a preparation for later applications. Instead of using a regression of y on X and a regression of y on X and Z, we use a regression of y on X, and then save the residual vector e from the first stage, and use this as the 'dependent variable' in a second regression of e on X and Z. Provided that X contains a column of ones to allow for an intercept, the sum, and hence the sample mean, of elements of e is zero, and the sum of squares of elements of e about the mean is therefore $e'e$. The significance of this result is that $e'e$ acts as the *total* sum of squares (TSS) for the second regression, and from the algebra presented earlier in this section, it is quite easy to show that the residual sum of squares (RSS) from the second regression is $\hat{u}'\hat{u}$. So *in terms of output from the regression of e on X and Z*, the F test statistic (3.22) can be written as

$$F = [(TSS - RSS)/g]/[RSS/(n-k)].$$

Dividing the numerator and denominator by TSS, it is easy to show that this is equivalent to

$$F = [R^2/g]/[(1-R^2)/(n-k)], \tag{3.25}$$

where R^2 refers to the reported value from the regression of e on X and Z.

There is one case in which (3.25) can be applied directly to the regression of y on X and Z. If the null hypothesis is that all slope parameters are zero, X corresponds to a single column of ones, and Z corresponds to all the genuine variables in the regression. In this case, there is no need to run a regression of y on X, since it can be shown that $e'e$ is equivalent to the total sum of squares computed directly from the elements of y, whilst $\hat{u}'\hat{u}$ is the residual sum of squares from the regression of y on X and Z. This means that (3.25) can be applied directly to any regression if the objective is to test the null hypothesis that *all* slope parameters are zero. The test statistic, which has $g = k - 1$ and $n - k$ degrees of freedom, is known as the *analysis of variance F test*, or the *regression F test*, and this is often provided as part of the standard output. For any other null hypothesis, (3.25) applies only to the regression of e on X and Z.

Apart from the special case mentioned above, (3.25) offers no real advantage over (3.22): both formulations require two regressions, and the regression of e on X and Z merely rearranges the information contained in a regression of y on X and Z. However, there is a large sample version of the variable addition test that does give a slightly simpler form. From (3.20), replacing the quadratic form in the numerator with $e'e - \hat{u}'\hat{u}$, we have

$$(e'e - \hat{u}'\hat{u})/\sigma^2 \sim \chi_g^2, \text{ under } H_0: \gamma = 0. \tag{3.26}$$

In a large sample, it can be argued that if σ^2 is replaced by any consistent estimator, the resulting statistic will still be approximately χ_g^2, under the null hypothesis. In particular, the restricted estimator $e'e/[n-(k-g)]$ is consistent under H_0, as indeed is $e'e/n$. If this last variant is used, then in terms of output from the regression of e on X and Z, we would have the statistic

$$\chi^2 = (e'e - \hat{u}'\hat{u})/(e'e/n)$$

$$= (TSS - RSS)/(TSS/n) = nR^2. \tag{3.27}$$

So a large sample version of the variable addition test may be obtained by running the regression of e on X and Z, recording the value of R^2 from this regression, and rejecting $H_0: \gamma = 0$ if the calculated value of nR^2 is greater than the critical value from a χ^2 distribution with g degrees of freedom, at the chosen level of significance.

Example 3.2

Equation (2.58) in section 2.5 shows a very simple version of the relationship between the average growth rate of per capita GDP (AVGR), the opening level of per capita GDP (GDP575L) and a human capital measure (SYRM75) for a sample of countries. The value of R^2 is 0.153 35. The regression F test considers the null hypothesis that both slope parameters are really zero, which is equivalent to saying that the estimated regression explains nothing about the behaviour of AVGR. The test statistic is

$$F = [R^2/(k-1)]/[(1-R^2)/(n-k)]$$

$$= [0.153\,35/(3-1)]/[(1-0.153\,35)/(102-3)]$$

$$= 8.966.$$

The 5% critical value for the F distribution with 2 and 99 degrees of freedom is 3.09, so the null hypothesis of zero slope parameters is rejected, though not strongly. Somewhat loosely, this may be interpreted as saying that the value $R^2 = 0.153\,35$ is significantly different from zero.

The RESET test

Variable addition tests of the type discussed in this section need not be applied only to new economic variables that may be thought to influence the behaviour of the dependent variable. The RESET test is a general procedure, designed primarily to detect the choice of an inappropriate functional form. The argument is that if the functional form is not consistent with the data, one might expect the square or some higher power of one or more of the regressors to improve the explanation of behaviour of the dependent variable. Since, in practice, one may not have a very clear idea as to which powers of which regressors are most relevant, and since one cannot afford to lose too many degrees of freedom by throwing in an arbitrary selection of terms, the solution suggested by the RESET test is to use powers of $\hat{Y}_t$, the predicted value series. A simple routine check is to use $\hat{Y}_t^2$ as an additional variable, and to test the significance of the parameter attached to this variable in the usual way.

One problem with the suggestion made above is that $\hat{Y}_t$ is random because it involves estimated values of the parameters of the underlying model. It follows that $\hat{Y}_t^2$ is also random, so classical assumptions cannot apply to the test regression

$$y = X\beta + Z\gamma + u, \tag{3.28}$$

where $z_t' = [\hat{Y}_t^2]$. The same argument applies if Z consists of observations on several powers of $\hat{Y}_t$. Consequently, we rely on a large sample justification of the test procedure, using methods to be developed in Chapter 4. If more than one power of $\hat{Y}_t$ is included, this would suggest a χ^2 test, possibly conducted using nR^2 from a regression of e on X and Z, as in (3.27). Alternatively, although we have not shown an exact small sample justification for doing so, one can in fact use the F test in any of its forms. Finally, if Z contains only the single power term $\hat{Y}_t^2$, the F test is equivalent to the square of a simple t test, applied to the parameter of the added variable $\hat{Y}_t^2$.

In practice, the RESET test may not be particularly good at detecting any specific alternative to a proposed model, and its usefulness lies in acting as a general indicator that something is wrong. For this reason, a test such as RESET is sometimes described as a test of *misspecification*, as opposed to a test of specification. This distinction is rather subtle, but the basic idea is that a specification test looks at some particular aspect of a given equation, with clear null and alternative hypotheses in mind, whilst a misspecification test can detect a range of alternatives, and indicate that something is wrong under the null, without necessarily giving clear guidance as to what alternative hypothesis is appropriate.

Example 3.3

This example again uses equation (2.58), as described in Example 3.2. Here, AVGR is Y, GDP575L is X_2 and SYRM75 is X_3. The RESET test, applied using the single added variable $\hat{Y}_t^2$, gives a test statistic of 6.02 for the nR^2 version, and 6.15 for the F test version. The 5% critical value for a χ^2 distribution with 1 degree of freedom is 3.84, whilst the 5% critical value for an F distribution with 1 and 98 degrees of freedom is 3.94, so both versions reject the null hypothesis of correct functional form (correct specification). Since only one power of $\hat{Y}_t$ is added here, the RESET test can be performed as a t test of the parameter associated with $\hat{Y}_t^2$ in the following regression:

$$\hat{Y}_t = \underset{(0.0317)}{0.0806} - \underset{(0.0048)}{0.0126X_{2t}} + \underset{(0.0100)}{0.0368X_{3t}} - \underset{(17.493)}{43.365\hat{Y}_t^2};$$

$$n = 102 \quad df = 98 \quad RSS = 5.3643 \times 10^{-2}.$$

The t test statistic is -2.479, and the 5% two-tailed critical value is approximately 1.96, so the null hypothesis is rejected. Note that in the case of a single added variable, both the t and F statistics and the corresponding critical values satisfy the relationship $t^2 = F$.

3.3 / Linear restrictions on parameters

In the preceding section, we made several comparisons between two models, which were written as

$$y = X\beta + u \tag{3.29}$$

and

$$y = X\beta + Z\gamma + u. \tag{3.30}$$

Equations (3.29) and (3.30) cannot both be true unless $\gamma = 0$. However, we can describe (3.29) as model (3.30) under the null hypothesis $\gamma = 0$ or, equivalently, we may say that (3.29) is (3.30) subject to the set of restrictions $\gamma = 0$.

The idea that one can take a model and add restrictions on the parameters is important, but we have so far considered only the special case of *exclusion* restrictions, where the effect of imposing the restrictions is to completely eliminate certain regressors from the model. In this section, we show that *any* feasible set of linear restrictions can be imposed by direct substitution, followed by a rearrangement of terms, to produce a version of the model from which restricted parameter estimates can be obtained by a standard regression calculation. The qualification of feasibility rules out the possibility of a contradictory set of restrictions, such as $\beta_2 = 1$, $\beta_3 = 1$ and $\beta_2 + \beta_3 = 1$.

At this point, we have a small difficulty with notation. It is awkward to use

$$y = X\beta + Z\gamma + u$$

to represent the unrestricted model when we are imposing a more general set of restrictions, since these may involve elements of both β and γ. For the purposes of this section, the model

$$y = X\beta + u$$

is treated as the unrestricted model, and

$$b = (X'X)^{-1}X'y$$

is now the unrestricted estimator. We also specify that X has k columns.

Now suppose that β is to be estimated subject to a set of g linear restrictions written as

$$H\beta = h.$$

We can exclude the possibility of inconsistent or redundant restrictions by requiring that the rows of H be linearly independent.

Imposing restrictions by substitution

The set of g restrictions $H\beta = h$ can be imposed by expressing g of the parameters in β in terms of the remaining $(k - g)$ parameters, and substituting directly into the equation

$$y = X\beta + u.$$

Formally, this requires partitioning H as $[H_1 H_2]$, where H_2 is $(g \times g)$ and non-singular. Partitioning in this way involves no loss of generality, since the ordering of variables and parameters is arbitrary. If β is split conformably into subvectors β_1 and β_2, then

$$H\beta = H_1\beta_1 + H_2\beta_2 = h$$

$$\Rightarrow \beta_2 = H_2^{-1}(h - H_1\beta_1). \tag{3.31}$$

If X is now partitioned in the same way as H, the model can be written as

$$y = X_1\beta_1 + X_2\beta_2 + u. \qquad (3.32)$$

In (3.32), X_1 has $(k - g)$ columns and X_2 has g columns. Using (3.31) to substitute for β_2, we obtain

$$y = X_1\beta_1 + X_2H_2^{-1}(h - H_1\beta_1) + u$$

or

$$(y - X_2H_2^{-1}h) = (X_1 - X_2H_2^{-1}H_1)\beta_1 + u.$$

A regression of $(y - X_2H_2^{-1}h)$ on $(X_1 - X_2H_2^{-1}H_1)$ produces a restricted estimator of β_1, which we shall write as b_{R1}. The restricted estimator of β_2 is obtained separately as

$$b_{R2} = H_2^{-1}(h - H_1 b_{R1}).$$

The purpose of the argument above is to demonstrate the *possibility* of imposing restrictions by substitution. In practice, it is often easy to see directly how the model should be rearranged for estimation when a restriction or set of restrictions has been imposed. For example, the restriction $\beta_2 + \beta_3 = 1$ can be imposed on the parameters of the model

$$Y_t = \beta_1 + \beta_2 X_{2t} + \beta_3 X_{3t} + u_t; \quad t = 1, \ldots, n$$

by writing

$$Y_t = \beta_1 + \beta_2 X_{2t} + (1 - \beta_2)X_{3t} + u_t$$

$$= \beta_1 + \beta_2(X_{2t} - X_{3t}) + 1(X_{3t}) + u_t$$

$$\Rightarrow (Y_t - X_{3t}) = \beta_1 + \beta_2(X_{2t} - X_{3t}) + u_t; \quad t = 1, \ldots, n.$$

A regression of $(Y_t - X_{3t})$ on $(X_{2t} - X_{3t})$, with an intercept, will produce restricted estimators of β_1 and β_2. The restricted estimator of β_3 is obtained separately from the condition $\beta_2 + \beta_3 = 1$.

Properties of restricted estimators

It has now been established that one can treat the set of restrictions $H\beta = h$ in much the same way as the special case of exclusion restrictions, in the sense that both can be imposed by direct substitution. The analogy can actually be pushed much further, in that the properties of restricted and unrestricted estimators parallel those obtained for exclusions, and a test of the validity of the restrictions $H\beta = h$ can be obtained by comparison of restricted and unrestricted values of the residual sum of squares, as in the version of the F test given in equation (3.24). Following the analogy through, we can state that the imposition of invalid linear restrictions will generally cause the restricted estimators to be biased, that restricted estimators will have variances which are less than or equal to the variances of the corresponding unrestricted estimators, and that a failure to impose valid restrictions will lead to the use of an inefficient estimator. For valid restrictions, it is the restricted estimator which is best linear unbiased under classical assumptions.

Testing a set of linear restrictions

Under the assumptions of the classical regression model, including normality of the disturbances, and a 'fixed regressor' assumption for X, the null hypothesis $H\beta = h$ can be tested against the alternative $H\beta \neq h$ by comparison of the residual sums of squares from two regressions, one subject to the restrictions, and one not subject to the restrictions. The test statistic is

$$F = [(S_R - S)/g]/[S/(n - k)] \tag{3.33}$$

where S_R denotes the residual sum of squares obtained from the restricted regression, and S is the residual sum of squares from the unrestricted regression. Under the null hypothesis, the statistic in (3.33) has an F distribution, with g and $(n - k)$ degrees of freedom. Assuming a 5% significance level, $H_0 : H\beta = h$ is rejected in favour of $H_1 : H\beta \neq h$ if the value of F calculated from the data is greater than the 5% critical value from an F distribution with g and $(n - k)$ degrees of freedom. Notice that k refers to the number of regressors in the *unrestricted* version of the model, and that g is the number of restrictions, corresponding to the number of linearly independent rows in $H\beta = h$.

The Lagrangian method

The procedures outlined above are quite adequate as a practical method for the imposition and testing of linear restrictions, but the theory of restricted estimation is usually approached somewhat differently. If the unrestricted least squares estimator is obtained by unconstrained minimisation of the sum of squares function, the restricted least squares estimator can be obtained by minimising the sum of squares function, subject to side conditions corresponding to the parameter restrictions. Given that the unrestricted model is

$$y = X\beta + u$$

and the set of g independent linear restrictions is

$$H\beta = h,$$

the appropriate Lagrangian function is

$$\phi = (y - X\beta)'(y - X\beta) - \lambda'(H\beta - h).$$

On differentiating ϕ with respect to β and λ, and setting the resulting derivatives to zero, we obtain the conditions

$$\partial\phi/\partial\beta = -2X'y + 2X'X\beta - H'\lambda = 0$$

$$\partial\phi/\partial\lambda = -(H\beta - h) = 0.$$

Premultiplying the first condition by $H(X'X)^{-1}$, and solving for λ, we get

$$\lambda = -2[H(X'X)^{-1}H']^{-1}(Hb - h)$$

where b is the unrestricted least squares estimator

$$b = (X'X)^{-1}X'y.$$

Then, on substituting for λ and solving for β, we obtain the restricted least squares estimator for β, which is written as b_R, and which is given by the expression

$$b_R = b - (X'X)^{-1}H'[H(X'X)^{-1}H']^{-1}(Hb - h). \tag{3.34}$$

If the restrictions $H\beta = h$ are valid and $E(u) = 0$, b_R is an unbiased estimator. If $H\beta \neq h$, b_R is generally biased. Whether b_R is biased or not, so long as $\text{var}(u) = \sigma^2 I$, the variance of b_R is given by the expression

$$\text{var}(b_R) = \text{var}(b) - \sigma^2(X'X)^{-1}H'[H(X'X)^{-1}H']^{-1}H(X'X)^{-1}. \tag{3.35}$$

To complete the formal analysis, we consider the logic behind the F test statistic given in (3.33). If the disturbances are normal, the unrestricted estimator b is normal, and

$$b \sim N[\beta, \sigma^2(X'X)^{-1}]$$

$$\Rightarrow (Hb - h) \sim N[H\beta - h, \sigma^2 H(X'X)^{-1}H'].$$

Under the null hypothesis $H\beta = h$, this gives

$$(Hb - h) \sim N[0, \sigma^2 H(X'X)^{-1}H']$$

and

$$(Hb - h)'[H(X'X)^{-1}H']^{-1}(Hb - h)/\sigma^2 \sim \chi_g^2. \tag{3.36}$$

Two steps remain before we are able to show exactly where (3.33) comes from. First, we use (3.34) to link b_R and b, and then note that

$$e_R = y - Xb_R$$

$$= y - Xb + X(X'X)^{-1}H'[H(X'X)^{-1}H']^{-1}(Hb - h).$$

Hence

$$e_R = e + X(X'X)^{-1}H'[H(X'X)^{-1}H']^{-1}(Hb - h).$$

On forming sums of squares on both sides of this equation, the cross-product vanishes, since $X'e = 0$, and

$$e_R'e_R = e'e + (Hb - h)'[H(X'X)^{-1}H']^{-1}(Hb - h)$$

or

$$S_R - S = (Hb - h)'[H(X'X)^{-1}H']^{-1}(Hb - h). \tag{3.37}$$

Consequently, the difference between restricted and unrestricted residual sums of squares is equal to the numerator quadratic form in (3.36), and

$$(S_R - S)/\sigma^2 \sim \chi_g^2, \text{ under } H_0: H\beta = h. \tag{3.38}$$

The arguments used to convert (3.38) to an F test statistic parallel those used in the preceding section. From section 2.4, we have

$$e'e/\sigma^2 = S/\sigma^2 \sim \chi_{n-k}^2.$$

Then, given normality of the disturbance distributions, the fact that $\mathrm{cov}(b, e) = 0$ is sufficient to show that $e'e$ and the quadratic form on the right of (3.37) are independent. Hence $(S_R - S)/\sigma^2$ and S/σ^2 are independent and, under $H_0: H\beta = h$,

$$F = [(S_R - S)/g]/[S/(n - k)] \sim F_{g,n-k}.$$

This confirms the result given in (3.33).

Large sample tests of restrictions

The F test procedure described above uses all the assumptions of the classical regression model, including normality of the disturbance distributions, but there are two important cases in which some relaxation of these assumptions is possible. If the disturbances are $IID(0, \sigma^2)$, but not normal, it is possible to argue that (3.38) holds approximately in a large sample. Hence, under $H_0: H\beta = h$, and for large n,

$$(S_R - S)/\sigma^2 \text{ is approximately } \chi_g^2. \tag{3.39}$$

The large sample theory that gives rise to (3.39) remains valid when σ^2 is replaced by any estimator that is consistent if H_0 is true, and this includes both the unrestricted estimator

$$\hat{\sigma}^2 = e'e/(n - k)$$

and the restricted estimator

$$\hat{\sigma}_R^2 = e'_R e_R/(n - k + g).$$

Since these estimators need only be consistent, it is not strictly necessary to adjust for degrees of freedom, and one could use n as the divisor in both cases, as with the nR^2 test at the end of the preceding section. On the other hand, the degrees of freedom adjustment does make some allowance for the uncertainty inherent in applying properties which hold in some limiting sense to results from a finite sample.

As well as arguing that (3.39) holds for nonnormal disturbances in a large sample, it can also be shown to hold in the same approximate sense if some columns of the X matrix are random, but are uncorrelated with the disturbances. The relevant large sample theory is discussed in Chapter 4, but we can give some pointers here. One important case is that of a dynamic model, discussed briefly at the end of section 2.4. It is generally possible to apply a large sample test based on (3.39) to such a model, but there must be no serial correlation of the disturbances and the underlying difference equation must be stable.

Although the large sample theory that gives rise to (3.39) does not strictly justify the application of an F test, it is quite common to find the standard F test used in place of the χ^2 test. If $\hat{\sigma}^2$ is used to estimate the disturbance variance in (3.39), the relationship between the F test statistic and the χ^2 test statistic is $gF = \chi^2$. At a given nominal significance level, the χ^2 test uses a critical value which is g times the critical value for $F_{g,\infty}$. Since this is less than the critical value for $F_{g,n-k}$, for any finite n, the F test rejects a true null hypothesis less frequently than the χ^2 test, and this provides some compensation for the fact that the true significance level in the χ^2 test is often greater than the nominal significance level suggested by the large sample theory.

Example 3.4

In section 2.5, we reported the following estimated equation, based on observations taken from data set 3. The variables are the implicit price of output (HUC), unit labour costs (ULC) and unit import costs (UMC):

$$\ln(\widehat{HUC_t}) = \begin{array}{l} 0.0252 \\ (0.0035) \end{array} + \begin{array}{l} 0.659\ln(ULC_t) \\ (0.034) \end{array} + \begin{array}{l} 0.062\ln(UMC_t) \\ (0.018) \end{array}$$

$$+ \begin{array}{l} 0.286\ln(HUC_{t-1}); \\ (0.023) \end{array} \qquad 1960-90 \qquad (2.57)$$

$$n = 31 \qquad df = 27 \qquad RSS = 1.7803 \times 10^{-3}$$

$$VAR = 6.594 \times 10^{-5} \quad R^2 = 0.9999 \quad DW = 1.99.$$

If Y is equated to $\ln(HUC)$, X_2 to $\ln(ULC)$ and X_3 to $\ln(UMC)$, the model on which this equation is based can be written as

$$Y_t = \beta_1 + \beta_2 X_{2t} + \beta_3 X_{3t} + \beta_4 Y_{t-1} + u_t; \ t = 1, \ldots, n.$$

Now consider a restriction which says that the sum of long-run elasticities is equal to 1, which implies that the output price is a linear homogeneous function of the input costs. This is equivalent to saying that $(\beta_2 + \beta_3)/(1 - \beta_4) = 1$, or that $\beta_2 + \beta_3 + \beta_4 = 1$. To impose such a restriction, one can substitute for any one of β_2, β_3 or β_4: if we choose to substitute for β_4, the restricted model is

$$Y_t = \beta_1 + \beta_2 X_{2t} + \beta_3 X_{3t} + (1 - \beta_2 - \beta_3) Y_{t-1} + u_t$$

or

$$(Y_t - Y_{t-1}) = \beta_1 + \beta_2 (X_{2t} - Y_{t-1}) + \beta_3 (X_{3t} - Y_{t-1}) + u_t; \quad t = 1, \ldots, n.$$

A regression of $(Y_t - Y_{t-1})$ on $(X_{2t} - Y_{t-1})$ and $(X_{3t} - Y_{t-1})$, with an intercept, will give restricted estimators of β_1, β_2 and β_3, and restricted residual sum of squares S_R.

Table 3.1 Restricted equation for the price of output

Sample based on observations 1960–90
Dependent variable is YT

Variable	Coefficient	Standard error	t value
INTER	0.021 729	0.003 111	6.9851
X2T	0.614 900	0.026 320	23.3590
X3T	0.091 046	0.009 559	9.5245

Degrees of freedom 28 from 31 observations

Residual SS	2.0245×10^{-3}
Total SS	7.9113×10^{-2}
Disturbance variance	7.2303×10^{-5}
R^2	0.9744
DW statistic	2.04

This methodology is applied, using observations from data set 3, to give the results shown in Table 3.1. The transformed versions of Y_t, X_{2t} and X_{3t} are named as YT, $X2T$ and $X3T$ respectively.

After cancelling powers of 10, the F test statistic for H_0: $\beta_2 + \beta_3 + \beta_4 = 1$ is

$$F = [(2.0245 - 1.7803)/1]/[1.7803/(31 - 4)] = 3.704.$$

There is an alternative approach to testing that $\beta_2 + \beta_3 + \beta_4 = 1$ which is sometimes useful. Introduce a new parameter δ such that under the alternative hypothesis,

$$\beta_2 + \beta_3 + \beta_4 = 1 + \delta,$$

so that testing that $\beta_2 + \beta_3 + \beta_4 = 1$ is equivalent to testing that $\delta = 0$. Substitute out for β_4 as before, to generate a reparameterisation of the unrestricted model as

$$(Y_t - Y_{t-1}) = \beta_1 + \beta_2(X_{2t} - Y_{t-1}) + \beta_3(X_{3t} - Y_{t-1}) + \delta Y_{t-1} + u_t; \quad t = 1, \ldots, n.$$

It is instructive to compare the results of estimating this equation with (2.57) above:

$$YT_t = 0.0252 + 0.659X2T_t + 0.062X3T_t + 0.006\,84\ln(HUC_{t-1}); \quad 1960\text{–}90$$
$$\quad (0.0035) \quad (0.034) \quad\quad (0.018) \quad\quad (0.003\,55)$$

$n = 31 \qquad df = 27 \qquad RSS = 1.7803 \times 10^{-3}$

$VAR = 6.594 \times 10^{-5} \qquad R^2 = 0.9775 \qquad DW = 1.99.$

All of the regression coefficients, apart from that attached to $\ln(HUC_{t-1})$, are the same as those of (2.57), as is RSS and VAR. R^2 is not the same, since the dependent variable is different in the two equations. The coefficient on $\ln(HUC_{t-1})$ is an estimate of δ, and thus of the extent to which the restriction is not satisfied. The estimate of δ should also equal 1 minus the sum of the slopes in equation (2.57), although there is a small rounding error in using the displayed values. The t value for a test of $\delta = 0$ is 1.92, and since the 5% critical value for a two-tailed test is 2.04, the restriction is accepted. Indeed, when the t value is accurately represented, its square is exactly equal to the F test statistic previously calculated.

Strictly speaking, the use of t and F tests is not justified here, since the presence of the lagged dependent variable on the right-hand side implies that there is at least one stochastic regressor. These tests are therefore informally corrected versions of $N(0, 1)$ and χ^2 tests, which can only be justified on large sample arguments. Since the sample size is only 31, one might have some reservations about the result, although the calculated value is well inside the acceptance region. Note also that the Durbin–Watson test procedure is not valid, again because of the inclusion of a lagged dependent variable in the list of regressors.

3.4 / Prediction and the forecast test

Suppose that the parameters of the model

$$y = X\beta + u$$

have been estimated by OLS, and that the model is to be used to predict y_f, a $(g \times 1)$ vector of dependent variable values that lie outside the original sample. The usual context for this problem is that of time series data, where y_f relates to a set of g periods which occur later in time than the data period, but similar ideas can be applied in the context of a cross-section. In order to make predictions for y_f, the corresponding regressor matrix X_f must be known or, in the case of a simulation exercise, specified by the user as an input. The analysis is therefore conditional on given values for X_f, and this excludes consideration of the fact that when the model is used for forecasting, as opposed to conditional prediction, it will often be necessary to forecast elements of X_f before using the model to generate forecasts for y_f.

The distinction between forecasting and prediction is a fine one, which is not always observed. The suggestion is that prediction is a mechanical exercise, whilst a forecast is a 'best guess' at future values, incorporating both a formal prediction and less formal judgemental adjustments. In fact, conventional usage is not entirely consistent, and terms such as 'forecast period' are used when strictly one should use the term 'prediction period' to refer to the set of g values for which predictions are to be made.

In section 2.3, predicted values of the dependent variable inside the data period were written as

$$\hat{y} = Xb$$

where b is the OLS estimator. It would therefore seem sensible to generate a prediction of y_f, for known X_f, as

$$\hat{y}_f = X_f b. \tag{3.40}$$

This method of prediction does have some optimal properties, but for the moment, our objective is to understand the broad nature of the prediction exercise, without worrying too much about alternative possibilities. Given that the estimator b is a random variable, it follows that $\hat{y}_f$ should be interpreted as a random variable, known as a *predictor*. One could certainly analyse the statistical properties of the predictor, but it is often more convenient to look at the *prediction error*, which we shall write as

$$f = y_f - \hat{y}_f = y_f - X_f b. \tag{3.41}$$

In everyday usage, a positive prediction error might be taken to indicate 'overshoot' in the prediction, and for this reason some authors reverse the order of y_f and $\hat{y}_f$ in (3.41). Our definition has the advantage of symmetry with the corresponding errors inside the sample, which are the residuals $e = y - Xb$. In fact, it does not really matter which definition we choose, but some care is needed when examining error plots in practical applications.

Before we can perform a statistical analysis of the prediction error, it is necessary to make some assumption about the process which generates y_f. If the model that holds for the data period also holds for the forecast period, then

$$y_f = X_f \beta + u_f, \tag{3.42}$$

where $E(u_f) = 0$, $\text{var}(u_f) = \sigma^2 I_g$ and $\text{cov}(u, u_f) = 0$, an $(n \times g)$ zero matrix. It follows that

$$
\begin{aligned}
f &= y_f - \hat{y}_f \\
&= X_f \beta + u_f - X_f b \\
&= X_f(\beta - b) + u_f.
\end{aligned}
\tag{3.43}
$$

Equation (3.43) shows that the prediction error is made up of two components, one due to the error of estimation inherent in the difference between the true value β and the estimator b, and the other due to the random disturbances in the forecast period. It is shown below that the two sources of error are uncorrelated; this occurs because b depends on the disturbances in the data period, which are contained in the vector u, and which by assumption are uncorrelated with the disturbances in the forecast period, contained in the vector u_f. Formally, we have

$$
\begin{aligned}
b &= (X'X)^{-1} X'y \\
&= (X'X)^{-1} X'(X\beta + u) \\
&= \beta + (X'X)^{-1} X'u \\
\Rightarrow X_f(\beta - b) &= -X_f(X'X)^{-1} X'u \\
\Rightarrow \text{cov}[X_f(\beta - b), u_f] &= -X_f(X'X)^{-1} X' \cdot \text{cov}(u, u_f) \\
&= 0; \quad \text{since } \text{cov}(u, u_f) = 0.
\end{aligned}
$$

Now consider the expectation and variance of the prediction error. From (3.43), we have

$$f = X_f(\beta - b) + u_f,$$

so

$$E(f) = X_f\beta - X_f E(b) + E(u_f)$$
$$= 0; \text{ if } E(b) = \beta \text{ and } E(u_f) = 0. \tag{3.44}$$

It is important to note that (3.44) holds conditionally on the assumption that the model continues to hold, with $E(u_f) = 0$, in the forecast period. If this condition is not satisfied, the expected prediction error is not zero and the prediction is biased. A second requirement for (3.44) to hold is that the OLS estimator b must be unbiased; violation of this condition will again lead to a biased prediction.

The evaluation of var(f) is simplified by the fact that we have already shown that the terms on the right of (3.43) have zero covariance, so

$$\text{var}(f) = \text{var}[X_f(\beta - b)] + \text{var}(u_f)$$
$$= \text{var}(-X_f b) + \text{var}(u_f); \text{ since } X_f\beta \text{ is nonrandom}$$
$$= (-X_f) \cdot \text{var}(b) \cdot (-X_f') + \text{var}(u_f)$$
$$= X_f \cdot \sigma^2 (X'X)^{-1} \cdot X_f' + \sigma^2 I_g$$
$$= \sigma^2 [I_g + X_f(X'X)^{-1} X_f']. \tag{3.45}$$

Again, there are several conditions that must be satisfied here, including var$(u_f) = \sigma^2 I_g$, var$(u) = \sigma^2 I_n$ and cov$(u, u_f) = 0$. Given that these conditions hold, var(f) reflects the two sources of error shown in (3.43); the first term in (3.45) is the variance due to random disturbances in the forecast period, and the second term is the variance that results from the use of b as an estimator for β.

Forecast test

In what follows, we describe what is formally an *ex post* test of prediction, although it is often described as the 'forecast test'. In this test, the assumption of normality is of vital importance and, rather unusually, the assumption cannot be relaxed for large samples. We therefore assume that the vectors u and u_f are jointly normal, and use (3.43) to show that the prediction error is normal since it is a linear function of u and u_f:

$$f = X_f(\beta - b) + u_f$$
$$= -X_f(X'X)^{-1} X'u + u_f. \tag{3.46}$$

Combining the normality of f with (3.44) and (3.45), we have

$$f \sim N(0, \sigma^2 [I_g + X_f(X'X)^{-1} X_f'])$$
$$\Rightarrow f'[I_g + X_f(X'X)^{-1} X_f']^{-1} f / \sigma^2 \sim \chi_g^2. \tag{3.47}$$

It is important to realise that (3.47) is conditional on the assumption that the model continues to hold in the forecast period, which is precisely what we wish to test. We therefore write the null hypothesis as

$$H_0: y_f = X_f\beta + u_f, \text{ with } E(u_f) = 0 \tag{3.48}$$

and say that (3.47) is the distribution under H_0. The nature of this null hypothesis is interesting in that it consists of a set of g stochastic restrictions on the elements of β. The model itself, written as $y = X\beta + u$, is a set of n such restrictions, and we are now proposing to test whether the model holds in the prediction period by adding and testing a further set of g restrictions. Note that these are *not* the same as the exact restrictions discussed in section 3.3.

In a small sample, (3.47) does not provide an operational test statistic because σ^2 is unknown. However, if σ^2 is replaced by the estimator

$$\hat{\sigma}^2 = e'e/(n-k),$$

it is possible to obtain a test statistic which has an F distribution under the null hypothesis. This follows because

$$e'e/\sigma^2 \sim \chi^2_{n-k} \tag{3.49}$$

and the χ^2 distributions in (3.47) and (3.49) are independent. To show independence, it is sufficient to show that $\mathrm{cov}(f, e) = 0$, because f and e are normal and zero covariance plus normality implies independence, both for f and e, and for the functions in (3.47) and (3.49). The problem is therefore reduced to showing that $\mathrm{cov}(f, e)$ is zero.

From equation (3.46), we have

$$f = -X_f(X'X)^{-1}X'u + u_f,$$

and from equation (2.43), in section 2.4,

$$e = My = M(X\beta + u) = Mu; \text{ where } M = I - X(X'X)^{-1}X'.$$

The covariance between f and e is now seen to be of the form

$$\mathrm{cov}(f, e) = \mathrm{cov}[(A_1 u + u_f), A_2 u],$$

which is equivalent to

$$A_1 \cdot \mathrm{var}(u) \cdot A_2' + \mathrm{cov}(u_f, u) \cdot A_2'.$$

Hence

$$\begin{aligned}
\mathrm{cov}(f, e) &= -X_f(X'X)^{-1}X' \cdot \mathrm{var}(u) \cdot M' + \mathrm{cov}(u_f, u) \cdot M' \\
&= -X_f(X'X)^{-1}X' \cdot \mathrm{var}(u) \cdot M'; \text{ since } \mathrm{cov}(u_f, u) = 0 \\
&= -\sigma^2 X_f(X'X)^{-1}X'M'; \text{ since } \mathrm{var}(u) = \sigma^2 I_n \\
&= 0; \text{ since } X'M' = X'M = 0.
\end{aligned}$$

Given that f and e are uncorrelated, and are independent under the normality assumption, it follows that the statistic

$$F = \{f'[I_g + X_f(X'X)^{-1}X_f']^{-1}f/g\}/[e'e/(n-k)] \tag{3.50}$$

has an F distribution, with g and $(n-k)$ degrees of freedom, under the null hypothesis (3.48). If the calculated value of this statistic is greater than the critical value $F_{g,n-k}^{0.05}$, H_0 is rejected at the 5% significance level. There are several possible explanations for rejection of the null hypothesis, but all indicate a failure that ought not to occur with a well-specified model.

Alternative forms for the forecast test

As presented above, the forecast test involves a quadratic form that is potentially awkward to calculate, but there are ways of conducting the test by running two regressions and comparing residual sums of squares. If S_D is the residual sum of squares from the original regression, using only observations from the data period, and S_{D+F} is the residual sum of squares from a regression combining observations from both the data and the forecast period, it can be shown that

$$S_{D+F} - S_D = f'[I_g + X_f(X'X)^{-1}X_f']^{-1}f.$$

Consequently, the F test statistic (3.50) can be written as

$$F = [(S_{D+F} - S_D)/g]/[S_D/(n-k)]. \tag{3.51}$$

Notice that n refers to the number of observations in the *data* period, and that $S_D/(n-k)$ is the disturbance variance estimator $\hat{\sigma}^2$, based on the data period only. This form of the F test does not require direct evaluation of the numerator quadratic form in (3.50), and can therefore be used when the computer program does not have a special subroutine for the forecast test.

A second variant involves the use of a special type of dummy variable. Dummy variables are discussed in detail in section 3.6. Here, all we need to know is that such a variable has observations that are either 0 or 1. Under the null hypothesis (3.48), observations for the data period and the forecast period are generated from the same model, so we can create a single data set, with $(n+g)$ observations, and write

$$\begin{bmatrix} y \\ y_f \end{bmatrix} = \begin{bmatrix} X \\ X_f \end{bmatrix} \beta + \begin{bmatrix} u \\ u_f \end{bmatrix}. \tag{3.52}$$

The application of least squares to this system produces the residual sum of squares already identified as S_{D+F}. Dropping the g observations in y_f and X_f produces the residual sum of squares S_D. However, instead of actually deleting observations, as in the previous version of the test, it is possible to *add* variables to (3.52), to give the system

$$\begin{bmatrix} y \\ y_f \end{bmatrix} = \begin{bmatrix} X & 0 \\ X_f & I_g \end{bmatrix} \begin{bmatrix} \beta \\ \gamma \end{bmatrix} + \begin{bmatrix} u \\ u_f \end{bmatrix}. \tag{3.53}$$

The new columns in (3.53) are dummy variables, created in such a way that the ith added variable takes the value one for observation i of the forecast period, and the value zero everywhere else. If least squares is applied to (3.53), element i of the least squares estimator $\hat{\gamma}$ can take whatever value is needed to set the ith residual in the forecast period to zero, leaving the least squares procedure to minimise the sum of squares:

$$(y - X\beta)'(y - X\beta).$$

It is obvious that this minimisation must produce the estimator

$$b = (X'X)^{-1}X'y$$

and

$$RSS = S_D = (y - Xb)'(y - Xb).$$

So least squares applied to (3.53) gives the estimator b and residual sum of squares S_D. If the role of $\hat{\gamma}$ is to allow the forecast period residuals from (3.53) to be zero, these residuals make no contribution to the value of S_D, and

$$y_f - X_f b - I_g \hat{\gamma} = 0$$
$$\Rightarrow \hat{\gamma} = y_f - X_f b = f.$$

There are now three different ways of performing the forecast test. The first is to run a regression on the n observations in the data period, and then to use (3.50) to obtain a value for the F test statistic. This involves direct evaluation of the numerator quadratic form. The second method is to run two regressions, one on the n observations in the data period, giving the residual sum of squares S_D, and one on the combined observations from the data and forecast periods, giving residual sum of squares S_{D+F}. The F test statistic can then be calculated using (3.51). Finally, one can set the number of observations at $(n + g)$, pooling observations from the data and forecast periods, and then run two regressions. One of these regressions includes dummy variables for each observation in the forecast period, and gives $RSS = S_D$. The other excludes the dummy variables, giving $RSS = S_{D+F}$. The test statistic is again as written in (3.51), but in this third case, the statistic can also be interpreted as a variable addition test of the null hypothesis that γ in (3.53) is zero. The residual sum of squares under $H_0: \gamma = 0$ is S_{D+F}, whilst under $H_1: \gamma \neq 0$, the residual sum of squares is S_D. The standard F test for the exact restrictions $\gamma = 0$ gives

$$F = [(S_{D+F} - S_D)/g]/\{S_D/[(n + g) - (k + g)]\}$$

which is identical to (3.51).

Large sample forecast test

There are two further variants of the forecast test that can be used in large samples. The first simply ignores the effect of estimating the disturbance variance, and is based on the proposition that if

$$f'[I_g + X_f(X'X)^{-1}X_f']^{-1}f/\sigma^2$$

is distributed as χ_g^2 under the null hypothesis, then replacing σ^2 by a consistent estimator will give a statistic that is asymptotically distributed as χ_g^2 under H_0. Hence, in a large sample, one can use the statistic

$$gF = f'[I_g + X_f(X'X)^{-1}X_f']^{-1}f/\hat{\sigma}^2 \tag{3.54}$$

which is tested against critical values from a χ^2 distribution. If gF is greater than $\chi_g^{2(0.05)}$, the null hypothesis in (3.48) is rejected, at a nominal significance level of 5%.

A second variant follows from the fact that in establishing large sample properties of estimators and test statistics, it is often assumed that the sample moments of the regressors converge in a particular manner. In the simplest case, in which the regressors are nonrandom, the standard assumption is that

$$\lim_{n \to \infty} (n^{-1}X'X) = Q; \text{ where } Q \text{ is nonsingular.}$$

If this condition is satisfied, we can examine the convergence of the quadratic form

$$f'[I_g + X_f(X'X)^{-1}X_f']^{-1}f = f'[I_g + n^{-1}X_f(n^{-1}X'X)^{-1}X_f']^{-1}f.$$

As the sample size in the data period is increased, $n^{-1}X'X$ converges to Q, whilst X_f still relates to g observations from the forecast period, and is therefore unchanged. Division by n ensures that the second term in the quadratic form converges to zero, so the quadratic form converges to $f'f$. Although this argument is somewhat informal, it does suggest that under the null hypothesis (3.48),

$$f'f/\hat{\sigma}^2 \text{ is approximately } \chi_g^2, \text{ for large } n. \tag{3.55}$$

This is very simple to compute as the sum of squared forecast errors divided by the estimated value of the disturbance variance. As before, the calculated value of the test statistic is compared with a critical value from the χ^2 distribution with g degrees of freedom.

The usual reason for considering large sample tests is that by doing so, one can allow some relaxation of the classical assumptions. Although the argument above assumes nonrandom regressors, this is not necessary, and equivalent arguments can often be used when some of the regressors are random. Thus, under certain conditions, one can apply the large sample forecast test to a dynamic model, though this will not be valid if there is a serial correlation of disturbances, or if the implied difference equation is unstable.

One relaxation that is not possible is the removal of the normality assumption. The numerator in (3.55) can only converge to a sum of squares of normal variables if the forecast period disturbances u_f are normal, and if $f'f$ does not converge to a sum of squares of normal variables, $f'f/\hat{\sigma}^2$ is not distributed as χ_g^2, no matter how large the sample size becomes.

Example 3.5

In Example 3.1, we estimated a version of the consumption function which includes an intercept, an income variable, an inflation variable and a liquid assets variable, using data from 1964–90. The relevant regression gave a residual sum of squares equal to 3.5516×10^{-3}. To test the null hypothesis that the model estimated for 1964–90 holds for the three additional periods 1991–93, we identify the residual sum of squares from the regression for 1964–90 as S_D. The same equation is then estimated using data for 1964–93, giving a residual sum of squares equal to 7.9724×10^{-3}. This is identified as S_{D+F}. Using the forecast F test written in equation (3.51), with n equal to the number of observations in the data period, k equal to the number of regressors and g equal to the number of observations in the forecast period, we have

$$F = [(7.9724 - 3.5516)/3]/[3.5516/(27 - 4)] = 9.543.$$

The 5% critical value for the F distribution with 3 and 23 degrees of freedom is 3.01, so H_0 is rejected in favour of the alternative that the model does not hold for 1991–93.

Failure in the prediction test may mean that the detailed specification used is simply not good enough, or it may reflect some underlying change in the economy which we ought to be able to model but which we have failed to reflect in the equation under test. In this particular case, the explanation seems to lie in the credit expansion and rise in the valuation of nonliquid assets that occurred in the United Kingdom during this period. Since this reflects behaviour which is 'newly learned', it is difficult to model using historical data; one could include a further explanatory variable in the model to capture this, but the introduction of a variable for just three periods smacks of fixing the model. We therefore accept predictive failure as a criticism of the current version of the model, though we note that the chosen forecast period does impose a rather severe test.

The calculation performed above can also be carried out by estimating the model for 1964–93, to give S_{D+F}, and then adding three dummy variables, DUM91, DUM92, and DUM93, constructed so that DUM91 has the value 1 in 1991 and zero elsewhere, with similar definitions for DUM92 and DUM93. The output shown in Table 3.2 demonstrates that the residual sum of squares from the regression with these variables added is equal to the value of S_D obtained above. The coefficients attached to the dummy variables are the forecast errors, f_{n+i}; $i = 1, 2, 3$, that arise when the equation estimated for 1964–90 is used to forecast for 1991–93.

Example 3.6

We may also consider the application of the forecast test procedure to the demand for money equation shown in Table 2.3 of section 2.5, but re-estimated over the period 1963–94. This gives an RSS of 8.662 29. Apparently, this now leaves no observations available to construct a forecast test, but there is no reason why the test cannot be turned in on an existing sample, defining S_{D+F} to be 8.6623, and re-estimating for a shorter period to give S_D. If the (new) data period is 1963–91, the null hypothesis

Table 3.2 Forecast test using dummy variables

Sample based on observations 1964–93
Dependent variable is LNRCONS

Variable	Coefficient	Standard error	t value
INTER	−0.356 27	0.083 89	−4.247
LNRPDI	0.886 39	0.029 57	29.974
DLPCONS	−0.055 58	0.067 80	−0.820
LNRLIQ	0.172 34	0.037 63	4.580
DUM91	−0.037 01	0.014 66	−2.526
DUM92	−0.065 70	0.014 66	−4.482
DUM93	−0.059 35	0.014 83	−4.001

Degrees of freedom 23 from 30 observations

Residual SS	3.5516×10^{-3}
Total SS	1.4178
Disturbance variance	1.5442×10^{-4}
R^2	0.9975
DW statistic	1.23

would be that the model as estimated for 1963–91 holds for 1992–94. The relevant information obtained from the estimation for 1963–91 is $n = 29$, $k = 3$, and $RSS = 8.102\,42$. The resulting F test statistic equals 0.5989 and the appropriate critical value is $F_{3,26}^{0.05} = 2.97$. Somewhat surprisingly, the null hypothesis of parameter stability appears to hold.

Before leaving these examples, it should be noted that in applying the forecast test, we have ignored the fact that some of the estimated equations exhibit low values for the Durbin–Watson statistic, and may on further examination reveal evidence of other violations of underlying assumptions. In practice, this would be of more consequence if the tests had suggested acceptance of the proposed models. As things stand, we have an indication of apparent failure, and we do not therefore risk acceptance of a model which violates underlying assumptions.

3.5 / Multicollinearity

Observations on economic variables are not generated under controlled conditions and, as a result, almost any correlation measure calculated between two or more columns of the regressor matrix X will produce a result different from zero. The name given to this phenomenon is multicollinearity.

As defined here, multicollinearity appears to exist when there is any departure from orthogonality in the set of regressors. This is certainly a possible definition, but it is convenient to distinguish between the usual 'centred' measures of correlation, calculated by subtracting sample means from the data, and 'noncentred' measures, calculated directly from the raw data. The regressors $X_j; j = 1, \ldots, k$ are orthogonal if

$$\sum X_{it} X_{jt} = 0; \ i \neq j; \ i, j = 1, \ldots, k. \tag{3.56}$$

If we assume the presence of an intercept, so that $X_{1t} = 1; \ t = 1, \ldots, n$, then (3.56) implies that the sample means are zero and that gross or noncentred sums of products are zero, for $X_2, \ldots, X_k$:

$$\sum X_{1t} X_{jt} = \sum X_{jt} = 0 \ \Rightarrow \ \bar{X}_j = 0; \ j = 2, \ldots, k$$

and

$$\sum X_{it} X_{jt} = 0; \ i \neq j; \ i, j = 2, \ldots, k.$$

A somewhat weaker condition is that deviation or centred sums of products are zero for $X_2, \ldots, X_k$:

$$\sum (X_{it} - \bar{X}_i)(X_{jt} - \bar{X}_j) = 0; \ i \neq j; \ i, j = 2, \ldots, k. \tag{3.57}$$

If (3.57) is true, then all zero-order correlation coefficients

$$r_{ij} = \frac{\sum (X_{it} - \bar{X}_i)(X_{jt} - \bar{X}_j)}{\sqrt{\sum (X_{it} - \bar{X}_i)^2} \sqrt{\sum (X_{jt} - \bar{X}_j)^2}}$$

are zero, for $i \neq j$ and $i, j = 2, \ldots, k$, and the regressor variables are said to exhibit zero measured correlation. Although a complete map of correlation in a given data set depends on partial and multiple correlation coefficients, as well as the zero-order coefficients defined above, it is true that if (3.57) holds for *all* $i \neq j$; $i, j = 2, \ldots, k$, then all centred partial and multiple correlations defined on $X_2, \ldots, X_k$ are also zero.

If we now say that multicollinearity exists whenever (3.57) is violated, that is, whenever the regressor variables do not have zero measured correlation, we are excluding the special case in which (3.57) is true but (3.56) is not. This case is a departure from orthogonality, but it is excluded from our definition because it has nothing to do with correlation between the regressors $X_2, \ldots, X_k$, in the usually understood sense of some centred correlation coefficient being different from zero.

It is important to realise that multicollinearity as defined here is a property of the data. There is no violation of the assumptions of the classical model, except in the extreme case in which one of the regressors, X_j, is an exact linear function of other regressors. If this happens, the matrix $X'X$ is singular and the regression calculation fails. So at one extreme the regressors are orthogonal and $X'X$ is diagonal. At the other extreme $X'X$ is singular. In between the extremes we have multicollinearity of some degree, or the rather unlikely special case in which (3.57) is true but (3.56) is not.

Since there is almost always some intercorrelation between regressor variables, multicollinearity is almost always present to some extent, but multiple regression recognises this fact and produces estimates accordingly. There are problems that arise when some of the measured correlations become very high, but before considering these problems, we need to know exactly how the regression calculation produces an estimator for a single parameter β_j. To answer this question, we shall use techniques similar to those employed in section 3.2, but with the different objective of finding an expression for a single coefficient, b_j, obtained from a multiple regression of y on X.

A single coefficient from a multiple regression

The regression of y on X produces the estimator vector

$$b = (X'X)^{-1}X'y.$$

A single coefficient, b_j, is clearly an element of b, but with a little algebra it is possible to extract a more useful expression for b_j.

If X is partitioned as $X = [X_1 X_2]$, where X_1 is $[n \times (k - g)]$ and X_2 is $(n \times g)$, and β is partitioned conformably so that β_1 is $[(k - g) \times 1]$ and β_2 is $(g \times 1)$, the single equation model can be written as

$$y = X_1\beta_1 + X_2\beta_2 + u. \tag{3.58}$$

Apart from a change in notation, (3.58) is identical to equation (3.2) in section 3.2, and the results of section 3.2 show that the OLS estimator of β_2 can be written as

$$b_2 = (X_2'M_1X_2)^{-1}X_2'M_1y \tag{3.59}$$

where $M_1 = I - X_1(X_1'X_1)^{-1}X_1'$. If X_1 and X_2 are nonrandom, and $\text{var}(u) = \sigma^2 I$, we also have

$$\text{var}(b_2) = \sigma^2(X_2'M_1X_2)^{-1}. \tag{3.60}$$

Now consider the special case in which X_2 contains only a single column, written as x_j. Since the numbering of variables and parameters is arbitrary, x_j can be any column from X, and X_1 would then contain all regressors in X apart from x_j. The subvector b_2 becomes a scalar quantity, written as b_j, and (3.59) becomes

$$b_j = (x_j'M_1x_j)^{-1}x_j'M_1y.$$

Since $M_1 = M_1' = M_1'M_1$, two alternative forms are

$$b_j = (x_j'M_1'M_1x_j)^{-1}x_j'M_1'y, \tag{3.61}$$

$$b_j = (x_j'M_1'M_1x_j)^{-1}x_j'M_1'M_1y. \tag{3.62}$$

Equation (3.61) suggests a regression of y on M_1x_j, whilst (3.62) suggests a regression of M_1y on M_1x_j. From the discussion at the end of section 2.3, it should be clear that M_1x_j represents the residuals from an auxiliary regression of x_j on X_1, which is equivalent to the regression of x_j on all other columns of X. Similarly, M_1y represents the residuals from a regression of y on all columns of X, except for x_j. So what the algebra shows is that the regression of y on M_1x_j and the regression of M_1y on M_1x_j both produce a result equivalent to a single coefficient from the *multiple* regression of y on X.

Since $M_1 y$ and $M_1 x_j$ are single columns, (3.61) and (3.62) can both be written in scalar form. For our purposes it is sufficient to look at (3.61). Let $\tilde{X}_{jt};\ t = 1, \ldots, n$ be the residuals from a regression on X_j on all other regressors in the model. Then (3.61) can be written as

$$b_j = \sum \tilde{X}_{jt} Y_t \Big/ \sum \tilde{X}_{jt}^2. \tag{3.63}$$

By similar arguments, one can show that equation (3.60) specialises to give

$$\mathrm{var}(b_j) = \sigma^2 \Big/ \sum \tilde{X}_{jt}^2. \tag{3.64}$$

It is now possible to see exactly what happens when a regression of y on X produces an estimator for a single parameter β_j. Instead of using all the information contained in the observations $X_{jt};\ t = 1, \ldots, n$, the multiple regression 'adjusts' X_j for the effect of other regressors, and uses only that part of the set of observations on X_j that cannot be 'explained' by the other regressors. This corresponds to the interpretation of the parameter β_j as the effect on Y of a unit change in X_j, *ceteris paribus*, that is, with all other regressors 'held constant'. Since changes in economic variables are almost always accompanied by changes in other economic variables, it is necessary to use an estimation method that attempts to isolate the effects of changes in X_j from the effects of changes in other regressors, and we now see that this is exactly what multiple regression attempts to do.

Regression using data in deviation form

Before returning to the discussion of multicollinearity, there is one other special case that can usefully be extracted from equation (3.59). If the submatrix X_1 is a single column, containing observations $X_{1t} = 1;\ t = 1, \ldots, n$, then X_2 contains all the regressors which are genuine variables, b_1 is the intercept and b_2 is the vector of slope coefficients. In this special case, X_1 can be written as the $(n \times 1)$ sum vector i, and M_1 is denoted by the matrix A. Hence

$$M_1 X_2 = [I - i(i'i)^{-1}i'] X_2$$
$$= A X_2;\ \text{where } A = I - i(i'i)^{-1}i'. \tag{3.65}$$

Since $(i'i) = n$, and $i' X_2$ is a row vector with elements equal to the sums $\sum X_{2t}, \ldots, \sum X_{kt}$, it follows that $A X_2$ is the matrix of observations on the regressors $X_2, \ldots, X_k$, 'adjusted for means', with elements $(X_{jt} - \bar{X}_j);\ j = 2, \ldots, k$ and $t = 1, \ldots, n$. Similarly, Ay is the vector of observations on the dependent variable, also adjusted for means, with elements $(Y_t - \bar{Y});\ t = 1, \ldots, n$. Equation (3.59) shows that the slope coefficients from a multiple regression can be expressed as

$$b_2 = (X_2' A X_2)^{-1} X_2' A y. \tag{3.66}$$

Given that $A = A' = A'A$, we can interpret this as saying that the slope coefficients can be obtained by first adjusting the data for means, to give Ay and AX_2, and then performing either the regression of Ay on AX_2 or the regression of y on AX_2.

Two useful insights follow from the discussion above. The first is that auxiliary regressions on the single 'variable' X_1 produce residuals which are deviations from sample means, provided of course that $X_{1t} = 1$, for $t = 1, \ldots, n$. The second relates to the concept of zero measured correlation: if equation (3.57) is satisifed, the matrix $X_2' A X_2$ is diagonal. This matrix contains deviation sums of squares and products for X_2 to X_k, and if (3.57) is satisfied, the least squares slope estimators $b_j; j = 2, \ldots, k$ simplify to

$$b_j = \sum (X_{jt} - \bar{X}_j)(Y_t - \bar{Y}) \Big/ \sum (X_{jt} - \bar{X}_j)^2.$$

These are identical to the slope coefficients from $(k - 1)$ 'two-variable' regressions of the form Y on X_1 and $X_j; j = 2, \ldots, k$.

Multicollinearity and data deficiency

Since it is very unlikely that zero measured correlation will ever arise in practice, there will generally be a difference between the 'two-variable' regression estimator, written now as

$$b_j^* = \sum (X_{jt} - \bar{X}_j)(Y_t - \bar{Y}) \Big/ \sum (X_{jt} - \bar{X}_j)^2$$

with

$$\mathrm{var}(b_j^*) = \sigma^2 \Big/ \sum (X_{jt} - \bar{X}_j)^2,$$

and the multiple regression estimator

$$b_j = \sum \tilde{X}_{jt} Y_t \Big/ \sum \tilde{X}_{jt}^2$$

with

$$\mathrm{var}(b_j) = \sigma^2 \Big/ \sum \tilde{X}_{jt}^2.$$

The cost associated with multicollinearity, at least as far as X_j is concerned, can be measured by comparing the actual variance from a multiple regression, $\mathrm{var}(b_j)$, with the ideal that would be attained in the absence of multicollinearity, which is $\mathrm{var}(b_j^*)$. The most convenient way of making this comparison is to use the measure

$$R_j^2 = 1 - \mathrm{var}(b_j^*)/\mathrm{var}(b_j)$$

$$= 1 - \sum \tilde{X}_{jt}^2 \Big/ \sum (X_{jt} - \bar{X}_j)^2. \tag{3.67}$$

The notation R_j^2 suggests a squared multiple correlation coefficient, and this turns out to be correct. In the auxiliary regression of X_j on all other regressors, $\sum (X_{jt} - \bar{X}_j)^2$ is the total sum of squares and $\sum \tilde{X}_{jt}^2$ is the residual sum of squares. So (3.67) is exactly analogous to the definition of R^2 given in section 2.3, the difference being that R_j^2 is the corresponding measure from the auxiliary regression of X_j on all other regressors in the model.

In the case in which $R_j^2 = 0$, b_j is identical to b_j^* and this corresponds to zero measured correlation in the specific context of the variable X_j. If *all* $R_j^2; j = 2, \ldots, k$ are zero, then we have zero measured correlation for all regressors $X_2, \ldots, X_k$, and this corresponds to the definition used earlier, since

$$R_j^2 = 0; \ j = 2, \ldots, k \Leftrightarrow r_{ij} = 0; \ i \neq j; \ i, j = 2, \ldots, k.$$

If any $R_j^2 > 0$, and $k > 2$, the multiple regression estimator b_j is used to avoid the omitted variables bias inherent in the two-variable estimator b_j^*. As R_j^2 approaches 1, the cost of using multiple regression becomes progressively higher as the effects of multicollinearity become more serious and $\mathrm{var}(b_j)$ becomes larger relative to $\mathrm{var}(b_j^*)$. In the limit, X_j is an exact linear function of the other regressors, $R_j^2 = 1$, and the regression calculation fails. This is the extreme of perfect multicollinearity, where the matrix $X'X$ becomes singular.

Since the maximum value in the set $R_j^2; j = 2, \ldots, k$ is greater than or equal to all other squared and centred correlation coefficients defined on the regressor matrix X, we can be sure that 'high' correlations of any kind will lead to at least one high R_j^2. We can therefore define serious multicollinearity as the situation in which at least one of the R_j^2 is close to 1, and we can guarantee the detection of serious multicollinearity by running all $(k-1)$ auxiliary regressions which define the R_j^2. Although this strategy may seem expensive, it is certainly cheaper than calculating all zero-order, partial and multiple correlations for the variables $X_2, \ldots, X_k$. When used in conjunction with other 'clues' to the existence of multicollinearity, which we discuss below, it is usually sufficient to run one or two well-chosen auxiliary regressions, and then only when one has reason to suspect that serious multicollinearity may be present.

It is important to note that multicollinearity is not the only reason why parameter estimators may have 'high' variance. If the model contains an intercept, then

$$\sum X_{jt}^2 \geq \sum (X_{jt} - \bar{X}_j)^2 \geq \sum \tilde{X}_{jt}^2. \tag{3.68}$$

In order to avoid a 'low' value of $\sum \tilde{X}_{jt}^2$, one must start with a sufficiently high value of $\sum X_{jt}^2$, and since this depends amongst other things on the number of observations, we can say that a first requirement is that the number of observations should not be too small. It is then necessary that each of regressors $X_2, \ldots, X_k$ should exhibit a reasonable amount of variation, for otherwise $\sum (X_{jt} - \bar{X}_j)^2$ will be small relative to $\sum X_{jt}^2$. Finally, multicollinearity must not be too serious, for otherwise $\sum \tilde{X}_{jt}^2$ will be small relative to $\sum (X_{jt} - \bar{X}_j)^2$. This identifies three possible sources of data deficiency, namely insufficient observations, insufficient variation and 'serious' multicollinearity. In all three cases, the result is a 'high' value of $\mathrm{var}(b_j)$.

'Extreme' data deficiency

For each of the three kinds of data deficiency, there is an extreme case in which $X'X$ is singular and the regression calculation fails. If $n < k$, then $\text{rank}(X) < k$, and there are not enough observations to estimate k parameters. If $n \geq k$, but one of the regressors $X_j; j = 2, \ldots, k$ is such that

$$\sum (X_{jt} - \bar{X}_j)^2 = 0,$$

then X_j does not vary at all and X_j is an exact linear function of the 'variable' X_1. Finally, if one or more of the R_j^2 is equal to 1, we have perfect or complete multicollinearity.

Multicollinearity, standard errors and the t test

Having made the point that all three kinds of data deficiency can have similar effects, we now avoid repetition by concentrating on the case in which we have serious but not complete multicollinearity.

The computer output does not give values for the theoretical variance, $\text{var}(b_j)$, but it does give standard errors

$$\text{se}(b_j) = \hat{\sigma}/\sqrt{\sum \tilde{X}_{jt}^2}.$$

Under classical assumptions, $\text{var}(b_j)$ is nonrandom, but $\text{se}(b_j)$ is random because it depends on the disturbance variance estimator

$$\hat{\sigma}^2 = \sum e_t^2/(n - k).$$

Provided that there are no omitted regressors, the distribution of $\hat{\sigma}^2$ is not influenced by multicollinearity, and the only way in which standard errors are affected is through the value of $\sum \tilde{X}_{jt}^2$. Since this affects all possible realisations of $\text{se}(b_j)$ in the same way, we can conclude that there is a systematic increase in the standard errors of variables for which R_j^2 is high. One immediate consequence is that confidence intervals are wider than would otherwise be the case.

If regressors are omitted from the equation to be estimated, the disturbance variance estimator is generally biased, and the bias is always positive, so that $E(\hat{\sigma}^2) > \sigma^2$. This means that 'high' standard errors may have nothing to do with multicollinearity or any other kind of data deficiency. If the problem is due to omitted variables, adding regressors will tend to make the standard errors smaller. If the problem arises because of multicollinearity, adding regressors will tend to make standard errors larger.

Now consider a test of the null hypothesis $\beta_j = 0$ against the alternative $\beta_j \neq 0$. Under the null hypothesis, the statistic

$$t_j = b_j/\text{se}(b_j)$$

has a t distribution with $(n - k)$ degrees of freedom, and the existence of multicollinearity does not alter this in any way. In particular, there is no effect on probability of Type I error. Under the alternative hypothesis, t_j has a noncentral distribution, which is described most conveniently in terms of the distribution of t_j^2. Under H_1: $\beta_j \neq 0$, t_j^2 has a noncentral F distribution, with noncentrality parameter $\lambda = \beta_j^2/2 \operatorname{var}(b_j)$. The probability of Type II error in the t test is a decreasing function of λ, and hence an increasing function of $\operatorname{var}(b_j)$, for given β_j. So the effect of multicollinearity is to increase the probability of Type II error relative to the case in which X_j is not correlated with other regressors. This makes it particularly dangerous to treat a failure to reject H_0: $\beta_j = 0$ as clear evidence that one should delete the variable X_j from the model in a situation where one has reason to suspect the existence of multicollinearity or any other kind of data deficiency.

Multicollinearity and the F test

In the more general case in which an F test is used to test H_0: $H\beta = h$ against H_1: $H\beta \neq h$, the distribution under H_1 is noncentral F, with noncentrality parameter

$$\lambda = (H\beta - h)'[H(X'X)^{-1}H']^{-1}(H\beta - h)/2\sigma^2. \tag{3.69}$$

This is equivalent to $gF/2$, with b and $\hat{\sigma}^2$ replaced by the true values β and σ^2. Since the probability of Type II error is a decreasing function of λ, we can examine the effect of multicollinearity on the performance of the F test by looking at the noncentrality parameter for each particular application.

Suppose that we wish to test the equality of two parameters, β_i and β_j. In this case, the noncentrality parameter reduces to

$$\lambda = (\beta_i - \beta_j)^2/2 \operatorname{var}(b_i - b_j)$$

where

$$\operatorname{var}(b_i - b_j) = \operatorname{var}(b_i) + \operatorname{var}(b_j) - 2\operatorname{cov}(b_i, b_j).$$

Now suppose that the regressors X_i and X_j have a strong positive correlation with each other, but relatively weak correlations with other regressors. This means that there will be a high positive value for the partial correlation between X_i and X_j, given other regressors, and it can be shown that this will lead to a negative value for $\operatorname{cov}(b_i, b_j)$. The result is a 'high' value for $\operatorname{var}(b_i - b_j)$, and a 'low' value for λ, leading to a high probability of Type II error in the F test. Under the conditions specified, it is difficult to estimate $\beta_i - \beta_j$, and when β_i is different from β_j it may be difficult to show that this is so.

Given the same conditions, it would be relatively easy to estimate the sum, $\beta_i + \beta_j$, and a test involving the sum would not be subject to the same difficulty. Thus one might test H_0: $\beta_i + \beta_j = 1$ against H_1: $\beta_i + \beta_j \neq 1$, and the existence of multicollinearity would actually reduce the Type II error probabilities for this test. By looking at the relevant noncentrality parameter, one can show that the same is true for a test of the joint hypothesis $\beta_i = 0$ and $\beta_j = 0$. The conclusion is that some F tests are adversely affected by multicollinearity, but others are not, and in some cases the probability of Type II error can actually be reduced.

Multicollinearity and 'near singularity'

If one or more of the R_j^2 approaches 1, or $\sum (X_{jt} - \bar{X}_j)^2$ is very small relative to $\sum X_{jt}^2$ for one or more of the regressors X_j; $j = 2, \ldots, k$, the matrix $X'X$ is said to exhibit 'near singularity'. In this situation, the estimated coefficients are very sensitive to small changes in the data, such as the correction of small errors, revisions to official data series, or changes in the price base used for expressing data in real, as opposed to current, price terms. A closely related problem is loss of accuracy in the computer calculation, whereby changes that ought not to affect the solution, such as the reordering of variables, do produce changes in the answers obtained. In order to deal with this problem, the writers of statistical and econometric software tend to use numerically stable algorithms, and most programs produce a warning of cases which are so nearly singular as to cause numerical problems. This is of some use in detecting extreme cases of data deficiency, but there are relatively few programs that provide an overall indicator of 'conditioning' in less extreme cases, and this puts the onus on the user to ensure that routinely executed regression calculations are not subject to serious data deficiency.

One measure that could usefully be calculated is the determinant of the matrix of zero-order correlation coefficients. If D is a diagonal matrix with elements

$$D_{ij} = \sqrt{\sum (X_{jt} - \bar{X}_j)^2}$$

and

$$D_{ij} = 0; \ i \neq j; \ i,j = 2, \ldots, k,$$

and C is the $(k-1) \times (k-1)$ matrix with elements

$$C_{jj} = 1, C_{ij} = r_{ij}; \ i \neq j; \ i,j = 2, \ldots, k,$$

then

$$C = D^{-1} \cdot (X_2' A X_2) \cdot D^{-1}, \tag{3.70}$$

where $X_2' A X_2$ is the matrix of deviation sums of squares and products used in equation (3.66). The value of $\det(C)$ lies between 0 and 1, with $\det(C) = 1$ corresponding to 'zero measured correlation' and $\det(C) = 0$ corresponding to either perfect multicollinearity or zero variation in one or more of the regressors. Very small values of $\det(C)$ indicate serious multicollinearity, but do not warn of 'serious' lack of variation. To provide an indicator which covers both problems, one can use a measure similar to (3.70), but defined in terms of gross rather than deviation sums of squares and products, and involving all regressors X_1 to X_k.

Estimation in the presence of multicollinearity

To conclude this section, we ask whether there is anything that can be done to mitigate the effects of multicollinearity. In theory, one can reduce estimator variances by imposing valid restrictions on the parameters, and one could also reduce the variances, at the cost of some bias, by imposing false restrictions. Intuitively, if the restrictions are 'almost valid', the resulting bias should be relatively small, and there are various techniques of variance reduction that attempt to exploit this fact. Such methods have not been widely used in applied econometrics, despite the existence of an extensive theoretical literature.

An alternative approach is to try to increase the information content of the data by choosing additional observations. Extending a time series that is dominated by multicollinearity will not help much if the new observations are subject to the same problem, but new data might break some previous pattern of association between regressors, and could certainly help to overcome problems caused by lack of variation or insufficient observations. In some cases, it may be possible to combine time series and cross-section data, provided that information obtained from the two sources is broadly compatible; there are methods for doing this which are rather more sophisticated than simply 'borrowing' cross-section estimates for use in a time series model.

It seems, after some discussion, that the only possible response to multicollinearity is to 'change the rules', either by adding to the information available, or by attempting something less ambitious than completely unrestricted estimation of all k parameters of the chosen model. The main reason for considering the effects of data deficiency is to alert the user to the dangers of making certain types of inference in the presence of relatively poor data. This warning is of particular importance when using a computer package that does not produce indices of data deficiency as part of the standard output.

3.6 / Dummy variables and quarterly data

It often happens that a set of data divides naturally according to the categories of some qualitative variable such as region, household type, 'policy on' or 'policy off', or the season of the year to which individual observations apply. In this section, we consider methods for including the effects of such variables in the single equation model. The discussion focuses on the problem of allowing for seasonal behaviour in quarterly time series data, so the qualitative variable is 'quarter' or 'season', but much of what is said would apply equally to any other qualitative variable.

Suppose that prior to any consideration of possible seasonal effects, it is assumed that some economic hypothesis is adequately represented by a two-variable regression model, written as

$$Y_t = \alpha + \beta X_t + u_t; \ t = 1, \ldots, n. \tag{3.71}$$

Although it is seldom realistic to argue that such a simple model is adequate, the use of (3.71) will enable us to concentrate on what is new in this section, without the distraction of a needlessly complex system of notation.

The most straightforward way of allowing for a seasonal effect in the behaviour of the dependent variable is to let the intercept α vary between quarters of the year. This suggests that Y has an additive seasonal component that has nothing to do with the behaviour of X, and in this case equation (3.71) becomes

$Y_t = \alpha_1 + \beta X_t + u_t$; in quarter 1

$Y_t = \alpha_2 + \beta X_t + u_t$; in quarter 2

$Y_t = \alpha_3 + \beta X_t + u_t$; in quarter 3

$Y_t = \alpha_4 + \beta X_t + u_t$; in quarter 4.

$$(3.72)$$

A second possibility is to let the slope β vary between seasons. This suggests that the way in which Y responds to changes in X is different in different quarters, and equation (3.71) becomes

$Y_t = \alpha + \beta_1 X_t + u_t$; in quarter 1

$Y_t = \alpha + \beta_2 X_t + u_t$; in quarter 2

$Y_t = \alpha + \beta_3 X_t + u_t$; in quarter 3

$Y_t = \alpha + \beta_4 X_t + u_t$; in quarter 4.

$$(3.73)$$

A third alternative is to let both parameters vary: leaving aside possible complications from lags or from the disturbance specification, this means that there are effectively four distinct equations, which do not have intercept or slope parameters in common, and which could therefore be estimated separately from data for different quarters:

$Y_t = \alpha_1 + \beta_1 X_t + u_t$; in quarter 1

$Y_t = \alpha_2 + \beta_2 X_t + u_t$; in quarter 2

$Y_t = \alpha_3 + \beta_3 X_t + u_t$; in quarter 3

$Y_t = \alpha_4 + \beta_4 X_t + u_t$; in quarter 4.

$$(3.74)$$

Finally, one could insist that α is the same in all four quarters and that β is the same in all four quarters, which means that (3.71) is applied as it stands to all the data: if this is done, $t = 1, \ldots, n$ counts quarterly observations.

There are two distinct cases in which (3.71) could be used. The first is where Y has no seasonal component, so the qualitative variable 'season' has nothing to explain. The second is where Y does have a seasonal component, but all seasonal behaviour in Y is fully explained by corresponding seasonal behaviour in X, leaving no additional effect to be modelled by varying the parameter values.

In order to choose which of the above specifications is most appropriate, the first and most obvious thing to do is to graph the data on Y and the data on X to see whether there is any visual evidence of a seasonal pattern. Unfortunately, such visual tests are seldom conclusive, and we also need a more formal method of testing between alternative specifications. This raises an apparent difficulty. We have not previously encountered a model with more than one equation, and we have certainly not considered how one might test restrictions that involve parameters from different equations. Fortunately, there is a simple trick that enables us to convert any of the specifications (3.72)–(3.74) into a single relationship. If this can be done, existing methods of testing restrictions can still be used.

Suppose that we create four dummy variables, denoted as Q_1, Q_2, Q_3, Q_4, or more compactly as Q_i; $i = 1, \ldots, 4$, and defined so that

$$Q_{it} = 1; \text{ in quarter } i$$

$$= 0; \text{ otherwise, } i = 1, \ldots, 4. \tag{3.75}$$

It is then possible to write the most general specification, which is (3.74), as

$$Y_t = \sum_i \alpha_i Q_{it} + \sum_i \beta_i Q_{it} X_t + u_t; \ t = 1, \ldots, n. \tag{3.76}$$

In quarter 1, $Q_{1t} = 1$, but Q_{2t}, Q_{3t} and Q_{4t} are all zero, so (3.76) reduces to the first equation in (3.74). A similar argument applies to each of the other quarters, showing that (3.74) and (3.76) are indeed identical.

Since it is possible to write (3.74) as a single equation, it must also be possible to write the alternative specifications in a similar fashion. If the β_i are all restricted to a single value β, (3.76) simplifies to

$$Y_t = \sum_i \alpha_i Q_{it} + \beta X_t + u_t; \ t = 1, \ldots, n. \tag{3.77}$$

This is clearly equivalent to (3.72). If the α_i are all restricted to a single value α, then (3.76) simplifies to

$$Y_t = \alpha + \sum_i \beta_i Q_{it} X_t + u_t; \ t = 1, \ldots, n, \tag{3.78}$$

which is equivalent to (3.73). If the α_i and β_i are both restricted to single values, (3.76) collapses to (3.71).

Now that all the alternative specifications are in a single equation format, it is possible to apply the F test for a set of exact linear restrictions to decide which specification is the most appropriate. Before doing this, it is convenient to rearrange equation (3.76), exploiting the fact that

$$Q_{1t} + Q_{2t} + Q_{3t} + Q_{4t} = 1; \ t = 1, \ldots, n.$$

By adding and subtracting terms to (3.76), we obtain

$$Y_t = \alpha_1(Q_{1t} + Q_{2t} + Q_{3t} + Q_{4t}) + (\alpha_2 - \alpha_1)Q_{2t} + (\alpha_3 - \alpha_1)Q_{3t} + (\alpha_4 - \alpha_1)Q_{4t}$$
$$+ \beta_1(Q_{1t} + Q_{2t} + Q_{3t} + Q_{4t})X_t + (\beta_2 - \beta_1)Q_{2t}X_t + (\beta_3 - \beta_1)Q_{3t}X_t$$
$$+ (\beta_4 - \beta_1)Q_{4t}X_t + u_t,$$

which simplifies to

$$Y_t = \alpha_1 + (\alpha_2 - \alpha_1)Q_{2t} + (\alpha_3 - \alpha_1)Q_{3t} + (\alpha_4 - \alpha_1)Q_{4t} + \beta_1 X_t + (\beta_2 - \beta_1)Q_{2t}X_t$$
$$+ (\beta_3 - \beta_1)Q_{3t}X_t + (\beta_4 - \beta_1)Q_{4t}X_t + u_t,$$

or

$$Y_t = \alpha_1 + \delta_2 Q_{2t} + \delta_3 Q_{3t} + \delta_4 Q_{4t} + \beta_1 X_t + \gamma_2 Q_{2t} X_t + \gamma_3 Q_{3t} X_t + \gamma_4 Q_{4t} X_t + u_t;$$

$$t = 1, \ldots, n, \tag{3.79}$$

where $\delta_i = \alpha_i - \alpha_1$ and $\gamma_i = \beta_i - \beta_1; i = 2, 3, 4$.

In equation (3.79), δ_i represents the *difference* between the intercept in quarter i and the intercept in quarter 1, for $i = 2, 3, 4$, and γ_i represents the difference between the slope in quarter i and the slope in quarter 1, again for $i = 2, 3, 4$. This is more convenient than (3.76) for two reasons. First, the restrictions which give rise to the alternative specifications are now exclusion rather than equality restrictions, and these can be imposed by simply omitting the relevant regressors from (3.79). Setting δ_2, δ_3 and δ_4 to zero restricts the intercept to equality between quarters, and setting γ_2, γ_3 and γ_4 to zero restricts the slope to equality between quarters. So restricted specifications equivalent to (3.77) and (3.78) are

$$Y_t = \alpha_1 + \delta_2 Q_{2t} + \delta_3 Q_{3t} + \delta_4 Q_{4t} + \beta_1 X_t + u_t; \ t = 1, \ldots, n \tag{3.80}$$

and

$$Y_t = \alpha_1 + \beta_1 X_t + \gamma_2 Q_{2t} X_t + \gamma_3 Q_{3t} X_t + \gamma_4 Q_{4t} X_t + u_t; \ t = 1, \ldots, n. \tag{3.81}$$

Strictly speaking, the subscripts on β in (3.80) and α in (3.81) are redundant, but they are left in place to show that these forms are obtained by imposing exclusion restrictions on (3.79).

A second reason why forms based on (3.79) are more convenient is that there is always a 'proper' intercept term, associated with a column of ones in the regressor matrix. Equation (3.76) has distinct intercepts for each quarter but no overall intercept associated with a column of ones. Some computer programs insert a column of ones automatically, and if this is done in a regression containing all four dummy variables, the result is an exact linear dependence between regressors, leading to a failure of the regression calculation. Equation (3.79) shows that it is not necessary to use all four dummy variables to identify the quarter to which an observation belongs, and one should never include Q_1, Q_2, Q_3 and Q_4 in an equation which has an overall intercept.

Now consider a model that is more general than that in (3.71). Suppose that the basic equation is

$$Y_t = \beta_1 + \beta_2 X_{2t} + \beta_3 X_{3t} + \beta_4 X_{4t} + u_t; \ t = 1, \ldots, n, \tag{3.82}$$

and that we wish to consider the possibility that β_1 and β_4 both vary from quarter to quarter. To allow for this, the variables Q_2, Q_3, Q_4, $Q_2 X_4$, $Q_3 X_4$ and $Q_4 X_4$ would be added to (3.82), and least squares applied to this equation would give $RSS = S$, with $n - (4 + 6)$ degrees of freedom. Under the null hypothesis of no seasonal difference in either β_1 or β_4, least squares would be applied to (3.82) as it stands, giving $RSS = S_R$, with $n - 4$ degrees of freedom. Since H_0 involves six restrictions (six parameters are set to zero under H_0), the F test statistic would be

$$F = [(S_R - S)/6]/[S/(n - 10)],$$

and a calculated value greater than $F_{6,n-10}^{0.05}$ would lead to rejection of H_0, in favour of the alternative that at least one of the parameters β_1, β_4 does change in at least one quarter. One could also test an equation which allows for shifts in β_1 against (3.82), or an equation which allows for shifts in β_4 against (3.82), or one could test for a shift in β_4 given that β_1 is allowed to change, or for a shift in β_1 given that β_4 is allowed to change.

The principles described above are quite general. We have already seen the application to testing for seasonal effects in a model with k regressors, and one can apply the same ideas to any other qualitative variable which takes values in one of m categories. Indeed, if one has sufficient data, there is no reason why one cannot introduce several qualitative variables. Apart from loss of degrees of freedom, which is not a problem with very large data sets, the only possible complication is that two qualitative variables might not act independently on Y, in which case one needs a separate dummy variable for each combination of categories, rather than for the individual categories of the two qualitative variables.

The Chow test

A special case of the procedure outlined above is a test which compares a 'most restricted' model, such as (3.82), with a 'least restricted' version in which *all* parameters are allowed to vary by the categories of some qualitative variable. If the model has k regressors and the qualitative variable has m categories, and there are n observations in total, the test statistic is

$$F = [(S_R - S)/(m - 1)k]/[S/(n - mk)]. \tag{3.83}$$

To obtain S_R, we would simply run a regression on the basic model, with no dummy variables included. To obtain S, we could add dummies for each parameter, but this is rather cumbersome. If *all* parameters are allowed to vary by the categories of the qualitative variable, one can apply the basic equation separately to data for each of the m categories, since the parameter estimates obtained in this way are identical to those derived from the estimation of a single equation with a full set of dummy variables. Moreover, if S_i represents the residual sum of squares from the regression on data in category i, the value S in (3.83) can be obtained as $S = \sum S_i$.

In this special case, the F test is often described as a Chow test, and the test statistic is written as

$$F = \left[\left(S_R - \sum S_i\right) \middle/ (m-1)k\right] \middle/ \left[\sum S_i/(n-mk)\right]. \tag{3.84}$$

The most common application of (3.84) is as a test of parameter stability between different time periods. Sometimes these correspond to an arbitrary split in the middle of a long run of data: in other cases, subsamples may correspond to different policy regimes. Under the null hypothesis, there is no change in parameter values between subsamples. Under the alternative, one (or more) of the parameters does change. To apply the test, each subsample must have at least k observations. If this condition is not satisfied, one has to treat any undersized subsample as a forecast period and apply the forecast test of section 3.4.

In the literature, some confusion is caused by the fact that the forecast test is also sometimes described as a Chow test. To avoid this difficulty, all that one has to do is to add the description – thus we can refer to the Chow parameter stability test (3.84), or to the (Chow) forecast test from section 3.4. The key difference between the two is that (3.84) tests a set of exact restrictions on parameters, whilst the forecast test tests a set of stochastic restrictions.

Disturbance assumptions

There is an important qualification to be added to the discussion above. When a model is written in terms of a single equation, it is implicitly assumed that the disturbances behave as in any other single equation model, and we have therefore taken for granted that, across the categories of any qualitative variable, the disturbances are uncorrelated, with common variance σ^2. If these assumptions are not satisfied, our methods of estimation and testing have to be modified accordingly. We consider this problem further in Chapters 5 and 7.

Deseasonalised data

In one respect, seasonality in quarterly or monthly data is different from other qualitative effects because it is possible to obtain data which have already been adjusted for known seasonal components. In some cases, two sets of data are available, one seasonally adjusted and one not adjusted. There is then a problem of choice as to which set of data should be used. The answer does depend on the particular situation under investigation, but we can give some guidance as to how the choice should be made.

Consider again the simple model used at the beginning of this section:

$$Y_t = \alpha + \beta X_t + u_t; \ t = 1, \dots, n.$$

If Y exhibits seasonal behaviour, but X does not, we could use adjusted data on Y, denoted as Y^d, and write the model as

$$Y_t^d = \alpha + \beta X_t + u_t; \ t = 1, \dots, n.$$

Official seasonal adjustments to the Y series are based on the past behaviour of Y, rather than on the behaviour of X, so if we believe that the seasonal behaviour of Y has nothing to do with the behaviour of X, it would be reasonable to use adjusted data for Y or, alternatively, to use unadjusted data with three dummy variables added to allow the intercept to vary by quarter. If we are correct in assuming that the seasonal pattern in Y is not associated with the behaviour of X, any differences between the two methods should be small.

A rather different situation holds if it is the response of Y to changes in X that varies by season. In this case, the use of deseasonalised data might well obscure the correct relationship, which is quite simple to model with unadjusted data and 'slope dummies' that allow β to vary by season. A similar argument holds in the case in which all seasonal behaviour in Y is fully explained by corresponding seasonal behaviour in X. If both series are adjusted, this would remove some of the variation in Y that is to be explained, and some of the variation in X that does the explaining. At the very least, this is likely to have an effect on estimator variances, and if only one series is adjusted the resulting model would simply be wrong. We therefore reach the tentative conclusion that, where possible, unadjusted data should be used because this gives the investigator the flexibility to discover the most appropriate representation of seasonality. In saying this, we do assume that allowance for seasonal effects should be a routine part of any modelling exercise involving the use of quarterly data.

Example 3.7

Following the discussion in this section, it is possible to relax the constraint of using only annual data in a time series context. However, since quarterly data series contain considerably more observations than a corresponding annual data set, it is rather tedious to enter the data and, for this reason, we make a single example serve for several different purposes. Data set 5 gives quarterly observations for the series previously defined as RCONS, RPDI and PCONS, together with a slightly modified real liquid assets series, RLIQ, for the United Kingdom from 1963 quarter 1 to 1995 quarter 2.

Before doing anything else, we examine a graph of real consumers' expenditure (RCONS) and real personal disposable income (RPDI) against time. The graph is shown in Figure 3.1, and the primary purpose of examining the graph is to look for the pattern of seasonal behaviour in the two series. It is immediately obvious that RCONS has a strong and regular seasonal pattern, so there is seasonal behaviour to be explained. The series RPDI also has a seasonal component, but this is less regular than that for RCONS. Since the seasonal regularity in RCONS is not entirely matched by corresponding behaviour in the income series, one might expect that seasonal dummy variables will be important.

In order to conduct a test for seasonality, we first estimate the parameters of the model

$$\ln(C_t) = \beta_1 + \beta_2 \ln(D_t) + \beta_3 \Delta_4 \ln(P_t) + \beta_4 \ln(L_{t-1}) + u_t; \quad t = 1, \ldots, n, \tag{3.85}$$

where $\Delta_4 \ln(P_t)$ is the year on year change in $\ln(P_t)$, defined as $\Delta_4 \ln(P_t) = \ln(P_t) - \ln(P_{t-4})$, with computer name D4LPCONS, and L is the real liquid assets variable RLIQ. At this stage, there is no interesting dynamic behaviour in the model: apart from the fact that P_{t-4} is a component of $\Delta_4 \ln(P_t)$, the model also involves $\ln(L_{t-1})$, but no lags in either consumers' expenditure or disposable income.

In earlier exercises, we found that even with annual observations, a purely static model fitted to time series data is unlikely to satisfy the conventional tests of model adequacy, and one would expect this problem to be rather more serious with the equivalent quarterly data. Nevertheless, our first exercise with quarterly data will

Data set 5 Consumers' expenditure and income by quarter, UK, 1963(1)–1995(2)

Year/quarter	RCONS	RPDI	PCONS	RLIQ
1963–1	39.559	43.537	0.117	149.8889
1963–2	42.967	46.009	0.119	148.8824
1963–3	43.707	47.608	0.118	152.9661
1963–4	44.641	48.272	0.120	153.8667
1964–1	41.500	46.380	0.120	154.8167
1964–2	44.122	48.131	0.123	153.4797
1964–3	44.597	48.859	0.123	155.7480
1964–4	45.825	49.877	0.126	155.4286
1965–1	42.306	47.735	0.126	156.4286
1965–2	44.524	49.105	0.129	156.2558
1965–3	45.346	49.440	0.129	158.2403
1965–4	46.317	50.718	0.131	159.0840
1966–1	43.296	51.094	0.132	160.1136
1966–2	46.064	49.924	0.134	158.9776
1966–3	45.710	49.462	0.135	159.3407
1966–4	46.480	50.727	0.137	158.4964
1967–1	43.327	48.900	0.137	160.0219
1967–2	46.217	51.025	0.137	163.7080
1967–3	47.378	51.899	0.138	164.9565
1967–4	49.063	52.347	0.139	167.9065
1968–1	46.489	51.895	0.140	167.7786
1968–2	46.729	52.332	0.144	166.0417
1968–3	48.066	51.369	0.145	167.1310
1968–4	49.925	52.176	0.148	167.1216
1969–1	45.467	51.750	0.150	166.7467
1969–2	47.682	52.411	0.151	167.0132
1969–3	48.494	52.139	0.152	167.4671
1969–4	50.723	53.384	0.155	166.5871
1970–1	46.228	52.180	0.157	165.6433
1970–2	48.922	54.774	0.160	165.1625
1970–3	50.435	54.814	0.162	166.7901
1970–4	52.288	55.907	0.166	168.0602
1971–1	47.254	52.680	0.170	167.7000
1971–2	50.353	55.011	0.175	166.0914
1971–3	52.035	55.422	0.177	167.9435
1971–4	54.497	57.231	0.179	171.2235
1972–1	50.173	55.665	0.182	171.6538
1972–2	53.405	60.776	0.184	172.6902
1972–3	55.138	59.748	0.188	172.9362
1972–4	58.036	62.555	0.192	172.9375
1973–1	54.685	60.741	0.195	172.9436
1973–2	56.166	64.388	0.199	175.8442
1973–3	57.861	64.355	0.203	178.4975
1973–4	59.903	64.845	0.211	179.7109
1974–1	53.065	61.683	0.220	176.4591
1974–2	55.198	61.929	0.232	171.7629
1974–3	57.026	64.359	0.240	170.7042

Data set 5 Continued

Year/quarter	RCONS	RPDI	PCONS	RLIQ
1974–4	60.028	64.389	0.252	169.4484
1975–1	53.859	64.634	0.268	164.1940
1975–2	55.667	62.971	0.289	159.0519
1975–3	56.462	63.599	0.299	158.9331
1975–4	58.592	62.610	0.311	156.8939
1976–1	53.509	62.457	0.323	154.5697
1976–2	55.260	62.657	0.332	154.3795
1976–3	57.050	65.244	0.340	155.1206
1976–4	59.847	62.654	0.354	151.2034
1977–1	53.426	59.836	0.373	146.6059
1977–2	54.469	60.748	0.387	146.1059
1977–3	56.523	62.293	0.393	147.7888
1977–4	60.474	64.818	0.397	151.5919
1978–1	56.839	63.696	0.409	151.8117
1978–2	57.523	66.206	0.420	152.1548
1978–3	60.163	67.571	0.429	154.4825
1978–4	62.384	68.452	0.438	156.0274
1979–1	58.697	67.670	0.451	155.9113
1979–2	62.282	69.552	0.467	155.9679
1979–3	61.533	69.617	0.497	152.2475
1979–4	64.700	74.245	0.511	154.7495
1980–1	61.087	70.661	0.531	153.1394
1980–2	59.936	70.901	0.557	152.4309
1980–3	62.511	72.051	0.569	153.8049
1980–4	63.651	71.798	0.583	157.5780
1981–1	60.104	71.891	0.595	159.7882
1981–2	60.409	70.604	0.620	159.7710
1981–3	62.403	70.129	0.633	160.0300
1981–4	64.486	70.552	0.645	160.1566
1982–1	59.964	70.098	0.659	160.5175
1982–2	60.271	70.096	0.677	161.9498
1982–3	63.352	70.640	0.682	164.3680
1982–4	66.265	70.888	0.691	168.1795
1983–1	62.549	70.836	0.697	172.5122
1983–2	63.135	72.193	0.708	173.6554
1983–3	66.658	72.648	0.715	174.1119
1983–4	68.858	73.527	0.722	176.8463
1984–1	63.958	73.532	0.728	180.5783
1984–2	65.077	74.662	0.746	182.0858
1984–3	66.738	74.369	0.751	184.1158
1984–4	70.713	77.193	0.757	189.3501
1985–1	65.886	75.454	0.768	190.5664
1985–2	66.822	78.173	0.785	192.5707
1985–3	70.092	77.299	0.791	194.6346
1985–4	73.942	78.895	0.798	198.2393
1986–1	69.431	79.078	0.802	204.5312
1986–2	71.929	81.482	0.814	208.0614

Data set 5 Continued

Year/quarter	RCONS	RPDI	PCONS	RLIQ
1986–3	75.874	81.383	0.819	210.0220
1986–4	78.388	81.679	0.832	211.5072
1987–1	72.642	80.877	0.841	210.3900
1987–2	74.897	83.307	0.849	215.6384
1987–3	80.127	84.492	0.853	216.8183
1987–4	83.568	86.026	0.866	218.5242
1988–1	78.377	85.572	0.873	225.0195
1988–2	80.349	88.419	0.892	227.4047
1988–3	86.593	89.389	0.900	233.8233
1988–4	89.272	91.247	0.912	235.5252
1989–1	82.052	90.440	0.925	238.3341
1989–2	84.045	92.824	0.943	241.1262
1989–3	88.490	93.867	0.953	244.2665
1989–4	90.819	94.545	0.968	247.1157
1990–1	83.175	93.370	0.985	248.9198
1990–2	85.015	94.010	0.990	257.6525
1990–3	88.774	95.057	1.003	259.8714
1990–4	90.563	95.888	1.020	260.5441
1991–1	81.798	92.870	1.035	265.7971
1991–2	82.469	94.712	1.076	263.5957
1991–3	86.415	94.579	1.086	265.5691
1991–4	89.233	95.808	1.095	265.6822
1992–1	80.719	92.537	1.108	271.4937
1992–2	82.451	97.206	1.129	272.6794
1992–3	86.870	98.005	1.128	275.7074
1992–4	89.497	99.056	1.131	278.1768
1993–1	82.840	95.924	1.147	281.7803
1993–2	84.149	98.331	1.169	281.7263
1993–3	89.217	98.322	1.169	283.6869
1993–4	92.241	100.548	1.168	286.1747
1994–1	85.608	96.481	1.181	289.1473
1994–2	86.438	98.022	1.198	287.3731
1994–3	91.738	99.839	1.196	289.8085
1994–4	94.446	101.394	1.197	290.4302
1995–1	87.396	98.440	1.214	293.9827
1995–2	88.726	100.530	1.234	293.5908

Key:
RCONS Real consumers' expenditure (£ billion, 1990 prices).
PCONS Implicit deflator, consumers' expenditure (1990 = 1.0).
RPDI Real personal disposable income (£ billion, 1990 prices).
RLIQA Real liquid asset holdings of personal sector (£ billion, 1990 prices).

Source: Derived from ONS database.

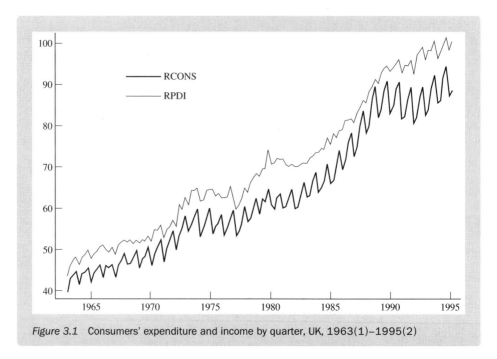

Figure 3.1 Consumers' expenditure and income by quarter, UK, 1963(1)–1995(2)

be to estimate (3.85), both as it stands and with seasonal dummy variables added. Table 3.3 gives basic information on both sets of results, using observations from 1964Q1 to 1995Q2.

If the parameters on the added dummy variables are identified as β_5, β_6 and β_7 (or in the notation of this section as δ_2, δ_3 and δ_4), we can test $H_0: \beta_5 = 0$ and $\beta_6 = 0$ and $\beta_7 = 0$ against the alternative that one or more of these parameters is not zero by using the following F test statistic:

$$F = [(1.2796 - 0.5576)/3]/[0.5576/(126 - 7)] = 51.362.$$

The 5% critical value for an F distribution with 3 and 119 degrees of freedom is approximately 0.70, so we find strong rejection of the null hypothesis of no seasonal effect in $\ln(C_t)$, over and above that explained by seasonal variation in income (or by any seasonal variation in inflation or liquid asset holdings). One can easily confirm that equivalent results, with the same residual sum of squares, are obtained by adding four seasonal dummies, but deleting the intercept. As a further exercise, one can also check on the effect of adding dummies in a form which gives seasonal variation in the consumption–income elasticity, β_2, rather than a shift in the intercept, β_1. This is achieved by adding products of Q_2, Q_3 and Q_4 with $\ln(D_t)$, instead of the simple dummies Q_2, Q_3 and Q_4. In this case, the resulting F test statistic is 52.44.

In evaluating the results obtained above, it should be observed that there is evidence of violation of the assumptions on which the test procedure is based. The Durbin–Watson statistic in version 2 is too low to accept the null hypothesis of no

Table 3.3 Quarterly consumption function

Sample based on observations 1964(1)–1995(2)
Dependent variable is LNRCONS

Version 1:

Variable	Coefficient	Standard error	t value
INTER	−0.1176	0.090 73	−1.296
LNRPDI	0.9648	0.026 88	35.896
D4LPCONS	−0.1582	0.079 50	−1.991
LNRLIQ(1)	0.0334	0.032 29	1.035

Degrees of freedom 122 from 126 observations

Residual SS	1.2796×10^{-1}
Total SS	6.6626
Disturbance variance	1.0489×10^{-3}
R^2	0.9808
DW statistic	1.64

Version 2:

Variable	Coefficient	Standard error	t value
INTER	−0.1775	0.060 94	−2.913
LNRPDI	0.9426	0.018 08	52.151
D4LPCONS	−0.1320	0.053 19	−2.483
LNRLIQ(1)	0.0575	0.021 69	2.650
Q2	0.0078	0.005 40	1.448
Q3	0.0380	0.005 50	6.949
Q4	0.0602	0.005 50	10.973

Degrees of freedom 119 from 126 observations

Residual SS	5.5765×10^{-2}
Total SS	6.6626
Disturbance variance	4.6861×10^{-4}
R^2	0.9916
DW statistic	0.98

serial correlation, and even if this were not the case, we should have some reservations, since DW is designed to detect correlation between successive residuals, whilst with quarterly data the most commonly observed phenomenon is correlation between residuals relating to the same quarter in successive years. The details of a more appropriate test for serial correlation are given in section 7.5.

Example 3.8

This example is intended to illustrate one of the problems that can arise with the use of dummy variables on cross-section data. The Barro–Lee data set, data set 4, is used for this purpose. It provides four regional dummy variables, $ASIAE$ for East Asian countries, $LAAM$ for Latin America, $OECD$ for OECD countries and $SAFRICA$ for sub-Saharan African countries.

An obvious criticism of equation (1.29),

$$AVGR_t = \beta_1 + \beta_2 GDP575L_t + \beta_3 SYRM75_t + u_t; \; t = 1, \ldots, 102,$$

is that it presumes that the parameter β_2, which governs the convergence rate, is the same over all countries. This does not seem very plausible, and it might be argued that only countries of a specific type, or in a specific region of the world, have common convergence rates. Permitting variation in the values of β_2 across types or regions then gives a common convergence rate only for countries of similar type or region. As possible variants on (1.29) utilising the regional dummy variables, we could consider appropriate versions of equations (3.79), (3.80) or (3.81), allowing for β_1 to shift for the chosen regions, or both β_1 and β_2, and finally only β_2. The argument above suggests that we are really only interested in the last two possibilities. In the results to follow, the $OECD$ dummy was not used.

Consider the most general model corresponding to (3.79):

$$AVGR_t = \beta_1 + \beta_2 GDP575L_t + \beta_3 SYRM75_t$$
$$+ \delta_1 ASIAE_t + \delta_2 LAAM_t + \delta_3 SAFRICA_t$$
$$+ \gamma_1 (ASIAE_t * GDP575L_t) + \gamma_2 (LAAM_t * GDP575L_t)$$
$$+ \gamma_3 (SAFRICA * GDP575L_t) + u_t; t = 1, \ldots, 102,$$

denoted Version 1. Excluding only the intercept dummies (and thus setting $\delta_1 = \delta_2 = \delta_3 = 0$) produces Version 2, whilst the exclusion only of the slope dummies (and thus setting $\gamma_1 = \gamma_2 = \gamma_3 = 0$) produces Version 3. There are then two issues: the statistical question of which of the additional variables are required in Version 1, and the impact of the additional variables on the estimated convergence rate. We focus on testing the inclusion of each of the two sets of dummies, and the convergence rates implied by the chosen version.

Equation (1.29) is the most restricted model, and Version 1 the least restricted. There are two possible ways of testing the restrictions which, when imposed on Version 1, generate equation (1.29). The first is to simply test the hypothesis that all of $\delta_1, \ldots, \delta_3, \gamma_1, \ldots, \gamma_3$ are zero. If rejection of this null hypothesis occurs, we don't know whether the rejection is due to the intercept shifts or the slope shifts or both. An alternative method is to perform two tests on Version 1: first that $\delta_1, \ldots, \delta_3$ are all zero, and then that $\gamma_1, \ldots, \gamma_3$ are all zero. In general, there is no reason why the results of the two separate tests should be consistent with the overall test that all six dummy coefficients are zero. However, it sometimes occurs that this procedure generates useful information, and this is the case here.

The basic information required for these tests is the residual sums of squares associated with the four models, and these are presented in Table 3.4. The 5% critical values required are 2.70 for an $F(3, 100)$ distribution, and 2.19 for an $F(6, 100)$ distribution. From Table 3.5, we can see that the hypothesis of excluding all the

Table 3.4 Residual sums of squares

	Model:			
	Version 1	Version 2	Version 3	Equation (1.29)
Residual SS	0.041 072	0.043 784	0.044 503	0.057 007
Number of parameters	9	6	6	3

dummies from Version 1 is rejected, although the exclusion of each set of dummies in turn from Version 1 is not rejected. The hypotheses of excluding each set of dummies in Version 2 and Version 3 are rejected, however. So, the most general version of equation (1.29) appears to be needed, although in testing the exclusion of each set of dummies from Version 1, we end up with the contradictory conclusion that each set of dummies individually can be excluded from Version 1, but not jointly.

Whilst this contradiction in inference can be resolved economically by saying that we need to use a model containing slope dummies (i.e. Version 2) in order to generate varying convergence rates, this does not cast light on the statistical explanation. It is not uncommon to encounter situations where there is high correlation between an intercept dummy and a slope dummy, especially when the variation of the variable whose parameter is being shifted by the dummy is not large. This is in fact the case here, for the simple correlation between $ASIAE$ and $ASIAE * GDP575L$ is 0.997 54, and the corresponding values are 0.997 23 and 0.995 85 for the other two pairings. So, we have a classically simple case of multicollinearity, where an intercept dummy and the corresponding slope dummy essentially carry the same information, leaving us with a choice of which variable to omit. A more refined examination of this point uses the determinant of the matrix of zero-order correlations for the explanatory variables in Version 1, as in section 3.5. The value of the determinant is 2.84E-08, which is quite close to zero, indicating serious multicollinearity.

Table 3.6 presents the coefficients of $GDP575L_t$ by region from estimation of Version 2, together with the implied convergence rates. The overall convergence rate from Version 2 of about 0.8% per year compares with that obtained from estimation of equation (1.29) of about 0.5% per year. What is significant, however,

Table 3.5 F statistics in Example 3.8

Hypothesis	Null model	Alternative model	Value of F	DF
No dummies	(1.29)	Version 1	6.0136	(6, 93)
No intercept dummies	Version 2	Version 1	2.0469	(3, 93)
No slope dummies	Version 3	Version 1	2.5986	(3, 93)
No slope dummies	(1.29)	Version 2	9.6642	(3, 96)
No intercept dummies	(1.29)	Version 3	8.9910	(3, 96)

Table 3.6 Convergence rates by region from Version 2

Region	Coefficient of GDP575L	Convergence rate
Overall	−0.007 74	0.008 052
ASIAE	−0.005 95	0.006 132
LAAM	−0.010 14	0.010 692
SAFRICA	−0.011 02	0.011 671

is the lower convergence rate of the East Asian or 'tiger' economies of about 0.6% per year, and the relatively more rapid rate of convergence of the poorer regions of Latin America and sub-Saharan Africa of about 1% per year. This conclusion seems to be entirely consistent with the 'absolute convergence' hypothesis mentioned in Chapter 1 in the initial discussion of the Barro–Lee data set, since these regions are starting from a lower base.

3.7 / Further reading

Goldberger (1991) and Greene (1993) again give detailed coverage, whilst Davidson and MacKinnon (1993) and Gourieroux and Monfort (1995) are still helpful.

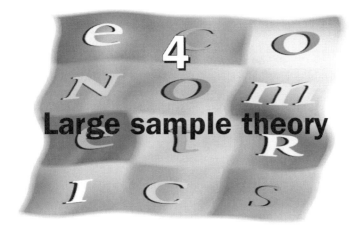

4

Large sample theory

4.1 / Introduction

Although much of the analysis of the preceding chapter was conducted under the rather restrictive assumptions of the classical regression model, many of the ideas that we have introduced can be applied, with some modification, to a much wider class of models. To complete the preparation for what could be described as 'proper' econometrics, as opposed to classical regression theory, we need to look at the way in which large sample methods are used to generate results that hold under conditions considerably weaker than those of the classical model.

As classical assumptions are relaxed, we encounter many cases in which OLS is no longer an optimal estimator, and two new principles are introduced in this chapter. These are maximum likelihood estimation and instrumental variable estimation. In both cases, large sample theory provides the rationale for choosing the method, and a means of obtaining the properties of estimators and test statistics.

At a formal level, large sample theory is not easy. If one looks for the weakest possible assumptions, it may be very difficult to check validity in the context of a specific model. If one goes for strong assumptions, it is easy to create the misleading impression that any relaxation or modification will remove a vital property, when this is not necessarily the case. In the next two sections, we provide some basic tools, but the general approach will be to illustrate what is typically true of a certain type of model, rather than to offer a completely rigorous analysis.

4.2 / Convergence in probability

As a first step, we consider the concept of convergence in probability, or, to be more accurate, the concept of weak convergence in probability. To initiate the discussion, we need to know what is meant by a random sequence. This is a sequence of random variables which depend in some way on the sample size n. A simple example is the sample mean for a set of observations $Y_1, \ldots, Y_n$. As n is increased, the sample mean is changed, so $\bar{Y}_1, \ldots, \bar{Y}_n$ is a random sequence, in this case a sequence of sample means. Questions of convergence are usually concerned with the behaviour of the sequence as $n \to \infty$.

Now let a_n represent a sequence of scalar random variables. The random sequence a_n is said to *converge in probability* to a constant a if, as $n \to \infty$,

$$\lim_{n \to \infty} \Pr(|a_n - a| > \delta) = 0; \quad \text{for any } \delta > 0. \tag{4.1}$$

Two alternative ways of stating the condition (4.1) are

$$a_n \xrightarrow{P} a \quad \text{and} \quad \text{plim}(a_n) = a,$$

where plim( ) is the probability limit operator introduced in Chapter 1. If a_n is a sequence of random vectors or random matrices, definition (4.1) would apply to each element.

In the case in which a_n is a sequence of estimators, convergence in probability to the true parameter means that the estimator is consistent. Again, this definition applies equally to a vector or matrix estimator.

One of the reasons for using convergence in probability is that the plim( ) operator has certain properties that are not shared by the expectation operator $E(\ )$. This makes it relatively easy to establish results involving probability limits in situations where it may be difficult, or perhaps impossible, to obtain results for expectations. The following rules summarise the properties of the plim( ) operator:

1. If $\text{plim}(a_n) = a$ and $g(\ )$ is a continuous function, and the rule defining $g(\ )$ does not involve n, then $\text{plim}[g(a_n)] = g(a)$.
2. If a_n and b_n are random sequences such that $\text{plim}(a_n)$ and $\text{plim}(b_n)$ both exist, then
   (a) $\text{plim}(a_n + b_n) = \text{plim}(a_n) + \text{plim}(b_n)$,
   (b) $\text{plim}(a_n - b_n) = \text{plim}(a_n) - \text{plim}(b_n)$,
   (c) $\text{plim}(a_n \cdot b_n) = \text{plim}(a_n) \cdot \text{plim}(b_n)$,
   (d) $\text{plim}(a_n/b_n) = \text{plim}(a_n)/\text{plim}(b_n)$, for $\text{plim}(b_n) \neq 0$.

It is useful to note that (2) above is really a special case of (1), since (1) holds for a sequence of random vectors or matrices. If a_n and b_n are interpreted as elements of a vector sequence, rules (2a)–(2d) are based on scalar-valued continuous functions of that sequence.

Having stated some basic properties of probability limits, we now introduce two results which are useful in establishing the existence of probability limits for certain special cases.

Khintchine's theorem

If $V_1, \ldots, V_n$ are IID random variables, with finite mean μ, then the sample mean $\bar{V}_n$ converges in probability to μ as $n \to \infty$. Alternatively, we may say that under the conditions specified, $\text{plim}(\bar{V}_n) = \mu$. Once the meaning is clear, we can drop the subscript on $\bar{V}$, and write $\text{plim}(\bar{V}) = \mu$.

Chebyshev lemma

If a_n is a random sequence such that, as $n \to \infty$, $\lim[E(a_n)] = a$ and $\lim[\text{var}(a_n)] = 0$, then $\text{plim}(a_n) = a$. This result can be proved by using the Chebyshev inequality (see, for example, Chow, 1983: 17). It is often quite straightforward to establish the expectation and variance of individual terms in a complex expression, but difficult to continue beyond this point using the expectation and variance operators. By using the Chebyshev lemma, one can convert to probability limits, and then prove consistency (or lack of consistency) in a relatively straightforward manner.

Convergence in probability to a random variable

For some purposes, it is useful to extend the concept of convergence in probability in the following manner. Suppose that the random sequence a_n is such that $\text{plim}(a_n - a) = 0$, where a is not a constant, but is instead a random variable with a distribution that does not depend on the sample size n. This can be described as convergence in probability to a random variable. It is important to note that, in this case, it is *not* true that $\text{plim}(a_n)$ is equal to a: it is the difference $(a_n - a)$ that converges in probability to a constant, which is equal to zero.

4.3 / Convergence in distribution

In most of the cases that we look at, it is not too difficult to establish convergence in probability, assuming of course that such convergence does take place. It is not always so easy to establish a second type of convergence, known as convergence in distribution.

Suppose that for the random sequence a_n, the sequence of distribution functions $F_n(\ )$ converges as $n \to \infty$ to a distribution function $F(\ )$, at all points at which $F(\ )$ is continuous. If this occurs $F(\ )$ is said to be the *limiting distribution* of the sequence a_n, and if a is a random variable having the distribution function $F(\ )$, a_n is said to *converge in distribution* to a.

It is often the case that we are concerned to establish that a sequence converges to a normal distribution, and this example can be used to illustrate the different ways in which results concerning convergence in distribution are stated. Suppose that η is a random variable distributed as $N(0, Q)$, and that as $n \to \infty$, the sequence a_n converges in distribution to η. We can write this as

$$a_n \xrightarrow{D} \eta \sim N(0, Q). \tag{4.2}$$

One disadvantage of the formal statement (4.2) is that it requires the explicit introduction of a variable corresponding to η. When the meaning is clear, a less formal statement is sometimes used, namely

$$a_n \xrightarrow{D} N(0, Q).$$ (4.3)

One could also write (4.2) as

$$a_n \overset{A}{\sim} N(0, Q),$$

indicating that a_n has an *asymptotic* normal distribution. Unfortunately, as explained in Chapter 1, this description is ambiguous, because it is often applied to a rescaled finite sample approximation, rather than to the sequence which is actually shown to converge in distribution.

As with convergence in probability, there are certain rules which can be used when trying to establish results concerning convergence in distribution:

1. If $\mathrm{plim}(a_n - b_n) = 0$, and b_n converges in distribution to a random variable b, then a_n also converges in distribution to b.

2. If $\mathrm{plim}(a_n) = 0$, and b_n converges in distribution to a random variable b, then $\mathrm{plim}(a_n b_n) = 0$.

3. If $\mathrm{plim}(a_n) = a$, where a is constant, and b_n converges in distribution to a random variable b, then

   (a) $(a_n + b_n) \xrightarrow{D} a + b$,

   (b) $(a_n b_n) \xrightarrow{D} ab$,

   (c) $(b_n / a_n) \xrightarrow{D} b/a$, provided $a \neq 0$.

4. If $b_n \xrightarrow{D} b$, $g(\ )$ is a continuous function, and the rule defining $g(\ )$ does not involve n, then $g(b_n) \xrightarrow{D} g(b)$.

5. If $b_n \xrightarrow{D} b$, $\mathrm{plim}(a_n - b_n) = 0$, $g(\ )$ is a continuous function, and the rule defining $g(\ )$ does not involve n, then $\mathrm{plim}[g(a_n) - g(b_n)] = 0$.

In these rules, a sequence which converges in distribution can be a sequence of random vectors, and a sequence which converges in probability can be a sequence of conformable scalars, vectors or matrices. For further details, see Rao (1973: 116 ff).

Cramér's theorem

A useful application of (3) above is Cramér's theorem, which states that if A_n is a matrix sequence such that $\mathrm{plim}(A_n) = A$, and b_n is a vector sequence such that $b_n \xrightarrow{D} b \sim N(0, Q)$, then $A_n b_n \xrightarrow{D} Ab \sim N(0, AQA')$.

The rules given above are important, but at the core of any argument concerning the limiting distribution of an estimator or test statistic, there must be a convergence theorem, analogous to the central limit theorem of elementary statistics. Unfortunately, the most commonly stated versions of the central limit theorem are not applicable, and it is usually necessary to construct a direct proof of convergence in distribution, in the context of some particular type of model. At this point, the formal analysis becomes more difficult, and our approach will be to sketch the argument and to state results which are 'generally true', without always giving the detailed technical conditions under which those results will hold.

4.4 / Least squares in large samples

In section 2.4, and at various points in Chapter 3, we mentioned large sample properties of least squares estimators and test statistics, without giving any formal justification for the procedures used. We have now explained the basic concepts of convergence in probability and convergence in distribution, and in this section we summarise what can be said about the large sample properties of the ordinary least squares estimator under various relaxations of classical assumptions.

Consistency

As a first step, we consider the model

$$y = X\beta + u; \ X \text{ nonrandom, with } u_t \sim IID(0, \sigma^2); \ t = 1, \ldots, n. \tag{4.4}$$

The only classical assumption that is missing here is that concerning normality of the disturbance distributions, and under these conditions, the least squares estimator b is still best linear unbiased, with

$$E(b) = \beta \text{ and } \text{var}(b) = \sigma^2 (X'X)^{-1}. \tag{4.5}$$

If it can be shown that, as $n \to \infty$, $\lim[\text{var}(b)] = 0$, then by the Chebyshev lemma, b is a consistent estimator of β.

To ensure that $\text{var}(b)$ does tend to zero as n is increased, we need some assumption concerning the limiting behaviour of the sample moments of the variables in X. One very common approach is to assume that, as $n \to \infty$,

$$\lim(n^{-1} X'X) = Q, \text{ where } Q \text{ is nonsingular.} \tag{4.6}$$

Here and in all subsequent uses in this chapter, $\lim(\ )$ is understood to mean $\lim_{n \to \infty}(\ )$. If condition (4.6) is satisfied, we can argue as follows:

$$\text{var}(b) = \sigma^2 (X'X)^{-1}$$
$$= n^{-1} \sigma^2 (n^{-1} X'X)^{-1}.$$

As $n \to \infty$, $(n^{-1} X'X) \to Q$, and by the properties of limits, $(n^{-1} X'X)^{-1} \to Q^{-1}$, provided Q is nonsingular. The term $n^{-1} \sigma^2$ tends to zero as n is increased, so

$$\text{var}(b) = n^{-1} \sigma^2 (n^{-1} X'X)^{-1}$$
$$\to 0 \cdot Q = 0, \text{ as } n \to \infty.$$

Assumption (4.6) is not a necessary condition for consistency, nor is it entirely innocent. What is implied is that, as $n \to \infty$, all sample moments of the form

$\sum X_{it} X_{jt}/n$ converge to finite limits. Clearly, there are some variables for which this assumption cannot hold. One simple example is a time trend, with observations $1, \ldots, n$; for this variable, the sum of squares is $n(n+1)(2n+1)/6$ and division by n is obviously not sufficient to ensure convergence. But this does not mean that a model involving a trend necessarily produces inconsistent estimators. If we take the example in which X is $(n \times 2)$, with $X_{1t} = 1$ and $X_{2t} = t$, $t = 1, \ldots, n$, it is easy to show that, as $n \to \infty$,

$$\lim[(X'X)^{-1}] = 0. \tag{4.7}$$

Since σ^2 does not vary as n increases, this weaker condition is sufficient to ensure that as $n \to \infty$, $\mathrm{var}(b) \to 0$, and if $E(b) = \beta$, then b is consistent.

Consistency of $\hat{\sigma}^2$

If b is a consistent estimator of β, it is usually straightforward to show that $\hat{\sigma}^2$ is a consistent estimator of σ^2. The vector of least squares residuals is

$$e = y - Xb = X(\beta - b) + u.$$

If X is nonrandom and b is consistent, each element of $(e - u)$ converges in probability to zero. This means that e_t converges in probability to the random variable u_t. The limiting behaviour of

$$\hat{\sigma}^2 = \sum e_t^2/(n-k)$$

is therefore equivalent to the limiting behaviour of $\sum u_t^2/(n-k)$, which is in turn equivalent to that of $\sum u_t^2/n$. The variables u_t^2; $t = 1, \ldots, n$ are IID, with $E(u_t^2) = \sigma^2$, so by Khintchine's theorem – see section 4.2 – it follows that $\mathrm{plim}(\sum u_t^2/n) = \sigma^2$. Hence we have shown that $\hat{\sigma}^2$ is a consistent estimator of σ^2.

Large sample distribution of b

Now consider the large sample distribution of b. Under the conditions of model (4.4), we can argue directly that

$$\mathrm{var}(X'u) = \sigma^2(X'X)$$

and

$$\mathrm{var}(n^{-1/2}X'u) = \sigma^2(n^{-1}X'X).$$

Given the 'standard' assumption (4.6),

$$\lim(n^{-1}X'X) = Q; \text{ where } Q \text{ is nonsingular,}$$

it follows that, as $n \to \infty$, $\mathrm{var}(n^{-1/2}X'u)$ tends to the limit $\sigma^2 Q$. The fact that this scaling has a finite nonzero variance for all values of n does not prove convergence in distribution, but it does suggest that such a result may hold. A formal proof can be obtained by considering the limiting behaviour of the characteristic function of

$n^{-1/2}X'u$ (see, for example, Theil, 1971: 380–1). The formal result is that, as $n \to \infty$,

$$n^{-1/2}(X'u) \xrightarrow{D} \eta \sim N(0, \sigma^2 Q). \tag{4.8}$$

Once a result corresponding to (4.8) is established, the remaining steps in a proof of convergence in distribution are relatively straightforward, and similar arguments are used for different estimators and in different models. The discussion below therefore serves as a prototype for other similar analyses which occur later in this chapter. Given assumption (4.6) and the result in (4.8), we have

$$
\begin{aligned}
b &= (X'X)^{-1}X'y \\
&= (X'X)^{-1}X'(X\beta + u) \\
&= \beta + (X'X)^{-1}X'u \\
\Rightarrow \quad \sqrt{n}(b - \beta) &= (n^{-1}X'X)^{-1} \cdot n^{-1/2}(X'u).
\end{aligned}
$$

As $n \to \infty$, $n^{-1/2}(X'u)$ converges in distribution to a random vector distributed as $N(0, \sigma^2 Q)$, $n^{-1}X'X$ converges to a finite limit Q, and by the properties of limits, $(n^{-1}X'X)^{-1} \to Q^{-1}$, provided Q is nonsingular. The limit of a nonrandom sequence can be considered as a special case of the probability limit, which gives

$$\text{plim}[(n^{-1}X'X)^{-1}] = Q^{-1}.$$

From the result identified earlier as Cramér's theorem, it follows that $\sqrt{n}(b - \beta)$ converges in distribution to a random vector $Q^{-1}\eta$, distributed as $N(0, \sigma^2 Q^{-1}QQ^{-1})$. Hence

$$\sqrt{n}(b - \beta) \xrightarrow{D} Q^{-1}\eta \sim N(0, \sigma^2 Q^{-1}). \tag{4.9}$$

It can then be argued that in a large finite sample, $\sqrt{n}(b - \beta)$ is *approximately* $N(0, \sigma^2 Q^{-1})$, and since the usual rules for the manipulation of expectation and variance would now apply, we can rescale to give

$(b - \beta)$ is approximately $N(0, \sigma^2 n^{-1} Q^{-1})$

and

b is approximately $N(\beta, \sigma^2 n^{-1} Q^{-1})$.

Since Q is the limit of the sequence $(n^{-1}X'X)$, and Q^{-1} is the limit of the sequence $(n^{-1}X'X)^{-1} = n(X'X)^{-1}$, an appropriate finite sample approximation for Q^{-1} is $n(X'X)^{-1}$. If this is used in place of Q^{-1}, we have

b is approximately $N[\beta, \sigma^2(X'X)^{-1}]$, for large n. \hfill (4.10)

Nonnormal disturbances

So far, all that we have done is to relax just one assumption from the classical model, and having done this, we have sought to provide an alternative justification for treating the OLS estimator as being approximately normal in a large sample, without having to assume normality of the disturbance distributions. This is useful, but the limitations of the analysis should be made clear. By using strong conditions, we automatically focus on those cases in which there is no strong incentive to change existing procedures. Thus we have said nothing about nonnormal disturbance distributions which do not possess first and second moments; this possibility is ruled out by the assumption that the disturbances are $IID(0, \sigma^2)$. On this, and related topics, see Harvey (1990: 116–20).

Exact linear restrictions

Having made the point that we are still operating under quite strong conditions, we now continue with the derivation of large sample versions of test statistics that would previously have been justified by the normality assumption. To test a set of independent linear restrictions $H\beta = h$, we proceed as follows. The formal convergence result that gives rise to (4.10) is

$$\sqrt{n}(b - \beta) \xrightarrow{D} Q^{-1}\eta \sim N(0, \sigma^2 Q^{-1})$$

$$\Rightarrow \sqrt{n}H(b - \beta) \xrightarrow{D} HQ^{-1}\eta \sim N(0, \sigma^2 HQ^{-1}H').$$

Under the null hypothesis $H\beta = h$, this becomes

$$\sqrt{n}(Hb - h) \xrightarrow{D} HQ^{-1}\eta \sim N(0, \sigma^2 HQ^{-1}H')$$

and

$$n(Hb - h)'[HQ^{-1}H']^{-1}(Hb - h)/\sigma^2 \xrightarrow{D} \chi^2 \sim \chi_g^2. \tag{4.11}$$

This last statement translates as convergence in distribution to a random variable denoted as χ^2, which has a χ^2 distribution with g degrees of freedom. The fact that we can move from a normal distribution to a χ^2 distribution in the same way as for a finite sample follows from rule (4) in section 4.3.

In a large finite sample, the matrix Q^{-1} is replaced by the approximation $n(X'X)^{-1}$, giving

$$(Hb - h)'[H(X'X)^{-1}H']^{-1}(Hb - h)/\sigma^2 \text{ is approximately } \chi_g^2, \text{ under } H_0: H\beta = h.$$

$$\tag{4.12}$$

From the discussion in section 3.3, we know that the quadratic form in (4.12) is usually calculated as the difference between restricted and unrestricted residual sums of squares. Hence

$$(S_R - S)/\sigma^2 \text{ is approximately } \chi_g^2, \text{ under } H_0: H\beta = h.$$

This result was stated earlier as equation (3.39); the discussion following this equation in section 3.3 explains the different ways in which a large sample test of restrictions can be carried out in practice.

Forecast test

A second test for which we gave a large sample variant is the forecast test, discussed in section 3.4. In this case, we did explain in an informal manner how the large sample version could be obtained. Here, we take a slightly different approach, which leads to the same conclusion. Equation (3.43) shows that the forecast error can be written as

$$f = X_f(\beta - b) + u_f.$$

If X_f is nonrandom, b is consistent, and the model continues to hold in the forecast period, we can argue that $(f - u_f)$ converges in probability to zero. This means that f converges in probability to the random vector u_f. It is then obvious that even with a very large sample in the data period, f can only be normal if u_f is normal. Since the normality of f is crucial to the logic of the forecast test, we see that, in this case, a large sample argument does not compensate for the removal of the normality assumption.

Random X matrix

We now consider the case in which some columns of the regressor matrix X are random. This is a much more fundamental relaxation of classical assumptions than nonnormality of disturbances, because it admits a very wide range of models with quite sharply differing properties. In many cases, the OLS estimator is no longer unbiased, consistent or asymptotically normal. Indeed, there is often little to be gained from analysis at this level of generality; for most purposes it is necessary to be specific as to the source and nature of the random behaviour in X. In the remainder of this section, we look briefly at what can be said of a linear model with a random X matrix.

Strong independence of X and u

If X has random components, and *all* random elements of X are distributed independently of *all* elements of u, the OLS estimator b is still unbiased:

$$b = (X'X)^{-1}X'y$$
$$= \beta + (X'X)^{-1}X'u,$$
$$E(b) = \beta + E[(X'X)^{-1}X']E(u)$$
$$= \beta; \text{ if } E(u) = 0. \tag{4.13}$$

For independent random variables, the expectation of a product is the product of expectations, and here we argue that if all elements of X are independent of all elements of u, then all elements of $(X'X)^{-1}X'$ are independent of all elements of u. Provided the expectation of $(X'X)^{-1}X'$ exists, b is shown to be unbiased.

Under the same conditions, if $\text{var}(u) = \sigma^2 I$, one can continue to show that

$$\text{var}(b) = \sigma^2 E[(X'X)^{-1}]. \tag{4.14}$$

In order to obtain (4.14), it is necessary to assume or prove that the expectation of $(X'X)^{-1}$ exists and, at this stage, the whole exercise becomes rather pointless. If X and u are completely independent, estimation and testing can be made conditional on given values for the elements of X, with no loss of information. All existing results stand, the difference being that all statements become conditional on X. Although it is of some value to know that b is unbiased if X and u are completely independent, there is little to be gained from trying to evaluate an unconditional variance for b: (4.14) holds only under a strong independence condition, it involves questions as to the existence of moments of the inverse matrix, and even when those moments do exist they are not always simple to evaluate. So, under the conditions assumed here, one would simply use the existing expression for $\text{var}(b)$ – see equation (4.5) – with the one modification that this is now interpreted as the conditional variance of b, for given X.

Consistency of b when X is random

If the X matrix contains some columns that are random, but we are able to assume or prove that

$$\text{plim}(n^{-1}X'X) = Q, \text{ nonsingular} \tag{4.15}$$

and

$$\text{plim}(n^{-1}X'u) = q = 0, \tag{4.16}$$

then the probability limit of the OLS estimator b can be found as follows:

$$b = (X'X)^{-1}X'y$$
$$= (X'X)^{-1}X'(X\beta + u)$$
$$= \beta + (X'X)^{-1}X'u$$
$$= \beta + (n^{-1}X'X)^{-1}n^{-1}X'u.$$

Since the inverse of a matrix is a continuous function of the elements, the rules for manipulating probability limits can be applied to give

$$\text{plim}(b) = \beta + \text{plim}[(n^{-1}X'X)^{-1}]\,\text{plim}(n^{-1}X'u)$$
$$= \beta + [\text{plim}(n^{-1}X'X)]^{-1}\,\text{plim}(n^{-1}X'u)$$
$$= \beta + Q^{-1}q = \beta, \text{ if } q = 0. \tag{4.17}$$

So if (4.15) and (4.16) are satisfied, b is consistent.

Assumption (4.15) replaces the earlier assumption (4.6) and requires that the sample moments of the variables in X converge in probability to give a nonsingular matrix Q. As before, this is convenient, but not always necessary. For some types of variable, an alternative scaling may have to be used. However, this is a detail; in the standard 'textbook' approach, the main factor which determines whether or not b is consistent is the value of q in (4.16).

If $\text{plim } n^{-1} \sum X_{jt} u_t = 0$; $j = 1, \ldots, k$, then q is a zero vector, and assuming for convenience that (4.15) does hold, it follows that b is consistent. If at least one of the variables in X is correlated with the disturbances, in the sense that

$$\text{plim } n^{-1} \sum X_{jt} u_t \neq 0,$$

then q is not a zero vector and b is inconsistent. What is at issue here is a limiting form of covariance between X_{jt} and u_t. Although the disturbances cannot be observed, it is possible to consider a measure corresponding to the sample covariance

$$\sum (X_{jt} - \bar{X}_j)(u_t - \bar{u})/n = \sum X_{jt} u_t/n - \bar{X}_j \bar{u}. \tag{4.18}$$

Since $E(u_t) = 0$, it seems reasonable to replace $\bar{u}$ by its expected value, and if this is done (4.18) reduces to $\sum X_{jt} u_t/n$. Hence (4.16) states that the sample covariance between X_{jt} and u_t converges in probability to zero, for all $j = 1, \ldots, k$. We shall describe this as the situation in which X_{jt} and u_t are *uncorrelated in the limit* as $n \to \infty$.

In practice, it is not reasonable to simply assume that (4.15) and (4.16) will hold, without being more specific as to the type of model under investigation. Thus, if we have a simple dynamic model

$$Y_t = \beta Y_{t-1} + u_t; \ u_t \sim IID(0, \sigma^2); \ t = 1, \ldots, n,$$

the least squares estimator of β would be

$$b = \sum Y_{t-1} Y_t / \sum Y_{t-1}^2$$
$$= \beta + \sum Y_{t-1} u_t / \sum Y_{t-1}^2.$$

It is argued in Chapter 7 that if $|\beta| < 1$, one can prove that $\text{plim}(\sum Y_{t-1} u_t/n) = 0$ and that $\text{plim}(\sum Y_{t-1}^2/n)$ exists and is nonzero. So in this simple dynamic model the least squares estimator is consistent, and subject to some further conditions on any additional regressors that may be present, this conclusion holds for other stable dynamic models with IID disturbances. In other cases, investigation of a specific model may show that (4.15) and (4.16) do not hold.

Large sample distribution of b when X is random

If it can be shown that

$$\text{plim}(n^{-1} X'X) = Q, \ Q \text{ is nonsingular}$$

and

$$n^{-1/2}(X'u) \xrightarrow{D} \eta \sim N(0, \sigma^2 Q),$$

then, as before, it follows that

$$\sqrt{n}(b - \beta) \xrightarrow{D} Q^{-1}\eta \sim N(0, \sigma^2 Q^{-1}). \tag{4.19}$$

It is by no means always true that least squares estimators in the random X model have the property shown in (4.19), and where this result does hold, the proof may not be simple. If it is possible to establish (4.19), the arguments leading to a large sample test of exact restrictions do follow, but the large sample forecast test is more problematic. The forecast error is still

$$f = X_f(\beta - b) + u_f,$$

but X_f is now random. Although it seems likely that where b is consistent, f will converge in probability to the random vector u_f, we need to look at particular cases to establish a formal proof. In fact, this is now generally true. There is little more that one can do in the context of the random X model, without specifying which of the many possible variants we are looking at. In some cases, least squares will retain some desirable properties. In other cases, least squares is no longer acceptable, and some other principle will have to be used. In the next section, we look at the first of these alternatives, which is maximum likelihood estimation.

4.5 / Maximum likelihood estimation

Although the reason for introducing maximum likelihood estimation is to provide a method of greater generality than ordinary least squares, it is convenient to start in the familiar territory of the classical regression model. If

$$y = X\beta + u; \quad X \text{ is nonrandom}; \quad u \sim N(0, \sigma^2 I), \tag{4.20}$$

the joint density function for the endogenous variable observations is

$$p(y) = (2\pi\sigma^2)^{-n/2} \exp[-(y - X\beta)'(y - X\beta)/2\sigma^2].$$

The density function is interpreted as a function of y for given values of the parameters β and σ^2. The likelihood function has the same form, but is interpreted as a function of parameters, for given observations. To capture this point, we should strictly write the density function as $p(y; \beta, \sigma^2)$ and the likelihood function as $L(\beta, \sigma^2; y)$. Hence

$$L(\beta, \sigma^2; y) = (2\pi\sigma^2)^{-n/2} \exp[-(y - X\beta)'(y - X\beta)/2\sigma^2]. \tag{4.21}$$

For convenience, we shall often abbreviate to $L(\beta, \sigma^2)$ or, where the meaning is clear, to L.

Since y is continuous, some care is needed when interpreting what the likelihood function tells us. It is not true that $L(\beta, \sigma^2; y)$ is the probability associated with a point value of y, but $L(\beta, \sigma^2; y)$ is proportional to the probability associated with a small region around y. By maximising the likelihood over possible values of β and

σ^2, we choose as estimators those values of the parameters which maximise the probability associated with a small region around the y vector actually observed, so we are effectively choosing parameter values which make most likely what we obtain as data. At an intuitive level, this would seem to be a very reasonable principle of estimation, and, under quite general conditions, it is possible to show that maximum likelihood (ML) estimators do have desirable properties.

To illustrate the mechanics of obtaining ML estimators for a given model, we shall maximise the likelihood function given in (4.21). In doing this, it is convenient to work with the log likelihood function $\ln[L(\beta, \sigma^2)]$: since $\ln(\ )$ is a monotonically increasing function, choosing values of β and σ^2 which maximise $\ln L = \ln[L(\beta, \sigma^2)]$ is equivalent to choosing values which maximise $L = L(\beta, \sigma^2)$. From (4.21), the log likelihood is

$$\ln L = \ln\{(2\pi\sigma^2)^{-n/2} \exp[-(y - X\beta)'(y - X\beta)/2\sigma^2]\}$$
$$= -(n/2)\ln(2\pi) - (n/2)\ln(\sigma^2) - (y - X\beta)'(y - X\beta)/2\sigma^2$$
$$= -(n/2)\ln(2\pi) - (n/2)\ln(\sigma^2) - S(\beta)/2\sigma^2,$$

where $S(\beta)$ is the sum of squares function $S(\beta) = (y - X\beta)'(y - X\beta)$. On differentiating with respect to β and σ^2, we obtain

$$\partial \ln L/\partial \beta = -[\partial S(\beta)/\partial \beta]/2\sigma^2 = 0$$
$$\Rightarrow \partial S(\beta)/\partial \beta = 0 \qquad (4.22)$$

and

$$\partial \ln L/\partial \sigma^2 = -n/2\sigma^2 + S(\beta)/2\sigma^4 = 0$$
$$\Rightarrow \sigma^2 = S(\beta)/n = (y - X\beta)'(y - X\beta)/n. \qquad (4.23)$$

From (4.22), it is clear that under classical regression assumptions, the conditions to be satisfied by the ML estimator of β are the same as those for the least squares estimator, and the two estimators are therefore identical. Equation (4.23) shows the value of σ^2 that maximises the likelihood for a given value of β, and by inserting the ML estimator of β, we can obtain the ML estimator for σ^2. Using $\tilde{\beta}$ and $\tilde{\sigma}^2$ to denote the ML estimators, we have

$$\tilde{\beta} = (X'X)^{-1}X'y \text{ (if } X'X \text{ is nonsingular)}$$
$$\tilde{\sigma}^2 = (y - X\tilde{\beta})'(y - X\tilde{\beta})/n. \qquad (4.24)$$

Notice that the ML estimator $\tilde{\sigma}^2$ is different from the least squares estimator $\hat{\sigma}^2$, the difference being that the ML estimator has no correction for degrees of freedom. As the sample size increases, this difference disappears. To complete the example, the reader should use second-order conditions to verify that we are indeed maximising the likelihood function, rather than finding some other turning point.

Regularity conditions

We now look at maximum likelihood estimation in a more general context. Suppose that $p(y; \theta, X)$ is the joint density function for a model in which y is a vector of endogenous variable observations, X is a nonstochastic matrix of exogenous variable observations and θ is an $(m \times 1)$ vector of parameters. Corresponding to $p(y; \theta, X)$, we write the likelihood function as $L(\theta; y, X)$, abbreviated to $L(\theta)$, or sometimes to L.

In what follows, it is assumed that the likelihood function has first and second derivatives with respect to θ, and that these derivatives are continuous in y. This enables the log derivatives to be treated as continuous random variables, as shown below.

It is often the case that ML estimation does not lead to an explicit expression for the estimator. Rather, by maximising the log likelihood, we obtain the conditions

$$\partial \ln L(\theta)/\partial \theta = (1/L)\, \partial L(\theta)/\partial \theta = 0. \tag{4.25}$$

If (4.25) gives equations which are nonlinear in θ, an iterative solution method is used to generate a value for the ML estimator $\tilde{\theta}$. Since we then have no explicit expression for $\tilde{\theta}$, the properties of the estimator have to be analysed indirectly, and the derivative in (4.25) plays an important role. For convenience of notation, we write

$$D \ln L(\theta) = \partial \ln L(\theta)/\partial \theta = (1/L)\, \partial L(\theta)/\partial \theta.$$

If $\tilde{\theta}$ is the maximum likelihood estimator, it must satisfy the first-order conditions, so $D \ln L(\tilde{\theta}) = 0$.

Given the identity between the likelihood function and the density function, the integral of $L(\theta)$ over the sample space for y is equal to 1 for any admissible value of θ:

$$\int L(\theta)\, dy = 1. \tag{4.26}$$

Provided the bounds of integration do not depend on θ, it is possible to differentiate (4.26) under the integral sign, to give

$$\frac{\partial}{\partial \theta} \int L(\theta)\, dy = \int \partial L(\theta)/\partial \theta\, dy = \int \partial \ln L(\theta)/\partial \theta \cdot L \cdot dy = 0. \tag{4.27}$$

Since L is formally identical to the density function $p(y; \theta, X)$, the third term of (4.27) corresponds to the expectation of the log derivative. Writing the log derivative as $D \ln L(\theta)$, we have

$$E[D \ln L(\theta)] = 0. \tag{4.28}$$

By differentiating (4.27) again, we can also find an expression for the variance of $D \ln L(\theta)$.

To ensure that dimensions are correctly maintained, recall that the operator $\partial^2(\ )/\partial \theta\, \partial \theta'$ is equivalent to $\partial(\ )/\partial \theta'$ applied to a column vector of first derivatives.

Differentiating again in (4.27), this gives

$$\frac{\partial}{\partial \theta'} \int \partial \ln L(\theta)\, \partial \theta \cdot L \cdot \mathrm{d}y = 0$$

$$\Rightarrow \int [\partial^2 \ln L(\theta)/\partial \theta\, \partial \theta' \cdot L + \partial \ln L(\theta)/\partial \theta \cdot \partial L(\theta)/\partial \theta']\, \mathrm{d}y = 0$$

$$\Rightarrow \int \partial^2 \ln L(\theta)/\partial \theta\, \partial \theta' \cdot L \cdot \mathrm{d}y + \int \partial \ln L(\theta)/\partial \theta \cdot \partial \ln L(\theta)/\partial \theta' \cdot L \cdot \mathrm{d}y = 0. \qquad (4.29)$$

The first term on the left of (4.29) is the expectation of the second log derivative; this is an $(m \times m)$ matrix, written as $E[\mathrm{D}^2 \ln L(\theta)]$. The second term is $E[\mathrm{D} \ln L(\theta) \cdot \mathrm{D} \ln L(\theta)']$, the $(m \times m)$ matrix of second moments of the first log derivative: since $E[\mathrm{D} \ln L(\theta)] = 0$, this is equivalent to the variance covariance matrix for the random vector $\mathrm{D} \ln (\theta)$. Hence

$$\mathrm{var}[\mathrm{D} \ln L(\theta)] = -E[\mathrm{D}^2 \ln L(\theta)]. \qquad (4.30)$$

Finally, we note that the matrix on the right of (4.30) is called the information matrix, for which we use the notation $I(\theta)$.

The analysis above looks rather daunting, but the main problem is one of interpretation. For any θ for which $p(y; X, \theta)$ is a valid density function, we have shown that, given certain conditions, $\mathrm{D} \ln L(\theta)$ is a random vector with zero mean and variance $I(\theta)$. On specifying a particular model, we would usually assume that there exists a unique 'true' value of θ, and once this is done, (4.28) and (4.30) should be applied only for that value of θ.

In order to justify (4.28) and (4.30), we imposed a condition which requires that the range of integration in (4.26) does not depend on θ. We also made some assumptions concerning the existence and continuity of derivatives. These are the so-called *regularity* conditions for ML estimation, and although these conditions are not always satisfied, there are many cases in which such assumptions are justified.

Large sample properties of ML estimators

In looking at the large sample properties of least squares estimators, we used rather strong assumptions, in order to convey the nature of the derivation and application of results which are 'typically true' for a certain type of model. An essentially similar approach is used here. All that we seek to do is to establish the plausibility of typical convergence results, so that we can understand the nature of the argument without becoming too involved in technicalities.

We have already shown that, under specified conditions, $\mathrm{D} \ln L(\theta)$ has zero mean and variance $I(\theta)$. For convenience, we write this as

$$\mathrm{D} \ln L(\theta) \sim [0, I(\theta)].$$

It follows immediately that, under two alternative scalings, we have

$$n^{-1/2}\mathrm{D}\ln L(\theta) \sim [0, n^{-1}I(\theta)]$$
$$n^{-1}\mathrm{D}\ln L(\theta) \sim [0, n^{-2}I(\theta)].$$

(4.31)

If we assume that as $n \to \infty$, $n^{-1}I(\theta)$ converges to a finite limit, equal to a positive definite matrix Q, then we have some idea as to the limiting behaviour of the random variables in (4.31). Since $n^{-1/2}\mathrm{D}\ln L(\theta)$ has zero mean and a variance which converges to a finite nonsingular matrix, our argument suggests (and does no more than suggest) that $n^{-1/2}\mathrm{D}\ln L(\theta)$ might converge in distribution to a random variable distributed as $N(0, Q)$. A more definite result is that $n^{-1}\mathrm{D}\ln L(\theta)$ has zero mean and variance $n^{-2}I(\theta)$, which converges to zero as $n \to \infty$. Hence, by the Chebyshev lemma (see section 4.2), $n^{-1}\mathrm{D}\ln L(\theta)$ converges in probability to zero.

Having indicated the likely pattern of convergence for $n^{-1/2}\mathrm{D}\ln L(\theta)$ and $n^{-1}\mathrm{D}\ln L(\theta)$, we now consider the relevance of these results for the properties of the ML estimator, which is found as a solution $\tilde{\theta}$ for which

$$\mathrm{D}\ln L(\tilde{\theta}) = 0.$$

(4.32)

In general, multiple solutions are possible and the algorithm used should ensure that the turning point chosen is the global maximum. Assuming this to be the case, we expand (4.32) in a Taylor series around the true value θ. This gives

$$\mathrm{D}\ln L(\tilde{\theta}) = 0 = \mathrm{D}\ln L(\theta) + \mathrm{D}^2\ln L(\theta) \cdot (\tilde{\theta} - \theta) + R_1.$$

Provided that the remainder term R_1 is relatively small and $\mathrm{D}^2\ln L(\theta)$ is nonsingular, we have

$$(\tilde{\theta} - \theta) \simeq -[\mathrm{D}^2\ln L(\theta)]^{-1}\mathrm{D}\ln L(\theta).$$

(4.33)

Equation (4.33) shows how one can overcome the difficulty inherent in not having an explicit expression for the ML estimator. However, before we can make use of (4.33), one further piece of information is needed. From equation (4.30), we have

$$E[-\mathrm{D}^2\ln L(\theta)] = I(\theta)$$
$$\Rightarrow E[-n^{-1}\mathrm{D}^2\ln L(\theta)] = n^{-1}I(\theta) \to Q, \text{ as } n \to \infty.$$

Although this is not sufficient to prove that $-n^{-1}\mathrm{D}^2\ln L(\theta)$ converges in probability to Q, it seems reasonable to argue that if the relevant probability limit exists, it is likely to be equal to the expected value. To show this formally, we would need some conditions on third derivatives of the likelihood function, but we again adopt the somewhat cavalier approach of simply assuming the result to be true. Hence we assert that, under 'standard' conditions,

$$\mathrm{plim}[-n^{-1}\mathrm{D}^2\ln L(\theta)] = \lim n^{-1}I(\theta) = Q.$$

(4.34)

If we accept the various arguments used above, then from equation (4.33) we have

$$(\tilde{\theta} - \theta) \simeq [-D^2 \ln L(\theta)]^{-1} D \ln L(\theta)$$

$$= [-n^{-1} D^2 \ln L(\theta)]^{-1} n^{-1} D \ln L(\theta)$$

$$\xrightarrow{P} Q^{-1} \cdot 0 = 0.$$

Provided that any remainder terms converge in probability to zero, it follows that $\text{plim}(\tilde{\theta} - \theta) = 0$ and hence that $\text{plim}(\tilde{\theta}) = \theta$. The ML estimator $\tilde{\theta}$ is therefore consistent.

With the alternative scaling,

$$\sqrt{n}(\tilde{\theta} - \theta) \simeq [-n^{-1} D^2 \ln L(\theta)]^{-1} N^{-1/2} D \ln L(\theta),$$

we have that if

$$n^{-1/2} D \ln L(\theta) \xrightarrow{D} \eta \sim N(0, Q)$$

and

$$-n^{-1} D^2 \ln L(\theta) \xrightarrow{P} Q,$$

then, by Cramér's theorem (see section 4.3),

$$\sqrt{n}(\tilde{\theta} - \theta) \xrightarrow{D} Q^{-1} \eta \sim N(0, Q^{-1} Q Q^{-1})$$

or

$$\sqrt{n}(\tilde{\theta} - \theta) \xrightarrow{D} Q^{-1} \eta \sim N(0, Q^{-1}).$$

Hence, in a large finite sample

$$\tilde{\theta} \text{ is approximately } N(\theta, n^{-1} Q^{-1}). \tag{4.35}$$

To use (4.35) in practice, it is necessary to replace $n^{-1} Q^{-1}$ with an appropriate finite sample approximation. This can be a source of confusion, so we list the steps in generating an appropriate measure below:

$n^{-1} I(\theta)$ is an approximation for Q

$n[I(\theta)]^{-1}$ is an approximation for Q^{-1}

$[I(\theta)]^{-1}$ is an approximation for $n^{-1} Q^{-1}$.

As it stands, this does not help very much because θ is unknown, but under the conditions assumed here, it is possible to show that $n[I(\tilde{\theta})]^{-1}$ is a consistent estimator of Q^{-1}, and this suggests using $[I(\tilde{\theta})]^{-1}$ to replace $n^{-1} Q^{-1}$ in (4.35). In practice, an estimate of the asymptotic variance matrix is usually obtained by inserting estimated parameter values into an analytic expression for the inverse information matrix, and this may be represented by writing $I^{-1}(\tilde{\theta})$ in place of the formally equivalent expression $[I(\tilde{\theta})]^{-1}$.

Asymptotic efficiency

Subject to certain conditions, we have 'shown' that the ML estimator $\tilde{\theta}$ is consistent and asymptotically normal, with variance of the limiting distribution of $\sqrt{n}(\tilde{\theta} - \theta)$ equal to Q^{-1}. To consider asymptotic efficiency, it is necessary to introduce some class of estimators, and this would typically consist of all estimators that are consistent and asymptotically normal. If $\theta_{(1)}$ and $\theta_{(2)}$ are two such estimators, with

$$\sqrt{n}(\theta_{(i)} - \theta) \xrightarrow{D} \eta_{(i)} \sim N(0, \Sigma_{(i)}); \ i = 1, 2,$$

$\theta_{(1)}$ is said to be asymptotically efficient relative to $\theta_{(2)}$ if $\Sigma_{(2)} - \Sigma_{(1)}$ is positive semidefinite (psd). The relevance of this to ML estimation is that under the usual 'fairly general conditions', all consistent and asymptotically normal estimators $\theta_{(i)}$ are such that $\Sigma_{(i)} - Q^{-1}$ is psd. In this sense, ML estimators are asymptotically efficient.

A closely related concept is that of the Cramér–Rao bound. Given regularity conditions of the kind assumed earlier, it can be shown that if an unbiased estimator of θ exists, its variance is greater than or equal to $[I(\theta)]^{-1}$, in the usual sense of the difference between two matrices being positive semidefinite. Since $[I(\theta)]^{-1}$ is a large finite sample approximation to the theoretical variance of the ML estimator, we can say that, in an asymptotic sense, the ML estimator attains the Cramér–Rao bound, and any unbiased estimator has a variance greater than or equal to that of the ML estimator.

Example 4.1

To show that ML theory can offer something new, even under the relatively strong conditions assumed here, consider the nonlinear regression model

$$y_t = f(x'_t, \beta) + u_t; \ u_t \sim NID(0, \sigma^2); \ t = 1, \ldots, n,$$

where $f(x'_t, \beta)$ is a function which is nonlinear in parameters, and the regressors in x'_t are nonrandom, satisfying appropriate convergence conditions on the sample moments. The log likelihood function is still of the form

$$\ln L = -(n/2)\ln(2\pi) - (n/2)\ln(\sigma^2) - S(\beta)/2\sigma^2,$$

but the sum of squares function is now

$$S(\beta) = \sum [y_t - f(x'_t, \beta)]^2 = \sum [u_t(\beta)]^2,$$

with $u_t(\beta)$ interpreted as a function of β. The second derivatives of the log likelihood are

$$\partial^2 \ln L/\partial\beta\,\partial\beta' = -[\partial^2 S(\beta)/\partial\beta\,\partial\beta']/2\sigma^2$$

$$\partial^2 \ln L/\partial(\sigma^2)^2 = n/2\sigma^4 - S(\beta)/\sigma^6$$

$$\partial^2 \ln L/\partial\beta\,\partial\sigma^2 = [\partial S(\beta)/\partial\beta]/2\sigma^4.$$

At the 'true' value β, $E[\partial^2 \ln L / \partial\beta \, \partial\sigma^2] = 0$, so the information matrix is block diagonal; this means that the large sample distribution of the ML estimator $\tilde{\beta}$ is uncorrelated with that of the ML estimator $\tilde{\sigma}^2$, and the two estimators can be analysed separately.

Focusing on the estimation of β, and using $I_{\beta\beta}^{-1}(\beta, \sigma^2)$ to denote the diagonal block of the inverse information matrix which corresponds to β, we have

$\tilde{\beta}$ is approximately $N[\beta, I_{\beta\beta}^{-1}(\beta, \sigma^2)]$

where

$$I_{\beta\beta}^{-1}(\beta, \sigma^2) = 2\sigma^2 \{E[\partial^2 S(\beta) / \partial\beta \, \partial\beta']\}^{-1}$$

$$= \sigma^2 \left[\sum (\partial u_t / \partial\beta \cdot \partial u_t / \partial\beta') \right]^{-1}.$$

To use this result in practice, we need an iterative method for finding a solution to the nonlinear equations $\partial S(\beta) / \partial\beta = 0$. In later applications, we shall use the Gauss–Newton procedure, which involves a series of regressions of currently estimated residuals $\hat{u}_t$ on derivatives $-\partial u_t / \partial\beta_j$; $j = 1, \ldots, m-1$. (This assumes m parameters in total, $m-1$ of which are elements of β, the other being the disturbance variance σ^2.) At each stage, the derivatives are evaluated using the current estimates $\hat{\beta}_j$, and the regressions produce revisions to the estimates of the form $(\tilde{\beta}_j - \hat{\beta}_j)$; $j = 1, \ldots, m-1$. The information matrix can be evaluated by inserting the final values of the derivatives $\partial u_t / \partial\beta_j$ into the expression

$$I_{\beta\beta}^{-1}(\beta, \sigma^2) = \sigma^2 \left[\sum (\partial u_t / \partial\beta \cdot \partial u_t / \partial\beta') \right]^{-1}.$$

The parameter σ^2 is estimated as $\tilde{\sigma}^2 = \sum \tilde{u}_t^2 / n$, where $\tilde{u}_t$; $t = 1, \ldots, n$ are residuals from the final iteration. For this procedure to be valid, the algorithm must be implemented in such a way as to locate the global minimum of $S(\beta)$.

Restricted ML estimation

As in the least squares case, one may wish to impose some restrictions on the parameters of a model that is to be estimated by maximum likelihood. It is often quite easy to do this by direct substitution; thus, if certain parameters are to be set to zero, the relevant restrictions are written into the model, and any redundant terms are removed. However, the formal theory of restricted estimation takes a different approach, and this is important in the next section when we discuss testing. It is therefore useful to add a brief review of the theory of ML estimation in the presence of restrictions.

Suppose that we wish to maximise the log likelihood subject to a set of g exact linear restrictions, written as $H\theta = h$. To do this, we set up the Lagrangian function

$$\phi = \ln L(\theta) - \lambda'(H\theta - h)$$

where λ is a $(g \times 1)$ vector of Lagrange multipliers. On differentiating ϕ with respect to β and λ, and setting the resulting derivatives to zero, we obtain the conditions

$$\partial\phi/\partial\theta = \mathrm{D}\ln L(\theta) - H'\lambda = 0$$
$$\partial\phi/\partial\lambda = -(H\theta - h) = 0. \qquad (4.36)$$

The equations in (4.36) are typically nonlinear in θ and, as before, an iterative solution method would be used. However, our concern here is not with the mechanics, but rather with the relevant large sample theory. As one might imagine, there are detailed analytic conditions to be satisfied, but the 'typical' convergence result is that if the restrictions are valid:

$$\sqrt{n}(\tilde{\theta}_{\mathrm{R}} - \theta) \xrightarrow{D} P\eta \sim N(0, P). \qquad (4.37)$$

In (4.37), $\tilde{\theta}_{\mathrm{R}}$ denotes the restricted ML estimator, $\eta \sim N(0, Q)$,

$$P = Q^{-1} - Q^{-1}H'[HQ^{-1}H']^{-1}HQ^{-1} \qquad (4.38)$$

and

$$PQP = P.$$

As before, $Q = \lim n^{-1}I(\theta)$. This bears a remarkable similarity to that for the formal restricted least squares estimator discussed in section 3.3. This is not surprising, since the derivation is based on approximations which use only leading (linear) terms. For details of the derivation, see Silvey (1970: 79–81).

One rather obvious implication of these results is that a restricted estimator is consistent, provided the restrictions are valid. If this is not the case, the restricted estimator is inconsistent, and there are certain problems associated with the concept of the limiting distribution. Some details are given in Chow (1983: 289).

When obtaining (4.37) and (4.38), Silvey actually argues in the more general context of a set of nonlinear restrictions, written in implicit form as $h_i(\theta) = 0$; $i = 1, \ldots, g$, or written together as the elements of the $(g \times 1)$ vector equation $h(\theta) = 0$. To apply the results above to this case, define $H(\theta)$ to be the $(g \times m)$ matrix $\partial h(\theta)/\partial\theta'$, with element (i, j) equal to $\partial h_i(\theta)/\partial\theta_j$, and then use $H(\theta)$ in place of H in (4.38). In the special case of exact linear restrictions, H and $H(\theta)$ are identical.

Quasi-ML estimators

In showing how maximum likelihood estimation is applied in the classical regression model, the normality assumption was used to write down the likelihood function, but it was not used when establishing the large sample distribution of the ML estimator. This enables us to define what may be called quasi-maximum likelihood estimators (sometimes known as pseudo-ML estimators), where a normal likelihood function is used but the disturbance distributions are not actually normal. The idea is that one might suspect nonnormality, without necessarily being able to specify the correct likelihood function. Alternatively, one might use the quasi-ML estimator for simplicity. In some cases, the large sample distribution is the same as that for the correct ML estimator, but this is not an inviolate rule. The cost of approximation is revealed more readily by computer simulation of the estimation process in a finite sample. This will usually show a loss of efficiency relative to the true ML estimator, and it may also reveal other problems not apparent from large sample results.

4.6 / Test principles

The econometrics literature of the past decade contains many articles which deal with the systematic testing of models, and in this literature, three basic test principles are of prime importance. These are known respectively as Wald (W), likelihood ratio (LR) and Lagrange multiplier (LM) tests.

In the discussion which follows, the test principles are explained in the context of maximum likelihood estimation. This provides a motivation, and shows the likely large sample behaviour in each case, but both Wald- and LM-type tests are often based on other estimators. This may arise because some other estimator is equivalent to that obtained by maximising the likelihood function, or because the estimator is an approximation to maximum likelihood. In other cases, the basic principles of the Wald or LM approach are used to suggest a test statistic, which is then justified by direct investigation of its properties, rather than by reference to maximum likelihood theory.

Wald test

The first test principle is already quite familiar because it corresponds to the method previously used to derive a test of exact linear restrictions, and we use this again as a convenient example. The objective is to test the validity of a set of g independent linear restrictions, written as $H\theta = h$, where θ is an $(m \times 1)$ vector of parameters. Our fundamental assumption is that we have a model which satisfies whatever conditions are necessary to establish that

$$\sqrt{n}(\tilde{\theta} - \theta) \xrightarrow{D} Q^{-1}\eta \sim N(0, Q^{-1}) \tag{4.39}$$

where $Q = \lim n^{-1}I(\theta)$. By a sequence of steps which parallel those used in section 4.4 in the context of least squares estimation we have

$$\sqrt{n}H(\tilde{\theta} - \theta) \xrightarrow{D} HQ^{-1}\eta \sim N(0, HQ^{-1}H'),$$

and under $H_0: H\theta = h$:

$$\sqrt{n}(H\tilde{\theta} - h) \xrightarrow{D} HQ^{-1}\eta \sim N(0, HQ^{-1}H')$$

$$\Rightarrow n(H\tilde{\theta} - h)'[HQ^{-1}H']^{-1}(H\tilde{\theta} - h) \xrightarrow{D} \chi^2 \sim \chi_g^2$$

$$\Rightarrow (H\tilde{\theta} - h)'[H(n^{-1}Q^{-1})H']^{-1}(H\tilde{\theta} - h) \xrightarrow{D} \chi^2 \sim \chi_g^2. \tag{4.40}$$

In practice, $n^{-1}Q^{-1}$ is replaced by $I^{-1}(\tilde{\theta})$, and using W to denote the resulting Wald-type test statistic, this gives

$$W = (H\tilde{\theta} - h)'[HI^{-1}(\tilde{\theta})H']^{-1}(H\tilde{\theta} - h) \text{ is approximately } \chi_g^2, \text{ under } H_0\colon H\theta = h.$$

(4.41)

The most important characteristic of the test above is that it is based entirely on unrestricted parameter estimates, and it is this that distinguishes Wald-type tests from the other types that we consider below.

Nonlinear restrictions

One simple and useful extension of the argument above is that we can consider a test of nonlinear restrictions by making the following modifications. Suppose first that the null hypothesis consists of g restrictions, written in implicit form as $h_i(\theta) = 0$; $i = 1, \ldots, g$, or written together as the elements of the $(g \times 1)$ vector equation $h(\theta) = 0$. Then define $H(\theta)$ to be the $(g \times m)$ matrix $\partial h(\theta)/\partial\theta'$, with element (i,j) equal to $\partial h_i(\theta)/\partial\theta_j$. A Taylor series expansion of $h(\tilde{\theta})$ about θ gives

$$h(\tilde{\theta}) \simeq h(\theta) + H(\theta) \cdot (\tilde{\theta} - \theta),$$

and if the restrictions $h(\theta) = 0$ are valid, we have

$$h(\tilde{\theta}) \simeq H(\theta) \cdot (\tilde{\theta} - \theta).$$

From this point on, the argument is very similar to that used above, and

$$W = h(\tilde{\theta})'[H(\theta)I^{-1}(\theta)H(\theta)']^{-1}h(\tilde{\theta}) \text{ is approximately } \chi_g^2, \text{ under } H_0\colon h(\theta) = 0.$$

(4.42)

In practice, $H(\theta)$ and $I^{-1}(\theta)$ are both replaced by the corresponding functions of $\tilde{\theta}$. This is a reasonably general method for testing nonlinear restrictions, although there is one theoretical problem, in that the outcome is not invariant to different ways of expressing a given set of nonlinear restrictions – see Lafontaine and White (1986).

Likelihood ratio (LR) test

To motivate the likelihood ratio test, suppose that we have a set of g restrictions which are feasible and which contain no redundancies. These may be linear restrictions of the form $H\theta = h$, or nonlinear restrictions of the kind discussed above. The null hypothesis H_0 is that the restrictions are valid. Then let $L(\tilde{\theta}_R)$ denote the maximised likelihood when the model parameters are made to satisfy the restrictions, and let $L(\tilde{\theta})$ be the maximised likelihood for the unrestricted model. The likelihood ratio, λ, is defined as $L(\tilde{\theta}_R)/L(\tilde{\theta})$, where, clearly, $0 \le \lambda \le 1$. The likelihood ratio test statistic is

$$LR = -2\ln\lambda = 2\ln L(\tilde{\theta}) - 2\ln L(\tilde{\theta}_R).$$

(4.43)

To obtain the limiting distribution of LR under H_0, we proceed in two steps. First, we use a Taylor series expansion of $\ln L(\tilde{\theta}_R)$ about $\tilde{\theta}$:

$$\ln L(\tilde{\theta}_R) \simeq \ln L(\tilde{\theta}) + D \ln L(\tilde{\theta})'(\tilde{\theta}_R - \tilde{\theta}) + \tfrac{1}{2}(\tilde{\theta}_R - \tilde{\theta})'D^2 \ln L(\tilde{\theta})(\tilde{\theta}_R - \tilde{\theta}).$$

If H_0 is true, $\tilde{\theta}_R$ should be relatively close to $\tilde{\theta}$, and higher-order terms should be negligible in the limit. So, given that $D \ln L(\tilde{\theta}) = 0$, we have

$$
\begin{aligned}
LR &= 2 \ln L(\tilde{\theta}) - 2 \ln L(\tilde{\theta}_R) \\
&\simeq (\tilde{\theta}_R - \tilde{\theta})'[-D^2 \ln L(\tilde{\theta})](\tilde{\theta}_R - \tilde{\theta}) \\
&= (\tilde{\theta} - \tilde{\theta}_R)'[-D^2 \ln L(\tilde{\theta})](\tilde{\theta} - \tilde{\theta}_R).
\end{aligned}
\tag{4.44}
$$

To investigate the limiting distribution of (4.44) under H_0, we need to ask what can be said about the limiting distribution of $\sqrt{n}(\tilde{\theta} - \tilde{\theta}_R)$.

In the preceding section, we argued that for valid restrictions, $\sqrt{n}(\tilde{\theta}_R - \theta)$ converges in distribution to a random variable distributed as $N(0, P)$, where

$$P = Q^{-1} - Q^{-1}H'[HQ^{-1}H']^{-1}HQ^{-1} \tag{4.45}$$

and

$$Q = \lim n^{-1}I(\theta).$$

The formal statement is that under H_0

$$\sqrt{n}(\tilde{\theta}_R - \theta) \xrightarrow{D} P\eta, \text{ where } \eta \sim N(0, Q),$$

whilst, for the unrestricted estimator,

$$\sqrt{n}(\tilde{\theta} - \theta) \xrightarrow{D} Q^{-1}\eta.$$

It follows that for the difference, $\sqrt{n}(\tilde{\theta} - \tilde{\theta}_R)$, we have

$$\sqrt{n}(\tilde{\theta} - \tilde{\theta}_R) \xrightarrow{D} (Q^{-1} - P)\eta \sim N[0, (Q^{-1} - P)Q(Q^{-1} - P)].$$

From the definition of P in (4.45), one can show that $PQP = P$ and $(Q^{-1} - P)Q(Q^{-1} - P) = Q^{-1} - P$. Although this matrix is typically singular, we can use a generalisation of the usual transition to the χ^2 distribution (see Rao, 1973: 524) to argue that, under H_0,

$$n(\tilde{\theta} - \tilde{\theta}_R)'Q(\tilde{\theta} - \tilde{\theta}_R) \xrightarrow{D} \chi^2 \sim \chi_g^2. \tag{4.46}$$

The reason why Q appears in the quadratic form on the left of (4.46) is that Q is a generalised inverse for $Q^{-1} - P$.

To compare (4.46) with the likelihood ratio test statistic, equation (4.44) is written as

$$LR \simeq n(\tilde{\theta} - \tilde{\theta}_R)'[-n^{-1}D^2 \ln L(\tilde{\theta})](\tilde{\theta} - \tilde{\theta}_R). \tag{4.47}$$

Under the conditions assumed, the matrix in square brackets on the right of (4.47) converges in probability to Q, and this means that, under H_0, LR has a limiting distribution identical to that in (4.46). This is also the limiting distribution of the Wald test statistic, so the LR and Wald (W) tests are asymptotically equivalent under H_0.

Lagrange multiplier (LM) test

As before, suppose that we have a set of g restrictions which are feasible and which contain no redundancies. The null hypothesis H_0 is that the restrictions are valid. Then consider the following test statistic, which uses quantities based on the restricted ML estimator $\tilde{\theta}_R$. The test statistic is

$$LM = D \ln L(\tilde{\theta}_R)'[I(\tilde{\theta}_R)]^{-1} D \ln L(\tilde{\theta}_R). \tag{4.48}$$

If H_0 is true, we would expect $\tilde{\theta}_R$ to be close to the unrestricted estimator $\tilde{\theta}$, and a Taylor series expansion of $D \ln L(\tilde{\theta}_R)$ about $\tilde{\theta}$ would give the approximation

$$D \ln L(\tilde{\theta}_R) \simeq D \ln L(\tilde{\theta}) + D^2 \ln L(\tilde{\theta})(\tilde{\theta}_R - \tilde{\theta}).$$

Since $D \ln L(\tilde{\theta}) = 0$, this suggests

$$D \ln L(\tilde{\theta}_R) \simeq D^2 \ln L(\tilde{\theta})(\tilde{\theta}_R - \tilde{\theta})$$

and

$$LM \simeq (\tilde{\theta}_R - \tilde{\theta})' D^2 \ln L(\tilde{\theta})'[I(\tilde{\theta}_R)]^{-1} D^2 \ln L(\tilde{\theta})(\tilde{\theta}_R - \tilde{\theta})$$

$$= (\tilde{\theta} - \tilde{\theta}_R)' D^2 \ln L(\tilde{\theta})'[I(\tilde{\theta}_R)]^{-1} D^2 \ln L(\tilde{\theta})(\tilde{\theta} - \tilde{\theta}_R). \tag{4.49}$$

Under the null hypothesis, $\tilde{\theta}_R$ and $\tilde{\theta}$ are both consistent estimators of θ and

$$\text{plim} \, n^{-1} I(\tilde{\theta}_R) = Q$$

$$\text{plim}[-n^{-1} D^2 \ln L(\tilde{\theta})] = Q.$$

From this, it follows that (4.49) is asymptotically equivalent to the quadratic form in (4.46), so if H_0 is true, LM has the same limiting distribution as the LR and Wald test statistics. Hence LM is approximately χ^2, with g degrees of freedom, under H_0.

As mentioned at the outset, the LM test statistic uses only values calculated under H_0, which means values based on the restricted estimator $\tilde{\theta}_R$. Bearing in mind that θ may contain parameters associated with the disturbance process, as well as the more obvious parameters from equations of a model, it is often true that the model under H_0 is much simpler to work with than the model under the alternative H_1. There may thus be a considerable advantage in using an LM test, rather than a Wald or LR test. The former uses only unrestricted estimators, which are appropriate under H_1, and the latter uses both restricted and unrestricted estimators to obtain both restricted and unrestricted values of the maximised log likelihood.

Example 4.2

If the Wald, LR and LM principles are applied to the problem of testing a set of g independent linear restrictions, $H\beta = h$, in the classical linear model, with normal disturbances, the resulting test statistics turn out to be

$$W = (Hb - h)'[H(X'X)^{-1}H']^{-1}(Hb - h)/\tilde{\sigma}^2$$

$$LR = n[\ln(\tilde{\sigma}_R^2/\tilde{\sigma}^2)] = n[\ln(S_R/S)]$$

$$LM = e_R'X(X'X)^{-1}X'e_R/\tilde{\sigma}_R^2.$$

It is simple to demonstrate, using the algebra of section 3.3, that the numerators in the W and LM statistics are identical, and consistency of the estimators $\tilde{\sigma}^2$ and $\tilde{\sigma}_R^2$ is all that is needed, over and above classical assumptions, to demonstrate that W and LM are indeed distributed as χ_g^2 in large samples under the null hypothesis. From the viewpoint of large sample theory, it is irrelevant whether one uses the ML estimators $\tilde{\sigma}^2$ and $\tilde{\sigma}_R^2$, or least squares variants which correct for degrees of freedom.

Turning to the LR statistic, we note that the monotonic transformation

$$(n - k)[\exp(LR/n) - 1]/g$$

is equivalent to the classical F test statistic

$$F = [(S_R - S)/g]/[S/(n - k)].$$

For this reason, the F test is often identified as the statistic which follows from the LR principle, the logic being that W involves only unrestricted (H_1) estimates, LM involves only restricted (H_0) estimates, whilst LR involves both sets of estimates. But in the context of the classical regression model, $(S_R - S)$ is a third algebraically equivalent variant of the numerator in the W and LM test statistics, and the statistic gF differs from W only in that it uses the least squares variant of the unrestricted disturbance variance estimator, rather than the ML variant $\tilde{\sigma}^2 = S/n$.

In the linear regression model, and in a number of other important cases, it is possible to establish the inequality

$$LM \leq LR \leq W. \tag{4.50}$$

The implication of this result is that if an LM test rejects the null hypothesis, or a Wald test fails to reject H_0, there will be no conflict between the three test principles.

4.7 / Instrumental variable estimation

Although maximum likelihood estimation offers obvious theoretical advantages, the properties obtained depend critically on being able to specify a complete and 'correct' model. In practice, it is often convenient to use a procedure that is less demanding in terms of the detail of specification that is required. This is particularly true for a data-based modelling strategy, where one has to work towards an acceptable specification through a series of preliminary experiments. In this section, we consider the alternative of instrumental variable (IV) estimation, which can be motivated as a modification of the least squares method, designed specifically to overcome the problems that arise when some regressors are correlated in the limit with corresponding elements of the disturbance vector.

Suppose that we have the single equation model

$$y = X\beta + u, \text{ with } u_t \sim IID(0, \sigma^2); t = 1, \ldots, n \tag{4.51}$$

where one or more of the columns of X has random elements. Then assume for convenience that

$$\text{plim}(n^{-1}X'X) = Q, \text{ nonsingular}$$

and

$$\text{plim}(n^{-1}X'u) = q.$$

It was shown in section 4.4 that if one or more of the variables in X is correlated in the limit with disturbances, in the sense that, for some X_j,

$$\text{plim } n^{-1} \sum X_{jt}u_t \neq 0,$$

then q is not a zero vector and the OLS estimator is inconsistent.

To find an estimator that is consistent, we may proceed as follows. Suppose that W is an $(n \times p)$ matrix of variables such that $p \geq k$ and

(a) $\text{plim}(n^{-1}W'u) = 0$
(b) $\text{plim}(n^{-1}W'X) = Q_{WX}$, where $\text{rank}(Q_{WX}) = k$ $\tag{4.52}$
(c) $\text{plim}(n^{-1}W'W) = Q_{WW}$, nonsingular.

The first condition requires that the columns of W are uncorrelated with u in the limit. The second condition is more technical but, amongst other things, it requires that there is some correlation in the limit between variables in X and W. However, this is an oversimplification, and a full explanation is given at a later stage. The third condition is the standard assumption concerning the convergence of sample moments for a set of regressor variables, applied here to the variables in W. The assumption of nonsingularity excludes the possibility that such a regression is subject to perfect multicollinearity in the limit as $n \to \infty$.

Now consider the mechanics of the IV method. Instead of a regression of y on X, we first regress the variables in X on the variables in W and take predicted values $\hat{X}$. We then regress y on $\hat{X}$, rather than X, to produce the IV estimator of β. If we are to do this, $W'W$ must be nonsingular in a finite sample, as well as in the limiting sense mentioned above. The process of forming predicted values, by regression of X on W, can be represented as

$$\hat{X} = W(W'W)^{-1}W'X = P_W X, \tag{4.53}$$

where $P_W = W(W'W)^{-1}W'$. The regression of y on $\hat{X}$ then gives the IV estimator, which we denote as $\tilde{b}$:

$$\tilde{b} = (\hat{X}'\hat{X})^{-1}\hat{X}'y. \tag{4.54}$$

Since $\hat{X} = P_W X$ and $P_W = P'_W = P'_W P_W$, the IV estimator can also be written as

$$\tilde{b} = (X' P'_W P_W X)^{-1} X' P'_W y$$

$$= (X' P_W X)^{-1} X' P_W y$$

or

$$\tilde{b} = [X' W (W' W)^{-1} W' X]^{-1} X' W (W' W)^{-1} W' y. \tag{4.55}$$

In a typical application, there are some columns of X that are still nonrandom, and possibly some columns which are random, but which are uncorrelated with u in the limit. In either case, these columns of X can be used as columns of W. If column j of X is identical to column i of W, the regression of X_j on $W_1, \ldots, W_p$ will produce the result

$$\hat{X}_{jt} = 0 W_{1t} + 0 W_{2t} + \ldots + 1 W_{it} + \ldots + 0 W_{pt}$$

$$= W_{it} = X_{jt}; \; t = 1, \ldots, n. \tag{4.56}$$

Equation (4.56) states that columns of X which are also columns of W have predicted values identical to observed values. This is very convenient for the algebra, since it enables us to represent the generation of predicted values as $\hat{X} = P_W X$, despite the fact that, in practice, some columns of X do not actually need to be replaced by predicted values.

So far, we have discussed IV estimation without saying exactly what is meant by a set of instrumental variables. In fact, this is rather awkward. Strictly speaking, the instrumental variables are the predicted values, denoted as $\hat{X}$ above, but the same term is often used for the variables in W, which are used to generate the predicted values. If ambiguity arises, we can talk about predicted values $(\hat{X})$ and generating or conditioning variables (W); alternatively, we can refer to the variables in $\hat{X}$ as instrumental variables and to the variables in W as *instruments*. Unfortunately, conventional usage is somewhat careless on this point, and it is quite common to find both sets of variables described as instrumental variables, or as instruments, without further qualification.

Choice of instruments

In discussing the choice of instruments, we can distinguish between the case in which one formulates a complete model, which purports to show why a given right-hand side variable is correlated with the disturbance term, and the more realistic case in which one wishes to consider the possibility of such correlation, without specifying a complete model.

As a first example, consider the textbook model in which consumers' expenditure C is taken to be a linear function of disposable income D, and D is expressed as the sum of consumers' expenditure and nonconsumption expenditure less taxes on income.

Suppose for convenience that nonconsumption expenditure less taxes on income is treated as a single exogenous variable Z. This simple model may be written as

$$C_t = \alpha + \beta D_t + u_t$$

$$D_t = C_t + Z_t; t = 1, \ldots, n.$$

Since C_t depends on u_t, and D_t depends on C_t, it follows that D_t and u_t are correlated, and under standard assumptions OLS applied to this model will produce inconsistent estimators for α and β. If Z is treated as an exogenous variable, the observations Z_t; $t = 1, \ldots, n$ can be considered to be nonrandom, and if we make standard assumptions about the convergence of $n^{-1} \sum Z_t^2$, and assume well-behaved disturbances, it is easy to show that $\operatorname{plim} n^{-1} \sum Z_t u_t = 0$. This means that Z_t is a suitable instrument, and a further candidate is the 'variable' associated with the intercept parameter α. An IV estimator can therefore be obtained by first regressing D_t on Z_t, with an intercept, taking predicted values $\hat{D}_t$; $t = 1, \ldots, n$, and then regressing C_t on $\hat{D}_t$, again with an intercept, to produce IV estimators for α and β.

By way of contrast, consider the problem of estimating a more realistic consumption function of the type discussed in Example 3.7. There is clearly the possibility of feedback from consumers' expenditure to disposable income, but the actual linkages are far less direct than in the textbook model considered above; and if the linkages are not specified, it is not clear what instruments one would use if IV estimation is to be attempted. In Example 4.3 at the end of this section, we show how one might go about finding an IV estimator in this less structured case.

Two-stage least squares

Since instrumental variable estimators are obtained by applying least squares in two consecutive steps, it is very tempting to describe the method as two-stage least squares. In fact, for historical reasons, this designation is associated with the specific case in which predicted values of right-hand side endogenous variables are generated by regression on all predetermined (exogenous and lagged endogenous) variables in a linear simultaneous equations model (see Chapter 8). This is exactly the rule followed in the first example above. In general, although the IV method is a two-stage procedure, it is not strictly accurate to describe it as two-stage least squares (2SLS), unless the variables in W are chosen by this specific rule.

'Simple' IV estimator

If $p = k$ and $\operatorname{rank}(W'X) = k$, the IV estimator

$$\tilde{b} = [X'W(W'W)^{-1}W'X]^{-1}X'W(W'W)^{-1}W'y$$

collapses to

$$\tilde{b} = (W'X)^{-1}W'y. \tag{4.57}$$

In the early literature on instrumental variables, (4.57) was the standard form for the IV estimator and, in order to distinguish between this special case and the general case (4.55), some authors use the term *generalised* IV estimator (GIVE) for (4.55), whereas (4.57) is a 'simple' IV estimator. This can be interpreted as providing one instrument in W for each variable in X.

Statistical properties

Given the conditions in (4.52), we now show formally that the IV estimator is consistent. Equation (4.55) presents $\tilde{b}$ as

$$\tilde{b} = [X'W(W'W)^{-1}W'X]^{-1}X'W(W'W)^{-1}W'y,$$

and, on substituting for y, we obtain the expression

$$\tilde{b} = \beta + [X'W(W'W)^{-1}W'X]^{-1}X'W(W'W)^{-1}W'u$$

$$= \beta + [n^{-1}X'W(n^{-1}W'W)^{-1}n^{-1}W'X]^{-1}n^{-1}X'W(n^{-1}W'W)^{-1}n^{-1}W'u.$$

Since each of the scaled terms has by assumption a finite probability limit, we have

$$\text{plim}(\tilde{b}) = \beta + [Q'_{WX}Q_{WW}^{-1}Q_{WX}]^{-1}Q'_{WX}Q_{WW}^{-1}0$$

$$= \beta + 0 = \beta. \tag{4.58}$$

This shows that, given suitable instruments, $\tilde{b}$ is consistent.

At the level of generality assumed here, it is difficult to be precise as to the most fundamental conditions under which $\tilde{b}$ is also asymptotically normal. We therefore assume what should really be proved, namely, that as $n \to \infty$, $n^{-1/2}W'u$ converges in distribution to a random vector η, distributed as $N(0, \sigma^2 Q_{WW})$. By Cramér's theorem (see section 4.3) it follows that

$$\sqrt{n}(\tilde{b} - \beta) \xrightarrow{D} [Q'_{WX}Q_{WW}^{-1}Q_{WX}]^{-1}Q'_{WX}Q_{WW}^{-1}\eta \sim N[0, \sigma^2(Q'_{WX}Q_{WW}^{-1}Q_{WX})^{-1}]. \tag{4.59}$$

Although the variance matrix in (4.59) looks complicated, it is not difficult to apply this result to a large finite sample because $Q'_{WX}Q_{WW}^{-1}Q_{WX}$ is the probability limit of $n^{-1}\hat{X}'\hat{X}$. So, in a large finite sample,

$$\tilde{b} \text{ is approximately } N[\beta, \sigma^2 n^{-1}(Q'_{WX}Q_{WW}^{-1}Q_{WX})^{-1}],$$

and $(Q'_{WX}Q'_{WW}Q_{WX})^{-1}$ can be replaced by the consistent estimator $n(\hat{X}'\hat{X})^{-1}$, giving

$$\tilde{b} \text{ is approximately } N[\beta, \sigma^2(\hat{X}'\hat{X})^{-1}], \text{ for large } n. \tag{4.60}$$

To make (4.60) operational, σ^2 must also be replaced by a consistent estimator. An obvious candidate is

$$\tilde{\sigma}^2 = \sum \tilde{e}_t^2/(n-k) \qquad \left[\text{or } \sum \tilde{e}_t^2/n\right] \tag{4.61}$$

where $\tilde{e}_t$; $t = 1, \ldots, n$ are IV residuals, elements of the vector $\tilde{e} = y - X\tilde{b}$. To avoid an extended notation, we have used the same symbol as for the ML estimator of σ^2; if there is any risk of confusion one could use $\tilde{\sigma}^2_{ML}$ and $\tilde{\sigma}^2_{IV}$ respectively.

For the purposes of consistency, it does not matter whether n or $(n - k)$ is used as the divisor in (4.61), but it is usually a good idea to correct for degrees of freedom, since this does make some allowance for the uncertainty inherent in applying asymptotic properties to estimates obtained from a finite sample.

Computation of IV estimates

It is clearly possible to obtain IV estimates by giving a standard regression procedure, first to generate the predicted values in $\hat{X}$, and then to carry out the regression of y on $\hat{X}$. This will give the correct IV estimates, but some of the other output statistics will not be correct, since the second-stage regression would automatically compute residuals as

$$\ddot{e} = y - \hat{X}\tilde{b} \tag{4.62}$$

whereas the correct IV residuals are

$$\tilde{e} = y - X\tilde{b}. \tag{4.63}$$

In (4.63), $\hat{X}$ is replaced by the original values in X, prior to computing the residual vector $\tilde{e}$. If an OLS procedure is used twice, the residuals will be computed as in (4.62), and standard errors, t values, R^2, and certain other statistics will not be calculated correctly. With a program specially designed for IV (or 2SLS) estimation, the residuals will be computed properly, as in (4.63). If this is done, most output statistics are as one would expect them to be, although it must be remembered that test procedures are only justified asymptotically, and there are one or two instances in which the uncritical application of procedures carried over from the least squares case can cause difficulty.

Identification

The IV method embodies certain assumptions about the number of instruments in the matrix W, and about the rank $W'W$ and $W'X$. Recall that W is $(n \times p)$ and that $\hat{X}$ is obtained by regressing the variables in X on the variables in W, and taking predicted values. This procedure requires that $\operatorname{rank}(W) = p$, for otherwise $(W'W)^{-1}$ does not exist. In the second stage, the matrix

$$\hat{X}'\hat{X} = X'W(W'W)^{-1}W'X$$

must be inverted, and this requires that $\operatorname{rank}(W'X) = k$. A necessary, but not sufficient, condition is $p \geq k$.

If W does not contain enough instruments, and $p < k$, the IV procedure will certainly fail. What actually happens is that columns of $\hat{X}$ will be linearly dependent, and the regression of y on $\hat{X}$ will exhibit the symptoms of perfect multicollinearity.

A more subtle problem arises when $\text{plim}(n^{-1}W'X) = Q_{WX}$ has $\text{rank}(Q_{WX}) < k$. This corresponds to a failure of what is known as the *rank* condition for identification, which can be traced back to some characteristic of the more elaborate model that must lie behind the equation $y = X\beta + u$, when one or more of the columns of X has random elements. At the level of generality used here, it is difficult to explain this phenomenon, but it will be discussed in Chapter 8. What is clear is that the necessary condition $p \geq k$ is of great importance: this is the so-called *order* condition for identification, and if it is violated the second stage of the IV estimation procedure cannot succeed.

Exact linear restrictions

To complete this section, we consider the problem of testing a set of g independent linear restrictions, written as $H\beta = h$, when parameter estimates are obtained by the instrumental variable method. Instead of the rather awkward expression used in (4.59), we simplify by writing

$$A = [Q'_{WX}Q^{-1}_{WW}Q_{WX}]^{-1}Q'_{WX}Q^{-1}_{WW}$$

and

$$\sqrt{n}(\tilde{b} - \beta) \xrightarrow{D} A\eta \sim N(0, \sigma^2 AQ_{WW}A')$$

$$\Rightarrow \sqrt{n}H(\tilde{b} - \beta) \xrightarrow{D} HA\eta \sim N(0, \sigma^2 HAQ_{WW}A'H').$$

Under the null hypothesis $H\beta = h$, this becomes

$$\sqrt{n}(H\tilde{b} - h) \xrightarrow{D} HA\eta \sim N(0, \sigma^2 HAQ_{WW}A'H')$$

and

$$n(H\tilde{b} - h)'[HAQ_{WW}A'H']^{-1}(H\tilde{b} - h)/\sigma^2 \xrightarrow{D} \chi^2 \sim \chi^2_g.$$

The expression $AQ_{WW}A'$ is the probability limit of $n(\hat{X}'\hat{X})^{-1}$, so in a large finite sample

$$(H\tilde{b} - h)'[H(\hat{X}'\hat{X})^{-1}H']^{-1}(H\tilde{b} - h)/\sigma^2 \text{ is approximately } \chi^2_g, \text{ under } H_0: H\beta = h.$$

(4.64)

If σ^2 is replaced by a consistent estimator, for example $\tilde{\sigma}^2$ from (4.61), this gives an operational large sample test.

Computation of test statistics

The test statistic in (4.64) is very similar to that obtained for OLS estimation and, as in the least squares case, it is possible to find a computationally convenient form. However, this is one of the places in which some care is needed. Whereas the OLS estimator minimises the sum of squares function $S(\beta) = (y - X\beta)'(y - X\beta)$, the IV estimator minimises

$$S_{\text{IV}}(\beta) = (y - X\beta)' W (W' W)^{-1} W'(y - X\beta)$$

$$= (y - X\beta)' P_W (y - X\beta). \qquad (4.65)$$

The first-order conditions for this minimisation are

$$X' P_W (y - X\beta) = 0$$

and the value of β that satisfies these conditions is the IV estimator (4.55). The orthogonality conditions for unrestricted IV estimation are $X' P_W \tilde{e} = \hat{X}' \tilde{e} = 0$, where $\tilde{e} = y - X\tilde{b}$ is the vector of unrestricted IV residuals.

If (4.65) is minimised subject to the conditions $H\beta = h$, it is possible to obtain the restricted IV estimator

$$\tilde{b}_{\text{R}} = \tilde{b} - (\hat{X}'\hat{X})^{-1} H'[H(\hat{X}'\hat{X})^{-1} H']^{-1}(H\tilde{b} - h).$$

Then, using $\tilde{e}_{\text{R}}$ to denote restricted IV residuals, we have

$$\tilde{e}_{\text{R}} = y - X\tilde{b}_{\text{R}}$$

$$= y - X\{\tilde{b} - (\hat{X}'\hat{X})^{-1} H'[H(\hat{X}'\hat{X})^{-1} H']^{-1}(H\tilde{b} - h)\}$$

$$= \tilde{e} + X(\hat{X}'\hat{X})^{-1} H'[H(\hat{X}'\hat{X})^{-1} H']^{-1}(H\tilde{b} - h). \qquad (4.66)$$

On forming the sum of squares $\tilde{e}_{\text{R}}'\tilde{e}_{\text{R}}$, the cross-product from the right of (4.66) does not disappear since, in general, $X'\tilde{e} \neq 0$. Consequently, the difference $\tilde{e}_{\text{R}}'\tilde{e}_{\text{R}} - \tilde{e}'\tilde{e}$ is not equal to the numerator in (4.64).

To obtain a short-cut formula similar to that for the least squares case, we have to consider the IV criterion function $S_{\text{IV}}(\beta) = (y - X\beta)' P_W (y - X\beta)$. The sum of squares corresponding to the criterion function does partition, to give

$$\tilde{e}_{\text{R}}' P_W \tilde{e}_{\text{R}} = \tilde{e}' P_W \tilde{e} + (H\tilde{b} - h)'[H(\hat{X}'\hat{X})^{-1} H']^{-1}(H\tilde{b} - h).$$

The quadratic form in the numerator of (4.64) can therefore be calculated as

$$S_{\text{IV}}(\tilde{b}_{\text{R}}) - S_{\text{IV}}(\tilde{b}) = \tilde{e}_{\text{R}}' P_W \tilde{e}_{\text{R}} - \tilde{e}' P_W \tilde{e}. \qquad (4.67)$$

If the computer program can evaluate (4.64) directly, only the unrestricted IV estimation is performed and the test routine takes care of the calculation of the test statistic. If no such procedure is available, but the program gives the unrestricted and restricted values of the IV criterion function, the left-hand side of (4.67) can be used to evaluate the numerator of (4.64). If all else fails, the value of the numerator can be obtained by performing both restricted and unrestricted IV estimation, saving $\tilde{e}_{\text{R}}$ and $\tilde{e}$, and regressing each in turn on the instruments in W. The expression on the right of (4.67) is equivalent to the difference between the sums of *predicted* values from these regressions.

At the risk of complicating the argument, we can add that if the computer program can be made to calculate the 'incorrect' residuals (4.62), and the equivalent 'incorrect' restricted residuals

$$\ddot{e}_{\mathrm{R}} = y - \hat{X}\tilde{b}_{\mathrm{R}},$$

then the numerator of the test statistic can be evaluated as $\ddot{e}'_{\mathrm{R}}\ddot{e}_{\mathrm{R}} - \ddot{e}'\ddot{e}$, since this difference can be shown to be algebraically equal to both sides of (4.67).

Example 4.3

In Example 3.7, we used OLS to estimate the parameters of the model

$$\ln(C_t) = \beta_1 + \beta_2 \ln(D_t) + \beta_3 \Delta_4 \ln(P_t) + \beta_4 \ln(L_{t-1}) + \beta_5 Q_{2t} + \beta_6 Q_{3t} + \beta_7 Q_{4t}$$
$$+ u_t; \; t = 1, \ldots, n,$$

where Q_2, Q_3 and Q_4 are quarterly dummy variables, and the other regressors are as defined in the earlier exercise. Although we found some problems with this equation, we can still use it to illustrate the *mechanics* of the IV method, in the case in which we do not have an explicit wider model from which to draw suitable instruments.

Suppose that we focus on the possibility that D_t is influenced by feedback from C_t; in the context of a wider model, this would make D_t endogenous, and possibly correlated with u_t. For the purposes of this exercise, we assume that all the other variables are not correlated in the limit with u_t. If this is so, the list of instruments must first include 1, $\Delta_4 \ln(P_t)$, $\ln(L_{t-1})$, Q_{2t}, Q_{3t} and Q_{4t}, where 1 is a shorthand for the variable that allows for an intercept term. But there must also be other instruments, which would be exogenous, or at least predetermined, in a wider model. There is clearly some arbitrariness in selecting likely variables; for the purposes of this exercise we have chosen the logarithms of real government expenditure, real exports, the average direct tax rate and labour productivity. There is no guarantee that these are acceptable instruments, and in due course we shall consider a test of validity, but they will suffice for the purposes of illustration. The results of the IV estimation are given in Table 4.1, and may be compared with the corresponding OLS results given as Version 2 in Table 3.3.

The fact that there is not a great deal of difference between the OLS and IV results suggests that, in this particular case, there may not have been a strong justification for using the IV method, though, as we see below, this is testable. The other main point to note is that we still do not have sufficient routine tests for OLS, let alone IV, and, if nothing else, this example is likely to exhibit serial correlation because it is an essentially static representation of the relationship between consumer's expenditure and income. Further details on the interpretation of the computer output from IV estimation are given in Chapter 7.

To conclude this section, we mention two further test procedures that are routinely used in conjunction with instrumental variable estimation. The first asks whether it is actually necessary to use the IV method, by testing the null hypothesis of 'exogeneity' of the variables for which predicted values (instrumental variables) would otherwise

Table 4.1 Quarterly consumption function

Sample based on observations 1964(1)–1995(2)

IV estimation:
Instrumental variables formed for: LNRPDI
Instruments used: INTER D4LPCONS LNRLIQ(−1) Q2 Q3 Q4 LNRGOV
LNRXPR LNDTR LNPRODY
Dependent variable is LNRCONS

Variable	Coefficient	Standard error	t value
INTER	−0.1767	0.061 20	−2.888
LNRPDI	0.9432	0.018 50	50.975
D4LPCONS	−0.1329	0.053 49	−2.484
LNRLIQ(1)	0.0569	0.022 09	2.574
Q2	0.0078	0.005 4	1.445
Q3	0.0380	0.005 5	6.945
Q4	0.0602	0.005 5	10.967

Degrees of freedom 119 from 126 observations

Residual SS	5.5765×10^{-2}
Total SS	6.6626
Disturbance variance	4.6861×10^{-4}
R^2	0.9916
IV objective function	2.4723×10^{-2}

be formed in the IV estimation. The second test assumes that IV estimation is used, and asks whether the chosen instruments are valid.

Hausman–Wu exogeneity test

If we anticipate a more explicit notation that is developed in Chapter 8, we can write any single equation for which IV estimation is contemplated as

$$y = X\beta + u = Y_1\alpha + Z_1\gamma + u, \tag{4.68}$$

where Y_1 contains r variables which are considered to be potentially correlated with disturbances and Z_1 contains $k - r$ variables which are taken without question to be uncorrelated with disturbances. Although the formal basis of the test is somewhat involved, we are concerned to ask whether $\text{plim}(n^{-1}Y_1'u) = \delta$ is such that $\delta = 0$. A relatively simple way of achieving this is to first estimate (4.68) by OLS, giving residual sum of squares S_0, and then to add the predicted values (instrumental variables) $\hat{Y}_1$ to this regression, estimating again by OLS, to give residual sum of squares S_1. There are several variants of the test statistic that are asymptotically equivalent under the null (assuming that no other 'problems' are present), but the general approach can be summarised by the statement

$$\chi^2(E) = (S_0 - S_1)/\hat{\sigma}^2 \text{ is approximately } \chi_r^2 \text{ under } H_0, \tag{4.69}$$

where $\chi^2(E)$ signifies that this is a χ^2 test of exogeneity, $\hat{\sigma}^2$ is any estimator of σ^2 that is consistent under the null hypothesis and r is the number of columns in Y_1. A large value of the test statistic rejects exogeneity, and shows that IV estimation is needed.

This procedure was first suggested by Wu (1973), who proposed implementation as an F test. It is also a special case of a more general test method suggested by Hausman (1978). For a discussion of the Hausman test and the various methods of implementation, see Godfrey (1988: 28–34, 191–9).

If the procedure suggested above is to be applied to the data used in Example 4.3, a second OLS regression is needed, which includes the single predicted value or instrumental variable corresponding to LNRPDI, as well as LNRPDI in original form. This regression gives $RSS = S_1 = 5.5754 \times 10^{-2}$, and if σ^2 is estimated from the original OLS regression, we obtain

$$\chi^2(E) = [(5.5765 - 5.5754) \times 10^{-2}]/4.6861 \times 10^{-4} = 0.2347.$$

Since only a single variable is under test, $r = 1$. The 5% critical value is 3.84, so that the null hypothesis of the exogeneity of income is accepted, and according to this test, OLS estimation is acceptable.

Sargan 'validity of instruments' test

If instrumental variable estimation is used, it is important to check the assumptions underlying the choice of instruments. In the example considered above, the specification of any linkage from consumers' expenditure to income is vague, but one can still check in a general way on the performance of instruments chosen.

The criterion function that is minimised by selecting an IV estimator is

$$S_{IV}(\beta) = (y - X\beta)'P_W(y - X\beta)$$

and the minimum value obtained is $\tilde{e}'P_W\tilde{e}$. The Sargan test statistic is formed from this as

$$\chi^2(V) = S_{IV}(\tilde{b})/\tilde{\sigma}^2 = \tilde{e}'P_W\tilde{e}/\tilde{\sigma}^2, \qquad (4.70)$$

where $\chi^2(V)$ signifies the validity of instruments test and $\tilde{\sigma}^2$ is the IV estimator of the disturbance variance. Under the null hypothesis that the instruments in W are valid (and the model is correctly specified), the test statistic $\chi^2(V)$ has an approximate χ^2 distribution with $(p - k)$ degrees of freedom, where p is the number of instruments and k is the number of regressors on the right of the equation to be estimated. A high value of $\chi^2(V)$ indicates rejection of the null hypothesis, and suggests in a rather nonspecific manner that there is something wrong with the model and/or the list of instruments used.

If the program used does not give the Sargan test or the minimum value of the IV criterion, it is possible to generate $\tilde{e}'P_W\tilde{e}$ by regressing the IV residual vector $\tilde{e}$ on W, and taking the sum of squares of predicted values. This quantity is the same as that used earlier when considering a test of exact restrictions. In the case of the IV estimation shown in Table 4.1, $p = 10$, $k = 7$ and $\chi^2(V) = 52.76$. The 5% critical value is

7.81, so this estimation rejects the null hypothesis, and fails the Sargan test. Given that the instruments were chosen in a rather arbitrary fashion, the result may not be too surprising, but there are several possible explanations for such a failure, given that we have not completed our development of the underlying equation.

4.8 / Further reading

The same texts as mentioned in Chapters 2 and 3 are useful, as also the standard reference, White (1984).

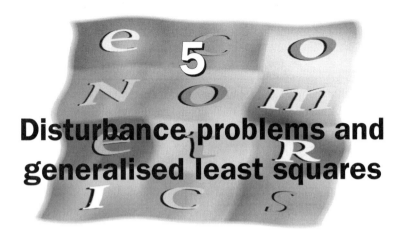

5
Disturbance problems and generalised least squares

5.1 / Introduction

Although we have now introduced maximum likelihood and instrumental variable estimation, as well as the least squares principle, we have assumed throughout our earlier discussion that individual elements of the disturbance vector are at least uncorrelated, and have constant variance. In this chapter, we consider the implications of the more general specification

$$\text{var}(u) = \Sigma, \text{ where } \Sigma \text{ is positive definite (pd).} \tag{5.1}$$

Two important theoretical problems are heteroscedasticity and serial correlation. Heteroscedasticity occurs when the disturbance variance is not constant for $t = 1, \ldots, n$, and implies that the diagonal elements of Σ are not identical. Serial correlation arises when at least one value of $\text{cov}(u_t, u_s)$ is nonzero, for $s \neq t$, and this implies that at least one off-diagonal element of Σ is nonzero. Further problems arise when we admit the possibility of a model containing more than one equation, because the disturbances from one equation may be correlated with disturbances from a second equation. In this chapter, the emphasis is on the topic of heteroscedasticity. The key question of testing is also considered: one can only take steps to deal with a 'problem' if that problem is known to exist, or is shown by a test to be present in a particular case. The topic of serial correlation is discussed in detail in Chapters 6 and 7, whilst multiple equation models are dealt with in Chapter 8.

Before considering how estimation methods are modified to allow for the new specification in (5.1), we should briefly explain why Σ is assumed to be positive definite. It is obvious that no random variable can have negative variance, and if Σ is not at least positive semidefinite (psd), one or more linear combinations of the elements of u would define new random variables with negative variance. The fact that Σ is assumed to be positive definite rather than just positive semidefinite is a convenience; at this stage, we do not want the added complexity of a singular covariance matrix.

Given that Σ is positive definite, it is always possible to find an $(n \times n)$ matrix L, such that $L'L = \Sigma^{-1}$, and $L\Sigma L' = I_n$. Such matrices are not unique, but one possibility is to make L lower triangular, and to use a process known as the Choleski decomposition to solve the equation system $L'L = \Sigma^{-1}$. This constitutes a proof by construction – the fact that a solution can be obtained proves that L exists, and for our purposes this is sufficient.

In some cases, there is a natural scale factor, corresponding to σ^2 in the simpler specification $\mathrm{var}(u) = \sigma^2 I$. If this is so, we can write

$$\mathrm{var}(u) = \Sigma = \sigma^2 V, \text{ where } V \text{ is pd}, \tag{5.2}$$

and the decomposition above is applied to V^{-1} rather than to Σ^{-1}. It is often more convenient to use this form, but there is no difficulty in switching because the decomposition of V^{-1} and the decomposition of Σ^{-1} produce L matrices which differ only by a scale factor equal to the positive square root of σ^2.

In the next section, we introduce the generalised least squares estimator, but before doing so we need to motivate by showing why the OLS estimator is now deficient. Given the model

$$y = X\beta + u; \ X \text{ nonrandom}; \ E(u) = 0;$$

$$\mathrm{var}(u) = \sigma^2 V, \text{ where } V \text{ is pd}, \tag{5.3}$$

the OLS estimator is

$$b = (X'X)^{-1}X'y$$

$$= \beta + (X'X)^{-1}X'u.$$

If $E(u) = 0$, b is still unbiased, but the variance of b is

$$\mathrm{var}(b) = (X'X)^{-1}X' \cdot \mathrm{var}(u) \cdot X(X'X)^{-1}$$

$$= \sigma^2 (X'X)^{-1}X'VX(X'X)^{-1}. \tag{5.4}$$

This means that the conventional least squares variance formula is now wrong; moreover, although (5.4) does not reveal the fact directly, the OLS estimator is no longer best linear unbiased (BLU). This we show indirectly in the next section by finding a different estimator which is BLU.

Continuing with our brief review of OLS when $\mathrm{var}(u) = \sigma^2 V$, note that if u is (multivariate) normal, b is still normal. But the disturbance variance estimator $\hat{\sigma}^2$ is now generally biased, and this compounds the error inherent in using conventional t and F tests. Although b is still an unbiased estimator, standard OLS inference procedures applied to a model corresponding to (5.3) could lead to quite seriously misleading results.

5.2 / Generalised least squares

In theory, the extension of the least squares principle to deal with the case in which $\mathrm{var}(u) = \sigma^2 V$ [or $\mathrm{var}(u) = \Sigma$] is straightforward. To start with, V is assumed to be a known positive definite matrix, and this means that we can find a nonsingular $(n \times n)$ matrix L, such that $L'L = V^{-1}$ and $LVL' = I_n$. Then, given the model

$$y = X\beta + u; \ X \text{ nonrandom}; \ E(u) = 0; \ \text{var}(u) = \sigma^2 V, \tag{5.5}$$

it is possible to transform to

$$Ly = LX\beta + Lu, \tag{5.6}$$

where LX is nonrandom, $E(Lu) = LE(u) = 0$ and

$$\text{var}(Lu) = L \cdot \text{var}(u) \cdot L' = L(\sigma^2 V)L' = \sigma^2 LVL' = \sigma^2 I.$$

Since (5.6) satisfies all the classical assumptions, it follows that least squares applied to (5.6) must give a best linear unbiased estimator. With reference to the *transformed* model, this estimator is indeed OLS, but with reference to the original model, it is not. Instead, we use the term *generalised* least squares (GLS), and we write the estimator as b_G. An expression for the estimator can be found by applying OLS to (5.6). This gives

$$b_G = [(LX)'(LX)]^{-1}(LX)'Ly$$

$$= (X'L'LX)^{-1}X'L'Ly$$

$$= (X'V^{-1}X)^{-1}X'V^{-1}y. \tag{5.7}$$

To analyse the properties of the estimator b_G, one can substitute for y in (5.7), and follow the steps used for the OLS estimator in section 2.4. However, this is not necessary; since GLS is equivalent to OLS applied to a transformed model which satisfies classical assumptions, b_G must be best linear unbiased, with

$$\text{var}(b_G) = \sigma^2[(LX)'(LX)]^{-1} = \sigma^2(X'V^{-1}X)^{-1}. \tag{5.8}$$

Moreover, if u is normal, b_G is normal, and analysis of the transformed model produces whatever other details we need. For example,

$$\hat{\sigma}_G^2 = (Ly - LXb_G)'(Ly - LXb_G)/(n-k)$$

must be an unbiased estimator of σ^2, and this corresponds to

$$\hat{\sigma}_G^2 = e_G'L'Le_G/(n-k) = e_G'V^{-1}e_G/(n-k), \tag{5.9}$$

where $e_G = y - Xb_G$ is the GLS residual vector.

Continuing in this way, one can find the GLS estimator subject to a set of g independent linear restrictions $H\beta = h$. This is done by applying the restricted OLS estimator (see section 3.3) to the transformed model, giving

$$b_{GR} = b_G - (X'L'LX)^{-1}H'[H(X'L'LX)^{-1}H']^{-1}(Hb_G - h)$$

$$= b_G - (X'V^{-1}X)^{-1}H'[H(X'V^{-1}X)^{-1}H']^{-1}(Hb_G - h). \tag{5.10}$$

An F test for the validity of the restrictions can be obtained by showing that the quadratic form

$$(Hb_G - h)'[H(X'V^{-1}X)^{-1}H']^{-1}(Hb_G - h)/\sigma^2 \qquad (5.11)$$

is distributed as χ_g^2 under $H_0: H\beta = h$, and then showing that the quadratic form is independent of $\hat{\sigma}_G^2$, defined in (5.9).

As before, we find that a computationally convenient form for a test of exact restrictions follows from showing that the numerator in (5.11) is equivalent to the difference between restricted and unrestricted values of the criterion function that is minimised to obtain the GLS estimator. If we seek to obtain the GLS estimator directly, rather than by application of OLS to the transformed model, we find that the unrestricted GLS estimator minimises the value of

$$S_G(\beta) = (y - X\beta)'V^{-1}(y - X\beta). \qquad (5.12)$$

The orthogonality conditions resulting from this minimisation are $X'V^{-1}e_G = 0$, and, using this condition, together with expression (5.10) for the restricted GLS estimator, one can show that

$$S_G(b_{GR}) - S_G(b_G) = e'_{GR}V^{-1}e_{GR} - e'_G V^{-1}e_G$$

$$= (Hb_G - h)'[H(X'V^{-1}X)^{-1}H']^{-1}(Hb_G - h),$$

where $e_{GR} = y - Xb_{GR}$. Consequently, a valid F test statistic for $H_0: H\beta = h$ can be written as

$$F = \{[S_G(b_{GR}) - S_G(b_G)]/g\}/[S_G(b_G)/(n - k)],$$

where

$$S_G(b_G) = e'_G V^{-1}e_G = e'_G L'Le_G$$

and

$$S_G(b_{GR}) = e'_{GR}V^{-1}e_{GR} = e'_{GR}L'Le_{GR}.$$

These are simply the unrestricted and restricted residual sums of squares computed from the transformed model. In short, the theoretical GLS estimator has properties which exactly parallel those of the OLS estimator, and correct expressions can always be obtained by applying the corresponding arguments for OLS estimation to the transformed equation (5.6).

It is perhaps surprising that one can state a simple condition under which the OLS and GLS estimators in the model (5.5) are actually *identical*. The implication is that when the condition holds, both the estimators are BLU. As might be imagined, this condition depends crucially on the natures of X and V, and can be generated by thinking of the GLS and OLS estimators as instrumental variable estimators. The 'simple' IV estimator (4.57) using instrument matrix $W_G = V^{-1}X$ generates the GLS estimator (5.7), whilst instrument matrix $W = X$ generates the OLS estimator b. For these two IV estimators to coincide, the required condition is that the instruments must be related by a nonsingular transformation

$W_G = WA$; A nonsingular

or

$$V^{-1}X = XA. \tag{5.13}$$

The logic of the condition is that $V^{-1}X$ in (5.7) can be replaced by XA, and then the matrix A is cancelled out to yield the OLS estimator b. This condition is largely of theoretical interest, although there is an application of this result in Chapter 8. The intuition behind the result is that W_G and W are effectively equivalent as instruments when (5.13) holds.

Feasible GLS

Unfortunately, in practice, things are not quite so easy. There is seldom any reason to suppose that V would consist entirely of known elements, and this means that estimation has to proceed in two steps. In the first step, unknown elements of V are estimated, usually from OLS residuals. In the second step, the estimated matrix $\hat{V}$ is used in place of V, giving the *feasible* GLS estimator

$$b_G = (X'\hat{V}^{-1}X)^{-1}X'\hat{V}^{-1}y. \tag{5.14}$$

Since GLS almost always implies feasible GLS, we shall not introduce special notation for the feasible GLS estimator, and b_G is now understood to imply feasible GLS, unless explicitly stated to be otherwise.

If elements of V have to be estimated, the transformed equation corresponding to (5.6) is now

$$\hat{L}y = \hat{L}X\beta + \hat{L}u \tag{5.15}$$

where $\hat{L}'\hat{L} = \hat{V}^{-1}$ and $\hat{L}\hat{V}\hat{L}' = I_n$. The transformation suggested by (5.15) has very different implications from that in (5.6), because $\hat{L}$ is random, and the application of least squares to (5.15) is equivalent to OLS when the regressor matrix has random elements. Finite sample analysis is far less straightforward than before, and the feasible GLS method is usually evaluated by looking at large sample properties. The following are 'standard' assumptions:

1. As $n \to \infty$, $\lim(n^{-1}X'V^{-1}X) = Q_V$, nonsingular;
2. $\text{plim}[n^{-1}X'(\hat{V}^{-1} - V^{-1})X] = 0$;
3. $\text{plim}[n^{-1/2}X'(\hat{V}^{-1} - V^{-1})u] = 0$.

Condition (1) is used together with the assumption that the elements of Lu are independent and identically distributed to ensure that the theoretical GLS estimator is consistent and asymptotically normal. Under conditions (2) and (3), the feasible GLS estimator b_G is asymptotically equivalent to the theoretical GLS estimator, and is therefore also consistent and asymptotically normal. In a large finite sample, this leads to the result

b_G is approximately $N[\beta, \sigma^2(X'\hat{V}^{-1}X)^{-1}]$. (5.16)

Standard inference procedures follow in the usual way. Essentially, these results mean that, in large samples, one can ignore the consequences of having to estimate elements of the V matrix. However, in a small finite sample, it is actually possible for feasible GLS to be less efficient than OLS.

ML and IV estimation

If maximum likelihood or instrumental variable estimation is applied to a model in which $\text{var}(u) = \sigma^2 V$ [or $\text{var}(u) = \Sigma$], both principles give straightforward and predictable results when V (or Σ) is known. Assuming that the model is as shown in (5.5), and that u is multivariate normal, the ML estimator of β is identical to the theoretical GLS estimator, and the ML estimator of σ^2 differs only in its use of n, rather than $(n - k)$, as a divisor. If X has random columns and an IV estimator is to be used, one can use arguments similar to those of section 4.7, except that one would first transform to give

$Ly = LX\beta + Lu$

and then generate instrumental variables for LX, rather than for X.

If V is not known, then elements of V become part of the parameter vector to be estimated by ML, and the ML estimator of β is no longer necessarily the same as the GLS estimator. In the case of IV estimation, the procedure adopted is analogous to feasible GLS rather than theoretical GLS. Since IV is justified by asymptotic arguments anyway, this should not, in principle, make much difference but, as always, there are detailed technical conditions to be satisfied.

To make progress with a more detailed discussion of feasible GLS, or alternatives such as ML or IV estimation, it is necessary to be more specific as to the particular problem which gives rise to a model such as (5.5). In the following section, we consider the specific problem of heteroscedasticity, leaving the issues of serial correlation to be dealt with in Chapter 7, and the disturbance problems that arise in the context of a model with more than one equation to Chapter 8.

5.3 / Heteroscedasticity

At one level, it could be argued that heteroscedasticity and homoscedasticity (constant disturbance variance) are simply alternative logical possibilities; so having given attention to the homoscedastic case, one must also consider heteroscedasticity. If this line of reasoning is followed, it would seem natural to include a test for heteroscedasticity as part of the standard toolkit for model evaluation. The only problem with such a strategy is that heteroscedasticity can take many forms, and it is not obvious which of these forms should be used to devise a standard test. This is clearly something that we need to consider, but first we look at an alternative reason for heteroscedasticity, namely, that its presence is suggested by 'theory', rather than by 'data'.

Suppose that we have a model which purports to represent the expenditure decisions of households. Then suppose that there are two households which are identical in terms of the level of income, and which also have identical values of any other explanatory variables considered to be relevant. If the expenditure behaviour of the two households is then seen to be different, the model would attribute this to random behaviour, as represented by the disturbance term. The question to be answered is whether all households have the same degree of 'randomness', as measured by the disturbance variance, or whether some households are 'more random' than others. One traditional argument is that high-income households have more discretion in choosing expenditure patterns than low-income households; if this is so, the disturbance variance would be linked to the level of income, and this suggests not only the presence of heteroscedasticity, but also the particular pattern required.

In practice, it must be admitted that the boundary between heteroscedasticity as suggested by examination of the data and heteroscedasticity as a theoretical property of a model does become blurred. In the example above, what happens is likely to depend crucially on the regressors that are present in the equation to be estimated; but this is also the case with an experimental strategy that would allow for heteroscedasticity in estimation only when all means of respecifying the main part of the model have been exhausted. Having made this point, we start our discussion from the traditional perspective of having some pattern of heteroscedasticity in mind, and examining the theoretical consequences of this for estimation.

Alternative patterns of heteroscedasticity

For convenience, we assume a linear model

$$y = X\beta + u$$

with X nonrandom and $E(u_t) = 0$. The first type of heteroscedastic behaviour that we consider is where var(u) is proportional to the value of some observable variable Z. This gives

$$\text{var}(u_t) = \sigma_t^2 = \delta Z_t; \ \delta > 0; \ t = 1, \ldots, n. \tag{5.17}$$

In the example discussed above, Z would be some measure of income. In other cases, Z can be any variable that is included in the regressor matrix X, or a transformation of such a variable, or a new variable, which does not appear in X. If (5.17) is used it is important that Z takes only positive values, preferably well away from zero. To avoid the obvious difficulties that would arise if (5.17) were to generate negative variances, one might decide to make Z equal to the square of some observable variable. Alternatively, one could write

$$\text{var}(u_t) = \sigma_t^2 = \delta Z_t^2; \ \delta > 0; \ t = 1, \ldots, n. \tag{5.18}$$

Continuing in this way, we can build up a whole series of possible specifications; some of the more common forms are listed below:

1. $\mathrm{var}(u_t) = \sigma_t^2 = \delta Z_t; \; \delta > 0; \; t = 1, \ldots, n;$
2. $\mathrm{var}(u_t) = \sigma_t^2 = \delta Z_t^2; \; \delta > 0; \; t = 1, \ldots, n;$
3. $\mathrm{var}(u_t) = \sigma_t^2 = \delta_1 + \delta_2 Z_t; \; \delta_1 > 0; \; t = 1, \ldots, n;$
4. $\mathrm{var}(u_t) = \sigma_t^2 = \exp(\delta_1 + \delta_2 Z_t); \; t = 1, \ldots, n;$
5. $\mathrm{var}(u_t) = \sigma_1^2; \; t = 1, \ldots, n_1;$
   $\qquad\quad = \sigma_2^2; \; t = n_1 + 1, \ldots, n.$

Specification (3) extends the proportionality hypothesis in (1) and (2) to a linear function of Z (where Z may actually be the square of some original variable), and admits the possibility of testing the null hypothesis of constant variance against the alternative of heteroscedasticity, by testing to see whether $\delta_2 = 0$. This case is known as *additive* heteroscedasticity. Specification (4) is similar, but represents heteroscedasticity in a *multiplicative* form:

$$\mathrm{var}(u_t) = \sigma_t^2 = \exp(\delta_1 + \delta_2 Z_t)$$
$$\Rightarrow \sigma_t^2 = \exp(\delta_1) \cdot \exp(\delta_2 Z_t); \; t = 1, \ldots, n. \tag{5.19}$$

Specification (5) is representative of the discrete switching case. In the particular example given, the disturbance variance is constant over observations 1 to n_1, and then switches to a new value for observations $n_1 + 1$ to n. A similar example can occur with quarterly data, when the disturbance variance is different in different quarters of the year, but is identical for observations relating to the same quarter of different years.

Some of the specifications above are clearly special cases of others, and discrete switching patterns can usually be accommodated within forms similar to (3) or (4), by use of dummy variables. Both (3) and (4) are readily extended to deal with more than one conditioning variable. Thus the linear or additive form can be extended to

$$\mathrm{var}(u_t) = \sigma_t^2 = \delta_1 + \delta_2 Z_{2t} + \ldots + \delta_p Z_{pt} \tag{5.20}$$

or

$$\mathrm{var}(u_t) = \sigma_t^2 = z_t' \delta; \; t = 1, \ldots, n,$$

where z_t' is a row vector with elements $1, Z_{2t}, \ldots, Z_{pt}$ and δ is a $(p \times 1)$ vector of parameters. Similarly, the multiplicative form can be extended to

$$\mathrm{var}(u_t) = \sigma_t^2 = \exp(\delta_1 + \delta_2 Z_{2t} + \ldots + \delta_p Z_{pt}) \tag{5.21}$$

or

$$\mathrm{var}(u_t) = \sigma_t^2 = \exp(z_t' \delta); \; t = 1, \ldots, n.$$

Theoretical GLS

Each of the specifications above shows how diagonal elements of V (or Σ) are determined. The off-diagonal elements are zero, and this means that the inverse matrix is also diagonal, with

$$(V^{-1})_{tt} = 1/V_{tt}.$$

A similar relationship holds for Σ and Σ^{-1}. Since theoretical GLS implies that both the form of heteroscedasticity and any parameters in the specification are known, it is very easy to obtain the theoretical GLS estimator. Suppose, for simplicity, that we have a two-variable model, written as

$$Y_t = \alpha + \beta X_t + u_t, \text{ with } E(u_t) = 0 \tag{5.22}$$

and

$$\text{var}(u_t) = \sigma_t^2 = \delta Z_t^2; \; t = 1, \ldots, n.$$

The variance specification in (5.22) can be written as $\text{var}(u) = \sigma^2 V$, with $\sigma^2 = \delta$ and $V_{tt} = Z_t^2$; or as $\text{var}(u) = \Sigma$, with $\Sigma_{tt} = \delta Z_t^2$. Of the two possible forms, the first is better, since δ could be treated as unknown. V^{-1} has diagonal elements $1/Z_t^2$, and from the relationship $L'L = V^{-1}$, we can deduce that L is also diagonal, with on-diagonal elements equal to the positive square root of $1/Z_t^2$. This suggests that the original model should be transformed as

$$(Y_t/Z_t) = \alpha(1/Z_t) + \beta(X_t/Z_t) + (u_t/Z_t) \tag{5.23}$$

where

$$\text{var}(u_t/Z_t) = \text{var}(u_t)/Z_t^2 = \delta = \sigma^2; \; t = 1, \ldots, n. \tag{5.24}$$

The transformed equation (5.23) is homoscedastic, and ordinary least squares applied to this equation defines the GLS estimator for the parameters of the original model (5.22). In the transformed model, there is no longer a 'variable' always equal to 1; the parameter α is now attached to the 'genuine' variable $(1/Z)$. Note also that the use of a two-variable model is simply a convenience – exactly the same transformation would be applied to all the regressors in the more general case.

Now consider one of the more elaborate specifications given above. This time, we assume that the underlying model has k regressors, and that the model is written in row form as

$$y_t = x_t'\beta + u_t; \; E(u_t) = 0; \; t = 1, \ldots, n.$$

The disturbance variance is given by

$$\text{var}(u_t) = \sigma_t^2 = \exp(\delta_1 + \delta_2 Z_{2t} + \ldots + \delta_p Z_{pt}); t = 1, \ldots, n.$$

If $\delta_1, \ldots, \delta_p$ were known, one would use this expression to calculate values for each σ_t^2; $t = 1, \ldots, n$, and then transform the original model as

$$(y_t/\sigma_t) = (x_t'/\sigma_t)\beta + (u_t/\sigma_t); \; t = 1, \ldots, n. \tag{5.25}$$

In practice, this cannot be done, but essentially the same transformation is used for the feasible GLS estimator, the difference being that the parameters $\delta_1, \ldots, \delta_p$ are first estimated from OLS residuals.

Testing for heteroscedasticity

Unfortunately, there is no one test that is accepted as the standard test for heteroscedasticity. Indeed, over the years, many possible approaches have been suggested. To give some idea of the issues involved, we look at two types of test, one using exact finite sample theory and the other based on large sample arguments.

To set the scene for the group of small sample tests, consider the following problem. Suppose that there are two subsamples of data, one with n_1 observations and the other with n_2 observations, where both n_1 and n_2 are greater than the number of regressors k. Then consider two separate regression models, corresponding to the two subsamples, where the models are written as

$$y_1 = X_1\beta_1 + u_1; \; u_1 \sim N(0, \sigma_1^2 I_1)$$

$$y_2 = X_2\beta_2 + u_2; \; u_2 \sim N(0, \sigma_2^2 I_2). \tag{5.26}$$

In (5.26), X_1 and X_2 are nonrandom, and I_1, I_2 are identity matrices with dimensions $(n_1 \times n_1)$ and $(n_2 \times n_2)$ respectively. The disturbance vectors u_1, u_2 are considered to be independent.

If OLS is applied separately to the two subsamples, giving residual sums of squares S_1 and S_2, then standard regression theory indicates that S_1/σ_1^2 and S_2/σ_2^2 both have χ^2 distributions, the first with $(n_1 - k)$ degrees of freedom and the second with $(n_2 - k)$ degrees of freedom. Moreover, since the two residual vectors are functions of u_1 and u_2, respectively, S_1 and S_2 are independent, and the two χ^2 distributions are independent. Under the null hypothesis $\sigma_1^2 = \sigma_2^2$, the statistic

$$F = [S_2/(n_2 - k)]/[S_1/(n_1 - k)] \tag{5.27}$$

has an F distribution with $(n_2 - k)$ and $(n_1 - k)$ degrees of freedom.

As it stands, (5.27) could be used to test whether $\sigma_1^2 = \sigma_2^2$, given that $\beta_1 \neq \beta_2$. If $\beta_1 = \beta_2$, the two subsamples would be pooled to give a single equation written as $y = X\beta + u$, and a test of $H_0 : \sigma_1^2 = \sigma_2^2$ would then be a test for a particular type of heteroscedasticity. Unfortunately, when the subsamples are pooled, least squares estimation gives a single residual vector

$$e = y - Xb = My = Mu; \; \text{where } M = I - X(X'X)^{-1}X',$$

and, even under the null hypothesis of no heteroscedasticity, subsets of this vector are not independent. If $\sigma_1^2 = \sigma_2^2 = \sigma^2$, the variance covariance matrix of e is

$$\text{var}(e) = \text{var}(Mu) = \sigma^2 MM' = \sigma^2 M.$$

The matrix $\sigma^2 M$ is not diagonal, and this indicates nonzero covariance and therefore lack of independence between elements of e. If we consider a statistic similar to (5.27), constructed from subvectors of residuals from a single regression, the resulting statistic does not have an F distribution.

To get around the lack of independence between elements of the least squares residual vector, various different approaches can be used. Some computer programs generate what are known as BLUS or LUS residuals. These are transformations of the least squares residual vector which remove the covariance between elements, and these could be used in an F test which is similar to (5.27), but which is based on BLUS or LUS residuals from a single regression.

A second possibility is to create an artificial division in the data from a single sample, in order to make use of (5.27). This is the basis of the Goldfeld–Quandt test, which we discuss below.

Goldfeld–Quandt test

Suppose that in the model $y = X\beta + u$, we believe that there is possible heteroscedasticity of the form

$$\text{var}(u_t) = \sigma_t^2 = \delta Z_t; \ \delta > 0; \ t = 1, \ldots, n \tag{5.28}$$

where Z is a single variable taken from the regressor matrix X, or some simple transformation, such as the square of the chosen variable. If the data are reordered according to the value of Z, and then split into two subsamples, separated by c observations from the middle of the ranked data set, one can perform two separate regressions, on the first $(n - c)/2$ and the last $(n - c)/2$ observations respectively. Obviously c should be chosen so that $(n - c)/2$ is an integer value.

Under the null hypothesis of no heteroscedasticity, the F statistic (5.27) simplifies to $F = S_2/S_1$. Under the alternative of heteroscedasticity in the form of (5.28), one would expect F to be large, because the data with high disturbance variance will fall in the second sample. The null hypothesis of no heteroscedasticity is therefore rejected at the 5% significance level if the calculated value of F is greater than the 5% critical value, for $[(n - c)/2] - k$ and $[(n - c)/2] - k$ degrees of freedom.

In the Goldfeld–Quandt test, the value of c is chosen to give some separation between the two subsamples, without losing too many degrees of freedom. Thus one might omit six observations when $n = 30$, perhaps ten or twelve when $n = 60$. One other point to note is that the test uses separate estimates of β for the two subsamples, even though the assumed model has the same value of β for all observations; this is done in order to exploit the relatively simple theory which gives rise to (5.27).

Regressions using squared residuals

A more general approach to testing for heteroscedasticity is based on the use of squared OLS residuals as a proxy for unobservable squared disturbances. To see the relevance of this idea, consider the specification

$$\text{var}(u_t) = \sigma_t^2 = \delta_1 + \delta_2 Z_{2t} + \ldots + \delta_p Z_{pt}; \ t = 1, \ldots, n.$$

If $E(u_t) = 0$, this can be written as

$$\text{var}(u_t) = E(u_t^2) = \delta_1 + \delta_2 Z_{2t} + \ldots + \delta_p Z_{pt}$$
$$= z_t' \delta; \ t = 1, \ldots, n. \tag{5.29}$$

There is a very close analogy between (5.29) and a standard regression model, written as

$$E(Y_t) = \beta_1 + \beta_2 X_{2t} + \ldots + \beta_k X_{kt}; \ t = 1, \ldots, n. \tag{5.30}$$

If the parameters $\beta_1, \ldots, \beta_k$ can be estimated from a regression of Y on $1, X_2, \ldots, X_k$ then, in principle, the parameters $\delta_1, \ldots, \delta_p$ could be estimated from a regression of u^2 on $1, Z_2, \ldots, Z_p$. Unfortunately, u^2 is unobservable, and squared OLS residuals e_t^2; $t = 1, \ldots, n$ have to be used instead. A moment's thought will show that these must be OLS rather than GLS residuals; prior to a test, we do not know whether feasible GLS will be needed and, as we shall see, a regression using squared residuals often forms part of the feasible GLS procedure.

If squared OLS residuals are regressed on $1, Z_1, \ldots, Z_p$, we obtain an estimated version of (5.29), which can be written as

$$e_t^2 = d_1 + d_2 Z_{2t} + \ldots + d_p Z_{pt} + \text{error}. \tag{5.31}$$

Since this regression is important in what follows, we emphasise that the first step is to run an OLS regression on the model $y = X\beta + u$; the second step is to save and square the residuals from this regression; and the final step is to run the regression shown in (5.31). Some computer packages automate this procedure, but it is still important to understand exactly what is done.

Breusch–Pagan test

If the parameters $\delta_2, \ldots, \delta_p$ in (5.29) are zero, $\text{var}(u_t)$ is a constant, equal to δ_1, and there is no heteroscedasticity in the disturbances to the original model $y = X\beta + u$. This suggests that one can test the null hypothesis of no heteroscedasticity by testing $H_0: \delta_2 = 0, \ldots, \delta_p = 0$. Even under the null hypothesis, the regression shown in (5.31) cannot satisfy all the classical assumptions and, in particular, the implied disturbances cannot possibly be normal if the disturbances to the original model are normal. However, under 'standard' assumptions, one can obtain a large sample test of restrictions which can be written as

$$LM(H) = (S_R - S)/(S_R/n). \tag{5.32}$$

In (5.32), S_R and S refer to the regression shown in (5.31), and the notation $LM(H)$ signifies that this is actually an LM test, of the type described in section 4.6, applied here to the problem of testing for heteroscedasticity. Since a regression which has $\delta_2, \ldots, \delta_p$ set to zero has residual sum of squares equal to total sum of squares, we can also write (5.32) as

$$LM(H) = (TSS - RSS)/(TSS/n) = ESS/(TSS/n) = nR^2.$$

Under the null hypothesis, $LM(H)$ is approximately χ^2 with $(p-1)$ degrees of freedom. So if the regression (5.31) has a value of nR^2 greater than the 5% critical value for a χ^2 distribution with $(p-1)$ degrees of freedom, the null hypothesis of no heteroscedasticity is rejected at a (nominal) 5% significance level.

We have sought to justify the test above from the perspective of least squares in a large sample. In fact, Breusch and Pagan (1980) obtained the test by direct application of the LM principle explained in section 4.6. Under the null hypothesis, their test statistic is asymptotically equivalent to (5.32), but the two are not exactly equivalent in a finite sample. The main difference is that under the null hypothesis $\text{var}(u_t) = \delta_1 = \sigma^2$, the disturbance variance corresponding to the regression (5.31) is actually equal to an expression involving the fourth moment of disturbances to the original model. If the original disturbances are normal, the required expression reduces to $2(\sigma^2)^2$. Hence (5.32) is replaced by

$$LM(H) = ESS/[2(\tilde{\sigma}^2)^2] \tag{5.33}$$

where

$$\tilde{\sigma}^2 = \sum e_t^2 / n.$$

In (5.33), $\tilde{\sigma}^2$ is the ML estimator of the constant disturbance variance that exists in the *original* model if H_0 is true, and $e_t; t = 1, \ldots, n$ are least squares residuals from the original regression. As before, the null hypothesis is rejected if the calculated value of the test statistic is greater than the 5% critical value for χ^2 distribution with $(p-1)$ degrees of freedom.

One final modification is that Breusch and Pagan suggest using $e^2/\tilde{\sigma}^2$ rather than e^2 as the dependent variable in (5.31). If this is done, the test statistic simplifies to $LM(H) = ESS/2$. It is interesting to note that one does not have to specify the exact form of heteroscedasticity to use the procedures outlined above. Breusch and Pagan show that if the linear hypothesis is written as

$$\text{var}(u_t) = \sigma_t^2 = z_t'\delta$$

the test will detect patterns based on any continuous function $h(z_t'\delta)$. In particular, a test based on the *linear* regression will detect multiplicative heteroscedasticity of the form

$$\text{var}(u_t) = \sigma_t^2 = \exp(z_t'\delta).$$

To use the Breusch–Pagan test, one has to specify a list of conditioning variables which are thought to determine $\text{var}(u_t)$ under the alternative hypothesis. If possible heteroscedasticity is suggested by the theory underlying the model, it is usually easy to do this. Alternatively, the nature of the data may help to suggest appropriate variables. Thus, with quarterly data, one might use seasonal dummy variables to check for a possible seasonal pattern in the disturbance variance.

If all else fails, there is one final possibility. The squared predicted values from the first-stage regression represent a general quadratic function of the original regressors, and if there is any pattern of association between the disturbance variance and some function of regressors, this should be detected by a test of $H_0: \delta_2 = 0$, based on the regression

$$e_t^2 = d_1 + d_2 \hat{Y}_t^2 + \text{error}; \quad t = 1, \ldots, n. \tag{5.34}$$

This procedure can be followed routinely, in cases where one has no other pattern of possible heteroscedasticity in mind. As before, the test may use nR^2, or any asymptotically equivalent χ^2 test, or an F test variant, which in this case would be equal to the square of the t value associated with d_2 in (5.34). Note that the justification for the F and t variants is based on an arbitrary correction to the large-sample χ^2 tests, and not on exact small-sample theory.

Example 5.1

This example uses the Barro–Lee data set (data set 4). The equation fitted as (2.58) was shown in Example 3.3 to be misspecified by applying the RESET test. Here, the regression of (2.58) is tested for heteroscedasticity using the Breusch–Pagan test in its variants (5.32) and (5.33). In the context of the model of (2.58), it is at least plausible that the variance of the average 1975–85 growth rate of per capita GDP (AVGR) is a function of the opening level of per capita GDP (GDP575L). The multiplicative form of heteroscedasticity of (5.19),

$$\text{var}(u_t) = \exp(\delta_1 + \delta_2 GDP575L_t),$$

will be used, since it guarantees positive variances, although as noted earlier, the Breusch–Pagan test would still be based on the *linear* form $\delta_1 + \delta_2 GDP575L_t$. The procedure adopted is therefore as follows.

The residuals e_t from the regression (2.58) are saved and squared, and the squared residuals are regressed on 1 and GDP575L. The total sum of squares (TSS) for this regression is $5.391\,10 \times 10^{-5}$, the residual sum of squares (RSS) $5.174\,81 \times 10^{-5}$ and $R^2 = 0.040\,12$. Since $n = 102$, the nR^2 form of the Breusch–Pagan test gives $nR^2 = 4.092\,24$. The null hypothesis sets $\delta_1 = 0$, so that $p - 1 = 1$. The 5% critical value for a χ^2 distribution with 1 degree of freedom is 3.84. Thus there is some evidence of heteroscedasticity, leading to the rejection of the null hypothesis of homoscedasticity. Although the value of the test is only just above the critical value, the sample size is reasonably large, giving some confidence in the conclusion.

To apply the form of test suggested in equation (5.33), we need to calculate the ML estimate of σ^2 under the null hypothesis. From (2.58), $RSS = 0.057\,007\,2$, so that $\tilde{\sigma}^2 = 0.057\,007\,2/102 = 5.588\,94 \times 10^{-4}$. From the regression results above, $ESS = (5.391\,10 - 5.174\,81) \times 10^{-5} = 2.162\,90 \times 10^{-6}$, giving

$$LM(H) = ESS/[2(\tilde{\sigma}^2)^2] = 3.462.$$

This value is smaller than the appropriate χ^2 critical value of 3.84, and would suggest acceptance of the null hypothesis. There is therefore a conflict in the test conclusions from the two versions of the Breusch–Pagan test. How can this conflict be reconciled?

There are two possibilities. One is that this version of the Breusch–Pagan test explicitly has to assume that the error terms are normally distributed, which may not be true here. However, we shall see later on that there appears to be no evidence of non-normality in the error terms of (2.58). Another possibility is to consider an alternative test. This is simply the routine F test that all slopes are zero in the regression using squared residuals: the value of the statistic is 4.1798, distributed approximately as $F(1, 100)$ under the null hypothesis. The 5% critical value is 3.94, leading to rejection of the null hypothesis again. The difficulty encountered here is common: different test procedures with identical large sample distributions may lead to conflicting test conclusions. The best that can be said here is simply that the rejections are relatively marginal.

The final test for heteroscedasticity is the Goldfeld–Quandt test. Here the observations are ordered by the variable PNST45a. The quantity c is set to 16, to put 43 observations in each group. In fact, the values of PNST45a for the first 43 observations are all less than 0.01, with many of the values actually equal to zero, whilst the last 43 observations have values of PNST45a greater than about 0.06. Since the maximum value of this variable is about 0.88, the second group of observations displays much greater instability than the first group. Calculating S_1 as the RSS from a regression based on the first 43 observations, and S_2 similarly from the last 43 observations gives $S_1 = 0.014\,410\,3$, $S_2 = 0.022\,354\,1$, with $F = S_2/S_1 = 1.551$. The 5% critical value here is 1.661, although this value is not available in Appendix B; there is no evidence of heteroscedasticity in average growth rates due to differing levels of political instability.

Feasible GLS

Having looked at theoretical GLS estimation and considered regressions using squared OLS residuals, we have much of the groundwork for feasible GLS estimation. For most purposes, multiplicative heteroscedasticity is the most appropriate specification, and we use this to summarise the feasible GLS procedure.

Suppose that we have performed the Breusch–Pagan test, and rejected the null hypothesis of no heteroscedasticity. In doing this, we will have used a *linear* regression of e^2 on $1, Z_2, \ldots, Z_p$. Having rejected the null hypothesis, we must decide on the exact functional form before proceeding to feasible GLS estimation. If we assume multiplicative heteroscedasticity, the procedure is as follows.

Step 1. Run a regression of $\ln(e^2)$ on $1, Z_2, \ldots, Z_p$, and save the predicted values from this regression. These are estimates of $\ln(\sigma_t^2)$, denoted as $\ln(\hat{\sigma}_t^2)$; $t = 1, \ldots, n$.

Step 2. Apply the exponential function to give

$$\hat{\sigma}_t^2 = \exp[\ln(\hat{\sigma}_t^2)]; \ t = 1, \ldots, n.$$

Step 3. Transform the original equation by dividing the dependent variable and all regressor observations by $\hat{\sigma}_t$, the positive square root of $\hat{\sigma}_t^2$, for $t = 1, \ldots, n$.

Step 4. Apply OLS to the transformed model.

Under 'standard' conditions, the feasible GLS estimators are asymptotically equivalent to theoretical GLS, and are therefore consistent and asymptotically efficient. However, one should be wary about rushing into feasible GLS estimation, since apparent heteroscedasticity may arise because the main part of the model is misspecified, rather than because of some intrinsic characteristic of the model. If misspecification does occur, the appropriate remedial action is to modify the main part of the model, rather than to attempt feasible GLS estimation.

If there is inherent heteroscedasticity, as opposed to apparent heteroscedasticity resulting from misspecification of the model, one could use ML estimation rather than feasible GLS. The key difference between ML and feasible GLS is that the ML procedure estimates all parameters simultaneously, whereas feasible GLS uses 'equation' parameters to estimate 'disturbance' parameters, and then uses the disturbance parameter estimates to produce new estimates of the equation parameters.

Both the feasible GLS and ML procedures require one to specify the pattern of heteroscedasticity, and the theoretical properties of the estimators depend upon this being correct. An alternative to either trying to respecify the main part of the model, or attempting feasible GLS, is to use the OLS estimator, recognising that if this is done when heteroscedasticity is present, the usual expression for the variance matrix of the OLS estimator is incorrect (see equation (5.4)). White (1980) suggests that, under certain conditions, the OLS variance matrix can be consistently estimated as

$$\text{var}(b) = (X'X)^{-1}X'\hat{\Sigma}X(X'X)^{-1}, \tag{5.35}$$

where the diagonal elements Σ_{tt} are simply replaced by the corresponding squared OLS residuals, giving $\hat{\Sigma}_{tt} = e_t^2; \ t = 1, \ldots, n$. This approach may be suitable when heteroscedasticity is detected by a routine diagnostic test, but where it proves to be difficult to pin down exactly why this occurs.

5.4 / Nonnormality and testing for normality

One of the standard pieces of diagnostic output from most econometric software packages is a test of normality. In this section, we shall try to indicate how the simplest of these tests is constructed, and why it might be important in practice to test for normality. If the test statistic leads to a rejection of the null hypothesis of normality, what might one do to respecify one's model? As a preliminary to a discussion of a certain type of heteroscedasticity called 'autoregressive conditional' heteroscedasticity, which will be discussed in some detail in Chapter 10, we shall show that some forms of heteroscedasticity can in fact lead to nonnormality.

The standard test for normality in econometrics is the Bera–Jarque test, which uses the fact that the normal distribution has a characteristic set of *moments*. That is, if $Z \sim N(0, 1)$,

$$E(Z) = 0$$

$$E(Z^2) = 1$$

$$E(Z^3) = 0$$

$$E(Z^4) = 3.$$

More generally, all odd moments are zero

$$E(Z^{2j+1}) = 0,$$

whilst even moments follow the pattern

$$E(Z^{2j}) = \frac{(2j)!}{2^j j!}.$$

If we use $W \sim N(0, \sigma^2)$, we can write

$$W = \sigma Z,$$

and deduce the third and fourth moments of W:

$$E(W^3) = 0, \quad E(W^4) = \sigma^4 E(Z^4) = 3\sigma^4.$$

As a shorthand, write

$$E(W^j) = \mu_j$$

for the jth moment of W.

The Bera–Jarque test

The Bera–Jarque test works by comparing the sample versions of the *coefficient of excess skewness*,

$$\gamma_1 = \frac{\mu_3}{(\sqrt{\mu_2})^3},$$

and the *coefficient of excess kurtosis*,

$$\gamma_2 = \frac{\mu_4}{\mu_2^2} - 3,$$

with their theoretical values of zero under normality. In fact, every symmetric distribution should have $\gamma_1 = 0$.

Although ideas of skewness and kurtosis are well known from elementary statistics, there is sometimes confusion over the relationship between these terms and the shape of a distribution. If an asymmetric distribution has its long tail on the right of the distribution, then there is positive skew, and $\gamma_1 > 0$. An example is the chi-squared distribution. Distributions with kurtosis different from that of the normal could have fatter tails (and hence a thinner centre) or thinner tails (and hence a fatter centre). A *platykurtic* distribution has $\gamma_2 \leq 0$, and is fatter in the centre than a normal, and thinner in the tails, whilst a *leptokurtic* distribution, with $\gamma_2 \geq 0$, is thinner in the centre and hence has fatter tails. In addition, a problem with using these definitions is that they do not always match visual inspection of the graphs of densities. For example, an $N(0,3)$ distribution appears to have fatter tails than the $N(0,1)$, but has exactly the same kurtosis.

For a given data set, $Y_1, \ldots, Y_n$, estimates of μ_2, μ_3 and μ_4 are obtained from sample moments: the jth sample moment is

$$m_j = \frac{1}{n} \sum_{t=1}^{n} (Y_t - \bar{Y})^j.$$

One could use a degrees of freedom correction $(n-1)$, but since the test is a large sample one, this can be ignored. Estimates of γ_1 and γ_2 are then obtained directly as

$$\hat{\gamma}_1 = \frac{m_3}{(\sqrt{m_2})^3}, \qquad \hat{\gamma}_2 = \frac{m_4}{m_2^2} - 3.$$

The large sample Bera–Jarque test for normality is based on the statistic

$$BJ = n\left(\frac{\hat{\gamma}_1^2}{6} + \frac{\hat{\gamma}_2^2}{24}\right) \xrightarrow{D} \chi_2^2.$$

This can be derived from the LM test principle by embedding the null hypothesis of a normal distribution for Y_t within a more general distributional form.

In econometrics, this statistic is used on least squares residuals e_t from regressions which usually contain constant terms. These residuals thus have sample mean zero, and the moment estimates are simply

$$m_j = \frac{1}{n} \sum_{t=1}^{n} e_t^j.$$

How effective is this test? Clearly, it examines only whether or not the third and fourth sample moments of the data are compatible with the third and fourth moments of a normal distribution. This is not quite the same as examining compatibility with a normal distribution – for example, the information in all the moments higher than four is being ignored. In addition, there is evidence that the large sample χ^2 distribution is not a very good approximation to the true distribution (under the null hypothesis) in finite samples: the test appears to reject too infrequently. Some software packages present different test statistics, for which the large sample χ^2 distribution is a better approximation.

Example 5.2

Here the Bera–Jarque test is performed on the residuals from equation (2.58). In principle, the outcome of the test would help us to decide which of the variants of the Breusch–Pagan test computed in Example 5.1 should be used to test for heteroscedasticity in (2.58). Using the residuals from (2.58), the coefficient of excess skewness γ_1 is estimated as $-0.037\,837$, and the estimate of the coefficient of excess kurtosis γ_2 is $-0.307\,931$. This gives the value of the Bera–Jarque statistic as

$$BJ = 102\left[\frac{(-0.037\,837)^2}{6} + \frac{(-0.307\,931)^2}{24}\right] = 0.427\,33.$$

The 5% critical value of a χ^2 distribution with 2 degrees of freedom is 5.99, so that the null hypothesis that the excess skewness and kurtosis of the distribution of the residuals from (2.58) is zero is not rejected. This result, together with the dubious reliability of the Bera–Jarque test, does nothing to resolve the difficulties with the heteroscedasticity tests in Example 5.1.

What should one do if the test rejects? Sometimes nothing! Part of the reasoning behind the use of large sample properties of estimators and large sample test procedures is that one is freed from the need to assume normality in order to make things work. However, it may be that rejection of normality forces one to think more carefully about the type of model that is appropriate for the data at hand. Indeed, this is the main reason for conducting diagnostic tests. If something wrong is detected with the model, it does not immediately follow that one has to modify it to reflect the apparent alternative hypothesis of the test being used. Rather, there needs to be a deeper consideration of how the model should change; this is not always obvious.

Conditional variance models and nonnormality

One way in which nonnormality can be generated by a model is described here. The discussion makes use of the ideas of conditional expectation and variance, and the 'law of iterated expectation' outlined in Appendix A. It will be enough to work with a two-variable model, in which we want to create a particular type of heteroscedasticity. We shall assume initially only that the disturbances have mean zero. It will be enough to treat the explanatory variable X_t as 'fixed', although we only need it to be conditionally fixed. In any case, it will play a minor role in what follows. Let v_t be a nonstochastic quantity, and put

$$Y_t = \alpha + \beta X_t + v_t u_t.$$

As a result, Y_t is heteroscedastic:

$$\text{var}(Y_t) = \sigma^2 v_t^2.$$

The discussions of heteroscedasticity so far in this chapter have investigated possible ways of generating v_t in order to capture the patterns of heteroscedasticity that have been observed empirically.

Suppose next that v_t is a random variable independent of u_s, for every s and t. Conditional on the value of v_t,

$$\text{var}(Y_t|v_t) = \sigma^2 v_t^2,$$

whilst the unconditional variance is, from the definition,

$$\text{var}(Y_t) = E(\sigma^2 v_t^2) + \text{var}[E(Y_t|v_t)] = \sigma^2 E(v_t^2),$$

since

$$E(Y_t|v_t) = \alpha + \beta X_t$$

from the independence of v_t and u_t. Put

$$\varepsilon_t = v_t u_t \tag{5.36}$$

with conditional and therefore unconditional mean zero, and

$$\text{var}(\varepsilon_t) = \text{var}(Y_t) = \sigma^2 E(v_t^2).$$

One area of application in which one expects to encounter nonnormality is in finance, particularly asset return distributions, which typically have rather thick-tailed distributions, One traditional approach to dealing with this has been to abandon the use of models based around the normal distribution, and use, for example, a t distribution as an error distribution. The approach discussed here, of allowing the variance of a regression error term to be random in a certain sense, provides another way in which nonnormality can arise. It seems in some cases that it is not enough empirically to combine normality with 'random variances' in this way – nonnormal error distributions also seem to be required.

To see how 'random variances' generate thick-tailed distributions for ε_t and Y_t, write

$$Y_t = \alpha + \beta X_t + v_t u_t$$
$$= \alpha + \beta X_t + \varepsilon_t$$

and treat u_t as conditionally normally distributed:

$$u_t|v_t \sim N(0, \sigma^2).$$

The point of the exercise is to show that under these conditions, ε_t is conditionally normally distributed, but not unconditionally. The evidence for the latter is that the fourth moment of ε_t is larger than it would be if it were actually normal. Clearly, given the assumptions, ε_t is conditionally heteroscedastic:

$$\varepsilon_t|v_t \sim N(0, \sigma^2 v_t^2).$$

What is the fourth moment of ε_t? Using conditional expectation arguments from Appendix A,

$$E(\varepsilon_t^4) = E[E(\varepsilon_t^4 | v_t)]$$
$$= E[E(u_t^4 v_t^4 | v_t)]$$
$$= E[v_t^4 E(u_t^4 | v_t)]$$
$$= E(v_t^4) E(u_t^4)$$
$$= 3\sigma^4 E(v_t^4).$$

The last statement uses the conditional normality of u_t. To see whether this fourth moment is too large for normality, suppose that ε_t is normal *unconditionally*:

$$\varepsilon_t \sim N[0, \mathrm{var}(\varepsilon_t)]$$

with

$$\mathrm{var}(\varepsilon_t) = \sigma^2 E(v_t^2).$$

Under this assumption,

$$E(\varepsilon_t^4) = 3[E(\varepsilon_t^2)]^2$$
$$= 3\sigma^4 [E(v_t^2)]^2.$$

The question then amounts to asking if

$$E(v_t^4) \geq [E(v_t^2)]^2.$$

It is easy to answer this question, since in general for some random variable W,

$$\mathrm{var}(W^2) = E(W^4) - [E(W^2)]^2 \geq 0,$$

$$E(W^4) \geq [E(W^2)]^2.$$

All together this gives us

$$E(\varepsilon_t^4) = 3\sigma^4 E(v_t^4) \geq 3\sigma^4 [E(v_t^2)]^2$$

with equality only when

$$v_t^2 = \text{constant}.$$

In summary, the unconditional fourth moment of ε_t is bigger than that implied by a normal distribution, and thus its unconditional distribution is more fat-tailed (leptokurtic) than a normal.

Notice that this discussion has not depended on the nature of the distribution of the random variable v_t^2 which generates the conditional heteroscedasticity and unconditional nonnormality. There are clearly a large range of possibilities: for example, it is not necessary to assume that the collection $v_1, \ldots, v_n$ are independent random variables. We shall see in Chapter 10 that the class of models discussed in Chapters 6 and 7 lead to the possibility that v_t^2 is generated from a dynamic model. One particular choice of model leads to the 'autoregressive conditional heteroscedasticity' or ARCH model.

5.5 / Further reading

Both Davidson and MacKinnon (1993) and Gourieroux and Monfort (1995) are worth looking at for the topics of this chapter. Goldberger (1991) and Greene (1993) give more traditional discussions.

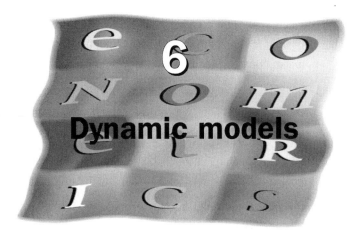

6

Dynamic models

6.1 / Introduction

Econometric models frequently incorporate some form of dynamic adjustment process, even when the underlying theory is essentially comparatively static in nature. This occurs because there is no reason to suppose that data are observed from a state of equilibrium, a fact which must be recognised when formulating the model, even though the primary objective may be to focus on long-run behaviour. At the very least, the econometrician must allow for the possibility of delays in the response of endogenous variables to changes in exogenous variables, and this may lead to the use of models involving lags in exogenous variables, or lags in endogenous variables, or both.

From the perspective of statistical modelling, it is useful to distinguish between the two kinds of lag that may arise. The models

$$Y_t = \beta_1 + \beta_2 X_t + \beta_3 X_{t-1} + u_t; \ t = 1, \ldots, n \tag{6.1}$$

and

$$Y_t = \beta_1 + \beta_2 X_t + \beta_3 Y_{t-1} + u_t; \ t = 1, \ldots, n \tag{6.2}$$

both involve lagged variables and delayed adjustment to changes in the exogenous variable, but the implications for estimation and hypothesis testing are rather different. In (6.1), if exogenous variable observations are considered to be non-random, there is no inherent reason for violation of the assumptions of the classical regression model. Indeed, the sequence $Y_t; \ t = 1, \ldots, n$ still consists of independent random variables if the assumption $u_t \sim IID(0, \sigma^2)$ is maintained. In (6.2), whatever assumption is made about the presample value Y_0, it is clear that Y_1 and all later terms in the Y_t sequence have random components. It follows that Y_{t-1}; $t = 2, \ldots, n$ are random, and classical assumptions cannot apply. Here, in contrast to (6.1), $Y_t; \ t = 1, \ldots, n$ are *not* independent random variables.

This is not the only way in which a failure of independence in $Y_t; \ t = 1, \ldots, n$ can arise. If the disturbances in a regression model are not independent, this property is

167

transmitted through to Y_t; $t = 1, \ldots, n$. This property usually comes under the heading of serial correlation, more formally described as a situation in which the disturbances in one period are correlated with disturbances from one or more of the preceding periods. Although an equivalent problem is sometimes found with ordered cross-section data, the vast majority of cases do arise in the context of time series.

As with heteroscedasticity, there are various reasons why serial correlation might occur. First, one could argue that serial correlation is simply a logical alternative to independence or zero covariance between disturbances. It is also possible that the equation used for estimation is obtained by a transformation of the original model, and there are transformations that can induce serial correlation. But the most persuasive argument is that there is no reason why the relationships between economic variables should be fully worked through within the unit time period chosen. Ideally, this would be represented by lags in the main part of the model, but it is clearly possible to have such effects spilling over to the disturbance term, which acts as a summary representation for all variables not included in the main part of the model.

There is a very fine dividing line between serial correlation as an intrinsic property of the disturbances, and serial correlation as evidence that the main part of the model is misspecified. In practice, it is often the case that apparent serial correlation can be removed by respecification of the main part of the model. So although we do need to review the theory of 'pure' serial correlation, it is important to remember that using an estimator appropriate to serially correlated disturbances is not always the answer to apparent serial correlation, as revealed by a routine diagnostic test.

Although econometric theory has a great deal to say about the processing of time series data, there is a narrower definition of time series modelling, in which one or more series are modelled exclusively in terms of their own past behaviour. Not surprisingly, the models found in this literature are also called 'time series models'. The key observation to be made here is that these can be used either as models for error terms exhibiting dependence, or as prototype models underlying (6.2). To illustrate this point, a simplified version of (6.2) is the 'autoregressive model'

$$Y_t = \phi_1 Y_{t-1} + u_t; \ u_t \sim IID(0, \sigma^2); \ t = 1, \ldots, n.$$

The corresponding model for disturbances is

$$u_t = \phi_1 u_{t-1} + \varepsilon_t; \ \varepsilon_t \sim IID(0, \sigma^2); \ t = 1, \ldots, n$$

in which u_t; $t = 1, \ldots, n$ are independent random variables. These 'time series models' will be presented initially as models for observed time series, and the implications of these models for correlated disturbances will be examined later.

6.2 / Stochastic processes

Suppose that we have a time-ordered sequence of random variables, each in principle associated with its own probability distribution. Since the observations are not usually independent, the set of observations Y_t; $t = 1, \ldots, n$ is characterised as a realisation of a joint distribution, with joint density function $p(Y_1, \ldots, Y_n)$. Without the notion of time sequencing, this is simply a probability model for a set of random variables; with the notion of time sequencing added, we have a stochastic process.

To be useful for the modelling of observations outside the sample period, the concept of a stochastic process must extend backwards and forwards in time. Consequently, we argue that the process, which may be written as $\{Y_t\}$, has a joint distribution in any 'time slice' of n observations, wherever this is located in real time. The question as to whether the distribution for $Y_1, \ldots, Y_n$ is identical to that for $Y_{1+s}, \ldots, Y_{n+s}$ is considered in the next section. If the time slices do have identical distributions, the process is said to be strictly stationary. In practice, we use a slightly weaker definition. A stochastic process is said to be wide-sense or covariance stationary if the means, variances, and covariances of the process are constant through time. This is usually what is meant by saying, without qualification, that a process is stationary. Hence we require that

$$E(Y_t) = E(Y_{t+s}); \text{ for all } s, t$$

$$\text{var}(Y_t) = \text{var}(Y_{t+s}); \text{ for all } s, t \tag{6.3}$$

$$\text{cov}(Y_t, Y_{t+k}) = \text{cov}(Y_{t+s}, Y_{t+k+s}); \text{ for all } k, s, t.$$

Since covariances play an important role in time series modelling, we shall examine the covariance terms in more detail. Let γ_{kt} be the covariance between Y_t and Y_{t+k}, that is,

$$\gamma_{kt} = \text{cov}(Y_t, Y_{t+k})$$

$$= E\{[Y_t - E(Y_t)][Y_{t+k} - E(Y_{t+k})]\}. \tag{6.4}$$

Because these are 'self' covariances between different observations on the same time series, the values γ_{kt} are known as *autocovariances*. The assumption of wide-sense stationarity implies that

$$\gamma_{kt} = \gamma_k; \text{ all } k, t$$

and also that

$$\gamma_k = \gamma_{-k}; \text{ all } k.$$

This last result follows from shifting the expression in (6.4) back through k periods; given stationarity, this time shift cannot alter the value of γ_k, but after shifting, (6.4) defines γ_{-k}. Hence, for a stationary series, $\gamma_k = \gamma_{-k}$, for all k.

A further point to note is that γ_{0t} is the variance of the process, since

$$\gamma_{0t} = \text{cov}(Y_t, Y_t) = \text{var}(Y_t).$$

Given stationarity, we have $\gamma_{0t} = \gamma_0$ for all t.

The collection of correlations obtained from the autocovariances as

$$\rho_{kt} = \frac{\text{cov}(Y_t, Y_{t+k})}{\sqrt{\text{var}(Y_t)}\sqrt{\text{var}(Y_{t+k})}}; \text{ for all } k, t$$

are called *autocorrelations*. If the process is stationary, $\rho_{kt} = \rho_k = \rho_{-k}$. Hence, for a stationary series,

$$\rho_k = \gamma_k/\gamma_0; \text{ for all } k. \tag{6.5}$$

MA processes

The simplest model of a stationary stochastic process exhibiting nonzero autocorrelations is the *moving average* process, or more accurately, the *moving average process of order 1*, or MA(1) process:

$$Y_t = \delta + u_t - \theta_1 u_{t-1}; \ u_t \sim IID(0, \sigma^2); \text{ all } t. \tag{6.6}$$

The mean of the process in (6.6) is easily seen to be $E(Y_t) = \delta$. To obtain the variance, we have

$$\mathrm{var}(Y_t) = \mathrm{var}(u_t) + \theta_1^2 \, \mathrm{var}(u_{t-1}) - 2\theta_1 \, \mathrm{cov}(u_t, u_{t-1}).$$

Since $\mathrm{cov}(u_t, u_{t-1}) = 0$ and $\mathrm{var}(u_t) = \mathrm{var}(u_{t-1})$, it follows that

$$\mathrm{var}(Y_t) = \mathrm{var}(u_t)(1 + \theta_1^2) = \sigma^2(1 + \theta_1^2).$$

It is easy to see that

$$\mathrm{cov}(Y_t, Y_{t-1}) = E(u_t - \theta_1 u_{t-1})(u_{t-1} - \theta_1 u_{t-2}).$$

Of the four terms in this expression, only $-\theta_1 E(u_{t-1}^2)$ is nonzero, and this term is equal to $-\theta_1 \mathrm{var}(u_{t-1}) = -\theta_1 \sigma^2$. Hence,

$$\gamma_1 = \mathrm{cov}(Y_t, Y_{t-1}) = -\theta_1 \sigma^2.$$

By similar arguments one can show that all other covariances $\gamma_k; \ k > 1$, are zero, giving

$$\rho_1 = \frac{\gamma_1}{\gamma_0} = -\frac{\theta_1}{(1 + \theta_1^2)}$$

and

$$\rho_k = 0; \ k > 1.$$

It is clear that this process is stationary, for any values of the parameters δ and θ_1.

A natural generalisation of the MA(1) process is the MA(q) process, in which lags of u_t up to u_{t-q} appear in the equation:

$$Y_t = \delta + u_t - \theta_1 u_{t-1} - \ldots - \theta_q u_{t-q}; \ u_t \sim IID(0, \sigma^2); \text{ all } t. \tag{6.7}$$

The autocovariances and autocorrelations of this process can be found in exactly the same way as the MA(1) process, although they have a more complicated expression. In this case,

$$\mathrm{cov}(Y_t, Y_{t-j}) = 0$$

if $j > q$, that is, if the lag exceeds the order of the process. Just as in the MA(1), the autocovariances and autocorrelations do not depend on t, showing that the MA(q) process is stationary.

6.3 / Autoregressive processes

Another example of a stochastic process which is stationary, under some conditions, is the *autoregressive process* of order 1, or AR(1) process,

$$Y_t = \delta + \phi_1 Y_{t-1} + u_t; \; u_t \sim IID(0, \sigma^2); \text{ all } t. \tag{6.8}$$

A special case in which $\delta = 0$ was used in section 6.1. The process is called *autoregressive* because we are regressing Y_t on an intercept and its own past value Y_{t-1}.

An AR(1) process is not guaranteed to be stationary. However, by imposing stationarity when calculating the mean, variances and autocovariances, it should be possible to find conditions ensuring that an AR(1) process is stationary. First,

$$E(Y_t) = \delta + \phi_1 E(Y_{t-1}) + E(u_t).$$

If $E(Y_t)$ is to be constant for all t,

$$E(Y_t) = \mu; \text{ all } t,$$

then it must be true that

$$\mu = \delta + \phi_1 \mu,$$

that is,

$$\mu = \frac{\delta}{1 - \phi_1}.$$

This automatically rules out $\phi_1 = 1$ as an admissible value of ϕ_1 under stationarity.

Finding the autocovariances relies on the observation that under the assumption

$$u_t \sim IID(0, \sigma^2),$$

u_t and Y_{t-1} are independent, simply because Y_{t-1} only depends on $u_{t-1}, u_{t-2}, \ldots$. In other words, because the error terms are independent, the 'present', u_t, is independent of the 'past', $Y_{t-1}, Y_{t-2}, \ldots$. Then, from (6.8),

$$\text{var}(Y_t) = \phi_1^2 \text{var}(Y_{t-1}) + \text{var}(u_t). \tag{6.9}$$

Under stationarity,

$$\text{var}(Y_t) = \text{var}(Y_{t-1}),$$

which makes (6.9)

$$\gamma_0 = \phi_1^2 \gamma_0 + \sigma^2$$

in autocovariance notation. Solving for γ_0 gives

$$\gamma_0 = \sigma^2 \frac{1}{1 - \phi_1^2}. \tag{6.10}$$

It is clear that

$$\phi_1 = \pm 1$$

cannot be considered as admissible values of ϕ_1 under stationarity, since γ_0 will not be finite. However, if $|\phi_1| > 1$, the variance γ_0 will be negative. Summarising, the demand that the AR(1) process (6.8) be stationary has so far ruled out values of the parameter ϕ_1 which satisfy $|\phi_1| \geq 1$.

To evaluate the autocovariance γ_1, we have

$$\begin{aligned}
\mathrm{cov}(Y_t, Y_{t-1}) &= \mathrm{cov}(\delta + \phi_1 Y_{t-1} + u_t, Y_{t-1}) \\
&= \phi_1 \mathrm{cov}(Y_{t-1}, Y_{t-1}) + \mathrm{cov}(u_t, Y_{t-1}) \\
&= \phi_1 \mathrm{var}(Y_{t-1}) \\
&= \phi_1 \gamma_0.
\end{aligned}$$

By similar arguments, one can show the general results

$$\gamma_k = \mathrm{cov}(Y_t, Y_{t-k}) = \phi_1^k \gamma_0$$

and

$$\rho_k = \frac{\gamma_k}{\gamma_0} = \phi_1^k; \ k = 0, 1, 2, \ldots.$$

The condition that $|\phi_1| < 1$ thus guarantees that the process (6.8) has a constant mean and variance. It is clear that this condition also guarantees that the autocovariances and autocorrelations are constant, and that $|\rho_k| \leq 1$, as is required for a correlation. Therefore, the AR(1) process (6.8) is stationary when the parameter ϕ_1 is restricted to satisfy $|\phi_1| < 1$.

Higher-order processes

In the same way that the MA(q) process is obtained from the MA(1) process by increasing the number of lags of u_{t-j}, an autoregressive process of order p, or AR(p) process, is obtained by increasing the number of lags of Y_t:

$$Y_t = \delta + \phi_1 Y_{t-1} + \ldots + \phi_p Y_{t-p} + u_t; \ u_t \sim IID(0, \sigma^2); \text{ all } t. \tag{6.11}$$

This process is similarly not guaranteed to be stationary: details of the precise conditions for stationarity are postponed until the next section.

Correlated disturbances

The discussion has focused on models for observed time series, although it was noted in section 6.1 that such models could be used as models for correlated disturbances.

Since disturbances are normally expected to have mean zero, one could write

$$u_t = \phi_1 u_{t-1} + \ldots + \phi_p u_{t-p} + \varepsilon_t; \ \varepsilon_t \sim IID(0, \sigma^2)$$

as an AR(p) process for regression disturbances, and similarly,

$$u_t = \varepsilon_t - \theta_1 \varepsilon_{t-1} - \ldots - \theta_q \varepsilon_{t-q}; \ \varepsilon_t \sim IID(0, \sigma^2)$$

as an MA(q) process. Sections 5.1 and 5.2 discuss a general framework for dealing with correlated disturbances: we now examine how disturbances generated from autoregressive or moving average processes fit into this framework.

Consider now the model given in equation (5.3):

$$y = X\beta + u; \ X \text{ nonrandom}; \ E(u) = 0;$$

$$\text{var}(u) = \sigma^2 V, \text{ where } V \text{ is pd.}$$

If the elements of u are generated by a stationary process, the covariances between these elements, $\text{cov}(u_{t-i}, u_{t-j})$, have the form

$$\text{cov}(u_{t-i}, u_{t-j}) = \gamma_{|i-j|}.$$

This creates the characteristic structure of the covariance matrix for such a process:

$$\Omega = \begin{bmatrix} \gamma_0 & \gamma_1 & \cdots & \cdots & \gamma_{n-2} & \gamma_{n-1} \\ \gamma_1 & \gamma_0 & \gamma_1 & \cdots & & \gamma_{n-2} \\ \vdots & \ddots & \ddots & \ddots & & \vdots \\ & & & \ddots & \ddots & \\ \vdots & & & \ddots & \ddots & \gamma_1 \\ \gamma_{n-2} & \cdots & \cdots & & \ddots & \gamma_1 \\ \gamma_{n-1} & \cdots & \cdots & \cdots & \gamma_1 & \gamma_0 \end{bmatrix}.$$

Factoring out γ_0 creates a matrix of autocorrelations,

$$\Omega = \gamma_0 \begin{bmatrix} 1 & \rho_1 & \cdots & \cdots & \rho_{n-2} & \rho_{n-1} \\ \rho_1 & 1 & \rho_1 & \cdots & & \rho_{n-2} \\ \vdots & \ddots & \ddots & \ddots & & \vdots \\ & & & \ddots & \ddots & \\ \vdots & & & \ddots & \ddots & \rho_1 \\ \rho_{n-2} & \cdots & \cdots & & \ddots & \rho_1 \\ \rho_{n-1} & \cdots & \cdots & \cdots & \rho_1 & 1 \end{bmatrix}.$$

Notice the contrast between the factor σ^2 given in the description of the regression model and the factor γ_0 given here. Notice also the structure of this covariance matrix: it is symmetric in above and below diagonal bands, and is called a band-symmetric, centrosymmetric or Toeplitz matrix.

The classic simple example of such a matrix is that generated from the AR(1) process, in which, as discovered above,

$$\gamma_0 = \frac{\sigma^2}{1 - \phi_1^2}$$

and

$$\rho_j = \phi_1^j.$$

In this case,

$$\Omega = \sigma^2 V,$$

or

$$\Omega = \frac{\sigma^2}{1 - \phi_1^2} \begin{bmatrix} 1 & \phi_1 & \cdots & \cdots & \phi_1^{n-2} & \phi_1^{n-1} \\ \phi_1 & 1 & \phi_1 & \cdots & \cdots & \phi_1^{n-2} \\ \vdots & \ddots & \ddots & \ddots & & \vdots \\ \vdots & & \ddots & \ddots & \ddots & \vdots \\ \phi_1^{n-2} & \cdots & \cdots & \ddots & \ddots & \phi_1 \\ \phi_1^{n-1} & \cdots & \cdots & \cdots & \phi_1 & 1 \end{bmatrix}. \tag{6.12}$$

To construct the generalised least squares estimator, as given in equation (5.7), it is necessary either to find an inverse for V, or to factor this inverse: that is, find a non-singular matrix C such that

$$C'C = V^{-1},$$

from which it follows that

$$CVC' = I_n.$$

Only in the case of the AR(1) process is there a simple expression for the inverse and for the factor C. It is easy to check that the matrix

$$C = \begin{bmatrix} \sqrt{1 - \phi_1^2} & 0 & \cdots & \cdots & \cdots & 0 \\ -\phi_1 & 1 & \ddots & & & \vdots \\ 0 & -\phi_1 & 1 & \ddots & & \vdots \\ \vdots & & \ddots & \ddots & \ddots & \vdots \\ \vdots & & & \ddots & \ddots & 0 \\ 0 & \cdots & \cdots & 0 & -\phi_1 & 1 \end{bmatrix} \tag{6.13}$$

has the desired property. The effect of premultiplying the vector y by C is to create the vector

$$\begin{bmatrix} \sqrt{1 - \phi_1^2}\, Y_1 \\ Y_2 - \phi_1 Y_1 \\ \vdots \\ Y_n - \phi_1 Y_{n-1} \end{bmatrix}.$$

If the regression model corresponds to a two-variable model,

$$Y_t = \alpha + \beta X_t + u_t; \quad t = 1, \ldots, n,$$

the transformation generates the new model

$$Y_t - \phi_1 Y_{t-1} = (1 - \phi_1)\alpha + \beta(X_t - \phi_1 X_{t-1}) + \varepsilon_t \tag{6.14}$$

for the last $n - 1$ observations. Even in this simple case a difficulty arises: the parameter ϕ_1 is usually unknown, and will have to be estimated for this transformation to be feasible. Further discussion is postponed until section 7.4 in the next chapter.

6.4 / The lag operator and stationary processes

It is very convenient to introduce the idea of the lag operator L. This is defined by the property that

$$LY_t = Y_{t-1},$$

and a repeated application shows that

$$L^2 Y_t = LY_{t-1} = Y_{t-2}.$$

It is sometimes called the backshift operator, for the obvious reason. More complicated operators can be constructed from L using the ordinary rules of algebra. For example, the (first) difference of Y_t used in section 2.5 can be written as

$$\Delta Y_t = Y_t - Y_{t-1} = (1 - L)Y_t.$$

Following this logic, one can define polynomials in the lag operator: for example, suppose that

$$\phi(L) = 1 - \phi_1 L,$$

and apply to Y_t to produce

$$\phi(L)Y_t = Y_t - \phi_1 Y_{t-1}.$$

This reasoning gives a simple way of representing an AR(1) process

$$Y_t - \phi_1 Y_{t-1} = \delta + u_t$$

as

$$\phi(L)Y_t = \delta + u_t.$$

More generally, let

$$\phi(L) = 1 - \phi_1 L - \ldots - \phi_p L^p,$$

which has the effect

$$\phi(L)Y_t = Y_t - \phi_1 Y_{t-1} - \ldots - \phi_p Y_{t-p}.$$

The AR(p) process (6.11) then becomes simply

$$\phi(L)Y_t = \delta + u_t. \tag{6.15}$$

Equally, the lag polynomial

$$\theta(L) = 1 - \theta_1 L - \ldots - \theta_q L^q$$

produces a similarly succinct expression for the MA(q) process (6.7):

$$Y_t = \delta + \theta(L)\varepsilon_t.$$

We can associate with each polynomial in the lag operator, $\phi(L)$, an ordinary polynomial in the complex variable z,

$$\phi(z) = 1 - \phi_1 z - \ldots - \phi_p z^p.$$

Algebraic operations on $\phi(z)$ can then be transferred back to the corresponding lag polynomial $\phi(L)$. The following discussion illustrates this point very well.

The remainder theorem for polynomials (see for example Stoll, 1952: 160, or Hartley and Hawkes, 1970: 41) implies that there exists a unique polynomial $q(z)$ such that

$$\phi(z) = \phi(1) + (1 - z)q(z). \tag{6.16}$$

The uniqueness of $q(z)$ then implies that there exists a unique polynomial $p(z)$ such that

$$\phi(z) = \phi(1)z + (1 - z)p(z), \tag{6.17}$$

and also a unique polynomial $r(z)$ such that

$$\phi(z) = \phi(1)z^k + (1 - z)r(z)$$

for a positive integer k. Indeed, it is easy to show that

$$r(z) = q(z) + (1 + z + z^2 + \ldots + z^{k-1}).$$

For an example, suppose that

$$\phi(z) = 1 - \phi_1 z - \phi_2 z^2 \tag{6.18}$$

and we seek $\psi(z)$ satisfying

$$\phi(z) = \phi(1)z + (1 - z)\psi(z),$$

that is, satisfying

$$1 - \phi_1 z - \phi_2 z^2 = (1 - \phi_1 - \phi_2)z + (1 - z)\psi(z).$$

It is intuitively clear that $\psi(z)$ should be of the form

$$\psi(z) = \psi_0 + \psi_1 z.$$

Multiplying out the right-hand side of (6.17) produces

$$1 - \phi_1 z - \phi_2 z^2 = (1 - \phi_1 - \phi_2)z + \psi_0 + (\psi_1 - \psi_0)z - \psi_1 z^2.$$

Equating coefficients of like powers of z on both sides of the equality then gives

$$\psi_0 = 1,$$

$$\psi_1 = \psi_0 - (1 - \phi_1 - \phi_2) - \phi_1 = \phi_2,$$

so that equating coefficients on z^2 is redundant. The desired $\psi(z)$ is therefore

$$\psi(z) = 1 + \phi_2 z.$$

Carrying over the reasoning to the lag polynomial $\phi(L)$ corresponding to (6.18), we can write

$$\phi(L) = \phi(1)L + (1 - L)\psi(L), \tag{6.19}$$

in which $\psi(L)$ is the AR(1) lag polynomial

$$\psi(L) = 1 + \phi_2 L.$$

The AR(2) process generated by $\phi(L)$,

$$\phi(L)Y_t = \delta + u_t; \ u_t \sim IID(0, \sigma^2); \ \text{all } t,$$

can then be written as

$$(1 + \phi_2 L)(1 - L)Y_t = (1 + \phi_2 L)\Delta Y_t = \delta - \phi(1)Y_{t-1} + u_t. \tag{6.20}$$

Only when the term in Y_{t-1} vanishes, that is, when $\phi(1) = 0$, will this AR(2) process become an AR(1) process in ΔY_t. For the AR(p) process (6.15), the analogous decomposition of $\phi(L)$ according to (6.19) produces

$$\psi(L)\Delta Y_t = \delta - \phi(1)Y_{t-1} + u_t,$$

in which $\psi(L)$ can be shown to be an AR($p - 1$) lag polynomial. The significance of these decompositions of AR lag polynomials will become much clearer in sections 6.6 and 6.7 of this chapter.

Stationarity

The condition for the stationarity of the AR(1) process (6.8), $|\phi_1| < 1$, can be expressed in terms of the roots of the lag polynomial

$$\phi(L) = 1 - \phi_1 L,$$

or, more precisely, the roots of the polynomial

$$\phi(z) = 1 - \phi_1 z.$$

Solving $\phi(z) = 0$ shows that the root, z_1 say, is

$$z_1 = \frac{1}{\phi_1},$$

so that the stationarity condition can be expressed as

$$|z_1| > 1.$$

When is the AR(p) process stationary? The corresponding polynomial $\phi(z)$ can always be factorised as

$$\phi(z) = (1 - \lambda_1 z) \dots (1 - \lambda_p z)$$

for some λ_i; $i = 1, \dots, p$, so that if $z_1, \dots, z_p$ are the roots of the equation

$$\phi(z) = 1 - \phi_1 z - \dots - \phi_p z^P = 0,$$

it must be true that

$$z_i = \frac{1}{\lambda_i}; \ i = 1, \dots, p.$$

The stationarity condition for the AR(p) process is then that

$$|z_i| > 1; \ i = 1, \dots, p,$$

or that the roots of $\phi(z) = 0$ must lie 'outside the unit circle', or have modulus exceeding 1, whether they are real or complex. This condition is equivalent to demanding that the quantities λ_i; $i = 1, \dots, p$ lie inside the unit circle. For brevity, when this condition holds, we shall say that the polynomial $\phi(z)$ is *stable*.

Invertibility

It is also possible to find the inverse of the lag polynomial $\phi(L)$, denoted $\phi^{-1}(L)$, such that

$$\phi(L)\phi^{-1}(L) = 1.$$

This inverse is a series expression, or infinite polynomial, in L. The simplest illustration uses

$$\phi(L) = 1 - \phi_1 L$$

whose inverse is

$$\phi^{-1}(L) = \frac{1}{1 - \phi_1 L} = \sum_{j=0}^{\infty} \phi_1^j L^j, \qquad (6.21)$$

as is easily verified by multiplying out the product

$$(1 - \phi_1 L)(1 + \phi_1 L + \phi_1^2 L^2 + \phi_1^3 L^3 + \dots)$$

and cancelling out terms. This manipulation is clearly true irrespective of the value of ϕ_1.

Applying this to the stationary AR(1) process

$$(1 - \phi_1 L) Y_t = \delta + u_t,$$

we obtain

$$Y_t = \phi^{-1}(L)(\delta + u_t) = \phi^{-1}(L)\delta + \sum_{j=0}^{\infty} \phi_1^j u_{t-j}.$$

The second term on the right-hand side of this equation is the limit of the sequence of random variables,

$$w_n = \sum_{j=0}^{n} \phi_1^j u_{t-j},$$

in the sense that (Hamilton, 1994: app. 3A)

$$E\left(w_n - \sum_{j=0}^{\infty} \phi_1^j u_{t-j}\right)^2 \to 0$$

as $n \to \infty$. For this convergence to hold, the condition

$$\sum_{j=0}^{\infty} \phi_1^{2j} < \infty$$

must be satisfied. This is guaranteed by the assumed stationarity, since $|\phi_1| < 1$ ensures that the condition is met. In addition, when $|\phi_1| < 1$, the expression $\phi^{-1}(L)\delta$ represents a finite and therefore well-defined quantity. We can then write, using $L\delta = \delta$,

$$\phi^{-1}(L)\delta = (1 + \phi_1 L + \phi_1^2 L^2 + \phi_1^3 L^3 + \dots)\delta$$

$$= (1 + \phi_1 + \phi_1^2 + \phi_1^3 + \dots)\delta$$

$$= \frac{\delta}{1 - \phi_1}$$

$$= \frac{\delta}{\phi(1)}.$$

The result is

$$Y_t = \frac{\delta}{\phi(1)} + \sum_{j=0}^{\infty} \phi_1^j u_{t-j}. \tag{6.22}$$

Because (6.22) involves an infinite number of lagged IID errors, it resembles a moving average process, and is called the infinite moving average representation of the AR(1) process. Infinite order moving average representations of an AR(1) process are often obtained by 'solving out': repeatedly substituting for the term Y_{t-j}; $j = 1, 2, \ldots$ on the right-hand side in the AR(1) process

$$Y_t = \delta + \phi_1 Y_{t-1} + u_t$$

will eventually produce the infinite moving average representation above.

This representation is often used as a method of generating the autocovariances for a stationary AR(1) process, since, for example,

$$\text{cov}(Y_t, Y_{t-1}) = \text{cov}\left(\sum_{j=0}^{\infty} \phi_1^j u_{t-j}, \sum_{r=0}^{\infty} \phi_1^r u_{t-1-r} \right)$$

$$= \sum_{r=0}^{\infty} \phi_1^{2r+1} \text{var}(u_{t-1-r})$$

$$= \phi_1 \sigma^2 \sum_{r=0}^{\infty} \phi_1^{2r}$$

$$= \frac{\phi_1 \sigma^2}{1 - \phi_1^2}$$

$$= \phi_1 \text{var}(Y_t),$$

where (6.10) has been used. The role played by the condition $\sum_{r=0}^{\infty} \phi_1^{2r} < \infty$ in ensuring that the autocovariances are finite is easy to see.

The same principle can be applied to write an MA(1) process as an infinite order autoregressive process. Write the MA(1) process

$$Y_t = \delta + u_t - \theta_1 u_{t-1}; \ u_t \sim IID(0, \sigma^2); \ \text{all } t$$

as

$$Y_t = \delta + (1 - \theta_1 L) u_t.$$

Then,

$$(1 - \theta_1 L)^{-1}(Y_t - \delta) = u_t.$$

To ensure that $(1 - \theta_1 L)^{-1}\delta$ and $(1 - \theta_1 L)^{-1} Y_t$ are well defined, the condition $|\theta_1| < 1$ is required. Then,

$$Y_t = \frac{\delta}{1 - \theta_1} - \sum_{j=1}^{\infty} \theta_1^j Y_{t-j} + u_t,$$

which is clearly an autoregressive model. The extra condition $|\theta_1| < 1$ imposed on the MA(1) is called the 'invertibility' condition.

An inverse for the lag polynomial of an AR(p) process can also be found. Its general form is

$$\phi^{-1}(L) = \sum_{j=0}^{\infty} f_j L^j \qquad (6.23)$$

where the f_j coefficients can be found through a recursion following from the demand that

$$\phi(L)\phi^{-1}(L) = 1.$$

This will then produce an infinite moving average representation for Y_t,

$$Y_t = \phi^{-1}(L)(\delta + u_t)$$

$$= \frac{\delta}{\phi(1)} + \sum_{s=0}^{\infty} f_s u_{t-s}.$$

To ensure the existence of the mean

$$E(Y_t) = \frac{\delta}{\phi(1)} = \delta \sum_{s=0}^{\infty} f_s,$$

the variance

$$\text{var}(Y_t) = \sigma^2 \sum_{s=0}^{\infty} f_s^2$$

and the autocovariances

$$\text{cov}(Y_t, Y_{t-j}) = \sigma^2 \sum_{s=0}^{\infty} f_s f_{s+j}; \ j \geq 1,$$

the condition

$$\sum_{j=0}^{\infty} |f_j| < \infty$$

must hold. This can be shown to be equivalent to demanding that the AR(p) process be stationary. In other words, the condition for the invertibility of an AR(p) process into infinite moving average form is that the roots of the equation $\phi(z) = 0$ lie outside the unit circle.

This line of argument also shows the conditions under which an MA(q) process,

$$Y_t = \delta + (1 - \theta_1 L - \ldots - \theta_q L^q)u_t; \ u_t \sim IID(0, \sigma^2); \ \text{all } t$$

is invertible: the roots of the polynomial

$$\theta(L) = 1 - \theta_1 L - \ldots - \theta_q L^q$$

must lie outside the unit circle. Summarising, invertibility of a lag polynomial is equivalent to saying that the lag polynomial is stable.

Autoregressive–moving average processes

For completeness, it is useful to mention how the features of an AR(p) and an MA(q) process can be combined into a single process. Suppose that Y_t follows an AR(p) process,

$$\phi(L)Y_t = \delta + u_t,$$

but instead of being $IID(0, \sigma^2)$, u_t now follows an MA(q) process:

$$u_t = \theta(L)\varepsilon_t; \quad \varepsilon_t \sim IID(0, \sigma^2); \text{ all } t.$$

The combined model is the *autoregressive–moving average* process of order (p, q), or ARMA(p, q) model:

$$\phi(L)Y_t = \delta + \theta(L)\varepsilon_t; \quad \varepsilon_t \sim IID(0, \sigma^2); \text{ all } t.$$

It is stationary under the same conditions that the AR(p) process is stationary, and will have an infinite MA representation. If the roots of $\theta(L)$ lie outside the unit circle, the moving average part will be invertible and so an infinite autoregressive representation will exist. For simple versions, like the ARMA($1, 1$) process, it is easy to find the autocovariances explicitly.

When does a process start?

It has been assumed above that the AR and MA processes have been running for all time, for example

$$Y_t = \delta + \phi_1 Y_{t-1} + u_t; \quad u_t \sim IID(0, \sigma^2); \text{ all } t.$$

This assumption allows us to write an infinite moving average representation for the stationary AR(1) process. However, the assumption does not seem very realistic in practice, and so one might consider a process starting at $t = 1$:

$$Y_t = \delta + \phi_1 Y_{t-1} + u_t; \quad u_t \sim IID(0, \sigma^2); \quad t = 1, 2, \ldots .$$

But, at $t = 1$,

$$Y_1 = \delta + \phi_1 Y_0 + u_1,$$

yet Y_0 is apparently not part of the process. This value is the starting value or presample value for an AR(1) process.

How is Y_0 generated? Is it random or fixed? If it is fixed, is its value known? An AR(1) process generated from a fixed presample value Y_0 in this way cannot be stationary in the sense used in section 6.2. It is, however, asymptotically stationary in the sense that as $t \to \infty$, the variances and covariances of the process approach those of a stationary AR(1) process, provided that $|\phi_1| < 1$. Also, if Y_0 is treated as random, it is possible to deduce the values of the mean and variance of Y_0 necessary to ensure that the process

$$Y_t = \delta + \phi_1 Y_{t-1} + u_t; \quad u_t \sim IID(0, \sigma^2); \quad t = 1, 2, \ldots$$

generates the same means, variances and autocovariances as the corresponding stationary process.

This discussion also has implications for dealing with samples of data, $Y_1, \ldots, Y_n$. Does the sample come from the stationary or the asymptotically stationary process? For theoretical purposes, it is convenient to pretend that the sample comes from the stationary process, implicitly running for all time. In large sample arguments, it generally does not matter which process is used, although it is still true that the stationary process makes the results easier to obtain.

As we shall see when discussing estimation of an AR(1) process, it is often convenient to use a fixed and known presample value Y_0, which is equivalent to assuming that the available sample of observations runs from $t = 0, 1, \ldots, n$. However, in other cases, it is more convenient to assume that the process starts at $t = 2$, with Y_1 used as the fixed and known presample value. The available sample of observations is then $t = 1, \ldots, n$. We shall use whichever perspective is more convenient, since the distinction is only a matter of notation.

6.5 / Dynamic properties of models

Equation (6.2) combines a static regression model with the lagged dependent variable Y_{t-1} associated with the AR(1) process. A more general version of (6.2) is

$$Y_t - \phi_1 Y_{t-1} - \ldots - \phi_p Y_{t-p} = \delta + \beta_0 X_t + \beta_1 X_{t-1} + \ldots + \beta_s X_{t-s} + u_t;$$

$$t = 1, \ldots, n, \tag{6.24}$$

which can be seen as an autoregressive model for Y_t augmented by the current and lagged values of the explanatory variable X_t. It is usually called an *autoregressive distributed lag model*: since there are p lags of Y_t and s lags of X_t, it is an ADL(p, s) model. When $\phi_1 = \ldots = \phi_p = 0$, this is simply the *distributed lag* model

$$Y_t = \delta + \beta_0 X_t + \beta_1 X_{t-1} + \ldots + \beta_s X_{t-s} + u_t; \ t = 1, \ldots, n. \tag{6.25}$$

Models like (6.24) are nonstationary because the presence of the explanatory variables $X_t, \ldots, X_{t-s}$ makes $E(Y_t)$ different for each t. Despite this nonstationarity, the properties of lag polynomials can be used to investigate the short- and long-run properties of (6.24).

Multipliers

In the distributed lag model (6.25), the response of Y_t to a change in current or past X_{t-j} equals β_j, for $j \leq s$. Another way of putting this is that the effect of a change in X_t will have died out after $s + 1$ periods:

$$\frac{\partial Y_{t+s+1}}{\partial X_t} = 0.$$

In contrast, in the ADL model, a change in X_t affects all future values of Y_t, and this effect dies out slowly, under certain conditions. This is easy to see in the ADL(1, 1) model,

$$Y_t = \delta + \phi_1 Y_{t-1} + \beta_0 X_t + \beta_1 X_{t-1} + u_t, \tag{6.26}$$

where a change in X_t directly affects Y_t, which will then affect Y_{t+1}, Y_{t+2} and so on. Using lag polynomials, the model is

$$(1 - \phi_1 L) Y_t = \delta + (\beta_0 + \beta_1 L) X_t + u_t$$

or

$$\phi(L) Y_t = \delta + \beta(L) X_t + u_t.$$

The formal solution is

$$Y_t = \frac{\delta}{(1 - \phi_1)} + \frac{(\beta_0 + \beta_1 L)}{(1 - \phi_1 L)} X_t + \frac{u_t}{(1 - \phi_1 L)}.$$

The existence of this solution depends on the existence of the inverse to $\phi(L)$, which requires that the roots of

$$\phi(L) = 0$$

lie outside the unit circle and thus that $\phi(L)$ is stable. More simply, the condition is $|\phi_1| < 1$.

Applying the inverse of $\phi(L)$ from equation (6.21) and collecting terms in X_{t-1}, X_{t-2} and so on produces

$$Y_t = \phi^{-1}(1)\delta + \sum_{j=0}^{\infty} \phi_1^j L^j (\beta_0 + \beta_1 L) X_t + \phi^{-1}(L) u_t$$

$$= \frac{\delta}{1 - \phi_1} + \beta_0 X_t + \sum_{j=1}^{\infty} (\phi_1^j \beta_0 + \phi_1^{j-1} \beta_1) X_{t-j} + \phi^{-1}(L) u_t.$$

In this expression, the direct impact of X_t on Y_t, the *impact multiplier*, is clearly β_0. Each component of the next term represents the indirect effects of X_{t-j} on the current Y_t, the first term being the effect via Y_{t-j} and the second the effect via Y_{t-j+1}. It is clear, at least in principle, that values of X_{t-j} from the far distant past have an effect on the current Y_t. These effects are the *dynamic multipliers*,

$$\frac{\partial Y_t}{\partial X_{t-1}} = (\beta_1 + \phi_1 \beta_0),$$

$$\frac{\partial Y_t}{\partial X_{t-2}} = \phi_1 (\beta_1 + \phi_1 \beta_0),$$

with general term

$$\frac{\partial Y_t}{\partial X_{t-j}} = \phi_1^{j-1} (\beta_1 + \phi_1 \beta_0).$$

This analysis looks into the past from time t to see how a change in the past X_{t-j} affects the current Y_t. It is sometimes more useful to examine the impact of a change in the current X_t on future values of Y_t. Take

$$\frac{\partial Y_t}{\partial X_{t-j}} = \phi_1^{j-1}(\beta_1 + \phi_1\beta_0),$$

put $t - j = s$ and regard s as the current period. Then, the derivative becomes

$$\frac{\partial Y_{s+j}}{\partial X_s} = \phi_1^{j-1}(\beta_1 + \phi_1\beta_0).$$

One can see that the effect of a change in X_s ultimately dies out at a rate determined by ϕ_1: provided that $|\phi_1| < 1$, the effect goes to zero. The impact multiplier, the effect of a change in X_s on Y_s, is not affected by this change in time perspective, and is still given by the value β_0.

Economists are often interested in the cumulative effect of the change in X_s: that is,

$$\sum_{j=0}^{\infty} \frac{\partial Y_{s+j}}{\partial X_s} = \beta_0 + \sum_{j=1}^{\infty} \phi_1^{j-1}(\beta_1 + \phi_1\beta_0)$$

$$= \frac{\beta_1 + \beta_0}{1 - \phi_1}.$$

This is called the *long-run* multiplier. An *interim* multiplier is a partial sum of the long-run multiplier. The long-run multiplier for the ADL(1, 1) model (6.26) is also the ratio of the lag polynomials $\phi(L)$ and $\beta(L)$, evaluated at $L = 1$:

$$\frac{\beta(1)}{\phi(1)} = \frac{\beta_0 + \beta_1}{1 - \phi_1}.$$

The expression on the left also gives the long-run multiplier in the general ADL(p, s) model. The assumption that $\phi(L)$ is stable ensures the existence of the long-run multiplier by eliminating the possiblity that $\phi(1) = 0$.

Dynamic multipliers are important because different sequences of dynamic multipliers (and hence interim multipliers) can lead to the same long-run effect. In one sequence, the effects may be concentrated in the first few terms of the sequence, and in the other, a slow cumulation may occur. One historically important scenario is the devaluation of sterling in 1967, where a change in an explanatory variable initially reduced the values of Y, and only as time passed did a long-run positive effect show through. The multiplier responses implied by different models may thus be important if they are to be used for policy purposes.

Equilibrium

Stationary equilibrium in economics occurs when the value of a dependent variable has fully adjusted to the values of determining variables. So, if the values of the determining variables are constant, the value of the dependent variable is constant.

In the ADL$(1, 1)$ model (6.26), assuming that the error term has temporarily disappeared (as was assumed above for the purpose of calculating multipliers), this is

$$Y = \delta + \phi_1 Y + \beta_0 X + \beta_1 X,$$

and solving for Y,

$$Y = \frac{\delta}{1 - \phi_1} + \frac{\beta_0 + \beta_1}{1 - \phi_1} X. \tag{6.27}$$

The equilibrium, or comparative static, effect of a change in X upon Y is then

$$\frac{\partial Y}{\partial X} = \frac{\beta_0 + \beta_1}{1 - \phi_1}.$$

This coincides, as it should in general, with the long-run multiplier obtained above.

One can interpret the role of the lagged dependent variables in the ADL model as embodying the adjustment of Y_t to the long-run equilibrium value. However, in the ADL model, the precise nature of the long-run equilibrium and the adjustment pattern are well hidden, as we have seen.

6.6 / A small catalogue of dynamic models

One argument for including lagged variables in models estimated from time series data is simply that this will lead to a more convincing explanation of observed behaviour than a purely static formulation. We have also suggested that there are advantages in starting from a relatively free dynamic specification, because this will enable us to capture the essential features of the dynamic linkage between an endogenous variable Y and an exogenous variable X, without incurring the penalty of serial correlation. By careful testing, it may then be possible to isolate a more specific mechanism, or at least to rule out some of the competing hypotheses that could give rise to a general dynamic model. In this section, we consider some of these alternatives. In practice, it is likely that there will be several exogenous variables, but the essence of the argument can be illustrated by considering special cases of the ADL$(1, 1)$ model

$$Y_t = \delta + \phi_1 Y_{t-1} + \beta_0 X_t + \beta_1 X_{t-1} + u_t; \quad u_t \sim IID(0, \sigma^2); \quad t = 1, \dots, n. \tag{6.28}$$

By suitably restricting the values of ϕ_1, β_0 and β_1 to be zero, we can obtain a variety of special cases: for example, a distributed lag model ($\phi_1 = 0$); a purely static model ($\phi_1 = \beta_1 = 0$); an autoregressive process ($\beta_0 = \beta_1 = 0$). More complicated parameter restrictions are required to obtain other well-known models as special cases.

Partial adjustment

If the desired or target value of the variable Y is determined as

$$Y_t^* = \alpha + \beta X_t + u_t; \quad t = 1, \dots, n \tag{6.29}$$

and the actual adjustment is always some fixed proportion of the desired adjustment

$$(Y_t - Y_{t-1}) = \delta(Y_t^* - Y_{t-1}); \ 0 < \delta \leq 1, \tag{6.30}$$

then, by substitution,

$$Y_t = \delta\alpha + \delta\beta X_t + (1 - \delta)Y_{t-1} + \delta u_t; \ t = 1, \ldots, n. \tag{6.31}$$

If u_t is $IID(0, \sigma^2)$ in (6.29), it will be in (6.31). In this model, $\delta\beta$ is the short-run response of Y to a unit change in X, and β is the long-run response.

If a second well-behaved disturbance is added to the partial adjustment process (6.30), the resulting composite disturbance in (6.31) will still not exhibit serial correlation, and the analysis above stands. The simple partial adjustment model therefore specialises (6.28) by setting $\beta_1 = 0$, with no inherent reason for serial correlation.

Adaptive expectations

Now suppose that Y_t is determined by what is expected to happen to X in period $t + 1$, that is,

$$Y_t = \alpha + \beta X_{t+1}^* + u_t; \ t = 1, \ldots, n. \tag{6.32}$$

In (6.32), X_{t+1}^* represents the expected or anticipated value of X in period $t + 1$. In using such a model, one has the choice between trying to observe X_{t+1}^* directly from anticipations data, or forming a subsidiary hypothesis about the way in which expectations are generated. The adaptive expectations hypothesis suggests that expectations are revised by some fixed proportion of the extent to which expectations are not realised in the current period:

$$(X_{t+1}^* - X_t^*) = (1 - \lambda)(X_t - X_t^*); \ 0 \leq \lambda < 1. \tag{6.33}$$

In lag operator notation, this is

$$(1 - \lambda L)X_{t+1}^* = (1 - \lambda)X_t,$$

with formal solution

$$X_{t+1}^* = \frac{(1 - \lambda)}{(1 - \lambda L)} X_t.$$

Substitution into (6.32) produces

$$Y_t = \alpha + \frac{(1 - \lambda)}{(1 - \lambda L)} \beta X_t + u_t.$$

Although estimation of dynamic models has not been discussed yet, one way of estimating the parameters in this model is to multiply through this equation by $(1 - \lambda L)$, producing

$$(1 - \lambda L)Y_t = (1 - \lambda)\alpha + (1 - \lambda)\beta X_t + (1 - \lambda L)u_t.$$

On expansion of the lag polynomial, this looks very similar to (6.31) and the ADL(1, 1) model, but the composite disturbance, say v_t, can be written as

$$v_t = (1 - \lambda L)u_t,$$

which is an MA(1) process if u_t is $IID(0, \sigma^2)$.

Common factors

Consider a static, two-variable regression model,

$$Y_t = \alpha + \beta X_t + u_t; \ t = 1, \ldots, n,$$

where the disturbance follows an AR(1) process,

$$u_t = \rho_1 u_{t-1} + \varepsilon_t; \ \varepsilon_t \sim IID(0, \sigma^2); \ \text{all } t.$$

As seen earlier in (6.14), attempting to transform the model to eliminate the serial correlation produces a model of the form

$$Y_t - \rho_1 Y_{t-1} = (1 - \rho_1)\alpha + \beta(X_t - \rho_1 X_{t-1}) + \varepsilon_t; \ t = 2, \ldots, n,$$

or, after rearrangement,

$$Y_t = \rho_1 Y_{t-1} + (1 - \rho_1)\alpha + \beta(X_t - \rho_1 X_{t-1}) + \varepsilon_t; \ t = 2, \ldots, n.$$

Comparing this with the ADL(1, 1) model (6.26) gives

$$\delta = (1 - \rho_1)\alpha, \quad \phi_1 = \rho_1, \quad \beta_0 = \beta, \quad \beta_1 = -\beta\rho_1.$$

The four parameters in the ADL model depend on the three parameters in the underlying static regression model with an autoregressive error. If the parameters of the ADL model satisfy the restriction

$$\beta_1 = -\phi_1 \beta_0, \tag{6.34}$$

the ADL model collapses to the underlying static model.

The source of the name 'common factors' can be easily seen using lag polynomials: write the ADL model as

$$(1 - \phi_1 L)Y_t = \delta + (\beta_0 + \beta_1 L)X_t + u_t,$$

in which u_t is $IID(0, \sigma^2)$. If the 'common factor' restriction (6.34) holds,

$$(\beta_0 + \beta_1 L) = \beta_0(1 - \phi_1 L)$$

so that the model becomes

$$(1 - \phi_1 L)Y_t = \delta + \beta_0(1 - \phi_1 L)X_t + u_t,$$

and dividing through by the 'common factor' $1 - \phi_1 L$ gives

$$Y_t = \frac{\delta}{1 - \phi_1} + \beta_0 X_t + \frac{u_t}{(1 - \phi_1 L)}.$$

Putting

$$v_t = \frac{u_t}{(1 - \phi_1 L)}$$

is equivalent to writing

$$(1 - \phi_1 L)v_t = u_t,$$

that is, v_t follows an AR(1) process. Apart from the parameterisation of the intercept, the resulting model is a static regression with AR(1) errors.

Error correction mechanism

As stated earlier, one could justify using an ADL(1, 1) model like (6.26) or (6.28) by arguing that the presence of lagged variables makes allowance for the fact that data are not observed in a state of equilibrium. However, one can choose a parameterisation of the ADL(1, 1) model (6.26) or (6.28) that displays the long-run equilibrium parameters of (6.27),

$$\mu_0 = \frac{\delta}{1 - \phi_1}, \quad \mu_1 = \frac{\beta_0 + \beta_1}{1 - \phi_1}$$

directly. The adjustment to equilibrium is then captured within the short-run dynamics, giving rise to the name 'error correction mechanism'. Recent developments in macroeconomics have emphasised the need to test hypotheses about long-run relationships, and such a parameterisation can facilitate this.

There are several ways of creating this parameterisation. The simplest employs lag polynomial notation and the decomposition of a lag polynomial shown in (6.19). We can, in fact, deal with the more general ADL(p, s) model

$$\phi(L)Y_t = \delta + \beta(L)X_t + u_t \tag{6.35}$$

where $\phi(L)$ is the AR(p) polynomial and

$$\beta(L) = \beta_0 + \beta_1 L + \ldots + \beta_s L^s.$$

Following (6.19), let

$$\phi(L) = L\phi(1) + (1 - L)\psi(L),$$

$$\beta(L) = L\beta(1) + (1 - L)g(L).$$

Substituting these expressions into the ADL model, and rearranging, gives

$$\psi(L)\Delta Y_t = \delta - \phi(1)Y_{t-1} + \beta(1)X_{t-1} + g(L)\Delta X_t + u_t$$

$$= -\phi(1)\left[Y_{t-1} - \frac{\delta}{\phi(1)} - \frac{\beta(1)}{\phi(1)}X_{t-1}\right] + g(L)\Delta X_t + u_t$$

$$= -\phi(1)(Y_{t-1} - \mu_0 - \mu_1 X_{t-1}) + g(L)\Delta X_t + u_t. \tag{6.36}$$

The long-run multiplier μ_1 exists if $\phi(L)$ is invertible. In the case of the ADL$(1,1)$ model (6.26), it is easy to show that

$$\psi(L) = 1,$$
$$g(L) = \beta_0, \tag{6.37}$$
$$\Delta Y_t = -\phi(1)(Y_{t-1} - \mu_0 - \mu_1 X_{t-1}) + \beta_0 \Delta X_t + u_t.$$

The *error correction model* (6.37) depicts changes in Y as driven by changes in X, and by the extent to which Y and X in the preceding period fail to satisfy the long-run equilibrium relationship (6.27). If $|\phi_1| < 1$, as is required even to be able to talk about the existence of the long-run multiplier μ_1, the error correction model incorporates negative feedback, which attempts to correct for the previous errors in aiming at the supposed long-run relationship between Y and X.

6.7 / Unit roots

All the arguments so far have been based on the assumption that autoregressive lag polynomials have roots outside the unit circle. This assumption implies that an autoregressive process is at least asymptotically stationary, and that long-run multipliers exist in an ADL model. What happens if this assumption fails? The most obvious comment is that the autoregressive process is then 'nonstationary', although there are many possible forms of nonstationarity.

It is best to examine the consequences of this in the simple case of an AR(1) process without intercept, starting from time $t = 1$:

$$Y_t = \phi_1 Y_{t-1} + u_t; \; u_t \sim IID(0, \sigma^2); \; t \geq 1. \tag{6.38}$$

The condition for this process to be asymptotically stationary is that the roots of the polynomial $1 - \phi_1 L$ lie outside the unit circle, which is equivalent to the demand that $|\phi_1| < 1$. Roots of $1 - \phi_1 L$ inside the unit circle therefore correspond to $|\phi_1| \geq 1$.

Without making any assumption about the value of ϕ_1, express Y_t in terms of the fixed and known presample value Y_0 by repeated substitution. That is, in (6.38), replace Y_{t-1} by $\phi_1 Y_{t-2} + u_{t-1}$, and so on:

$$\begin{aligned} Y_t &= \phi_1 Y_{t-1} + u_t \\ &= \phi_1(\phi_1 Y_{t-2} + u_{t-1}) + u_t \\ &= \phi_1^2 Y_{t-2} + \phi_1 u_{t-1} + u_t \\ &= \phi_1^3 Y_{t-3} + \phi_1^2 u_{t-2} + \phi_1 u_{t-1} + u_t \\ &\;\;\vdots \\ &= \phi_1^t Y_0 + \phi_1^{t-1} u_1 + \ldots + \phi_1 u_{t-1} + u_t. \end{aligned} \tag{6.39}$$

Just as in section 6.4, the mean and variance of Y_t can be computed from this representation, as also the covariances between Y_t and Y_{t-s}:

$$E(Y_t) = \phi_1^t Y_0; \ t \geq 1$$

$$\text{var}(Y_t) = \sigma^2 \left(1 + \phi_1^2 + \phi_1^4 + \ldots + \phi_1^{2(t-1)}\right); \ t \geq 1 \qquad (6.40)$$

$$\text{cov}(Y_t, Y_{t-s}) = \phi_1^s \, \text{var}(Y_{t-s}); \ 1 \leq s \leq t - 1.$$

Since all these quantities depend on t, this process is nonstationary, irrespective of the value of ϕ_1.

If $|\phi_1| < 1$, however, it is clear that as $t \to \infty$

$$E(Y_t) \to 0$$

$$\text{var}(Y_t) \to \frac{\sigma^2}{1 - \phi_1^2}$$

$$\frac{\text{cov}(Y_t, Y_{t-s})}{\text{var}(Y_t)} \to \phi_1^s.$$

These are the values expected for a stationary AR(1) process, confirming the claim of asymptotic stationarity.

For the case $|\phi_1| \geq 1$, the problem is that the sum defining $\text{var}(Y_t)$ diverges, so that the values of the process wander increasingly far from the mean. When $\phi_1 = 1$, this mean is constant at Y_0, but if $\phi_1 > 1$, the mean itself will explode unless $Y_0 = 0$. If $\phi_1 < -1$, this explosion will be oscillatory. On a priori grounds, then, such explosive behaviour seems to preclude the application of a process with $|\phi_1| > 1$ to economic data in general. Perhaps surprisingly, given that $\text{var}(Y_t)$ diverges, the case of $\phi_1 = 1$ is actually of great importance in economics.

The random walk

The special case of (6.38) where $\phi_1 = 1$ is usually called the random walk process,

$$Y_t = Y_{t-1} + u_t; \ u_t \sim IID(0, \sigma^2); \ t \geq 1.$$

Here the root is on the unit circle. The analysis leading to (6.39) yields

$$Y_t = Y_0 + (u_t + \ldots + u_1). \qquad (6.41)$$

The cumulated errors

$$\sum_{j=1}^{t} u_j$$

will be referred to as a *stochastic trend*: the reasoning behind this terminology will be explained below. What is clear though is that every error from the start of the process has an impact on the current value of Y_t: the jargon for this is that the errors are *persistent*. The implication is that shocks due to wars or oil crises, for example, have permanent effects on the evolution of the economy. This behaviour can be contrasted with that of a stationary AR(1) process in its infinite moving average form (6.22). Here, all past errors have an impact on Y_t, but this impact dies out as one goes further into the past.

The mean and variance in a random walk are, by specialising (6.40),

$$E(Y_t) = Y_0,$$

$$\text{var}(Y_t) = t\sigma^2.$$

Unlike the explosive case, the mean of Y_t is constant, and the variance increases linearly with t – in the explosive case, it increases geometrically. Again, this process is nonstationary.

The autocovariances are easily computed directly from (6.41):

$$\text{cov}(Y_t, Y_{t-s}) = E(Y_t - Y_0)(Y_{t-s} - Y_0)$$

$$= E\left(\sum_{j=1}^{t} u_j\right)\left(\sum_{r=1}^{t-s} u_r\right)$$

$$= (t - s)\sigma^2. \tag{6.42}$$

Notice that the covariance depends both on the time difference (s) and directly on the calendar time – a complete contrast to the stationary case.

Now consider the correlations between Y_t and Y_{t-s}:

$$\text{corr}(Y_t, Y_{t-s}) = \frac{\text{cov}(Y_t, Y_{t-s})}{\sqrt{\text{var}(Y_t)\,\text{var}(Y_{t-s})}}$$

$$= \sqrt{\frac{t-s}{t}}$$

$$= \sqrt{1 - \frac{s}{t}}.$$

Hold s constant and let $t \to \infty$: then, $\text{corr}(Y_t, Y_{t-s}) \to 1$. That is, observations any finite distance apart, but sufficiently far into the future relative to the starting time of the process, are perfectly correlated.

By changing the time origin, one can see that

$$\text{corr}(Y_{t+s}, Y_t) = \sqrt{\frac{t}{t+s}},$$

from which one can deduce that for t fixed, $\text{corr}(Y_{t+s}, Y_t) \to 0$ as $s \to \infty$. It is easy to see from numerical experiments with values of t and s that the rate of convergence to zero is very slow, especially as t increases. For example, for $t = 100$, the correlation declines from 0.995 at $s = 1$ to 0.913 for $s = 20$. This long-memory property is characteristic of the random walk process.

These results contrast markedly with the asymptotically stationary AR(1) case, for which

$$\text{corr}(Y_t, Y_{t-s}) \to \phi_1^s; \ t \to \infty$$

and $|\phi_1^s| < 1$. In a stationary AR(1) process, it is also true that for t fixed, $\text{corr}(Y_{t+s}, Y_t) = \phi_1^s$: as $s \to \infty$, this correlation goes to zero, and much faster than the random walk case. In other words, observations generated from a stationary AR(1) process that are sufficiently far apart in time are effectively uncorrelated. To illustrate, for $\phi_1 = 0.95$, the correlation declines from 0.95 at $s = 1$ to 0.358 at $s = 20$.

The random walk with drift

This is simply the random walk process with a nonzero intercept:

$$Y_t = \delta + Y_{t-1} + u_t; \ u_t \sim IID(0, \sigma^2); \ t \geq 1.$$

Re-examining the repeated substitution argument of (6.39) shows that

$$Y_t = Y_0 + \delta t + \sum_{j=1}^{t} u_j. \tag{6.43}$$

The random walk with drift has a mean,

$$E(Y_t) = Y_0 + \delta t,$$

which is a linear trend, and has an autocorrelation structure that coincides with that of the random walk process.

The representation just given for the random walk with drift reveals that it can be considered as the sum of a deterministic linear trend and a drift-free random walk, or equivalently, as the sum of a deterministic trend and a stochastic trend. The persistence of past error terms encountered with the random walk is therefore also present here.

The random walk and random walk with drift processes are examples of integrated processes, this referring to the 'cumulative summation' required to solve the models for the time path of Y_t. Recall that the (first) difference of a series is defined to be

$$\Delta Y_t = Y_t - Y_{t-1}.$$

It is clear that in each model, the first difference of Y_t follows a stationary process

$$\Delta Y_t = u_t,$$

$$\Delta Y_t = \delta + u_t,$$

since an $IID(0, \sigma^2)$ process is stationary. They are also unit root processes, in the sense that they are AR(1) processes where the polynomial $\phi(z)$ has a root equal to 1.

Figure 6.1 displays 120 out of a sample of 130 observations from an asymptotically stationary AR(1) process, a random walk and a random walk with drift. These are some of the series from data set 7, a collection of computer-generated series. The

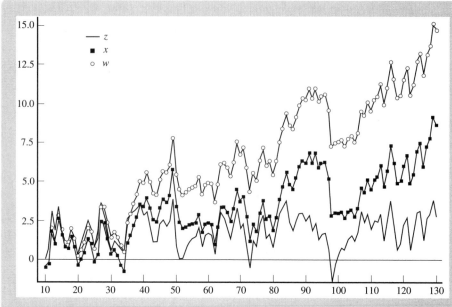

Figure 6.1 Observations from an asymptotically stationary AR(1) process (z), a random walk (x), and a random walk with drift (w)

first 10 observations for each series were discarded. The models are

$$z_t = 0.5 + 0.7z_{t-1} + u_t; \ u_t \sim NID(0,1); \ t = 10, \ldots, 130,$$

$$x_t = x_{t-1} + u_t; \ u_t \sim NID(0,1); \ t = 10, \ldots, 130,$$

$$w_t = 0.05 + w_{t-1} + u_t; \ u_t \sim NID(0,1); \ t = 10, \ldots, 130,$$

all with zero presample values. Each process is generated from the same set of drawings $u_1, \ldots, u_{130}$, which accounts for the broadly similar pattern of variation displayed in the graphs.

The mean of the stationary version of the z_t process is $0.5/(1-0.7) = 1.6667$, and the series for z_t in the graph clearly fluctuates about this level in a bounded way. In contrast, the random walk series x_t drifts upwards, justifying the idea of a stochastic trend component, although there are also periods in which the series drifts downwards. The random walk with drift, w_t, shows a relatively persistent upward trend, arising both from its deterministic trend component $0.05t$, as well as from the stochastic trend component inherited from x_t.

Autoregressive processes with a unit root

The lag polynomial $\phi(L)$ for an AR(p) process

$$\phi(L)Y_t = \delta + u_t; \ u_t \sim IID(0, \sigma^2); \ \text{all } t \tag{6.44}$$

may also contain one or more unit roots. That is,

$$\phi(z) = 0$$

is satisfied for $z = 1$. The decomposition (6.19) then shows that (6.44) can be written as an $AR(p-1)$ process in ΔY_t,

$$\psi(L)\Delta Y_t = \delta + u_t; \ u_t \sim IID(0,\sigma^2); \ \text{all } t.$$

If there were only a single root of $\phi(z)$ on the unit circle, this would be a stationary process for the *differences* ΔY_t. What sort of properties does such a process imply for Y_t? One might expect to see features associated with the random walk with drift, given the presence of the unit root. Revealing these features, when the process starts at $t = 1$ for comparability with the random walk process, is best done by changing the framework slightly.

Suppose that Y_t is generated by a random walk process with fixed presample value Y_0,

$$\Delta Y_t = v_t; \ t \geq 1, \tag{6.45}$$

and v_t is generated from the *stationary* $AR(p-1)$ process

$$\psi(L)v_t = \delta + u_t; \ u_t \sim IID(0,\sigma^2); \ \text{all } t, \tag{6.46}$$

so that

$$\psi(L)\Delta Y_t = \delta + u_t; \ u_t \sim IID(0,\sigma^2); \ t \geq 1.$$

From (6.45),

$$Y_t = Y_0 + \sum_{j=1}^{t} v_j; \ t \geq 1$$

and from (6.46),

$$v_t = \psi^{-1}(L)(\delta + u_t); \ \text{all } t.$$

Combining the two equations produces

$$Y_t = Y_0 + \psi^{-1}(1)\delta t + \psi^{-1}(L)\sum_{j=1}^{t} u_j.$$

One can see within this expression the deterministic linear trend component of the random walk with drift, but the stochastic trend component $\sum_{j=1}^{t} u_j$ does not appear in the same manner as in that model. One way of separating out the stochastic trend component is to argue that the infinite series $\psi^{-1}(L)$ can be decomposed like (6.16), as

$$\psi^{-1}(L) = \psi^{-1}(1) + (1-L)\eta(L)$$

in which $\eta(L)$ is itself an infinite series in the lag operator. The coefficients in $\eta(L)$ are obtained by multiplying out the right-hand side, and equating coefficients of like powers of L on both sides of the equality sign. Substitution of $\psi^{-1}(L)$ together with the observation that

$$(1 - L) \sum_{j=1}^{t} u_j = u_t - u_0$$

produces

$$Y_t = Y_0 + \psi^{-1}(1)\delta t + \psi^{-1}(1) \sum_{j=1}^{t} u_j + \eta(L)(u_t - u_0). \tag{6.47}$$

This is the Beveridge–Nelson decomposition for an autoregressive process with a unit root. Comparing this with the corresponding expression for the random walk with drift, (6.43), one can see that the deterministic and stochastic trend terms have been modified by the constant factor $\psi^{-1}(1)$, which will usually exceed 1, so that past error terms are more persistent than in the random walk case. In addition, there is an error term generated by the process

$$\eta(L)(u_t - u_0) = \sum_{j=0}^{\infty} \eta_j (u_{t-j} - u_{-j}).$$

This can be written in the form

$$\sum_{j=0}^{\infty} \kappa_j u_{t-j};$$

a process generated from this quantity will be stationary, given that $\psi(L)$ is invertible, although this is not easy to show. Whilst the Beveridge–Nelson decomposition (6.47) has been obtained for an $AR(p)$ process generated in a particular way, for simplicity, its structure does carry over to the general case of an $AR(p)$ process with a single root of $+1$ on the unit circle.

Integrated processes and series

An $AR(p)$ process with a unit root, like the random walk and the random walk with drift, is an integrated process. Yet, when expressed as an $AR(p-1)$ process in ΔY_t, the process for ΔY_t is at least asymptotically stationary. The process for Y_t is then an $I(1)$ process, the '1' suggesting 'differencing once' for (asymptotic) stationarity. One could imagine a process containing two unit roots, and this would require differencing twice to become asymptotically stationary. This would be an $I(2)$ process. The same sort of logic suggests that a process which is (asymptotically) stationary is $I(0)$. Often, these labels are applied to a series generated by an integrated process, so that an $I(1)$ process generates an $I(1)$ series. The first difference of such a series would then be an $I(0)$ series. In turn, one can ask the question empirically: Is a (data) series $I(1)$ or $I(0)$? This question enables us to return to the distinction between deterministic and stochastic trends.

Deterministic and stochastic trends

There are several ways in which one could summarise the behaviour of an upwardly trending series Y_t; $t = 1, \ldots, n$. A purely data-based approach could be to compute the sequence of data growth rates

$$g_t = \frac{Y_t - Y_{t-1}}{Y_{t-1}} \tag{6.48}$$

and plot them. Equivalently, one could use $\Delta \ln(Y_t)$ as an approximation to g_t (for small g_t). A sample mean of these data growth rates would then give some overall indication of the rate of growth in the sample.

An alternative model-based approach would be to consider trend models. For example, one could fit a linear trend model

$$Y_t = \alpha + \beta t + u_t; \ u_t \sim IID(0, \sigma^2); \ t = 1, \ldots, n$$

or even an exponential trend in its semi-logarithmic form,

$$\ln(Y_t) = \alpha + \beta t + u_t; \ u_t \sim IID(0, \sigma^2); \ t = 1, \ldots, n.$$

In the linear trend, Y_t increases on average by the same absolute amount β each period, while in the exponential trend model, it grows at a constant rate β each period, using the instantaneous rate of growth definition $\partial \ln(Y_t)/\partial t$. In both these models, the variations about the growth path for Y_t are directly due to the current error term u_t.

To highlight the contrasts between such deterministic trend models and the component $\sum_{j=1}^{t} u_j$ of random walk models that was described as a stochastic trend, we shall concentrate on the case where $\ln(Y_t)$ follows a random walk with drift. Then, the linear trend in

$$\ln(Y_t) = \ln(Y_0) + \delta t + \sum_{j=1}^{t} u_j; \ u_t \sim IID(0, \sigma^2); \ t \geq 1 \tag{6.49}$$

corresponds to the deterministic exponential trend for Y_t. It is clear that all the current and past error terms affect $\ln(Y_t)$ in a cumulative way. This means that shocks have permanent effects on the time path of Y_t, in contrast to the exponential trend model, where there is no such effect.

If the error terms in the semi-logarithmic trend are dependent, say a stationary AR(1) process, then there will be slow changes in $\ln(Y_t)$ around this growth path, due to the impact of past shocks. However, as noted above, the effect of past shocks on the current $\ln(Y_t)$ will eventually die out – they are not persistent. Until recently, this picture of *stationary* fluctuations about a deterministic growth path was the standard perception of how quantities like GDP should be evolving over the longer term.

To motivate the notion of a stochastic trend, consider the random walk process for $\ln(Y_t)$:

$$\ln(Y_t) = \ln(Y_0) + u_t + u_{t-1} + \ldots + u_1; \ u_t \sim IID(0, \sigma^2); \ t \geq 1.$$

The expected value of the cumulated shocks is zero, yet the effect of a sequence of positive shocks is to drive the value of $\ln(Y_t)$ above its expected value. One could say, using ordinary language, that the *current trend is upwards*, yet this trend could be reversed if a sequence of sufficiently large negative shocks is encountered, as illustrated in Figure 6.1 for the series x_t. This intuitive argument is largely responsible for the interpretation of the cumulative sum of errors as a *stochastic trend*. In a random walk with drift, the effect of a positive sequence of cumulated shocks can be to drive the series above its long-term trend path $Y_0 + \delta t$. The same sort of interpretation can be given in the case of the AR(p) process with a unit root, although the factor $\psi^{-1}(1)$ will tend to magnify the effect of a sequence of positive or negative shocks.

These remarks are of great practical significance. For example, consider the economics of business cycles. Here, the traditional view is that the economy tends to grow along a smooth trend path, and that business cycles are the short-term cyclical fluctuations or shocks which temporarily disturb this trend. A simple characterisation of this might be an exponential trend for GDP,

$$\ln(Y_t) = \alpha + \beta t + u_t$$

in which the disturbances u_t capturing the cyclical fluctuations follow some stationary process, so that their influence eventually dies out. But, if $\ln(Y_t)$ follows a random walk with drift, the cyclical fluctuations or shocks persist and thus influence all future levels of GDP. Another way of putting this is that some part of the apparently short-term variation in GDP contributes to a change in the long-term trend.

Another perspective on the contrast between deterministic and stochastic trends comes from recognising a random walk with drift process for $\ln(Y_t)$ as a model for the growth rate of Y_t. This stems from the observation above that

$$\Delta \ln(Y_t)$$

is an approximation to the (data) growth rate g_t as defined in (6.48). The random walk with drift process for $\ln(Y_t)$ asserts that

$$g_t \cong \Delta \ln(Y_t) = \delta + u_t; \ u_t \sim IID(0, \sigma^2); \ t \geq 1.$$

This is a model of a constant expected (data) growth rate, with zero mean shocks generating the observed growth rate. In contrast, the exponential trend model has a constant expected (instantaneous) growth rate, but the shocks affect $\ln(Y_t)$ directly. In (6.49), δ also has the status of an instantaneous growth rate, because it is the coefficient on a linear trend term in a semi-logarithmic model.

We can now see that treating random walk processes for variables in logarithms as models for growth rates enables us to interpret the random walk as a model of a stochastic trend around an expected growth rate of zero. In the random walk with drift, there is a stochastic trend around a nonzero expected growth rate. It is clear that similar sorts of considerations apply to more general autoregressive models for $\ln(Y_t)$, if they contain a unit root.

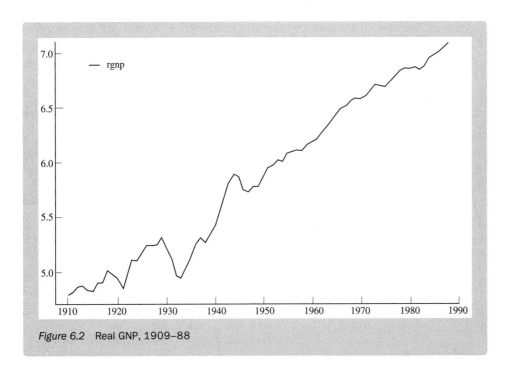

Figure 6.2   Real GNP, 1909–88

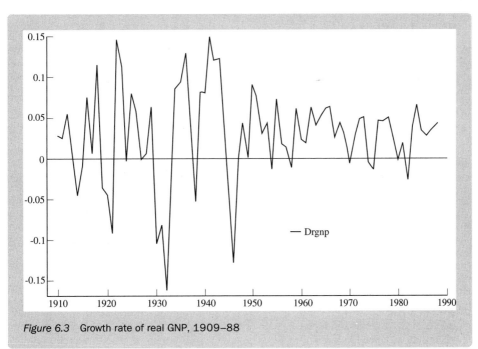

Figure 6.3   Growth rate of real GNP, 1909–88

Partly as a result of these sorts of issues, and partly as a result of considerations discussed in the next chapter, there has been considerable interest in establishing whether macroeconomic series like GDP, inflation, exports, and exchange rates (amongst others) are generated by processes that contain unit roots – that is, are integrated series. Without more formal inferential procedures, it is not that easy to tell from the graph of a series or its logarithm if the process generating the series contains a unit root. To illustrate, Figures 6.2 and 6.3 display the log of US real GNP over the period 1909–88, and its growth rate (that is, the first difference of log real GNP), the series being taken from a data set more fully discussed in the next chapter. Examining these graphs, it is not easy to see whether real GNP contains a unit root. The first differences fluctuate quite a lot around an apparently nonzero mean, which is suggestive, but no substitute for a formal procedure.

6.8 / Further reading

Of the texts so far mentioned, Davidson and MacKinnon (1993) is still helpful. Hamilton (1994) is a standard and comprehensive reference for all the topics of this chapter. Hendry (1995) is excellent on the economic modelling aspects, and also covers the technical material, as well as expounding Hendry's views on econometric methodology.

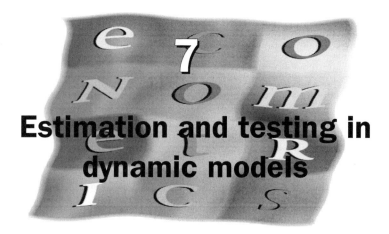

7

Estimation and testing in dynamic models

7.1 / Introduction

The range of models considered in the previous chapter creates a number of different types of estimation problem. AR models and ADL models for an observable Y_t appear to be linear regression models, with error terms that are supposed to satisfy classical assumptions. Despite the presence of lagged dependent variables, these might be expected to be amenable to OLS estimation. The properties of the OLS estimator in these models where the dynamics are stable are considered in some detail in sections 7.2 and 7.3.

AR and MA processes also function as models for serially correlated disturbances in a regression model, and the parameters of these processes will have to be estimated alongside the regression parameters. Nonlinear estimators like maximum likelihood are often employed in this case, and we shall see that such estimators can be computed iteratively via a sequence of linear estimation problems in which OLS is used.

Estimation of an AR or ADL model by maximum likelihood, discussed in section 7.4, is a useful prelude to the generation of Lagrange multiplier tests for serial correlation. It is intuitively obvious that failing to model correctly the dynamics of Y_t in an AR or ADL model ensures that the disturbance term cannot have classical properties. Tests for dependence in the disturbance thus take on the role of (mis)specification tests, a point that was made in Chapters 1 and 2. Section 7.5 discusses the Durbin–Watson test used so far for this purpose, as well as a more general Lagrange multiplier test.

The other main distinction made in the previous chapter was that between stationary and unit root or integrated processes: this distinction has a dramatic effect on the behaviour of OLS estimators even in the simplest dynamic model, the AR(1) model. We can carry over the discussion of the properties of OLS estimators of sections 7.2 and 7.3 to the case of a random walk or a random walk with drift in section 7.6. Providing test procedures for the existence of a unit root in an AR(p) process is an important issue discussed in section 7.7.

If explanatory variables in regression models can be random, as in sections 4.4 and 4.7, there is no reason why they cannot be generated by some kind of dynamic process. If the explanatory variable process is at least asymptotically stationary, this has no real impact on the large sample properties of OLS estimators in a regression model, provided that the explanatory variables are uncorrelated with the error terms, as noted in section 4.4. However, if in the supposed model

$$Y_t = \alpha + \beta X_t + u_t; \ u_t \sim IID(0, \sigma^2); \ t = 1, \dots, n,$$

Y_t and X_t are completely independent $I(1)$ variables, it is possible for an investigator to be misled by the OLS estimation results into concluding that there really is a relationship between Y_t and X_t. This is the very serious problem of *spurious regressions*. If the two series are *cointegrated* in the sense defined in section 7.8, then this spurious regression problem can be avoided by an appropriate estimation method. One cannot guarantee that two $I(1)$ series are cointegrated, and thus a suitable test procedure is necessary. Two possible tests are outlined in section 7.8.

One feature common to all dynamic models is easily illustrated using the AR(1) process

$$Y_t = \phi_1 Y_{t-1} + u_t; \ u_t \sim IID(0, \sigma^2); \ t = 1, \dots, n, \tag{7.1}$$

in which $|\phi_1| < 1$. The sequence of values of the *dependent variable*, $Y_1, \dots, Y_n$, are not independent random variables. Indeed, one could say that $Y_1, \dots, Y_n$ are *dependent random variables* in this sense, although the conflict of terminology is confusing. This property of dependence in a dynamic model can be contrasted with the *independence* for $Y_1, \dots, Y_n$ inherited from the independence of the error terms in a classical regression model

$$Y_t = \beta_1 + \beta_2 X_{2t} + u_t; \ u_t \sim IID(0, \sigma^2); \ t = 1, \dots, n.$$

The lack of independence in $Y_1, \dots, Y_n$ in (7.1) has to be taken into account in establishing the large sample properties of the estimator of ϕ_1, and makes the analysis a little more complex than that discussed in section 4.4.

Ideally, one would like to discuss estimation in the context of the simplest dynamic economic model for Y_t, the ADL(1, 1) model,

$$Y_t = \delta + \phi_1 Y_{t-1} + \beta_0 X_t + \beta_1 X_{t-1} + u_t; \ u_t \sim IID(0, \sigma^2); \ t = 1, \dots, n. \tag{7.2}$$

However, the presence of the explanatory variables X_t and X_{t-1} complicate the analysis, and add no new insights to the results. We shall therefore concentrate on the pure AR(1) model with no intercept of equation (7.1) under the assumption that $|\phi_1| < 1$. All of the properties that can be deduced for the least squares estimator of ϕ_1 in (7.1) can be carried over to the more general ADL models.

7.2 / OLS estimation in linear dynamic models

Since the disturbances in (7.1) have classical properties, it is reasonable to consider the use of the ordinary least squares estimator for ϕ_1. In constructing the OLS estimator $\hat{\phi}_1$, there is a choice here of considering equation (7.1) as a stationary process running for all time, and obtaining a sample of n observations from this process, or as a process starting at $t = 1$, with the presample value Y_0 known. In the latter asymptotically stationary case, one obtains in effect a sample of $n + 1$ observations, including the presample value Y_0. The discussion below will attempt to combine the stationary and asymptotically stationary cases.

The OLS estimator of ϕ_1 in (7.1) is

$$\hat{\phi}_1 = \left(\sum Y_{t-1}^2 \right)^{-1} \sum Y_{t-1} Y_t.$$

In the stationary case the sums run from 2 to n, and in the asymptotically stationary case, the sums run from 1 to n. The sampling error of the estimator is

$$\hat{\phi}_1 = \phi_1 + \left(\sum Y_{t-1}^2 \right)^{-1} \sum Y_{t-1} u_t, \tag{7.3}$$

which can also be written as

$$\hat{\phi}_1 = \phi_1 + \sum \left(\frac{Y_{t-1}}{\sum Y_{t-1}^2} \right) u_t. \tag{7.4}$$

If all observations on Y_t were independent of all disturbances, for $t = 1, \ldots, n$, then it would clearly be possible to take separate expectations for $Y_{t-1}/\sum Y_{t-1}^2$ and u_t. Since this is clearly not the case (because the model expresses Y_t as a function of disturbances), we cannot proceed in any simple way to evaluate the expectation of the second term in (7.3). In fact, in an autoregressive model with IID disturbances, least squares estimators are biased, though the bias does become smaller as the sample size is increased. What is true is that $\hat{\phi}_1$ is consistent and asymptotically normal, provided that $|\phi_1| < 1$ and any relevant moments of the disturbance distribution exist.

A complete derivation of asymptotic properties in an autoregressive model involves analytic niceties that are beyond the scope of this book, but it is possible to sketch some of the details here. The reward for doing this is that the AR(1) case is a prototype for more general cases. Examination of some details here also has a payoff in understanding what happens in the unit root case of section 7.6.

To establish the consistency of $\hat{\phi}_1$ we need to show that

$$\text{plim} \frac{1}{n} \sum Y_{t-1}^2 = c \neq 0, \tag{7.5}$$

$$\text{plim} \frac{1}{n} \sum Y_{t-1} u_t = 0. \tag{7.6}$$

In the classical regression model discussed in section 4.4, an assumption equivalent to (7.5) was made: for example, equation (4.15). In addition, the Chebyshev lemma was used to verify the equivalent of (7.6). There are a number of ways of proceeding here to verify these two requirements: it is probably easiest to start with (7.6).

Here, the key issue is the independence of Y_{t-1} and u_t. To see that Y_{t-1} and u_t are independent, use the expression of (6.39),

$$Y_t = \phi_1^t Y_0 + \phi_1^{t-1} u_1 + \ldots + \phi_1 u_{t-1} + u_t.$$

In this expression, Y_0 is being treated as fixed, so that the random variable Y_t depends on $u_1, \ldots, u_t$. Consider Y_{t-1}: this depends on $u_1, \ldots, u_{t-1}$, and by the independence of the error terms, is independent of u_t. It then follows that

$$E(Y_{t-1} u_t) = E(Y_{t-1}) E(u_t) = 0,$$

as well as the more obvious result for $t = 1$, since Y_0 is fixed. In the stationary case, use of (6.22), with δ in that expression set to zero, shows that the independence of Y_{t-1} and u_t still holds. As a result,

$$E\left(\frac{1}{n} \sum Y_{t-1} u_t\right) = 0. \tag{7.7}$$

The independence of Y_{t-1} and u_t also implies that

$$\operatorname{var}(Y_{t-1} u_t) = E(Y_{t-1} u_t)^2$$
$$= E(Y_{t-1}^2) E(u_t^2).$$

If we can now show that

$$\operatorname{var}\left(\frac{1}{n} \sum Y_{t-1} u_t\right) \to 0 \quad \text{as } n \to \infty, \tag{7.8}$$

we could claim that (7.6) holds using Chebyshev's lemma.

Given (7.7),

$$\operatorname{var}\left(\frac{1}{n} \sum Y_{t-1} u_t\right) = E\left(\frac{1}{n} \sum Y_{t-1} u_t\right)^2$$
$$= \frac{1}{n^2} \sum_s \sum_t E(Y_{t-1} Y_{s-1} u_s u_t).$$

Although this expression looks complicated, we need only consider the behaviour of the term

$$E(Y_{t-1} Y_{s-1} u_s u_t)$$

in three distinct cases:

$$s > t; \quad s < t; \quad s = t.$$

When $s > t$, u_s is independent of Y_{t-1}, Y_{s-1}, and u_t, since all the latter terms are in the past relative to u_s. As a result,

$$E(Y_{t-1} Y_{s-1} u_s u_t) = E(u_s) E(Y_{t-1} Y_{s-1} u_t) = 0.$$

Similarly, when $s < t$, Y_{t-1}, Y_{s-1}, and u_s are in the past relative to u_t, so that the independence property of u_t produces

$$E(Y_{t-1}Y_{s-1}u_su_t) = E(u_t)E(Y_{t-1}Y_{s-1}u_s) = 0.$$

For $s = t$, u_t is still independent of Y_{t-1}, so that

$$E(Y_{t-1}Y_{s-1}u_su_t) = E(u_t^2)E(Y_{t-1}^2) = \sigma^2 E(Y_{t-1}^2).$$

Putting these results together shows that

$$\text{var}\left(\frac{1}{n}\sum Y_{t-1}u_t\right) = \frac{\sigma^2}{n} \cdot \frac{1}{n}\sum E(Y_{t-1}^2). \tag{7.9}$$

Again we have to distinguish between the stationary and asymptotically stationary cases. In the former case, $E(Y_{t-1}^2)$ is also $\text{var}(Y_{t-1})$, which equals γ_0 for every t. There will be $n - 1$ terms in the sum, so that

$$\text{var}\left(\frac{1}{n}\sum Y_{t-1}u_t\right) = \frac{\sigma^2}{n} \cdot \frac{(n-1)\gamma_0}{n}, \tag{7.10}$$

and since

$$\frac{\sigma^2}{n} \to 0$$

as $n \to \infty$, (7.8) will hold.

In the asymptotically stationary case, $E(Y_{t-1}^2)$ varies with t. From equation (6.39), one can show that

$$E(Y_t^2) = \sigma^2\left(\frac{1 - \phi_1^{2t}}{1 - \phi_1^2}\right) + \phi_1^{2t}Y_0^2,$$

and given that $|\phi_1| < 1$, it is clear that this approaches γ_0 as $t \to \infty$. We can then show that (7.8) holds in this case as well.

To establish (7.5), we can see from the previous discussion that

$$\frac{1}{n}\sum E(Y_{t-1}^2)$$

should converge to a limit in either case. In the stationary case, this would be the process variance, γ_0: it would then be possible to appeal to a stationary process version of Khinchine's theorem given in section 4.2 to show that

$$\text{plim}\,\frac{1}{n}\sum_{t=1}^{n} Y_{t-1}^2 = \gamma_0. \tag{7.11}$$

In the asymptotically stationary case, the same result holds, although the details are more involved than can be given here.

To summarise this rather technical section, we have seen that the probability limit of the OLS estimator of ϕ_1 in (7.1) can be written as

$$\text{plim}\,\hat{\phi}_1 = \phi_1 + \left(\text{plim}\,\frac{1}{n}\sum Y_{t-1}^2\right)^{-1}\text{plim}\,\frac{1}{n}\sum Y_{t-1}u_t.$$

The independence of the error terms and the fact that $|\phi_1| < 1$ has been assumed leads to the result that

$$\text{plim } \hat{\phi}_1 = \phi_1 + (\gamma_0)^{-1} \cdot 0 = \phi_1,$$

confirming the consistency of this OLS estimator in a stationary or asymptotically stationary AR(1) process.

7.3 / Extensions

As implicitly suggested, these results carry over to the ADL model, for example the ADL$(1,1)$ model (7.2), when $|\phi_1| < 1$ is assumed. The details are more messy, but provided that the errors are IID, Y_{t-1} and u_t are still independent. The analysis which shows that

$$\text{var}\left(\frac{1}{n}\sum Y_{t-1}u_t\right) \to 0$$

still holds provided that

$$\frac{1}{n}\sum E(Y_{t-1}^2) < \infty.$$

If X_t is also independent of u_t for each t, the least squares estimators of δ, ϕ_1, β_0 and β_1 in (7.2) are consistent under the stated conditions.

What happens if the errors are correlated, specifically if in (7.1), the errors are assumed to follow a stationary AR(1) process? Suppose that Y_t is generated by the model

$$Y_t = \phi_1 Y_{t-1} + u_t$$

$$u_t = \rho u_{t-1} + \varepsilon_t; \ \varepsilon_t \sim IID(0, \sigma^2); \ t = 1, \dots, n \tag{7.12}$$

in which $|\phi_1| < 1$ and $|\rho| < 1$. Suppose also that the serial correlation of u_t is ignored and the OLS estimator of ϕ_1 from (7.1) is used. Then, the properties obtained above for $\hat{\phi}_1$ no longer hold. Because Y_{t-1} and u_t both depend on u_{t-1}, Y_{t-1} and u_t are now correlated, and

$$\text{plim } \frac{1}{n}\sum Y_{t-1}u_t \neq 0.$$

The probability limit of the OLS estimator $\hat{\phi}_1$ can be shown to be

$$\text{plim}(\hat{\phi}_1) = \frac{\phi_1 + \rho}{1 + \phi_1\rho} \neq \phi_1,$$

which only collapses to ϕ_1 when $\rho = 0$.

Ignoring the serial correlation here has led to the inconsistency of the OLS estimator. Can a consistent estimator of ϕ_1 and ρ be found for (7.12)? There is actually no point in looking for one, because there is an identification problem associated with this particular model. One way of showing this is to write the error process in lag operator form as

$$(1 - \rho L)u_t = \varepsilon_t.$$

Transforming

$$Y_t = \phi_1 Y_{t-1} + u_t$$

by $(1 - \rho L)$ converts the serially correlated error u_t into the independent error ε_t, and some rearrangement then gives

$$Y_t = (\phi_1 + \rho) Y_{t-1} - \phi_1 \rho Y_{t-2} + \varepsilon_t, \tag{7.13}$$

an AR(2) process in which the parameters ϕ_1 and ρ appear in a perfectly symmetrical fashion. Thus, $\phi_1 = 0.6$ and $\rho = 0.4$ would clearly generate the same observations as $\phi_1 = 0.4$ and $\rho = 0.6$: no amount of data could distinguish between these possibilities.

Use of the lag polynomial form for the error process enables us to see the inconsistency of the OLS estimator of ϕ_1 from another perspective. This estimator is obtained by regressing Y_t on Y_{t-1}, yet the 'true model' (7.12) is equivalent to a model in which Y_t depends on both Y_{t-1} and Y_{t-2}. That is, the inconsistency of $\hat{\phi}_1$ is the consequence of the large sample equivalent of omitted variables bias discussed in section 3.2.

More general models

Inconsistency of the OLS estimator due to serial correlation can be seen to carry over to the ADL model on exactly the same grounds of omitted variables bias. However, in models with more than one parameter to estimate, there is the implication that all the parameter estimators are inconsistent, just as in section 3.2.

The implications of this observation are important. To repeat: in a model containing lagged dependent variables, if the errors are serially correlated, the least squares estimators of all the parameters are inconsistent. These least squares estimators are usually consistent for something – they will generally have probability limits (under weak conditions), but these plims will not be the parameters of interest. The strength of the need to test a fitted regression model for serial correlation of the residuals thus increases.

Dependence and large sample normality

A standard property one expects the OLS estimator of a regression parameter to have is normality, for this underpins the use of the t test of significance. For this normality to hold, the error terms have to be normally distributed. If the error terms are not normally distributed, one can only establish large sample normality for the OLS estimator, as expressed in equations (4.9) and (4.19). Ultimately, this large sample normality property in the classical regression model underpins the use of large sample tests of various kinds.

To obtain a large sample normality property for the OLS estimator $\hat{\phi}_1$ of ϕ_1 in (7.1), write the sampling error (7.3) in the form

$$\sqrt{n}(\hat{\phi}_1 - \phi_1) = \left(\frac{1}{n}\sum Y_{t-1}^2\right)^{-1}\frac{1}{\sqrt{n}}\sum Y_{t-1}u_t.$$

As in section 4.4, the first part of the argument is to claim that $(1/\sqrt{n})\sum Y_{t-1}u_t$ converges in distribution to some random variable, say Z, which has a normal distribution. This is the same as saying that $(1/\sqrt{n})\sum Y_{t-1}u_t$ has a large sample normal distribution, with zero mean and some variance to be determined. The fact that $Y_1,\ldots,Y_n$ are dependent random variables (see section 7.1) makes the claim of convergence in distribution harder to justify, although we need not worry about the details in this book. The next step is to show that $(1/n)\sum Y_{t-1}^2$ converges in probability to some (nonzero) limit c. The convergence in distribution arguments of section 4.3 then allow us to claim that

$$\sqrt{n}(\hat{\phi}_1 - \phi_1) \xrightarrow{D} \frac{Z}{c} \sim N(0, v^2),$$

where the variance v^2 is to be determined.

This variance, v^2, is determined by the limit of the variance of $(1/\sqrt{n})\sum Y_{t-1}u_t$ and by c. From (7.10), we can see, assuming that there are $n-1$ terms in the summation, that

$$\text{var}\left(\frac{1}{\sqrt{n}}\sum Y_{t-1}u_t\right) = \sigma^2\frac{1}{n}\sum E(Y_{t-1}^2) = \sigma^2\cdot\frac{(n-1)\gamma_0}{n}, \tag{7.14}$$

which will converge to $\sigma^2\gamma_0$ as $n \to \infty$. Taking this in conjunction with the claim of (7.11), it will follow that

$$\sqrt{n}(\hat{\phi}_1 - \phi_1) \xrightarrow{D} \frac{Z}{\gamma_0} \sim N\left(0, \frac{\sigma^2}{\gamma_0}\right).$$

Given the nature of γ_0 for an AR(1) process from (6.10), the variance of the limiting distribution simplifies to

$$\frac{\sigma^2}{\gamma_0} = 1 - \phi_1^2,$$

so that

$$\sqrt{n}(\hat{\phi}_1 - \phi_1) \xrightarrow{D} N(0, 1 - \phi_1^2).$$

An immediate application of this result is to generate a simple test that $\phi_1 = 0$. Under this null hypothesis, the distribution collapses to

$$\sqrt{n}\hat{\phi}_1 \xrightarrow{D} N(0, 1),$$

so that a simple test of $\phi_1 = 0$ consists of multiplying the OLS estimate by the square root of the sample size and comparing the result to the appropriate critical value from standard normal tables. This is an alternative to the usual t test procedure: if T is the t statistic associated with $\hat{\phi}_1$, it is still true that

$$\sqrt{n}T \xrightarrow{D} N(0,1),$$

under the null hypothesis that $\phi_1 = 0$.

The discussion in this subsection concerns a very simple model, the AR(1). However, the essence of the result carries over to the more general AR and ADL models, providing a large sample normality result for the least squares estimators which exactly parallels that given in (4.10) for the standard regression model.

7.4 / Estimation with serially correlated errors

It is helpful to distinguish, for purposes of estimation, between serial correlation in a static regression model written in the matrix form

$$y = X\beta + u \tag{7.15}$$

and serial correlation in the type of dynamic model, for example (7.1), discussed in this chapter. Suppose that the elements of the disturbance vector in (7.15) follow a stationary AR(1) process,

$$u_t = \rho u_{t-1} + \varepsilon_t; \ \varepsilon_t \sim IID(0,\sigma^2), \tag{7.16}$$

so that $|\rho| < 1$. The covariance matrix of u then has the form of (6.12), with ρ replacing ϕ_1. Under the assumption that X is nonrandom, it is independent of u, so that the OLS estimator of β in (7.15) is unbiased (as noted in section 5.1) and consistent. As we saw in the previous section, the OLS estimator of ϕ_1 in (7.1) is inconsistent when the errors are serially correlated. This suggests that different approaches to estimation in static and dynamic models may be needed when serial correlation is present.

In the static model, if ρ were known, GLS would be a possible estimator, as noted in section 6.3. In practice, ρ is not known, and GLS can only be made feasible if a suitable consistent estimator of ρ can be found. Many of the estimation procedures that have been suggested for both the static and dynamic cases require at some stage the use of a consistent estimator of ρ, so we start the discussion off by describing how such an estimator may be obtained.

An instrumental variable estimator

In section 4.7, we suggested the use of an instrumental variable (IV) estimator when one or more regressors are correlated with disturbances in the limit. This is exactly the situation here. We therefore consider how IV estimation can be applied to the model

$$Y_t = \phi_0 + \phi_1 Y_{t-1} + \beta_0 X_t + u_t; \ t = 1,\ldots,n$$
$$u_t = \rho u_{t-1} + \varepsilon_t; \ \varepsilon_t \sim IID(0,\sigma^2); \text{ all } t. \tag{7.17}$$

In its simplest form, the IV method consists of finding an instrumental variable for each of the existing regressors in (7.17). If X is exogenous and X_t; $t = 1, \ldots, n$ are non-random, it follows that $\mathrm{plim}(n^{-1} \sum X_t u_t) = 0$, so X_t can act as its own instrumental variable. However, $\mathrm{plim}(n^{-1} \sum Y_{t-1} u_t) \neq 0$, and we need to find an instrumental variable that is correlated with Y_{t-1}, but is uncorrelated with u_t in the limit. Since Y_t is partly explained by X_t, it follows that Y_{t-1} is partly explained by X_{t-1}, and this suggests using X_{t-1} as an instrumental variable for Y_{t-1}. The 'simple' IV estimator defined in equation (4.57) would then be

$$\tilde{b} = (W'X)^{-1} W'y \tag{7.18}$$

where the typical row of W is $w_t' = [1 \quad X_t \quad X_{t-1}]$ and the typical row of X is $x_t' = [1 \quad X_t \quad Y_{t-1}]$.

In practice, it is more convenient to find $\tilde{b}$ by a two-stage procedure, as represented by the formula

$$\tilde{b} = [X'W(W'W)^{-1}W'X]^{-1} X'W(W'W)^{-1}W'y. \tag{7.19}$$

At face value, this suggests that all the variables in the matrix X are replaced by corresponding predicted values (instrumental variables), but the regression of X on W has no effect on columns of X which are also columns of W. In this example, Y_{t-1} is the only variable which does not appear in both X and W, so the IV estimator can be obtained by first regressing Y_{t-1} on X_t and X_{t-1}, with an intercept, and taking predicted values $\hat{Y}_{t-1}$, and then regressing Y_t on X_t and $\hat{Y}_{t-1}$, again with an intercept, to obtain the IV estimators of ϕ_0, ϕ_1 and β_0. Since we assume for convenience that suitable presample values are available, these regressions can use data for $t = 1, \ldots, n$.

The attraction of this IV estimator is that it is consistent in circumstances in which the OLS estimator would be inconsistent. The consistency of estimation of $\tilde{b}$ has a useful implication: a consistent estimator of ρ can be generated from the IV residuals

$$\tilde{u}_t = Y_t - \tilde{\phi}_0 - \tilde{\phi}_1 Y_{t-1} - \tilde{b}_0 X_t; t = 1, \ldots, n.$$

This estimator $\tilde{\rho}$ is obtained by the simple expedient of regressing $\tilde{u}_t$ on $\tilde{u}_{t-1}$ for $t = 2, \ldots, n$. A convenient interpretation is that u_t and u_{t-1} in (7.16) are being replaced by the corresponding IV residuals, so that

$$\tilde{\rho} = \frac{\sum_{t=2}^{n} \tilde{u}_t \tilde{u}_{t-1}}{\sum_{t=2}^{n} \tilde{u}_{t-1}^2}. \tag{7.20}$$

It is possible to construct a large sample normal distribution for $\tilde{b}$ following the reasoning given in Chapter 4 which would have to allow for the fact that the covariance matrix of u differs from the classical case. Since we have no need for such a result, we shall not do this.

Feasible GLS

In section 6.3, it was shown that the inverse of the covariance matrix for the vector of error terms u in (7.16) could be factored using the matrix C of (6.13), replacing ϕ_1

there by ρ. The effect of the transformation by C on the model (7.15) is

$$Cy = CX\beta + Cu$$

and OLS estimation of this model corresponds to GLS estimation of (7.15). In terms of observations, the transformed model is, for the first observation,

$$\sqrt{(1 - \rho^2)}\, Y_1 = \sqrt{(1 - \rho^2)}\, x_1'\beta + \sqrt{(1 - \rho^2)}\, u_1,$$

and for the remaining observations,

$$
\begin{aligned}
Y_t - \rho Y_{t-1} &= (x_t - \rho x_{t-1})'\beta + (u_t - \rho u_{t-1}) \\
&= (x_t - \rho x_{t-1})'\beta + \varepsilon_t; \quad t = 2, \ldots, n.
\end{aligned}
\tag{7.21}
$$

Neglecting the first of the transformed observations and applying OLS to the remaining $n - 1$ transformed observations would result in a small loss of efficiency in finite samples.

To make this approach feasible, that is, constructing the feasible GLS estimator described in section 5.2, a suitable estimator of ρ has to be found. As noted above, in this static regression model, the OLS estimator of the vector β is still consistent, and this consistency can be shown to be inherited by estimators generated from the OLS residuals e_t. The procedure leading up to (7.20) can be adapted for use with OLS residuals to yield a consistent estimate of ρ from the regression of e_t on e_{t-1},

$$e_t = \rho e_{t-1} + \text{error}; \quad t = 2, \ldots, n, \tag{7.22}$$

$$\hat{\rho} = \frac{\sum_{t=2}^{n} e_t e_{t-1}}{\sum_{t=2}^{n} e_{t-1}^2}.$$

The feasible GLS estimator involves the substitution of $\tilde{\rho}$ into the covariance matrix Ω and its (inverse) factor C. In practice, this value is simply substituted into (7.21), and the resulting OLS estimator of β is virtually identical to the feasible GLS estimator in reasonably sized samples. The attraction of this procedure is that this estimator of β will, as indicated in section 5.2, have the large sample properties of the GLS estimator of β assuming ρ is known.

Maximum likelihood

The disadvantage of methods like feasible GLS in estimating (7.15) is that there are separate procedures for estimating ρ and β. In contrast, the attraction of the maximum likelihood estimator for models like (7.15) is that the likelihood function is maximised with respect to all the parameters β, σ^2 and ρ. In principle, then, a maximum likelihood estimator of ρ emerges just as naturally as the estimator for β.

In order to use ML estimation, we have to be specific as to the distribution of the disturbance vector u, and this can be derived from assumptions concerning the ε process. If, in addition to $\varepsilon_t \sim IID(0, \sigma^2)$, we assume that the ε_t are normal, the distribution of u is

$$u \sim N(0, \sigma^2 V) \tag{7.23}$$

where the matrix V has the form shown in equation (6.12), with ρ replacing ϕ_1. The log likelihood function is then

$$\ln L = -(n/2)\ln(2\pi) - (1/2)\ln[\det(\sigma^2 V)] - S_G(\beta)/2\sigma^2 \tag{7.24}$$

where $S_G(\beta)$ is the generalisation of the sum of squares function, shown in equation (5.12) to be $S_G(\beta) = (y - X\beta)' V^{-1}(y - X\beta)$.

Since it can be shown analytically that $\det(V) = (1 - \rho^2)^{-1}$, (7.24) can be written as

$$\ln L = -(n/2)\ln(2\pi) - (n/2)\ln(\sigma^2) + (1/2)\ln(1 - \rho^2) - S_G(\beta)/2\sigma^2. \tag{7.25}$$

If $\ln L$ is now maximised partially with respect to β and σ^2, we obtain solutions which are functions of ρ, which can be written as

$$\tilde{\beta}(\rho) = [X' V^{-1}(\rho) X]^{-1} X' V^{-1}(\rho) y$$

$$\tilde{\sigma}^2(\rho) = S_G[\tilde{\beta}(\rho)]/n = [y - X\tilde{\beta}(\rho)]' V^{-1}(\rho)[y - X\tilde{\beta}(\rho)]/n.$$

Here $V^{-1}(\rho)$ is used to signify that V^{-1} is also a function of ρ. For any given value of ρ, the form of the estimator for β is that of the full GLS estimator, and the estimator for σ^2 differs only in using n rather than $(n - k)$ as a divisor. By substituting these expressions in (7.25), we obtain the concentrated likelihood function

$$\ln L^* = -(n/2)\ln(2\pi) - (n/2)\ln[\tilde{\sigma}^2(\rho)] + (1/2)\ln(1 - \rho^2) - (n/2)$$

$$= \text{const} - (n/2)\ln\{S_G[\tilde{\beta}(\rho)]/(1 - \rho^2)^{1/n}\}. \tag{7.26}$$

Maximising the log likelihood function is therefore equivalent to choosing estimates of β, σ^2 and ρ so as to minimise $S_G(\beta)/(1 - \rho^2)^{1/n}$. Since an iterated feasible GLS estimator minimises $S_G(\beta)$, the ML criterion is not the same as that for feasible GLS, and even when the feasible GLS estimator is iterated to convergence, it is not the same as the ML estimator in a finite sample. However, under standard assumptions, the two estimators do typically have the same asymptotic distribution.

The difficulty here is that one cannot obtain an explicit expression for the ML estimator of ρ, and hence of β and σ^2. We shall see a little later that an iterative method of maximising the log likelihood can be used, and that this casts some light on the nature of these estimators. As a step in this direction, we now consider maximum likelihood estimation of a dynamic model.

Maximum likelihood in dynamic models

The likelihood function L in (7.24) is of course the joint density $p(y; \theta, X)$ of the multivariate normal distribution of the observations in the vector y. Ultimately this depends on the normal distribution (7.23), which embodies the assumption of stationarity of the error process.

In estimating a dynamic model such as an AR(1), we will use the asymptotically stationary version, where the process starts at $t = 1$, with a known presample value Y_0. This has a number of advantages, as we shall see. The process

$$Y_t = \phi_1 Y_{t-1} + u_t; \ t = 1, \ldots, n$$

can be viewed as specifying the *conditional* distribution of Y_t, given its own past. If it is assumed that

$$u_t \sim NID(0, \sigma^2),$$

this conditional distribution is also normal:

$$Y_t | Y_{t-1}, \ldots, Y_1, Y_0 \sim N(\phi_1 Y_{t-1}, \sigma^2).$$

The decomposition of a joint density into a product of conditional densities, here,

$$
\begin{aligned}
p(Y; \theta, Y_0) &= p(Y_n, \ldots, Y_1; \theta, Y_0) \\
&= p(Y_n | Y_{n-1}, \ldots, Y_1; \theta, Y_0) p(Y_{n-1}, \ldots, Y_1; \theta, Y_0) \\
&= \ldots \\
&= \prod_{t=1}^{n} p(Y_t | Y_{t-1}, \ldots, Y_1; \theta, Y_0),
\end{aligned}
$$

provides a representation of the log likelihood function for this model as a sum of the logs of these conditional densities. Note that this is a different perspective from that underlying the log likelihood function (7.24), which was computed directly from the joint distribution of the observations. In addition, there was no need for a presample value Y_0 in that log likelihood function.

The conditional normal density of Y_t is

$$p(Y_t | Y_{t-1}, \ldots, Y_1; \theta, Y_0) = (2\pi\sigma^2)^{-1/2} \exp\left(-\frac{(Y_t - \phi_1 Y_{t-1})^2}{2\sigma^2} \right)$$

so that the log likelihood function is

$$\ln L = -\frac{n}{2}\ln(2\pi) - \frac{n}{2}\ln(\sigma^2) - \frac{1}{2\sigma^2} \sum_{t=1}^{n} (Y_t - \phi_1 Y_{t-1})^2.$$

Inspecting this carefully, we can see that maximising $\ln L$ with respect to ϕ_1 is equivalent to minimising the sum of squares function

$$
\begin{aligned}
S(\phi_1) &= \sum_{t=1}^{n} (Y_t - \phi_1 Y_{t-1})^2 \\
&= \sum_{t=1}^{n} u_t^2,
\end{aligned}
$$

which was implicitly used to find the OLS estimator of ϕ_1 in the model of (7.1). Under normality, then, this maximum likelihood estimator of ϕ_1 is also the OLS estimator. Sometimes, this estimator is called a 'conditional' least squares estimator to emphasise the dependence on the presample value Y_0.

This simple result for the maximum likelihood estimator based on conditional distributions will carry over to ADL models like (7.2), provided that the disturbances are $NID(0, \sigma^2)$. When serial correlation of the disturbances is allowed, the maximum likelihood estimator is more complex. To see this, consider as a second example the estimation of the model

$$Y_t = \phi_1 Y_{t-1} + \beta_0 X_t + u_t; \ t = 1, \ldots, n \tag{7.27}$$

$$u_t = \rho u_{t-1} + \varepsilon_t; \ \varepsilon_t \sim NID(0, \sigma^2), \ \text{all } t. \tag{7.28}$$

To generate maximum likelihood estimators using the arguments above, one has to find the conditional distribution of Y_t given X_t and the past values of Y_t implied by the model. Transforming (7.27) by the lag polynomial $(1 - \rho L)$ gives

$$Y_t - \rho Y_{t-1} = \phi_1 (Y_{t-1} - \rho Y_{t-2}) + \beta_0 (X_t - \rho X_{t-1}) + \varepsilon_t \tag{7.29}$$

which can also be written as

$$Y_t = \phi_1 Y_{t-1} + \beta_0 X_t + \rho (Y_{t-1} - \phi_1 Y_{t-2} - \beta_0 X_{t-1}) + \varepsilon_t.$$

These equations can be compared with the results of the GLS transform in (7.21).

Here, if we assume that a presample value Y_0 is available to start up (7.27), (7.29) can only run from $t = 2$, since Y_1 and Y_0 are required to start up what is now a second-order process for Y_t. The conditional densities will now start at $t = 2$, so that the log likelihood function is

$$\ln L = -\frac{(n-1)}{2} \ln(2\pi) - \frac{(n-1)}{2} \ln(\sigma^2)$$

$$- \frac{1}{2\sigma^2} \sum_{t=2}^{n} [Y_t - \phi_1 Y_{t-1} - \beta_0 X_t - \rho(Y_{t-1} - \phi_1 Y_{t-2} - \beta_0 X_{t-1})]^2.$$

We can again see that the maximisation of the log likelihood function with respect to ϕ_1, β_0 and ρ requires the minimisation of the sum of squares function

$$S(\phi_1, \beta_0, \rho) = \sum_{t=2}^{n} [Y_t - \phi_1 Y_{t-1} - \beta_0 X_t - \rho(Y_{t-1} - \phi_1 Y_{t-2} - \beta_0 X_{t-1})]^2$$

$$= \sum_{t=2}^{n} (u_t - \rho u_{t-1})^2$$

$$= \sum_{t=2}^{n} \varepsilon_t^2. \tag{7.30}$$

This 'shorthand' representation as a sum of squares of the ε_t is useful because all the derivatives of the log likelihood function can be expressed in terms of the derivatives of

$$\varepsilon_t = u_t - \rho u_{t-1}$$
$$= Y_t - \phi_1 Y_{t-1} - \beta_0 X_t - \rho(Y_{t-1} - \phi_1 Y_{t-2} - \beta_0 X_{t-1})$$

with respect to the parameters.

It is valuable to display these derivatives to see that the first-order conditions cannot be solved explicitly for the estimators of ϕ_1, β_0 and ρ, and that an iterative procedure for their solution is required. In addition, the derivatives provide the input to the construction of a Lagrange multiplier test of serial correlation, or more precisely in the current context, a test that $\rho = 0$.

The derivatives are

$$\frac{\partial S}{\partial \phi_1} = -2 \sum_{t=2}^{n} \frac{\partial \varepsilon_t}{\partial \phi_1} \varepsilon_t = -2 \sum_{t=2}^{n} (Y_{t-1} - \rho Y_{t-2})(u_t - \rho u_{t-1}), \qquad (7.31)$$

$$\frac{\partial S}{\partial \beta_0} = -2 \sum_{t=2}^{n} \frac{\partial \varepsilon_t}{\partial \beta_0} \varepsilon_t = -2 \sum_{t=2}^{n} (X_t - \rho X_{t-1})(u_t - \rho u_{t-1}), \qquad (7.32)$$

$$\frac{\partial S}{\partial \rho} = -2 \sum_{t=2}^{n} \frac{\partial \varepsilon_t}{\partial \rho} \varepsilon_t = -2 \sum_{t=2}^{n} u_{t-1}(u_t - \rho u_{t-1}). \qquad (7.33)$$

Since the u_t and u_{t-1} in these expressions depend on ϕ_1 and β_0 it is clear that (7.31)–(7.33), as first-order conditions, cannot be solved explicitly, and that an iterative method will be required.

Nonlinear least squares

Nonlinear least squares involves minimising a sum of squares which is a nonlinear function of parameters, like the sum of squares function (7.30). Here, the nonlinear least squares estimator of ϕ_1, β_0 and ρ would be equivalent to a maximum likelihood estimator, because of the assumptions about the presample value Y_0 (and Y_1).

Many computer packages offer nonlinear least squares procedures, and, in general, one can assume that such procedures will not only generate estimators for ϕ_1, β_0 and ρ, but also give valid expressions for standard errors and associated test statistics. However, it is worth looking at this point in a little more detail, because the choice of algorithm does have a bearing on how results needed for inference emerge from the calculation.

One very common approach is to use the Gauss–Newton method. This involves the regression of residuals obtained at each iteration, which are

$$\hat{\varepsilon}_t = Y_t - (\hat{\phi}_1 + \hat{\rho})Y_{t-1} + \hat{\phi}_1\hat{\rho}Y_{t-2} - \hat{\beta}_0 X_t + \hat{\beta}_0\hat{\rho}X_{t-1}$$

on variables defined as

$$-\partial \varepsilon_t / \partial \phi_1, \quad -\partial \varepsilon_t / \partial \beta_0 \quad \text{and} \quad -\partial \varepsilon_t / \partial \rho,$$

evaluated at current parameter estimates. By differentiating ε_t with respect to each parameter in turn, as in equations (7.31)–(7.33), the variables in question are seen to be $\hat{Y}_{t-1}^*$, $\hat{X}_t^*$ and $\hat{u}_{t-1}^*$, where

$$\hat{Y}_{t-1}^* = Y_{t-1} - \hat{\rho}Y_{t-2},$$

$$\hat{X}_t^* = X_t - \hat{\rho}X_{t-1}, \tag{7.34}$$

$$\hat{u}_{t-1}^* = Y_{t-1} - \hat{\phi}_1 Y_{t-2} - \hat{\beta}_0 X_{t-1}.$$

At each iteration, the estimates $\hat{\phi}_1$, $\hat{\beta}_0$ and $\hat{\rho}$ are revised, and this means that the transformed variables $\hat{Y}_{t-1}^*$, $\hat{X}_t^*$ and $\hat{u}_{t-1}^*$ are also revised. The coefficients attached to $\hat{Y}_{t-1}^*$, $\hat{X}_t^*$ and $\hat{u}_{t-1}^*$ are revisions to the estimates of ϕ_1, β_0 and ρ, so the updating at each iteration is

$$\hat{\phi}_{1\text{new}} = \hat{\phi}_{1\text{old}} + \text{coefficient of } \hat{Y}_{t-1}^*$$

$$\hat{\beta}_{0\text{new}} = \hat{\beta}_{0\text{old}} + \text{coefficient of } \hat{X}_t^* \tag{7.35}$$

$$\hat{\rho}_{\text{new}} = \hat{\rho}_{\text{old}} + \text{coefficient of } \hat{u}_{t-1}^*.$$

If the Gauss–Newton procedure is iterated to convergence, the final values of $\hat{Y}_{t-1}^*$, $\hat{X}_t^*$ and $\hat{u}_{t-1}^*$ can be used as though they were regressors in a linear least squares calculation, to produce an estimated variance covariance matrix of the form $\hat{\sigma}^2(\hat{X}_*'\hat{X}_*)^{-1}$, where the columns of $\hat{X}_*$ are the final values of $\hat{Y}_{t-1}^*$, $\hat{X}_t^*$ and $\hat{u}_{t-1}^*$, and $\hat{\sigma}^2$ is given as

$$\hat{\sigma}^2 = \sum \hat{\varepsilon}_t^2 / n.$$

Any iterative procedure needs some initial estimates to start the process off. These can be obtained as simple IV estimates of ϕ_1 and β_0, written as $\tilde{\phi}_1$ and $\tilde{\beta}_0$, with the initial estimate of ρ formed as

$$\tilde{\rho} = \frac{\sum \tilde{u}_t \tilde{u}_{t-1}}{\sum \tilde{u}_{t-1}^2}$$

where

$$\tilde{u}_t = Y_t - \tilde{\phi}_1 Y_{t-1} - \tilde{\beta}_0 X_t; \quad t = 2, \ldots, n$$

are the simple IV residuals. Alternatively, one can go straight into the Gauss–Newton iterations, using $\tilde{\phi}_1$ and $\tilde{\beta}_0$ as initial estimates of ϕ_1 and β_0, with the initial estimate of ρ set equal to zero.

A variant of the method described above involves the cancellation of some terms in the iterative regression. Instead of using the residuals $\hat{\varepsilon}_t$ as the dependent variable, we define

$$\hat{Y}_t^* = Y_t - \hat{\rho}Y_{t-1}$$

and regress $\hat{Y}_t^*$ on $\hat{Y}_{t-1}^*$, $\hat{X}_t^*$ and $\hat{u}_{t-1}^*$ at each stage. In this case, the coefficients of $\hat{Y}_{t-1}^*$ and $\hat{X}_t^*$ give new estimates of ϕ_1 and β_0 directly, without the need for updating shown in (7.35). The coefficient of $\hat{u}_{t-1}^*$ is still a revision, and $\hat{\rho}$ is still updated as in (7.35).

If necessary, one could implement either version of the Gauss–Newton NLS procedure as a two-step method. This makes no difference to the asymptotic properties, although there may be some difference in performance in finite samples. It is also true that the NLS procedure could entail some loss of finite sample performance relative to a full ML estimation, because of the difference in the treatment of starting values. However, the Gauss–Newton estimator does offer a significant advantage over other possible two-step estimators, because the estimation of ρ is treated symmetrically with that of ϕ_1 and β_0. From a formal analysis of ML estimation with this model (see, for example, Hatanaka, 1974), it is clear that estimates of ϕ_1 and β_0 are not independent. By including $\hat{u}_{t-1}^{*}$ in the iterative regression, this dependence is recognised and the resulting estimators are consistent and asymptotically efficient.

The method used above can be extended in an obvious way to allow for higher-order AR schemes. The transformed variables would involve higher-order generalised differences, and additional lagged disturbance terms could be included in the iterative regression.

7.5 / Testing for serial correlation

The traditional test for serial correlation is the Durbin–Watson (DW) test, which is based on the statistic

$$DW = d = \sum_{t=2}^{n}(e_t - e_{t-1})^2 \Big/ \sum_{t=1}^{n} e_t^2 \qquad (7.36)$$

where e_t; $t = 1, \ldots, n$ are least squares residuals. We have already used DW as a general indicator of misspecification: we now consider the statistic in its formal role as a test for serial correlation.

Unfortunately its use is only appropriate for nondynamic models, that is, models without any lagged dependent variables. So, the following discussion is restricted initially to the case

$$Y_t = x_t'\beta + u_t; \; u_t \sim NID(0, \sigma^2); \; t = 1, \ldots, n, \qquad (7.37)$$

and e_t are the OLS residuals from this model.

Even under the null hypothesis of no serial correlation, the distribution of (7.36) is not entirely straightforward, as it depends on the observed regressor matrix X. However, it is possible to obtain upper and lower bounds for critical values, which depend only on the number of observations (n) and the number of regressors (k). Table C4 in Appendix C gives lower bounds (d_L) and upper bounds (d_U) for selected values of n and k: somewhere between these bounds, there exists a critical value c such that $\Pr(d < c) = 0.05$, under the null hypothesis of no serial correlation. As shown below, this can be used to conduct a one-tailed test that will detect certain specific departures from the null hypothesis.

Suppose that we consider the alternative of first-order serial correlation of the AR(1) type, which we can write as

$$u_t = \rho u_{t-1} + \varepsilon_t; \ t = 1, \ldots, n. \tag{7.38}$$

In this context, the null hypothesis of no serial correlation is $\rho = 0$, whilst if $\rho > 0$ we have positive serial correlation and if $\rho < 0$ we have negative serial correlation. Although d is a random variable, it is known to lie between 0 and 4, and positive serial correlation tends to be associated with small values of d, whilst negative serial correlation is associated with large values. Values of d in a region around 2 are consistent with the absence of serial correlation.

To conduct a formal test to detect positive serial correlation, we set up the null hypothesis $H_0: \rho = 0$ and the alternative $H_1: \rho > 0$. If the calculated value of d is less than d_L, H_0 is rejected in favour of H_1. If d is greater than d_U, H_0 is not rejected. If d lies between d_L and d_U, the test is inconclusive.

If the test is to be used to detect negative serial correlation, the null hypothesis is $H_0: \rho = 0$ as before, but the alternative is now $H_1: \rho < 0$. In this case, a calculated value of d greater than $4 - d_L$ leads to rejection of H_0, a value less than $4 - d_U$ means that H_0 is not rejected and a value between $4 - d_U$ and $4 - d_L$ is inconclusive.

The Durbin–Watson test will detect certain other patterns of serial correlation, and it can also be used as an indicator of misspecification in the main part of the model. Unfortunately, it is not entirely reliable in either of these roles. The upper and lower bounds shown in Appendix C are based on the assumption that the regressor matrix X is nonrandom, with a column of ones to allow for an intercept term. With random regressors, and particularly in the presence of lagged endogenous variables on the right-hand side, the test is unreliable. Even when the assumptions are satisfied, the test statistic may fail to indicate the presence of higher-order serial correlation. Finally, although it is often the case that a 'low' value of d indicates at least one missing variable, rather than serial correlation as a genuine characteristic of the disturbance process, it is not always true that missing variable problems are picked up in this way.

Some effort has been put into modifications of the DW test and into tabulating bounds for variants of the basic test procedure, but there is an increasing tendency to turn to tests which are based on large sample theory. This is not unreasonable, since higher-order patterns of serial correlation are more likely to occur with frequently observed data, where the number of observations does tend to be large. In particular, when quarterly data are used, one should look carefully for serial correlation involving lags at multiples of four periods.

The Durbin–Watson test in dynamic models

Strictly speaking, we should have addressed the question of testing for serial correlation in a dynamic model before describing an estimation method which is appropriate if serial correlation is present. In this context, the main point to note is that one should not use the Durbin–Watson test. The assumptions underlying the DW test are not satisfied, and it has been demonstrated that the presence of a lagged endogenous variable biases the DW statistic towards acceptance of the null hypothesis of no serial correlation. In contrast, the LM test described in the next subsection is still valid, and since no routinely applicable small sample test is available, the LM test provides an acceptable alternative.

For the record, we should also mention the Durbin h test. This applies specifically to testing for first-order serial correlation, and it is therefore less flexible than the LM test. But the value of Durbin h is sometimes reported, so an explanation is needed. The test statistic is

$$h = (1 - 0.5d)\sqrt{\{n/[1 - \text{var}(\hat{\phi}_1)]\}} \qquad (7.39)$$

where d is the Durbin–Watson statistic and $\text{var}(\hat{\phi}_1)$ represents the estimated variance of the parameter associated with Y_{t-1}, when OLS is applied directly to a dynamic model. Under the null hypothesis of no serial correlation, the h test statistic is distributed asymptotically as $N(0, 1)$. In the spirit of the DW test procedure, the h test is often used as a one-tailed test against the alternative of positive serial correlation. In this case H_0 is rejected at the 5% significance level if $h > 1.645$. Against the alternative of negative serial correlation, H_0 is rejected if $h < -1.645$.

Lagrange multiplier tests for serial correlation

The discussion of maximum likelihood estimation of the model (7.27) and (7.28) provides the basis for a Lagrange multiplier test of the hypothesis that $\rho = 0$, which corresponds to a test of the independence of the error terms u_t. The Lagrange multiplier test statistic of (4.48) requires the formal derivative vector

$$D \ln L(\theta)$$

evaluated at the estimate of θ from the null hypothesis model. The derivatives (7.31), (7.32), and (7.33) can be used to construct

$$D \ln L(\theta) = \frac{1}{\sigma^2}[(y_{-1} - \rho y_{-2}) : (x - \rho x_{-1}) : u_{-1}]'(u - \rho u_{-1})$$

$$= \frac{1}{\sigma^2} Z'(u - \rho u_{-1}).$$

Here, y_{-1}, y_{-2}, x and x_{-1} are the $(n - 1) \times 1$ vectors of observations formed from Y_{t-1}, Y_{t-2}, X_t and X_{t-1}, and u_{-1} represents the $(n - 1) \times 1$ vector of lagged disturbances u_{t-1}.

Under the null hypothesis that $\rho = 0$, the restricted maximum likelihood estimator $\tilde{\theta}_R$ is the OLS estimator, and evaluation of the derivatives at $\tilde{\theta}_R$ generates an OLS residual vector of $n - 1$ elements, here denoted $\tilde{u}$. Notice that the usual presample value problem applies here: if the computed residuals are $\tilde{u}_2, \ldots, \tilde{u}_n$, what is the value of the lag of $\tilde{u}_2$? A standard approach is to set $\tilde{u}_1 = 0$, but a possible alternative is to use only the last $n - 2$ available residuals. Either way, if $\tilde{Z}$ is Z evaluated at $\tilde{\theta}_R$, so that

$$\tilde{Z} = [y_{-1} : x : \tilde{u}_{-1}],$$

the last column contains the lagged residuals $\tilde{u}_{t-1}$, and

$$D \ln L(\tilde{\theta}_R) = \frac{1}{\tilde{\sigma}^2} \tilde{Z}' \tilde{u}.$$

Here, $\tilde{\sigma}^2$ is the OLS variance estimator contained in $\tilde{\theta}_R$.

To construct the information matrix component of the LM statistic (4.48), $I(\tilde{\theta}_R)$, requires more analysis than can be presented here: suffice it to say that

$$\frac{1}{\tilde{\sigma}^2} \tilde{Z}' \tilde{Z}$$

is a suitable estimator. This generates the Lagrange multiplier test statistic as

$$LM = \frac{1}{\tilde{\sigma}^2} \tilde{u}' \tilde{Z} (\tilde{Z}' \tilde{Z})^{-1} \tilde{Z}' \tilde{u}, \qquad (7.40)$$

exactly in the form of the Lagrange multiplier test for linear restrictions in a classical regression model discussed in Example 4.2. In fact, the discussion surrounding (3.25) and (3.26) reveals that this test statistic can be considered as a test of the exclusion of $\tilde{u}_{-1}$ in the OLS regression

$$\tilde{u} = Z_1 a + \tilde{u}_{-1} r + \text{error} \qquad (7.41)$$

where Z_1 is the $(n-1) \times 2$ matrix consisting of the first two columns of $\tilde{Z}$. Z_1 is also the last $n-1$ rows of the matrix of observations on the explanatory variables in (7.28).

This test procedure can be generalised in a number of ways. Leaving aside the justification based on maximum likelihood, it is applicable to the model (7.37) in which x_t may now contain lags of Y_t, and where u_t can follow an AR(p) process. The matrix Z_1 in (7.41) then consists of the matrix of observations corresponding to x_t. Defining the vector $\tilde{u}_{-j}$ to contain the observations on $\tilde{u}_{t-j}$, a matrix $\tilde{U}$ with columns $\tilde{u}_{-1}, \ldots, \tilde{u}_{-p}$ is used in (7.41) instead of $\tilde{u}_{-1}$, producing the test regression

$$\tilde{u} = Z_1 a + \tilde{U} r + \text{error} \qquad (7.42)$$

in which one tests the exclusion of $\tilde{U}$. The number of observations used in this regression depends on the number of lags of Y_t, the number of presample values of Y_t available, and p. As in the previous case, zeros can be used for the initial values of the lagged residuals if desired.

If the parameters of the AR(p) process for the errors are denoted $\rho_1, \ldots, \rho_p$, the null hypothesis under test is that all these parameters are zero. The Lagrange multiplier test statistic is usually taken to have an approximate χ_p^2 distribution under this null hypothesis, and can be calculated as nR^2 from the test regression if desired. This will be denoted $LM(nR^2)$. Another version of the test in common use is simply the usual F statistic for exclusion of $\tilde{U}$ in the test regression, denoted $LM(F)$ when displayed in regression output. Here, the F distribution is used as an alternative approximation to the true distribution of the test statistic. In this version, the variance estimator $\tilde{\sigma}^2$ is implicitly being replaced by the residual variance estimate from the test regression (7.42). An attraction of the test regression perspective is that it shows that t tests performed on the elements of the r vector will be asymptotically valid when compared with critical values from the standard normal distribution. Such tests can be useful if the joint test rejects the null hypothesis, and one wishes to get an idea of which lag or lags of $\tilde{u}_t$ are possibly responsible for the rejection.

It is interesting to compare the test regressions (7.41) and (7.42) with the regression (7.22) used to construct an initial estimator of ρ from OLS residuals. The only difference is in the inclusion of the regressors Z_1 from the original model in the test regression. In fact, if there are no lagged values of Y_t in the regressor set x_t of (7.37), an alternative test regression is simply

$$\tilde{u} = \tilde{u}_{-1}r + \text{error}$$

for the first-order case or

$$\tilde{u} = \tilde{U}r + \text{error}$$

in the more general case.

A final point concerns alternatives to the AR specification for the errors. One can show (Godfrey, 1988: 114–15) that the same test procedure is valid against $MA(p)$ errors, or even ARMA errors where the maximum lag on the AR or MA part is p. In this sense then, the Lagrange multiplier test is a test against general serial correlation of a relatively unspecified kind.

Example 7.1

In Example 3.7, we estimated the parameters of the model

$$\ln(C_t) = \beta_1 + \beta_2 \ln(D_t) + \beta_3 \Delta_4 \ln(P_t) + \beta_4 \ln(L_{t-1}) + \beta_5 Q_{2t} + \beta_6 Q_{3t}$$
$$+ \beta_7 Q_{4t} + u_t; \ t = 1, \dots, n$$

using the quarterly observations provided in data set 5. Since this model contains no dynamic behaviour for the consumption and income variables, there is a strong presumption that apparent serial correlation might occur, and Table 7.1 gives the results needed to construct an LM test of the null hypothesis of no serial correlation up to order 4.

From the reported value for R^2 in the regression of residuals (RESID) on the existing regressors plus lagged residuals [RESID(−1) to RESID(−4)], we find $nR^2 = 126(0.4108) = 51.761$. The 5% critical value for a χ^2 distribution with $p = 4$ degrees of freedom is 9.49, so the null hypothesis of no serial correlation is quite strongly rejected. From the t values associated with individual lagged residuals, we observe that the strongest effect seems to relate to four-period lagged residuals, with a smaller but still marked effect at a lag of one period.

This version of the LM test has set the values of RESID to zero for the period 1963(1)–1963(4), so that the presample values of RESID(−1), . . . , RESID(−4) are

Table 7.1 LM test for serial correlation

Sample based on observations 1964(1)–1995(2)
Dependent variable is RESID

Variable	Coefficient	Standard error	t value
INTER	−0.000 26	0.047 62	−0.005
LNRPDI	−0.010 66	0.014 19	−0.751
D4LPCONS	−0.009 81	0.041 60	0.236
LNRLIQ(1)	0.008 51	0.016 99	0.501
Q2	6.8601E-05	0.004 23	0.016
Q3	8.0563E-05	0.004 27	0.019
Q4	0.000 16	0.004 28	0.037
RESID(−1)	0.285 81	0.087 61	3.262
RESID(−2)	0.165 20	0.091 68	1.802
RESID(−3)	0.011 86	0.091 87	0.129
RESID(−4)	0.343 47	0.087 79	3.912

Degrees of freedom 115 from 126 observations

Residual SS	3.2854×10^{-2}
Total SS	5.5765×10^{-2}
Disturbance variance	2.8569×10^{-4}
R^2	0.4108
DW statistic	1.91

zero. If the test regression is computed instead over the period 1965(1)–1995(2), so that the values of RESID for 1964(1)–1964(4) are used as presample values, the nR^2 value is $122(0.4263) = 52$. The F test version of the LM test, over the period 1964(1)–1995(2), uses $RSS = 5.5765 \times 10^{-2}$ from the Version 2 equation in Table 3.3 as S_R and $RSS = 3.2854 \times 10^{-2}$ from Table 7.1 as S to produce

$$LM(F) = [(5.5765 - 3.2854)/4]/(3.2854/115) = 20.049.$$

Since the 5% critical value of the F distribution with 4 and 115 degrees of freedom is approximately 2.46, the same test conclusion is obtained.

Several further experiments can be performed with these data. If we attempt to allow for some of the apparent serial correlation by including four-period lags of both the consumption variable and the income variable – by adding $\ln(C_{t-4})$ and $\ln(D_{t-4})$ – the value of $LM(nR^2)$ is reduced to 40.40. This is still significant, but we have evidence from earlier exercises that consumer behaviour in the United Kingdom is difficult to model in the last few years of the sample period.

Example 7.2

Another example which illustrates a number of aspects of the material of sections 7.6 and 7.7 uses data set 1, and estimates a number of variants of an annual consumption function. The liquid assets variable LNRLIQ, in both current or lagged form, has been excluded from the analysis because t tests showed that it was insignificant.

As well as parameter estimates and t values, Table 7.2 gives the DW statistic and the $LM(F)$ statistic, which here tests only for first-order serial correlation. The 5% critical values for $LM(F)$ are between 4.20 and 4.26 for the degrees of freedom given in Table 7.2, so that only Version 5 is free of serial correlation. The 5% critical value for the h statistic is 1.96, indicating that Versions 3–5 all suffer from serial correlation.

An interesting aspect of these results is that whilst Version 4 appears to be the 'best' of the models considered, this would not be detected by a forward search, starting from Version 1. The insignificant coefficient on $\ln(D_{t-1})$ in Version 2 would lead one to drop this variable, whilst $\ln(C_{t-1})$ would be retained in Version 3. In a backward search, starting from the most general model, you would immediately accept Version 5.

One other point to note is the relative stability of the estimate of the long-run consumption–income elasticity over the different dynamic specifications. Using the methods outlined in section 6.5 applied to the parameter estimates, one can compute long-run elasticities of consumption with respect to income for Versions 1–5.

Version 1: 0.9877

Version 2: $1.0526 - 0.0648 = 0.9878$

Version 3: $0.6478/(1 - 0.3437) = 0.9870$

Version 4: $(0.8239 - 0.5402)/(1 - 0.7125) = 0.9868$

Version 5: $(0.7748 - 0.4240)/(1 - 0.8275 - 0.1866) = -24.8794$.

The difficulty with Version 5 is simple: the denominator of the multiplier is negative. This, together with the insignificance of $\ln(C_{t-2})$ in Version 5, indicates that it is not an economically acceptable model.

LM tests for serial correlation and instrumental variables

An obvious question is whether the Lagrange multiplier test procedure above can be adapted to the case of IV estimation. Without going into the theoretical details, a simple and direct adaptation of the test regression method using (7.42) is possible. However, the residual $\tilde{u}$ has to be interpreted as an IV residual vector, computed as

$$\tilde{u} = y - X\tilde{b}, \tag{7.43}$$

using the IV estimator $\tilde{b}$ of the parameter vector of a model like (7.27) and (7.28). The test regression (7.42) uses the appropriate number of lags of $\tilde{u}$, but has to be estimated by IV using the same set of instruments that were used to find $\tilde{b}$. Finally, test the inclusion of the p lags of $\tilde{u}$ in $\tilde{U}$, using the analogue of (4.64).

Table 7.2 Annual consumption function with lagged variables

Sample based on observations	1964–94	1964–94	1964–94	1964–94	1965–94

OLS estimation

Dependent variable in all versions is LNRCONS
Values in brackets are *t* values

Regressor	Version 1	Version 2	Version 3	Version 4	Version 5
INTER	−0.0178	−0.0206	0.0048	0.0059	0.0209
	(−0.219)	(−0.249)	(0.065)	(0.098)	(0.338)
LNRPDI	0.9877	1.0526	0.6478	0.8239	0.7748
	(68.984)	(7.410)	(5.124),	(7.389)	(6.867)
DLPCONS	−0.2161	−0.2045	−0.2211	−0.1298	−0.1433
	(−3.039)	(−2.676)	(−3.440)	(−2.282)	(−2.545)
LNRPDI(−1)		−0.0648		−0.5402	−0.4240
		(−0.459)		(−3.926)	(−2.729)
LNRCONS(−1)			0.3437	0.7125	0.8275
			(2.702)	(5.120)	(5.491)
LNRCONS(−2)					−0.1866
					(−1.657)
RSS × 10^{-3}	8.8399	8.7714	6.9582	4.3681	3.8362
Degrees of freedom	28	27	27	26	24
R^2	0.9943	0.9944	0.9955	0.9972	0.9973
DW statistic	0.71	0.79	0.69	1.26	1.40
Durbin's *h*			5.17	3.26	2.91
LM(F)	19.297	19.662	21.943	7.6871	3.6398

The procedure described above sounds very straightforward, but there are some details to consider. Constructing the IV estimate $\check{b}$ requires y and X to be regressed on the set of instruments, so that estimation of (7.42) by IV also requires this for $\tilde{u}$ and $\tilde{U}$. There are p additional variables in (7.42) compared with the model underlying (7.43), so that there must be an apparent surplus of at least p instruments in obtaining $\check{b}$. For the purposes of this test, the residuals in (7.43) are considered as restricted, whilst the residuals from (7.42) are unrestricted. If the IV residuals from (7.42) form the vector $\tilde{\tilde{u}}$, the test statistic

$$LM(IV) = \frac{\tilde{u}' P_W \tilde{u} - \tilde{\tilde{u}}' P_W \tilde{\tilde{u}}}{\tilde{\sigma}_0^2} \tag{7.44}$$

is approximately distributed as χ_p^2, under the null hypothesis of no serial correlation, and where p is the maximum order of serial correlation under the alternative hypothesis. In (7.44), $\tilde{\sigma}_0^2$ is the disturbance variance estimate under the null hypothesis; an alternative form uses the variance estimate $\tilde{\sigma}^2$ from the test regression. This is the large sample analogue of the F test of inclusion of $\tilde{U}$, and parallels the $LM(F)$ form of the Lagrange multiplier test for serial correlation: it will be denoted $LM(IV\text{-}F)$. This form of test still uses the χ_p^2 distribution as an approximation to the distribution of the test statistic.

The quantities in the numerator of (7.44) are the restricted and unrestricted minimum values of the IV objective function, so that (7.44) is easy to calculate if these values are available. If not, the methods of calculation discussed in section 4.7 will have to be used.

Now consider the problem of choosing appropriate instruments for the procedure outlined above. If the equation to be estimated has k variables on the right-hand side and we are testing for serial correlation of up to order p, we need at least $p + k$ instruments. These cannot all be independent of the error term, since they would not be correlated with lagged residuals, and this violates the requirement that instruments be correlated to some extent with the variables for which predicted values are required. Some lags of the dependent variable or explanatory variables which are correlated with the error term must therefore be included in the instrument set.

This last point can cause some confusion, since in the presence of serial correlation, these variables are not valid instruments. However, the test statistic is constructed under the assumptions of the null hypothesis, and this means that for the purpose of the test, they are valid instruments.

Example 7.3

Using the column labelled Version 3 in Table 7.2, the evidence of serial correlation and the presence of a lagged dependent variable indicates that OLS estimators of this model are inconsistent. This inconsistency arises from the correlation between the lagged dependent variable and the error term. A simple IV estimator must therefore find at least one instrumental variable for lagged consumption: one possibility is lagged income. On the other hand, if one wishes to test for serial correlation using IV estimates, further variables would be required to act as instruments for the lagged residuals in the test regression, although this leads to the loss of observations. Here, we use two lags of income and one lag of DLPCONS as instruments for lagged consumption, so that there are six instruments in total. The results for IV estimation of Version 3 of Example 7.2 over the period 1965–94 are, noting that the quantities in brackets are t values,

$$\ln(\hat{C}_t) = -0.0098 + 0.9596\ln(D_t) - 0.2199\Delta\ln(P_t) + 0.0273\ln(C_{t-1});$$

$$(-0.1098) \quad (4.9805) \qquad\quad (-2.9600) \qquad\qquad (0.1407)$$

$$1965\text{–}94 \quad (7.45)$$

$n = 30 \quad RSS = 8.5374 \times 10^{-3} \quad IVOBJ = 7.5402 \times 10^{-4} \quad R^2 = 0.9940$

$df = 26 \quad VAR = 3.2836 \times 10^{-4} \qquad\qquad\qquad\qquad DW = 0.702$

IVOBJ is the minimum value of the IV objective function. With the value of the IV residual $\tilde{u}_t$ in 1964 set to 0 for convenience, the IV estimates of the test regression (7.42) using the same set of instruments are

$$\tilde{u}_t = \quad 0.0670 \; - \; 0.4395 \ln(D_t) \; - \; 0.0332\Delta \ln(P_t) \; + \; 0.4379 \ln(C_{t-1})$$

$$(t) \quad (0.5774) \quad (1.0574) \qquad\quad (-0.3687) \qquad\qquad (1.0539)$$

$$+1.2498\tilde{u}_{t-1}; \quad 1965\text{--}94$$

$$(1.2538)$$

$$n = 30 \quad RSS = 1.1031 \times 10^{-2} \quad IVOBJ = 6.0346 \times 10^{-5} \quad R^2 = -0.2921$$

$$df = 25 \quad VAR = 4.4125 \times 10^{-4} \qquad\qquad\qquad\qquad DW = 1.198$$

Comparing the results in (7.45) with the corresponding column of Table 7.2, one sees an increase in the coefficient on $\ln(D_t)$, a decrease in the coefficient on $\ln(C_{t-1})$, a reduction in the t values for these variables and for $\Delta \ln(P_t)$. The long-run consumption–income elasticity is 0.9865, not so very different from those computed in Example 7.2. Looking at the test regression results, the t value on $\tilde{u}_{t-1}$ would suggest that this variable can be excluded from the regression, and hence that there is no evidence of serial correlation in Version 3 when fitted by instrumental variables. Computing the $LM(IV)$ test statistic, this is

$$LM(IV) = (7.5402 \times 10^{-4} - 6.0346 \times 10^{-5})/(3.2836 \times 10^{-4}) = 2.1125,$$

whereas the $LM(IV\text{-}F)$ version equals 1.5721. Both of these statistics have a χ_1^2 distribution under the null hypothesis of no serial correlation: since the 5% critical value is 3.84, the acceptance of the null hypothesis is confirmed. This conclusion clearly contradicts that from Example 7.2. The explanation for this may lie in the interpretation of an LM test for serial correlation as a misspecification test, just like the DW statistic. In the current example, inconsistent estimates of the parameters will result if the instruments are correlated with the equation error terms for (7.45). Given the nature of the instruments chosen here, this is a possibility.

A passing comment should be made about the appearance of a negative R^2 in the residual-based regression above. As with many pieces of software, the standard definition of R^2 is used, despite the fact that OLS estimation is not being used here. The properties of the R^2 defined in equation (2.34) hold only for equations containing an intercept and which are estimated by OLS. In any other circumstances, negative R^2 is certainly possible.

7.6 / Estimation in nonstationary models

At the end of Chapter 6, it was noted that many macroeconomic time series display nonstationary behaviour. If this is the case, then the analysis so far in this chapter would appear to be of little relevance. Fortunately, this is not so. The discussion of estimator properties in sections 7.2 and 7.3 provides a useful contrast to the properties to be discussed in this section.

Linear trend models

One of the distinctions made at the end of Chapter 6 was that between a stochastic trend, generated by an AR process with a unit root, and a deterministic trend. A simplified linear trend model,

$$Y_t = \beta t + u_t; \ u_t \sim IID(0, \sigma^2); \ t = 1, \ldots, n, \tag{7.46}$$

contains the nonstochastic explanatory variable t, and so one would expect the large sample theory of section 4.4 to be applicable. In particular, from (4.9), one would expect the least squares estimator $\hat{\beta}$ of β to have a large sample normal distribution,

$$\sqrt{n}(\hat{\beta} - \beta) \xrightarrow{D} N(0, v^2)$$

with v^2 given by σ^2 times the inverse of

$$\lim \frac{1}{n} \sum_{t=1}^{n} t^2.$$

The problem with this claim is that $(1/n) \sum_{t=1}^{n} t^2$ actually diverges as $n \to \infty$, since

$$\sum_{t=1}^{n} t^2 = \frac{n(n+1)(2n+1)}{6}.$$

In fact, $\hat{\beta}$ does have a large sample normal distribution, but not scaled by $\sqrt{n}$. To see what the scaling ought to be, we need to look at the sampling error of $\hat{\beta}$,

$$\hat{\beta} - \beta = \left(\sum_{t=1}^{n} t^2 \right)^{-1} \sum_{t=1}^{n} t u_t, \tag{7.47}$$

where

$$\mathrm{var}\left(\sum_{t=1}^{n} t u_t \right) = \frac{\sigma^2 n(n+1)(2n+1)}{6}.$$

Given that the highest-order term in this variance is n^3, it will follow that

$$\mathrm{var}\left(n^{-3/2} \sum_{t=1}^{n} t u_t \right) \to \frac{\sigma^2}{3} \quad \text{as } n \to \infty.$$

We can then claim, as in section 4.4, that $n^{-3/2} \sum_{t=1}^{n} t u_t$ converges in distribution to some random variable Z with a normal distribution:

$$n^{-3/2} \sum_{t=1}^{n} t u_t \xrightarrow{D} Z \sim N\left(0, \frac{\sigma^2}{3} \right).$$

The other term in the sampling error (7.47) has a limit,

$$n^{-3} \sum_{t=1}^{n} t^2 \to \frac{1}{3},$$

so that by Cramér's theorem,

$$n^{3/2}(\hat{\beta} - \beta) \xrightarrow{D} 3Z \sim N(0, 3\sigma^2).$$

The point about this discussion is that the sampling error $\hat{\beta} - \beta$ needs to be scaled by a different power of n than in the usual case in order to establish large sample normality, and that this need is driven by the characteristics of the explanatory variable.

The random walk model

The issue of the scaling of the sampling error is also found in the random walk model. Suppose that we fit the AR(1) model by estimating ϕ_1 in

$$Y_t = \phi_1 Y_{t-1} + u_t; \; u_t \sim IID(0, \sigma^2); \; t = 1, \ldots, n,$$

where it is known that $\phi_1 = 1$, and a presample value Y_0 is available. We can then ask, what are the properties of the least squares estimator $\hat{\phi}_1$ in this nonstationary model?

Here, the sampling error is

$$\hat{\phi}_1 - 1 = \left(\sum_{t=1}^{n} Y_{t-1}^2 \right)^{-1} \sum_{t=1}^{n} Y_{t-1} u_t.$$

Since u_t is independent of Y_{t-1}, the argument underlying (7.9) and the covariance properties of the random walk process described in (6.42) yield

$$\text{var}\left(\sum_{t=1}^{n} Y_{t-1} u_t \right) = \sigma^2 \sum_{t=1}^{n} [(t-1)\sigma^2 + Y_0^2]$$

$$= \sigma^2 \left(\sum_{s=0}^{n-1} s\sigma^2 + nY_0^2 \right)$$

$$= \frac{1}{2} n(n-1)\sigma^4 + n\sigma^2 Y_0^2.$$

Given this information, it is clear that

$$\text{var}\left(\frac{1}{n} \sum_{t=1}^{n} Y_{t-1} u_t \right) = \frac{1}{2} \frac{(n-1)}{n} \sigma^4 + \frac{\sigma^2 Y_0^2}{n} \to \frac{\sigma^4}{2} \tag{7.48}$$

$$\text{var}\left(\frac{1}{\sqrt{n}} \sum_{t=1}^{n} Y_{t-1} u_t \right) = \frac{\sigma^4}{2}(n-1) + \sigma^2 Y_0^2 \to \infty, \tag{7.49}$$

both as $n \to \infty$. These conclusions can be contrasted with the stationary and asymptotically stationary AR(1) cases of section 7.2, where by (7.10),

$$\mathrm{var}\left(\frac{1}{n}\sum_{t=1}^{n} Y_{t-1}u_t\right) \to 0$$

and by (7.14),

$$\mathrm{var}\left(\frac{1}{\sqrt{n}}\sum_{t=1}^{n} Y_{t-1}u_t\right) \to \sigma^2\gamma_0 = \frac{\sigma^4}{1-\phi_1^2}.$$

There are clearly some very odd things going on here, which require a more detailed investigation than can be given in this book. A very good and reasonably accessible discussion of the details is given in Hamilton (1994: ch. 17). For our purposes, it is enough to observe that the large sample distribution of $\hat{\phi}_1$ is driven by the result that

$$\frac{1}{\sqrt{n}}\sum_{j=1}^{n} u_j \xrightarrow{D} N(0,\sigma^2)$$

under the IID assumption for the errors of the random walk process. As a consequence of this, the scaled numerator

$$\frac{1}{n}\sum_{t=1}^{n} Y_{t-1}u_t$$

and the scaled denominator

$$\frac{1}{n^2}\sum_{t=1}^{n} Y_{t-1}^2$$

in the sampling error $\hat{\phi}_1 - 1$ both have nondegenerate limit distributions when $\phi_1 = 1$. Neither of these are normal distributions, Note that scaling by $1/n$ and $1/n^2$ is required to obtain these limit distributions. The most important feature of these results is that the denominator has a limit distribution. This is in contrast to the stationary case, where when divided by n rather than n^2, it converges in probability to a constant.

The consequence of this discussion is that the limit distribution of

$$n(\hat{\phi}_1 - 1) = \frac{(1/n)\sum_{t=1}^{n} Y_{t-1}u_t}{(1/n^2)\sum_{t=1}^{n} Y_{t-1}^2}$$

is that of a random variable $\mathcal{W}$ with a *nonnormal* distribution:

$$n(\hat{\phi}_1 - 1) \xrightarrow{D} \mathcal{W}. \tag{7.50}$$

Notice that nothing has been said about the *consistency* of the OLS estimator $\hat{\phi}_1$ in this case. In general, for a consistent estimator $\hat{\theta}$ with a large sample normal distribution,

$$\sqrt{n}(\hat{\theta} - \theta) \xrightarrow{D} N(0, v^2),$$

an application of result (2) in section 4.3 with

$$a_n = 1/\sqrt{n} \quad \text{and} \quad b_n = \sqrt{n}(\hat{\theta} - \theta)$$

reproduces the presumed consistency of $\hat{\theta}$. For, by that result,

$$\text{plim } a_n b_n = \text{plim}(\hat{\theta} - \theta) = 0.$$

A purely intuitive argument for this is that as n increases, the range of $a_n b_n$ gets smaller and smaller. The value of a_n can be roughly interpreted as measuring the rate of convergence of $\hat{\theta}$ to θ. For the case of the simplified linear trend model (7.46), this rate of convergence would be $n^{-3/2}$, which goes to zero faster than $n^{-1/2}$ as $n \to \infty$. Estimators with the property of converging to the true value at a rate faster than $n^{-1/2}$ are called *superconsistent*, and it is clear from (7.50) that $\hat{\phi}_1$ has this property in the case of the random walk process, but not in the case of the stationary or asymptotically stationary AR(1) process.

The random walk with drift

Here, we estimate the model

$$Y_t = \delta + \phi_1 Y_{t-1} + u_t; \ u_t \sim IID(0, \sigma^2); \ t = 1, \ldots, n, \tag{7.51}$$

again under the presumption that we know that $\phi_1 = 1$, and with a presample value Y_0 being available. Recall from (6.43) that the behaviour of Y_t is given by

$$Y_t = Y_0 + \delta t + u_t + u_{t-1} + \ldots + u_1$$

where the sum of error terms represents the stochastic trend component.

The least squares estimator of ϕ_1 is given by

$$\tilde{\phi}_1 = \frac{\sum_{t=1}^{n}(Y_{t-1} - \bar{Y}_{-1})Y_t}{\sum_{t=1}^{n}(Y_{t-1} - \bar{Y}_{-1})^2} = 1 + \frac{\sum_{t=1}^{n}(Y_{t-1} - \bar{Y}_{-1})u_t}{\sum_{t=1}^{n}(Y_{t-1} - \bar{Y}_{-1})^2}.$$

Without going into details, the deterministic trend component in Y_t is sufficient to dominate the stochastic trend component, as $n \to \infty$, and one can show (see Hamilton, 1994: 497) that the large sample distribution of $\tilde{\phi}_1$ is given by

$$n^{3/2}(\tilde{\phi}_1 - 1) \xrightarrow{D} N\left(0, \frac{12\sigma^2}{\delta^2}\right). \tag{7.52}$$

Here the distribution is normal, and the scaling is that appropriate to the trend case. Notice that this normal distribution is not the one that would be obtained for the large sample distribution of $\tilde{\phi}_1$ in (7.51) if $|\phi_1| < 1$, and also the presence of the intercept parameter δ in the variance expression.

7.7 / Testing for unit roots

The discussion in section 6.7 gave a number of reasons why an economist might be interested in asking whether a series Y_t contains a unit root. If it does, the series will contain a stochastic trend, and thus imply behaviour rather different from that implied by the presence of a deterministic trend. In particular, shocks to the series will persist over time.

The discussion in the previous section shows that there are some statistical consequences as well: the large sample distributions of estimators in an AR(1) model differ according to whether $\phi_1 = 1$ or $|\phi_1| < 1$, and are sensitive to the precise specification of the model in the former case. Although not mentioned above, these distributional features carry over to the t statistic associated with the estimator of ϕ_1 as well. Given that we can never know what the 'true' model generating Y_t is, these differences create some practical inferential difficulties. In the next section, a somewhat more dramatic consequence of the presence of unit roots in a series will be illustrated.

The initial discussion of tests for a unit root will be conducted within a rather narrow framework. If the series Y_t contains a unit root, it will be assumed to be generated by a pure random walk:

$$Y_t = Y_{t-1} + u_t; \; u_t \sim IID(0, \sigma^2); \; t = 1, \ldots, n; \tag{7.53}$$

or equivalently by an AR(1) process with $\phi_1 = 1$:

$$Y_t = \phi_1 Y_{t-1} + u_t; \; u_t \sim IID(0, \sigma^2); \; t = 1, \ldots, n. \tag{7.54}$$

In this latter model, a 'test of a unit root' can be phrased as a test of the null hypothesis $\phi_1 = 1$, with the alternative hypothesis being $\phi_1 < 1$.

However, the tests proposed in the literature do not always consider (7.54) to be the model for generating test statistics. It is not that easy to understand why this is so. Consider (7.53): the mean of this process will be the starting value, Y_0, for all t. But, if $\phi_1 < 1$ in (7.54), the mean of Y_t is, from (6.40),

$$E(Y_t) = \phi_1^t Y_0$$

which will eventually approach zero. The argument is then that under the alternative hypothesis, (7.54) cannot capture the nonzero mean generated by (7.53), unless $Y_0 = 0$. To ensure that the 'alternative hypothesis' model can account for this, an intercept is introduced:

$$Y_t = \delta + \phi_1 Y_{t-1} + u_t; \; u_t \sim IID(0, \sigma^2); t = 1, \ldots, n. \tag{7.55}$$

This model is then used to generate the estimator of ϕ_1 and implied t statistic for testing the null hypothesis $\phi_1 = 1$ in (7.54). In effect, the model for generating the test statistic, the 'test model' or 'test regression', is different from the model within which the null hypothesis is embedded. One can see that the null hypothesis model (7.53) is the special case of (7.55) where

$$\delta = 0 \quad \text{and} \quad \phi_1 = 1,$$

yet it is conventional to test only the hypothesis $\phi_1 = 1$. Tests of this joint hypothesis have been developed, but they are not discussed here.

Denote the estimator of ϕ_1 from (7.55) by $\hat{\phi}_1$: it can be shown that both the sampling error $n(\hat{\phi}_1 - 1)$ and the t statistic $t_{(\hat{\phi}_1 - 1)}$ have different, but related, limiting nonnormal distributions under the null hypothesis model (7.53) (see, for example, Banerjee *et al.*, 1993: ch. 4; or Hamilton, 1994: ch. 17). Critical values for 5% tests are given in Tables 7.3 and 7.4; the use of these will shortly be explained.

Drift under the null hypothesis

If it is likely that the series to be investigated for a unit root has a nonzero mean, it would seem natural to use the random walk with drift as the analogue of (7.53),

$$Y_t = \delta + Y_{t-1} + u_t; \ u_t \sim IID(0, \sigma^2); \ t = 1, \ldots, n, \tag{7.56}$$

and

$$Y_t = \delta + \phi_1 Y_{t-1} + u_t; \ u_t \sim IID(0, \sigma^2); \ t = 1, \ldots, n, \tag{7.57}$$

as the analogue of (7.54).

In section 7.6, it was stated that the OLS estimator of ϕ_1 in (7.57) had the normal limiting distribution (7.52) if $\phi_1 = 1$, arising from the dominant deterministic trend component of Y_t. This suggests that if Y_t is generated by a random walk with drift, the t statistic for testing $\phi_1 = 1$ should be compared with critical values from an $N(0, 1)$ distribution. The difficulty with this argument is the way in which δ enters the distribution (7.52), and in fact, if $\delta = 0$, the limiting distribution of the t statistic is nonnormal. This is tricky, if we do not know whether the true model generating Y_t actually contains an intercept.

An alternative approach to testing for a unit root where there is possibly drift adapts the argument leading to (7.55) as the test regression. When $\phi_1 < 1$, (7.57) cannot capture deterministic trend behaviour in the series Y_t. The logic of the argument leading to (7.55) suggests that a test regression for this case can be constructed simply by adding a deterministic trend component to (7.55):

$$Y_t = \delta + \phi_1 Y_{t-1} + \beta t + u_t; \ u_t \sim IID(0, \sigma^2); \ t = 1, \ldots, n. \tag{7.58}$$

Denote the estimator of ϕ_1 from (7.58) by $\tilde{\phi}_1$, and the t statistic by $t_{(\tilde{\phi}_1 - 1)}$. It can be shown (Banerjee *et al.*, 1993: ch. 4; or Hamilton, 1994: ch. 17) that $n(\hat{\phi}_1 - 1)$ has the same nonnormal limiting distribution under either of the null hypothesis models (7.53) or (7.56). The same feature is true for $t_{(\tilde{\phi}_1 - 1)}$, although its distribution is different from that of $n(\tilde{\phi}_1 - 1)$. In turn, these two distributions are different from the corresponding distributions of $n(\hat{\phi}_1 - 1)$ and $t_{(\hat{\phi}_1 - 1)}$. The fact that the limiting distributions of $n(\tilde{\phi}_1 - 1)$ and $t_{(\tilde{\phi}_1 - 1)}$ are therefore independent of δ resolves the difficulty arising from testing for a unit root in (7.57).

However, this independence of δ means that the test regression (7.58) can also be used to generate a test of $\phi_1 = 1$ against $\phi_1 < 1$ in (7.54). We therefore have two alternative tests to choose between in this case. One way of deciding which of the test regressions (7.54)–(7.58) to use with a particular series is simply to examine the graph of the series. If the series appears to have a zero mean and no trend, (7.54) could be used as the test regression. If there appears to be a nonzero mean, but no trend, (7.55) can be used, whilst if there is a trend, (7.58) can be used. This does

Table 7.3 Dickey–Fuller tests: lower-tail critical values for scaled sampling errors

Distribution of	Test regressions	Case	Lower-tail critical values		
			1%	5%	10%
$n(f_1 - 1)$	(7.54)	No constant, no trend	−13.8	−8.1	−5.7
$n(\hat{\phi}_1 - 1)$	(7.55), (7.59)	Constant, no trend	−20.7	−14.1	−11.3
$n(\tilde{\phi}_1 - 1)$	(7.58), (7.60)	Constant and trend	−29.5	−21.8	−18.3

Source: Fuller (1976), table 8.5.2.

not resolve the difficulty over the choice between (7.55) or (7.58) when there is no trend. Ultimately one has to hope that the two test procedures deliver the same test conclusion. We now turn to the details of the test procedures.

Dickey–Fuller tests

Consider first the use of the distributions of the sampling errors $n(\hat{\phi}_1 - 1)$ from (7.55) and $n(\tilde{\phi}_1 - 1)$ from (7.58). Under the alternative hypothesis $\phi_1 < 1$, the values of these sampling errors are expected to be negative, so that a lower one-tailed test is required. Table 7.3 displays the appropriate critical values. The first row displays the critical values appropriate to the distribution of the estimator of ϕ_1, denoted f_1, obtained from (7.54). The columns marked 'Test regressions' and 'Case' are for easy reference when using the tables.

If t values are used, a lower one-tailed test is also required, for which the critical values are given in Table 7.4. Again to provide a contrast, the corresponding critical values from a standard normal are presented. These would be appropriate if the null hypothesis model was a (asymptotically) stationary AR(1) process.

It would be convenient if the test regressions (7.55) and (7.58) could be modified so that the correct t values for testing ϕ_1 were automatically generated in the regression output. A simple way of doing this is to subtract Y_{t-1} from both sides of the test

Table 7.4 Dickey–Fuller tests: lower-tail critical values for t values

Distribution of	Test regressions	Case	Lower-tail critical values		
			1%	5%	10%
$N(0, 1)$			−2.33	−1.645	−1.28
$t_{(f_1 - 1)}$	(7.54)	No constant, no trend	−2.58	−1.95	−1.62
$t_{(\hat{\phi}_1 - 1)}$	(7.55), (7.59), (7.64), (7.62)	Constant, no trend	−3.43	−2.86	−2.57
$t_{(\tilde{\phi}_1 - 1)}$	(7.58), (7.60), (7.65)	Constant and trend	−3.96	−3.41	−3.12

Source: Fuller (1976), table 8.5.2.

regressions, producing

$$\Delta Y_t = \delta + \gamma Y_{t-1} + u_t; \; u_t \sim IID(0, \sigma^2); \; t = 1, \dots, n \tag{7.59}$$

and

$$\Delta Y_t = \delta + \gamma Y_{t-1} + \beta t + u_t; \; u_t \sim IID(0, \sigma^2); \; t = 1, \dots, n, \tag{7.60}$$

in which $\gamma = \phi_1 - 1$, which is zero under the null hypothesis that $\phi_1 = 1$ and negative under the alternative that $\phi_1 < 1$.

Dickey–Fuller tests for unit roots then consist of comparing the t value for γ against the critical values in Table 7.4. If they are too large and negative, the null hypothesis of a unit root is rejected. Otherwise, the null hypothesis is accepted, and it is concluded that the series contains a unit root.

Example 7.4

The belief that unit roots are prevalent in macroeconomic time series data stems from the seminal paper of Nelson and Plosser (1982). The data set used by Nelson and Plosser has been used as an example for many procedures for testing unit roots, and it is used here. The original version of the data set consisted of annual observations on a number of US macroeconomic time series, with different starting points but ending in 1970; the series selected for use here are real GNP per capita (PCRGNP), unemployment rate (UNEMP), the difference of consumer prices (DCPI), and stock prices (SP500). All the selected variables are in logs, so that the difference of consumer prices is approximately the annual inflation rate. The version of the data set used here is that employed by Schotman and van Dijk (1991), which extends to 1988, and is contained in data set 8.

Figures 7.1–7.4 display the graphs of the selected series. Of the four series, PCRGNP and SP500 appear to be trending, whilst UNEMP and DCPI, roughly speaking, seem to fluctuate around a constant nonzero level. This suggests that test regression (7.60) is appropriate for PCRGNP and SP500, whereas (7.59) is not appropriate. This test regression would seem to be applicable only to UNEMP and DCPI, although there is no reason why (7.60) cannot be used with these variables. One would hope that the two different test regressions give the same test conclusions for these variables, whereas one would expect different conclusions for PCRGNP and SP500.

Table 7.5 displays the results of the two test regressions for the selected variables. The numbers in brackets are t values, and 5% critical values from Table 7.4 are shown. The null hypothesis being tested here is that $\gamma = 0$ or $\phi_1 = 1$: examining the results for PCRGNP, the t values for both test regressions exceed (algebraically) the corresponding critical values, and are thus evidence in favour of the null hypothesis of a unit root. In the case of UNEMP, the two t values are more negative than the critical values, and this would indicate rejection of the null hypothesis of a unit root. Since UNEMP is actually the unemployment rate, perhaps this is not too surprising. For SP500, the t values exceed the critical values, providing evidence for a unit root.

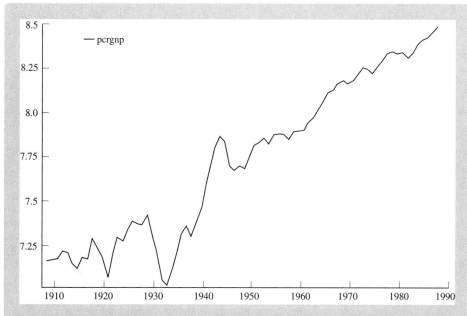

Figure 7.1 PCRGNP: logarithm of real GNP per capita, United States, 1909–88

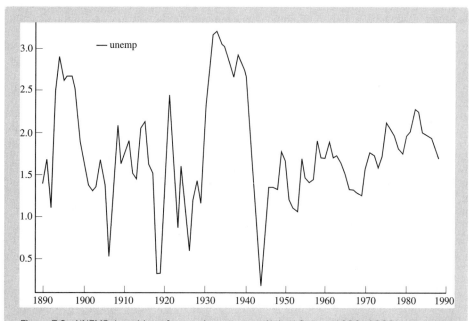

Figure 7.2 UNEMP: logarithm of unemployment rate, United States, 1890–1988

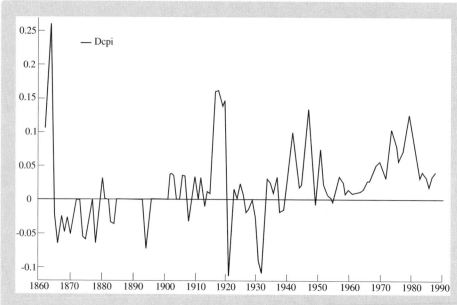

Figure 7.3 DCPI: logarithm of difference of consumer price index, United States, 1861–1988

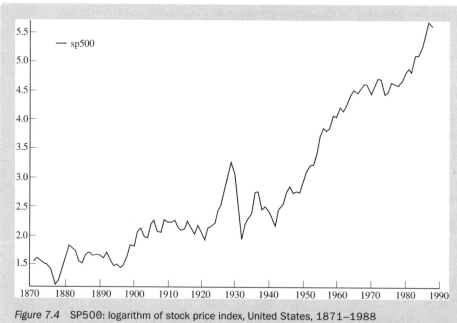

Figure 7.4 SP500: logarithm of stock price index, United States, 1871–1988

Table 7.5 Unit root tests, Nelson–Plosser data set

Dependent variable	Coefficient on			5% critical value	Sample period	n
	Constant	Trend	Y_{t-1}			
DPCRGNP	0.0234		−0.0008		1914–88	75
	(0.188)		(−0.0508)	−2.86		
DPCRGNP	0.9301	0.0032	−0.1563		1914–88	75
	(2.626)	(2.718)	(−2.6392)	−3.41		
DUNEMP	0.3992		−0.2347		1895–1988	94
	(3.324)		(−3.6538)	−2.86		
DUNEMP	0.3461	0.0006	−3.627		1895–1988	94
	(1.962)	(0.413)	(−3.6268)	−3.41		
DSP500	0.0126		0.0083		1876–1988	113
	(0.322)		(0.6542)	−2.86		
DSP500	0.0134	0.0028	−0.0650		1876–1988	113
	(0.350)	(2.196)	(−1.8249)	−3.41		
DDCPI	0.0126		−0.3655		1916–88	73
	(2.161)		(−3.9921)	−2.86		
DDCPI	−0.0040	0.0002	−0.3803		1916–88	73
	(−0.179)	(0.762)	(−4.0520)	−3.41		

For DCPI, the t values are smaller than the critical values, indicating rejection of the null hypothesis of a unit root.

Some software packages use critical values that differ from those used here. They make use of the results of the extensive investigations in the literature of the finite sample distributions of these test statistics to provide critical values that vary with sample size, and there will be cases where the difference between these and the large sample critical values is the difference between concluding that a unit root is or is not present.

Augmented Dickey–Fuller tests

One feature that is present in all of the above discussion is the proposition that the error term u_t is an $IID(0, \sigma^2)$ random variable. The absence of any other variables than Y_{t-1} and perhaps an intercept in the null model is rather unrealistic from an empirical viewpoint.

A natural extension of the idea of testing for a unit root in an AR(1) process is to consider an AR(p) process for Y_t,

$$\phi(L)Y_t = \delta + u_t; \ u_t \sim IID(0, \sigma^2); \ t \geq 1.$$

The decomposition of $\phi(L)$ given in (6.19) enables us to write this as

$$[\phi(1)L + (1 - L)\psi(L)]Y_t = \delta + u_t; \ u_t \sim IID(0, \sigma^2); \ t \geq 1,$$

or as

$$\psi(L)\Delta Y_t = \delta - \phi(1)Y_{t-1} + u_t; \ u_t \sim IID(0, \sigma^2); \ t \geq 1. \tag{7.61}$$

Here, $\psi(L)$ is the lag polynomial of an AR$(p-1)$ process,

$$\psi(L) = 1 + \psi_1 L + \ldots + \psi_{p-1}L^{p-1},$$

which shows that (7.61) is equivalent to

$$\Delta Y_t = \delta - \phi(1)Y_{t-1} - \psi_1 \Delta Y_{t-1} - \ldots - \psi_{p-1}\Delta Y_{t-p+1} + u_t. \tag{7.62}$$

In the special case of $\phi(L)$ being an AR(1), $\psi(L)$ should be an AR(0), that is $\psi(L) = 1$, so that $\psi_1 = \ldots = \psi_{p-1} = 0$ in (7.62) gives test regression (7.59).

If there is only one root of $\phi(z) = 0$ on the unit circle, and this equals $+1$, so that

$$\phi(1) = 0,$$

then $\psi(1) \neq 0$. If there is no unit root, $\phi(1)$ can have any sign, although if all the roots are positive (and thus exceed 1), it can be shown that $\phi(1) > 0$. Testing for a unit root here then is testing that $\phi(1) = 0$. Under the null hypothesis of a unit root, (7.61) becomes

$$\psi(L)\Delta Y_t = \delta + u_t. \tag{7.63}$$

If one could assert that $\phi(1) > 0$ under the alternative, it would be natural to use a lower one-tailed alternative in (7.61). In writing (7.61) as

$$\psi(L)\Delta Y_t = \delta + \gamma Y_{t-1} + u_t \tag{7.64}$$

with $\gamma = -\phi(1)$, one would conventionally use a lower one-tailed test on the assumption that $\gamma < 0$ is the appropriate alternative to $\gamma = 0$.

An investigator looking to test for the presence of a unit root in a series believed to be generated by an AR(p) process with drift could therefore employ (7.62) or (7.64) as a test regression in the same manner as (7.59). The presence or absence of a drift term in the test regression would be argued in the same way as before, as also the issue of a trend in the test regression. A variant on (7.64) is therefore

$$\psi(L)\Delta Y_t = \delta + \beta t + \gamma Y_{t-1} + u_t. \tag{7.65}$$

Perhaps surprisingly, the distribution of the t value on Y_{t-1} in (7.64), under the null hypothesis of a unit root, is the same as that from (7.59), so the corresponding entry in Table 7.4 provides large sample critical values. Exactly the same point applies to the pairing of (7.60) and (7.65). The test procedure is therefore exactly the same.

This test procedure is called the *augmented Dickey–Fuller* test. In comparison with (7.59) and (7.60), the additional terms in ΔY_{t-j} in (7.64) and (7.65) appear because of the additional serial correlation in the Y_t series arising from the AR(p) assumption. In many cases, an investigator will not want to have a firm hypothesis about the model generating Y_t under the null hypothesis of a unit root. Instead of explicitly asserting that an AR(p) process generates the serial correlation in Y_t, he or she will simply 'allow' for possible serial correlation in conducting the unit root test by including an appropriate number of lags of ΔY_t in (7.59) and (7.60), thus generating the test regressions (7.64) and (7.65) in a more informal way than done here.

Both approaches have to deal with the practical problem that we may not know what order of AR process to employ, or how many lags of ΔY_{t-j} to include in (7.64) and (7.65). One possible procedure is equivalent to testing the order of an AR process. Working with (7.62), start with a suitably high value of $p - 1$ and adopt a t test procedure on the parameters $\psi_{p-1}, \ldots, \psi_1$ one by one. The first null hypothesis in the sequence to be tested would be

$$\psi_{p-1} = 0$$

with alternative $\psi_{p-1} \neq 0$: if the hypothesis $\psi_{p-1} = 0$ is accepted, proceed to test

$$\psi_{p-2} = 0$$

and so on. When the hypothesis

$$\psi_{p-j} = 0$$

is first rejected, decide to include the terms $\Delta Y_{t-1}, \ldots, \Delta Y_{t-p+j}$ in the test model. Given that nonnormal distributions appear to arise in models where there is supposed to be a unit root, there is an issue of what distribution should be used for these t tests. One has to use the distribution that would hold under the null hypothesis of a unit root: fortunately, one can show that these t values are asymptotically $N(0, 1)$.

Having identified the appropriate order of augmentation, the test can be carried out as before. There is considerable evidence to suggest that augmented Dickey–Fuller tests are not very powerful in general, so that their ability to detect the absence of a unit root when one is not present is not large. In addition, it is known that these tests do not work well when the serial correlation is of the moving average variety, and a more specific test, not described here, has been developed to deal with this.

The results of applying these test procedures to the PCRGNP variable from the Nelson–Plosser data set are given in Table 7.6. The maximum number of lags of DPCRGNP included in the test regression (7.65), which is appropriate since PCRGNP appears to be trending, has been chosen as 4.

Following the procedure of identifying the order of augmentation prior to carrying out the unit root test, we need to start with the column where $p - 1 = 4$, in which the t value for DPCRGNP(−4) is seen to be insignificant compared with the 5% critical value for a two-sided test from the $N(0, 1)$ distribution, ± 1.96, which is also the approximate 5% critical value from the t distribution with 68 to 72 degrees of freedom. Similarly, DPCRGNP(−3) is insignificant in the $p - 1 = 3$ column, as is DPCRGNP(−2) in the $p - 1 = 2$ column. In the second column of the table, DPCRGNP(−1) is significant, indicating the apparent presence of first-order serial correlation for DPCRGNP. We then compare the t value on PCRGNP(−1) with the Dickey–Fuller test critical value from Table 7.4: since the t value is less than the critical value, we reject the null hypothesis that a unit root is present. This overturns the conclusion obtained from Table 7.5, and shows that some care is required in using the Dickey–Fuller test procedure. It is also interesting to note that the estimate

Table 7.6 Augmented Dickey–Fuller tests

Sample based on observations 1914–88

Dependent variable in all versions is DPCRGNP
Values in brackets are t values

Regressor	p – 1 values			
	1	2	3	4
INTER	1.2168	1.2724	1.2161	1.2095
	(3.665)	(3.558)	(3.181)	(3.008)
TREND	0.0041	0.0042	0.0041	0.0040
	(3.676)	(3.585)	(3.241)	(3.085)
DPCRGNP(−1)	0.4105	0.3981	0.3913	0.3898
	(3.894)	(3.625)	(3.507)	(3.380)
DPCRGNP(−2)		0.0507	0.0621	0.0613
		(0.434)	(0.516)	(0.503)
DPCRGNP(−3)			−0.0510	−0.0494
			(−0.435)	(−0.408)
DPCRGNP(−4)				−0.0067
				(−0.057)
PCRGNP(−1)	−0.2041	−0.2135	−0.2040	−0.2029
	(−3.6780)	(−3.5687)	(−3.1906)	(−3.0167)
Critical value	−3.41	−3.41	−3.41	−3.41

of ϕ_1 implied by these test regressions is around 0.8, a value that would not seem close to 1, so that the test conclusion looks reasonable.

The results for the other three variables considered in Example 7.4 can be quickly summarised: the same data periods as in Example 7.4 were used. A unit root in UNEMP can be tested against using either of the test regressions (7.64) and (7.65). In both cases, augmentations of three lags of DUNEMP is required, and both test regressions indicate that the null hypothesis of a unit root is rejected, with t values of −3.9252 and −3.8933 for (7.64) and (7.65). For SP500, (7.65) with two lags of DSP500 is called for, but the t value on SP500(−1) of −2.3463 indicates the presence of a unit root, as before. An augmentation of one lag is appropriate for DCPI, and the Dickey–Fuller t value of −4.6602 confirms the earlier conclusion.

7.8 / Cointegration

The discussion in section 7.6 reveals that the presence of a unit root in an AR process can have a number of different effects on the distribution of the least squares estimators, depending very critically on the precise case. There are, however, a number of more serious problems arising from unit roots. These are associated with the fact, as noted in section 6.7, that many macroeconomic time series, even in logs – for example, real GDP, real non-durable consumption, inflation, money supply – all appear to behave as if the process that generates them contains a unit root. That is, they are all integrated processes, mostly $I(1)$, although there is some evidence that the price level is $I(2)$, which is compatible with inflation being $I(1)$. Due to the inadequacies of test procedures for unit roots, not all of these variables will behave as $I(1)$ in all countries over all sample periods, however.

Spurious regressions

To illustrate the nature of one of the problems, consider the following example using data set 9 which consists of a sample of 150 observations on variables Y and X generated by computer from two completely independent random walks. Figure 7.5 shows that these two series drift over time in apparently independent ways. If we estimate the regression

$$Y_t = \beta_0 + \beta_1 X_t + u_t \tag{7.66}$$

we get apparently sensible results (see Table 7.7).

By conventional standards, the R^2 is not great, yet the two t values are very significant. If this were a practical application and the origins of Y and X were unknown, one could imagine trying to improve the fit by considering other possible explanatory

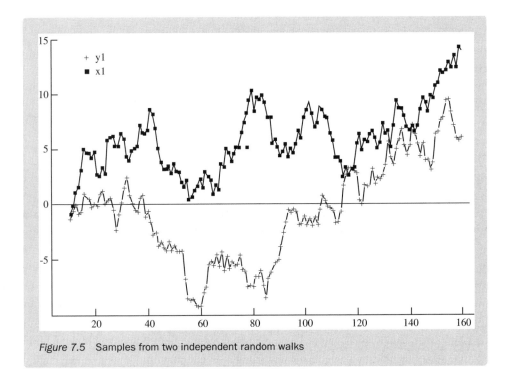

Figure 7.5 Samples from two independent random walks

Table 7.7 Regression results: independent $I(1)$ series

Sample based on observations 1 to 150
Dependent variable is Y

Variable	Coefficient	Standard error	t value
INTER	0.746 62	0.694 16	−7.382
X	−5.124 2	0.105 02	7.110

Degrees of freedom 148 from 150 observations

Residual SS	2242.6195
Disturbance variance	15.1528
R^2	0.2546
DW statistic	0.0947

variables. This perspective is reinforced by considering a few diagnostic tests:

Serial correlation: $LM(F) = 1347.3$ (first order)

$$LM(F) = 675.25 \text{ (second order)}$$

RESET :   0.8333

Normality BJ $= 7.25$

Here, both of the $LM(F)$ statistics are highly significant, regarded as having $F(1, 148)$ and $F(2, 147)$ distributions, for which the 5% critical values are 3.84 and 3.00 respectively. The RESET test is not significant, using the $F(1, 148)$ critical value, but the Bera–Jarque normality test is, since the 5% critical value of χ_2^2 is 5.99. In the face of these difficulties, it would be tempting to respecify (7.66) to try to eliminate the misspecifications.

The apparent relationship contained in the regression results of Table 7.7, and any subsequent analyses, is entirely *spurious* since we know that Y and X are unrelated. This apparent relationship arises simply because both variables follow random walks and thus contain a stochastic trend. It is important to stress that this trend is *not* common to both series because they are known to be unrelated. Phillips (1986) has provided a theoretical analysis of such spurious regressions in the current context. A summary of his results is instructive: all of the following quantities arising from estimation of (7.66) have limiting distributions, which in general are *not* normal:

1. $\hat{\beta}_1$;
2. $n^{-1/2}\hat{\beta}_0$;
3. $n^{-1/2}t_{\hat{\beta}_1}$;
4. R^2.

The implications of these results are interesting, and need to be considered in the light of the superconsistency discussion of section 7.6. First, $\hat{\beta}_0$ and $\hat{\beta}_1$ are *necessarily* inconsistent in the ordinary sense – they do not possess constant probability limits.

To see this, observe that $\hat{\beta}_1$ does *not* converge in probability to a constant, but a random variable. Next,

$$n^{-1/2}\hat{\beta}_0$$

converges in distribution to a random variable. To obtain the large sample behaviour of $\hat{\beta}_0$ from this, one would have to multiply by a quantity, $n^{1/2}$, which explodes as $n \to \infty$, and thus reveals that $\hat{\beta}_0 \to \infty$. It is also quite startling to see the same divergence implication for the t value. The idea that R^2 is, in the limit, obtained as a random drawing from some probability distribution is also quite striking.

The main point here is that one can easily fit such regressions using *levels* of macroeconomic, 'trending' variables and find reasonable goodness of fit and heavy serial correlation. However, such relationships may well be *spurious*, and one must guard against their production. The symptoms mentioned above are the important ones to look for. One can emphasise the importance of avoiding spurious regressions by considering the implications for macroeconomics of the statement that the observed relationship between aggregate log real consumption and log real income is a spurious regression. Consider again the evidence of the regression results presented in (2.54): the R^2 is 0.9904, the t value for $\ln(D_t)$ is 51.825, the $LM(F)$ statistic for second-order serial correlation is 18.341 (the 5% critical value of $F(2, 24)$ is 3.40), the RESET statistic is 23.315 (the 5% critical value of $F(1, 25)$ is 4.22), although the Bera–Jarque normality test statistic is only 0.99 (the 5% critical value of χ_2^2 is 5.99). Compared with Table 7.6, this evidence is at least suggestive.

This suggestion that an annual consumption function is actually a spurious relationship is not to be taken too seriously. What it does suggest is that detecting spurious relationships, and by implication, nonspurious relationships, is an important practical issue, to which we now turn.

Cointegration

Suppose that variables Y_t and X_t contain common stochastic trends: for simplicity, suppose that X_t follows a random walk. In this case, a regression relationship between Y_t and X_t might not be spurious. If in fact Y_t and X_t are related by the model

$$Y_t = \beta_0 + \beta_1 X_t + u_t; \ u_t \sim IID(0, \sigma^2), \tag{7.67}$$

then the stochastic trend in Y_t is a consequence of the stochastic trend in X_t. In this particular example, Y_t and X_t are $I(1)$, yet the linear combination of Y_t and X_t given by $Y_t - \beta_1 X_t$ is $I(0)$, since $\beta_0 + u_t$ is $IID(\beta_0, \sigma^2)$, and is therefore stationary. This linear combination is said to be *cointegrated*.

In general, an arbitrary linear combination of two $I(1)$ series, Y_t and X_t,

$$\alpha_1 Y_t + \alpha_2 X_t \tag{7.68}$$

will itself be $I(1)$, as in the spurious regression example (7.66). However, under certain circumstances, the coefficients α_1 and α_2 may be such as to make the linear combination $I(0)$, as in (7.67), where $\alpha_1 = 1$ and $\alpha_2 = -\beta_1$. In this case, (7.68) is a

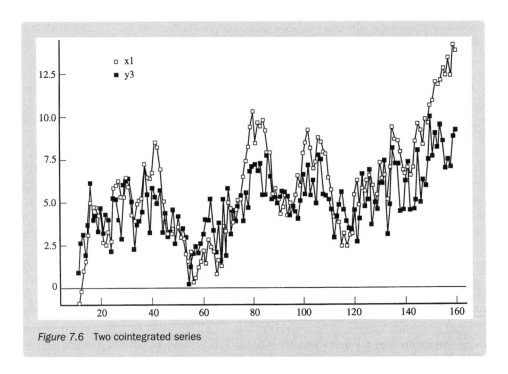

Figure 7.6 Two cointegrated series

cointegrating linear combination, and Y_t and X_t are again cointegrated. In contrast, if $\alpha_2 \neq -\beta_1$, the linear combination

$$Y_t - \alpha_2 X_t = Y_t - \beta_1 X_t + (\beta_1 - \alpha_2) X_t$$

is $I(1)$, for there are two components, the first of which is $I(0)$ and the second $I(1)$ since X_t is $I(1)$. When the variable generated by (7.68) is $I(0)$, it can be said, loosely speaking, to be stationary. A variable generated by such a process will not diverge or wander away indefinitely from its mean, so that the time paths of the cointegrated Y_t and X_t are tied to each other by this stationary process. If Y_t and X_t are not cointegrated, their time paths will tend to diverge from each other over substantial periods of time, as seen in Figure 7.5. Figure 7.6 displays the situation in which variables Y_t and X_t are cointegrated: in this example, the variables are tied quite closely to each other over the sample period.

In economics (and finance), cointegration captures the idea that there might be long-run relationships between integrated variables Y and X. If so, their values cannot diverge persistently over time, since the divergence would ultimately destroy the cointegration relationship. With such long-run relationships, there can only be *stationary* deviations about the cointegrating relationship, so that in

$$Y_t = \beta_0 + \beta_1 X_t + u_t$$

u_t follows a stationary process, rather than necessarily being $IID(0, \sigma^2)$.

This discussion relates to one of the major problems in econometrics. Long-run models tend to suggest static economic relationships, yet it is obvious empirically that models involving lagged values of both dependent and explanatory variables are required. These lags are usually supposed to capture the short-run dynamics. Where in such models can the long-run relationship be found? To say that the long-run multiplier displays this information is to be restricted to a stationary world, given the conditions for existence of the long-run multiplier.

At this point it is necessary to look further ahead. Consider the ADL(1, 1) model

$$Y_t = \delta + \phi_1 Y_{t-1} + \beta_0 X_t + \beta_1 X_{t-1} + u_t \tag{7.69}$$

in which X_t is $I(1)$ and $|\phi_1| < 1$. This will make Y_t $I(1)$ since X_t is assumed $I(1)$, but if $\phi_1 = 1$, the equation can be rewritten with ΔY_t on the left-hand side, and this would make Y_t an $I(2)$ variable.

Using the lag polynomials

$$\phi(L) = 1 - \phi_1 L, \quad \beta(L) = \beta_0 + \beta_1 L,$$

and assuming that $|\phi_1| < 1$, (7.69) can be written in a sort of 'error correction' form

$$\phi_1 \Delta Y_t = -\phi(1)\left[Y_t - \frac{\delta}{\phi(1)} - \frac{\beta(1)}{\phi(1)} X_t\right] - \beta_1 \Delta X_t + u_t. \tag{7.70}$$

The implied long-run relationship between Y_t and X_t is contained in the large bracket,

$$Y = \mu_0 + \mu_1 X$$

given that ΔY_t and ΔX_t should be $I(0)$. A static regression which captures the long-run relationship is

$$Y_t = \mu_0 + \mu_1 X_t + \varepsilon_t$$

which can be compared with the rearrangement of (7.70) as

$$Y_t - \frac{\delta}{\phi(1)} - \frac{\beta(1)}{\phi(1)} X_t = \frac{-1}{\phi(1)} (\phi_1 \Delta Y_t + \beta_1 \Delta X_t - u_t). \tag{7.71}$$

The terms on the right-hand side of this equation represent ε_t, and are $I(0)$ given the assumptions about X_t and the model (7.69). By definition, then, Y_t and X_t are cointegrated. This argument shows that cointegration embeds long-run relationships between integrated variables within the apparently short-run dynamics of an ADL(1, 1) model.

In general, a vector y_t of $I(1)$ variables is said to be *cointegrated* if there exists a vector α such that

$$\alpha' y_t$$

is $I(0)$ – loosely speaking, stationary. We can interpret this as saying that the elements of y_t might share a stochastic trend component, making y_t $I(1)$, but forming the linear combination $\alpha' y_t$ eliminates this common component. The idea of cointegration can in principle be extended to deal with variables of different order of integration: for example, if Z_t is an $I(2)$ variable, ΔZ_t is $I(1)$, and this can be cointegrated with other $I(1)$ variables. However, for our purposes, it is sufficient to consider combinations of $I(1)$ variables that cointegrate to an $I(0)$ variable. Later, in Chapter 9, we shall discuss the issues of how many *cointegrating* combinations of y_t can be formed, and thus how many *common trends* there might be, whether they are unique, how they are found and so on. For the moment, there are a number of statistical issues to discuss.

Testing for cointegration: the Engle–Granger approach

An answer to the question of whether a relationship like

$$Y_t = \beta_0 + \beta_1 X_t + u_t, \tag{7.72}$$

the *cointegrating regression*, is spurious, if Y_t and X_t are $I(1)$ variables, is equivalent to asking if Y_t and X_t are cointegrated. If they are not cointegrated, the disturbance u_t should be $I(1)$ and thus contain a unit root, since it is equal to the zero mean component of the noncointegrating linear combination of $I(1)$ variables

$$Y_t - \beta_1 X_t.$$

A natural procedure would be to use the Dickey–Fuller-type unit root test on the residuals e_t from least squares estimation of (7.72). The simplest Dickey–Fuller test regression would then be

$$\Delta e_t = \gamma e_{t-1} + \text{error}. \tag{7.73}$$

Testing that $\gamma = 0$ is equivalent to testing that e_t contains a unit root, and thus that Y_t and X_t are *not* cointegrated. One therefore wishes to reject the null hypothesis of a unit root, and accept the alternative $\gamma < 0$, which implies that u_t is $I(0)$ and thence that Y_t and X_t are cointegrated. The test procedure is exactly the same as before, including the logic for using augmented Dickey–Fuller tests, where the augmentation will consist of adding terms in Δe_{t-j} to (7.73).

One question to be answered is which of the types of Dickey–Fuller tests are appropriate here. Even then, there is still a more fundamental question: is the distribution of the t value for e_{t-1} unchanged under the null hypothesis, given that we are working with residuals that contain the effects of estimated parameters? Not every potential cointegrating regression will contain only two variables: does the distribution change with the number of variables that are supposed to be cointegrated? A final issue: supposing the variables to be integrated, is standard inference using normal and chi-squared distributions possible on the parameters of the cointegrating regression? Attempts to answer all these questions will be made below.

The distribution of the t value for e_{t-1} from (7.73) does unfortunately differ from that in the case of the pure unit root test, and also differs according to the number of variables included in the cointegrating regression. However, if the cointegrating relationship is known exactly, so that there is no need for estimation, then the usual Dickey–Fuller critical values can be used. An example might be a situation where it was hypothesised that

$$Y_t - X_t$$

was $I(0)$.

Whilst this *Engle–Granger* approach for testing cointegration is quite simple and straightforward, it does not work all that well in some circumstances. More specifically, the test appears to be biased in finite samples, in the sense that it can reject rather more frequently than the nominal 5% of the time. An alternative test is described later in this section.

It is important to stress that there can be a difference between the nature of the processes that actually generate X_t and Y_t, and the process for Y_t implied by the cointegrating regression (7.72). For example, X_t and Y_t may be zero mean $I(1)$ processes, resulting in the cointegrating combination $\alpha_1 X_t + \alpha_2 Y_t$ being a zero mean $I(0)$ process. Nonetheless, we can use (7.72), in which the intercept β_0 is assumed nonzero, to generate residuals for an augmented Dickey–Fuller test. Hamilton (1994: 591–8) discusses the distribution of test statistics when there is such a conflict.

MacKinnon's approach

Given this extra degree of complexity in the distribution of the t statistic from (7.73), a different approach to the provision of critical values is needed. In a series of papers, MacKinnon (1991, 1994, 1996) (see also Banerjee *et al.*, 1993) has used a response surface approach which provides a formula for generating critical values and p values for these tests. Here, we use the version for critical values. The general formula for generating the critical values is

$$CV = \lambda_\infty + \lambda_1 n^{-1} + \lambda_2 n^{-2},$$

where the parameters in this formula differ according to the particular test circumstances and the size of the test required. Table 7.8(a) gives three different sets of the coefficients required for the computation of 5% critical values.

Consider the three models

$$Y_t = \beta_1 X_t + u_t, \tag{7.74}$$

$$Y_t = \beta_0 + \beta_1 X_t + u_t, \tag{7.72}$$

$$Y_t = \beta_0 + \beta_1 X_t + \beta_2 t + u_t. \tag{7.75}$$

In MacKinnon's approach, these may represent the 'true' cointegrating relationship, but they may also be used as the cointegrating regression for generating residuals e_t for use in a possibly augmented version of (7.73),

$$\Delta e_t = \gamma e_{t-1} + \psi_1 \Delta e_{t-1} + \ldots + \psi_q \Delta e_{t-q} + \text{error}. \tag{7.76}$$

The 5% critical value for the t test that $\gamma = 0$ in this equation depends on whether, taken together, the 'true' cointegrating relationship and the cointegrating regression contain neither intercept nor trend, only an intercept, or both an intercept and trend.

Table 7.8 Coefficient for MacKinnon's response surfaces

(a)

No constant, no trend	λ_∞	λ_1	λ_2
$k = 1$	−1.9393	−0.3980	0.0000

(b)

Constant, no trend	λ_∞	λ_1	λ_2
$k = 1$	−2.8621	−2.7380	−8.3600
$k = 2$	−3.3377	−5.9670	−8.9800
$k = 3$	−3.7429	−8.3520	−13.410
$k = 4$	−4.1000	−10.745	−21.570
$k = 5$	−4.4185	−13.641	−21.160

(c)

Constant, trend	λ_∞	λ_1	λ_2
$k = 1$	−3.4126	−4.0390	−17.830
$k = 2$	−3.7809	−9.4210	−15.060
$k = 3$	−4.1193	−12.0240	−13.130
$k = 4$	−4.4294	−14.501	−19.540
$k = 5$	−4.7154	−17.432	−16.500

For example, the 'constant and trend' case may arise if the true cointegrating relationship is (7.72), and we use (7.75) as the cointegrating regression, or if the true cointegrating relationship is (7.74), but we use (7.75) as the cointegrating regression.

To complicate matters, in computing the t value from (7.76), we can include an intercept and/or trend if they have not already been included in the cointegrating regression. If these variables were included in the cointegrating regression, there is no need to include them in the test regression, since the residuals already allow for this effect, as (7.76) indicates. In practice, an intercept is usually included in the cointegrating regression, as in (7.72), and a trend might also be included if it was felt that Y_t behaved like a random walk with drift, whereas X_t might be just a random walk. There is some evidence, from Hansen (1995), that the inclusion of a trend in either the cointegrating regression (7.75) or test regression (7.76) reduces the power of the test. This suggests that the combination of (7.72) and (7.76) will be adequate in practice, so that the 'constant, no trend' component of Table 7.8 is the one to use.

In Table 7.8, k is the total number of variables (apart from intercept and trend) appearing in the cointegrating regression. The case of $k = 1$ corresponds to zero right-hand-side variables, and is equivalent to the case of testing for a unit root with a single variable. The principle of using the tables is that the coefficient λ_∞ gives the asymptotic critical value, which will be sufficient for most purposes, whilst the coefficients λ_1 and λ_2 allow a correction for sample size. With this in mind, the $k = 1$ values can be compared with the numbers in the 5% column of Table 7.4. It can be seen that the 'no constant, no trend' case matches the $t_{(f_1-1)}$ row of Table 7.4, whilst the 'constant, no trend' case matches the $t_{(\hat{\phi}_1-1)}$ row. In a number of popular econometric packages, these critical values are automatically generated, for both pure unit root tests and cointegration tests.

As an example, choosing the 'constant, trend' case with $n = 75$ and $k = 1$, the critical value would be

$$CV = -3.4126 - (4.0390/75) - (17.830)(1/75)^2 = -3.469\,62$$

which provides a more refined critical value for use in the second equation of Table 7.5, although it does not change the test conclusion. Obviously, the impact of the sample size correction factors λ_1 and λ_2 will be greater for smaller sample sizes. Apart from the use of residuals and different critical values, the test procedure is exactly the same as the pure unit root case.

Example 7.5

The speculation that the annual consumption function (2.54) is actually a spurious regression can now be subjected to formal test. A necessary preliminary is confirmation that both $\ln(C_t)$ and $\ln(D_t)$ are both $I(1)$ series, which was implicitly assumed in proposing that (2.54) might be spurious. Augmented Dickey–Fuller tests for this example are sensitive to the precise period and number of observations used, as might be expected with such a small sample but, for the period 1965–90, the test results give t values of 1.0541 and 0.5439 for $\ln(C_t)$ and $\ln(D_t)$ respectively using test regression (7.59), and -2.2853 and -3.0979 for test regression (7.60). Since the asymptotic critical value is -2.86 for test regression (7.59), and -3.41 for (7.60), these results confirm that $\ln(C_t)$ and $\ln(D_t)$ do appear to be $I(1)$ series, so that we can go ahead with a test for the cointegration of $\ln(C_t)$ and $\ln(D_t)$. The test results quoted come from test regressions which include an intercept, but no augmentation.

Taking e_t to represent the residuals of (2.54), which was estimated over the period 1963–90, we use (7.73) augmented with up to three lags of Δe_t to carry out the test. Presample values for the residuals were set to zero. Using the 'testing down' procedure used in Table 7.6, we find that none of these lags are significant, so that the test regression used is (7.73), and the t value attached to e_{t-1} is found to be -1.884. Since (2.54), treated as a cointegrating regression, is of the form (7.72), the 5% critical value computed using MacKinnon's response surface should use the 'constant, no trend' subsection with $k = 2$ and $n = 28$, giving

$$CV = -3.3377 - 5.9670(1/28) - 8.9800(1/28)^2 = -3.552\,08.$$

Since the t value exceeds this critical value, we accept the null hypothesis that the disturbances of (2.54) contain a unit root, which implies that $\ln(C_t)$ and $\ln(D_t)$ in that equation are not cointegrated, and that the relationship is spurious.

One can test a number of other versions of this annual consumption function, by including the inflation variable $\ln(\Delta P_t)$ and the liquid asset variable $\ln(L_t)$ as further explanatory variables, or by including a trend in the test regression (7.73), or by varying the sample period to use all available observations, and still reach the same test conclusion. What is at fault here, the underlying economic theory or the test procedure? First, note that a very small sample size is being used, despite the correction for sample size in the critical values. Second, the underlying Dickey–Fuller test procedure is not very powerful, as noted previously in section 7.7. Thirdly, the static regression (7.72), even when augmented by other explanatory variables, is unlikely to capture adequately the dynamics in the relationship. One can see from the version (7.71) of the ADL(1, 1) model that such dynamics are automatically included in the disturbance of the static regression (7.72), and it is likely that such a misspecification of the underlying ADL model affects the outcome of the test procedure. This suggests that a test for cointegration built directly around the estimation of an ADL model may be better than the Engle–Granger test.

Cointegration and the ADL(1, 1) model

There is a powerful link between the ADL model and cointegration, which will be seen more fully in Chapter 9. The ADL(1, 1) model (7.69) has an 'error correction form', (6.37), repeated here for convenience,

$$\Delta Y_t = -\phi(1)(Y_{t-1} - \mu_0 - \mu_1 X_{t-1}) + \beta_0 \Delta X_t + u_t. \tag{7.77}$$

The term in brackets represents the relationship between Y_t and X_t in a 'long-run stationary equilibrium', whose existence requires $|\phi_1| < 1$. If X_t is $I(1)$, such a 'long-run stationary equilibrium' cannot exist, since X_t will never be stationary in this sense. But, constructing the error correction form of the ADL model is an algebraic exercise, and does not depend on the nature of X_t. So, we can still interpret the term in brackets as the 'long-run' relationship between Y_t and X_t when X_t is $I(1)$, and draw the analogy between this and a cointegrating linear combination of Y_t and X_t. The ADL model itself makes Y_t $I(1)$ and cointegrated with X_t, provided that $\phi(1) = 1 - \phi_1 \neq 0$. If $\phi_1 = 1$, it can be seen from the ADL form that ΔY_t would be $I(1)$ through X_t, and Y_t would then be $I(2)$. As a result, Y_t and X_t cannot be cointegrated, although it may be possible for ΔY_t and X_t to be cointegrated. To see that Y_t may be $I(2)$ when $\phi_1 = 1$ from the error correction form is not so easy because the parameters μ_0 and μ_1 are not defined when $\phi_1 = 1$.

Estimation under cointegration

This discussion leads quite naturally into the issues of estimation of the ADL model under cointegration, and will in fact lead us into the discussion of an additional test for cointegration. The first estimation procedure is called the Engle–Granger two-step procedure, which starts from the supposed cointegrating relation

$$Y_t = \mu_0 + \mu_1 X_t + \varepsilon_t. \tag{7.78}$$

Here, X_t is supposed to be an $I(1)$ process, for example a random walk, or perhaps a process with more general dependence like an $AR(p)$ with a unit root. Drift in the X_t

process is also allowed. For (7.78) to be compatible with the ADL model (7.69), ε_t will contain the disturbance u_t of (7.69) and factors involving ΔY_t and ΔX_t, as in (7.71). The disturbance ε_t is unlikely to be $IID(0, \sigma^2)$, although it is expected to follow an $I(0)$ process, and possibly even to be a stationary process.

The Engle–Granger two-step procedure proposes that μ_1 is estimated directly from (7.78) by OLS, and the resulting estimator $\hat{\mu}_1$ is plugged into the ADL model (7.77) to give

$$\Delta Y_t = \delta - \phi(1)(Y_{t-1} - \hat{\mu}_1 X_{t-1}) + \beta_0 \Delta X_t + u_t, \tag{7.79}$$

in which the remaining unknown parameters, δ, $-\phi(1)$ and β_0, are then estimated directly by OLS. Many discussions of this procedure do not allow for the presence of an intercept in the cointegrating regression (7.78) or the ADL model (7.77): in these cases, the substitution of $\hat{\mu}_1$ into the ADL model would make the term $Y_{t-1} - \hat{\mu}_1 X_{t-1}$ equal to the lagged residual from the cointegrating regression (7.78). For this interpretation to work in the presence of intercepts, the OLS estimates of both μ_0 and μ_1 from (7.78) would have to be substituted into the error correction form (7.77) to produce

$$\Delta Y_t = -\phi(1)(Y_{t-1} - \hat{\mu}_0 - \hat{\mu}_1 X_{t-1}) + \beta_0 \Delta X_t + u_t, \tag{7.80}$$

leaving the parameters $-\phi(1)$ and β_0 to be estimated by OLS.

Why does this procedure appear to 'work'? It can be shown (for example, see Hamilton, 1994: 587–8) that both

$$\sqrt{n}(\hat{\mu}_0 - \mu_0) \quad \text{and} \quad n(\hat{\mu}_1 - \mu_1)$$

have limiting, nonnormal distributions, and thus $\hat{\mu}_1$ is 'superconsistent' in the sense used previously in section 7.6. The distributional implication of this for the estimators $\hat{\delta}$, $-\hat{\phi}(1)$ and $\hat{\beta}_0$ from OLS estimation of (7.79) is that $\hat{\mu}_1$ can be treated as if it were identical to the true parameter μ_1. Since the ADL model contains only $I(0)$ variables under cointegration, the limit distributions of the estimators $\hat{\delta}$, $-\hat{\phi}(1)$ and $\hat{\beta}_0$ are normal distributions, so that inference on the values of these parameters can proceed as usual.

A number of caveats need to be made here. First, there is evidence to suggest that the estimate of μ_1 suffers from finite sample biases associated with the dynamic effects that are relegated to the error term. Secondly, the superconsistency property of $\hat{\mu}_1$ holds under the range of circumstances mentioned following (7.78), but the precise nature of the limiting distribution of $n(\hat{\mu}_1 - \mu_1)$ varies from case to case. For example, in the simple model where

$$Y_t = \mu_1 X_t + u_t; \ u_t \sim IID(0, \sigma_u^2)$$

$$\Delta X_t = v_t; \ v_t \sim IID(0, \sigma_v^2)$$

and the errors u_t and v_t are *not* independent, the limiting distribution is nonnormal. But if, in fact, u_t and v_t are independent, it can be shown that

$$n(\hat{\mu}_1 - \mu_1) \xrightarrow{D} N\left(0, \frac{\sigma_v^2}{\sigma_u^2}\right).$$

It will follow that the t value for testing that $\mu_1 = 0$ is also normal in this case. This is established in Banerjee *et al.* (1993: 174–6), where it is also established that if X_t follows a random walk with drift parameter η,

$$\Delta X_t = \eta + v_t,$$

then

$$n^{3/2}(\hat{\mu}_1 - \mu_1) \xrightarrow{D} N\left(0, \, 3\frac{\sigma_v^2}{\eta^2}\right).$$

The power of n involved here is the same as that for estimation in a random walk with drift process – see (7.52).

An alternative estimation procedure starts from the observation that direct estimation of the error correction form (7.77) of the ADL model (7.69) has to deal with the fact that the parameters $-\phi(1)$ and μ_0, μ_1 enter nonlinearly through the products $-\phi(1)\mu_0$ and $-\phi(1)\mu_1$. This is not a serious nonlinearity, and is easy to deal with using nonlinear estimation techniques similar to that discussed in Example 4.1. However, a two-step approach which is different from that of Engle–Granger can be used, and has the attraction of generating a test of cointegration based on direct estimation of the ADL model (7.69). This method is based on the observation that the long-run parameters μ_0 and μ_1 are functions of the ADL parameters through

$$\mu_0 = \frac{\delta}{\phi(1)}, \quad \mu_1 = \frac{\beta(1)}{\phi(1)}. \tag{7.81}$$

Comparing the error correction form of the ADL model, (7.69), with the cointegrating regression (7.78), we see that (7.69) 'contains' (7.78), along with some short-run dynamics. Direct estimation of (7.69) thus implies estimators of the long-run parameters as

$$\tilde{\mu}_0 = \frac{\hat{\delta}}{\hat{\phi}(1)}, \quad \tilde{\mu}_1 = \frac{\hat{\beta}(1)}{\hat{\phi}(1)}$$

which can be substituted into the error correction form (7.77) to produce an equation like (7.80). The remaining parameters $-\phi(1)$ and β_0 are estimated by OLS as before. This type of estimation procedure for error correction models has been popularised via the software package *PcGive*.

Another test of cointegration

To describe how this test arises requires the error correction form (6.36) of the ADL(p, s) model (6.35): these equations are reproduced here for convenience,

$$\psi(L)\Delta Y_t = -\phi(1)(Y_{t-1} - \mu_0 - \mu_1 X_{t-1}) + g(L)\Delta X_t + u_t \tag{7.82}$$

$$\phi(L)Y_t = \delta + \beta(L)X_t + u_t. \tag{7.83}$$

Here $\psi(L)$ and $g(L)$ are lag polynomials of order $p - 1$ and $s - 1$ respectively.

In (7.82), put

$$\mu_1 = 1 + \lambda_1$$

and use (7.81), so that (7.82) becomes

$$\psi(L)\Delta Y_t = \delta - \phi(1)(Y_{t-1} - X_{t-1}) + \phi(1)\lambda_1 X_{t-1} + g(L)\Delta X_t + u_t.$$

Suppose that the model

$$\psi(L)\Delta Y_t = \delta + \gamma_1(Y_{t-1} - X_{t-1}) + \gamma_2 X_{t-1} + g(L)\Delta X_t + u_t \qquad (7.84)$$

is estimated by OLS. The estimate of γ_1 is then a direct estimate of $-\phi(1)$, in contrast to the estimate of $\phi(1)$ deduced from the ADL model (7.83), which will depend on the estimates of $\phi_1, \ldots, \phi_p$. In (7.84), there are

$$p - 1 + 1 + 1 + 1 + s - 1 = p + s + 1$$

parameters, exactly the same number as in the ADL model (7.83). There is in fact a nonsingular linear transformation connecting the variables and the parameters of the two models. Thus, the estimates from (7.84) will be exactly equal to this linear transformation of the estimates from (7.83), and the estimate of $\phi(1)$ will be the same from both models, as well as from (7.82). It should be noted that in general the computed standard error for the estimate of $\phi(1)$ from (7.82) will differ from that in (7.84), since fewer explanatory variables are present.

The test of cointegration is then simply a t test that

$$\gamma_1 = 0$$

in (7.84), against the alternative

$$\gamma_1 \neq 0.$$

There are a number of points that can be made about this test. Since $\gamma_1 = -\phi(1)$, $\gamma_1 = 0$ corresponds to a unit root. As noted above, this would imply that Y_t is $I(2)$ and thus not cointegrated with the $I(1)$ variable X_t. If $\gamma_1 \neq 0$, $\phi(L)$ is a stable or invertible lag polynomial, and this means that Y_t is $I(1)$ only through the ADL model linking the two variables. This is the same as saying that Y_t and X_t are cointegrated through the ADL relationship (7.83). If in the ADL model, X_t is a *vector* of $I(1)$ variables, the same principles apply. It is hoped that Y_t and all the variables in the vector X_t are cointegrated, and the evidence for or against this is still the value of $\phi(1)$, since this provides the dynamic link between Y_t and X_t.

The t test on γ_1 has a nonnormal limiting distribution, which depends partly on a Dickey–Fuller-type distribution. Tables of the critical values do not seem to be available outside the *PcGive* software (Doornik and Hendry, 1994), which automatically calculates the correct critical values for 5% and 1% tests. The test is referred to as the '*PcGive* unit root test' in the output of that software. The test seems to perform well when the estimators of the parameters of the cointegrating relationship perform well.

Example 7.6

This follows on from Example 7.5: here the ADL-based cointegration test is applied to a version of (2.54). An ADL model has to be estimated first: an ADL(1, 1) model for $\ln(C_t)$ (LNRCONS) and $\ln(D_t)$ (LNRPDI) is estimated over the period 1964–90, as being the nearest feasible period to that used in (2.54). The results are (standard errors in brackets)

$$\ln(\hat{C}_t) = -0.0651 + 0.898\ln(C_{t-1}) + 0.808\ln(D_t) - 0.695\ln(D_{t-1})$$

$$(0.072) \quad (0.145) \quad\quad\quad (0.115) \quad\quad\quad (0.130)$$

$$n = 27 \quad RSS = 3.7915 \times 10^{-3} \quad R^2 = 0.9960 \quad 1964-90$$

$$df = 23 \quad VAR = 1.6485 \times 10^{-4}.$$

The long-run relationship implied by the model is

$$\ln(C) = -0.639\,49 + 1.106\ln(D)$$

with an approximate t value of 5.33 for the coefficient of $\ln(D)$. Despite the apparent significance of this long relationship, it does not seem very plausible to suggest that, in the long run, C has an 'income' elasticity greater than 1. This suggests that the estimated relationship is not very satisfactory from an economic viewpoint. The $LM(F)$ statistic for second-order serial correlation here has the value 1.5239, so that there is no apparent evidence of serial correlation. The estimated version of (7.84) is

$$\Delta\ln(\hat{C}_t) = -0.0651 - 0.102\ln(C_{t-1} - D_{t-1}) + 0.808\Delta\ln(D_t)$$

$$(0.072) \quad (0.145) \quad\quad\quad\quad\quad (0.115)$$

$$+ 0.0108\ln(D_{t-1})$$

$$(0.013)$$

$$n = 27 \quad RSS = 3.7915 \times 10^{-3} \quad R^2 = 0.7341 \quad 1964-90$$

$$df = 23 \quad VAR = 1.6485 \times 10^{-4}.$$

The estimated value of $\phi(1)$ is thus 0.102, with standard error 0.145: the cointegration test statistic is then

$$-\hat{\phi}(1)/\mathrm{se}[\hat{\phi}(1)] = -0.7034,$$

which exceeds the critical value according to *PcGive*. This leads to acceptance of the null hypothesis $\phi(1) = 0$, and confirms the judgement of the Engle–Granger test procedure, that the annual consumption function is spurious.

Example 7.7

To show that cointegrating relationships do appear to exist empirically, another example is given, based on a well-known and well-used data set. The data set originates with Hendry and Ericcson (1991) and is used by Hendry (1995) and Harris (1995): it is data set 10. The data set consists of UK quarterly, seasonally adjusted observations from 1963(1) to 1989(2) on the differential between the three-month local authority bill rate and the retail sight deposit interest rate adjusted for 'learning', denoted $\ln(R_t)$, and the logarithms of the nominal money supply M1, real total final expenditure, and the deflator of total final expenditure, denoted $\ln(M_t)$, $\ln(Y_t)$ and $\ln(P_t)$ respectively. The precise details of the interest rate variable r_t are given in Hendry and Ericcson (1991) and Hendry (1995: 584). The model fitted for this data set is deliberately chosen to be an ADL(2, 2) connecting the derived variable $\ln(M_t/P_t Y_t)$, the logarithm of the inverse velocity of money, with the interest rate variable so as to provide a connection with some of the results of Chapter 9. Denoting $M_t/P_t Y_t$ by I_t, the empirical results of fitting such a model over the period 1963(3)– 1989(2) are (standard errors in brackets)

$$\ln(I_t) = 0.008 + 0.617 \ln(I_{t-1}) + 0.285 \ln(I_{t-2}) - 0.789 \ln(R_t)$$
$$(0.006) \quad (0.096) \qquad\qquad (0.089) \qquad\qquad (0.144)$$
$$- 0.032 \ln(R_{t-1}) + 0.088 \ln(R_{t-2})$$
$$(0.229) \qquad\qquad (0.156)$$

$n = 104 \quad RSS = 3.6316 \times 10^{-2} \quad R^2 = 0.9925 \quad 1963(3)-1989(2)$

$df = 98 \quad VAR = 3.7058 \times 10^{-4}.$

The $LM(F)$ statistic for fifth-order serial correlation is 1.9147, so that there is no evidence of serial correlation. Looking at the standard errors for $\ln(I_{t-2})$ and $\ln(R_{t-2})$, one would not want to reduce the order of the ADL model to $(1, 1)$, although omission of $\ln(R_{t-2})$ would be acceptable. This possible simplification is not adopted here. The long-run relationship implied by this model would correspond, on the presumption that the two variables are $I(1)$, to a potential cointegrating relationship,

$$\ln(I_t) = \mu_0 + \mu_1 \ln(R_t).$$

The estimates of μ_0 and μ_1 implied by the estimated ADL(2, 2) model are

$$\ln(I_t) = 0.0862 - 7.512 \ln(R_t).$$

Both the Engle–Granger and ADL-based cointegration tests are employed to see if the data are consistent with $\ln(I_t)$ and $\ln(R_t)$ being cointegrated.
  If the model is written in the form

$$\phi(L) \ln(I_t) = \delta + \beta(L) \ln(R_t) + u_t, \tag{7.85}$$

the estimates of the sums of the coefficients in the lag polynomials $\phi(L)$ and $\beta(L)$ are

$$\hat{\phi}(1) = 0.097\,555\,6, \quad \hat{\beta}(1) = -0.732\,844, \tag{7.86}$$

from which the estimate of μ_1 above is obtained. The transformation of (7.85) which parallels the transformation of the ADL(p, s) model (7.83) into the model (7.84) is

$$\Delta \ln(I_t) = \delta + \gamma_1 [\ln(I_{t-1}) - \ln(R_{t-1})] + g_0 \Delta \ln(R_t) + \gamma_2 \ln(R_{t-1}) + u_t.$$

Estimation by least squares delivers an estimate of $\phi(1)$ via the estimate of γ_1 which is the same as that in (7.86), and with a standard error of 0.014 041 4, generating the value of the *PcGive* cointegration test statistic as -6.9477. According to *PcGive*, the value is significant at the 5% level, enabling one to reject the null hypothesis of no cointegration.

The static regression required for the Engle–Granger cointegration test is

$$\ln(I_t) = -0.2027 - 3.9361 \ln(R_t)$$

$$\quad\quad\quad (0.040) \ (\quad 0.418)$$

$$n = 104 \quad RSS = 2.5867 \times 10^1 \quad R^2 = 0.4654 \quad 1963(3) - 1989(2)$$

$$df = 102 \quad VAR = 2.5360 \times 10^{-2}$$

which gives a very different long-run relationship to the ADL(2, 2) model above. There is considerable evidence of serial correlation in the residuals, the $LM(F)$ statistic for fifth-order serial correlation being 151.54 in comparison with the 5% critical value of $F(5, 97)$, which is approximately 2.46. Using the residuals e_t from this model in the Engle–Granger test regression (7.76) over the period 1965(1)–1989(2), with augmentation set at 5 lags of Δe_t, the standard order-testing procedure reveals that the augmentation is unnecessary. Using only the basic Engle–Granger test regression (7.73) over the period 1963(4)–1989(2) (103 observations), the t value on e_{t-1} is -1.895. This can be compared with the critical value deduced from Table 7.8(b), $k = 2$, as

$$CV = -3.3377 - (5.9670/103) - (8.9800)(1/103)^2 = -3.396,$$

and leads to a conclusion which contrasts with that from the *PcGive* unit root test, that $\ln(I_t)$ and $\ln(R_t)$ are not cointegrated. We shall be able to re-examine this issue using yet another test for cointegration in Chapter 9.

Example 7.8

Yet another example is presented here, requiring the use of an ADL model with several explanatory variables. It is also the major example to be used in Chapter 9, and some useful preliminary results can be presented here. The example relates to the empirical IS/LM model presented in Johansen and Juselius (1994), but using UK seasonally adjusted data from 1963(1) to 1994(2) instead of the Australian data used in the article. The variables used are a broad money measure, a real GDP measure, the corresponding GDP deflator in index form as a measure of the price level, and a short and long interest rate, with the first three variables used in logarithmic form. In this example, M4 is used as the broad money measure (LNM4 or m_t), the expenditure measure of deflated GDP, GDP(E), at factor cost as the GDP measure (LNRGDP or y_t), and the implied deflator of GDP(E) at factor cost, $1990 = 100$ (LNPGDP or p_t). The short interest rate is taken to be the yield on Treasury bills (TBILL or r_t), and the long interest rate is the yield on a 20 year British Government stock (B20 or b_t). The main difference between the example presented here and the model of Johansen and Juselius (1994) is that the first difference of the GDP deflator (DLNPGDP or Δp_t) is used rather than the level. This is equivalent to using a measure of inflation rather than the price level. The short forms of some of the variable names are used below to save space.

The intention is to construct an ADL model linking M4 with RGDP, DLNPDGP, B20 and TBILL. Some experimentation shows that an $ADL(2,2,2,2,2)$ model is satisfactory in terms of absence of fifth-order serial correlation, although not so in terms of other diagnostic tests like heteroscedasticity or normality. The choice of a two-lag model is partly governed by the analysis in Chapter 9, so that this model will be used anyway. The results are displayed in Table 7.9.

Table 7.9 Example 7.8: $ADL(2,2,2,2,2)$ model for LNM4

Sample based on observations 1963(3)–1994(2)
Dependent variable is LNM4

Variable	Coefficient	Standard error	t value
INTER	−0.245 55	0.163 725	−1.500
LNM4(−1)	1.575 3	0.079 589 2	19.793
LNM4(−2)	−0.584 52	0.078 317 7	−7.463
LNRGDP	0.011 21	0.071 881 3	0.156
LNRGDP(−1)	0.123 46	0.089 107 1	1.386
LNRGDP(−2)	−0.082 61	0.073 343 2	−1.126
DLNPGDP	0.063 68	0.098 783 5	0.645
DLNPGDP(−1)	−0.020 49	0.098 468 3	−0.208
DLNPGDP(−2)	−0.092 47	0.090 062 6	−1.027
B20	−0.001 61	0.001 740 29	−0.927
B20(−1)	−0.000 067	0.002 438 39	−0.027
B20(−2)	0.002 43	0.001 757 87	1.383
TBILL	0.000 84	0.000 910 529	0.927
TBILL(−1)	−0.000 005 8	0.001 235 31	−0.005
TBILL(−2)	−0.000 76	0.000 913 570	−0.832

Degrees of freedom 109 from 124 observations

Residual SS	1.1112×10^{-2}
Total SS	1.7229×10^{2}
Disturbance variance	1.0195×10^{-4}
R^2	0.9999
DW statistic	2.21

The long-run relationship implied by the fitted model is

$$m_t = -26.71 + 5.663y_t - 5.361\Delta p_t + 0.0817b_t + 0.0085r_t,$$

which could be interpreted as a money demand relationship. Although the details are not presented, all the variables used in the model appear to be $I(1)$ using suitable augmented Dickey–Fuller tests. There is some evidence of $I(2)$ behaviour for LNM4, but this issue is neglected, for simplicity. This suggests that the long-run relationship could be a cointegrating relationship: here, only the *PcGive* unit root test is used. The model corresponding to (7.84) for generating the test statistic has the form

$$\psi(L)\Delta m_t = \delta + \gamma(m_{t-1} - y_{t-1} - \Delta p_{t-1} - b_{t-1} - r_{t-1})$$

$$+ g_1(L)\Delta y_t + g_2(L)\Delta^2 p_t + g_3(L)\Delta b_t + g_4(L)\Delta r_t$$

$$+ \gamma_1 y_{t-1} + \gamma_2 \Delta p_{t-1} + \gamma_3 b_{t-1} + \gamma_4 r_{t-1} + u_t.$$

Estimating this over the same period as the results in Table 7.9 produces an estimate of γ as -0.0092 with standard error $0.005\,56$, giving the *PcGive* cointegration test statistic as -1.6521, which is apparently not significant. This indicates, contrary to the supposition, that the long-run relationship implied by the ADL model is not a cointegrating relationship. We shall see in Chapter 9 that there are some cointegrating relationships between the set of variables used in the ADL model, but that there are reasons for believing that this single equation approach is incapable of revealing them.

7.9 / A brief overview

The discussion of estimation and inference in this chapter appears to separate neatly into two distinct cases: stable or stationary processes, and nonstationary or unit root processes. Indeed, the differences in the results obtained seem to confirm this separation. However, the final topic of cointegration draws the results for the two cases together in the following way. Cointegration is a property of a set of integrated or unit root processes, and so a preliminary to verifying the presence of cointegration between a set of variables requires us to test for a unit root in each series. Establishing the existence of cointegration uses an adapted version of a unit root test. We then resort to an error correction model to explain one of the variables in terms of the others. Because only $I(0)$ variables appear in the error correction model, the properties of estimators, and in particular the large sample distribution theory, of the stable ADL model apply. This perspective takes us from the end of the chapter towards the beginning, and is of course a very simplified view.

Cointegration is extremely important in modern time series econometrics for a number of reasons. One reason that can be emphasised is the resolution of the spurious regressions problem. No investigator would wish to be told that his or her empirical results are spurious: the presence of cointegration can be then seen as a satisfactory assurance that the regression is not spurious. This line of reasoning is not entirely valid, since the assurance depends on a number of heroic assumptions. Are the tests for unit roots sufficiently powerful to detect correctly that a series is $I(1)$, or that a group of series are cointegrated? We have already noted that the precise nature of the limiting distributions of some estimators and test statistics in the presence of a unit root is sensitive to small changes in the estimated model. How do these properties change if the data are seasonal? The inclusion of seasonal dummies will affect the distribution of the test statistics in as yet unknown ways. A further potential complication is the concept of 'seasonal integration' in which a process for a quarterly series contains a factor $(1 - L^4)$ containing a unit root, as well as the corresponding concept of 'seasonal cointegration', neither of which can be investigated here. Harris (1995) gives a nontechnical discussion of these ideas.

There are alternatives to the basic idea of integration. It may be argued that a concept called *fractional integration* (Hamilton, 1993: 447) is a better empirical description for some macroeconomic series: with this notion, a series might be described for example as $I(0.8)$ rather than $I(1)$, since the process will contain a factor $(1 - L)^{0.8}$ in this case. 'Unbalanced' regressions, in which the order of integration of the dependent variable does not match that of the explanatory variables, seem to show some of the characteristics of spurious regressions (see Banerjee *et al.*, 1993: 164–8). This seems to be a likely possibility with fractional integration.

Another observation, easily seen in Figure 7.1, is that structural changes in a series, for example the impact of wars, oil crises or stock market crashes, can appear to be the random shocks that create a stochastic trend in a series. Such structural changes may also have a permanent or persistent effect on a series for reasons which have nothing to do with the series being $I(1)$. A similar line of reasoning leads to the idea of 'broken trends': a series may follow a deterministic trend, which shifts over time due to structural changes. A good discussion of these ideas is found in Stock (1994: 2805–21).

It is now appropriate to look ahead a little. A cointegrating relationship may connect any number of integrated variables. Each of these variables is assumed to be generated by some stochastic process, so that cointegrating regressions have stochastic explanatory variables. How much does one need to know about the processes generating these explanatory variables? Is it necessary to build models for these variables? If so, we are immediately put into the multiple equation framework mentioned in section 1.2. In the next chapter, we discuss such models as generalisations of the static regression model, postponing issues of dynamics until Chapter 9, where we shall be able to re-examine some of the issues just mentioned.

7.10 / Further reading

Further reading for this chapter is the same as that for Chapter 6. It will be useful also to follow up the references given in the text of the chapter.

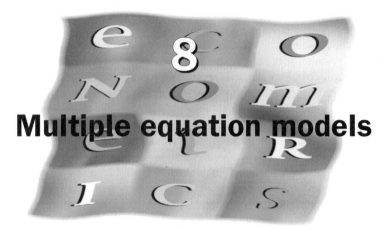

8
Multiple equation models

In this chapter, we deal with models that explain the behaviour of many dependent variables. Initially, we consider the extension of the static regression model written in row form as

$$y_t = x_t'\beta + u_t; \ u_t \sim IID(0, \sigma^2); \ t = 1, \dots, n \tag{8.1}$$

to the case where there are just two dependent variables y_{1t} and y_{2t} to be explained. The assumption that the vector of explanatory variables x_t is nonstochastic will be maintained. Without spelling out the details yet, it is clear that we can presume a model similar to (8.1) for each of these variables, and thus we are automatically working with a two-equation model.

There are many circumstances in economics where multiple equation models arise. For example, it is possible to build models based on utility maximisation principles to explain the quantities demanded by a household of a number of commodities. In the case of two commodities, these would be y_{1t} and y_{2t}, dependent on commodity prices, the household's income and possibly demographic factors like the number of working adults or the number of children in the household. This is an example where there are 'multiple' dependent variables per agent, and a common set of explanatory variables for each equation.

Another type of example is where the same variable y is observed over time on two or more agents, which might be households, firms or even countries, as in the case of the Barro–Lee data set (data set 4) of Chapter 2. In this case, y_{1t} and y_{2t} would represent the observations on the particular variable for each of the two agents at time t, and it would be the behaviour of the agents over time that would be modelled. A classic example is the Grunfeld–Griliches investment model which postulates a simple gross investment function for five large US corporations over the period 1935–54 (see, for example, Greene, 1993: 445). The five dependent variables

$y_{1t}, \ldots, y_{5t}$ are the values of gross investment for the five corporations in year t, to be explained by factors like the market value and the value of the stock of capital equipment of the corporation, each at the end of the previous year. Here, there are different explanatory variables in each of the five equations, so that it is being assumed for example that the market value of corporation i does not affect the value of gross investment of corporation j. Each equation has the form of (8.1), with potentially five different parameter vectors $\beta_1, \ldots, \beta_5$ in the system. It is possible, however, that the corporations have common behavioural responses to changes in market value or capital stock, which is the same as saying that the parameter vectors $\beta_1, \ldots, \beta_5$ coincide. Common parameters across equations would not be expected in a demand system, however.

Even if the explanatory variables for agent i have no impact on the dependent variable for agent j, it is possible that the behaviour of the agents is interrelated through correlation of the equation errors. In the case of the demand for a number of commodities by a single household, the demands are subject to the overall household budget constraint and this would ensure that the disturbances for commodity i are correlated with commodity j at time t. Sections 8.2 and 8.4 describe models embodying this feature of 'contemporaneously' correlated disturbances to be estimated by appropriate versions of OLS or GLS. Section 8.3 examines estimation of these models by maximum likelihood under an explicit normality assumption. This latter material is a useful preliminary to some of the issues discussed in Chapter 9.

As observed in section 1.2, there are circumstances where a dependent variable y_{1t} may actually help to explain the behaviour of another dependent variable y_{2t}. The converse may also be true: y_{2t} may partly explain the behaviour of y_{1t}. This is very common in macroeconomics, where in a certain naïve sense, 'everything depends on everything else'. Here, for example, y_{1t} becomes one of the explanatory variables in the version of (8.1) for y_{2t}, and (8.1) now contains a stochastic explanatory variable. As noted in section 4.4, a key issue is whether the stochastic explanatory variable y_{1t} is correlated with the disturbance term for y_{2t}, for if it is, the least squares estimator of the parameters of the y_{2t} model will be inconsistent. Models with this type of 'simultaneous' interdependence also tend to have 'contemporaneously' correlated disturbances, and it is this which makes the stochastic explanatory variables in an equation correlated with the disturbance in that equation. The precise nature of this type of model, the 'simultaneous equations' model, is discussed in sections 8.5 and 8.6, and techniques for consistent estimation in this model are discussed in sections 8.7 and 8.8. Section 8.7 also contains an empirical example of a simultaneous equations model, the 'Klein model 1' dating from 1950, and thus one of the earliest simultaneous equations models.

Only occasionally in this chapter will lagged variables be allowed as explanatory variables. Bearing in mind the issues raised in Chapter 7, the use of such variables will have no impact on the theoretical analysis in this chapter. A full discussion of the issues raised by such variables in multiple equation and simultaneous equations models is postponed until Chapter 9.

8.2 / The multivariate regression model

To formalise some of the ideas of the previous section, suppose that the two dependent variables y_{1t} and y_{2t} depend on the same set of explanatory variables in the $k \times 1$ vector x_t. A notation change here will help in later sections, so the appropriate versions of (8.1) are

$$y_{1t} = x_t'\pi_1 + u_{1t}; \ u_{1t} \sim IID(0, \sigma_{11}); \ t = 1, \ldots, n, \qquad (8.2)$$

$$y_{2t} = x_t'\pi_2 + u_{2t}; \ u_{2t} \sim IID(0, \sigma_{22}); \ t = 1, \ldots, n. \qquad (8.3)$$

Calling this model a *multivariate* regression model is intended to point to the branch of statistics called *multivariate analysis*, which deals with the statistical analysis of *vectors* of random variables, rather than single random variables. This perspective would therefore force us to think in terms of a vector containing y_{1t} and y_{2t}, which may be a row vector or a column vector. Which choice we make has some interesting consequences for the way in which the two-equation model (8.2) and (8.3) is analysed.

To start with, we need to think of a vector random variable analogue of the IID assumption for the two disturbances u_{1t} and u_{2t} taken individually. Let

$$u_t = \begin{bmatrix} u_{1t} \\ u_{2t} \end{bmatrix},$$

and assume that $E(u_t) = 0$. The assumption that the random vectors $u_t; \ t = 1, \ldots, n$ are independent implies that the random variables $u_{j1}, \ldots, u_{jn}$ are independent of each other, for each $j = 1, 2$, and also that u_{1s} and u_{2t} are independent, for $s \neq t$, $s, t = 1, \ldots, n$. It does not imply that u_{1t} and u_{2t} are independent of each other, for each t. The alternative name sometimes given to models of this type, 'seemingly unrelated regressions', stresses a possible 'hidden' dependence between y_{1t} and y_{2t} created by this potential correlation between u_{1t} and u_{2t}.

The covariance forms of the independence statements are

$$E(u_s u_t') = 0; \ s \neq t; \ s, t = 1, \ldots, n$$

and

$$E(u_t u_t') = \begin{bmatrix} E(u_{1t}^2) & E(u_{1t}u_{2t}) \\ E(u_{1t}u_{2t}) & E(u_{2t}^2) \end{bmatrix}$$

$$= \mathrm{var}(u_t)$$

$$= \begin{bmatrix} \sigma_{11} & \sigma_{12} \\ \sigma_{21} & \sigma_{22} \end{bmatrix}$$

$$= \Sigma. \qquad (8.4)$$

The covariance σ_{12} is usually called a 'contemporaneous covariance' to distinguish it from the intertemporal dependence found in dynamic models. It is the presence or absence of this contemporaneous covariance which creates the characteristic results found in multivariate regression models.

There are a number of different ways in which the two equations (8.2) and (8.3) can be arranged in vector and matrix form, each useful in particular situations. First, combine the dependent variables y_{1t} and y_{2t} into a column vector to match the structure of u_t. This turns (8.2) and (8.3) into an equation with a vector-dependent variable,

$$\begin{bmatrix} y_{1t} \\ y_{2t} \end{bmatrix} = \begin{bmatrix} \pi'_1 \\ \pi'_2 \end{bmatrix} x_t + \begin{bmatrix} u_{1t} \\ u_{2t} \end{bmatrix}. \tag{8.5}$$

The first thing to notice in this is the appearance of a $2 \times k$ *matrix* of parameters,

$$\Pi = \begin{bmatrix} \pi'_1 \\ \pi'_2 \end{bmatrix},$$

in which the parameter vectors of the two multiple regression models (8.2) and (8.3) appear as rows. Labelling the vectors, (8.5) can be written as

$$y_t = \Pi x_t + u_t; \ u_t \sim IID(0, \Sigma); \ t = 1, \ldots, n, \tag{8.6}$$

where Σ is the covariance matrix given in (8.4). This is the most natural form of the multivariate regression model for expressing the nature of the assumptions made about the disturbance vector.

If attention were focused on one of the equations (8.2) or (8.3), it would be natural to write it in the standard matrix form of a classical multiple regression model,

$$y_j = X\pi_j + u_j; \ j = 1, 2, \tag{8.7}$$

where the elements of the $n \times 1$ vectors y_j and u_j are y_{jt} and u_{jt} respectively, and the rows of the $n \times k$ matrix X are $x'_t; \ t = 1, \ldots, n$. Putting y_{1t} and y_{2t} into a row vector produces a link with this classical form:

$$[y_{1t} \quad y_{2t}] = x'_t[\pi_1 \quad \pi_2] + [u_{1t} \quad u_{2t}]; \ t = 1, \ldots, n \tag{8.8}$$

can be recognised as

$$y'_t = x'_t\Pi' + u'_t; \ t = 1, \ldots, n.$$

If the matrix X has rows x'_t, we can analogously define $n \times 2$ matrices Y and U whose rows are y'_t and u'_t respectively. This enables us to write (8.8) as

$$Y = X\Pi' + U, \tag{8.9}$$

a very compact notation. Comparing (8.9) with (8.7), it is apparent that Y and U can be expressed by columns as

$$Y = [y_1 \quad y_2], \qquad U = [u_1 \quad u_2]$$

and this provides the link between the standard matrix forms of (8.7) and (8.9), since the two columns of Π' are precisely the two parameter vectors from (8.7). The presence of the transposed matrix Π' is an indication of a conflict in notation: what is conveniently written in one form of the model can be inconvenient in another.

There is a final matrix form of (8.1) and (8.2) which utilises the notion of a Kronecker product, described in Appendix A. This version arranges or 'stacks' the two $n \times 1$ vectors of observations y_1 and y_2 into a 'long' vector of length $2n$, and thus 'stacks' the two equations of (8.7) into

$$\begin{bmatrix} y_1 \\ y_2 \end{bmatrix} = \begin{bmatrix} X & 0 \\ 0 & X \end{bmatrix} \begin{bmatrix} \pi_1 \\ \pi_2 \end{bmatrix} + \begin{bmatrix} u_1 \\ u_2 \end{bmatrix}, \tag{8.10}$$

or

$$\bar{y} = (I_2 \otimes X)\pi + \bar{u}. \tag{8.11}$$

This form shows the system arranged apparently as a single regression equation with $2n$ observations rather than n, and a matrix of regressors with a particular block diagonal structure. In addition, the parameter vector π has also increased in length to $2k \times 1$ to contain both sets of regression parameters. Since the elements of u_1 and u_2 are individually IID,

$$\mathrm{var}(u_j) = \sigma_{jj} I_n; \ j = 1, 2,$$

and the same logic shows that u_1 and u_2 are correlated,

$$\mathrm{cov}(u_1, u_2) = \sigma_{12} I_n.$$

The covariance matrix of $\bar{u}$ can then be written as

$$\mathrm{var}(\bar{u}) = \begin{bmatrix} \mathrm{var}(u_1) & \mathrm{cov}(u_1, u_2) \\ \mathrm{cov}(u_1, u_2) & \mathrm{var}(u_2) \end{bmatrix} = \begin{bmatrix} \sigma_{11} I_n & \sigma_{12} I_n \\ \sigma_{21} I_n & \sigma_{22} I_n \end{bmatrix} = (\Sigma \otimes I_n) \tag{8.12}$$

using Kronecker product notation. It is clear that this covariance matrix is not diagonal, confirming the correlation between u_1 and u_2. Using the analogy with the single equation regression model, this would suggest that estimation of (8.11) by OLS would be inefficient.

All of these forms can be generalised to multiple equation models with any number of equations, or equivalently, any number of dependent variables y_{jt}, say, $j = 1, \ldots, m$. In the general case, the vectors y_t and u_t in (8.6) become m vectors

$$y_t' = [y_{1t} \ldots y_{mt}], \qquad u_t' = [u_{1t} \ldots u_{mt}],$$

and the covariance matrix of u_t will now be $m \times m$, still denoted Σ. The matrices Π', Y and U become

$$\Pi' = [\pi_1 \ldots \pi_m], \qquad k \times m,$$

$$Y = [y_1 \ldots y_m], \qquad U = [u_1 \ldots u_m], \qquad n \times m.$$

The long vectors $\bar{y}$ and $\bar{u}$ formed from these two matrices will now have m subvectors, as also the vector π, and the covariance matrix of $\bar{u}$ will be

$$\mathrm{var}(\bar{u}) = (\Sigma \otimes I_n) = \|\sigma_{ij} I_m\|; \ i, j = 1, \ldots, m. \tag{8.13}$$

Estimation

If the correlation between the disturbance vectors u_1 and u_2 in (8.7) was ignored, estimation of the multivariate regression model by OLS would be quite natural, since u_1 and u_2 satisfy classical assumptions. But, the form (8.11) confirms the need for GLS estimation, given the form of the covariance matrix (8.12). The comparison of OLS and GLS estimators made in sections 5.1 and 5.2 indicates that theoretically the GLS estimator would be preferred to OLS, and that an estimator of $\mathrm{var}(\bar{u})$ in (8.12) would be required to generate a feasible GLS estimator. One possibility here is to use the OLS estimators in (8.7) (or equivalently, (8.11)) to provide such an estimate.

The OLS estimators from (8.7) are

$$\hat{\pi}_j = (X'X)^{-1}X'y_j; \; j = 1, 2,$$

and have the classical property of being unbiased, with covariance matrices

$$\sigma_{jj}(X'X)^{-1}.$$

One can see from the definitions of Π' and Y that $\hat{\pi}_1$ and $\hat{\pi}_2$ generate a matrix estimator of Π',

$$\hat{\Pi}' = [\hat{\pi}_1 \quad \hat{\pi}_2] = (X'X)^{-1}X'Y, \tag{8.14}$$

so that although the estimators are obtained one equation at a time, in fact one is estimating all the parameters of the system (8.9). This matrix representation of the OLS estimator of Π' is very convenient when the system is expressed as (8.9) and (8.6).

From the form of the GLS estimator given in (5.7), the GLS estimator of π in (8.11) is

$$\tilde{\pi}_G = [(I_2 \otimes X')(\Sigma^{-1} \otimes I_n)(I_2 \otimes X)]^{-1}(I_2 \otimes X')(\Sigma^{-1} \otimes I_n)\bar{y}.$$

Use of the properties of Kronecker products shows that this can be written as

$$\tilde{\pi}_G = [(\Sigma^{-1} \otimes X'X)]^{-1}(\Sigma^{-1} \otimes X')\bar{y}$$

$$= [I_2 \otimes (X'X)^{-1}X']\bar{y}. \tag{8.15}$$

Comparison of the subvectors in $\tilde{\pi}_G$,

$$(X'X)^{-1}X'y_j,$$

with the OLS estimator

$$\hat{\pi} = \begin{bmatrix} \hat{\pi}_1 \\ \hat{\pi}_2 \end{bmatrix} \tag{8.16}$$

shows that in this case the GLS and OLS estimators coincide. The implication is that despite ignoring the correlation of the disturbance vectors u_1 and u_2, OLS is just as efficient as GLS. It is clear that this proposition will generalise to the case of m-equation systems.

This result can be seen as a consequence of the condition (5.13) for the equivalence of OLS and GLS estimators in a multiple regression model. Translating (5.13) to the current notation requires us to find a nonsingular matrix A satisfying

$$(\Sigma^{-1} \otimes I_n)(I_2 \otimes X) = (I_2 \otimes X)A$$

and the obvious choice is $(\Sigma^{-1} \otimes I_k)$.

Estimation of Σ

It is convenient to discuss the estimation of Σ here. Using the OLS estimator $\hat{\pi}$, the diagonal elements of Σ, σ_{jj}, can be estimated from the residual sums of squares associated with each $\hat{\pi}_j$, since this is the standard procedure in a multiple regression model. Denoting the corresponding residual vectors by $\hat{u}_j$, the estimator is

$$\hat{\sigma}_{jj} = \frac{\hat{u}'_j \hat{u}_j}{n},$$

ignoring a degrees of freedom correction. The covariance term can be estimated in an analogous way by

$$\hat{\sigma}_{12} = \frac{\hat{u}'_1 \hat{u}_2}{n}.$$

If we write the $n \times 2$ matrix of residuals as

$$\hat{U} = [\hat{u}_1 \quad \hat{u}_2],$$

the implied estimator of Σ can be expressed as

$$\hat{\Sigma} = \frac{\hat{U}'\hat{U}}{n}. \tag{8.17}$$

For the m-equation case, this formula remains valid.

Since the covariance matrix of $\hat{\pi} = \tilde{\pi}_G$ will be, from (8.15),

$$\text{var}(\tilde{\pi}_G) = \left(\Sigma^{-1} \otimes X'X\right)^{-1} = \Sigma \otimes (X'X)^{-1},$$

standard errors for the elements of $\hat{\pi} = \tilde{\pi}_G$ can be calculated using the estimator of $\hat{\Sigma}$ in (8.17).

8.3 / Maximum likelihood estimation

In the spirit of setting up a simple prototype for ideas to follow, we consider the maximum likelihood estimation of the model of section 8.1, and try to establish which of its various forms (8.6)–(8.8) is the most useful for this purpose. The discussion will be phrased in terms of an m-dimensional system, for later reference, but setting $m = 2$ will enable us to see how the maximum likelihood estimator relates to the OLS and GLS estimators just discussed. To set up a log likelihood function, we add the assumption

$$u_t \sim NID(0, \Sigma) \tag{8.18}$$

to (8.6). The density function of such a random vector is

$$p(u_t) = \left[(2\pi)^m \det(\Sigma)\right]^{-1/2} \exp\left(-\frac{1}{2}u_t'\Sigma^{-1}u_t\right),$$

from which the density of y_t in (8.6) follows as

$$p(y_t) = \left[(2\pi)^m \det(\Sigma)\right]^{-1/2} \exp\left[-\frac{1}{2}(y_t - \Pi x_t)'\Sigma^{-1}(y_t - \Pi x_t)\right].$$

The log likelihood function then involves sums of logarithms of these terms:

$$\ln L = -\frac{nm}{2}\ln 2\pi - \frac{n}{2}\log\det(\Sigma) - \frac{1}{2}\sum_{t=1}^{n}(y_t - \Pi x_t)'\Sigma^{-1}(y_t - \Pi x_t). \tag{8.19}$$

Using a result on the trace of a matrix in Appendix A, the whole of the summation term can be expressed as

$$\text{trace}\left[\Sigma^{-1}(Y - X\Pi')'(Y - X\Pi')\right],$$

giving

$$\ln L = -\frac{nm}{2}\ln 2\pi - \frac{n}{2}\log\det(\Sigma) - \frac{1}{2}\text{trace}\left[\Sigma^{-1}(Y - X\Pi')'(Y - X\Pi')\right]. \tag{8.20}$$

This is the standard form in which the log likelihood function for a multivariate regression model is presented, a form that will reappear later in this chapter and in Chapter 9. The traditional argument for finding the maximum likelihood estimators is to differentiate this log likelihood function with respect to the columns of the matrix Π' and the distinct elements of Σ, and solve the resulting first-order conditions. Finding the derivatives is a little involved, although solving the first-order conditions is not. Since our immediate objective is to show that the maximum likelihood estimators of Π' and Σ are precisely the OLS estimators $\hat{\Pi}$ and $\hat{\Sigma}$, we resort to a simpler approach.

This uses the log likelihood function associated with the multivariate regression model in the form (8.11). Under the normality assumption (8.18), it follows that

$$\bar{u} \sim N(0, \Sigma \otimes I_n)$$

so that

$$\bar{y} \sim N[(I_2 \otimes X)\pi, \Sigma \otimes I_n].$$

The log likelihood function $\ln L$ for (8.11) can now be constructed along the lines of (7.24), noting that there are in effect $2n$ observations (rather than n) in the model for $\bar{y}$, and that $m = 2$:

$$\ln L = -\frac{2n}{2}\ln 2\pi - \frac{1}{2}\log\det(\Sigma \otimes I_n)$$

$$-\frac{1}{2}[\bar{y} - (I_2 \otimes X)\pi]'(\Sigma^{-1} \otimes I_n)[\bar{y} - (I_2 \otimes X)\pi]. \tag{8.21}$$

In section 5.2, it was shown that a GLS estimator minimises the quantity $S_G(\beta)$ of (5.12). The translation of the notation of that section to the regression model (8.11) defines the corresponding quantity,

$$S_G(\pi) = [\bar{y} - (I_2 \otimes X)\pi]'(\Sigma^{-1} \otimes I_n)[\bar{y} - (I_2 \otimes X)\pi],$$

and it is clear that maximising $\ln L$ with respect to π is equivalent to minimising the corresponding $S_G(\pi)$. The maximum likelihood estimator of π in (8.11) is therefore the GLS estimator, which is also the OLS estimator, and this is of course the OLS estimator for (8.9) as well. The estimator of Σ derived from $\hat{\pi}$, (8.17), is the maximum likelihood estimator derived from (8.14). It is worth reiterating that these conclusions carry over directly to the case of m equations.

8.4 / The seemingly unrelated regression model

When a multiple equation model is constructed to explain a particular dependent variable for a number of agents over time, it is often presumed that all these agents have the same behavioural responses to changes in the explanatory variables. In the context of section 8.1, this is equivalent to saying that $\pi_1 = \pi_2$. This is unlikely to be true in general, and indeed there may be different sets of explanatory variables for different agents. In the other case of many dependent variables for the same agent, it would be somewhat surprising if there were a common set of explanatory variables for each of the dependent variables: it is more likely, intuitively, that there is a different set for each. In the context of the models of (8.7), the common regressor set X would be replaced by regressor sets X_1 and X_2:

$$y_1 = X_1\pi_1 + u_1,$$
$$y_2 = X_2\pi_2 + u_2. \tag{8.22}$$

It is possible to write this in a form equivalent to (8.9) by redefining the matrix X to include all the distinct variables in X_1 and X_2. Then, the columns of Π' in (8.9) must contain some zero elements in order to capture the exclusion of certain variables expressed by (8.22). One perspective therefore is that (8.22) is a restricted version of (8.9), and that estimation subject to restriction is required, for example via the log likelihood function (8.21).

Although the name 'seemingly unrelated regression model' is sometimes applied to the multivariate regression model of section 8.2, it is more commonly applied to the model (8.22). These two equations may appear as two unrelated regression models in terms of their dependent variables, explanatory variables and parameters. But, if u_1 and u_2 are correlated at each point in time, there is a hidden relationship between the two equations, leading to the description 'seemingly unrelated regressions'. Exploitation of this hidden relationship enables one to obtain estimators that are more efficient than OLS, as we shall now see.

A simple approach to estimation of (8.22) is to write it in a form similar to (8.10),

$$\begin{bmatrix} y_1 \\ y_2 \end{bmatrix} = \begin{bmatrix} X_1 & 0 \\ 0 & X_2 \end{bmatrix} \begin{bmatrix} \pi_1 \\ \pi_2 \end{bmatrix} + \begin{bmatrix} u_1 \\ u_2 \end{bmatrix},$$

or, adapting (8.11),

$$\bar{y} = \bar{X}\bar{\pi} + \bar{u}. \tag{8.23}$$

Here $\bar{X}$ has a block diagonal structure which is similar to that of (8.10),

$$\bar{X} = \begin{bmatrix} X_1 & 0 \\ 0 & X_2 \end{bmatrix}, \tag{8.24}$$

but it does not have a Kronecker product form. The covariance matrix of the error term $\bar{u}$ is unchanged:

$$\mathrm{var}(\bar{u}) = \Sigma \otimes I_n.$$

Formal GLS estimation then produces

$$\tilde{\bar{\pi}}_G = \left[\bar{X}'(\Sigma^{-1} \otimes I_n)\bar{X} \right]^{-1} \bar{X}'(\Sigma^{-1} \otimes I_n)\bar{y}. \tag{8.25}$$

As noted in section 5.2, when Σ is known, this will be the best linear unbiased estimator and therefore will show a gain in efficiency over the OLS estimator from (8.23),

$$\hat{\bar{\pi}} = (\bar{X}'\bar{X})^{-1}\bar{X}'\bar{y},$$

unless the equivalent of the condition (5.13) holds. Whether or not this condition holds depends on the nature of $\bar{X}$ and $(\Sigma^{-1} \otimes I_n)$: in general, for Σ an arbitrary positive definite matrix and $\bar{X}$ of the form (8.24), this condition will not hold. So, the GLS estimator (8.25) will not collapse to the OLS estimator $\hat{\bar{\pi}}$ except under special conditions. We have already seen one of them in section 8.2: when (in a general m-equation model)

$$\bar{X} = I_m \otimes X.$$

Another circumstance is when Σ is actually diagonal, for then, the matrix $\Sigma^{-1} \otimes I_n$ is diagonal,

$$\bar{X}'(\Sigma^{-1} \otimes I_n)\bar{X}$$

is block diagonal and $\tilde{\bar{\pi}}_G$ reduces to equation by equation OLS. Here, any efficiency gains due to restrictions on Π' are localised in each equation by the diagonality of Σ.

There are several efficiency comparisons that arise in estimating (8.23). The first follows from the fact that (8.23) is a restricted version of (8.9) or (8.10), so that the GLS estimator in (8.23) is a restricted GLS estimator of (8.10). Because true restrictions are being imposed, the GLS estimator from (8.23) is more efficient than the 'unrestricted' GLS estimator in (8.10), which is the GLS and hence OLS estimator $\hat{\pi}$ of (8.16). The second concerns the comparison between the GLS and OLS estimators of the restricted model (8.23): as noted above, the results of sections 5.1 and 5.2 apply here to claim that the GLS estimator is more efficient than the OLS estimator. To see the intuition behind this, note that because of the form of $\bar{X}$, the OLS estimator $\hat{\hat{\pi}}$ can be obtained by OLS estimation of (8.22) one equation at a time. Any efficiency gains that arise from having imposed true restrictions on an equation, or equivalently, having fewer 'free' parameters to be estimated in that equation, are therefore not transmitted to the other equations of the system by the OLS estimator $\hat{\hat{\pi}}$. In contrast, the restricted GLS estimator $\tilde{\tilde{\pi}}_{\mathrm{G}}$ exploits the contemporaneous correlation of the disturbances to transmit efficiency gains from equation to equation. Finally, it does not follow that the 'restricted' OLS estimator $\hat{\hat{\pi}}$ of (8.23) is more efficient than the unrestricted OLS estimator of (8.10), which is the OLS estimator $\hat{\pi}$ of (8.9). Without going into details, suffice it to say that whether or not this is true depends on the relative sizes of the two efficiency gains just mentioned.

As always, efficiency gains from GLS cannot be realised unless the covariance matrix Σ can be estimated in a suitable manner. Fortunately, this is easy here. OLS estimation of each equation in (8.22) generates both $\hat{\hat{\pi}}$ and a matrix of residuals, say $\hat{\hat{U}}$, which can be used to construct an estimator of Σ paralleling (8.17),

$$\hat{\hat{\Sigma}} = \frac{\hat{\hat{U}}' \hat{\hat{U}}}{n}. \tag{8.26}$$

In turn, this can then be used to create the 'feasible' GLS estimator

$$\tilde{\tilde{\pi}}_{\mathrm{G}} = \left[\bar{X}'(\hat{\hat{\Sigma}}^{-1} \otimes I_n) \bar{X} \right]^{-1} \bar{X}'(\hat{\hat{\Sigma}}^{-1} \otimes I_n) \bar{y}. \tag{8.27}$$

Making a degrees of freedom correction to ensure that the estimator of Σ is unbiased is not easy when there are different numbers of explanatory variables in different equations (see Greene (1993: 489) for more details). In practice, software packages adopt an assortment of simple degrees of freedom corrections.

The discussion of maximum likelihood estimation in the multivariate regression model leading up to (8.21) can be easily adapted for the seemingly unrelated regression case. It is only necessary to replace the matrix $(I_2 \otimes X)$ of (8.11) by $\bar{X}$ instead of (8.24), and if Σ were known, the maximum likelihood estimator of π would coincide with $\tilde{\tilde{\pi}}_{\mathrm{G}}$. However, the maximum likelihood estimator of Σ here, $\tilde{\tilde{\Sigma}}$ say, depends on $\tilde{\tilde{\pi}}_{\mathrm{G}}$, and conversely, so that there is a nonlinear estimation problem to be solved. The iterative procedures typically employed create a sequence of estimators like $\tilde{\tilde{\pi}}_{\mathrm{G}}$ and $\tilde{\tilde{\Sigma}}$ at each iteration, using the previous iterations' estimate of Σ and residuals. In general, the solution of these iterations for π will not coincide with the value of the feasible GLS estimator of π.

Example 8.1

This example is based on the Grunfeld–Griliches investment model data set (data set 12) mentioned in section 8.1. One of the objectives of the example is to show that there is a tension between system estimation (and inference) and the behaviour of individual equations. This shows itself most directly through the issues of goodness of fit and diagnostic tests for individual equations and for the system as a whole. The model can be written as

$$y_{it} = \pi_{i1} + \pi_{i2}x_{2it} + \pi_{i3}x_{3it} + u_{it}; \quad i = 1, \ldots, 5; \quad t = 1, \ldots, 20,$$

where y_{it} is the value of gross investment for corporation i in year t, x_{2it} is the market value and x_{3it} the value of the capital equipment of the corporation, both in the previous year.

Tables 8.1 and 8.3 give the OLS and GLS coefficient estimates for this model, along with standard errors, residual variance estimates and R^2 values. The GLS calculations use the estimate of Σ given in Table 8.2, which corresponds to (8.27). It can be seen that there are some substantial differences in the regression coefficients, and that all of the GLS standard errors are smaller than their OLS counterparts. In Table 8.1, the usual degrees of freedom correction is made for the residual variance estimates, and this feeds through to the standard errors of the coefficients. As a result, these residual variance estimates are different from those in Table 8.2. The GLS estimates are computed as if Table 8.2 represents the true, known covariance matrix of u_{it}; $i = 1, \ldots, 5$, and thus the residual variance estimates presented coincide with the diagonal elements of the matrix of Table 8.2. This matrix is also used in computing the standard errors of the GLS estimates.

Given a matrix of residuals $\breve{U}_G$ based on $\breve{\pi}_G$, a (feasible) GLS estimator of Σ, $\breve{\Sigma}_G$, can be computed just as in (8.27), and this is shown in Table 8.4. As with the

Table 8.1 OLS coefficient estimates

Dependent variable is value of gross investment
Standard errors in brackets

Corporation	Constant	Value of firm	Capital stock	Residual variance	R^2
General Motors	−149.78 (105.84)	0.1193 (0.0258)	0.3714 (0.0371)	8423.88	0.9214
Chrysler	−6.1900 (13.506)	0.0779 (0.0200)	0.3157 (0.0288)	176.32	0.9136
General Electric	−9.9563 (31.374)	0.0266 (0.0156)	0.1517 (0.0257)	777.446	0.7053
Westinghouse	−0.5093 (8.015)	0.0529 (0.0157)	0.0924 (0.056)	104.308	0.7444
US Steel	−30.369 (157.05)	0.1566 (0.0789)	0.4239 (0.1552)	10 466.4	0.4403

Table 8.2 OLS covariance matrix estimate: $\hat{\Sigma}$

$$
\begin{bmatrix}
7160.29 & -282.76 & 607.53 & 126.18 & -2222.06 \\
-282.76 & 149.87 & -21.38 & 13.31 & 418.08 \\
607.53 & -21.38 & 660.83 & 176.45 & 904.95 \\
126.18 & 13.31 & 176.45 & 88.66 & 546.19 \\
-2222.06 & 418.08 & 904.95 & 546.19 & 8896.42
\end{bmatrix}
$$

regression coefficients, there are some differences between the OLS and GLS estimates of Σ. It is possible to make degrees of freedom corrections for the individual equation GLS residual variance estimates, and this would produce values different from the diagonal elements of Table 8.4.

The R^2 values given in Table 8.3 are calculated exactly as in (2.34), but using the GLS residuals for each equation rather than the OLS residuals. This is not strictly correct, and there is no reason in general why these R^2 values should lie between 0 and 1. Given that a system estimator is being used to produce Table 8.3, one might expect the most natural goodness of fit measure to be a systemwide measure. There appears to be no general agreement in the literature and hence in software packages as to which is the best measure: some more comments on this are made later.

System inference and goodness of fit

In evaluating these regression results, one might expect to examine some diagnostic test statistics, and perform some hypothesis tests on the parameters. At one level, had the models been estimated by maximum likelihood, the standard likelihood

Table 8.3 GLS coefficient estimates

Dependent variable is value of gross investment
Standard errors in brackets

Corporation	Constant	Value of firm	Capital stock	Residual variance	R^2
General Motors	−162.36 (89.459)	0.1205 (0.0216)	0.3827 (0.0328)	7160.29	0.9207
Chrysler	−0.5043 (11.513)	0.0695 (0.0169)	0.3085 (0.0259)	149.87	0.9119
General Electric	−22.439 (25.519)	0.0373 (0.0122)	0.1308 (0.0220)	660.829	0.6876
Westinghouse	1.0888 (6.259)	0.0570 (0.0114)	0.0415 (0.0412)	88.662	0.7264
US Steel	85.4239 (111.88)	0.1015 (0.0548)	0.4000 (0.1278)	8896.42	0.4220

Table 8.4 GLS covariance matrix estimate: $\hat{\Sigma}_G$

$$
\begin{bmatrix}
7216.04 & -313.70 & 605.34 & 129.89 & -2686.52 \\
-313.70 & 152.85 & 2.05 & 16.66 & 455.09 \\
605.34 & 2.05 & 700.46 & 200.32 & 1224.41 \\
129.89 & 16.66 & 200.32 & 94.91 & 652.73 \\
-2686.52 & 455.09 & 1224.41 & 652.73 & 9188.15
\end{bmatrix}
$$

ratio test statistic of equation (4.43) could be used. However, given the emphasis on the use of feasible GLS estimation, we focus on inference procedures and goodness of fit statistics appropriate for this estimator.

A test on an individual parameter would use the computed standard errors in the standard way, but for several parameters, a generalisation of the F statistic of (5.11) would be required. The estimator $\breve{\pi}_G$ of (8.27) minimises the quantity

$$
S_G(\bar{\pi}) = [\bar{y} - \bar{X}\bar{\pi}]'(\hat{\Sigma}^{-1} \otimes I_n)[\bar{y} - \bar{X}\bar{\pi}], \tag{8.28}
$$

so that if $S_G(\bar{\pi})$ is minimised subject to restrictions on $\bar{\pi}$, a restricted estimator $\breve{\pi}_{GR}$ will be obtained. A comparison of the values $S_G(\breve{\pi}_G)$ and $S_G(\breve{\pi}_{GR})$ then gives a suitable large sample test statistic:

$$
S_G(\breve{\pi}_{GR}) - S_G(\breve{\pi}_G) \sim \chi^2, \text{ approximately,}
$$

with degrees of freedom equal to the number of restrictions being tested, or equivalently, to the difference in the number of the parameters being estimated. The quantities $S_G(\breve{\pi}_G)$ and $S_G(\breve{\pi}_{GR})$ appear to be quite complicated, but can be expressed (see Greene, 1993: 490–1) in terms of the estimators of Σ which follow from $\breve{\pi}_G$ and $\breve{\pi}_{GR}$. These estimators use the implied residual matrices to construct an estimator of Σ as in equation (8.26). Denoting the estimators as $\breve{\Sigma}_G$ and $\breve{\Sigma}_{GR}$ it can be shown that

$$
S_G(\breve{\pi}_G) = n \operatorname{trace}(\hat{\Sigma}^{-1}\breve{\Sigma}_G), \quad S_G(\breve{\pi}_{GR}) = n \operatorname{trace}(\hat{\Sigma}^{-1}\breve{\Sigma}_{GR}).
$$

The large sample test statistic then becomes

$$
n \operatorname{trace}[\hat{\Sigma}^{-1}(\breve{\Sigma}_{GR} - \breve{\Sigma}_G)]. \tag{8.29}
$$

Notice that the use of a common estimator of Σ in the two versions of (8.28) is critical for this.

A natural application is to testing that all ten slopes in the Grunfeld model are zero. Under this null hypothesis, feasible GLS estimation of the model

$$
y_{it} = \pi_{i1} + u_{it}; \ i = 1, \ldots, 5; \ t = 1, \ldots, 20
$$

is required, using the covariance matrix estimate $\hat{\Sigma}$ of Table 8.2. Here, there are common explanatory variables to every equation (i.e. the intercept), so that the GLS estimators of π_{i1} are simply the OLS estimators, the sample means of y_{it} for each i. This means that the restricted GLS residuals are simply the mean deviations of y_{it}, and the implied estimator of Σ, $\breve{\Sigma}_{GR}$, is the sample covariance matrix S_{yy} of the y_{it}:

$$(\breve{\sigma}_{ij})_{GR} = \frac{1}{n}\sum_{t=1}^{n}(y_{it} - \bar{y}_i)(y_{jt} - \bar{y}_j) = s_{ij}.$$

In Example 8.1,

$$S_{yy} = \begin{bmatrix} 91\,044.63 & 11\,185.14 & 11\,761.10 & 4778.05 & 24\,043.44 \\ 11\,185.14 & 1\,734.20 & 1\,504.85 & 611.00 & 3\,824.95 \\ 11\,761.10 & 1\,504.85 & 2\,242.43 & 806.11 & 4\,633.94 \\ 4\,778.05 & 611.00 & 806.11 & 346.93 & 1\,972.43 \\ 24\,043.44 & 3\,824.95 & 4\,633.94 & 1972.43 & 15\,895.32 \end{bmatrix}$$

and using $\hat{\Sigma}$ from Table 8.2 and $\breve{\Sigma}_G$ from Table 8.4 gives a value for (8.29) of 633.11. The 5% critical value of 18.31 should come from a χ^2 distribution with 10 degrees of freedom, so that the null hypothesis is easily rejected. This should come as no surprise bearing in mind the t values implicit in Table 8.3.

This discussion is also relevant to the question of goodness of fit. The normal definition of R^2 is closely related to the F test that all the slopes in a regression model are zero, so a system R^2 might be expected to involve the quantities in

$$\text{trace}\left[\hat{\Sigma}^{-1}(S_{yy} - \breve{\Sigma}_G)\right]$$

in some way. One possible definition which parallels the usual definition directly is

$$R_I^2 = 1 - \frac{\text{trace}(\hat{\Sigma}^{-1}\breve{\Sigma}_G)}{\text{trace}(\hat{\Sigma}^{-1}S_{yy})},$$

whilst Greene (1993: 491) gives the definition

$$R_*^2 = 1 - \frac{m}{\text{trace}(\breve{\Sigma}_G^{-1}S_{yy})}.$$

Their values in Example 8.1 are 0.8707 and 0.8687 respectively, which contrast quite strongly with the individual equation R^2's of Table 8.3.

The same conflict between individual equation information and system information appears when discussing diagnostic tests. Consider a test for first-order serial correlation for each equation which would use the appropriate column of the (feasible) GLS residual matrix $\breve{U}_G$ in constructing a test regression like (7.42). This would involve a regression of $\breve{u}_{itG}$ on an intercept, x_{2it}, x_{3it} and $\breve{u}_{it-1,G}$ for each i, testing the inclusion of $\breve{u}_{it-1,G}$. Conventionally, least squares is used for this regression, even though (feasible) GLS residuals are being used. Table 8.5 shows the t values associated with each of the five test regressions for Example 8.1: since this is a large sample test procedure, critical values from the $N(0,1)$ distribution should be used. Since the 5% critical value is ± 1.96, it is clear that three out of the five equations show some evidence of first-order serial correlation.

Table 8.5 OLS estimation of test regressions for Example 8.1

t values for lagged GLS residuals

General Motors	Chrysler	General Electric	Westinghouse	US Steel
2.124	−0.080	2.175	1.139	2.703

The idea of a system test for serial correlation really involves looking ahead to Chapter 9, since this is concerned with dynamic systems. Suffice it to say here that the appropriate system version of serial correlation amounts to assuming that every element in the disturbance vector u_t in (8.6) depends on all the elements in u_{t-1}, with the implication that an individual equation test regression should include, in the case of Example 8.1, all five lagged (feasible) GLS residuals rather than just one. In addition, the system of test regressions should be estimated by feasible GLS using the covariance matrix estimate $\hat{\Sigma}$ of (8.26). The test procedure then involves an application of the appropriate version of (8.29). The estimate of Σ under the null hypothesis of no (system) serial correlation is $\breve{\Sigma}_G$ (from Table 8.4), whilst the estimate implied by the system of test regressions can be denoted $\breve{\Sigma}_{GT}$. There is too much output from the test system to display all the results, so that Table 8.6 simply gives $\breve{\Sigma}_{GT}$. Computing the value of test statistic gives 34.697, distributed approximately as χ^2_{25}, since there are five explanatory variables to be excluded from each of five equations. The 5% critical value is no smaller than 36.42, so that the null hypothesis of no serial correlation is accepted. This contrasts with the conclusions from the individual equation tests.

8.5 / The simultaneous equations model

In this chapter so far, a model has consisted of a collection of standard regression equations, maintaining the restrictive assumption that all right-hand-side variables are exogenous and nonrandom. This assumption excludes the possibility that the left-hand-side or dependent variable in one equation also appears on the right of some other equation. A dependent variable is necessarily endogenous and must

Table 8.6 Estimate of Σ from residuals of test regression system

$$
\begin{bmatrix}
4251.71 & -246.77 & 446.34 & 134.17 & -860.96 \\
-246.77 & 137.63 & 99.56 & 37.44 & 533.47 \\
446.34 & 99.56 & 313.56 & 111.45 & 696.21 \\
134.17 & 37.44 & 111.45 & 63.56 & 365.71 \\
-860.96 & 533.47 & 696.21 & 365.71 & 4570.33
\end{bmatrix}
$$

include a random component; so allowing such variables to appear on the right of other equations means that we cannot treat all right-hand-side variable observations as nonrandom quantities.

In what follows, the important distinction to be made is between endogenous and exogenous variables, rather than between left-hand-side and right-hand-side variables. Unfortunately, these terms are not unambiguously defined, and there are particular difficulties with the concept of exogeneity. One can certainly start by thinking of endogenous variables as those whose behaviour is determined by the model, whilst exogenous variables are taken as given. This is a reasonable working definition for some purposes, but it must be recognised that such a classification rests on prior assumptions. If one treats exogeneity as a testable proposition, the situation becomes more complicated.

Two concepts that are reasonably easy to understand are *predeterminedness* and so-called *strict* exogeneity. A variable Z is predetermined in a given equation if Z_t is independent of current and future values of the disturbance to that equation. An example is provided by an equation which includes a lagged endogenous variable in the set of regressors. If $Z_t = Y_{t-1}$, and there is no serial correlation in the model, then Z_t will be independent of u_t and all future disturbances, u_{t+s}; $s > 0$. So, in the absence of serial correlation, lagged endogenous variables are predetermined.

For strict exogeneity, the requirement is that Z_t be independent of all current, future and past disturbances to a particular equation; in this case, lagged endogenous variables will not satisfy the condition because they will depend on past disturbances. The situation in which *all* regressors in a given equation are strictly exogenous corresponds to what, for want of a better term, was described as 'strong independence' in section 4.4.

Predeterminedness and strict exogeneity are clearly relevant to estimation theory, but alternative definitions are needed for a formal treatment which embraces estimation, testing and uses of the model, including policy simulation (see Engle, Hendry and Richard, 1983). We shall use predeterminedness and strict exogeneity when we discuss estimation, but for our initial discussion of simultaneous equation models, where the classification of variables is predefined, we shall continue to use the terms 'endogenous' and 'exogenous' in a rather loose way, treating endogenous variables as those whose behaviour is determined by the model, whilst exogenous variables are taken as given.

Since the initial discussion does not involve testing of the assumed classification of variables, nothing is lost by treating strictly exogenous variable observations as non-random quantities. If a variable is predetermined but not strictly exogenous, the observations must be treated as realisations of random variables.

An example

To illustrate these and other ideas relevant to the use of a simultaneous equation model, consider the following example. Suppose that quantity demanded for some commodity (Q^d) is a function of income (Y) and the relative price of the commodity

(P), whilst quantity supplied (Q^s) is a function of relative price and some other variable (Z). If the model is formulated as

$$Q_t^d = \alpha_1 + \alpha_2 P_t + \alpha_3 Y_t + u_{1t}$$

$$Q_t^s = \beta_1 + \beta_2 P_t + \beta_3 Z_t + u_{2t}$$

$$Q_t^d = Q_t^s = Q_t; \ t = 1, \dots, n, \tag{8.30}$$

the market-clearing assumption may be used to give

$$Q_t = \alpha_1 + \alpha_2 P_t + \alpha_3 Y_t + u_{1t} \tag{8.31}$$

$$Q_t = \beta_1 + \beta_2 P_t + \beta_3 Z_t + u_{2t}; \ t = 1, \dots, n. \tag{8.32}$$

The equations in (8.30) define a three-equation model. The equations in (8.31) and (8.32) represent the same model with the market-clearing identity eliminated, leaving only equations which have random disturbances. By using the market-clearing assumption, we have also removed Q^d and Q^s, which are typically unobservable.

Now assume that Y and Z are (strictly) exogenous. The logic of the model is that Q_t and P_t are jointly determined by solution of the equations in (8.31) and (8.32), for given values of Y_t and Z_t. It is easy to obtain this solution algebraically, as

$$Q_t = \pi_{11} + \pi_{12} Y_t + \pi_{13} Z_t + v_{1t};$$

$$P_t = \pi_{21} + \pi_{22} Y_t + \pi_{23} Z_t + v_{2t}; \ t = 1, \dots, n, \tag{8.33}$$

where

$$\pi_{11} = (\alpha_1 \beta_2 - \alpha_2 \beta_1)/(\beta_2 - \alpha_2)$$

$$\pi_{12} = \alpha_3 \beta_2/(\beta_2 - \alpha_2)$$

$$\pi_{13} = -\alpha_2 \beta_3/(\beta_2 - \alpha_2)$$

$$\pi_{21} = (\alpha_1 - \beta_1)/(\beta_2 - \alpha_2)$$

$$\pi_{22} = \alpha_3/(\beta_2 - \alpha_2) \tag{8.34}$$

$$\pi_{23} = -\beta_3/(\beta_2 - \alpha_2)$$

$$v_{1t} = (\beta_2 u_{1t} - \alpha_2 u_{2t})/(\beta_2 - \alpha_2)$$

$$v_{2t} = (u_{1t} - u_{2t})/(\beta_2 - \alpha_2).$$

The equations in (8.33) represent the *reduced form*, which is the solution for current endogenous variables in terms of predetermined variables. In general, the set of predetermined variables includes strictly exogenous and lagged endogenous variables, but here only exogenous variables appear on the right of (8.33). Notice that the 'variable' that allows for an intercept is treated formally as one of the exogenous variables.

Although Q_t appears on the left-hand side of both (8.31) and (8.32), this is merely a convenience, and one could easily select an alternative normalisation in which P_t appears on the left. On the other hand, it would not be particularly useful to write an exogenous variable on the left-hand side, since this would create a misleading impression of what the model is supposed to determine.

If we consider estimation of either (8.31) or (8.32), it follows from the reduced form that P_t depends directly on both u_{1t} and u_{2t}, and given the existence of the relevant probability limits, it is relatively simple to show that OLS estimators will be inconsistent. Estimation is discussed further in sections 8.6 and 8.7, but it seems from the example given above that there is at least a potential problem in estimating the parameters of an equation which has a current endogenous variable on the right-hand side. It remains to be seen whether all models with a current endogenous variable on the right lead to the same conclusion.

Now suppose that the model is changed, so that supply depends on price in the preceding period. This gives

$$Q_t^d = \alpha_1 + \alpha_2 P_t + \alpha_3 Y_t + u_{1t}$$

$$Q_t^s = \beta_1 + \beta_2 P_{t-1} + \beta_3 Z_t + u_{2t}$$

$$Q_t^d = Q_t^s = Q_t; \; t = 1, \ldots, n,$$

or

$$Q_t = \alpha_1 + \alpha_2 P_t + \alpha_3 Y_t + u_{1t}$$

$$Q_t = \beta_1 + \beta_2 P_{t-1} + \beta_3 Z_t + u_{2t}; \; t = 1, \ldots, n. \tag{8.35}$$

In (8.35), there is a clear causal sequence, or, more accurately, an order of precedence, which runs from P_{t-1} to Q_t to P_t. This means that (8.35) is not a simultaneous model. The second equation is already in reduced form, and the reduced form equation for P_t is

$$P_t = \pi_{21} + \pi_{22} Y_t + \pi_{23} Z_t + \pi_{24} P_{t-1} + v_{2t}; \; t = 1, \ldots, n$$

where

$$\pi_{21} = (\beta_1 - \alpha_1)/\alpha_2$$

$$\pi_{22} = -\alpha_3/\alpha_2$$

$$\pi_{23} = \beta_3/\alpha_2$$

$$\pi_{24} = \beta_2/\alpha_2$$

$$v_{2t} = (u_{2t} - u_{1t})/\alpha_2.$$

Given that the solution sequence in (8.35) runs from Q_t to P_t, there is a case for rewriting the first equation as

$$P_t = \gamma_1 + \gamma_2 Q_t + \gamma_3 Y_t + u_{3t}; \; t = 1, \ldots, n \tag{8.36}$$

where $\gamma_1, \ldots, \gamma_3$ are functions of $\alpha_1, \ldots, \alpha_3$, and u_{3t} is a rescaled version of u_{1t}. Now something rather curious occurs. Despite that fact that, in terms of the models as a whole, Q_t is a current endogenous variable, it is not necessarily true that the use of

OLS will lead to inconsistent estimators of the parameters of (8.36). If u_{1t} and u_{2t} are neither contemporaneously nor serially correlated, Q_t is actually independent of u_{1t}, and hence of u_{3t}. This suggests that the parameters of (8.36) can be consistently estimated by OLS, and that the presence of a current endogenous variable on the right of an equation does not always lead to the problem that arose with our first example.

What is happening here is that in terms of the *model* that we use in the second example, Q_t is a current endogenous variable. However, in terms of the specific *equation* shown in (8.36), Q_t also satisfies the formal definition of predeterminedness, since it is independent of current and future disturbances to that equation. In the next section, when we discuss the formal structure of a simultaneous model, we make categories of variable mutually exclusive by taking predetermined to mean not current endogenous, even though, as our example shows, it is possible for a current endogenous variable to satisfy the formal definition of predeterminedness within an individual equation.

To conclude this introduction, we need to make clear what is meant when we refer to simultaneous equation models which are linear in endogenous variables. An alternative to (8.31) and (8.32) which is not linear in this sense is

$$\ln(Q_t) = \alpha_1 + \alpha_2 \ln(P_t) + \alpha_3 \ln(Y_t) + u_{1t}$$
$$Q_t = \beta_1 + \beta_2 P_t + \beta_3 Z_t + u_{2t}; \ t = 1, \ldots, n. \tag{8.37}$$

If this model used $\ln(Q)$ and $\ln(P)$ throughout, it would still be linear in appropriately defined endogenous variables, namely $\ln(Q)$ and $\ln(P)$. The problem in (8.37) is that the linear and log forms are mixed and, as a result, (8.37) is nonlinear in endogenous variables. In practice, models are often nonlinear in this sense, and it is as well to bear this in mind when reviewing the conventional textbook treatment of simultaneous models, which does tend to focus on the linear case.

The linear simultaneous equations model

A linear simultaneous model can be written formally as

$$Ay_t = \Gamma z_t + u_t; \ t = 1, \ldots, n, \tag{8.38}$$

where y_t is a $(G \times 1)$ vector of current observations on endogenous variables, z_t is a $(K \times 1)$ vector of observations on predetermined variables, u_t is a $(G \times 1)$ vector of disturbances to each of the G equations at time t, and A and Γ are matrices of parameters, with dimensions $(G \times G)$ and $(G \times K)$ respectively. In the absence of serial correlation of disturbances, the set of predetermined variables includes current and lagged exogenous variables, and lagged endogenous variables.

For convenience, we have adopted a slightly different convention to that normally used, in that the term Γz_t is written on the right of (8.38). This avoids an unnecessary proliferation of minus signs when applied to examples written directly with one endogenous variable on the left, and all other variables on the right.

To illustrate the application of this notation, consider the example given in equations (8.31) and (8.32). In the standard notation, this is written as in (8.38), with

$$A = \begin{bmatrix} 1 & -\alpha_2 \\ 1 & -\beta_2 \end{bmatrix}, \qquad \Gamma = \begin{bmatrix} \alpha_1 & \alpha_3 & 0 \\ \beta_1 & 0 & \beta_3 \end{bmatrix} \qquad (8.39)$$

and

$$y'_t = [Q_t \quad P_t], \qquad z'_t = [1 \quad Y_t \quad Z_t], \qquad u'_t = [u_{1t} \quad u_{2t}].$$

Turning now to the disturbance specification, we assume initially that the disturbance vector u_t is multivariate *IID*, that is,

$$u_t \sim IID(0, \Sigma); \quad t = 1, \ldots, n. \qquad (8.40)$$

The diagonal elements of Σ are variances for the individual elements of u_t, written as σ_i^2, or as σ_{ii}, for $i = 1, \ldots, G$. The off-diagonal elements are contemporaneous covariances between the disturbances to different equations; in general, these are not assumed to be equal to zero.

The supposed logic of the model is that the system is solved for y_t, for given z_t (and given values of A, Γ and u_t). The solution is

$$y_t = A^{-1}\Gamma z_t + A^{-1}u_t$$

or

$$y_t = \Pi z_t + v_t; \quad t = 1, \ldots, n. \qquad (8.41)$$

It is assumed here that A is nonsingular. In other contexts, one might wish to consider the possibility of an economy with multiple solutions, but we shall assume that the solution is unique. The form shown in (8.41) is the reduced form – the solution for y_t – whereas (8.38) is the *structural form*, which is a form that follows naturally from consideration of the relevant economic theory. It is easy to confirm the reduced form parameter expressions of (8.34) using the matrix formulation of the model in (8.39) and the derivation leading to (8.41).

8.6 / Identification

The notion of identification can be a little hard to grasp. It is an issue which usually appears in the theory of the simultaneous equations model, yet often appears not to be terribly important in practice. In order to get to grips with the idea, consider the model of (8.31) and (8.32), and its reduced form (8.33). In the structural form (8.31) and (8.32), there are six parameters, α_1, α_2, α_3, β_1, β_2, β_3, and similarly six parameters in the reduced form (8.33). It is reasonable to assume, on the face of it, that if the reduced form parameters are known, the six equations (8.34) can be solved for the structural form parameters. However, we do not know this for sure, without attempting to solve the equations.

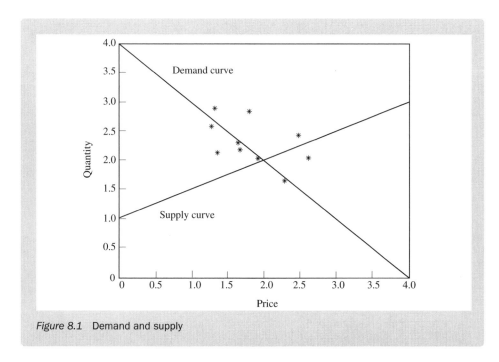

Figure 8.1 Demand and supply

A graphical argument

To see what can happen, consider the structural form (8.31) and (8.32) where $\alpha_3 = \beta_3 = 0$. Then, the model matches the simple demand and supply diagram of Figure 8.1, where the demand curve is defined by

$$Q = \alpha_1 + \alpha_2 P,$$

and the supply curve by

$$Q = \beta_1 + \beta_2 P.$$

The scatter of points represents the impact of the disturbances u_{1t} and u_{2t}, which creates a scatter about the equilibrium price–quantity combination. A least squares regression line of Q on P would resemble neither the demand curve nor the supply curve. In ordinary language, we cannot 'identify' either the demand curve or the supply curve from these data. In the reduced form (8.33), when $\alpha_3 = \beta_3 = 0$, there are now only two parameters, π_{11} and π_{21}, but still four structural form parameters. In the equations relating the reduced form and structural form parameters, (8.34), there are now two equations in four unknowns, and hence no solutions. 'Identifying' a demand or supply curve from the data on Q and P is now linked to the existence of a solution for the structural form parameters in (8.34).

To pursue this idea further, consider what happens if only α_3 is set equal to zero in (8.31) and (8.32). The variable Z_t is free to shift around, and as it does so, the supply curve will move up and down the demand curve, creating a scatter of points roughly

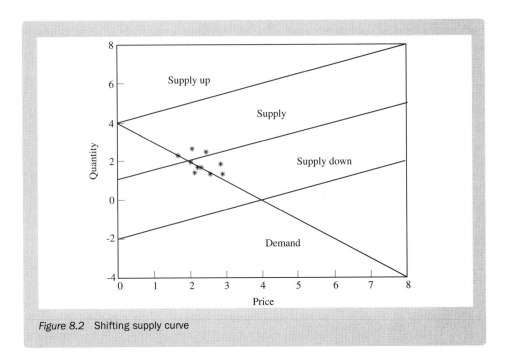

Figure 8.2 Shifting supply curve

along the demand curve (see Figure 8.2). Fitting a regression line to the scatter should generate a line which resembles the demand curve, and can therefore be considered as an estimate of the demand curve. Thus, fitting a regression line allows us to 'identify' the demand curve. How does this reasoning relate to the relevant equations in (8.34)? We have to solve the equations for π_{11}, π_{13}, π_{21}, and π_{23} for the parameters α_1, α_2, β_1, β_2, β_3. There are four equations to determine five unknowns, so that there cannot be solutions for all five parameters. However, it may be possible to find solutions for some of them: one can show that

$$\alpha_2 = \frac{\pi_{13}}{\pi_{23}}, \qquad \alpha_1 = \pi_{11} - \pi_{21}\alpha_2.$$

Solving the reduced form equations for α_1 and α_2 but not for β_1, β_2, β_3 is equivalent to saying that we have identified the demand curve, but not the supply curve.

It is easy to see now what might happen if in (8.32), $\beta_3 = 0$, maintaining $\alpha_3 \neq 0$ in (8.31). The demand curve shifts along the supply curve as Y_t shifts, producing a scatter along the supply curve, which is now identified. Using the relevant reduced form equations in (8.34) shows that there is a solution for the parameters of the supply function,

$$\beta_2 = \frac{\pi_{12}}{\pi_{22}}, \qquad \beta_1 = \pi_{11} - \pi_{21}\beta_2,$$

but not for the parameters of the demand function.

The problem with this approach is that it can be extremely tedious to solve subsets of (8.34), and even harder to distinguish between the nonexistence of a solution and an algebraic error in trying to find a solution. A simpler procedure that enables one to decide whether equations like (8.34) have a solution for some or all of the structural form parameters is clearly needed.

The *F* method

The basis of one particular procedure is the observation that the transformation of the structural form (8.38) by the nonsingular matrix F produces a new structural form

$$FAy_t = F\Gamma z_t + Fu_t; \ t = 1, \ldots, n, \tag{8.42}$$

but which has exactly the same reduced form (8.41) as the structural form (8.38), since

$$y_t = (FA)^{-1}F\Gamma z_t + (FA)^{-1}Fu_t$$

$$= A^{-1}F^{-1}F\Gamma z_t + A^{-1}F^{-1}Fu_t$$

$$= A^{-1}\Gamma z_t + A^{-1}u_t; \ t = 1, \ldots, n.$$

For the model of equations (8.31) and (8.32), $F = \|f_{ij}\|$ is any 2×2 nonsingular matrix, and we can interpret the action of transformation by F on this model as multiplying one equation by a scalar and adding it to a scalar multiple of the other equation. This is the same as forming a linear combination of the two equations. For example, the result of multiplying (8.31) by f_{11} and (8.32) by f_{12} yields the new equation

$$(f_{11} + f_{12})Q_t = (f_{11}\alpha_1 + f_{12}\beta_1) + (f_{11}\alpha_2 + f_{12}\beta_2)P_t + f_{11}\alpha_3 Y_t$$

$$+ f_{12}\beta_3 Z_t + (f_{11}u_{1t} + f_{12}u_{2t}). \tag{8.43}$$

If we then take $f_{21} = 0$ and $f_{22} = 1$, we have a new system in which the supply curve (8.32) is unchanged. This new system is very different from (8.31) and (8.32), since it includes both Y_t and Z_t in (8.43), whereas (8.31) carefully excluded Z_t. Even if we normalise (8.43) by dividing through by $(f_{11} + f_{12})$ to make Q_t the dependent variable, as in (8.31), the new system is still different. Setting the coefficient on Q_t to one in this way is called a *normalisation rule*.

From any given structural form then, we can generate an infinity of structural forms having a common reduced form. If our objective is to ensure that there is a one-to-one relationship between a reduced form and a structural form, this does not seem very helpful. But, economic arguments often imply the exclusion of certain variables from certain equations. Demanding that these *exclusion restrictions* (and normalisation rules) be preserved under the transformation F may reduce the number of structures that can be generated right down to one, as we shall see.

If there exist structural forms generated by linear combination that share the same exclusion restrictions and normalisation rules as the model of (8.31) and (8.32), then the latter model is not identified, since there is then more than one structural form being associated with the same reduced form. If there are no structural forms other than (8.31) and (8.32) satisfying the exclusion restrictions and normalisation rules, then these serve to distinguish, or identify, the structural form (8.31) and (8.32) from others that generate the reduced form (8.33). The nonexistence of such a generated structural form is equivalent to the use of *trivial* linear combinations $f_{11} = f_{22} = 1, f_{12} = f_{21} = 0$ applied to (8.31) and (8.32).

For example, if we impose $\beta_3 = 0$ in (8.32), and use the linear combination leading to (8.43), then after normalisation on Q_t, (8.43) has the same structure as the demand function (8.31) but with a different set of parameters. That is, if the supply function does not contain Z_t, adding a multiple of the supply function to the demand function yields, after normalisation, another version of the demand function, sharing the same restrictions as (8.31). This implies that (8.31) is not identified.

Again, in the system (8.31) and (8.32), any linear combination other than the trivial one will introduce, for example, Y_t into the supply function, or Z_t into the demand function, and thus produce different demand or supply functions. Thus we can argue that there is a single structural form associated with the reduced form of that model, which is therefore identified.

These arguments can now be expressed more generally. The linear transformation producing (8.42) replaces the equations of the original structure (8.38) with a set of G linear combinations of the form

$$f_i' A y_t = f_i' \Gamma z_t + f_i' u_t; \ i = 1, \ldots, G; \ t = 1, \ldots, n,$$

where f_i' is the ith row of F. But this creates a potential problem. If we consider the observations on y_t as being generated by the reduced form, such data would be consistent with both (8.38) and (8.42). In the absence of further information, there is no way of telling whether an estimation method applied to (8.38) would actually be estimating the parameters of (8.38), or the parameters of a set of linear combinations, such as (8.42). In fact, one cannot hope to estimate the parameters of a linear simultaneous equations model, unless there are sufficient restrictions on the elements of A and Γ to distinguish the possible structures generated from (8.42). When there are enough restrictions, we will have identified the parameters of each equation of the model. In passing, we note that restrictions on Σ may also be used for this purpose.

Within the discussion of the model of (8.31) and (8.32), three main methods of checking identification have been mentioned. They may appear different superficially, but are in fact formally equivalent. In terms of (8.42), they are as follows.

Method 1 (the 'F' method)

If (8.42) is to be considered as an acceptable alternative structure, any restrictions on A and Γ must also be satisfied by FA and $F\Gamma$, for otherwise (8.42) does not satisfy the a priori restrictions that lead to the specification (8.38). These restrictions impose conditions on the rows of F, and if it can be shown that f_i' must be equal to row i of a $(G \times G)$ identity matrix, then the parameters of equation i are identified. If there are more conditions than are needed to show that f_i' is equal to row i of an identity matrix, the parameters of equation i are said to be overidentified. This is the general statement of the method used in the example above.

Method 2 (the informal F method)

With small models, it is often possible to simply look at each equation, to decide whether the equation can or cannot be distinguished from possible linear combinations. This 'quick and dirty' method was used to motivate the F method.

Method 3 (solution for structural parameters)

From (8.41), we see that the connection between structural form parameters and reduced form parameters is

$$\Pi = A^{-1}\Gamma \quad \text{or} \quad A\Pi = \Gamma. \tag{8.44}$$

If it is possible to solve for nonzero elements of A and Γ from given values of the elements of Π, then all parameters of the model are identified. If it is possible to solve for nonzero elements of row i of A and Γ, then the parameters of equation i are identified. If there is more than one way of expressing the elements of row i of A and Γ in terms of elements of Π, the parameters of equation i are said to be overidentified.

Method 4 (rank and order conditions)

Since all the methods given above involve the solution of sets of linear equations, it is not surprising that formal conditions for solution can be expressed in terms of the rank of an appropriately defined matrix. When looking at the rank of any matrix, there are necessary conditions associated with the dimensions of the matrix, and these are known as *order* conditions. Necessary and sufficient conditions are obtained by direct evaluation of the rank of the matrix in question, and these are known as *rank* conditions.

The starting point of method 4 is the model (8.38), without any restrictions imposed. Let $A = ||\alpha_{ij}||$, $\Gamma = ||\gamma_{ij}||$. For the model of (8.31) and (8.32), these matrices would be

$$A = \begin{bmatrix} \alpha_{11} & \alpha_{12} \\ \alpha_{21} & \alpha_{22} \end{bmatrix}, \qquad \Gamma = \begin{bmatrix} \gamma_{11} & \gamma_{12} & \gamma_{13} \\ \gamma_{21} & \gamma_{22} & \gamma_{23} \end{bmatrix},$$

whose restricted versions are given in (8.39). The restrictions on the elements of A and Γ have to be expressed in the form given in section 3.3: defining

$$\beta_1 = \begin{bmatrix} \alpha_{11} \\ \alpha_{12} \\ \gamma_{11} \\ \gamma_{12} \\ \gamma_{13} \end{bmatrix}, \qquad \beta_2 = \begin{bmatrix} \alpha_{21} \\ \alpha_{22} \\ \gamma_{21} \\ \gamma_{22} \\ \gamma_{23} \end{bmatrix},$$

the restricted versions of these vectors are

$$\beta_1 = \begin{bmatrix} 1 \\ -\alpha_2 \\ \alpha_1 \\ \alpha_3 \\ 0 \end{bmatrix}, \qquad \beta_2 = \begin{bmatrix} 1 \\ -\beta_2 \\ \beta_1 \\ 0 \\ \beta_3 \end{bmatrix}.$$

We have to find matrices H_1, H_2 and vectors h_1, h_2 that can represent these restrictions. It is easy to see that for the model of (8.31) and (8.32) these matrices and vectors are

$$H_1 = \begin{bmatrix} 1 & 0 & 0 & 0 & 0 \\ 0 & 0 & 0 & 0 & 1 \end{bmatrix}, \quad h_1 = \begin{bmatrix} 1 \\ 0 \end{bmatrix}, \quad H_2 = \begin{bmatrix} 1 & 0 & 0 & 0 & 0 \\ 0 & 0 & 0 & 1 & 0 \end{bmatrix}, \quad h_2 = \begin{bmatrix} 1 \\ 0 \end{bmatrix}.$$

More generally, consider a particular equation of the model (8.38), say the first, and arrange the elements of the first row of A and Γ into a column vector β_1. This is the same as defining the matrix

$$B' = \begin{bmatrix} A' \\ \Gamma' \end{bmatrix}, \qquad (G+K) \times G,$$

and taking β_1 to be the first column of B'. Suppose that the restrictions imposed on the parameters of the first equation, including the normalisation rule, are given by

$$H_1 \beta_1 = h_1.$$

If there are p_1 restrictions, then H_1 is $p_1 \times (G+K)$, and h_1 is $p_1 \times 1$. The relationship (8.44) in the transposed form

$$\Pi' A' + \Gamma' = 0$$

is equivalent to writing

$$[\Pi' \quad I_K] B' = 0,$$

and this reveals that β_1 satisfies the equation

$$[\Pi' \quad I_K] \beta_1 = 0.$$

Put

$$Q = [\Pi' \quad I_K].$$

Whether or not the first equation of the model (8.38) is identified turns on whether there is a unique solution to the pair of equations

$$H_1 \beta_1 = h_1 \quad \text{and} \quad Q \beta_1 = 0,$$

that is, whether there is a unique solution to the equation

$$\begin{bmatrix} H_1 \\ Q \end{bmatrix} \beta_1 = \begin{bmatrix} h_1 \\ 0 \end{bmatrix}.$$

As noted in Appendix A, this requires the $(p_1 + K) \times (G + K)$ matrix

$$S_1 = \begin{bmatrix} H_1 \\ Q \end{bmatrix}$$

to have full column rank $(G + K)$. This is then a *rank* condition for the identification of the first equation, and is necessary and sufficient. A necessary condition is that S_1 has more rows than columns, that is $p_1 \geq G$: this is the *order* condition for identification.

Since rank is preserved by multiplication by nonsingular matrices, we can post-multiply S_1 by a cleverly chosen matrix to create an equivalent and simpler rank condition. If

$$C' = \begin{bmatrix} 0 \\ I_K \end{bmatrix}, \quad (G + K) \times K$$

the matrix

$$[B' \quad C'] = \begin{bmatrix} A' & 0 \\ \Gamma' & I_K \end{bmatrix}$$

is nonsingular, since A' is nonsingular. Then,

$$S_1[B' \quad C'] = \begin{bmatrix} H_1 B' & H_1 C' \\ 0 & I_K \end{bmatrix}$$

on using the definition of Q and (8.44). Since the rank of S_1 is not changed by the postmultiplication, we have

$$\text{rank}(S_1) = \text{rank}(H_1 B') + K,$$

or

$$\text{rank}(H_1 B') = G.$$

This is an alternative necessary and sufficient condition for identification. Before applying this to the example above, note that the principle applies to each equation of the model, simply by using the appropriate matrix of restrictions, and that it is not restricted simply to exclusion restrictions, although this is the most common case. In using this rank condition, the restricted parameters appear in the matrix B', since we are interested in the question of whether the restrictions on a particular equation distinguish that equation uniquely from the other equations of the system.

Consider the first equation of the model (8.31) and (8.32): we need to calculate the rank of the matrix

$$H_1 B' = \begin{bmatrix} 1 & 0 & 0 & 0 & 0 \\ 0 & 0 & 0 & 0 & 1 \end{bmatrix} \begin{bmatrix} 1 & 1 \\ -\alpha_2 & -\beta_2 \\ \alpha_1 & \beta_1 \\ \alpha_3 & 0 \\ 0 & \beta_3 \end{bmatrix} = \begin{bmatrix} 1 & 1 \\ 0 & \beta_3 \end{bmatrix},$$

using the expressions for the parameter matrices from (8.39). This matrix clearly has rank $G = 2$, so that the equation is (just) identified.

Usually the row of a restriction matrix, say H, which represents the normalisation rule is excluded from consideration. The required rank of HB' is reduced by 1 to compensate: this makes the rank condition

$$\text{rank } HB' = G - 1.$$

This procedure may seem very involved, but there is a quick way to construct the matrix HB' for any given equation, and which is best seen using the model (8.31) and (8.32). Comparing the transpose of H_1B', BH_1', with (8.39), we see that its columns are simply the columns of $B = [A \quad \Gamma]$ corresponding to the restricted elements of the first row of this latter matrix. According to this principle, the matrix BH_2' for the second equation in this example would be

$$BH_2' = \begin{bmatrix} 1 & \alpha_3 \\ 1 & 0 \end{bmatrix}$$

which is easily verified. It has rank 2 provided that $\alpha_3 \neq 0$, so that the second equation is identified. Ignoring the normalisation rule means ignoring the first column of this matrix, so that the rank of the corresponding matrix is $G - 1 = 2 - 1 = 1$.

To illustrate these ideas, we consider a simple linearised version of the textbook IS–LM model. If this is written in a manner which is consistent with the standard notation, we have

$$C_t = \gamma_{11} - \alpha_{14}Y_t + u_{1t}$$

$$I_t = \gamma_{21} - \alpha_{23}R_t + u_{2t}$$

$$R_t = -\alpha_{34}Y_t + \gamma_{32}M_t + u_{3t}$$

$$Y_t = C_t + I_t + Z_t; \; t = 1, \dots, n \tag{8.45}$$

or

$$Ay_t = \Gamma z_t + u_t; \; t = 1, \dots, n$$

where

$$A = \begin{bmatrix} 1 & 0 & 0 & \alpha_{14} \\ 0 & 1 & \alpha_{23} & 0 \\ 0 & 0 & 1 & \alpha_{34} \\ -1 & -1 & 0 & 1 \end{bmatrix}, \quad \Gamma = \begin{bmatrix} \gamma_{11} & 0 & 0 \\ \gamma_{21} & 0 & 0 \\ 0 & \gamma_{32} & 0 \\ 0 & 0 & 1 \end{bmatrix},$$

$y_t' = [C_t \quad I_t \quad R_t \quad Y_t]$, $z_t' = [1 \quad M_t \quad Z_t]$ and $u_t' = [u_{1t} \quad u_{2t} \quad u_{3t} \quad 0]$. The variables are C, consumers' expenditure, I, gross investment, R, a rate of interest, Y, total income, M, the money stock and Z autonomous expenditure. C, I, R and Y are considered to be endogenous, whilst M, Z and the intercept 'variable' are considered to be exogenous. The model is extremely naïve, but it does serve to illustrate the various methods of checking for identification. Note that, in (8.45), it is simply a convenience to write each equation with a different endogenous variable on the left-hand side. Some normalisation rule is needed, but it need not be the particular rule chosen here.

To apply the 'F method' of checking for identification, we ask whether there exists any alternative structure of the form

$$FAy_t = F\Gamma z_t + Fu_t; \ t = 1, \ldots, n$$

which satisfies the same restrictions as those on A and Γ in the model given above. Taking the consumption function first, we make the first rows of FA and $F\Gamma$ satisfy restrictions identical to those in the first rows of A and Γ. If f_1' is the first row of F, we have $f_1' = [f_{11} \quad f_{12} \quad f_{13} \quad f_{14}]$, and the conditions on the first rows of FA and $F\Gamma$ give

$$f_{11} - f_{14} = 1, \qquad f_{12} - f_{14} = 0,$$

$$f_{12}\alpha_{23} + f_{13} = 0, \qquad f_{13}\gamma_{32} = 0, \qquad f_{14} = 0.$$

From these equations, we can deduce that $f_{11} = 1, f_{12} = 0, f_{13} = 0$ and $f_{14} = 0$. This means that having considered the set of possible linear combinations

$$f_1'Ay_t = f_1'\Gamma z_t + f_1'u_t$$

that may or may not be distinguishable from the consumption function, we find that only those for which $f_1' = [1 \quad 0 \quad 0 \quad 0]$ are actually admissible – in other words, the only acceptable linear combination is the trivial case in which the combination has a weight of one on the consumption function and zeros on the other functions; such a 'combination' is of course the consumption function itself. Notice that we have one restriction more than is actually needed to show that $f_1' = [1 \quad 0 \quad 0 \quad 0]$. This means that the consumption function is overidentified.

Proceeding in a similar fashion, we can show that the investment function and the interest rate function are also overidentified. We need not bother about the fourth equation, which is an identity. Identities do not involve unknown parameters and, not surprisingly, identities are always identified.

A less formal application of the F method would proceed as follows. To see whether the consumption function is identified, we consider those linear combinations of the equations in (8.45) which include the consumption function. If the interest rate function is included, the combination would involve M. If the identity is included, the combination would involve Z. Since the consumption function involves neither of these variables, it is distinct from all combinations considered so far. If the combination includes the investment function, it would involve I and R. The variables I and R could be taken out again by adding particular multiples of the interest rate function and the identity, but we have already decided that combinations involving these equations are not admissible. The consumption function is therefore identified; in fact, it is overidentified, since there are more than enough conditions to rule out possible linear combinations.

The informal F method may seem more complicated than the formal version, but looking directly for admissible combinations is actually a rather versatile approach to the problem of checking the identifiability of parameters in a more general class of models and, with a little practice, the informal method becomes quite easy to use.

The third method mentioned above involves solution from reduced form parameters. This is actually very tedious, and we shall not attempt to apply this method to the model given in (8.45).

Finally we consider the rank and order conditions. This time, we consider the identifiability of the interest rate function. To do this, we use the quick method and form a matrix $B'H$ from those elements of A and Γ which are in the columns associated with zeros in the third row (the interest rate equation row) of A and Γ. Since the normalisation rule is ignored by focusing on the zeros, this gives

$$\begin{bmatrix} 1 & 0 & \gamma_{11} & 0 \\ 0 & 1 & \gamma_{21} & 0 \\ 0 & 0 & 0 & 0 \\ -1 & -1 & 0 & 1 \end{bmatrix}.$$

What we require is that the rank of this matrix be equal to the number of equations (G) minus 1. Here $G - 1 = 3$, and by inspection, the rank is indeed 3. Clearly, the third row can be deleted without changing the rank, and it is more usual to exclude the row corresponding to the equation being checked, to give

$$\begin{bmatrix} 1 & 0 & \gamma_{11} & 0 \\ 0 & 1 & \gamma_{21} & 0 \\ -1 & -1 & 0 & 1 \end{bmatrix}. \tag{8.46}$$

Since the number of columns in the matrix above is equal to the number of restrictions on the parameters of the interest rate equation (excluding the normalisation rule), a necessary condition is that the number of restrictions is greater than or equal to $G - 1$. This is the order condition for identification.

If, as in the example given above, the only restrictions other than the normalisation rule are exclusions, the order condition for equation i can be written as

$$R_i \geq G - 1 \;\Rightarrow\; (K - K_i) + (G - G_i) \geq G - 1$$
$$\Rightarrow\; K - K_i \geq G_i - 1, \tag{8.47}$$

where R_i is the number of restrictions in equation i, apart from the normalisation rule, K_i is the number of predetermined variables in equation i and G_i is the number of endogenous variables in equation i. As before, G and K refer to the number of endogenous and predetermined variables in the model. In our example, $K = 3$, $K_i = 1$, $G = 4$ and $G_i = 2$. Since $(3 - 1)$ is strictly greater than $(2 - 1)$, the equation is overidentified. Notice that the order condition is necessary but not sufficient and, strictly speaking, the rank condition should be checked before using the order condition to reveal overidentification. In practice, there are relatively few cases in which the order condition is satisfied when the rank condition is not and, in such cases, a direct search for linear combinations will usually make it quite obvious why the equation in question is not identified.

Nonexclusion restrictions

The equations of the model (8.45) are all identified by exclusion restrictions. A second example reveals that this is not always the case. Consider the model

$$C_t = \gamma_{11} - \alpha_{13}(Y_t - T_t) + u_{1t}$$

$$T_t = \gamma_{21} - \alpha_{23}Y_t + u_{2t}$$

$$Y_t = C_t + Z_t; \; t = 1, \ldots, n, \tag{8.48}$$

where T_i represents taxes on income. The consumption function in this model is identified by the fact that Z_t is excluded ($\gamma_{12} = 0$), and by the implicit restriction that the parameter on T is the negative of the parameter on Y. If this restriction is relaxed, to give

$$C_t = \gamma_{11} - \alpha_{13}Y_t - \alpha_{12}T_t + u_{1t} \tag{8.49}$$

the resulting equation is not identified.

To reveal correctly that the restriction $\alpha_{12} = -\alpha_{13}$ is needed for identification of the consumption function, the order condition must be written as $R_i \geq G - 1$, and $\alpha_{12} = -\alpha_{13}$ must be included in the restriction count. With this restriction, $R_i = 2$ and $G - 1 = 2$. Without the extra restriction, $R_i = 1$, and the consumption function is not identified.

To apply the rank condition to the example given above, one must first write the new restriction as $\alpha_{12} + \alpha_{13} = 0$, and then add a column corresponding to this restriction to the matrix which contains one column for each exclusion restriction. If the restriction $\gamma_{12} = 0$ generates a column with elements γ_{22} and γ_{32}, the restriction $\alpha_{12} + \alpha_{13} = 0$ generates a column with elements $\alpha_{22} + \alpha_{23}$ and $\alpha_{32} + \alpha_{33}$. Noting that $\gamma_{22} = 0$, $\gamma_{32} = 1$, $\alpha_{22} = 1$, $\alpha_{32} = 0$ and $\alpha_{33} = 1$, this gives the matrix

$$\begin{bmatrix} 0 & 1 + \alpha_{23} \\ 1 & 1 \end{bmatrix}.$$

As required, this has rank $G - 1 = 2$, unless $\alpha_{23} = -1$. This can be discounted as it would imply a marginal tax rate of 100%!

One final comment concerns the use of a nonhomogeneous restriction, such as $\alpha_{13} = 1$. Since this has no meaning without reference to a particular normalisation rule, we handle such restrictions as before, with the one crucial modification that the normalisation rule is now included in the restriction count, and both rank and order conditions use G in place of $G - 1$.

At the start of this section, it was suggested that one should not overstate the importance of formal methods of checking for identification in the linear model, since many models are actually nonlinear in endogenous variables, and even in the linear case, it is difficult to apply formal methods to anything other than relatively small-scale models. This argument is strengthened by the observation that the methods used above for checking identification assume that the model is correctly specified, an idea which does not fit at all easily with the concept of progressive refinement in the light of evidence from the data. Although it is important to understand the nature of the identification problem, one should perhaps restrict the amount of time spent on mastering formal methods which are limited in scope.

8.7 / Estimation: single equation methods

From the outset, it should be made clear that in the context of a simultaneous equation model, a 'single equation method' is one which sets out to estimate the parameters of just one equation, whilst recognising that the equation in question does come from a larger model.

To apply such methods, it is not necessary to specify the remaining equations in detail. Indeed, the rest of the model may be left implicit. We proceed on the assumption that variables known to be in the remainder of the model can be categorised as endogenous or exogenous, but such assumptions are testable, and both the list and classification of variables may be revised during a sequence of experiments. Hence we use only limited information concerning the structure of the remaining equations; in fact, the term *limited information* methods is a rather more accurate description of what this section is about.

Notation

If the focus of attention is a single equation from a larger model, that equation may be written for the purposes of estimation as

$$y = X\beta + u; \ E(u) = 0; \ \text{var}(u) = \sigma^2 I, \tag{8.50}$$

where y is an $(n \times 1)$ vector of observations on the endogenous variable that we choose to write on the left-hand side, X is an $(n \times k)$ matrix of observations on both right-hand-side endogenous variables and all the predetermined variables that are included in the target equation, β is an appropriately dimensioned parameter vector and u is an $(n \times 1)$ vector of disturbances to the target equation.

If the target equation is equation i from the larger model, then σ^2 is equivalent to σ_i^2 (or σ_{ii}), and k is equal to $K_i + G_i - 1$. The disturbance properties in (8.50) follow directly from (8.40).

For some purposes, it is necessary to split X between the current endogenous and predetermined variables, and this can be achieved by rewriting (8.50) as

$$y = Y_1\alpha + Z_1\gamma + u; \ E(u) = 0; \ \text{var}(u) = \sigma^2 I, \tag{8.51}$$

where Y_1 is the $[n \times (G_i - 1)]$ matrix of observations on current endogenous variables that appear on the right of equation i, Z_1 is the $(n \times K_i)$ matrix of observations on predetermined variables included in equation i, and α and γ are the corresponding parameter vectors. The relationship between X and β in (8.50) and Y_1, Z_1, α and γ in (8.51) is

$$X = [Y_1 \quad Z_1], \qquad \beta = \begin{bmatrix} \alpha \\ \gamma \end{bmatrix}.$$

Using the conventions given above, the matrix of all current endogenous variable observations in the model is $Y = [y \quad Y_1 \quad Y_2]$ and the matrix of all predetermined (exogenous and lagged endogenous) variable observations is $Z = [Z_1 \quad Z_2]$. Obviously, Y_2 and Z_2 represent variables excluded from the equation to be estimated. The representation of the reduced form equation (8.41) in terms of matrices of observations is that implied by (8.9):

$$Y = Z\Pi' + V \tag{8.52}$$

where Y is $(n \times G)$, Z is $(n \times K)$, Π' is $(K \times G)$ and V is $(n \times G)$. To obtain an expression for Y_1, the matrix of current endogenous variables on the right of (8.51), we write

$$Y_1 = Z(\Pi')_1 + V_1, \tag{8.53}$$

where $(\Pi')_1$ contains the appropriate selection of $(G_i - 1)$ columns from Π', and V_1 is the corresponding selection of columns from V.

The properties of v_t, and hence those of V and V_1, follow from the disturbance assumptions in (8.40):

$$v_t = A^{-1}u_t, \text{ where } u_t \sim IID(0, \Sigma)$$

$$\Rightarrow v_t \sim IID[0, A^{-1}\Sigma(A^{-1})']. \tag{8.54}$$

The relationship between v_t' and u_t' is $v_t' = u_t'(A^{-1})'$, which implies that $V = U(A^{-1})'$, where U is an $(n \times G)$ matrix, with typical row u_t'. Hence $V_1 = U[(A^{-1})']_1$, where $[(A^{-1})']_1$ is the appropriate selection of $G_i - 1$ columns from $(A^{-1})'$.

Ordinary least squares

Now consider the application of OLS to (8.50) or, equivalently, to (8.51). Given that all necessary probability limits exist, the behaviour of the OLS estimator follows from showing that

$$\text{plim}(n^{-1}X'X) = Q_{XX}, \text{ nonsingular} \tag{8.55}$$

whilst

$$\text{plim}(n^{-1}X'u) = q \neq 0. \tag{8.56}$$

The OLS estimator is

$$b = (X'X)^{-1}X'y = \beta + (X'X)^{-1}X'u$$

and

$$\text{plim}(b) = \beta + [\text{plim}(n^{-1}X'X)]^{-1}\text{plim}(n^{-1}X'u)$$

$$= \beta + Q_{XX}^{-1}q \neq \beta. \tag{8.57}$$

Equation (8.57) states that b is an inconsistent estimator for β, at least under the conditions assumed here.

The argument presented above falls well short of a formal proof; results concerning the observation matrix X should be derived from information about the constituent submatrices Y_1 and Z_1, and there is also the technical question as to whether the various probability limits do actually exist. Having outlined the basic reason for the inconsistency of the OLS estimator in a simultaneous equation model, we now examine the details of the argument.

Assuming first that there is no problem with the existence of probability limits, consider the interpretation of what has been said so far. Equation (8.56) suggests that some elements of X are correlated in the limit with corresponding elements of u. In scalar form, we have

$$\text{plim}\left(n^{-1} \sum X_{jt} u_t\right) \neq 0; \text{ for at least one } j; \, j = 1, \ldots, k. \tag{8.58}$$

As we shall see, the reason for this result is that the matrix X contains both predetermined and current endogenous variables.

For a predetermined variable, Z_h, there is no correlation between Z_{ht} and u_t, so it should certainly follow that there is zero correlation in the limit between Z_{ht} and u_t. Hence, for predetermined variables, we assume that

$$\text{plim}\left(n^{-1} \sum Z_{ht} u_t\right) = 0; \, h = 1, \ldots, K$$

or

$$\text{plim}(n^{-1} Z' u) = 0. \tag{8.59}$$

For current endogenous variables on the right of (8.51), the situation is different. From equation (8.53) we have

$$Y_1 = Z(\Pi')_1 + V_1$$

and

$$\text{plim}(n^{-1} Y_1' u) = \text{plim}\{n^{-1}[Z(\Pi')_1 + V_1]' u\}$$
$$= [(\Pi')_1]' \text{plim}(n^{-1} Z' u) + \text{plim}(n^{-1} V_1' u).$$

Since $\text{plim}(n^{-1} Z' u) = 0$, it follows that

$$\text{plim}(n^{-1} Y_1' u) = \text{plim}(n^{-1} V_1' u). \tag{8.60}$$

Equation (8.60) is concerned with a set of sample moments derived from the IID random vector u_t'. Such moments can be shown by Khintchine's theorem (see section 4.2) to converge in probability to the corresponding population moments. Here, the population moments in question are the covariances between the disturbance to the one structural equation of interest and the reduced form disturbances corresponding to right-hand-side endogenous variables. Since these covariances are clearly important, we look a little more closely at exactly what they represent.

For future reference, we denote $\text{plim}(n^{-1} V_1' u)$ by the parameter δ. This is a subvector drawn from one column of the matrix $A^{-1}\Sigma$; the selection of one column corresponds to focusing on the disturbance to one particular structural equation, and the selection of elements from this column focuses on those endogenous variables that appear on the right of the single structural equation (8.51). What we have shown is that if $\delta \neq 0$, then $\text{plim}(n^{-1}Y_1'u)$ is nonzero, $\text{plim}(n^{-1}X'u)$ is nonzero, and the OLS estimator β is inconsistent. If δ is zero, there is zero correlation in the limit between corresponding elements of Y_1 and u, which suggests that, at least in a limiting sense, the variables in Y_1 are predetermined. If this happens, there is clearly something unusual about the structure of the model, but in this case, OLS would actually be consistent.

Before leaving this argument, we should note that it was also assumed in (8.55) that $\text{plim}(n^{-1}X'X)$ exists, and is nonsingular. This can usually be shown to follow as a consequence of the more fundamental assumption that the moment matrix for predetermined variables converges, that is

$$\text{plim}(n^{-1}Z'Z) = Q_{ZZ}, \text{ nonsingular.} \tag{8.61}$$

However, for certain types of data, assumption (8.61) may prove untenable. There are then two possibilities. Convergence in probability may still be established if a different scaling is used, and might lead to the same answer as before. Alternatively, there may be some conditions under which the OLS estimator is not inconsistent, because convergence in probability operates in such a way as to lead to a different result. The obvious case in which (8.61) will not hold is where exogenous variables are represented by stochastic processes which do not satisfy stationarity conditions.

A further point is that, even if OLS is inconsistent, the extent of the inconsistency may not be large. But both this and the other qualifications made above are second-round arguments. What we have shown is that, under standard assumptions, the OLS estimator is generally inconsistent in a simultaneous model.

A simple example

To complement the rather technical arguments used above, consider a simple example, first introduced in section 4.7. This concerns the textbook model in which aggregate consumers' expenditure (C) is a function of disposable income (D), and disposable income is the sum of consumers' expenditure and a single exogenous variable (Z), which represents nonconsumption expenditure less taxes on income. For convenience, assume that Z has nonrandom observations. Finally, make the rather implausible assumption that this simple model will have well-behaved disturbances. In linear form, we have

$$C_t = \alpha + \beta D_t + u_t; \ u_t \sim IID(0, \sigma^2)$$
$$D_t = C_t + Z_t; \ t = 1, \dots, n. \tag{8.62}$$

Now consider the effect of a positive disturbance shock in (8.62). In the absence of the second equation, D_t could be treated as a fixed quantity, and a positive disturbance shock would increase only C_t, for a given value of D_t. As it is, the presence of the second equation leads to the reduced form

$$C_t = \alpha/(1 - \beta) + [\beta/(1 - \beta)]Z_t + u_t/(1 - \beta)$$

$$D_t = \alpha/(1 - \beta) + [1/(1 - \beta)]Z_t + u_t/(1 - \beta); \quad t = 1, \ldots, n. \tag{8.63}$$

These equations show that a positive disturbance shock now increases both C_t and D_t. Consequently, there is a tendency for positive disturbances to be associated with *relatively* higher values of D_t, and for negative disturbances to be associated with *relatively* lower values of D_t, and this has the effect of rotating the OLS regression line anticlockwise, thus overestimating the 'true' slope parameter. This corresponds to a positive inconsistency, which is exactly what emerges from applying probability limit arguments to (8.62).

Instrumental variable estimation

The problems inherent in OLS estimation of a single equation from a simultaneous model could well have been anticipated, in the light of the discussion in section 4.7, and this earlier discussion also provides an obvious solution, at least in the limited information context. To achieve consistency, we should employ an instrumental variable (IV) estimator. To do this, we require a set of instruments that are not correlated in the limit with the disturbances to (8.50). Such a set of instruments is readily available; if we assume that all the variables in Z satisfy the formal condition for predeterminedness, then subject only to the existence of the appropriate probability limits, we have

$$\mathrm{plim}(n^{-1}Z'u) = 0. \tag{8.64}$$

Consequently, we may apply the instrumental variable estimator, written in equation (4.54) as

$$\tilde{b} = (\hat{X}'\hat{X})^{-1}\hat{X}'y \tag{8.65}$$

or in (4.55) as

$$\tilde{b} = [X'W(W'W)^{-1}W'X]^{-1}X'W(W'W)^{-1}W'y, \tag{8.66}$$

where W is an $(n \times p)$ matrix of instruments or conditioning variables, and $\hat{X}$ is the $(n \times k)$ matrix of instrumental variables or predicted values, generated as

$$\hat{X} = P_W X = W(W'W)^{-1}W'X. \tag{8.67}$$

Since the variables in Z qualify as instruments, equations (8.65) through (8.67) may be rewritten with $W = Z$. This particular choice of instruments corresponds to two-stage least squares (2SLS). In fact, as we explained in Chapter 4, all IV estimators can be generated by a two-stage regression process, but the name 2SLS is historically reserved for the case in which the set of instruments consists of all the predetermined variables in a linear simultaneous model.

In this case, the predicted values are

$$\hat{X} = Z(Z'Z)^{-1}Z'[Y_1 \quad Z_1]$$

$$= [Z(\hat{\Pi}')_1 \quad Z_1] \tag{8.68}$$

showing that the OLS estimator $\hat{\Pi}'$ of the reduced form system (8.52) is being used.

A necessary condition for the application of the IV method is that the number of instruments (p) must be at least as great as k, the number of regressors in the equation to be estimated. In the context of 2SLS estimation of a single equation from a simultaneous equation model, the condition is

$$p = K \geq k = (G_i - 1) + K_i$$
$$\Rightarrow K - K_i \geq G_i - 1. \tag{8.69}$$

This was shown in (8.47) to be the necessary condition for identification, when only exclusion restrictions are used. If this condition is not satisfied, the 2SLS estimation procedure will fail, with symptoms equivalent to perfect multicollinearity in the second stage.

The distribution theory for 2SLS also follows from the analysis of section 4.7. In addition to (8.64), we require that

$$\text{plim}(n^{-1}Z'X) = Q_{ZX}, \text{ where rank}(Q_{ZX}) = k \tag{8.70}$$

and

$$\text{plim}(n^{-1}Z'Z) = Q_{ZZ}, \text{ nonsingular.} \tag{8.71}$$

Given these conditions, and convergence in distribution of $n^{-1/2}Z'u$ to a random vector η, distributed as $N(0, \sigma^2 Q_{ZZ})$, we have

$\tilde{b}$ is approximately $N[\beta, \sigma^2 n^{-1}(Q'_{ZX}Q_{ZZ}^{-1}Q_{ZX})^{-1}]$

or

$\tilde{b}$ is approximately $N[\beta, \sigma^2(\hat{X}'\hat{X})^{-1}]$, for large n. $\tag{8.72}$

To make (8.72) operational, σ^2 is replaced by the consistent estimator

$$\tilde{\sigma}^2 = \sum \tilde{e}_t^2/(n-k) \quad \left[\text{or } \sum \tilde{e}_t^2/n\right] \tag{8.73}$$

where $\tilde{e}_t$; $t = 1, \ldots, n$ are IV residuals, elements of the vector $\tilde{e} = y - X\tilde{b}$.

Given the large sample theory above, one can conduct tests of hypotheses concerning single parameters, or tests of exact linear restrictions, using the methods outlined in section 4.7. In this context, note that one should not attempt to test restrictions that are needed to achieve exact identification. Remember also that some care is needed when obtaining 'easily computed' versions of the relevant test statistics.

Apart from the fact that one can test sets of linear restrictions, using a modified version of the approach used in the least squares case, one can also employ the Hausman–Wu exogeneity test, to check on the assumed classification of variables, and the Sargan test, to check on the validity of the instruments used. Again, details are given in section 4.7. In the context of a linear simultaneous equation model, the Sargan test is equivalent to a test of restrictions over and above those needed to achieve exact identification.

Other limited information methods

Two-stage least squares is not the only consistent limited information method available, since one can vary the list of instruments without necessarily destroying the conditions needed for consistency. The instrument matrix W should certainly contain Z_1, the predetermined variables actually appearing in the equation to be estimated, but it need not contain every variable in Z_2. So long as there are sufficient additional variables to satisfy the condition $p \geq k$, omitting some columns of Z_2 from W does not destroy consistency, though it does alter the asymptotic variance matrix, and will generally lead to a loss of asymptotic efficiency.

It is also possible to generate limited information estimators by applying a different principle of estimation. The limited information maximum likelihood (LIML) estimator is obtained by maximising the likelihood function derived from a system consisting of one structural equation and the reduced form equations for the remaining endogenous variables. In contrast, the full information maximum likelihood estimator, which we discuss briefly in the next section, is based on a full specification of all structural equations in the model.

The asymptotic distribution of the LIML estimator is equivalent to that of the 2SLS estimator, and since 2SLS is more easily obtained in practice, the LIML estimator is not widely used, though it is of some interest in econometric theory, and is discussed a little more in section 8.7.

Example 8.2

Few investigators would now consider constructing even a small model which is entirely linear in endogenous variables, but there are historical examples, which have been widely used in the past to conduct experiments in the estimation and use of simultaneous models. In the example given below, we use Klein's model 1, an annual model for the US economy in the interwar years. The data are found in data set 13. The model consists of three behavioural equations, namely a consumption function, an investment function and a labour demand function, together with four identities. The equations of the model are

$$C_t = \alpha_1 + \alpha_2 P_t + \alpha_3 P_{t-1} + \alpha_4(W_t + W_t') + u_{1t}$$

$$I_t = \beta_1 + \beta_2 P_t + \beta_3 P_{t-1} + \beta_4 K_{t-1} + u_{2t}$$

$$W_t = \gamma_1 + \gamma_2 X_t + \gamma_3 X_{t-1} + \gamma_4 t + u_{3t}$$

$$Y_t + T_t = C_t + I_t + G_t$$

$$I_t = K_t - K_{t-1}$$

$$Y_t = W_t + W_t' + P_t$$

$$X_t = Y_t + T_t - W_t'; \quad t = 1, \ldots, n, \tag{8.74}$$

where C is consumers' expenditure (CONSUM), P is profit (PROFIT), W is the private wage bill (WAGEPR), W' is the government wage bill (WAGEGOV), K is the end period capital stock (CAPITAL), X is total private product (PRODUCT), I is net investment (INVEST), t is a time trend (TREND, measured as $1921 = 1$, etc.), G is government expenditure (GOVEXP), T is taxes (TAXES) and Y is income net of taxes. Y is not given a computer name, as it is not explicitly used in estimating the parameters of the model.

The variables C_t, I_t, W_t, Y_t, K_t, P_t and X_t are endogenous, whilst K_{t-1}, t, T_t, G_t, W'_t, P_{t-1}, X_{t-1} and 1, the intercept variable, are predetermined. The data needed for estimation are given as data set 13: since K_t is not needed directly, it is listed only in lagged form, under the heading CAPITAL(-1). To create lagged values of P and X, an additional observation is given for these variables.

The identification of each equation can be checked by any of the methods outlined in section 8.6. The simplest way to handle the implicit restriction on the coefficients of W and W' in the consumption function is to define an additional endogenous variable $(W + W')$, with computer name WAGETOT, together with an extra identity

$$(W_t + W'_t) = W_t + W'_t; \quad t = 1, \ldots, n. \tag{8.75}$$

Corresponding to this identity, we create the transformed variable WAGETOT = WAGEPR + WAGEGOV. There are then eight equations, eight current endogenous variables $(G = 8)$ and eight predetermined variables $(K = 8)$. The simplest way to check the order condition is to compare the number of regressors in each behavioural equation $(k = 4)$ with the number of instruments that would be used in 2SLS estimation $(p = K = 8)$. Since the order condition is easily satisfied, it would be rather surprising if the rank condition were not, and by checking the rank condition directly, or by looking for admissible linear combinations, we confirm that all three behavioural equations are overidentified, provided that all a priori restrictions are actually valid.

To obtain 2SLS estimates of the parameters of the three behavioural equations, the three current endogenous variables which appear on the right-hand side, P_t, $(W_t + W'_t)$ and X_t, are regressed on the eight predetermined variables which act as instruments, and predicted values (instrumental variables) are obtained. These are then used to replace the right-hand-side current endogenous variable observations in the second stage. Most computer packages automate the two stages to give the 2SLS (IV) estimates shown in Table 8.7.

In Table 8.7, the standard errors and t values are based on large sample approximations, and should be treated with some caution, since the sample size is only 21. Regressors that have been replaced by instrumental variables (predicted values) are indicated with the letters IV on the right of the printout. The definition used for R^2 is identical to that for OLS estimation, namely, $R^2 = 1 - RSS/TSS$. When this is applied to IV estimates, it is not based on a valid partition of sums of squares, and it is possible to find negative R^2 values when the degree of explanation achieved is very low.

The label 'IV objective function' gives a value equal to

$$S_{IV}(\tilde{b}) = \tilde{e}' P_W \tilde{e} = (y - X\tilde{b})' P_W (y - X\tilde{b}) \tag{8.76}$$

Table 8.7 2SLS estimation of Klein model 1

Sample based on observations 1921–41
Instrumental variable (2SLS) estimation

Dependent variable is CONSUM

Variable	Coefficient	Standard error	t value
INTER	16.55453	1.46787	11.2779
PROFIT	0.01735	0.13117	0.1323 IV
PROFIT(−1)	0.21619	0.11920	1.8137
WAGETOT	0.81018	0.04473	18.1117 IV

Degrees of freedom 17 from 21 observations

Residual SS	21.92281
Disturbance variance	1.28958
IV objective function	9.15826
Total SS	941.4295
R^2	0.9767
Sargan test	7.1018

Dependent variable is INVEST

Variable	Coefficient	Standard error	t value
INTER	20.30276	8.39466	2.4185
PROFIT	0.14975	0.19271	0.7771 IV
PROFIT(−1)	0.61613	0.18105	3.4031
CAPITAL(−1)	−0.15789	0.04020	−3.9273

Degrees of freedom 17 from 21 observations

Residual SS	29.06902
Disturbance variance	1.70994
IV objective function	2.52718
Total SS	252.3267
R^2	0.8848
Sargan test	1.4779

Dependent variable is WAGEPR

Variable	Coefficient	Standard error	t value
INTER	0.06592	1.15331	0.0572
PRODUCT	0.43887	0.03960	11.0837 IV
PRODUCT(−1)	0.14667	0.04316	3.3983
TREND	0.13039	0.03239	4.0260

Degrees of freedom 17 from 21 observations

Residual SS	10.00496
Disturbance variance	0.58853
IV objective function	5.95182
Total SS	794.9095
R^2	0.9874
Sargan test	10.1131

Table 8.8 Test regression results for Klein model 1

Equation	IV objective function	Residual variance	LM(IV)	LM(IV-F)
CONSUM	8.099 81	1.563 98	0.8208	0.6768
INVEST	0.278 45	2.767 15	1.3151	0.8126
WAGEPR	5.853 79	0.663 74	0.1666	0.1477

where $\tilde{e}$ is the vector of 2SLS residuals. As explained in section 4.7, this value can be used for a number of different hypothesis tests in the context of IV estimation. One example is the Sargan validity of instruments test, labelled simply as the Sargan test in Table 8.7 above, and defined in equation (4.70) as

$$\chi^2(V) = S_{IV}(\tilde{b})/\tilde{\sigma}^2 = \tilde{e}'P_W\tilde{e}/\tilde{\sigma}^2. \tag{8.77}$$

In the context of a fully defined model, this can be interpreted as a test of exclusion restrictions, over and above those needed for exact identification. This test involves $p - k$ degrees of freedom, where p is the number of instruments and k the number of regressors in a given equation. In each behavioural equation shown above, $p - k = 4$ and the 5% critical value for a χ^2 distribution with 4 degrees of freedom is 9.49. So the null hypothesis of valid instruments is not rejected for the first two equations, but it is rejected for the private wage equation.

Using the arguments leading up to (7.44), it is easy to construct an LM test for first-order serial correlation within each of the three behavioural equations. For each behavioural equation, regress the 2SLS or IV residuals on the explanatory variables of that equation together with the first lag of the residuals by instrumental variables, using the original set of instruments. As before, the initial values of the lagged residuals are set to zero. The simplest form of LM test is the $LM(IV\text{-}F)$ form, since this can be calculated, for first-order serial correlation, as the square of the t value attached to the lagged residual. Table 8.8 gives the IV objective functions and the residual variance estimates for the test regressions, and the values of the $LM(IV)$ and $LM(IV\text{-}F)$ test statistics. The critical values for the test statistics come from the χ_1^2 distribution whose 5% point is 3.84, and it is clear from the table that there is no evidence of first-order serial correlation in the Klein model 1.

8.8 / Estimation: complete system methods

In theory, limited information methods are not fully efficient, because they ignore the possibility that information concerning the structure of one equation in a system could be used to improve the efficiency of estimation of other equations in the system. As explained in section 8.4, this possibility exists in a multiple equation model that exhibits contemporaneous correlation of the disturbances. If

$$\text{cov}(u_{it}, u_{jt}) = \sigma_{ij} \neq 0, \text{ for at least one } i \neq j; \; i, j = 1, \ldots, G,$$

then there is a path of association between equations, quite apart from any such link established by observable variables. This gives the potential for efficiency gains to be realised if all equations are estimated together, using what may be called a complete system, or *full information* method of estimation.

An obvious requirement for a complete system method is that all equations must be fully specified. As usual, we proceed on the assumption that the specification is correct. Clearly, this assumption is much more demanding than the usual requirements for a single equation.

The economist's specification of a multiple equation model naturally leads to the form (8.38) in which the parameter matrices A and Γ contain various kinds of restrictions: this is clear in the example of the Klein model 1. These restrictions are then utilised in establishing the identification of the equations of the system. However, it is the reduced form (8.41) which generates the statistical properties of the system, in particular, the transformation from the distribution of the error vectors v_t, $t = 1, \ldots, n$, to the distribution of the observables y_t, $t = 1, \ldots, n$.

More specifically, if

$$v_t \sim NID(0, \Omega); \ t = 1, \ldots, n$$

then

$$y_t \sim NID(\Pi z_t, \Omega); \ t = 1, \ldots, n.$$

This suggests that the parameters to be estimated via a log likelihood function are the reduced form parameters, Π and Ω. Yet, it is clear that it is the structural form parameters that we wish to estimate. What is the connection between the structural form and reduced form parameters? It is exactly the relationship (8.44), here written as

$$\Pi A + \Gamma = 0. \tag{8.78}$$

Identification is, in one sense, designed to ensure that associated with every estimator of Π there is a unique estimator of A and Γ, satisfying the restrictions imposed a priori on A and Γ. This reasoning can be emphasised by collecting the unrestricted elements of A and Γ into a vector θ, and writing Π as a function of θ, $\Pi(\theta)$. When these elements of A and Γ are identified, it is possible to solve the equation

$$\Pi = \Pi(\theta) \tag{8.79}$$

uniquely for θ. The estimation problem is then how to estimate θ via estimation of Π.

Maximum likelihood estimation of the system requires the maximisation of a log likelihood function similar to (8.19) or (8.20), but modified to reflect the current notation of G equations,

$$\ln L = -\frac{nG}{2} \ln 2\pi - \frac{n}{2} \log \det(\Omega) - \frac{1}{2} \sum_{t=1}^{n} (y_t - \Pi z_t)' \Omega^{-1} (y_t - \Pi z_t), \tag{8.80}$$

subject to the constraints on Π embedded in (8.78). How many constraints are there? If we assume that the model contains only normalisation rules and exclusion restrictions, the order condition for identification (8.47) shows that there are $G_i - 1 + K_i$

parameters to estimate in each equation, and that the total number of reduced form parameters to be estimated is no more than GK, the number of elements of Π. There are thus

$$GK - \sum_{i=1}^{G}(G_i - 1 + K_i) \tag{8.81}$$

restrictions to be imposed on Π in estimation. Another way of viewing maximum likelihood estimation is to say that in (8.80), Π is actually $\Pi(\theta)$, and $\ln L$ has to be maximised with respect to θ and Ω. This view does not involve the idea of constrained maximisation, since maximisation takes place directly with respect to the $\sum_{i=1}^{G}(G_i - 1 + K_i)$ unrestricted parameters in θ.

Either way, the maximum likelihood estimation problem is a nonlinear estimation problem. Nonlinear estimation requires an iterative procedure, and it is for this reason that the 'full information maximum likelihood' (FIML) method cannot be fully described here. Fortunately, there is a simple estimator that is, under certain conditions, as asymptotically efficient as FIML, and this is described in the next subsection.

Setting out the log likelihood function in this way enables the LIML estimator to be put into context. Here, the $G - 1$ equations in reduced form contain unrestricted parameters, so that the only restrictions connecting the structural form parameters in A and Γ and the reduced form parameters in Π are the ones from the single overidentified equation under consideration. Since information is being discarded in constructing the LIML estimator, there is no reason for LIML and FIML to coincide unless the system has the peculiar structure assumed by LIML. This explains the efficiency loss incurred in the use of a limited information estimator in comparison with FIML.

Three-stage least squares

To write a complete model in a notation suitable for discussing estimation, we first delete all identities, and then suppose that the model consists of G linear equations, written as

$$y_i = X_i\beta_i + u_i; \ E(u_i) = 0; \ \text{var}(u_i) = \sigma_i^2 I_n; \quad \text{cov}(u_i, u_j) = \sigma_{ij} I_n; \ i, j = 1, \ldots, G. \tag{8.82}$$

In (8.82), y_i is the $(n \times 1)$ vector of observations on the endogenous variable that we choose to write on the left of equation i, X_i is the $(n \times k_i)$ matrix of regressors for equation i, which will contain both current endogenous and predetermined variables, β_i is the $(k_i \times 1)$ vector of parameters for equation i and u_i is the $(n \times 1)$ disturbance vector for equation i. The disturbance specification is still based on that shown in equation (8.40), which rules out serial correlation of any kind, but assumes that the disturbances to a simultaneous model will generally exhibit contemporaneous correlation.

As in section 8.3, the collection of G equations in (8.82) can be written in a 'stacked' form as

$$
\begin{bmatrix} y_1 \\ y_2 \\ \vdots \\ y_G \end{bmatrix} = \begin{bmatrix} X_1 & 0 & \cdots & 0 \\ 0 & X_2 & & 0 \\ \vdots & & \ddots & \\ 0 & 0 & & X_G \end{bmatrix} \begin{bmatrix} \beta_1 \\ \beta_2 \\ \vdots \\ \beta_G \end{bmatrix} + \begin{bmatrix} u_1 \\ u_2 \\ \vdots \\ u_G \end{bmatrix}
\tag{8.83}
$$

and directly identifying the vectors and matrices,

$$
\bar{y} = \bar{X}\bar{\beta} + \bar{u}.
\tag{8.84}
$$

Comparing the model (8.82) with (8.22), the covariance matrix of $\bar{u}$ is

$$
\mathrm{var}(\bar{u}) = \Sigma \otimes I_n
$$

so that a GLS estimator of $\bar{\beta}$ would be like (8.25):

$$
\bar{b}_G = [\bar{X}'(\Sigma^{-1} \otimes I_n)\bar{X}]^{-1}\bar{X}'(\Sigma^{-1} \otimes I_n)\bar{y}.
$$

However, this is an analogue of the OLS estimator discussed in the previous section, and would thus be inconsistent. A modification to correct for the presence of current endogenous variables is needed, as also a modification to create a feasible GLS estimator: the resulting estimator is the three-stage least squares estimator (3SLS).

To initiate three-stage least squares estimation, we start by applying 2SLS to each equation in (8.82). This generates predicted values

$$
\hat{X}_i = P_Z X_i = Z(Z'Z)^{-1}Z'X_i
\tag{8.85}
$$

and two-stage least squares residuals

$$
\tilde{e}_i = y_i - X\tilde{b}_i.
\tag{8.86}
$$

We can then use the predicted values $\hat{X}_i$ defined in (8.85) to replace the X_i on the right of (8.83). Remember that, in practice, this only changes current endogenous variables; premultiplication by P_Z has no effect on variables which appear in both X_i and Z. The unknown elements of Σ are replaced by estimates obtained from 2SLS residuals.

The disturbance variance estimates from 2SLS estimation of one particular equation were written earlier as

$$
\tilde{\sigma}^2 = \sum \tilde{e}_t^2/(n-k).
$$

It is convenient here to write the whole set of estimated variances and covariances as

$$
\tilde{\sigma}_{ij} = \sum \tilde{e}_{it}\tilde{e}_{jt}/n; \; i,j = 1, \ldots, G.
\tag{8.87}
$$

This suggests that we should now write the estimated version of Σ as $\tilde{\Sigma}$. Division by n avoids any difficulty caused by the fact that different equations may not have the same number of variables on the right-hand side. Since what we require are consistent estimators for the elements of Σ, it is not really necessary to make an adjustment for degrees of freedom.

It would be rather clumsy to apply the 'hat' symbol to $\bar{X}$, so we now use Kronecker product notation to show how $\bar{X}$ is transformed when individual regressor matrices, X_i, are replaced by predicted values $\hat{X}_i$. The operation can be represented as

$$
\begin{bmatrix} P_Z & 0 & \cdots & 0 \\ \vdots & P_Z & & \vdots \\ \vdots & & \ddots & 0 \\ 0 & \cdots & \cdots & P_Z \end{bmatrix}
\begin{bmatrix} X_1 & 0 & \cdots & 0 \\ \vdots & X_2 & & \vdots \\ \vdots & & \ddots & 0 \\ 0 & \cdots & \cdots & X_G \end{bmatrix}
=
\begin{bmatrix} \hat{X}_1 & 0 & \cdots & 0 \\ \vdots & \hat{X}_2 & & \vdots \\ \vdots & & \ddots & 0 \\ 0 & \cdots & \cdots & \hat{X}_G \end{bmatrix}
$$

or as $(I \otimes P_Z)\bar{X}$ where, as before, $P_Z = Z(Z'Z)^{-1}Z'$. Using this device, the three-stage least squares estimator can be written as

$$\tilde{b}_G = [\bar{X}'(I \otimes P_Z)'(\tilde{\Sigma} \otimes I)^{-1}(I \otimes P_Z)\bar{X}]^{-1}X'(I \otimes P_Z)'(\tilde{\Sigma} \otimes I)^{-1}\bar{y} \tag{8.88}$$

where $\tilde{b}_G$ is used in place of $\bar{b}_G$ to signify the IV component of 3SLS estimation.

One can see from (8.68) that all the columns of the OLS estimator $\hat{\Pi}'$ are being used in this estimator. In contrast to the FIML estimator, which generates an estimator of Π, A and Γ simultaneously, the 3SLS estimator is generating estimates of the unrestricted elements of A and Γ from a given initial estimator of Π.

There are actually several different forms for the 3SLS estimator; a more concise expression is obtained by applying the rules for manipulating Kronecker products, to give

$$\tilde{b}_G = [\bar{X}'(\tilde{\Sigma}^{-1} \otimes P_Z)\bar{X}]^{-1}\bar{X}'(\tilde{\Sigma}^{-1} \otimes P_Z)\bar{y}. \tag{8.89}$$

Although the details are omitted here, it should come as no surprise to find that under 'standard' assumptions, the 3SLS estimator is consistent and asymptotically normal, with a large sample approximation to $\text{var}(\tilde{b}_G)$ given by the expression

$$\text{var}(\tilde{b}_G) = [\bar{X}'(\tilde{\Sigma}^{-1} \otimes P_Z)\bar{X}]^{-1}. \tag{8.90}$$

However, this result is conditional on the assumption that the model is correctly specified; as mentioned earlier, this is much more demanding than the usual 'correctness' condition for a single equation.

The steps in obtaining the 3SLS estimator can be summarised as follows:

1. Use the reduced form equations to generate predicted values for all right-hand-side current endogenous variables, as in the first stage of 2SLS.

2. Apply 2SLS to each structural equation in turn, to obtain 2SLS residuals. Use these residuals to estimate the elements of the contemporaneous covariance matrix Σ.

3. Apply feasible GLS to the entire system, with right-hand-side current endogenous variable observations replaced by predicted values, and with elements of the unknown matrix Σ replaced by estimates obtained in stage (2).

Under certain circumstances, the 3SLS procedure can be simplified. If Σ is block diagonal, having a structure such as

$$\Sigma = \begin{bmatrix} \Sigma_{11} & 0 \\ 0 & \Sigma_{22} \end{bmatrix},$$

where Σ_{11} and Σ_{22} are square submatrices, then 3SLS can be applied separately to the corresponding subsets of equations. If Σ is completely diagonal, 3SLS is equivalent to 2SLS applied to each equation in turn. If Σ is neither diagonal nor block diagonal, it is still possible to simplify if some equations are just identified. The procedure is to apply 3SLS to the block of overidentified equations, and then to obtain estimates of just identified equations by applying a simple correction to 2SLS estimates of those equations (see, for example, Theil, 1971: 514). Finally, if all equations are just identified, 3SLS is again equivalent to 2SLS applied to each equation in turn.

An overview

A linear simultaneous equation model involves the parameter matrices A, Γ, Σ and Π. In order to achieve identification, exclusions and possibly other linear restrictions are imposed on A and Γ, and restrictions may also be imposed on Σ. The three-stage least squares procedure estimates Π at the first stage, when unrestricted reduced form regressions are used to generate predicted values for right-hand-side endogenous variables. The elements of Σ are estimated at the second stage, and final estimates of nonzero elements of A and Γ are obtained at the third stage.

As described here, the 3SLS procedure makes no attempt at reconciling estimates of the various parameter matrices. For a start, Π is related to A and Γ, and for any estimates $\hat{A}$, $\hat{\Gamma}$ which satisfy the prior restrictions, the derived estimate

$$\hat{\Pi} = \hat{A}^{-1}\hat{\Gamma}$$

is typically different from that obtained from unrestricted reduced form regressions. The 3SLS procedure does not iterate back to find a new estimate of Π, from which new predicted values (instrumental variables) could be generated. Nor does the procedure as stated above work back from estimates of nonzero elements of A and Γ to give a new estimate of Σ. This provides a simple way to explain the difference between 3SLS and FIML. The first-order conditions for FIML require iterative solution, and when these iterations converge, one will have completely reconciled estimates of A, Γ, Σ and Π.

To achieve the same reconciliation using the 3SLS approach, one would have to iterate on an inner loop of estimates for Σ, A and Γ, and then iterate again on an outer loop to obtain reconciled estimates of Σ, A, Γ and Π. If this is done, fully iterated 3SLS estimates are the same as FIML estimates, but this is not true if one only iterates between A, Γ and Σ. However, in most cases, the asymptotic distribution of even the noniterated 3SLS estimator is the same as that for the FIML estimator, so in terms of asymptotic efficiency, there is no reward for extra computational effort. As usual, one would expect there to be some advantage to FIML in terms of finite sample performance, though this conclusion depends crucially on having a correctly specified model.

In seeking to choose between 3SLS and FIML, it is easy to overlook a more important question, which is whether one should use any complete system approach. This question can be answered by making a distinction between two different types of exercise, namely, trying to estimate a complete system of equations derived formally from an underlying choice model, as is the case with a consumer demand or production system, and trying to estimate a model assembled from separate theoretical or empirical studies of the constituent parts, as is the case with most large-scale macroeconomic forecasting models.

In examples of the first kind, the theory leads to a very specific set of fully specified equations, and it makes sense to estimate and test in a systems context. In the latter case, there is often considerable uncertainty as to how the model should be formulated, and single equations are usually developed with rather limited information as to what the rest of the model will eventually look like. Apart from the impracticality of using a complete system method with a very large model, any theoretical gains in efficiency are likely to be offset by the effect of using what may turn out to be untenable assumptions concerning the structure of other equations.

8.9 / Further reading

In some ways, much of the material of this chapter is quite traditional, and thus will be found in some form in most econometric texts. Davidson and MacKinnon (1993), Greene (1993), Hamilton (1994) and Hendry (1995) all have useful discussions.

9

Dynamic systems

9.1 / Introduction

In this chapter, the single equation dynamic models of Chapter 7 are extended to the multivariate framework of Chapter 8. This extension yields multivariate or vector autoregressive models, which are dynamic versions of the multivariate regression model, and ultimately an explicitly dynamic version of the simultaneous equations model. The analysis of this chapter starts from the maintained assumption that all the variables in an economic system, apart from patently nonstochastic variables like the intercept, trends, and seasonal dummies, should be explicitly modelled by a dynamic process, specifically a vector autoregressive process. This contrasts with the simultaneous equations model, where the exogenous variables are explicitly not modelled.

The justification for this maintained assumption was originally given by Sims (1980). He argued that in simultaneous equations models many of the restrictions imposed on structural form parameters to obtain identification were 'incredible' relative to the data. His conclusion was that it would be better to use models which did not rely on the imposition of incorrect prior information. However, as we shall see at the end of the chapter, the wheel has now come full circle. In empirical applications of vector autoregressive processes, there are often variables which cannot be modelled effectively in this framework. In this situation, it is better to proceed conditionally on the values of these variables, if this is possible given the structure of the estimated vector autoregressive process.

Cointegration is the dominant topic in this chapter, reflecting its recent empirical importance. The resolution of the spurious regression problem through cointegration described in section 7.8 relied on the idea that explanatory variables in a regression may be generated by unit root AR(1) processes or, equivalently, a nonstationary vector autoregressive process. Going further, the presumption that all stochastic variables should be modelled by a vector autoregressive process, together with assertion that these variables are $I(1)$, then leads naturally into a discussion of cointegration between such variables.

The chapter is structured to tackle these issues. Section 9.2 discusses the conditions under which a vector autoregressive process is stationary, together with a brief discussion of estimation and inference for such processes. In section 9.3, a particular representation of the vector autoregressive process called the 'vector error correction' model is introduced, which has a number of similarities to the error correction model of section 6.6, equation (6.36). The central feature of this discussion is the 'Granger Representation Theorem', which draws out the implications of the existence of cointegrating relationships, as defined in section 7.8, between the variables generated by the model. The estimation of a vector error correction model by maximum likelihood is the subject of section 9.4. The details of this estimation procedure are undeniably complex, and this section is organised so that these details can be put aside initially. Some effort has to be made to examine the details, however, in order to understand properly the nature of Johansen's method (Johansen, 1991) for detecting the number of cointegrating relationships (if any) in a vector autoregressive model, which is discussed and illustrated in section 9.5. The method proposed for the estimation of a vector error correction model makes the structure of any cointegrating relationships completely data-determined, and these may not embody any known or presumed economic relationships. Recall from section 7.8 that cointegrating relationships are assumed to capture long-run relationships between the variables. It is possible to force the cointegrating relationships in a vector error correction model to satisfy prior restrictions which reflect presumed knowledge of the structure of these long-run relationships, and this is discussed in section 9.6. There are connections between the vector error correction model and the ADL model, as well as with the dynamic simultaneous equations model, and these are discussed in section 9.7, which concludes the chapter.

9.2 / The vector autoregressive process

In the previous chapter, multiple equation models were introduced as being collections of single equation models. This simple principle can be extended to dynamic models as well. Suppose that we are given two AR(1) processes,

$$y_{1t} = \pi_{11} y_{1t-1} + u_{1t}; \ u_{1t} \sim IID(0, \sigma_{11}); \ \text{all } t,$$

$$y_{2t} = \pi_{22} y_{2t-1} + u_{2t}; \ u_{2t} \sim IID(0, \sigma_{22}); \ \text{all } t.$$

Using the logic of section 8.2, these processes form the system

$$\begin{bmatrix} y_{1t} \\ y_{2t} \end{bmatrix} = \begin{bmatrix} \pi_{11} & 0 \\ 0 & \pi_{22} \end{bmatrix} \begin{bmatrix} y_{1t-1} \\ y_{2t-1} \end{bmatrix} + \begin{bmatrix} u_{1t} \\ u_{2t} \end{bmatrix}$$

or, analogously to (8.6),

$$y_t = \Pi_1 y_{t-1} + u_t; \ u_t \sim IID(0, \Sigma); \ \text{all } t. \tag{9.1}$$

However, the two AR(1) processes specify that there are restrictions on the matrix Π_1

which force it to be diagonal, and so (9.1) is really a version of the SUR model of section 8.4.

The generalisation of the univariate AR(1) process to multivariate regression model form would require the matrix Π_1 to be unrestricted, so that every element of the vector y_{t-1} appears in every equation of the model. In this case, a nondiagonal Π_1 would make (9.1) correspond to the models

$$y_{1t} = \pi_{11}y_{1t-1} + \pi_{12}y_{2t-1} + u_{1t}; \quad u_{1t} \sim IID(0, \sigma_{11}); \text{ all } t,$$

$$y_{2t} = \pi_{21}y_{1t-1} + \pi_{22}y_{2t-1} + u_{2t}; \quad u_{2t} \sim IID(0, \sigma_{22}); \text{ all } t,$$

in which lags of the other variable also influence the current value. Hidden in the form of (9.1) is the possibility that the two error terms are correlated, making $\sigma_{12} \neq 0$. In general, Π_1 and Σ in (9.1) will be taken to be nondiagonal unless there is strong prior information that the off-diagonal elements in one or other matrix are zero.

The model (9.1) is a (bivariate) *vector autoregressive* model of order 1, or VAR(1) process. From its form, it can be seen as the direct vector analogue of the AR(1) process (6.8), despite the absence of an intercept (vector) here. It is easy to introduce an intercept vector

$$\mu = \begin{bmatrix} \mu_1 \\ \mu_2 \end{bmatrix}$$

if required. It is not difficult to see that a (bivariate) vector analogue to the AR(p) process simply includes additional lags:

$$\begin{bmatrix} y_{1t} \\ y_{2t} \end{bmatrix} = \Pi_1 \begin{bmatrix} y_{1t-1} \\ y_{2t-1} \end{bmatrix} + \Pi_2 \begin{bmatrix} y_{1t-2} \\ y_{2t-2} \end{bmatrix} + \ldots + \Pi_p \begin{bmatrix} y_{1t-p} \\ y_{2t-p} \end{bmatrix} + \begin{bmatrix} u_{1t} \\ u_{2t} \end{bmatrix}.$$

In vector notation, this VAR(p) process is

$$y_t = \Pi_1 y_{t-1} + \ldots + \Pi_p y_{t-p} + u_t; \quad u_t \sim IID(0, \Sigma); \text{ all } t. \tag{9.2}$$

Just as in section 8.2, (9.1) and (9.2) can also be considered as the appropriate form for m-dimensional systems. In particular, (9.2) then carries the implication that in the equation for each $y_{it}, y_{1t-1}, \ldots, y_{1t-p}, \ldots, y_{mt-1}, \ldots, y_{mt-p}$ appear as 'explanatory variables'. This is the major difference between a univariate AR(p) process and a VAR(p) process.

Extensions

One can construct vector moving average (VMA) and vector autoregressive–moving average (VARMA) processes following the analogy by which the VAR(1) process (9.1) is constructed from a univariate AR(1) process. Here, the scalars Y_t, u_t and ϕ_1 of the AR(1) process are converted into the vectors y_t and u_t, and the matrix Π_1 of the vector autoregressive process. A VMA(1) process would then be, following (6.6),

$$y_t = u_t - \Theta_1 u_{t-1}; \quad u_t \sim IID(0, \Sigma); \text{ all } t,$$

in which Θ_1 is an $m \times m$ matrix. Introducing further lags of u_t and further parameter matrices Θ_j gives a VMA(q) process,

$$y_t = u_t - \Theta_1 u_{t-1} - \ldots - \Theta_q u_{t-q}; \ u_t \sim IID(0, \Sigma); \text{ all } t. \tag{9.3}$$

The tactic of treating the error term u_t in the VAR(p) process (9.2) as following a VMA(q) process, rather than being $IID(0, \Sigma)$, generates the vector analogue of the ARMA(p, q) process of section 6.4, the VARMA(p, q) process,

$$y_t = \Pi_1 y_{t-1} + \ldots + \Pi_p y_{t-p} + \varepsilon_t - \Theta_1 \varepsilon_{t-1} - \ldots - \Theta_q \varepsilon_{t-q};$$

$$\varepsilon_t \sim IID(0, \Sigma); \text{ all } t. \tag{9.4}$$

There is little use of these vector generalisations of MA and ARMA processes in the remainder of this chapter, although the VMA process does appear at one critical point in the next section.

It is convenient to mention here two further extensions of the VAR model, although these will not be discussed in detail until the end of the chapter. A univariate AR process augmented by the current and lagged values of nonstochastic explanatory variables becomes an ADL model. The same logic can be applied to a VAR(p) model, by extending (9.2) to include a vector of explanatory variables z_t and its lags:

$$y_t = N_0 z_t + N_1 z_{t-1} + \ldots + N_q z_{t-q} + \Pi_1 y_{t-1} + \ldots + \Pi_p y_{t-p} + u_t;$$

$$u_t \sim IID(0, \Sigma); \ t = 1, \ldots, n. \tag{9.5}$$

By collecting all of the vectors $z_t, z_{t-1}, \ldots, z_{t-q}, y_{t-1}, \ldots, y_{t-p}$, into a single large vector x_t, and all of the corresponding parameter matrices into a large matrix Π, (9.5) has the same form as (8.6) or (8.41), that is

$$y_t = \Pi x_t + u_t; \ u_t \sim IID(0, \Sigma); \ t = 1, \ldots, n. \tag{9.6}$$

The equation (8.41), which uses z_t rather than x_t, is the reduced form of the static simultaneous equations system (8.38): comparing this with (9.6) suggests a dynamic simultaneous equations system, in which both lags of y_t and z_t occur,

$$A_0 y_t = \Gamma_0 z_t + \Gamma_1 z_{t-1} + \ldots + \Gamma_q z_{t-q} + A_1 y_{t-1} + \ldots + A_p y_{t-p} + \varepsilon_t;$$

$$\varepsilon_t \sim IID(0, \Sigma); \ t = 1, \ldots, n. \tag{9.7}$$

The Klein model 1 of the previous chapter contained such dynamic elements, although these were restricted to lags of the endogenous variables in the system: there were no lags of the exogenous variables in that system. From this perspective, (9.5) is then the reduced form of (9.7), in which $u_t = A_0^{-1} \varepsilon_t$.

Despite these extensions, the philosophy behind the use of a VAR model admits no necessary association with a simultaneous equations model. That is, the VAR model is not considered to be the reduced form of an underlying dynamic simultaneous equations model. In most of the chapter, we shall follow this presumption, and only in the final section of the chapter will this issue be re-examined.

$$\phi(L) = 1 - \phi_1 L - \phi_2 L^2 - \cdots \phi_p L^r$$

The lag operator

The lag operator can be used with vectors, by applying it to each element of a vector; for example,

$$Ly_t = L\begin{bmatrix} y_{1t} \\ y_{2t} \end{bmatrix} = \begin{bmatrix} Ly_{1t} \\ Ly_{2t} \end{bmatrix} = \begin{bmatrix} y_{1t-1} \\ y_{2t-1} \end{bmatrix} = y_{t-1}.$$

The bivariate VAR(1) process (9.1) can then be expressed as

$$(I_2 - \Pi_1 L)y_t = u_t,$$

$$y_t = \Pi_1 y_{t-1} + u_t$$
$$\Downarrow$$
$$L y_t$$

or as

$$1 - \Pi_1 L - \Pi_2 L^2 \cdots \Pi_p L^p$$

$$\Pi(L)y_t = u_t,$$

where $\Pi(L)$ is now a *matrix* polynomial in the lag operator. It is easy to see how to generalise this to the VAR(p) m-dimensional case by defining

$$\Pi(L) = I_m - \Pi_1 L - \ldots - \Pi_p L^p. \tag{9.8}$$

There is an obvious definition for the matrix polynomial $\Theta(L)$ which allows the expression of the VMA model (9.3) as

$$y_t = \Theta(L)u_t$$

and the VARMA model (9.4) as

$$\Pi(L)y_t = \Theta(L)u_t.$$

The decomposition (6.19) for (univariate) polynomials in the lag operator can be used without change in this context, provided that in adapting the notation of (6.19) we remember that $\Pi(1)$ is an $m \times m$ matrix and $\Psi(L)$ an $m \times m$ matrix polynomial:

$$\Pi(L) = \Pi(1)L + (1 - L)\Psi(L). \tag{9.9}$$

For example, in the VAR(1) case,

$$\Pi(L) = I_m - \Pi_1 L,$$

$$\Pi(1) = I_m - \Pi_1,$$

and we can show quite easily that

$$\Psi(L) = I_m.$$

This gives

$$\Pi(L)y_t = (I_m - \Pi_1)y_{t-1} + (1 - L)y_t,$$

or, rearranging,

$$\Delta y_t = -\Pi(1)y_{t-1} + u_t.$$

For later work, we shall require the version of the decomposition suitable for a VAR(p) process,

$$\Pi(L) = \Pi(1)L^p + (1 - L)\Psi(L) \tag{9.10}$$

where $\Psi(L)$ is expected to be of the form

$$\Psi(L) = \Psi_0 + \Psi_1 L + \ldots + \Psi_{p-1}L^{p-1}.$$

The nature of the coefficient matrices in $\Psi(L)$ can be found as before, by expanding the right-hand side of (9.10) and equating the coefficients of like powers of L on each side of the equals sign.

Stationarity

To deduce the conditions under which a VAR(1) process with an intercept vector μ is stationary, it is best to start with the $m = 2$ case:

$$\begin{bmatrix} y_{1t} \\ y_{2t} \end{bmatrix} = \begin{bmatrix} \mu_1 \\ \mu_2 \end{bmatrix} + \begin{bmatrix} \pi_{11} & \pi_{12} \\ \pi_{21} & \pi_{22} \end{bmatrix} \begin{bmatrix} y_{1t-1} \\ y_{2t-1} \end{bmatrix} + \begin{bmatrix} u_{1t} \\ u_{2t} \end{bmatrix}; \text{ all } t. \tag{9.11}$$

Suppose that π_{12} and π_{21} are zero, and consider

$$\det(I_2 - \Pi_1 L).$$

The matrix polynomial is diagonal, so the determinant is easy to calculate as

$$\det(I_2 - \Pi_1 L) = (1 - \pi_{11}L)(1 - \pi_{22}L).$$

The components of the determinant are the underlying AR(1) polynomials for y_{1t} and y_{2t}, and the roots of these polynomials determine whether the process is stationary. In particular, these roots have to be outside the unit circle for stationarity. Here, then, by finding the roots of the determinental equation

$$\det(I_2 - \Pi_1 L) = 0$$

we find the roots for the univariate processes.

The same principle applies to the case where π_{12} and π_{21} are not necessarily zero: calculate the (two) roots of

$$\det(I_2 - \Pi_1 L) = 0.$$

If the roots are outside the unit circle, then this bivariate VAR(1) is stationary. These roots are actually the inverses of the eigenvalues of the matrix Π_1, and so the eigenvalues will be inside the unit circle if $\Pi(L) = (I_2 - \Pi_1 L)$ has roots outside the unit circle. Generalising, in the determinental equation

$$\det \Pi(L) = 0$$

corresponding to a bivariate VAR(2) process, $\det \Pi(L)$ has $4 = mp$ as the highest power of L, and each of the four roots must be outside the unit circle for stationarity.

In general, the VAR(p) process (9.2) is stationary if the mp roots of

$$\det \Pi(L) = 0$$

are all outside the unit circle, where $\Pi(L)$ is given by (9.8).

Given stationarity, we can attempt to find the mean, the covariance matrix and the autocovariance matrices generated from a VAR(1) process with intercept. Here,

$$Ey_t = \Pi_1 Ey_{t-1} + \mu + Eu_t,$$

and under stationarity,

$$Ey_t = Ey_{t-1},$$

which implies

$$Ey_t = (I_m - \Pi_1)^{-1}\mu$$
$$= [\Pi(1)]^{-1}\mu.$$

Can one be sure that $\Pi(1)$ is nonsingular? Suppose that $L = 1$ is a root of

$$\det(I_m - \Pi_1 L) = 0,$$

so that

$$\det(I_m - \Pi_1) = 0.$$

This implies that $(I_m - \Pi_1) = \Pi(1)$ is a singular matrix, and therefore has no inverse. The stationarity condition guarantees the nonsingularity of $\Pi(1)$, in the general case, and therefore in this example. We shall be returning to the issue of what happens when $\Pi(L)$ has a unit root: but, it is worthwile stressing that when $\Pi(L)$ has a unit root, $\Pi(1)$ will in general be a singular matrix.

As in the univariate case, y_{t-1} and u_t are independent of each other, given the assumptions about u_t, so that

$$\text{var}(y_t) = \Pi_1 \text{var}(y_{t-1})\Pi_1' + \text{var}(u_t).$$

Put $\text{var}(y_t) = V$. Then, to find $\text{var}(y_t)$, we have to solve the equation

$$V = \Pi_1 V\Pi_1' + \Sigma.$$

Although this equation looks difficult to solve, the use of Kronecker products and the arrangement of the elements of V into a long vector make solution possible. The autocovariances then follow in a natural way: for example,

$$\text{cov}(y_t, y_{t-1}) = \Pi_1 \text{var}(y_{t-1}) + \text{cov}(u_t, y_{t-1})$$
$$= \Pi_1 V.$$

It is worth noticing that

$$\text{cov}(y_{t-1}, y_t) = V'\Pi_1',$$

so that the two autocovariance matrices are not equal, but are transposes of each other.

Just as in the univariate case in section 6.4, it is often convenient to represent a VAR(p) process as an infinite order VMA process. The essential condition is that the VAR(p) process be stationary: let

$$[\Pi(L)]^{-1} = F(L) = \sum_{j=0}^{\infty} F_j L^j.$$

Then, the VMA(∞) representation of the VAR(p) process

$$\Pi(L)y_t = \mu + u_t; \; u_t \sim IID(0, \Sigma); \; \text{all } t$$

is

$$y_t = F(L)(\mu + u_t)$$

$$= [\Pi(1)]^{-1}\mu + \sum_{j=0}^{\infty} F_j u_{t-j},$$

provided that $\Pi(1)$ is nonsingular, which is guaranteed by the assumed stationarity.

Estimation and inference

The VAR(1) process is a natural analogue of the multivariate regression model of section 8.2. One would therefore expect that the estimation procedures for the latter model would carry over to the VAR case. It was shown in section 8.3 that in the multivariate regression model, the OLS estimator coincides with the maximum likelihood estimator: this model was characterised by the fact that all the explanatory variables in the system occurred in each equation of the system. In contrast, in the SUR model of section 8.4, the maximum likelihood estimator resembles a GLS estimator, except in special cases.

To see that the maximum likelihood estimator in a VAR process is the OLS estimator, the log likelihood function is required. For the VAR(1) process (9.1), this follows directly from the log likelihood function of the multivariate regression model (8.19) or (8.20). Assuming that a known vector of starting values, y_0, is available, the log likelihood function is then most naturally written as

$$\ln L = -\frac{nm}{2}\ln 2\pi - \frac{n}{2}\ln \det(\Sigma) - \frac{1}{2}\sum_{t=1}^{n}(y_t - \Pi_1 y_{t-1})'\Sigma^{-1}(y_t - \Pi_1 y_{t-1}). \qquad (9.12)$$

The form

$$\ln L = -\frac{nm}{2}\ln 2\pi - \frac{n}{2}\ln \det(\Sigma) - \frac{1}{2}\text{trace}[\Sigma^{-1}(Y - Y_1\Pi_1')'(Y - Y_1\Pi_1')], \qquad (9.13)$$

in which Y_1 is the $n \times m$ matrix of observations on y_{t-1}, reveals most clearly that the maximum likelihood estimator is the OLS estimator

$$\hat{\Pi}_1' = (Y_1'Y_1)^{-1}Y_1'Y \qquad (9.14)$$

in the model

$$Y = Y_1 \Pi_1' + U. \tag{9.15}$$

Again, the discussion of section 8.2 shows that this estimator can be constructed by fitting each equation of the VAR process separately. The estimator of Σ follows that obtained in (8.17) as

$$\hat{\Sigma} = \frac{(Y - Y_1 \hat{\Pi}_1')'(Y - Y_1 \hat{\Pi}_1')}{n}. \tag{9.16}$$

How many parameters are there to be estimated in a VAR(1) model? Since the parameter matrix Π_1 is $m \times m$, there are m^2 parameters. In a VAR(p) model, the number of parameters is pm^2; for example, with $p = 4$ and $m = 3$, this is 36. So, there are a lot of parameters to be estimated. Often, there are too many relative to the amount of information contained in the data set, and one strand of literature concerns sensible ways in which empirically acceptable restrictions can be imposed in order to reduce the number of free parameters (see Hamilton, 1994: 360–2).

The discussion of inference on parameters, goodness of fit and diagnostic tests in section 8.4 carries over directly to the VAR(p) model. Instead of using the large sample test statistic (8.29), the direct likelihood ratio test of (4.43) can be employed, given that maximum likelihood estimation is being used here. One hypothesis of considerable interest is testing the order of a VAR process. A natural procedure contains the following steps. Choose a maximum possible value for p, and then fit a VAR(p). Within the VAR(p) model, test that $\Pi_p = 0$. If the hypothesis is rejected, decide that p is the order of the process. If the hypothesis is accepted, conclude that the order of the VAR is less than or equal to $p - 1$, and proceed to fit a VAR($p - 1$), in which the hypothesis $\Pi_{p-1} = 0$ is to be tested. Continuing in this way, suppose that as a result of accepting in turn the hypotheses $\Pi_p = 0, \ldots, \Pi_{p-j+1} = 0$, the hypothesis $\Pi_{p-j} = 0$ is tested in a VAR($p - j$). If it is rejected, decide that the order of the VAR is $p - j$. This procedure of testing down the sequence of VAR models corresponds to imposing more and more restrictions on the VAR(p) process, since more and more of the matrices $\Pi_p, \Pi_{p-1}, \ldots, \Pi_1$ are being set to zero. In effect, this testing down procedure selects the order of the VAR as $p - j$, using the first j for which the hypothesis $\Pi_{p-j} = 0$ is rejected. Notice that this procedure is inherently systemwide, and needs system inference.

9.3 / Unit roots and cointegration in VAR models

As noted in the previous section, the m-dimensional VAR(p) process with intercept,

$$\Pi(L)y_t = \mu + u_t,$$

will be stationary if the roots of the determinental equation

$$\det \Pi(L) = 0$$

are outside the unit circle. We also saw that if $\Pi(1)$ is singular, then $L = 1$ will satisfy the determinental equation, and clearly the converse is also true. The root 1 lies *on* the unit circle, and therefore the VAR process is nonstationary. From section 6.7, one would expect y_t to be a vector of $I(1)$ variables, and Δy_t to be a vector of $I(0)$ variables. We also saw in section 7.8 that it is possible for linear combinations of $I(1)$ variables to be cointegrated, that is, $I(0)$.

All these ideas are linked through the *Granger Representation Theorem*, as stated by Johansen (1991). It is best to examine the issues in the VAR(1) model first, and then simply quote the extensions to the VAR(p) model. The VAR(1) model can be written as

$$(I_m - \Pi_1 L)y_t = \mu + u_t,$$

or, using the decomposition (9.9), as

$$\Delta y_t = -\Pi(1)y_{t-1} + \mu + u_t. \tag{9.17}$$

To start with, consider the implications of $\Pi(1)$ being nonsingular – that is, having rank m. Then,

$$\det \Pi(1) \neq 0,$$

and 1 cannot be a root of

$$\det \Pi(L) = 0,$$

so that the VAR(1) process is stationary and y_t is $I(0)$. Next, consider the implication of

$$\Pi(1) = 0,$$

which is equivalent to saying that $\Pi(1)$ has rank zero. In the VAR model above, this produces

$$\Delta y_t = \mu + u_t,$$

so that y_t follows a (vector) random walk with drift and is therefore $I(1)$.

Suppose next that rank $\Pi(1) = r < m$. Then, this is equivalent to saying that 1 is a repeated root of

$$\det \Pi(L) = 0,$$

the multiplicity being $m - r$. From Appendix A, there exist matrices H and J, $m \times r$, with full column rank, such that

$$\Pi(1) = HJ'. \tag{9.18}$$

These matrices play a very important role in what follows. The matrices H and J are not unique, for a given $\Pi(1)$, since

$$\Pi(1) = HF^{-1}FJ' = HJ' \tag{9.19}$$

for any nonsingular $r \times r$ matrix F. Sometimes this possibility is exploited in software for this problem by choosing F to be a diagonal matrix formed from the inverse of the elements $j_{11}, \ldots, j_{rr}$ of J, for then

$$J^* = JF \tag{9.20}$$

has unit elements on the diagonal. This is called the normalised or standardised form of J, and there is a corresponding normalised or standardised form of H given by

$$H^* = HF^{-1}$$

for the stated form of F.

To illustrate the argument, consider the bivariate VAR(1) model

$$\begin{bmatrix} y_{1t} \\ y_{2t} \end{bmatrix} = \begin{bmatrix} 1 - \pi_{12} & \pi_{12} \\ 0 & 1 \end{bmatrix} \begin{bmatrix} y_{1t-1} \\ y_{2t-1} \end{bmatrix} + \begin{bmatrix} u_{1t} \\ u_{2t} \end{bmatrix}.$$

Here, the matrix $\Pi(1)$ is

$$\Pi(1) = \begin{bmatrix} \pi_{12} & : -\pi_{12} \\ 0 & : 0 \end{bmatrix},$$

which clearly has rank 1, provided that $\pi_{12} \neq 0$. It would have rank 0 if $\pi_{12} = 0$. Then,

$$\Pi(1) = HJ' = \begin{bmatrix} \pi_{12} \\ 0 \end{bmatrix} [1 \quad -1], \tag{9.21}$$

in which the two matrices H and J (vectors in this case) have rank 1. Here, J is already in normalised or standardised form. Another example in a similar vein has

$$\Pi_1 = \begin{bmatrix} 1 - \pi_{11} & \pi_{12} \\ 0 & 1 \end{bmatrix}$$

and

$$\Pi(1) = \begin{bmatrix} \pi_{11} & : -\pi_{12} \\ 0 & : 0 \end{bmatrix} = \begin{bmatrix} 1 \\ 0 \end{bmatrix} [\pi_{11} \quad -\pi_{12}]. \tag{9.22}$$

The most general form of Π_1 for the bivariate case which generates a $\Pi(1)$ having rank 1 is

$$\Pi_1 = \begin{bmatrix} 1 - h_{11} j_{11} & -h_{11} j_{21} \\ -h_{21} j_{11} & 1 - h_{21} j_{21} \end{bmatrix},$$

for then

$$\Pi(1) = HJ' = \begin{bmatrix} h_{11} \\ h_{21} \end{bmatrix} [j_{11} \quad j_{21}]. \tag{9.23}$$

Thinking of the equations for y_{1t} and y_{2t} implied by the choice of Π_1 here,

$$y_{1t} = (1 - h_{11} j_{11}) y_{1t-1} - h_{11} j_{21} y_{2t-1} + u_{1t},$$

$$y_{2t} = -h_{21} j_{11} y_{1t-1} + (1 - h_{21} j_{21}) y_{2t-1} + u_{2t},$$

one can see that three out of the four underlying parameters $h_{11}, h_{21}, j_{11}, j_{12}$ enter each equation of the model in a nonlinear way.

The Granger Representation Theorem

This theorem relates to the model (9.17) in which $\Pi(1)$ satisfies (9.18). A formal statement and a proof of this theorem are available in Banerjee *et al.* (1993: 148–50), Hamilton (1994: ch. 19), and Johansen (1991, 1995). Two easily stated parts of this theorem are that

1. Δy_t is stationary, that is, $I(0)$;
2. $J' y_t$ is stationary, that is, $I(0)$.

The implication is that the matrix J' which appears in (9.18) actually provides the cointegrating combinations of y_t. It is precisely the existence of singularity or rank deficiency in $\Pi(1)$ that creates the existence of cointegration, and the two properties are equivalent. In the example of (9.21), the cointegrating combination is

$$y_{1t} - y_{2t},$$

whilst in the two following examples it is

$$\pi_{11} y_{1t} - \pi_{12} y_{2t}$$

and

$$j_{11} y_{1t} + j_{21} y_{2t}$$

respectively.

The next part of the theorem asserts that there exists a (vector) moving average representation for Δy_t:

$$\Delta y_t = C(L)(\mu + u_t), \tag{9.24}$$

in which $C(L)$ is of infinite order:

$$C(L) = \sum_{j=0}^{\infty} C_j L^j.$$

In addition, the theorem shows that $C(1)$, an $m \times m$ matrix, satisfies the properties

$$J'C(1) = 0, \quad C(1)H = 0,$$

and therefore has rank $m - r$. One can see from the form of $\Pi(1)$ in (9.18) that

$$\Pi(1)C(1) = 0 \quad \text{and} \quad C(1)\Pi(1) = 0.$$

In fact, these relationships define a form of duality between $\Pi(1)$ from the VAR model and $C(1)$ from the VMA model. Since $C(1)$ is singular if $\Pi(1)$ is, there is at least one unit root in the VMA form.

The advantage of the VMA model is that it enables us to reveal the trends that are responsible for the nonstationarity of y_t, and that these trends are in principle common to all the elements of y_t. One can decompose $C(L)$ through

$$C(L) = C(1) + (1 - L)C^*(L),\qquad(9.25)$$

which is similar to equation (6.16). Here, $C^*(L)$ has the form

$$C^*(L) = \sum_{j=0}^{\infty} C_j^* L^j.$$

Combining equations (9.24) and (9.25), the VMA form becomes

$$\Delta y_t = C(1)\mu + C(1)u_t + (1 - L)C^*(L)u_t,\qquad(9.26)$$

where the fact that $(1 - L)\mu = 0$ has been used. Given that u_t has mean zero, this implies that

$$E\Delta y_t = C(1)\mu.$$

Since

$$\sum_{j=1}^{t} \Delta y_j = y_t - y_0 \quad \text{and} \quad \sum_{j=1}^{t}(1 - L)u_j = u_t - u_0,$$

summing (9.26) gives

$$y_t = y_0 + [C(1)\mu]t + C(1)\left(\sum_{j=1}^{t} u_j\right) + C^*(L)(u_t - u_0).\qquad(9.27)$$

This is the vector analogue of the Beveridge–Nelson decomposition, equation (6.47), for an AR(p) process with unit root. From (9.27), y_t contains $m - r$ (linearly) independent deterministic linear trends, that is, the independent components of $C(1)\mu t$, and the same number of independent stochastic trends in

$$C(1)\left(\sum_{j=1}^{t} u_j\right).$$

Although it is not obvious, the remaining term is stationary.

This completes the propositions in the Granger Representation Theorem that are useful to us. One point needs to be made: implicitly, we have assumed that no *second differencing* is required to produce an $I(0)$ series. This rules out the possibility that there are any $I(2)$ series in the vector y_t. More explicit conditions for this are given in Banerjee *et al.* (1993), Johansen (1995) and Harris (1995).

There is only a slight difference between the VAR(1) version of the Granger Representation Theorem and the general VAR(p) case. Let

$$\Pi(L)y_t = \mu + u_t$$

represent the VAR(p), and use (9.10) to decompose $\Pi(L)$ as

$$\Pi(L) = \Pi(1)L^p + (1 - L)\Psi(L),$$

in which $\Psi(L)$ will be the matrix polynomial corresponding to a VAR$(p-1)$. It is not difficult, by equating coefficients on 'like powers' of L, to establish that

$$\Psi_j = I_m - \Pi_1 - \ldots - \Pi_j; \ j = 0, 1, \ldots, p - 1.$$

The VAR(p) can then be written as

$$\Psi(L)\Delta y_t = -\Pi(1)y_{t-p} + \mu + u_t$$

or

$$\Delta y_t = -\Psi_1 \Delta y_{t-1} - \ldots - \Psi_{p-1}\Delta y_{t-p+1} - \Pi(1)y_{t-p} + \mu + u_t. \tag{9.28}$$

Again, it is assumed that $\Pi(1)$ satisfies (9.18). The statement of the Granger Representation Theorem is then exactly the same, with the same stipulation that y_t must not contain any $I(2)$ variables.

It is possible to give an apparently different version of (9.28), which is used in some software. This uses the decomposition (9.9)

$$\Pi(L) = \Pi(1)L + (1 - L)\Psi(L)$$

for the VAR(p) process, giving

$$\Delta y_t = -\Psi_1 \Delta y_{t-1} - \ldots - \Psi_{p-1}\Delta y_{t-p+1} - \Pi(1)y_{t-1} + \mu + u_t. \tag{9.29}$$

Although the parameters Ψ_j are different across the two forms, the forms are equivalent since they are both reparameterisations of the underlying VAR model. It is easy to see that the two forms must be identical in the VAR(1) case.

The vector error correction model

The representation

$$\Delta y_t = -\Pi(1)y_{t-1} + \mu + u_t \tag{9.30}$$

of the VAR(1) model in the form

$$\Delta y_t = -HJ'y_{t-1} + \mu + u_t \tag{9.31}$$

using (9.18) is called the *vector error correction* model, or VEC(1) model. The extension to the VEC(p) case is straightforward: the representation (9.28) together with (9.18) gives

$$\Delta y_t = -\Psi_1 \Delta y_{t-1} - \ldots - \Psi_{p-1}\Delta y_{t-p+1} - HJ'y_{t-p} + \mu + u_t. \tag{9.32}$$

The alternative form derived from (9.29) would simply replace y_{t-p} with y_{t-1}.

The Granger Representation Theorem says that Δy_t and $J'y_t$ are $I(0)$ variables, so we can consider the long-run relationships implied by the VEC(1) model (9.31) when $\mu = 0$. In effect, we can try to calculate the implied long-run multipliers. Setting $\Delta y_t = 0$ and deleting the error term, we get

$$HJ'y_{t-1} = 0.$$

Since H has full column rank, it must follow that

$$J'y_{t-1} = 0. \tag{9.33}$$

Deleting the '$t-1$' subscript, these are the long-run relations implied by the underlying VAR model. It is the presence of the long-run relationships in the VEC model that accounts for its name, just as in the error correction form of the ADL model of Chapter 6.

In the examples of (9.21), (9.22) and (9.23), in which there is no intercept vector μ, the long-run relationships or error correction terms are simply

$$y_{1t} - y_{2t} = 0$$

$$\pi_{11}y_{1t} - \pi_{12}y_{2t} = 0$$

and

$$j_{11}y_{1t} + j_{21}y_{2t} = 0$$

respectively. Similarly, if the 'cointegrating regression' (7.72) used in the Engle–Granger approach to cointegration appeared in the VEC form of a VAR model, the long-run relationship would correspond to

$$y_t - \beta x_t = 0$$

if the intercept is ignored. A simple economic illustration of this states that log consumption is proportional to log income, in the long run.

In two of these examples, there is a natural normalisation on a particular element of y_t. The purpose of normalisation is to define an explicit dependent variable in a relationship. There is no reason why there has to be such a normalisation, yet economists do prefer to have relationships which have a single dependent variable. This issue also arises in the simultaneous equations model, and will recur later on in this chapter.

Equation (9.27) displays the deterministic and stochastic trend components of y_t, as well as the stationary component. Consider the VAR(1) model with intercept, (9.17), in its VMA form (9.26). As previously noted, it is the intercept vector μ which creates the deterministic trends in y_t. Suppose that in (9.26),

$$C(1)\mu = 0.$$

Then the deterministic trends would disappear from y_t in (9.27). The other implication from (9.26) is that

$$E\Delta y_t = 0.$$

For variables in logs, this means that the expected rates of growth generated for the variables in the system are all zero. This contrasts with the simple case of the RWD, or an AR(p) model with an intercept and a unit root, discussed in section 6.7, where the drift implies a nonzero expected growth rate.

The dual relationships between $C(1)$ and $\Pi(1)$ from the Granger Representation Theorem force the conclusion that if $C(1)\mu = 0$, then there must exist a vector α, say, such that

$$\mu = -H\alpha.$$

Then, the VEC form of the VAR(1) model (9.17) becomes

$$\Delta y_t = -H(\alpha + J'y_{t-1}) + u_t, \tag{9.34}$$

and the long-run relationship contains an intercept vector:

$$\alpha + J'y = 0.$$

Provided that an intercept only appears in the error correction term, then the system shows no growth.

It is easy to extend these ideas to the case where

$$\mu = -H\alpha + \tau, \tag{9.35}$$

so that τ functions as an overall intercept. From (9.27), τ will create a deterministic trend generating growth in the system. One can even introduce a deterministic trend in the VEC(1) model

$$\Delta y_t = -HJ'y_{t-1} + \mu + \delta t + u_t \tag{9.36}$$

where δ is a vector of parameters. If μ satisfies (9.35) and

$$\delta = -H\eta, \tag{9.37}$$

then the trend term t will only appear in the cointegrating relationship,

$$\Delta y_t = \tau - H(J'y_{t-1} + \alpha + \eta t) + u_t, \tag{9.38}$$

and will not appear in the corresponding VMA form. If the linear trend was not restricted only to enter the cointegrating relationship, (9.27) would imply that y_t contains a quadratic trend, which is empirically rather unlikely.

Let

$$w_t = J'y_t$$

represent the vector of cointegrating relationships. Then, the versions (9.21), (9.22) and (9.23) of the bivariate VAR(1) model have VEC(1) forms which are special cases of

$$\begin{bmatrix} \Delta y_{1t} \\ \Delta y_{2t} \end{bmatrix} = \begin{bmatrix} h_{11} \\ h_{21} \end{bmatrix} w_{t-1} + \begin{bmatrix} u_{1t} \\ u_{2t} \end{bmatrix}.$$

In the versions (9.21) and (9.22), $h_{21} = 0$, so that the single cointegrating relationship appears only in the first equation. In the version (9.23), this cointegrating relationship appears in both equations. Thinking of the error correction interpretation, agents are supposed to adjust the current value of y_{1t} in proportion to the extent of last periods' long-run disequilibrium measured by w_{t-1}. This means that the elements of H can be interpreted as adjustment coefficients, just as in section 6.6.

More generally, if we write a single equation from (9.31), say the first, as

$$\Delta y_{1t} = -\sum_{j=1}^{r} h_{1j} w_{jt-1} + \mu_1 + u_{1t}, \tag{9.39}$$

it is also clear from (9.39) that all of the cointegrating relationships appear in every equation, unless there is some specific structure in the H matrix, for example that

$$h_{1j} = 0; \; j = 2, \ldots, r.$$

This restriction would ensure that only the first cointegrating relationship appeared in the first equation, but would not prevent it from appearing in the remaining $m - 1$ equations. To ensure this,

$$h_{k1} = 0; \; k = 2, \ldots, m$$

would be required. This would give H the structure

$$H = \begin{bmatrix} h_{11} & 0' \\ 0 & H_{22} \end{bmatrix}. \tag{9.40}$$

In the case of only one cointegrating relationship,

$$H = \begin{bmatrix} h_{11} \\ 0 \end{bmatrix} \tag{9.41}$$

would still be required to ensure that the cointegrating relationship is located only in the first equation of the model, as in the examples (9.21) and (9.22).

9.4 / Estimation in VEC models: Johansen's method

A two-variable system can contain at most one cointegrating relation, since the number of cointegrating relationships is determined by rank $\Pi(1)$, and rank $\Pi(1) = 2$ corresponds to stationarity, whilst rank $\Pi(1) = 0$ corresponds to saying that the system is stationary in differences. In a VAR containing more than two variables, how many independent cointegrating relations are there? This is the same as asking, what is the rank of $\Pi(1)$, or, how many rows are there in J'? The now-standard empirical answer to this question is by means of a likelihood ratio test due to Johansen (1991). Johansen's method involves the maximum likelihood estimation of the VEC(p) model (9.28), with a normality assumption for the errors u_t, subject to the constraint (9.18) implied by a specific rank r for $\Pi(1)$. The likelihood ratio test then involves a comparison of the log likelihood function values obtained assuming specific values for r under null and alternative hypotheses. Estimation of the VEC model thus proceeds in two steps: identify the value of r, and then obtain estimates of H and J' conditional on this value.

The details of Johansen's method are very complex and involved, and yet it is in such widespread use that some attempt has to be made to see how it works. One possibility is to simplify the model that has to be estimated: here, only estimation of the VEC(1) model (9.31) (with μ set to zero) is considered in any detail. Even then, the details are quite complicated, and involve the use of generalised eigenvalues and vectors, which are briefly discussed in Appendix A. The reader who does not wish to see the details at this stage may omit the two subsections with 'optional details' in their titles, and jump ahead to the subsection entitled 'A summary'. This subsection also contains some indication of how the analysis is extended to the more general VEC(p) case.

As part of the attempt to simplify, the normal procedure of calculating maximum likelihood estimates by finding the derivatives of the log likelihood function and solving the resulting first-order conditions will not be followed. Instead, analogies with maximum likelihood estimation of the multivariate regression model from section 8.3 and of the VAR(1) process from section 9.2 will be exploited. The basis of the estimation procedure is still the log likelihood function: for the model

$$\Delta y_t = -HJ'y_{t-1} + u_t, \tag{9.42}$$

this is given by suitable modifications of (9.12) or (9.13),

$$\ln L = -\frac{nm}{2}\ln 2\pi - \frac{n}{2}\ln\det(\Sigma) - \frac{1}{2}\sum_{t=1}^{n}(\Delta y_t + HJ'y_{t-1})'\Sigma^{-1}(\Delta y_t + HJ'y_{t-1}),$$

or equivalently

$$\ln L = -\frac{nm}{2}\ln 2\pi - \frac{n}{2}\ln\det(\Sigma) - \frac{1}{2}\text{trace}[\Sigma^{-1}(\Delta Y + Y_1 JH')'(\Delta Y + Y_1 JH')]. \tag{9.43}$$

Here, ΔY is used for the matrix of observations on the differences Δy_t to avoid overburdening the notation further. The log likelihood function (9.43) corresponds to writing (9.42) in the form

$$\Delta Y = -Y_1 JH' + U \tag{9.44}$$

which matches the VAR(1) form (9.15).

Suppose first that J is actually known. Then, the maximum likelihood estimator of H' is, from sections 8.2, 8.3 and 9.2, the OLS estimator

$$\hat{H}' = -(J'Y_1'Y_1 J)^{-1}J'Y_1'\Delta Y. \tag{9.45}$$

Similarly, the estimator of Σ will match (9.16):

$$\hat{\Sigma} = \frac{(\Delta Y + Y_1 J\hat{H}')'(\Delta Y + Y_1 J\hat{H}')}{n}$$

$$= \frac{\Delta Y'\Delta Y - \Delta Y'Y_1 J(J'Y_1'Y_1 J)^{-1}J'Y_1'\Delta Y}{n}, \tag{9.46}$$

where the second expression comes from expanding the numerator of $\hat{\Sigma}$ and using (9.45).

This shows that the difficult part of the problem will be determining the estimator of J so as to maximise the log likelihood function. When the maximum likelihood estimator of J is found, say, $\hat{J}$, it will be substituted into the OLS forms for $\hat{H}'$ and $\hat{\Sigma}$, producing the maximum likelihood estimators of H' and Σ.

The standard way to proceed here is to express the log likelihood function solely in terms of J, and then maximise the log likelihood function as a function of J. This procedure is called *concentrating* the log likelihood function. It is equivalent, although simpler in this case, to finding the derivatives of the log likelihood function with respect to H', J and Σ, and then solving the resulting first-order conditions.

Maximising the log likelihood function: optional details

The idea of concentrating the log likelihood function is straightforward: try to express the log likelihood function solely in terms of the parameters that are the most difficult to estimate. The next stages in the procedure show that maximising the log likelihood function is equivalent to the maximisation (or minimisation) of the simpler function. Eventually we reduce the problem to the minimisation of a function where the solution is known.

It is not difficult to show that

$$\text{trace}[\hat{\Sigma}^{-1}(\Delta Y + Y_1 J \hat{H}')'(\Delta Y + Y_1 J \hat{H}')] = n \, \text{trace} \, I_m.$$

Substituting the estimator of H into the log likelihood function (9.43) then produces the *concentrated* log likelihood function,

$$\ln L^c = -\frac{nm}{2}\ln 2\pi - \frac{n}{2}\ln \det(\hat{\Sigma}) - \frac{nm}{2} \tag{9.47}$$

in which $\hat{\Sigma}$ is a function of J through (9.46). Maximising this concentrated log likelihood function with respect to J involves minimising, because of the minus sign and (9.46),

$$\ln \det(\hat{\Sigma}) = \ln \det \frac{1}{n}[\Delta Y' \Delta Y - \Delta Y' Y_1 J (J' Y_1' Y_1 J)^{-1} J' Y_1' \Delta Y]. \tag{9.48}$$

At this point, we need to use a result from Appendix A concerning the determinant of a partitioned matrix. If the partitioned matrix is considered to be

$$\frac{1}{n}\begin{bmatrix} \Delta Y' \Delta Y : \Delta Y' Y_1 J \\ J' Y_1' \Delta Y : J' Y_1' Y_1 J \end{bmatrix},$$

its determinant can be represented as

$$\det \frac{1}{n}(J' Y_1' Y_1 J) \det \frac{1}{n}[\Delta Y' \Delta Y - \Delta Y' Y_1 J (J' Y_1' Y_1 J)^{-1} J' Y_1' \Delta Y]$$

or equivalently as

$$\det \frac{1}{n}(\Delta Y' \Delta Y) \det \frac{1}{n}[J' Y_1' Y_1 J - J' Y_1' \Delta Y (\Delta Y' \Delta Y)^{-1} \Delta Y' Y_1 J]. \tag{9.49}$$

This shows that the log-determinant on the right of (9.48) is equal to

$$\ln \det \frac{1}{n}(\Delta Y'\Delta Y)$$

$$+ \ln \left\{ \frac{\det(1/n)[J'Y_1'Y_1J - J'Y_1'\Delta Y(\Delta Y'\Delta Y)^{-1}\Delta Y'Y_1J]}{\det(1/n)(J'Y_1'Y_1J)} \right\}. \tag{9.50}$$

Minimising the ratio of determinants in this expression with respect to J is, surprisingly, a well-known problem with a well-known solution (see, for example, Johansen, 1995: 224). The minimum value of the ratio is obtained by choosing the r columns of J to be the r (generalised) eigenvectors $\hat{\psi}_j$ corresponding to the r smallest (generalised) eigenvalues $\hat{\xi}_j$ of the $m \times m$ matrix

$$\frac{1}{n}[Y_1'Y_1 - Y_1'\Delta Y(\Delta Y'\Delta Y)^{-1}\Delta Y'Y_1] \tag{9.51}$$

in the metric of $(1/n)Y_1'Y_1$. The generalised eigenvalues are the roots of the determinental equation

$$\det \frac{1}{n}\{[Y_1'Y_1 - Y_1'\Delta Y(\Delta Y'\Delta Y)^{-1}\Delta Y'Y_1] - \hat{\xi}Y_1'Y_1\} = 0. \tag{9.52}$$

By rearranging this expression as

$$(-1)^m \det \frac{1}{n}[Y_1'\Delta Y(\Delta Y'\Delta Y)^{-1}\Delta Y'Y_1 - (1 - \hat{\xi})Y_1'Y_1] = 0,$$

one can see that $\hat{\xi}$ in (9.52) is directly related to $\hat{\lambda}$ in the following determinantal equation

$$\det \frac{1}{n}[Y_1'\Delta Y(\Delta Y'\Delta Y)^{-1}\Delta Y'Y_1 - \hat{\lambda}Y_1'Y_1] = 0 \tag{9.53}$$

by $\hat{\xi} = 1 - \hat{\lambda}$.

If the roots of (9.52) and (9.53) are ordered as $\hat{\xi}_1 \geq \ldots \geq \hat{\xi}_m$ and $\hat{\lambda}_1 \geq \ldots \geq \hat{\lambda}_m$ respectively, one can see that the r smallest roots of (9.52) correspond to the r largest roots $\hat{\lambda}_1, \ldots, \hat{\lambda}_r$ of (9.53). As a result, J can also be expressed in terms of the generalised eigenvectors corresponding to the r largest roots of (9.53). It is more usual to work with the roots of (9.53) rather than those of (9.52).

Summarising, the generalised eigenvalues $\hat{\lambda}_j$ and eigenvectors $\hat{\psi}_j$ satisfy the equation

$$\frac{1}{n}Y_1'\Delta Y(\Delta Y'\Delta Y)^{-1}\Delta Y'Y_1\hat{\psi}_j = \frac{1}{n}\hat{\lambda}_j Y_1'Y_1\hat{\psi}_j, \tag{9.54}$$

or, equivalently,

$$\frac{1}{n}[Y_1'Y_1 - Y_1'\Delta Y(\Delta Y'\Delta Y)^{-1}\Delta Y'Y_1]\hat{\psi}_j = (1 - \hat{\lambda}_j)\frac{1}{n}Y_1'Y_1\hat{\psi}_j, \tag{9.55}$$

for each $j = 1, \ldots, m$. As is usual in eigenvalue problems, the generalised eigenvectors have to be normalised for uniqueness: here the condition is that

$$\frac{1}{n}\hat{\psi}_i'Y_1'Y_1\hat{\psi}_j = \begin{cases} 1 & \text{if } i = j \\ 0 & \text{if } i = j \end{cases} \quad i,j = 1, \ldots, m. \tag{9.56}$$

The generalised eigenvalues and eigenvectors are sample quantities since they depend on the sample matrices ΔY and Y_1.

Having found the maximum likelihood estimator of J as

$$\hat{J}' = [\hat{\psi}_1, \ldots, \hat{\psi}_r],$$

satisfying the normalisation rule (9.56) in the form

$$\frac{1}{n}\hat{J}'Y_1'Y_1\hat{J} = I_r,$$

we can find the estimator of H'. This is obtained by substituting $\hat{J}$ into (9.45) and taking into account the normalisation, giving

$$\hat{H}' = -\frac{1}{n}\hat{J}'Y_1'\Delta Y. \tag{9.57}$$

The maximum value of ln L: optional details

To find the maximum value of the log likelihood function (9.43), we need to find the minimum value of $\ln\det(\hat{\Sigma})$ in (9.48) or (9.50). This is slightly involved, but not difficult, and very important to the issues of inference on the number of cointegrating relationships which is going to be discussed in the next section.

Consider the ijth element of the matrix

$$\frac{1}{n}\hat{J}'[Y_1'Y_1 - Y_1'\Delta Y(\Delta Y'\Delta Y)^{-1}\Delta Y'Y_1]\hat{J} \tag{9.58}$$

appearing in (9.49): this is

$$\frac{1}{n}\hat{\psi}_i'[Y_1'Y_1 - Y_1'\Delta Y(\Delta Y'\Delta Y)^{-1}\Delta Y'Y_1]\hat{\psi}_j; \ i,j = 1, \ldots, r.$$

From (9.55), this equals

$$(1 - \hat{\lambda}_j)\frac{1}{n}\hat{\psi}_i'Y_1'Y_1\hat{\psi}_j; \ i,j = 1, \ldots, r,$$

which is zero if $i \neq j$, and is $(1 - \hat{\lambda}_j)$ for $i = j$, using (9.56). In short, matrix (9.58) is a diagonal matrix, with determinant equal to

$$\prod_{j=1}^{r}(1 - \hat{\lambda}_j). \tag{9.59}$$

Because of the normalisation (9.56), this is also the minimum value of the determinant ratio in (9.50).

The results (9.48), (9.50) and (9.59) now enable us to write out the maximum value of $\ln L$ in (9.47) as

$$\ln L = -\frac{nm}{2}\ln 2\pi - \frac{n}{2}\ln\det\left(\frac{\Delta Y'\Delta Y}{n}\right) - \frac{nm}{2} - \frac{n}{2}\sum_{j=1}^{r}\ln(1 - \hat{\lambda}_j). \tag{9.60}$$

One can see that the value of the log likelihood function will vary with the choice of r, and it is exactly this feature that permits the construction of test statistics for hypotheses about the value of r. These will be discussed in section 9.5.

A summary

Before summarising the results of the two preceding optional sections, note that some of the equations obtained there are restated in this subsection, *with the original numbers*. Some equations in this subsection will appear out of order: this should not cause too much confusion.

One of the steps in finding the maximum likelihood estimator $\hat{J}$ of J in (9.44) requires the computation of all m generalised eigenvectors $\hat{\psi}_j$; $j = 1, \ldots, m$ and generalised eigenvalues $\hat{\lambda}_j$; $j = 1, \ldots, m$ satisfying the equation

$$\frac{1}{n} Y_1' \Delta Y (\Delta Y' \Delta Y)^{-1} \Delta Y' Y_1 \hat{\psi}_j = \frac{1}{n} \hat{\lambda}_j Y_1' Y_1 \hat{\psi}_j. \tag{9.54}$$

The generalised eigenvalues are found as the roots of the determinental equation

$$\det \frac{1}{n} [Y_1' \Delta Y (\Delta Y' \Delta Y)^{-1} \Delta Y' Y_1 - \hat{\lambda} Y_1' Y_1] = 0. \tag{9.53}$$

Given the choice of r, the log likelihood function (9.43) is maximised by choosing as the estimator of J, the r generalised eigenvectors $\hat{\psi}_j$ corresponding to the r largest generalised eigenvalues $\hat{\lambda}_j$:

$$\hat{J} = [\hat{\psi}_1 \ldots \hat{\psi}_r]. \tag{9.61}$$

In order to find a unique $\hat{J}$ maximising the concentrated log likelihood function (9.47), $\hat{J}$ is made to satisfy a normalisation rule,

$$\frac{1}{n} \hat{J}' Y_1' Y_1 \hat{J} = I_r. \tag{9.56}$$

This choice of $\hat{J}$ also ensures that

$$\frac{1}{n} \hat{J}' [Y_1' Y_1 - Y_1' \Delta Y (\Delta Y' \Delta Y)^{-1} \Delta Y' Y_1] \hat{J} \tag{9.58}$$

is a diagonal matrix, with diagonal elements $1 - \hat{\lambda}_j$. Taking the normalisation rule (9.56) into account, substituting $\hat{J}$ into (9.45) then produces the maximum likelihood estimator of H' as

$$\hat{H}' = -\hat{J}' Y_1' \Delta Y. \tag{9.57}$$

Substituting both $\hat{H}$ and $\hat{J}$ into (9.46) gives the maximum likelihood estimator of Σ.

It should be clear from (9.61) that these estimators depend critically on the rank r chosen initially. Different values of r will require a larger or smaller selection of the m generalised eigenvectors $\hat{\psi}_j$ and will thus generate different estimators of J, H' and Σ. Note, however, that the matrices $(1/n) Y_1' \Delta Y (\Delta Y' \Delta Y)^{-1} \Delta Y' Y_1$ and $(1/n) Y_1' Y_1$ from which the generalised eigenvalues and generalised eigenvectors are being computed do not change as r changes.

The maximised value of the log likelihood function (9.43) is shown in the previous subsection to depend directly on the values of the r largest generalised eigenvalues $\hat{\lambda}_j$ from (9.54), as well as other quantities not depending on the value of r:

$$\ln L_r = -\frac{nm}{2}\ln 2\pi - \frac{n}{2}\ln\det\left(\frac{\Delta Y'\Delta Y}{n}\right) - \frac{nm}{2} - \frac{n}{2}\sum_{j=1}^{r}\ln(1-\hat{\lambda}_j). \tag{9.60}$$

The fact that the value depends directly on r, emphasised now by the subscript on L, suggests the possibility of using a likelihood ratio test for inference on the value of r. This will be discussed in section 9.5, where it is seen that the testing procedure in effect generates an estimator of r.

A special case

What happens to the results of the derivation above if the value of r chosen to construct the estimators is $r = m$? In (9.18), the two matrices H and J will be square and nonsingular. In turn, the estimator of J in (9.61) will use all m (generalised) eigenvectors $\hat{\psi}_1, \ldots, \hat{\psi}_m$. Ignoring the fact that $\hat{J}$ has been normalised through (9.56), the expression for $\hat{H}'$ in (9.45) then simplifies to

$$\hat{H}' = -\hat{J}^{-1}(Y_1'Y_1)^{-1}Y_1'\Delta Y,$$

giving the implied estimator of $-\Pi(1)$ as

$$\hat{J}\hat{H}' = -\hat{J}\hat{J}^{-1}(Y_1'Y_1)^{-1}Y_1'\Delta Y.$$

This is simply the OLS estimator of $\Pi(1)$ ignoring the cointegrating relationships. In this case, then, the estimator of $\Pi(1)$ is not restricted by the demand that

$$\operatorname{rank}\Pi(1) = m.$$

The VEC(p) case

To complete the discussion of Johansen's method, the extension to the VEC(p) version of the VAR(p) model

$$\Delta y_t = -\Psi_1\Delta y_{t-1} - \ldots - \Psi_{p-1}\Delta y_{t-p+1} - HJ'y_{t-p} + u_t \tag{9.62}$$

is needed. In terms of observation matrices, this model is

$$\Delta Y = -\Delta Y_1\Psi_1' - \ldots - \Delta Y_{p-1}\Psi_{p-1}' - Y_pJH' + U,$$

in which the observations on the lagged values of Δy_t are collected in the matrices $\Delta Y_1, \ldots, \Delta Y_{p-1}$. To keep things notationally simple, define the matrix X and the parameter matrix K' as

$$X = [\Delta Y_1 \ldots \Delta Y_{p-1}], \quad n \times m(p-1), \tag{9.63}$$

$$K' = -\begin{bmatrix} \Psi_1' \\ \vdots \\ \Psi_{p-1}' \end{bmatrix}, \quad m(p-1)\times m. \tag{9.64}$$

Then, the VEC(p) model (9.62) can be written as

$$\Delta Y = XK' - Y_p JH' + U. \tag{9.65}$$

In the log likelihood function (9.43), instead of the term $\Delta Y + Y_1 JH'$, there will be the term

$$\Delta Y - XK' + Y_p JH', \tag{9.66}$$

and thought has to be given to the estimation of the parameters in K'. Using the same argument as before, if *both* H and J were known, the maximum likelihood estimator of K' would be the least squares estimator for the model

$$\Delta Y + Y_p JH' = XK' + U,$$

that is,

$$\hat{K}' = (X'X)^{-1}X'(\Delta Y + Y_p JH'). \tag{9.67}$$

The principle of concentrating the log likelihood function mentioned earlier would lead to $\hat{K}'$ being substituted back into the log likelihood function, from which H, J and Σ have to be estimated. This substitution would create the term

$$\Delta Y - X\hat{K}' + Y_p JH'.$$

Inserting the expression for $\hat{K}$ into this and rearranging introduces matrices of residuals $\Delta \tilde{Y}$ and $\tilde{Y}_p$ from regressions of ΔY and Y_p on X:

$$\Delta \tilde{Y} = \Delta Y - X(X'X)^{-1}X'\Delta Y, \quad \tilde{Y}_p = Y_p - X(X'X)^{-1}X'Y_p.$$

The insertion of $\hat{K}'$ into (9.65) then produces the 'model'

$$\Delta \tilde{Y} = -\tilde{Y}_p JH' + \text{error}, \tag{9.68}$$

so that the component $\Delta Y - X\hat{K}' + Y_p JH'$ appearing in the log likelihood function becomes simply

$$\Delta \tilde{Y} + \tilde{Y}_p JH'.$$

This takes us to the starting point of the previous analysis, the estimation of H presuming that J is known, where (9.68) is analogous to (9.44), except that the variables are now matrices of residuals. The remainder of the analysis follows as before, apart from the replacement of ΔY and Y_1 by $\Delta \tilde{Y}$ and $\tilde{Y}_p$ everywhere. So, for example, the maximised value of the log likelihood function would become

$$\ln L_r = -\frac{nm}{2}\ln 2\pi - \frac{n}{2}\ln \det\left(\frac{\Delta \tilde{Y}'\Delta \tilde{Y}}{n}\right) - \frac{nm}{2} - \frac{n}{2}\sum_{j=1}^{r}\ln(1 - \hat{\lambda}_j), \tag{9.69}$$

where the dependence of the maximised value on r is again explicitly shown.

Estimation with intercept

There are two further issues of estimation to investigate for VEC models: both are concerned with the presence of deterministic explanatory variables like the intercept or a linear trend. There are two issues because, as noted in equations (9.34), (9.35) and (9.38), such variables can be restricted to enter only the cointegrating relationship or error correction term. Consider first the variant of (9.62) in which an overall intercept is included,

$$\Delta y_t = -\Psi_1 \Delta y_{t-1} - \ldots - \Psi_{p-1} \Delta y_{t-p+1} - HJ' y_{t-p} + \mu + u_t.$$

In terms of observation matrices, the version of (9.38) which will be employed is

$$\Delta Y = 1_n \mu' - \Delta Y_1 \Psi_1' - \ldots - \Delta Y_{p-1} \Psi_{p-1}' - Y_p JH' + U, \qquad (9.70)$$

where 1_n is an n-vector of ones. If we redefine X in equation (9.63) and K' in (9.64) to allow for the intercept,

$$X = [1_n \quad \Delta Y_1 \quad \ldots \quad \Delta Y_{p-1}], \qquad n \times [1 + m(p-1)],$$

$$K' = - \begin{bmatrix} -\mu' \\ \Psi_1' \\ \vdots \\ \Psi_{p-1}' \end{bmatrix}, \qquad [1 + m(p-1)] \times m, \qquad (9.71)$$

then (9.70) has the same form as (9.65) and is estimated in exactly the same way.

For the case where the deterministic terms are restricted to appear in the error correction term only, we use the model

$$\Delta Y = -\Delta Y_1 \Psi_1' - \ldots - \Delta Y_{p-1} \Psi_{p-1}' - (Y_p J + 1_n \alpha') H' + U \qquad (9.72)$$

which is the VEC(p) version of (9.34), using observation matrices. In this case, we use the matrices X of (9.63) and K' of (9.64), and define Y_p^a, J^a as

$$Y_p^a = [Y_p \quad 1_n], \qquad J^a = \begin{bmatrix} J \\ \alpha' \end{bmatrix}. \qquad (9.73)$$

Then, (9.72) can also be written in a form similar to (9.65) as

$$\Delta Y = XK' - Y_p^a J^a H' + U. \qquad (9.74)$$

We can then repeat the concentration of the log likelihood with respect to K' to produce the variant of (9.68),

$$\Delta \tilde{Y} = - \tilde{Y}_p^a J^a H' + \text{error}, \qquad (9.75)$$

where the tilde represents residuals from regression of ΔY and Y_p^a on the X of (9.63). The estimation of H' and J^a then follows the same pattern as the estimation of (9.44), with $\Delta \tilde{Y}$ replacing ΔY and $\tilde{Y}_p^a$ replacing Y_1.

Because $\tilde{Y}_p^a$ now has $m+1$ columns, the estimation procedure will produce $m+1$ generalised eigenvalues and vectors. The smallest of these eigenvalues will always be zero, and the corresponding generalised eigenvector can be ignored. The reason for this has to do with the dimensions and ranks of the matrices in the determinantal equation

$$\det[\tilde{Y}_p^{a\prime}\Delta\tilde{Y}(\Delta\tilde{Y}'\Delta\tilde{Y})^{-1}\Delta\tilde{Y}'\tilde{Y}_p^a - \hat{\lambda}\tilde{Y}_p^{a\prime}\tilde{Y}_p^a] = 0$$

which is analogous to (9.53). The $(m+1) \times (m+1)$ matrix

$$\tilde{Y}_p^{a\prime}\Delta\tilde{Y}(\Delta\tilde{Y}'\Delta\tilde{Y})^{-1}\Delta\tilde{Y}'\tilde{Y}_p^a$$

is singular since $\Delta\tilde{Y}'\tilde{Y}_p^a$ is an $m \times (m+1)$ matrix, and thus has maximum rank m. On the other hand, $\tilde{Y}_p^{a\prime}\tilde{Y}_p^a$ is a nonsingular $(m+1) \times (m+1)$ matrix. The clash of ranks can only be reconciled by one of the roots of the determinantal equation being equal to zero.

The argument presented can be adapted to the case of both an intercept and trend restricted to belong to the error correction term by including $\mathbf{t}$, an n-vector of observations on a linear trend in the term $(Y_p J + \mathbf{1}_n \alpha')H'$, changing it to

$$(Y_p J + \mathbf{1}_n \alpha' + \mathbf{t}\eta')H'.$$

Another point concerns estimation of a model containing an intercept where, as in (9.35), one component appears in the error correction term and one part unrestrictedly. This would have the effect of using a model like (9.74), but where X is defined by (9.71) and Y_p^a by (9.73). Concentrating the likelihood function by regressing ΔY and Y_p^a on X will produce a matrix of residuals $\tilde{Y}_p^a$ with a zero column corresponding to $\mathbf{1}_n$, since the intercept in X will explain perfectly the intercept in Y_p^a. Attempting to estimate the equivalent of (9.75) will fail as a result of the exact multicollinearity arising from the zero column in $\tilde{Y}_p^a$.

Example 9.1

This example is based on the IS/LM model of Johansen and Juselius (1994), but using UK seasonally adjusted data from 1963(1) to 1994(2) instead of the Australian data used in the article. The data are exactly as used in Example 7.8.

The general objective here is to see if there are any cointegrating relationships within a VAR model for the five variables LNM4, LNRGDP, DLNPGDP, B20 and TBILL, and then attempt to interpret them in economic terms. This contrasts with the single equation investigation of this issue in Example 7.8. It is indicated in that example that all the series appear to be $I(1)$, although there is some evidence of $I(2)$ behaviour for LNM4. The analysis of cointegration for a group of series of which some are $I(1)$ and some are $I(2)$ is much more complicated than the $I(1)$ case discussed here, and thus these issues will be ignored, even though they will undoubtedly have an effect on the empirical results for the example. See Johansen (1995) or Harris (1995) for further details.

The next step is to fit a VAR model with unrestricted intercept to the five series, followed by some diagnostic testing. Johansen and Juselius choose a VAR(2), although if one uses a testing down procedure from some suitably high value for

Table 9.1 Unrestricted ML estimates of $\Pi(1)$

	LNM4	LNRGDP	DLNPGDP	B20	TBILL
LNM4	−0.009 92	0.009 90	−0.020 63	−0.720 99	−0.816 67
(s.e.)	(0.0050)	(0.0069)	(0.0050)	(0.3264)	(0.6241)
LNRGDP	0.056 57	−0.058 56	0.114 37	4.1830	5.4833
	(0.0304)	(0.0413)	(0.03009)	(1.9680)	(3.7634)
DLNPGDP	−0.102 82	−0.097 32	−0.655 64	0.814 60	−11.105
	(0.1080)	(0.1469)	(0.1069)	(6.9934)	(13.373)
B20	0.001 06	0.000 42	0.002 26	−0.084 28	0.031 68
	(0.0007)	(0.0009)	(0.0006)	(0.0424)	(0.0811)
TBILL	−0.000 10	−0.001 30	0.000 02	0.028 15	−0.1469
	(0.0005)	(0.0007)	(0.0005)	(0.0317)	(0.0605)

the order p of the VAR like $p = 4$, the VAR(2) model is rejected in favour of a VAR(3). Notwithstanding this, the VAR(2) is used in the results presented below, since the example is meant to illustrate the techniques and possibilities rather than be a perfect piece of econometrics.

This VAR(2) model contains altogether $(2 \times 5 \times 5) + 5 = 55$ parameters, the first part of the calculation being the parameters in Π_1 and Π_2 and the next the five intercept parameters. There are therefore far too many results to display, and only selected parts will be displayed. Table 9.1 displays the implied estimate of $\Pi(1)$ from this VAR(2) system: it has a pair of complex conjugate eigenvalues and three real eigenvalues, all inside the unit circle, indicating the rank of the estimated $\Pi(1)$ is 5 and that the estimated VAR(2) process is stationary. The VEC form of this VAR(2) model is a version of (9.29).

$\Delta y_t = -\Psi_1 \Delta y_{t-1} - \Pi(1) y_{t-2} + \mu + u_t$. Direct estimation of this model produces the same numerical estimates of $\Pi(1)$ as those derived from estimation of the VAR(2) model, but also provides standard errors of the estimates, which are presented in Table 9.1.

Implementation of the Johansen estimation procedure requires some presumed value of r: given this choice, the estimates of H and J' are deduced from the generalised eigenvalues and generalised eigenvectors obtained from (9.53) and (9.54). This corresponds to maximum likelihood estimation of the model

$$\Delta y_t = -\Psi_1 \Delta y_{t-1} - HJ' y_{t-2} + \mu + u_t \tag{9.76}$$

in which r is also unknown. The generalised eigenvalues and eigenvectors do not depend on the value of r chosen by the investigator, and it is usual to present all of these. For the example, the five generalised eigenvalues and generalised eigenvectors are given in Table 9.2. Table 9.3 displays the implied estimate of the 5×5 matrix H under the assumption that $r = 5$. If we chose instead $r = 1$ as the presumed rank of $\Pi(1)$, the first columns in Tables 9.2 and 9.3 would contain the estimates of J and

Table 9.2 Generalised eigenvalues and eigenvectors

Eigenvalues $\hat{\lambda}$	0.290 95	0.180 85	0.092 81	0.052 37	0.003 96
Eigenvectors $\hat{\psi}$					
LNM4	−3.173 92	−2.726 06	−3.195 42	1.858 43	−0.650 12
LNRGDP	17.764 97	14.558 84	18.723 76	−13.086 93	9.971 62
DLNPGDP	−114.893 43	−13.002 08	23.447 57	−24.231 35	−0.340 75
B20	0.424 84	−0.006 31	−0.492 44	−0.317 71	−0.100 69
TBILL	−0.113 62	0.365 88	0.155 24	0.349 14	−0.067 29

Table 9.3 Estimate of H

LNM4	0.001 03	0.001 61	−0.000 17	−0.001 64	−0.000 33
LNRGDP	0.001 08	−0.003 95	−0.000 25	0.000 76	−0.000 58
DLNPGDP	0.005 45	0.001 54	−0.000 13	0.000 29	0.000 13
B20	0.032 25	−0.000 52	0.196 61	0.004 03	−0.001 09
TBILL	0.201 06	−0.279 79	0.203 59	−0.148 25	0.023 35

H respectively. Table 9.4 gives the implied estimate of the 5×5 matrix $\Pi(1)$ based on the assumption that $r = 1$. These results are only illustrative at the moment, since we do not know whether the hypothesis that $r = 1$ is acceptable with this data set.

In examining these results, we can start by comparing the unrestricted estimates of $\Pi(1)$ in Table 9.1 and the restricted estimates assuming that $\Pi(1)$ has rank 1 in Table 9.4. As one might expect, there are cells in the two tables that are not very different, whilst others differ quite a lot. The 'eigenvector' columns of Table 9.2 contain the coefficients in the cointegrating combinations of the variables. It would be natural to try and interpret these combinations from an economic viewpoint. However, we shall postpone this, since the issues of interpretation depend on the correctness of the presumed rank r, and are often easier using normalised or standardised generalised eigenvectors. The next section tackles the issues of estimating r and conducting inference on its value.

Table 9.4 Estimates of $\Pi(1)$ given that $r = 1$

$\Pi(1)$	LNM4	LNRGDP	DLNPGDP	B20	TBILL
LNM4	0.003 25	−0.018 21	0.117 77	−0.000 44	0.000 12
LNRGDP	0.003 44	−0.019 26	0.124 56	−0.000 46	0.000 12
DLNPGDP	0.017 28	−0.096 73	0.625 60	−0.002 31	0.000 62
B20	0.102 35	−0.572 85	3.704 86	−0.013 70	0.003 66
TBILL	0.638 15	−3.571 82	23.100 45	−0.085 42	0.022 84

9.5 / Testing for cointegration in the VEC model

Having established the nature of the maximised log likelihood function (9.60) for the VEC(1) model and (9.69) for the VEC(p) model, it can now be used for testing hypotheses about the number of cointegration relations r, or equivalently, the rank of $\Pi(1)$. It is natural to use the likelihood ratio test statistic of (4.43): as a reminder, a log likelihood function

$$\ln L(\theta)$$

is evaluated at an estimate $\tilde{\theta}_R$ obtained under the truth of a null hypothesis, and then at an estimate $\tilde{\theta}$ ignoring this hypothesis. The test statistic is then

$$LR = -2[\ln L(\tilde{\theta}_R) - \ln L(\tilde{\theta})].$$

Unfortunately, in its application for testing the rank of $\Pi(1)$, it fails to have the usual central χ^2 distribution under the null hypothesis. As with the unit root tests and the cointegration tests discussed in sections 7.7 and 7.8, it has a non-standard distribution, although suitable tables of critical values for the tests have been calculated.

Trace and max statistics

Suppose that we wished to test the hypothesis

$$H_r\text{: the rank of }\Pi(1)\text{ is }r \tag{9.77}$$

against the alternative that

$$H_m\text{: the rank of }\Pi(1)\text{ is }m. \tag{9.78}$$

We can do this for any value of r from 0 to $m-1$. Under the alternative hypothesis H_m, $\Pi(1)$ is unrestricted, so that H_r corresponds to the imposition of some number of restrictions on $\Pi(1)$.

In constructing the likelihood ratio statistic using either (9.60) or (9.69), we would use the difference of $\ln L_r$ and $\ln L_m$, since these formally correspond to $\ln L(\tilde{\theta}_R)$ and $\ln L(\tilde{\theta})$. One can see from (9.69) that the only term that differs between $\ln L_r$ and $\ln L_m$ is the last term, so that the likelihood ratio statistic would be

$$-2(\ln L_r - \ln L_m) = n \sum_{j=1}^{r} \ln(1 - \hat{\lambda}_j) - n \sum_{j=1}^{m} \ln(1 - \hat{\lambda}_j)$$

$$= -n \sum_{j=r+1}^{m} \ln(1 - \hat{\lambda}_j). \tag{9.79}$$

This is called the *trace* statistic, for the following reason. The term

$$\sum_{j=1}^{r} \ln(1 - \hat{\lambda}_j)$$

in the first line of the likelihood ratio statistic above is the trace of the matrix appearing in (9.58), under the supposition that rank $\Pi(1) = r$. Similarly, the second term involves the same matrix assuming that rank $\Pi(1) = m$. Despite the non-standard distribution of the statistic (9.79), large values are evidence against the null hypothesis.

If it were true that the (generalised) eigenvalues $\hat{\lambda}_j$ were zero for $j = r+1, \ldots, m$, the value of the trace test statistic would be zero. This suggests that it is really a test that the population quantities corresponding to $\hat{\lambda}_j$, say, λ_j, are zero for $j = r+1, \ldots, m$. If these quantities are taken as indicators of the rank *deficiency* of $\Pi(1)$, then it can be seen that H_r is really a hypothesis about the rank deficiency of $\Pi(1)$. This alternative perspective will appear the most natural when tables of critical values are examined shortly.

Admitting that the true value of rank $\Pi(1)$ is unknown makes it clear that this integer-valued quantity has to be estimated. Testing the hypothesis that rank $\Pi(1) = r < m$ against the alternative that rank $\Pi(1) = m$ for a specified value r provides us with some information about the true value of rank $\Pi(1)$. But, we need to do more than simply test a single hypothesis. Estimation of rank $\Pi(1)$ is what is called a *multiple decision problem*: decide that r is 0 or 1 or 2 or … or m. There are a number of possible ways of approaching this problem, but most of them involve a sequence of hypothesis tests. Using the hypotheses (9.77) and (9.78) above, consider testing H_r against H_m in turn, for $r = 0, \ldots, m-1$. If we reject H_0, here the hypothesis that $r = 0$, we can conclude intuitively that r is greater than 0, even though the true value may not actually be the m indicated by the alternative hypothesis. Proceeding up the sequence

$$r = 0, 1, 2, \ldots, m-1,$$

suppose for example we reject H_2 against H_m and accept H_3 against H_m. Then, the implied estimate of r would be 3.

In this argument, the use of H_m as the alternative hypothesis at each step seems a little strange. The sequence of null and alternative hypotheses seems to be equivalent to asking at each step, 'Should we choose r or $r+1$ as the estimate of rank $\Pi(1)$?' If so, we should be testing H_r against H_{r+1} for $r = 0, 1, \ldots, m-1$. The likelihood ratio statistic for this is

$$-2(\ln L_r - \ln L_{r+1}) = -n\ln(1 - \hat{\lambda}_{r+1}).$$

This is called the $\lambda_{\max}$ statistic, with a different distribution to that of the trace statistic. Different authors use different notation for the roots λ, but all refer to the statistic as a *max* statistic. As with the trace statistic procedure, we perform a sequence of tests: H_0 against H_1, H_1 against H_2, and so on. If for example we reject H_2 against H_3 and accept H_3 against H_4, we accept the estimate of rank $\Pi(1)$ as 3.

It is clear from both procedures that the estimate of rank $\Pi(1)$ is the value determined by the first accepted hypothesis. As always with two different but related test procedures, it is possible to have conflicts in the conclusions drawn from the two procedures.

Table 9.5 95% critical values for rank deficiency test

Trace

m − r	Case 1	Case 1.1*	Case 1*	Case 2	Case 2*
1	3.76	8.18	9.24	3.74	12.25
2	15.41	17.95	19.96	18.17	25.32
3	29.68	31.52	34.91	34.55	42.44
4	47.21	48.28	53.12	54.64	62.99
5	68.52	70.60	76.07	77.74	87.31
6	94.15	85.18	102.14	104.94	114.90

λ_{max}

m − r	Case 1	Case 1.1*	Case 1*	Case 2	Case 2*
1	3.76	8.18	9.24	3.74	12.25
2	14.07	14.90	15.67	16.87	18.96
3	20.97	21.07	22.00	23.78	25.54
4	27.07	27.14	28.14	30.33	31.46
5	33.46	33.32	34.40	36.41	37.52
6	39.37	39.43	40.30	42.48	43.97

Source: Osterwald-Lenum (1992)

The critical values for each test are displayed in Table 9.5. There are five separate cases for each of the trace and λ_{max} statistics, but only one case is of immediate relevance. The two tables make it clear that the distribution of the test statistic depends *only* on the *rank deficiency* $m - r$ of $\Pi(1)$, not the dimensionality of the model m or the *rank* r of $\Pi(1)$.

In the unit root tests and cointegration tests of sections 7.7 and 7.8, it was noted that there was a difference between a model which was used to construct the test statistics (the *test model*) and the model that was supposed to hold under the null hypothesis of a unit root. The different cases arise here for the same reasons.

To see the significance of the various cases, consider the VEC(1) model

$$\Delta y_t = -HJ'y_{t-1} + \mu + u_t,$$

in which

$$\mu = -H\alpha + \tau,$$

producing

$$\Delta y_t = -H(\alpha + J'y_{t-1}) + \tau + u_t.$$

Case 1 in the table corresponds to using this model to generate the likelihood ratio test statistics, and also that it is the model under the null hypothesis of a specific rank for $\Pi(1)$. Case 1.1* again uses this as the test model, but assumes that the model under the null hypothesis has $\tau = 0$, so that the effect of an intercept is located solely in the error correction term. Case 1* assumes that both the test model and the model under null

Table 9.6 Example 9.1: inference on rank $\Pi(1)$

Assumed value of r under null hypothesis	Rank deficiency $m - r$	Value of In L_r	Value of trace statistic for null value of r	Value of λ_{max} statistic for null value of r
0	5	835.628	86.611*	42.634*
1	4	856.945	43.976	24.737
2	3	869.314	19.240	12.078
3	2	875.352	7.162	6.670
4	1	878.688	0.492	0.492
5	0	878.934		

hypothesis have $\tau = 0$. Case 1 is appropriate for the model of Example 9.1, in which the intercept is estimated unrestrictedly. It is not forced to belong only to the cointegration space. However, it is arguable that Case 1.1* is also appropriate: one may believe that there should be an intercept only in the error correction term, but not enforce this in estimation. Cases 2 and 2* correspond to the inclusion of both an intercept and a trend in the VAR and VEC model. Case 2 allows the intercept and trend to be unrestricted, and Case 2* allows an unrestricted intercept but forces the trend to be only in the error correction term. In both of these cases, the model used to generate the likelihood ratio test statistics is also considered to be the model generating the data under the null hypothesis of a specific rank for $\Pi(1)$.

The model underlying Example 9.1 is a VAR(2), but the basic information required for carrying out inference on the value of rank $\Pi(1)$ is still the set of generalised eigenvalues from Table 9.2, and the associated likelihood values. Table 9.6 summarises this information. The values in the trace column are equivalent to minus twice the difference between ln L_r and ln L_m, as in (9.79), although they were calculated directly from the values of the generalised eigenvalues. The values in the λ_{max} column are minus twice the difference of ln L_r and ln L_{r+1}.

Comparing the values of the test statistic with the critical values in Table 9.5, Case 1, those marked with an asterisk exceed the critical value. Looking at the column for the trace statistic, 68.52 is the critical value for testing (9.77) with $r = 0$ against the alternative (9.78) that $r = m = 5$. This null hypothesis is rejected, so we proceed to test (9.77) with $r = 1$ against (9.78): since the critical value is 47.21, the null hypothesis is accepted. Tentatively, we select 1 as the estimate of r. Following through the same procedure for the λ_{max} test statistic, we reject $r = 0$ against $r = 1$, but accept $r = 1$ against $r = 2$. This is a case in which the two test statistics give the same conclusions, although it is not unusual for conflicting conclusions to occur.

For this choice, the first column in Table 9.2 is the generalised eigenvector which is taken as the estimate of the matrix J of (9.44), and the second column of Table 9.7 gives the estimate of the normalised or standardised version of J, denoted J^* in the table – see (9.20). The estimate of H implied by choosing $r = 1$ is the first column of Table 9.3, and the corresponding 'standardised' estimate H^* is also given in Table 9.7.

Table 9.7 Example 9.1: estimates of standardised H and J for r = 1

	$\hat{H}^*$	$\hat{J}^*$
LNM4	−0.003 25	1.000 00
LNRGDP	−0.003 44	−5.597 17
DLNPGDP	−0.017 28	36.199 20
B20	−0.102 35	−0.133 85
TBILL	−0.638 15	0.035 80

The reasoning which leads to the presentation of the standardised cointegration vectors in the columns of $\hat{J}^*$, rather than simply relying on the estimates of J from Table 9.2, is that interpretation of the estimated cointegration vectors becomes easier. Using (9.33), the normalisation on LNM4 suggests immediately that the single cointegration vector is a long-run nominal money demand relationship,

$$\text{LNM4} = 5.597\text{LNRGDP} - 36.2\text{DLNPGDP} + 0.134\text{B20} - 0.036\text{TBILL}, \qquad (9.80)$$

in which the demand for money is strongly influenced by real GDP and the inflation rate, and rather weakly by B20 and TBILL. The structure of $\hat{H}^*$ suggests that this cointegrating relationship appears in each equation of the VEC model, and the size of the elements seems to indicate it affects B20 and TBILL more than LNM4, LNRGDP or DLNPGDP. However, this would need to be confirmed by suitable hypothesis tests, an issue discussed in the next section.

Example 9.2

This example uses the same data set, the same sample period and VAR(2) model as Example 9.1, but forces the constant term to appear only in the cointegrating relation. The VEC model to be estimated is then a version of (9.76) in which

$$\mu = -H\alpha :$$
$$\Delta y_t = -\Psi_1 \Delta y_{t-1} - H(\alpha + J' y_{t-2}) + u_t$$
$$= -\Psi_1 \Delta y_{t-1} - HJ^{a'} y^a_{t-2} + u_t, \qquad (9.81)$$

using the notation of (9.73) for augmenting J and y_{t-2} to take account of the presence of the intercept in the cointegrating relation.

Table 9.8 displays the values of the log likelihood function and the values of the trace and $\lambda_{\max}$ statistics for deciding on the value of rank $\Pi(1)$. In this example, Case 1* from Table 9.5 provides the relevant critical values, the pattern of rejections being summarised by the asterisks in the last two columns of Table 9.8. Here there is a slight conflict between the test conclusions from the trace and $\lambda_{\max}$ statistics, but for $r = 2$, the trace statistic only just exceeds its critical value of 34.91, so that we can safely work with the conclusion that rank $\Pi(1) = 2$. The standardised estimators $\hat{H}^*$ and $\hat{J}^{a*}$ are presented in Table 9.9, and are 5×2 and 6×2 respectively.

Table 9.8 Example 9.2: inference on rank $\Pi(1)$

Assumed value of r under null hypothesis	Rank deficiency $m - r$	Value of In L_r	Value of trace statistic for null value of r	Value of λ_{max} statistic for null value of r
0	5	823.367	111.779*	44.433*
1	4	845.260	67.346*	31.983*
2	3	861.252	35.363*	17.198
3	2	869.851	18.165	11.896
4	1	875.799	6.269	6.269
5	0	878.933		

The first column of $\hat{J}^{a*}$ in Table 9.9 gives a cointegrating relationship which is not too dissimilar from that given in equation (9.80), but now has a constant term with value −26.506:

$$\text{LNM4} = -26.506 + 5.543\text{LNRGDP} - 33.1\text{DLNPGDP} + 0.125\text{B20}$$
$$- 0.021\text{TBILL}.$$

The second cointegrating vector gives another long-run relationship as

$$\text{LNRGDP} = 4.342 + 0.214\text{LNM4} - 7.672\text{DLNPGDP} + 0.026\text{B20}$$
$$- 0.071\text{TBILL}.$$

Whilst one could maintain the interpretation of the first cointegrating vector as a nominal money demand relationship, the second can perhaps be interpreted as an excess demand relationship. These cointegrating vectors can be compared with the long-run relationship found for Example 7.8 using a single equation ADL approach, although no evidence of cointegration was found using the ADL model. That long-run relationship resembles the first cointegrating relation here for the intercept and LNRGDP variables, but not for the other three variables. Another comparison between these long-run relationships is made in the next section, in connection with the implications of restrictions on the elements of H and H^*.

Table 9.9 Example 9.2: estimates of standardised H and J^a for $r = 1$

	$\hat{H}^*$		$\hat{J}^{a*}$	
LNM4	−0.007 96	0.012 20	1.000 00	−0.213 85
LNRGDP	−0.004 36	−0.005 63	−5.543 23	1.000 00
DLNPGDP	−0.017 69	−0.001 91	33.081 90	7.671 59
B20	−0.076 87	−0.101 26	−0.124 89	−0.025 75
TBILL	−0.291 95	−1.429 75	0.020 76	0.071 04
CONSTANT			26.506 26	−4.342 49

9.6 / Structure and cointegration

The decomposition of (9.18),

$$\Pi(1) = HJ',$$

provides a way in which long-run economic relationships can be embedded within a VAR model. However, the estimation procedures described in section 9.4 assume that all variables in the VAR model will automatically appear in each of the long-run cointegrating relationships, and in turn that each cointegrating relationship will appear in each equation of the VAR model in VEC form. As in the case of the simultaneous equations model of Chapter 8, natural economic specifications can lead to the exclusion of particular variables from an equation. In the VEC model, these exclusions can apply to both H and J. For example, excluding TBILL from (9.80) removes that variable from the long-run relationship for LNM4. Equation (9.41) shows that a particular structure of H for the case of $r = 1$ ensures that the cointegrating relationship appears *only* in the first equation of the VEC model. Economists often have quite strong views about the long-run relationships that are expected to hold between certain macroeconomic variables. There is then the question of whether these are compatible with the estimate of J, whether it is possible to test these relationships, or even force the model to satisfy them.

There are two general cases to consider. The first is where the nature of the restrictions imposed on H and/or J leads to estimators of the general form (9.57) for H and (9.61) for J'. The normalisation rule (9.56) in effect guarantees the uniqueness of the estimator of J', from which that of H follows (through (9.57)). We shall see that tests of such restrictions are easy to carry out by means of a likelihood ratio test. The second case is where the nature of the restrictions does not lead to the same type of estimators, and where a separate argument for uniqueness of the estimators is required. This corresponds exactly to the issue of identification in the simultaneous equations model in Chapter 8, and has, perhaps surprisingly, a similar solution. The implication is that some restrictions are required for identification, and that only 'overidentifying' restrictions are testable.

Uniform restrictions

These are restrictions whose structure is the same for each column of the matrix of parameters, be this H or J. The model of Example 9.2 will be used to illustrate, since H has five rows, and J six rows, each having two columns in this case. Technically, the J for Example 9.2 is an augmented matrix, but this detail will be ignored.

One simple example is

$$H^1 = \begin{bmatrix} h_{11} & h_{12} \\ 0 & 0 \\ h_{31} & h_{32} \\ 0 & 0 \\ h_{51} & h_{52} \end{bmatrix}, \tag{9.82}$$

which ensures that the cointegrating relationships do not appear in equations 2 and 4 of the VEC model. Another example is

$$H^2 = \begin{bmatrix} h_{11} & h_{12} \\ -h_{11} & -h_{12} \\ h_{31} & h_{32} \\ -h_{31} & -h_{32} \\ h_{51} & h_{52} \end{bmatrix}.$$

For H^1, both columns have the same pattern of zeros, that is, have common restrictions imposed, that both rows 2 and 4 are zero. For H^2, each column has a common pattern of restrictions linking element 1 with element 2, and element 3 with element 4. A particular way of expressing these restrictions is useful here. In H^1, the elements of each column depend on the elements of a corresponding smaller dimensional vector, whose columns can be collected into a matrix H_R:

$$H^1 = \begin{bmatrix} \begin{bmatrix} 1 & 0 & 0 \\ 0 & 0 & 0 \\ 0 & 1 & 0 \\ 0 & 0 & 0 \\ 0 & 0 & 1 \end{bmatrix} \begin{bmatrix} h_{11} \\ h_{31} \\ h_{51} \end{bmatrix} & \begin{bmatrix} 1 & 0 & 0 \\ 0 & 0 & 0 \\ 0 & 1 & 0 \\ 0 & 0 & 0 \\ 0 & 0 & 1 \end{bmatrix} \begin{bmatrix} h_{12} \\ h_{32} \\ h_{52} \end{bmatrix} \end{bmatrix}$$

$$= \begin{bmatrix} 1 & 0 & 0 \\ 0 & 0 & 0 \\ 0 & 1 & 0 \\ 0 & 0 & 0 \\ 0 & 0 & 1 \end{bmatrix} \begin{bmatrix} h_{11} & h_{12} \\ h_{31} & h_{32} \\ h_{51} & h_{52} \end{bmatrix} = M_H^1 H_R. \tag{9.83}$$

The uniformity comes from the way in which the parameters in each column of H^1 depend on the corresponding column of H_R in the same way via the common matrix M_H^1. For H^2, it is easy to see that

$$H^2 = \begin{bmatrix} 1 & 0 & 0 \\ -1 & 0 & 0 \\ 0 & 1 & 0 \\ 0 & -1 & 0 \\ 0 & 0 & 1 \end{bmatrix} \begin{bmatrix} h_{11} & h_{12} \\ h_{31} & h_{32} \\ h_{51} & h_{52} \end{bmatrix} = M_H^2 H_R.$$

For J, an example of uniform restrictions might be one in which TBILL (which corresponds to row 5 of J) is excluded from both cointegrating relationships:

$$J = \begin{bmatrix} j_{11} & j_{12} \\ j_{21} & j_{22} \\ j_{31} & j_{32} \\ j_{41} & j_{42} \\ 0 & 0 \\ j_{61} & j_{62} \end{bmatrix}$$

$$= \begin{bmatrix} 1 & 0 & 0 & 0 & 0 \\ 0 & 1 & 0 & 0 & 0 \\ 0 & 0 & 1 & 0 & 0 \\ 0 & 0 & 0 & 1 & 0 \\ 0 & 0 & 0 & 0 & 0 \\ 0 & 0 & 0 & 0 & 1 \end{bmatrix} \begin{bmatrix} j_{11} & j_{12} \\ j_{21} & j_{22} \\ j_{31} & j_{32} \\ j_{41} & j_{42} \\ j_{61} & j_{62} \end{bmatrix} = M_J J_R. \tag{9.84}$$

Such restrictions still have to ensure that rank H = rank J = r, so that the rank of both H_R and J_R will still have to be r. This requires the number of rows in each, say s_H and s_J, to exceed r, but still be smaller than m:

$$r \leq s_H \leq m, \quad r \leq s_J \leq m.$$

Estimation under uniform restrictions

Suppose first that only J is restricted, satisfying the restriction

$$J = M_J J_R$$

in the VEC(1) model of (9.44): then the restricted model is

$$\Delta Y = -Y_1 M_J J_R H' + U. \tag{9.85}$$

Put

$$Y_1^J = Y_1 M_J,$$

so that (9.85) becomes

$$\Delta Y = -Y_1^J J_R H' + U, \tag{9.86}$$

which is the same as (9.44) apart from the replacement of Y_1 by Y_1^J. The estimation procedure for the VEC(1) model then proceeds as in section 9.4, and the extension to a VEC(p) model also carries over.

In the case where H is restricted, things are more complicated, whether or not J is also restricted. Suppose that both H and J satisfy the uniform restrictions $H = M_H H_R$ and $J = M_J J_R$: then the VEC(1) model of (9.44) becomes

$$\Delta Y = -Y_1 M_J J_R H_R' M_H' + U$$
$$= -Y_1^J J_R H_R' M_H' + U. \qquad (9.87)$$

The presence of the term M_H' creates the difficulty: even when J_R is known, there is no simple form for the OLS estimator of H_R'. However, it is possible to fit this estimation problem into the same format as the previous case. Let Q_H and $\bar{M}_H$ be matrices with the property that

$$M_H' Q_H = 0, \quad M_H' \bar{M}_H = I_r.$$

Postmultiplication of (9.87) by Q_H eliminates the effect of Y_1^J completely, whilst postmultiplication of (9.87) by $\bar{M}_H$ eliminates M_H':

$$\Delta Y \bar{M}_H = -Y_1^J J_R H_R' + U \bar{M}_H.$$

This looks similar in form to (9.86), but this is not the full story. One has to regress $\Delta Y \bar{M}_H$ and Y_1^J on $\Delta Y Q_H$, generating residual matrices $\Delta \tilde{Y}_R$ and $\tilde{Y}_{1R}^J$: estimates of J_R and H_R are then obtained by interpreting the relation

$$\Delta \tilde{Y}_R = -\tilde{Y}_{1R}^J J_R H_R' + \text{error}$$

as if it were the underlying VEC(1) model. This is reminiscent of the way in which estimates of a VEC(p) model were obtained using the reasoning for a VEC(1) model in section 9.4. Indeed, the reasoning described here can be adapted directly to the case of a VEC(p) model subject to uniform restrictions on H and J, by starting from (9.68) rather than (9.44).

Testing uniform restrictions

In all of these cases, the maximised value of the restricted log likelihood function has the form of (9.60) for the VEC(1) case and (9.69) for the VEC(p) case. More specifically, when there are restrictions on H, the determinant terms in these maximised log likelihood functions still involve ΔY or $\Delta \tilde{Y}$, rather than $\Delta \tilde{Y}_R$. Denote the generalised eigenvalues appearing in the appropriate maximised log likelihood function for the restricted problem by $\hat{\lambda}_j^R, j = 1, \ldots, r$: then the restricted analogue of (9.60) is

$$\ln L^R = -\frac{nm}{2} \ln 2\pi - \frac{n}{2} \ln \det \left(\frac{\Delta Y' \Delta Y}{n} \right) - \frac{nm}{2} - \frac{n}{2} \sum_{j=1}^{r} \ln(1 - \hat{\lambda}_j^R).$$

A likelihood ratio test of uniform restrictions in the VEC(1) model of (9.44) then

Table 9.10 Example 9.2: testing uniform restrictions

Generalised eigenvalues for $r = 2$	$\hat{\lambda}_1^{R}$	$\hat{\lambda}_2^{R}$	Value of maximised L	Value of LR
Unrestricted	0.301 16	0.227 35	861.2521	
(9.83) imposed	0.296 18	0.220 57	860.2708	1.963
(9.83) and (9.84) imposed	0.295 56	0.191 16	857.9191	6.666

follows the general case of (4.43) as

$$LR = 2(\ln L - \ln L^{R})$$

$$= -n\left[\sum_{j=1}^{r}\ln(1 - \hat{\lambda}_j) - \sum_{j=1}^{r}\ln(1 - \hat{\lambda}_j^{R})\right]$$

$$= -n\sum_{j=1}^{r}\ln\left[\frac{(1 - \hat{\lambda}_j)}{(1 - \hat{\lambda}_j^{R})}\right].$$

The statistic has the same form in the general VEC(p) case.

An important issue is the distribution of this test statistic under the null hypothesis that the restrictions hold, and given that rank $\Pi(1) = r$. It is perhaps fortunate that the LR is approximately distributed as χ^2 (in large samples) under the null hypothesis, with degrees of freedom equal to the number of restrictions tested. If the restrictions are

$$H = M_H H_R$$

where M_H is $m \times s_H$, then there are $(m - s_H)r$ restrictions being imposed. Similarly, if

$$J = M_J J_R$$

where M_J is $m \times s_J$, there are $(m - s_J)r$ restrictions.

For the example of (9.83), $m = 5$, $s_H = 3$, $r = 2$, giving four restrictions, which can also be counted up from the structure of the matrix H^1 in (9.82). In the case of the exclusion of TBILL from J of (9.84), here $s_J = 4$, giving two restrictions. If both sets of restrictions are imposed on the model of Example 9.2 there will be six restrictions imposed overall. Table 9.10 displays the generalised eigenvalues $\hat{\lambda}_1^{R}$ and $\hat{\lambda}_2^{R}$ obtained by imposing (9.83) on the VEC model of Example 9.2, and also by imposing both (9.83) and (9.84). The 5% critical values from χ_4^2 and χ_6^2 are 9.49 and 12.59 respectively, so that both sets of restrictions are accepted.

Identification and restrictions on H and J

It is important to remember that in decomposing $\Pi(1)$ as (9.18),

$$\Pi(1) = HJ',$$

we are interested in the conclusion of the Granger Representation Theorem that $J'y_t$ is $I(0)$. But, any nonsingular transformation $FJ'y_t$ of $J'y_t$ would also be $I(0)$. In order to maintain equality in (9.18) under such a transformation, the matrix H would have to change, as noted in (9.19):

$$\Pi(1) = HF^{-1} \cdot FJ'. \tag{9.88}$$

This feature is reminiscent of the way in which the reduced form parameters of a simultaneous equations model are related to the structural form parameters. Bearing in mind the fact that the long-run relationships implicit in the underlying VAR model are given by the rows of $J'y_t$, this ability to change the long-run relationships by premultiplication by an arbitrary nonsingular matrix is a little disconcerting.

The Johansen estimation procedure evades this difficulty by choosing its estimate of J to uniquely satisfy the conditions implicit in (9.56) and (9.58). Indeed, these equations subject the $m \times r$ matrix J to r^2 restrictions, leaving in effect only $(m-r)r$ unrestricted elements. These restrictions come from setting the off-diagonal elements to zero and the diagonals to 1 in (9.56), giving $(1/2)r(r+1)$ restrictions, and setting the off-diagonal elements to zero in (9.58), giving $(1/2)r(r-1)$ restrictions. In total, there are r^2 restrictions. The result of these restrictions is a unique estimate of J. This is sometimes expressed by saying that the Johansen procedure gives a unique estimate of the space of cointegrating vectors.

The restrictions in (9.56) and (9.58) are data-dependent in that they depend on the data matrices ΔY and Y_1. However, if (9.56) is replaced by

$$J'E(Y_1'Y_1)J = I_r \tag{9.89}$$

and (9.58) by

$$J'E[Y_1'Y_1 - Y_1'\Delta Y(\Delta Y'\Delta Y)^{-1}\Delta Y'Y_1]J = \text{diagonal matrix}, \tag{9.90}$$

'population' restrictions are obtained. The point about the uniqueness argument is that no transformation of J' by an arbitrary nonsingular F can satisfy the conditions in (9.89) and (9.90) unless $F = I_r$. This reasoning corresponds very closely to that discussed in section 8.6 for the simultaneous equations model.

Even with the imposition of uniform restrictions on H and/or J, it is still possible that the structure of the cointegrating relationships and the way they appear in the equations of the VEC model may not match the prior views of economists. For example, in the context of Example 9.2, it may be felt that whilst TBILL can be excluded from the first cointegrating relationship, it cannot reasonably be excluded from the second (notwithstanding the empirical results in Table 9.10). Thus, J cannot satisfy purely uniform restrictions. Equally, it may be felt that only one of the two cointegrating relationships can be excluded from a particular equation of the model: H cannot then satisfy purely uniform relationships. We shall therefore have to consider more general types of restrictions on H and J. It turns out that estimation of a VEC model subject to nonuniform restrictions on H and J by maximum likelihood does not follow the pattern described in section 9.4, and specifically the estimator of J does not arise as the solution to a generalised eigenvalue problem:

see Johansen (1995) for further details. The implication of this is that the restrictions embodied in (9.89) and (9.90) do not ensure in particular that J is identified, and that a unique estimator emerges.

Instead, we will have to ensure the identification of J (and ultimately H) by other means. The idea is exactly the same as that of the simultaneous equations model: the restrictions imposed by the economist's specification must ensure that there is only one pairing of H and J that can generate a specific value of the 'reduced form' parameter matrix $\Pi(1)$. Equivalently, what nonsingular transformations F of J' preserve the restrictions imposed on J'? If the only such transformation is $F = I_r$, then the elements of J' are identified, and one can expect to obtain unique estimates of these parameters. If this is so, the elements of H are automatically identified. It is possible to imagine cases where it is the pattern of restrictions on H and J' together that serves to ensure that the only 'admissible' transformation of H and J' is $F = I_r$, although such cases will not be investigated here.

Consider the following example of a J' matrix, appropriate for Example 9.2:

$$J' = \begin{bmatrix} 1 & j_{21} & j_{31} & j_{41} & 0 & j_{61} \\ j_{12} & 1 & j_{32} & j_{42} & 0 & j_{62} \end{bmatrix}. \tag{9.91}$$

Again the fact that this reflects the inclusion of a constant term in the cointegrating relationship and that (9.91) is therefore the augmented matrix $J^{a'}$ of (9.73) will be ignored. Recall that Example 9.2 is a five-equation system with cointegrating rank $r = 2$. The corresponding long-run relationship is

$$\alpha + J'y_t = \begin{bmatrix} y_{1t} + j_{21}y_{2t} + j_{31}y_{3t} + j_{41}y_{4t} + j_{61} \\ y_{2t} + j_{12}y_{1t} + j_{32}y_{3t} + j_{42}y_{4t} + j_{62} \end{bmatrix}.$$

Note that in (9.91) there is exactly one zero restriction and one normalisation per row of J'. Following the technique of section 8.6, put $FJ' = J^{*'}$, satisfying the same pattern of zeros and ones as (9.91). Here, F is a 2×2 matrix. Equating the 11, 15, 22 and 25 elements of J' and $J^{*'}$ gives four equations from which to determine the four unknown elements of F. Unfortunately, equating the 15 and 25 elements produces equations which place no restriction on the elements of F, and hence we cannot conclude that the only solution to these four equations is $F = I_2$. Thus the elements of J' in (9.91) are not identified.

For another example, let

$$J' = \begin{bmatrix} 1 & j_{21} & j_{31} & j_{41} & 0 & j_{61} \\ j_{12} & 1 & 0 & j_{42} & j_{52} & j_{62} \end{bmatrix}. \tag{9.92}$$

Here, y_{5t} is excluded only from the first cointegrating relationship, and y_{3t} from the second. Now, the 11, 15, 22 and 23 elements of J' and $J^{*'}$ are equated. The equations implied by the 23 and 15 elements give $f_{21} = 0$ and $f_{12} = 0$, and then the 11 and 22 elements imply that $f_{11} = 1$ and $f_{22} = 1$: that is, $F = I_2$, and J' in (9.92) is identified. Just as in the simultaneous equations case, one can see from this example that one would need at least two restrictions in each row of J', one of which must be a normalisation rule. This corresponds to an order condition: in the general case, there must be

$$r - 1$$

restrictions per row of J', plus a normalisation rule, as a necessary condition for identification.

The 'informal F-method' for checking identification of section 8.6 works well here. It is possible to form a linear combination of the two rows of (9.91) which is indistinguishable from the first row, possibly after renormalising the resulting linear combination, and hence the first row of (9.91) is not identified. A similar argument applies to the second row. The rows of (9.92) are *just*-identified, since there are just enough restrictions imposed to ensure that $F = I_2$. An example with overidentification is

$$J' = \begin{bmatrix} 1 & j_{21} & j_{31} & j_{41} & 0 & j_{61} \\ j_{12} & 1 & 0 & 0 & j_{52} & j_{62} \end{bmatrix}, \tag{9.93}$$

in which there is one additional restriction in the second row. We could say here that the first cointegrating vector is just-identified, and the second, over-identified.

An example of an H matrix embodying nonuniform restrictions is

$$H = \begin{bmatrix} 0 & h_{12} \\ 0 & 0 \\ h_{31} & 0 \\ 0 & 0 \\ 0 & h_{52} \end{bmatrix}. \tag{9.94}$$

Although rows 2 and 4 have common restrictions in each column, rows 1, 3 and 5 do not. These restrictions have the effect of confining the first cointegrating relationship to the third equation of the model, and the second one to the first and last equations. No equation of the model contains both cointegrating vectors. One consideration to be borne in mind in imposing restrictions on H is that the restrictions must not compromise the presumption that H has rank r. For example, one cannot have

$$H = \begin{bmatrix} h_{11} & 0 \\ 0 & 0 \\ 0 & 0 \\ 0 & 0 \\ 0 & 0 \end{bmatrix}$$

corresponding to J' in (9.93), since this H has rank 1.

There are two other special types of restriction that may be mentioned. Sometimes the prior knowledge of economists is sufficiently informative to suggest that a complete row of J' is known. This corresponds to the case in which a cointegrating relationship is completely known a priori. Such a row is automatically identified, and the restrictions embodied within it can usually be tested. Another possibility is to write J' in the form

$$J' = \begin{bmatrix} 1 & 0 & j_{31} & j_{41} & j_{51} & j_{61} \\ 0 & 1 & j_{32} & j_{42} & j_{52} & j_{62} \end{bmatrix},$$

which is just-identified according to the reasoning above. This provides a kind of 'reduced form' structure for the cointegrating relationships,

$$\alpha + J'y_t = \begin{bmatrix} y_{1t} + j_{31}y_{3t} + j_{41}y_{4t} + j_{51}y_{5t} + j_{61} \\ y_{2t} + j_{32}y_{3t} + j_{42}y_{4t} + j_{52}y_{5t} + j_{62} \end{bmatrix},$$

corresponding to solving out the cointegrating relations for y_{1t} and y_{2t}.

Testing the restrictions

It is important to remember that the log likelihood values for just-identified versions of the same model are the same, so that just-identifying restrictions are not testable. One way of seeing this is to compare the number of free parameters in J' to be estimated imposing only the restrictions in (9.92), compared with the number actually estimated by the Johansen method. Suppose that m_a is the number of rows of J', to allow for the possibility that it is actually a $J^{a'}$ matrix, as in Example 9.2. In general there would be $(m_a - r)r$ elements of J' estimated by the Johansen method – that is, $m_a - r$ per row. In (9.92) there are $m_a - r = (6 - 2) = 4$ elements per row, so that the Johansen estimate and (9.92) are just-identified versions of the same model.

In the absence of further restrictions on H, estimation imposing only the restrictions in (9.92) would produce the same log likelihood value as the estimates of J and H arising from the Johansen procedure. A likelihood ratio test of the restrictions would automatically deliver a value of zero, so that the restrictions imposed on J in (9.92) are not testable. Now consider (9.93): the second row of J' contains one more restriction than is required for just-identification, and this should make the log likelihood function for a model with this set of restrictions differ from that arising from the Johansen procedure. A likelihood ratio test is therefore possible, treating the more restricted J' as corresponding to the null hypothesis. Which restriction on J in (9.93) is being tested? That is, what is the structure of J' under the alternative hypothesis? The normalisation rule is indispensable, so the restriction being tested must be either $j_{32} = 0$ or $j_{42} = 0$. Relaxing either one of these gives a just-identified model with the same log likelihood value. This discussion shows that one cannot know which out of a set of over-identifying restrictions are being tested.

As noted in the discussion of uniform restrictions, likelihood ratio tests of over-identifying restrictions on H and/or J have large sample or approximate χ^2 distributions, with degrees of freedom equal to the excess number of restrictions over the minimum required for just-identification. In the case of (9.93), this would be 1. If both (9.93) and (9.94) are imposed, there would be an additional 7 restrictions imposed, making the degrees of freedom 8.

Table 9.11 Example 9.2: restricted standardised estimates of H and J^a

(9.93) Imposed	$\hat{H}^*$		$\hat{J}^{a*}$	
LNM4	−0.005 88	0.025 77	1.000	−0.193 32
LNRGDP	−0.006 57	−0.018 43	−5.499	1.000
DLNPGDP	−0.020 76	−0.018 11	28.84	0.0000
B20	−0.111 86	−0.278 98	−0.108 76	0.0000
TBILL	−0.716 05	−3.928	0.0000	0.027 93
CONSTANT			26.18	−4.603
ln L			861.245 5	

It is possible to give a general formula for the degrees of freedom of likelihood ratio tests of the over-identifying restrictions on J. Presuming that a normalisation has been applied to each row of J', let k_i denote the number of restrictions applied to row i of J', excluding the normalisation rule. Then, the number of over-identifying restrictions applied to J' is simply

$$\sum_{i=1}^{m}(k_i - r + 1),\tag{9.95}$$

or

$$\sum_{i=1}^{m}[(k_i + 1) - r],$$

when expressed in terms of the total number of restrictions (including normalisation rule) and the total number of identifying restrictions required.

We can examine the imposition of the restrictions embodied in (9.93) and (9.94) on the model of Example 9.2. From Table 9.10, the unrestricted log likelihood function value is 861.2521, so that the value of LR for the restrictions in (9.93) is, from Table 9.11, 0.0132. For the combined set of restrictions (9.93) and (9.94), the value of LR is, using Table 9.12, 5.535. The degrees of freedom are 1 and 8 respectively, with 5%

Table 9.12 Example 9.2: restricted standardised estimates of H and J^a

(9.93) and (9.94) imposed	$\hat{H}^*$		$\hat{J}^{a*}$	
LNM4	0.000 0	0.033 35	1.000 00	−0.193 28
LNRGDP	0.000 0	0.000 0	−5.454	1.000 00
DLNPGDP	−0.018 55	0.000 0	35.62	0.000 0
B20	0.000 0	0.000 0	−0.117 11	0.000 0
TBILL	0.000 0	−2.568	0.000 0	0.024 54
CONSTANT			26.13	−4.538
ln L			858.484 6	

critical values 3.84 and 15.51, so that the null hypothesis that the restrictions are satisfied holds in each case.

In each case, the structures of the cointegrating vectors in $\hat{J}^{a*}$ are not so very different, and do not differ dramatically from the unrestricted estimates in Table 9.10. The same is broadly true for the estimates $\hat{H}^*$, despite the effect of imposing zero restrictions in Table 9.12.

Two-stage estimation

It is easy to see from the discussion of the previous sections that the emphasis in estimation and inference is on the parameter matrices H and J, simply because they capture the effects of cointegration. What about the parameter matrices $\Psi_1, \ldots, \Psi_{p-1}$ that appear in a VEC(p) model? Equation (9.67) shows how the estimators of $\Psi_1, \ldots, \Psi_{p-1}$ are related to the estimators $\hat{H}$ and $\hat{J}$ of H and J. In principle, then, a maximum likelihood estimation procedure for the VEC model ought to generate estimates of $\Psi_1, \ldots, \Psi_{p-1}$ as well as H and J. In practice, however, a two-step procedure is adopted, which resembles the estimation method for the single equation error correction model of (7.80) and Example 7.7. This is most easily explained in the context of the model used in Example 9.2, equation (9.81). This example restricts the intercept in the VEC model to lie wholly in the cointegrating relationship, but the discussion is easily extended to cover the case of an unrestricted intercept.

The two-step procedure for (7.80) amounts to simply replacing the unknown parameters in the error correction term by suitable estimates, and estimating the remaining parameters as if these estimates are the true values. Here, one would replace only J and α in (9.81) by the maximum likelihood estimates $\hat{J}$ and $\hat{\alpha}$, and then estimate Ψ_1 and H from the model

$$\Delta y_t = -\Psi_1 \Delta y_{t-1} - H(\hat{\alpha} + \hat{J}' y_{t-2}) + \text{error}. \tag{9.96}$$

This differs from the procedure embodied in (9.67), since the estimator of Ψ_1 implied by that equation would be from the model

$$\Delta y_t - \hat{H}(\hat{\alpha} + \hat{J}' y_{t-2}) = -\Psi_1 \Delta y_{t-1} + \text{error}.$$

One can see that the estimate of H from (9.96) will differ (hopefully only slightly) from the maximum likelihood estimator $\hat{H}$, and will not satisfy any restrictions imposed on $\hat{H}$, unless (9.96) is estimated subject to these restrictions. As a result of the difference between the two estimators of H, there is no reason for the maximum likelihood estimator of Ψ_1 implied by (9.81) to coincide with that from (9.96).

These points can be illustrated with results from Example 9.2. Interpreting J in (9.96) as the standardised value J^* with $(1, 1)$ and $(2, 2)$ elements normalised to 1, the maximum likelihood estimates of H^*, J^* and α are given in Table 9.9. OLS estimation of (9.96) gives the results in Table 9.13.

Because the estimation takes place using the VEC form, all the variables are differenced. The variables CI1_2 and CI2_2 are the two cointegrating relationships, lagged twice, defined by linear combination of the variables of the model of Example 9.2

Table 9.13 Example 9.2: two-step estimation of H^* and Ψ_1

Equation	Variable	DLNM4_1	DLNRGDP_1	DDLNPGDP_1	DB20_1	DTBILL_1	CI1_2	CI2_2
DLNM4		0.63927	0.14775	-0.04267	-0.00224	0.00107	-0.00796	0.01224
(t)		(9.115)	(2.300)	(-0.471)	(-1.343)	(1.223)	(-2.687)	(3.655)
DLNRGDP		0.23964	-0.15548	-0.07395	-0.00028	-0.00027	-0.00431	-0.00560
(t)		(2.423)	(-1.716)	(-0.565)	(-0.119)	(-0.221)	(-1.032)	(-1.185)
DDLNPGDP		-0.14364	0.07068	-0.72173	0.00067	0.00113	-0.01776	-0.00183
(t)		(-2.074)	(1.114)	(-7.878)	(0.408)	(1.301)	(-6.071)	(-0.553)
DB20		2.2519	-1.5533	1.3033	0.04716	0.10675	-0.10084	-0.07715
(t)		(0.482)	(-0.363)	(0.211)	(0.424)	(1.821)	(-0.452)	(-0.391)
DTBILL		26.831	-9.4655	-4.5484	-0.00283	0.04350	-0.29247	-1.4275
(t)		(3.077)	(-1.185)	(-0.394)	(-0.014)	(0.398)	(-0.794)	(-3.428)

Table 9.14 Example 9.2: two-step estimates of H^* where J satisfies only (9.93)

Equation	CI1_2	CI2_2
DLNM4	−0.004 86	0.016 73
(t)	(−1.356)	(1.469)
DLNRGDP	−0.002 78	−0.051 66
(t)	(−0.575)	(−3.366)
DDLNPGDP	−0.022 23	−0.005 10
(t)	(−6.333)	(−0.457)
DB20	−0.120 10	−0.208 46
(t)	(−0.499)	(−0.273)
DTBILL	−0.692 92	−4.126 0
(t)	(−1.544)	(−2.893)

using the two columns of $\hat{J}^{a*}$ given in Table 9.9. There are a number of interesting points in Table 9.13. Comparing the coefficients on CI1_2 and CI2_2 with the columns of Table 9.9 corresponding to $\hat{H}^*$, we see that the two estimates of H^* are similar, but not the same. Although it is possible to compute standard errors and hence t values for the maximum likelihood estimators of H and H^*, these are not always presented by software packages. The two-step procedure does have the advantage of generating these automatically. Examining the t values in the columns of Table 9.13 for CI1_2 and CI2_2, we infer that h^*_{11}, h^*_{12}, h^*_{31} and h^*_{52} are significant, whilst h^*_{21}, h^*_{22}, h^*_{32}, h^*_{41}, h^*_{42} and h^*_{51} are insignificant. This is almost the same as the pattern of exclusions imposed by (9.94) on the H and H^* of Example 9.2, apart from setting h^*_{11} equal to zero.

It is interesting to note that if the exercise is repeated using the restricted estimator of J satisfying (9.93), the estimated H^* matrix (given in Table 9.14) still satisfies some of the restrictions of (9.94). Only the behaviour of h^*_{12} and h^*_{21} is now inconsistent with (9.94).

What is the theoretical justification for this two-step procedure? In Chapter 7, such a procedure was justified by arguing that the estimators of the slopes in the long-run relationship or error correction term were superconsistent in the sense used in section 7.6. The same is true for the estimators of J and J^*: a reference for this is Johansen (1995: 183).

9.7 / The relationship between VEC, ADL and dynamic simultaneous equations models

The attraction of cointegration in a VAR model is very simple: hidden within the model are both the nonstationary and stationary components of the system. Formulating a VAR in vector error correction form displays this separation very neatly.

Next, moving from the use of Johansen's orthogonality conditions to identify the cointegrating relations in J to the imposition of normalisation rules, exclusion restrictions and other constraints reveals the possibility of a structural formulation of the long-run relationships embedded within the VAR. This line of reasoning points ultimately to a relationship in general between a VEC model and a simultaneous equations model. Initially, however, we restrict consideration to the relationship, if any, between one equation from a bivariate VEC(1) model and an ADL$(1,1)$ model in the error correction form (6.37) or (7.77).

To see how this works, suppose that Y_t and X_t are scalar random variables following a VAR(1) process with an intercept,

$$\begin{bmatrix} Y_t \\ X_t \end{bmatrix} = \begin{bmatrix} \mu_1 \\ \mu_2 \end{bmatrix} + \begin{bmatrix} \pi_{11} & \pi_{12} \\ \pi_{21} & \pi_{22} \end{bmatrix} \begin{bmatrix} Y_{t-1} \\ X_{t-1} \end{bmatrix} + \begin{bmatrix} u_{1t} \\ u_{2t} \end{bmatrix}, \tag{9.97}$$

where $u_t \sim IID(0, \Sigma)$. The change in notation here is intended for compatibility with Chapter 7. The VEC(1) form of this model is the bivariate form of (9.34), with the presumption that rank $H = $ rank $J = 1$:

$$\begin{bmatrix} \Delta Y_t \\ \Delta X_t \end{bmatrix} = \begin{bmatrix} \mu_1 \\ \mu_2 \end{bmatrix} - \begin{bmatrix} h_{11} \\ h_{21} \end{bmatrix} \begin{bmatrix} 1 & j_{21} \end{bmatrix} \begin{bmatrix} Y_{t-1} \\ X_{t-1} \end{bmatrix} + \begin{bmatrix} u_{1t} \\ u_{2t} \end{bmatrix}. \tag{9.98}$$

In addition, we shall assume that the intercept appears only in the single cointegrating relationship, giving (9.98) the form

$$\begin{bmatrix} \Delta Y_t \\ \Delta X_t \end{bmatrix} = - \begin{bmatrix} h_{11} \\ h_{21} \end{bmatrix} (Y_{t-1} + \alpha + j_{21} X_{t-1}) + \begin{bmatrix} u_{1t} \\ u_{2t} \end{bmatrix}. \tag{9.99}$$

The first equation of (9.99) is

$$\Delta Y_t = -h_{11}(Y_{t-1} + \alpha + j_{21} X_{t-1}) + u_{1t}, \tag{9.100}$$

which can be compared with the error correction form (7.77),

$$\Delta Y_t = -\phi(1)(Y_{t-1} - \mu_0 - \mu_1 X_{t-1}) + \beta_0 \Delta X_t + v_t \tag{9.101}$$

in which the error term u_t from (7.77) has been changed to avoid a notational conflict. Apart from other notational changes, the major contrast is between the presence of the 'dependent variable' ΔX_t in (9.101) as an explanatory variable, and its absence in (9.100). The VAR model in VEC form would then seem to be incompatible with an ADL model. We can also interpret (9.101) as the first equation of a bivariate simultaneous equations model, if it is considered that ΔX_t is correlated with v_t. The implication here is then that the VAR(1) model (9.97) and its VEC form (9.98) are reduced forms of two related simultaneous equations models, the model corresponding to the VEC form being

$$\begin{bmatrix} 1 & a_{12} \\ a_{21} & 1 \end{bmatrix} \begin{bmatrix} \Delta Y_t \\ \Delta X_t \end{bmatrix} = - \begin{bmatrix} \gamma_{11} \\ \gamma_{21} \end{bmatrix} (Y_{t-1} + \alpha + j_{21} X_{t-1}) + \begin{bmatrix} \varepsilon_{1t} \\ \varepsilon_{2t} \end{bmatrix}. \tag{9.102}$$

There are two main points to note about the system (9.102). Necessarily, the cointegrating relationship is left unchanged by the transformation to and from the structural form. It can then be interpreted as part of the 'structure' in the structural form which remains 'structural' in the reduced form. Secondly, ΔX_t is an endogenous variable in the system, and thus will be correlated with ε_{1t}, unless ε_{1t} and ε_{2t} are independent of each other. In turn, if the error correction model (9.101) is interpreted as being the first equation of (9.102), so that v_t and ε_{1t} coincide, then ΔX_t is correlated with v_t. Unless v_t is independent of ε_{2t}, then, the OLS estimation method used in Chapter 7 is inappropriate.

A conditional model

There is an alternative approach which does not rely on a link to a simultaneous equations model. Suppose that the errors in (9.99) have a joint normal distribution. Then, (9.99) makes the joint distribution of ΔY_t and ΔX_t (conditional on their past values) normal. In this distribution, as indicated in Appendix A, we can find the distribution of ΔY_t conditional on the values of ΔX_t (and the past values of X_t and Y_t) as a normal distribution with mean given by

$$E(\Delta Y_t | \Delta X_t, X_{t-1}, Y_{t-1}) = (-h_{11} - \sigma_{12}\sigma_{22}^{-1}h_{21})(Y_{t-1} + \alpha + j_{21}X_{t-1})$$
$$+ \sigma_{12}\sigma_{22}^{-1}\Delta X_t, \tag{9.103}$$

and a variance ω^2 independent of t. Recall that the covariance matrix of the joint distribution is $\Sigma = ||\sigma_{ij}||$. A conditional model for ΔY_t is then defined by writing

$$\Delta Y_t = E(\Delta Y_t | \Delta X_t, X_{t-1}, Y_{t-1}) + v_t,$$

in which $E(v_t | \Delta X_t, X_{t-1}, Y_{t-1}) = 0$, with variance ω^2. This is equivalent to writing

$$\Delta Y_y = (-h_{11} - \sigma_{12}\sigma_{22}^{-1}h_{21})(Y_{t-1} + \alpha + j_{21}X_{t-1}) + \sigma_{21}\sigma_{22}^{-1}\Delta X_t + v_t \tag{9.104}$$

which has the form of the error correction model (9.101).

Careful inspection of this apparently complex expression is needed. The second equation of the VEC model (9.99),

$$\Delta X_t = -h_{21}(Y_{t-1} + \alpha + j_{21}X_{t-1}) + u_{2t}, \tag{9.105}$$

shows how ΔX_t evolves. All the parameters in this equation also appear in (9.104). Also, it is the dependence between the error terms u_{1t} and u_{2t} in the VAR(1) process that creates the presence of ΔX_t in (9.104). If these disturbances were independent, σ_{12} would be zero and ΔX_t would not appear; ΔX_t is automatically independent of the error term v_t in (9.104) by construction (see Appendix A), and similarly v_t and u_{2t} are independent by construction. In terms of the discussion of section 8.5, ΔX_t is a strictly exogenous variable in (9.104).

The equations (9.104) and (9.105) are simply transformed versions of (9.99) and therefore equivalent to them. Yet, the independence of the transformed errors suggests that (9.104) and (9.105) could be estimated independently of each other. This would cause some loss of efficiency in estimation since the same parameters appear in both equations. The loss in efficiency would arise from the failure to impose the valid cross-equation restrictions in the model defined by (9.104) and (9.105). For this loss of efficiency not to occur, we would have to be able to localise the parameters into the separate equations. If $h_{21} = 0$, the cointegrating relation or error correction

$$Y_{t-1} + \alpha + j_{21}X_{t-1}$$

would only appear in the first equation of the model, thus ensuring that (9.104) becomes

$$\Delta Y_t = -h_{11}(Y_{t-1} + \alpha + j_{21}X_{t-1}) + \beta_0 \Delta X_t + v_t \tag{9.106}$$

on putting $\beta_0 = \sigma_{12}\sigma_{22}^{-1}$. This has exactly the same form as the error correction model (9.101). The restriction $h_{21} = 0$ in a bivariate model therefore implies that the cointegrating relation can be estimated efficiently from (9.101) by the methods outlined in section 7.8, without the need for the complications of the Johansen procedure.

One can see from this last observation that the structure of the H matrix in the VEC model has implications for whether the single equation estimation of cointegrating relations discussed in section 7.8 is valid. If the structure of H does not lead to a localisation of the cointegrating relationships into specific equations, then the system estimation discussed above is required. This can be seen in the discussion of the results for Example 9.2 presented in Tables 9.13 and 9.14. In the latter case, only a single cointegrating relationship appears in the first equation of the model, and this could justify a single equation estimation approach.

Example 9.3

To illustrate the conditioning approach, the data set of Example 7.7 is used, but deliberately fitting a bivariate VAR(2) model in VEC form. This will correspond to the estimation of an ADL(2, 2) model to explain the variable $\ln(I_t)$ in terms of $\ln(R_t)$. In effect, this connects the logarithm of the inverse velocity of money with a learning-adjusted interest rate – see Example 7.7 for more details. There was mixed evidence in this example for a cointegrating relationship, the *PcGive* unit root test indicating cointegration, whilst the Engle–Granger procedure indicated a lack of cointegration. The estimated long-run relationship from the ADL(2, 2) model is repeated here:

$$\ln(I_t) = 0.0862 - 7.512 \ln(R_t).$$

In trying to apply the Johansen estimation and inference procedure to this data set in order to provide a contrast with the single equation estimation of Chapter 7, it is necessary to use the alternative representation (9.29) of the VEC form of a VAR(p) model. This makes the cointegrating relationships, if any, appear with lag 1 in the VEC form, which is then comparable with the standard error correction model form (6.36). Choosing a VAR(2) model for $\ln(I_t)$ and $\ln(R_t)$ for comparability with the ADL(2, 2) model of Example 7.7, and using the same sample period, produces Table 9.15, analogous to Table 9.6. The intercept in the VEC model here is restricted to belong to the cointegrating relations only. The computed generalised

Table 9.15 Example 9.3: inference on rank $\Pi(1)$

Assumed value of r under null hypothesis	Rank deficiency $m - r$	Value of ln L_r	Value of trace statistic for null value of r	Value of λ_{max} statistic for null value of r
0	2	539.904	59.68*	56.56*
1	1	568.183	3.126	3.126
2	0	569.746		

eigenvalues are 0.419 477 8 and 0.029 609 84. The critical values employ Case 1.1* from Table 9.5, rows $m - r = 2$ and 1 respectively. This gives critical values 17.95 and 8.18 for the trace statistic, and 14.90 and 8.18 for the λ_{max} statistic. It is clear that $r = 1$ is the conclusion from this analysis. The 'Unrestricted' block of Table 9.16 gives the estimates of H^* and J^*, and from which it is seen that the elements of $\hat{J}^*$ are similar to those in the long-run equation from the ADL$(2, 2)$ model.

If the second element in H^* is forced to satisfy the restriction $h_{21} = 0$, the matching with the estimated long-run relation is even closer. This restriction is acceptable in this data set, with long likelihood value 567.376, and LR value 1.614: here LR would be distributed approximately as χ_1^2, with 5% critical value of 3.84. This is the critical restriction: it ensures that the single cointegrating relationship appears only in the equation for $\ln(I_t)$.

In turn, this would justify the construction of a conditional model, which would here coincide with the error correction form of the ADL$(2, 2)$ model. Although the numerical results have not been presented, the unrestricted VAR(2) model underlying the cointegration analysis of Table 9.15 has as estimated error variance covariance matrix

$$\hat{\Sigma} = \begin{bmatrix} 0.000\,479 & -0.000\,141\,911 \\ -0.000\,141\,911 & 0.000\,179\,874 \end{bmatrix}.$$

From this one obtains

$$\hat{\sigma}_{12}\hat{\sigma}_{22}^{-1} = -0.788\,95,$$

Table 9.16 Example 9.3: estimates of H^* and J^* – unrestricted and restricted

Variable	Unrestricted		Restricted	
	$\hat{H}^*$	$\hat{J}^*$	$\hat{H}^*$	$\hat{J}^*$
$\ln(I_t)$	0.087 363	1.0	0.097 504	1.0
$\ln(R_t)$	0.010 322	7.692	0.0	7.513
Constant		-0.102 09		-0.086 286

which is remarkably close to the coefficient of $\Delta \ln(R_t)$, -0.789, in the estimated error correction model given in Example 7.7.

Single equation estimation

The version of Example 9.2 which leads to Tables 9.9 and 9.13, with only normalisation rules applied to J', has both cointegrating relationships present in the first equation of the VEC form of the model. Leaving aside the question of whether the structure of the H matrix localises these cointegrating relationships solely into the first equation, there is the question of what is being estimated by a single equation error correction version of that equation. Intuitively, the two cointegrating relationships are combined into one in the estimation process, so that the estimated long-run relationship corresponds to a linear combination of the two true cointegrating vectors. This can be illustrated by forming the linear combination of the two columns for $\hat{J}^{a*}$ using the two coefficients $-0.007\,96$ and $0.012\,20$ in the first row of $\hat{H}^*$ in Table 9.9, and renormalising them so that the new column has first element equal to $+1$. Interpreted as a cointegrating relationship, this is

$$\text{LNM4} = -24.98 + 5.33\text{LNRGDP} - 16.05\text{DLNPGDP} + 0.064\text{B20}$$

$$+ 0.066\text{TBILL},$$

which is reasonably close to the long-run relationship obtained for Example 7.8, despite the apparent absence of cointegration in that example. At its simplest, single equation estimation of an ADL model cannot reveal the existence of two long-run or cointegrating relationships. System estimation is required for this.

Conditional systems

More generally, maintaining the normality assumption, the discussion leading up to (9.103) can be generalised so that the scalar ΔY_t and ΔX_t of (9.103) become subvectors Δy_{1t} and Δy_{2t} of the dependent variable vector Δy_t of (9.31). One could therefore write a conditional VEC(1) model as

$$\Delta y_{1t} = -(H_1 - \Sigma_{12}\Sigma_{22}^{-1}H_2)J'y_{t-1} + \Sigma_{12}\Sigma_{22}^{-1}\Delta y_{2t} + v_t,$$

where H and Σ have been partitioned as

$$H = \begin{bmatrix} H_1 \\ H_2 \end{bmatrix}, \quad \Sigma = \begin{bmatrix} \Sigma_{11} & \Sigma_{12} \\ \Sigma_{21} & \Sigma_{22} \end{bmatrix}$$

to match the partitioning of Δy_t into Δy_{1t} and Δy_{2t}. Here, the vector error term v_t has a multivariate normal distribution such that

$$E(v_t|y_{t-1}, \Delta y_{2t}) = 0$$

and is independent of Δy_{2t} (under normality). This again carries the implication that Δy_{2t} is (strictly) exogenous in the sense used in section 8.5.

If $H_2 = 0$, the cointegrating relations $J'y_{t-1}$ are localised into the Δy_{1t} equations, and do not appear in the Δy_{2t} block. Making this assumption, and putting

$$\Sigma_{12}\Sigma_{22}^{-1} = S,$$

this conditional VEC(1) model can be written as

$$\Delta y_{1t} = -H_1 J' y_{t-1} + S\Delta y_{2t} + v_t, \tag{9.107}$$

which is very like the reduced form (9.5) of the dynamic simultaneous equations system (9.7).

One of the other justifications advanced for conditional systems is easily presented in this more general framework. Quite often, in using two-step estimation for a VEC model, there are some equations where, in effect, there is no explanatory power. An example of this is the equation for DB20 in Table 9.13, where none of the explanatory variables, including the estimated cointegrating relationships, are significant. One could explain this by saying that DB20 is explained by variables outside the model under consideration. In a loose sense, such variables are 'exogenous' to the system, although this does not automatically make them exogenous in the sense used in section 8.6. If we identify DB20 with a component of Δy_{2t} in (9.107) we can then see that proceeding conditionally on the values of these variables automatically makes them exogenous in the sense of being independent of v_t.

A dynamic simultaneous equations system like (9.7) can be obtained by premultiplying (9.107) by a matrix A,

$$A\Delta y_{1t} = -AH_1 J' y_{t-1} + AS\Delta y_{2t} + Av_t,$$

and redefining parameters as

$$A\Delta y_{1t} = A_1 J' y_{t-1} + \Gamma \Delta y_{2t} + \varepsilon_t, \tag{9.108}$$

where $A_1 = -AH_1, \Gamma = AS$. The important point to notice here is that the cointegrating relationships are preserved under the transformation to and from the reduced form (9.107). This observation serves to reinforce the comment made earlier about the structural nature of the cointegrating relationships, provided that structural restrictions, rather than Johansen's orthogonality conditions (9.56) and (9.58), are used. In addition, it also emphasises the idea that cointegrating structure has to be discovered in what would be considered as the reduced form of a dynamic simultaneous equations model, and that this requires prior investigation before the specification of a structural form model compatible with any cointegrating restrictions.

The need to use conditional models derived from a VAR system also casts a little light on the proposition of Sims (1980) mentioned at the beginning of the chapter. One cannot simply rely on VAR models to provide an adequate model for all the variables under consideration. In any case, there is also the need to ensure that the parameter matrices A, A_1 and Γ are identified in (9.108).

Overview

An extensive collection of ideas is involved in estimation and inference for cointegrated systems. One can see from the structure of this chapter that one has to unite ideas from the preceding three chapters, unit roots, cointegration, single equation error correction models, and simultaneous equations models to add to those of vector autoregressive models and vector error correction models. Despite these complications, cointegration is such a pervasive idea in current time series econometrics because it resolves the spurious regressions problem for $I(1)$ variables discussed in Chapter 7. Associated with the resolution by cointegration is a cluster of valuable properties. One of these is the ability to separate out the short- and long-run components of a model, which is extremely important to economists, simply because many economic theories are phrased in terms of the long run. Being able to test restrictions on the specification of the long-run or cointegrating relations is also important in this context. The link to a simultaneous equations system via the idea of a conditional model again emphasises the structural aspects of cointegration. The invariance of the cointegrating relationships across the structural and reduced forms of a system is also quite striking.

9.8 / Further reading

The literature in this area is extensive and still growing. The recent texts by Banerjee *et al.* (1993), Harris (1995), Hamilton (1994) and Hendry (1995) provide a wealth of additional detail and insight on all of the topics of this chapter. Johansen (1995) provides a fairly high-level, but still readable, study of the technical details of his methodology.

10 Extension and review

ECONOMETRICS

10.1 Introduction

The purpose of this final chapter is to add some further detail to what has gone before, to show first that one can apply the general principles developed so far to new types of model, and then to consider whether the methodology implicit in our earlier discussion is really adequate for the practice of good applied econometrics. In section 10.2, we introduce the class of limited dependent variable (LDV) models, in which observations on the dependent variable are restricted in some way, possibly to zero-one categories of a dummy variable, or to some bounded range of continuous variation. Although this type of model is new, and there are details that are specific to individual variants within the LDV class, no fundamentally new principle of estimation is involved. In the same spirit, section 10.3 presents a brief discussion of a popular class of models in finance, 'autoregressive conditional heteroscedasticity' or ARCH models.

Having shown at least one example of extension to a novel area, we turn to a reconsideration of the framework within which one should use existing material. In recent years, econometricians have paid great attention to questions of methodology, and a brief review of this topic is provided in section 10.3. We also add some observations on computer software, to give some idea of the range of options available. In section 10.4, we return to a theme mentioned at the outset, which sees an exercise in the application of econometric methods as a composite of economic theory, statistical modelling, computer implementation and intelligent use of the data, and we offer some final reflections on this theme.

10.2 Limited dependent variable models

All the models considered in earlier chapters have 'left-hand-side' or dependent variables which, if not actually continuous, have so many discrete values that continuity is not an unreasonable approximation. Moreover, no explicit limits have been imposed on the range of variation of the dependent variable. This means that one could, in principle, generate negative values for a variable such as aggregate consumers' expenditure. In practice, this is highly unlikely, because such values are far away from the observed experience of a real economy.

If we were to disaggregate consumers' expenditure, to look at individual commodities and individual consumers or households, the concept of bounds on observable behaviour becomes much more relevant. For many commodities, there will be some households that do not purchase at all in a given period, either because as a matter of taste they never consume that commodity, or because they consume existing stocks during the period for which purchases are recorded.

This example can be used to illustrate both major forms of limited dependent variable. A household either does or does not make purchases during the recording period. Hence 'purchase' can be a zero-one dummy variable (also known as a *qualitative* or *categorical* variable). If this were to act as the dependent variable in an equation, we would have a dummy (qualitative, categorical) dependent variable.

Now suppose that purchases are recorded in cash terms. Although technically discrete, we may treat purchase value as continuous, but negative values cannot be recorded unless we include returns, and there will be a bunch of zero values corresponding to nonpurchase for reasons of taste, and perhaps also to nonpurchase because of stock holding. Now the dependent variable observations are limited to values greater than or equal to zero, and in some applications, it is very important to alter the model to recognise this fact.

Our example suggests that the material in this section is more relevant to the analysis of disaggregated data than to the aggregate time series approach that characterises much of applied macroeconomics. The data used are often in the form of a cross-section, or in the form of a set of cross-section samples taken through time, and the relevant economic theory is often microeconomic.

In what follows, we often refer to 'individual t', taken from a sample which is indexed as $t = 1, \dots, n$. This may mean an individual person, or a household, firm, or any other unit in a cross-section. Also, when discussing a two-category dummy variable, we often refer to the presence or absence of an *attribute*. This has to be interpreted appropriately; the attribute is more likely to be 'nonzero purchase recorded' than 'having red hair', but these examples are identical in form, since both can be coded using a zero-one dummy variable.

From the outset, it should be made clear that we offer only a very brief introduction to LDV models, which represent an important and rapidly growing area of econometric analysis. For further details, it is necessary to consult the specialist literature (see, for example, Maddala, 1983).

The linear probability model

The starting point for a discussion of modelling 'yes/no' responses is the linear probability model, in which the dependent variable is a zero-one dummy, with zero representing the absence of an attribute (no), and one representing the presence of the attribute (yes). The model describes the behaviour of the dummy dependent variable in terms of a linear regression on nonrandom explanatory variables contained in the row vector x_t'. Hence

$$y_t = x_t'\beta + u_t; \ t = 1, \ldots, n,$$

where

$$y_t = 1 \text{ for 'yes'}-\text{attribute present}$$

$$= 0 \text{ for 'no'}-\text{attribute absent.} \tag{10.1}$$

In (10.1), the term $x_t'\beta$ represents those characteristics of individual t that make it more or less likely that individual t has the attribute in question. A natural interpretation is that $x_t'\beta$ is the *probability* that individual t has this attribute. In later models, $\Pr(y_t = 1)$ will be seen to depend on $x_t'\beta$, but not to be directly equal to $x_t'\beta$.

The probability $\Pr(y_t = 1)$ is only part of the story. In (10.1), the question as to whether individual t actually has the attribute is decided both by the probability and by the value taken by the random disturbance u_t.

Since y_t can only take the values 0 and 1, the disturbance can only take the values $-x_t'\beta$ and $1 - x_t'\beta$. Clearly, the disturbance distribution is not continuous and is certainly not normal. The probability that u_t is equal to $1 - x_t'\beta$ is equal to the probability that $y_t = 1$, which we have taken to be $x_t'\beta$. The probability that u_t is equal to $-x_t'\beta$ is equal to the probability that $y_t = 0$, which is $1 - x_t'\beta$. So the probability distribution for u_t is

u_t	$\Pr(u_t)$
$-x_t'\beta$	$(1 - x_t'\beta)$
$1 - x_t'\beta$	$x_t'\beta$

Although the distribution shown above has zero mean, it does not have constant variance. To see this, note that

$$E(u_t) = (-x_t'\beta)(1 - x_t'\beta) + (1 - x_t'\beta)(x_t'\beta) = 0,$$

$$\mathrm{var}(u_t) = (-x_t'\beta)^2(1 - x_t'\beta) + (1 - x_t'\beta)^2(x_t'\beta)$$

$$= x_t'\beta(1 - x_t'\beta). \tag{10.2}$$

It follows that the disturbances are heteroscedastic, and if OLS is applied to (10.1), the estimator for β will be inefficient. Moreover, standard small sample inference procedures are invalid, both because of the heteroscedasticity, and because the disturbances are nonnormal.

It is possible to devise a feasible GLS procedure, using OLS to estimate β, and then using estimated probabilities $\hat{P}_t = x_t'b$ to reweight observations as

$$y_t/[\hat{P}_t(1 - \hat{P}_t)]^{1/2} \quad \text{and} \quad X_{jt}/[\hat{P}_t(1 - \hat{P}_t)]^{1/2} = 1, \ldots, k; \ t = 1, \ldots, n. \tag{10.3}$$

OLS applied to this transformed data set will produce the required feasible GLS estimator. However, there is a problem. It is theoretically possible for $x_t'\beta$ to take values outside the range 0 to 1, and this conflicts with the interpretation of $x_t'\beta$ as the probability that $y_t = 1$. And one could certainly find *estimated* probabilities outside the range 0 to 1. If this happened, the feasible GLS procedure would fail.

As it happens, the most serious problem with the linear probability model is not to do with estimation, but, rather, with the model itself. The difficulty is that the model sets $\Pr(y_t = 1)$ equal to $x_t'\beta$, rather than specifying that $\Pr(y_t = 1)$ is determined as some transformation of $x_t'\beta$. This can be remedied by reformulating the model to incorporate a more sensible transformation rule.

Before considering alternative models, we note that the linear probability model is often used as a starting point for more elaborate methods. It is also closely related to a technique known as linear *discriminant* analysis; here, the objective is to find a linear function which can be used to assign new individuals to one of two groups. The criterion for success is correct assignment, rather than correct evaluation of probabilities, but in the simplest case the two methods produce effectively the same result.

Now suppose that the mapping of values of $x_t'\beta$ to probabilities is achieved by some function $h(\ )$, rather than by direct equality. Suppose also that $h(\ )$ is chosen so that it maps onto the 0, 1 interval for any value of the argument. An obvious choice is a cumulative distribution function (cdf). If the cdf for a standard normal distribution is used, we have what is known as the *probit* model. If the cdf for a standard logistic is used, we have the *logit* model.

Logit and probit models

The logit and probit models are not usually specified directly in terms of the transformation of $x_t'\beta$ into probabilities. Instead, we retain a linear regression model, but argue that this determines the value of a *latent* or unobserved variable, y_t^*, which in turn determines the outcome observed for the zero-one dummy y_t. Hence

$$y_t^* = x_t'\beta + u_t; \ t = 1, \ldots, n$$

and

$$y_t = 1 \quad \text{if } y_t^* > 0$$
$$= 0 \quad \text{otherwise.} \tag{10.4}$$

Since y_t^* is not constrained to equal 0 or 1, there is now no reason why u_t cannot be associated with a continuous distribution, and we can specify that u_t is $IID(0, \sigma^2)$.

In (10.4), the probability that $y_t = 1$ is equal to the probability that $y_t^* > 0$, which in turn is equal to the probability that $x_t'\beta + u_t$ is greater than 0. Hence

$$P_t = \Pr(y_t = 1) = \Pr(y_t^* > 0)$$
$$= \Pr(x_t'\beta + u_t > 0)$$
$$= \Pr(u_t > -x_t'\beta) = 1 - F(-x_t'\beta). \tag{10.5}$$

In (10.5), $F(\ )$ is the cumulative distribution function (cdf) for u_t. If the chosen cdf is symmetric about zero, then $F(\ )$ has the property

$$1 - F(-x_t'\beta) = F(x_t'\beta).$$

It follows that

$$P_t = \Pr(y_t = 1) = F(x_t'\beta). \tag{10.6}$$

Equation (10.6) shows that the latent variable model (10.4) maps values of $x_t'\beta$ onto probabilities by using the cumulative distribution of u_t as the transformation function $h(\ )$. Since y_t is invariant to a change of scale in y_t^*, the model can be standardised to give $\text{var}(u_t) = \sigma^2 = 1$, or any other convenient value. This means that σ^2 is not an unknown parameter. If u_t is standard normal, then $F(\ )$ is the standard normal cdf, and we have the probit model. If u_t has a standard logistic distribution (which actually has $\sigma^2 = \pi^2/3$), then $F(\ )$ is the standard logistic cdf, which is also known simply as the logistic function.

In practice, there is usually little difference between the results from the probit model and those from the logit model, but the latter is easier to work with, because the normal cdf can only be expressed as an integral. The standard logistic cdf is given by the expression

$$F(\ ) = \exp(\ )/[1 + \exp(\ )].$$

Hence, with argument $x_t'\beta$, we have

$$F(x_t'\beta) = \exp(x_t'\beta)/[1 + \exp(x_t'\beta)]. \tag{10.7}$$

Estimation

Suppose that our data consist of a sample of n individuals, for whom we have recorded the vector observation x_t', and 0 or 1 for the value of y_t. We assume throughout that the first element of x_t' is 1, to allow for a constant term.

Since what we really want to do is to estimate probabilities, it seems natural to apply the maximum likelihood principle here. Having observed some individuals with a certain attribute, and others without, and knowing that $\Pr(y_t = 1)$ depends on the unknown parameter vector β, we select that estimate of β which maximises the probability of observing what we have actually observed – in other words, we maximise the likelihood function.

For a particular ordered sample, the likelihood function is

$$L(\beta) = L(\beta; y_1, \ldots, y_n)$$

$$= \Pr(y_1, \ldots, y_n | x_1', \ldots, x_n'; \beta)$$

$$= \left[\prod_1 P_t \right]\left[\prod_0 (1 - P_t) \right]$$

where $\prod_1$ signifies a product over observations for which $y_t = 1$ and $\prod_0$ signifies a product over observations for which $y_t = 0$. The log likelihood function is

$$\ln L(\beta) = \sum_1 \ln(P_t) + \sum_0 \ln(1 - P_t) \tag{10.8}$$

where $\sum_1$ and $\sum_0$ are sums relating to observations for which $y_t = 1$ and $y_t = 0$ respectively.

To maximise (10.8) with respect to β, we first differentiate $\ln(P_t)$ and $\ln(1 - P_t)$ with respect to β, and then use these intermediate results to find the derivative of $\ln L(\beta)$ with respect to β. From (10.6) and (10.7)

$$\ln(P_t) = \ln\{\exp(x_t'\beta)/[1 + \exp(x_t'\beta)]\}$$

$$= \ln[\exp(x_t'\beta)] - \ln[1 + \exp(x_t'\beta)]$$

$$= x_t'\beta - \ln[1 + \exp(x_t'\beta)].$$

Hence

$$\partial \ln(P_t)/\partial\beta = x_t - [\exp(x_t'\beta)]x_t/[1 + \exp(x_t'\beta)]$$

$$= (1 - P_t)x_t. \tag{10.9}$$

Note that the derivative in (10.9) is a column vector; this accords with the rules of differentiation given in Appendix A.

By a similar argument, we can show that

$$\partial \ln(1 - P_t)/\partial\beta = -[\exp(x_t'\beta)]x_t/[1 + \exp(x_t'\beta)]$$

$$= -P_t x_t. \tag{10.10}$$

Using these results to differentiate (10.8) with respect to β, we have

$$\partial \ln L(\beta)/\partial\beta = \sum_1 (1 - P_t)x_t + \sum_0 (-P_t x_t)$$

$$= \sum_1 x_t - \sum P_t x_t. \tag{10.11}$$

The symbol $\sum$ without a subscript signifies summation over the whole sample.

Setting the derivative (10.11) equal to zero gives the conditions for a turning point. The second-order conditions show that a solution obtained in this way is a maximum, which actually turns out to be the global maximum. The equations to be solved are nonlinear in β, so an iterative solution algorithm is required.

In Chapter 4, we argued that for 'well-behaved' problems, the maximum likelihood estimator is consistent and asymptotically normal. The asymptotic variance matrix can be obtained from the information matrix

$$I(\beta) = -E[\partial^2 \ln L(\beta)/\partial\beta \, \partial\beta'].$$

To evaluate $I(\beta)$, we need to differentiate (10.11) again with respect to β, and to do this, we need to find $\partial P_t/\partial\beta$.

From (10.9), we have

$$\partial \ln(P_t)/\partial\beta = [\partial \ln(P_t)/\partial P_t]\partial P_t/\partial\beta = (1/P_t)\partial P_t/\partial\beta$$

$$= (1 - P_t)x_t$$

$$\Rightarrow \partial P_t/\partial\beta = P_t(1 - P_t)x_t.$$

Hence, from (10.11)

$$\partial^2 \ln(P_t)/\partial\beta \, \partial\beta' = -\sum P_t(1 - P_t)x_t x_t'.$$

If x_t is nonrandom, the expectation operator leaves this expression unchanged, and the information matrix is

$$I(\beta) = \sum P_t(1 - P_t)x_t x_t'. \tag{10.12}$$

This can be expressed as $I(\beta) = X'VX$, where X is a matrix of all regressor observations and V is a diagonal matrix, with diagonal elements $P_t(1 - P_t)$; $t = 1, \ldots, n$. The final result needed for inference concerning β is that for the maximum likelihood estimator $\tilde{\beta}$, in a large sample

$$\tilde{\beta} \text{ is approximately } N[0, (X'VX)^{-1}]. \tag{10.13}$$

In practice, the unknown elements of V are replaced by estimated values.

The calculation of logit estimates does require an iterative solution procedure, but several standard computer packages now offer logit and probit estimation. In both models, the significance of individual parameters can be tested using asymptotic t ratios, based on reported standard errors. In the case of the logit model, these are derived from (10.13).

One problem that does cause some difficulty is the question of prediction from logit and probit models. If the explanatory variable vector for a new individual is fed into the estimated version of the linear equation in (10.4), one obtains a prediction of the latent variable for that individual. In fact, it is much more relevant to calculate the estimated probability that the individual has the attribute measured by the dummy dependent variable. For the logit model, the probability for individual $n + 1$ is

$$\hat{y}_{n+1} = \hat{P}_{n+1}$$

$$= F(x_{n+1}'\tilde{\beta})$$

$$= \exp(x_{n+1}'\tilde{\beta})/[1 + \exp(x_{n+1}'\tilde{\beta})]. \tag{10.14}$$

Much the same problem arises in measuring goodness of fit. There is a considerable literature on the appropriate way to do this with a dummy dependent variable; one simple way is to calculate in-sample estimated probabilities, which are equivalent to predicted values of the dummy variable, and then to calculate R^2 as

$$R^2 = 1 - \left[\sum(y_t - \hat{y}_t)^2 / \sum(y_t - \bar{y})^2 \right].$$ (10.15)

Given that the predicted values are continuous on the $0, 1$ interval, whilst actual values of y_t are 0 or 1, even very good fits cannot give R^2 values which are too close to 1. It is also relevant to note that, even in conventional regression analysis, cross-section data will seldom generate the sort of R^2 values that one sees regularly in time series analysis of aggregate 'levels' data.

There is one part of the post-estimation analysis that does use the estimated linear function, at least implicitly. It is often the case that one would like to compare the results from different approaches, and this can be done by presenting estimated linear functions in much the same way as in a regression analysis. However, there are two important caveats. First, it is *not* correct to write out the linear function with the dummy dependent variable on the left-hand side – what $x_t'\tilde{\beta}$ determines is the predicted value of the latent variable y_t^*. Next, the coefficients obtained from the logit, probit and linear probability models are not directly comparable, because each model has a different disturbance variance, and thus a different scaling of the underlying parameters.

In the standard probit model, the disturbance variance is $\sigma^2 = 1$. In the standard logit model, $\sigma^2 = \pi^2/3$. Finally, the linear probability model has heteroscedastic disturbances, with

$$\sigma_t^2 = \mathrm{var}(u_t) = P_t(1 - P_t).$$ (10.16)

If the probit model is taken as the reference point, logit estimates must be divided by $\pi/\sqrt{3}$ (multiplied by 0.5513). However, some authors use Amemiya's suggestion that 0.625 is a better multiplying factor. Linear probability model estimates must be divided by the square root of (10.16), for a 'typical' value of P_t. Using $P_t = 0.8$ implies dividing linear probability model estimates by 0.4 (multiplying by 2.5).

Finally, we have to allow for the fact that the linear probability model directly predicts probabilities, whilst the linear functions from the logit and probit models act as the argument for a cumulative distribution function – which is a rather complex way of saying that the constant terms are not comparable. Assuming that the constant terms have already been adjusted to allow for different variances, as described in the previous paragraph, one must make an additional adjustment by subtracting 1.25 from the constant term obtained from the linear probability model.

Censored and truncated regression models

Instead of using a latent variable to code an observed zero-one dummy, we now consider the case in which it is possible to observe values of the latent variable within a certain range, but not outside that range. An example is the *Tobit* model

$$y_t = y_t^* \quad \text{if } y_t^* > 0$$
$$ = 0 \quad \text{otherwise,}$$

where

$$y_t^* = x_t'\beta + u_t; \ u_t \sim NID(0, \sigma^2); \ t = 1, \ldots, n. \tag{10.17}$$

Here y_t^* is observed, and $y_t = y_t^*$, if $y_t^* > 0$; otherwise y_t^* is not observed, and all that one sees is the value $y_t = 0$. It is important to note that nonpositive values of the latent variable are presumed to exist, even though such values are not available to the observer.

In the application originally considered by Tobin, the dependent variable was expenditure on automobiles. Positive and zero expenditures were revealed, but zero-revealed expenditure includes both nonusers and those drawing down their available stock of automobile services. The latent variable y^* would be interpreted as something like 'current affordable need' or 'current affordable desired service', which could be negative for stock users, or for certain levels of income. Without more detailed recording of individual behaviour, negative values of y_t^* would not be available to the observer. Hence we have a *censored* model of the kind shown in (10.17).

This interpretation of the Tobin example could be challenged, since it assumes that positive levels of affordable need or desire automatically translate into expenditures. If we insist that y^* and y both relate to actual expenditure, then, strictly speaking, negative values are impossible, and the Tobit model misrepresents the true decision-making process.

Turning now to estimation, it is immediately obvious that attempting to estimate the parameters of the Tobit model by a simple regression of y_t on the variables in x_t' will cause problems. Instead of a spread of negative values of y_t, corresponding to values of the explanatory variables which would lead to negative affordable need, we have a bunch of zero values. In the two-variable case, this would obviously distort an estimated regression; for positive true slope, the effect would be to lower the estimated slope relative to the true slope. For a k vector of explanatory variable observations, there would be a similar distortion of the k dimensional regression plane.

If zero and negative values of y_t were discarded, leaving a renumbered sample of n_1 observations, we would have the implied model

$$y_t = x_t'\beta + u_t; \ t = 1, \ldots, n_1. \tag{10.18}$$

Unfortunately, the disturbances in (10.18) do not have zero mean, because values of u_t less than $-x_t'\beta$ are not allowed. If the disturbances in (10.17) are independent normal, the disturbances (10.18) have nonidentical truncated normal distributions, with means which depend on β, σ^2 and x_t', and which therefore vary from observation to observation. It is not surprising to find that this leads to bias and inconsistency in

OLS estimators of the parameters of (10.18). The simple intuition is that observations with $x_t'\beta$ close to zero cannot have large negative disturbances, and this distorts the scatter of observed values around the true regression plane.

To overcome these problems, we need an estimation technique that can incorporate information about the implied disturbance distribution, and this again leads us to maximum likelihood estimation. If we think in terms of generation of the latent variable, as in (10.17), then positive and negative values of y_t^* are generated from disturbances which are $NID(0, \sigma^2)$, but only positive values of y_t arise in this way. The zero values of y_t arise from zero or negative values of y_t^*. The probability element for a positive y_t is therefore

$$\Pr(y_t) = (2\pi\sigma^2)^{-1/2} \exp[-(y_t - x_t'\beta)^2/2\sigma^2] \cdot dy_t.$$

This can be expressed in terms of the *standard* normal density as

$$\Pr(y_t) = \sigma^{-1} p[(y_t - x_t'\beta)/\sigma] \cdot dy_t$$

where

$$p(\ ) = (2\pi)^{-1/2} \exp[-(\ )^2/2].$$

The probability for a zero value of y_t depends on the corresponding value of $x_t'\beta$; specifically, it is

$$\Pr(u_t \le -x_t'\beta) = \Pr(u_t/\sigma \le -x_t'\beta/\sigma) = F(-x_t'\beta/\sigma)$$

where $F(\ )$ is the standard normal cdf. It follows that the likelihood function for the observed sample of y_t values is

$$L(\beta, \sigma^2) = \prod_1 \sigma^{-1} p[(y_t - x_t'\beta)/\sigma] \cdot \prod_0 F(-x_t'\beta/\sigma) \tag{10.19}$$

where $\prod_1$ signifies a product for observations with positive y_t and $\prod_0$ signifies a product for observations with $y_t = 0$.

Maximisation of the log likelihood derived from (10.19) will lead to a set of equations in β and σ^2; these equations are again nonlinear, and an iterative solution procedure is required. As mentioned earlier, there are computer packages which allow for this and other limited dependent variable problems, and given that such programs can estimate parameters of the Tobit model, and give the necessary information for inference procedures to be carried out, we shall not give further details here.

The Tobit model is only one of a whole class of censored regression models. A single censoring point need not be equal to zero, and one might have censoring above some point, or censoring both above and below the observed sample. Models of this kind often arise when we request both the decision to undertake some activity, and the return that follows from a positive decision to participate. Examples can be found in the consumer demand literature, and in the econometric analysis of labour markets. The details of individual models differ, but typically ML estimation is used, and appropriate large sample inference procedures follow from this choice of estimation method.

To complete our very brief introduction to limited dependent variable methods, we look quickly at the difference between a censored regression model and a *truncated* regression model. Truncated models arise when we require a sample of observations with values of the dependent variable in a certain range, but where eligible members of the sample can only be identified after measurement has taken place. Noneligible observations are discarded, and the investigator receives neither dependent nor explanatory variable observations for noneligible individuals. In a censored model, dependent variable values are not observed beyond the censoring points, but the corresponding explanatory variable observations are available, and do form part of the data set used for estimation.

Without pursuing the details, we can again argue that truncation will distort the scatter of observed points, and will cause OLS estimators from the truncated sample to be biased and inconsistent. If maximum likelihood estimation is used, the likelihood function must reflect both the probability of generating an eligible observation, and the distribution of observations that are retained.

Suppose that the latent variable y^* is used to represent dependent variable observations before truncation, and that

$$y_t^* = x_t'\beta + u_t; \ u_t \sim NID(0, \sigma^2). \tag{10.20}$$

If the retained sample includes only observations with $y_t^* < c$, the probability element for observed y_t is

$$\Pr(y_t) = \Pr(y_t^*|y_t^* < c).$$

If this is written in terms of standard normal density $p(\ )$ and standard normal cdf $F(\ )$, we have

$$\Pr(y_t) = \{\sigma^{-1}p[(y_t - x_t'\beta)/\sigma]/F[(c - x_t'\beta)/\sigma]\} \cdot dy_t$$

and the likelihood function is

$$L(\beta, \sigma^2) = \prod \{\sigma^{-1}p[(y_t - x_t'\beta)/\sigma]/F[(c - x_t'\beta)/\sigma]\}, \tag{10.21}$$

where $\prod$ is the product over eligible observations. Maximisation of the corresponding log likelihood produces ML estimates of β and σ^2.

10.3 / Autoregressive conditional heteroscedasticity

This can be regarded as the use of the dynamic models of Chapters 6 and 7 to generate models for heteroscedasticity. This is done by adapting the discussion of section 5.4 of a situation in which the error term ε_t of a two-variable regression model

$$Y_t = \alpha + \beta X_t + \varepsilon_t$$

has a distribution which is conditional on the value of a random variable v_t. This conditional distribution has mean zero and variance $\sigma^2 v_t^2$. If it is also a normal distribution, the unconditional distribution of ε_t cannot be normal, simply because its kurtosis is too large.

Dependence in ε_t

Heteroscedastic error terms are usually expected to be independent, even if not identically distributed. However, in the current case, the error terms need not be independent, although they may be uncorrelated. To see why this might be so, put

$$\varepsilon_t = v_t u_t; \ t = 1, \ldots, n,$$

as in (5.36), where u_t are independent random variables, and v_t is independent of u_s, for every s and t. Then,

$$E(\varepsilon_t \varepsilon_{t-1}) = E(v_t u_t v_{t-1} u_{t-1})$$
$$= E(v_t u_{t-1} v_{t-1}) E(u_t)$$
$$= 0,$$

using the independence properties of u_t again. This type of argument can be repeated for any autocovariance. It is clear that $\varepsilon_t; \ t = 1, \ldots, n$ are uncorrelated, and that this claim depends on the independence of the u_t's, together with their independence from the v_t's, since no assumption has so far been made about the independence, or otherwise, of the v_t's. But, if the v_t's are independent, as well as being independent of all the u_s's, $\varepsilon_t; \ t = 1, \ldots, n$ will be independent.

Without making the assumption that the v_t's are independent, one can show that there is a possibility of correlation between ε_t^2 and ε_{t-1}^2. Using the assumed independence between v_t and u_s, consider the covariance between ε_t^2 and ε_{t-1}^2:

$$\mathrm{cov}(\varepsilon_t^2, \varepsilon_{t-1}^2) = E(\varepsilon_t^2 \varepsilon_{t-1}^2) - E(\varepsilon_t^2) E(\varepsilon_{t-1}^2)$$
$$= E(v_t^2 v_{t-1}^2) E(u_t^2) E(u_{t-1}^2) - \sigma^4 E(v_t^2) E(v_{t-1}^2)$$
$$= \sigma^4 \mathrm{cov}(v_t^2, v_{t-1}^2).$$

So, if the squares of the v_t process are correlated, the squares of the ε_t process are correlated, even though $\varepsilon_t; \ t = 1, \ldots, n$ is uncorrelated. If this seems an unusual argument, note that if v_t is a stationary process, the autocorrelations of v_t^2 are the *squares* of those of v_t, under certain conditions. This proposition merely serves to stress the fact that dependence in the v_t series creates dependence in the ε_t series. One can go a little further: under the stationarity of the v_t series, $E(v_t^2)$ is constant, and

$$\mathrm{var}(\varepsilon_t) = \sigma^2 E(v_t^2)$$

is also constant. In this case, $\varepsilon_t; \ t = 1, \ldots, n$ are uncorrelated, and have constant variance, but will not be identically distributed, since the 'drawings' may not actually be from a common distribution.

ARCH models

It is the nature of the process determining the values of the conditioning variable v_t which gives ARCH models their characteristic properties. For example, if we could construct an AR(1) type of model for v_t^2, we could create the dependence that makes ε_t; $t = 1, \ldots, n$ uncorrelated but not independent. Since v_t^2 is proportional to the conditional variance

$$\text{var}(\varepsilon_t | v_t) = \sigma^2 v_t^2,$$

creating a dynamic model for v_t^2 is also creating a dynamic conditional variance model. There are some slight complications to be dealt with before we can do this directly. Since ε_t has conditional mean zero,

$$E(\varepsilon_t^2 | v_t) = \text{var}(\varepsilon_t | v_t),$$

and then we can define a new random variable η_t with conditional mean zero to make

$$\varepsilon_t^2 = \text{var}(\varepsilon_t | v_t) + \eta_t.$$

This means that a model for v_t^2 is also a model for $\text{var}(\varepsilon_t | v_t)$ and for ε_t^2. Indeed, it is conventional to strengthen these connections by setting $\sigma^2 = 1$ to make

$$v_t^2 = \text{var}(\varepsilon_t | v_t) = h_t.$$

The final notation is simply a shorthand.

The simplest model embodying this type of dependence is the *autoregressive conditional heteroscedasticity* model of order 1, or ARCH(1) model, in which

$$h_t = \text{var}(\varepsilon_t | \varepsilon_{t-1}) = E(\varepsilon_t^2 | \varepsilon_{t-1}) = \alpha_0 + \alpha_1 \varepsilon_{t-1}^2, \tag{10.22}$$

so that the conditioning variable is the lagged error term from the regression model. Equation (10.22) can be expressed as

$$\varepsilon_t^2 = \alpha_0 + \alpha_1 \varepsilon_{t-1}^2 + \eta_t, \tag{10.23}$$

in which η_t has conditional mean zero:

$$E(\eta_t | \varepsilon_{t-1}) = 0.$$

In the h_t notation,

$$\varepsilon_t^2 = h_t + \eta_t, \tag{10.24}$$

so that (10.22) is also equivalent to

$$h_t = \alpha_0 + \alpha_1 h_{t-1} + \alpha_1 \eta_{t-1}. \tag{10.25}$$

Using the squared error term ε_t^2 as a dependent variable makes (10.23) look like an AR(1) in the squared error terms. On the other hand, (10.25), with the conditional variance h_t as dependent variable, looks more like an ARMA(1, 1) model. Yet, both represent the same model, (10.22).

One detail to be careful about is the need to ensure that these time series models generate positive (conditional) variances. If we suppose that ε_0 is known, and $\alpha_0 > 0$, $\alpha_1 \geq 0$, the sequence of conditional variances generated by (10.22) will be positive, as required. Applying the iterated expectation argument to $E(\varepsilon_t^2 | \varepsilon_{t-1})$, we obtain

$$E(\varepsilon_t^2) = \alpha_0 + \alpha_1 E(\varepsilon_{t-1}^2).$$

Despite generating heteroscedastic conditional variances, it is possible for this ARCH process to be stationary. If we assume stationarity and thus demand

$$E(\varepsilon_t^2) = \sigma^2$$

for each t, then if $\alpha_1 < 1$,

$$\sigma^2 = \frac{\alpha_0}{1 - \alpha_1}.$$

This is an example of a model with unconditional homoscedasticity, and conditional heteroscedasticity. In principle, if this ARCH process is used as an error process for a standard regression model

$$y_t = \beta_0 + \beta_1 x_t + \varepsilon_t,$$

and if stationarity for ε_t is assumed, then ε_t would satisfy the usual least squares assumptions!

The model of (10.22) is an analogue of an AR(1) process, with only one conditioning variable. An easy way of creating dependence on several conditioning variables is to generalise (10.22) to be the analogue of an AR(p) process,

$$h_t = \mathrm{var}(\varepsilon_t | \varepsilon_{t-1}, \ldots, \varepsilon_{t-p}) = \alpha_0 + \alpha_1 \varepsilon_{t-1}^2 + \ldots + \alpha_p \varepsilon_{t-p}^2. \tag{10.26}$$

This is the ARCH(p) process. Again, taking $\alpha_0 > 0$ and $\alpha_j \geq 0$ is enough to make $\mathrm{var}(\varepsilon_t | \varepsilon_{t-1}, \ldots, \varepsilon_{t-p}) > 0$; provided that

$$1 - \alpha_1 - \ldots - \alpha_p > 0,$$

the iterated expectations argument makes

$$E(\varepsilon_t^2) = \sigma^2 = \frac{\alpha_0}{1 - \alpha_1 - \ldots - \alpha_p}.$$

Writing (10.26) as

$$\varepsilon_t^2 = \alpha_0 + \alpha_1 \varepsilon_{t-1}^2 + \ldots + \alpha_p \varepsilon_{t-p}^2 + \eta_t \tag{10.27}$$

shows that it is really an AR process in squared errors.

Generalised ARCH processes

It would be natural to look for the ARMA generalisation of the ARCH process: such a generalisation has turned out to be useful in practice. To do this, note that (10.26) has the form of an MA model, in that there are no lags in h_t present (at least, in this form). The generalisation to the *generalised* ARCH or GARCH model puts these lags in:

$$h_t = \alpha_0 + \alpha_1 \varepsilon_{t-1}^2 + \ldots + \alpha_p \varepsilon_{t-p}^2 + \delta_1 h_{t-1} + \ldots + \delta_q h_{t-q}. \qquad (10.28)$$

This would be a GARCH(p, q) model – p lags in ε_t^2 and q lags in h_t. The form paralleling (10.27) comes by substituting

$$h_t = \varepsilon_t^2 - \eta_t$$

and rearranging:

$$\varepsilon_t^2 = \alpha_0 + (\alpha_1 + \delta_1)\varepsilon_{t-1}^2 + \ldots + (\alpha_p + \delta_p)\varepsilon_{t-p}^2 + \delta_{p+1}\varepsilon_{t-p-1}^2 + \ldots + \delta_q \varepsilon_{t-q}^2$$
$$+ \eta_t - \delta_1 \eta_{t-1} - \ldots - \delta_q \eta_{t-q} \qquad (10.29)$$

if $p < q$, and something similar if $p > q$. In the former case, this is like an ARMA(q, q) model in ε_t^2, and in the latter an ARMA(p, q). The rearrangement of (10.28) into (10.29) shows that the conditioning variables are simply lagged ε_t's, apparently up to $\max(p, q)$ lags.

The most common version of (10.28) is the GARCH$(1, 1)$ model,

$$h_t = \alpha_0 + \alpha_1 \varepsilon_{t-1}^2 + \delta_1 h_{t-1}, \qquad (10.30)$$

or

$$\varepsilon_t^2 = \alpha_0 + (\alpha_1 + \delta_1)\varepsilon_{t-1}^2 + \eta_t - \delta_1 \eta_{t-1},$$

which will require

$$\alpha_0 > 0, \quad \alpha_1 \geq 0, \quad \delta_1 \geq 0$$

for positive conditional variances, and

$$1 - \alpha_1 - \delta_1 > 0$$

for stationarity.

It is possible to imagine nonstationary versions of GARCH models. Consider the GARCH$(1, 1)$ model in which

$$\alpha_1 + \delta_1 = 1.$$

A simple rearrangement of (10.30) produces

$$h_t = \alpha_0 + h_{t-1} + \alpha_1 \eta_{t-1},$$

with a structure rather like a random walk with drift for the conditional variance. This model is both conditionally and unconditionally heteroscedastic, and is often called the IGARCH or *integrated* GARCH model. There has been some interest in such models simply because many empirical studies seem to produce estimates of α_1 and δ_1 with sum near to 1.

Estimation and inference for ARCH models

In principle, estimation of ARCH models by maximum likelihood follows the same pattern as the estimation of any heteroscedastic regression model by maximum likelihood. Using the current notation, suppose that the error term ε_t in the two-variable model

$$Y_t = \beta_0 + \beta_1 X_t + \varepsilon_t; \; t = 1, \ldots, n \tag{10.31}$$

has a (conditional) $NID(0, h_t)$ distribution, and where the conditional variance is some (as yet unspecified) function of two parameters, for simplicity:

$$h_t = h_t(\alpha_0, \alpha_1). \tag{10.32}$$

Then, the log likelihood function is given by

$$\ln L = -\frac{n}{2} \ln 2\pi - \frac{1}{2} \sum_{t=1}^{n} \ln h_t(\alpha_0, \alpha_1) - \frac{1}{2} \sum_{t=1}^{n} \left[\frac{(Y_t - \beta_0 - \beta_1 X_t)^2}{h_t(\alpha_0, \alpha_1)} \right].$$

Deriving maximum likelihood estimates then follows the standard procedure discussed in section 4.5. However, in ARCH models there is a complication in that

$$h_t = \alpha_0 + \alpha_1 (y_{t-1} - \beta_0 - \beta_1 x_{t-1})^2$$

and this makes the regression parameters appear nonlinearly in the log likelihood function.

An alternative approach to estimation employs the idea of regressions using squared residuals discussed in section 5.4. This exploits the fact that in the ARCH(1) case, h_t is linear in α_0 and α_1. Start by estimating (10.31) by OLS: denote the least squares residuals by $\hat{\varepsilon}_t$ and then fit

$$\hat{\varepsilon}_t^2 = \alpha_0 + \alpha_1 \hat{\varepsilon}_{t-1}^2 + \text{error} \tag{10.33}$$

by OLS. The fitted values from this regression are actually estimates of h_t: $\hat{h}_t$. With the aid of these estimates of h_t, weighted least squares estimates $\tilde{\beta}_0, \tilde{\beta}_1$ can be obtained as in equation (5.25). Substituting these estimates into (10.31) produces a new set of residuals,

$$\tilde{\varepsilon}_t = Y_t - \tilde{\beta}_0 - \tilde{\beta}_1 X_t.$$

The underlying model

$$\varepsilon_t^2 = \alpha_0 + \alpha_1 \varepsilon_{t-1}^2 + \eta_t$$

has error terms whose conditional variance is (assuming conditional normality) $2h_t^2$, which suggests that a weighted least squares procedure is more appropriate in the regressions using $\tilde{\varepsilon}_t^2$. So, fit by weighted least squares using $\hat{h}_t$ as weights,

$$\frac{\tilde{\varepsilon}_t^2}{\hat{h}_t} = \frac{1}{\hat{h}_t} \alpha_0 + \frac{\tilde{\varepsilon}_{t-1}^2}{\hat{h}_t} \alpha_1 + \text{error} \tag{10.34}$$

to re-estimate the α's, producing say $\tilde{\tilde{\alpha}}_j$. This procedure should give consistent estimates of the parameters. In principle, we can repeat the steps of the method until the estimates have converged, but the estimators generated in this way are not equivalent to the maximum likelihood estimates.

The properties of the two-stage estimators $\tilde{\beta}_0$, $\tilde{\beta}_1$, $\tilde{\alpha}_0$, and $\tilde{\alpha}_1$ are interesting, in comparison with the maximum likelihood ones. Suppose that ε_t is conditionally normal: then the maximum likelihood estimator will be consistent and asymptotically efficient. The latter is equivalent to saying that there is no more efficient estimator than maximum likelihood, although there may be estimators which are as good. The two-stage estimator produces consistent estimators of all the parameters, but $\tilde{\beta}_0$ and $\tilde{\beta}_1$ are inefficient compared to maximum likelihood. However, the two-stage estimators of α_0 and α_1 *are* asymptotically efficient.

The equation (10.33) can be used as the basis of a test for ARCH(1) effects, since as a test regression it has the same form as (5.31). The procedure is easily generalised to the ARCH(2) case, where

$$h_t = \alpha_0 + \alpha_1 \varepsilon_{t-1}^2 + \alpha_2 \varepsilon_{t-2}^2.$$

It is easy to follow through the arguments above to generate the test regression

$$\varepsilon_t^2 = \alpha_0 + \varepsilon_{t-1}^2 a_1 + \varepsilon_{t-2}^2 a_2 + \text{error}$$

before replacement of disturbances by residuals. Here, the test for homoscedasticity would consist in testing that both a_1 and a_2 are zero. It is less obvious that a test regression for the GARCH(1,1) case of (10.30) is equivalent to that for the ARCH(1) case, but this is in fact true.

As noted earlier, ARCH models have found widespread application in the area of finance, typically using very high frequency observations, often daily, on asset prices, exchange rates or interest rates. The attraction of these models is that they capture some of the fluctuations in the conditional variance, which can be regarded as measuring volatility and therefore risk in these markets. Using aggregate quarterly data and typical macroeconomic variables, it is often difficult to find a regression model for which there is a simple ARCH or GARCH model generating the conditional variances. In this type of application, the attraction of ARCH is in generating yet another diagnostic test, picking up the impact of certain kinds of model misspecifications. The advantage of these tests is that they are explicitly dynamic, and are often associated with failures of normality.

Further reading for ARCH

The literature on ARCH models and their refinements is vast. There are many, many variations on the theme: models that can capture asymmetry in volatility, multivariate models, models in continuous time and so on. The most readily available reference to this literature is Bollerslev, Engle and Nelson (1994) and Engle (1995).

10.4 / Some questions of methodology

The material in the preceding section illustrates the extension of earlier ideas to a new type of model, but still reflects the fact that the econometric theory is developed under strong assumptions concerning the model specification. For some time, econometricians have recognised the contrast that exists between the typical theoretic description of an estimation exercise, and the realities of live research in applied econometrics. The essence of the problem is that we employ a statistical model that assumes that we know far more about a given specification than is actually the case in practice. This has led to attempts to construct models of the *research process*, as distinct from models which relate to the estimation of a single equation, and has caused a sometimes fierce debate on the whole question of an appropriate methodology for econometrics.

One of the less appealing ideas used throughout our earlier discussion is the concept of a 'true' model. This immediately reflects the tension between a construct needed for estimation theory, and the objective of a modelling exercise, which is to obtain an approximation to 'reality' of sufficient quality for the particular purpose to hand. To overcome such difficulties, David Hendry has suggested the concept of the *data generating process* or DGP (see, for example, Hendry and Richard, 1982). The DGP is a higher-level model, embodying the assumption that the data are generated from a probability distribution, but imposing no other conditions at this stage. The DGP can be represented as the joint probability density for all sample observations, and this in turn can be expressed as a product of conditional densities. Thus, if x_t is the $(k \times 1)$ column vector of observations on all variables at time t, and X_{t-1} is the $[(t-1) \times k]$ matrix with rows $x'_1, \ldots, x'_{t-1}$, the DGP is

$$\text{DGP} = \prod_{t=1}^{n} p(x_t | X_{t-1}; \theta) \tag{10.35}$$

where θ is a vector of parameters and $\prod$ signifies the product over indices $t = 1, \ldots, n$. The objective of the modelling exercise is then to find an acceptable approximation to the DGP.

Hendry and his co-workers have been very specific as to what is involved in finding appropriate simplifications of the data-generating process. The variables in x_t are partitioned as $x'_t = [y'_t \; z'_t \; w'_t]$, where y_t contains endogenous variables, z_t contains (weakly) exogenous variables and w_t represents a set of variables which are irrelevant for the purposes of modelling the behaviour of y_t. By 'removing' the irrelevant variables, and conditioning endogenous variables on exogenous variables, one obtains a simplified representation

$$\prod_{t=1}^{n} p(y_t | Y_{t-1}; Z_t, \phi) \tag{10.36}$$

where Y_{t-1}, Z_t are matrices defined by the same conventions as X_{t-1} in (10.35) and ϕ is the parameter vector in the new, simplified form. The essence of the exercise is then to find a version of (10.36) that is *adequate* rather than *correct* in any absolute sense, and various criteria are suggested for selecting the model that will serve as the approximation. These criteria are listed in Hendry and Richard (1983), and interpreted further in a very readable paper by Gilbert (1986). The criteria include consistency with both 'data' and 'theory' (by which we mean *economic* theory), and a requirement for what is known as the *encompassing* of rival models. A proposed model is said to encompass an alternative model if the proposed model can explain results generated from the alternative model.

An important part of the Hendry philosophy is the need for exhaustive testing, using a range of different procedures, many of which we have outlined at various stages through the earlier chapters of this book. Although few econometricians would dispute the importance of testing, Hendry's methodology has been criticised, and it does leave some questions unanswered. An alternative viewpoint is that of Edward Leamer – see, for example, Leamer (1978, 1983), a comparative survey in Pagan (1987), and the Hendry–Leamer debate in Hendry, Leamer and Poirier (1990).

Leamer does not disagree with Hendry about the weakness of traditional methods – what Gilbert disarmingly calls the *average economic regression* or AER – but the Leamer response to undercritical presentation of results is different. At the outset of a Leamer exercise, the investigator must specify objectives by designating parameters of interest. A careless data analysis may fail to reveal that inferences concerning these parameters are sensitive to the specification of other variables in the model, and the operational procedures in the Leamer approach are designed to uncover any such sensitivity.

What is less clear is Leamer's attitude to economic theory. Where Hendry sees competition between competing theories as being subject to resolution by careful testing, Leamer sees prior belief as something much wider than a predisposition to one theory rather than another, and has little respect for the concept of an objective DGP. Although Leamer's methods are by no means exclusively 'Bayesian', subjectivity is important to Leamer's view of the modelling process, and there are stages at which prior belief would be formalised by using Bayesian methods. It is also true that the operational procedures of the Leamer approach are less common-place than the ingredients of the Hendry methodology, and there are certainly fewer examples in which Leamer's methods have been used in practice.

A somewhat different perspective is provided by the work of Christopher Sims – see, for example, Sims (1980). In section 9.1, we mentioned the Sims view that many structural econometric models involve prior restrictions that owe more to tradition than to rigorous empirical testing. The suggested answer to this is to use a freely specified multivariate time series model, typically in vector autoregressive (VAR) form, and to allow conclusions about causality and precedence to flow from experiments with the model. If we must categorise this on a 'theory' versus 'data' spectrum, it would tend to discount at least received theory in favour of evidence from the data.

Since none of the protagonists mentioned above has accorded a similar discounting to the data, we round off with a slightly unfair characterisation of what one might call the complete system model (CSM) school of applied econometrics. Our prototype member of the CSM school will typically be concerned to estimate a system of consumer demand equations, production functions, or perhaps a general equilibrium model of an entire economy. In such an exercise, the main interest lies in the fact that the underlying economic theory has been formalised to the extent that it is possible to estimate parameters, often using highly sophisticated estimation methods, in a full system context. But testing is often confined to specific postulates of the theory, rather than to the adequacy of the model as a whole. Such exercises are interesting and intellectually demanding, but could be criticised for putting too much weight on theory, at the expense of data. Within any given exercise, there is no discrimination between competing theories, since only one 'truth' is ever considered.

This brings us back to the starting point. If the theory is mistrusted, or too specific, the obvious reaction is to use the data as the guiding light in model specification. But the quality of the data is often suspect, and it is virtually impossible to conduct a totally free search over alternative specifications, without some guidance from economic theory. We therefore find ourselves between a rock and a hard place, forced to find some position on the line between two imperfect sources of information. It is from this perspective that the debate on methodology has emerged. No one disputes the need for great care in drawing inferences from econometric models; the point at issue is the appropriate methodology for achieving this end.

There are one or two other points that we should mention in passing. Nothing has been said so far about the problem of *pretesting*: a pretest estimator is one which recognises that you arrive at a certain stage only because you have conducted a sequence of earlier experiments. All econometricians are aware of this problem, and of the fact that the true significance level after a sequence of tests is not that of the last test performed, but it is difficult to devise an estimator that recognises several stages of pretesting, and neither pretest estimators nor corrected significance levels have been widely used in practice.

Another question that has concerned econometricians is the *direction* in which one should search for an acceptable model. Should one start with a relatively simple formulation, which captures the basic relationships under investigation, and then augment this in the light of evidence of misspecification, or should one start with as full a specification as possible, and then test down to remove unnecessary detail? In Hendry's terminology, we have to choose between *specific to general* modelling, which is sometimes called forward searching, and *general to specific* modelling, or backward searching. Hendry unambiguously favours the latter, on the grounds that a forward search necessarily means passing through a sequence of 'wrong', that is unacceptable, versions, with all the resulting problems of inference from a misspecified model. A general to specific search might involve inefficient estimation in the early stages, but it avoids the systematic distortion inherent in a seriously underspecified model.

In a specification search which follows a definite direction, all tests will be concerned with *nested* hypotheses, in which the null is a special case of the alternative. This idea underlies all the different forms of variable addition test that we have used;

in each case, the test concerns a maintained model

$$H_1: y = X\beta + Z\gamma + u \tag{10.37}$$

and a model under the null hypothesis $\gamma = 0$, which is

$$H_0: y = X\beta + u. \tag{10.38}$$

Notice that there is a slight shift in terminology here, in that H_1 and H_0 refer to models, rather than to the distinguishing conditions $\gamma \neq 0$ versus $\gamma = 0$. If we now consider the alternative to H_0 to be

$$H_1: y = Z\gamma + u, \tag{10.39}$$

then we have *non-nested* hypotheses, and we need to devise tests of H_0 against H_1 and of H_1 against H_0.

There are various approaches that can be used here, and some computer packages now give a variety of non-nested test procedures (see below). One simple way out of the problem is to artificially nest (10.38) and (10.39) by adding nonredundant columns of Z to X, or vice versa. This is known as the encompassing test. For this and other non-nested test procedures, see Godfrey (1984), McAleer and Pesaran (1986).

One final comment. The literature on methodology is very revealing, but also somewhat intimidating for the applied economist, who is left with the feeling that whatever he or she may do, there will inevitably be some departure from a currently fashionable model of research activity. The answer is to read, digest and learn, but not to allow the research model to stifle creativity.

Computer software

At a more mundane level, the detail of the way in which one conducts a model building exercise is likely to be influenced by the computer software used. Given the wide choice now available, one is not often prevented from using a particular technique because there is no suitable program. Indeed, there is nothing more galling to the writer of a textbook than finding that the latest version of program X provides facilities that are omitted from the text for reasons of space, taste or discretion, and then finding that students are using program X, demanding to know why they have not been instructed in the use of some 'vital' procedure.

Traditionally, econometric software was dominated by large command-driven mainframe packages, of which TSP and SHAZAM are amongst the best-known examples. Both packages have been ported to the personal computer environment, but their origins are obvious. When using a command-driven program, one has to initiate action by typing an instruction in a format recognisable to the program, or by submitting a prepared file of commands in what is known as batch mode. With a good help facility, a great deal of learning can be done at the computer terminal, but the basic characteristic of a command-driven design is that nothing will happen unless you can communicate with the program, using the recognised conventions.

In contrast, programs which are designed from scratch for an interactive environment tend to be menu or dialogue driven. Provided that you understand the questions asked, or the menu that is on offer (or even that you make random selections), something will happen. For this reason, a genuinely interactive program will usually enable you to get started more easily. This offers definite advantages in a teaching environment, but interactive programs can be frustrating when one is in production mode, repeating a job with minor variations as experiments proceed. It is therefore useful when interactive programs have an optional batch facility.

Virtually any program that you choose will produce numerically sound least squares and IV estimates, a range of test statistics and some form of graphical display. It will also provide for data entry, sample and variable selection, data transformation and some form of data management, allowing you to import and export preprepared data files. Many packages now offer extensions to areas such as ARIMA modelling and probit and logit estimation, but programs designed for estimation do not always offer facilities for model solution and simulation.

There is also considerable variation in the degree of provision for nonlinear estimation. You may well be offered a clearly defined algorithm such as Gauss–Newton estimation for AR disturbances, or FIML for some specific model type, but it is difficult to provide full flexibility in nonlinear procedures without resorting to user-written subroutines. To exploit this type of facility, you must have some knowledge of a standard or purpose-written programming language, and such extensions usually require considerably more skill than selecting a standard option.

Turning now to a few specific examples, we note that all programs have strengths and weaknesses. It is not our purpose here to conduct an exhaustive survey, or to enthuse about the matters of detail such as graphics support. All that we want to do is to indicate something of the range of choice available.

Amongst the brand leaders, TSP allows a wide range of estimation techniques and provides for model solution as well as for estimation. Successive versions of SHAZAM have always been timely in providing for new developments, particularly in the range of tests available. RATS is a more recent contender, with particular strengths in the estimation of dynamic models, including VAR models of the type mentioned in section 9.1. LIMDEP has a traditional command-driven structure, offering both conventional techniques and a wide range of limited dependent variable options. PC-GIVE is envisaged as the computer implementation of many of David Hendry's ideas, and again has particular strengths in dynamic modelling. Finally Micro-FIT (formerly Data-FIT) illustrates well the advantages of a menu-driven package, offering a particularly good range of automatically produced test statistics, and some less widely available features such as non-nested testing.

Apart from packages intended exclusively for econometrics, we should also mention statistical software such as SPSS and MINITAB, which allow for some econometric procedures, and program suites such as SAS, which offers the econometrics and time series module SAS/ETS. Finally, there are special purpose languages such as Gauss and Matlab, which operate at a higher level than Pascal, Fortran or more recently C and C++. These packages enable one to create tailor-made programs to perform a specific task, and thus offer great flexibility, but clearly require more investment in learning than a standard econometrics package.

In recent years, the appearance of multifunctional spreadsheet packages has brought to every personal computer user basic statistical and regression facilities. Whilst these facilities are often quite poor in comparison with those offered by specialist packages, they do have some advantages. Anyone who can use a spreadsheet can also perform regression analyses: the estimated results (usually to a high degree of numerical accuracy) are immediately available for further calculations or for graphical work. Another useful feature of some spreadsheets is the ability to compute values of various statistical distribution functions and inverse distribution functions, which are valuable in performing hypothesis tests. Spreadsheets also provide a relatively standardised data storage format with high levels of portability.

10.5 / A final perspective

At the end of this book, it is appropriate to have returned to a point at which one can stress again the integration of economic theory, statistical modelling, computer implementation and the manipulation and quality control of the data. However, we should be realistic about the extent to which it is possible to do justice to these component skills within the scope of a single text. At various points, we have given numerical examples, most of which are based on current data, but which necessarily provide a very partial snapshot of the model building process. For reasons of exposition, we usually followed what amounts to a forward search. In most cases, the experiments were curtailed before reaching a finally acceptable specification, and no example was ever subjected to all the tests that eventually became available to us. However, most of the data sets would support further experimentation, and we did show quite clearly that results from simple models should never be taken at face value, without asking why those results arise. Where an apparently acceptable model is found, it is often the case that a more extensive diagnosis is needed before one can have any real confidence in the inferences to be made. Where very poor results are found, one needs to understand why this may be, before dismissing the underlying theory as unsupportable.

It is sometimes felt that statistics and econometrics can be taught simply by teaching students how to use an appropriate software package. Nothing could be further from the truth. One has to know at least something about the theory behind the techniques in order to understand the significance of the computer output, and to recognise when there are problems with the results. If nothing else, this text shows that there are often many different ways of implementing the same basic idea, for example Lagrange multiplier tests. It is often very unclear from the software's documentation exactly how a technique is implemented, and so one can be in the difficult position of obtaining conflicting results from two different pieces of software. Quite often, some experimentation is required in order to deduce how a particular technique has been implemented.

Turning to econometric theory, it is important to realise that we have been concerned with basic principles, and have often omitted technical details. For the user of econometric methods, it is perhaps sufficient to understand what particular techniques can achieve, and perhaps more importantly, to recognise the limitations. In many ways, the user's task has been greatly simplified by the availability of robust and powerful computer software, but it is a great mistake to believe that being able to call upon sophisticated methods necessarily makes for good results. Unfortunately, good practice in applied econometrics tends to follow from experience, guided by the good, bad and indifferent examples to be found in the literature.

If by now you have acquired a taste for econometrics, then it is certainly time to move beyond the confines of this book. With the wisdom of hindsight, it is easy to overlook the importance of individual contributions to the literature, but each step rests on someone's intellectual effort, and is based on detailed technical knowledge. Given the growth in the scope of econometric theory, the backlog of important economic issues to be resolved and the progressive availability of bigger and better data sets, together with the availability of more and more powerful computing resources, further study of econometrics is likely to prove rewarding. There is certainly no shortage of work to be done.

Appendix A: Matrix algebra

A matrix is a rectangular array of numbers. If the matrix has n rows and m columns, it is said to be an $(n \times m)$ matrix. An $(n \times 1)$ matrix is a column vector, and a $(1 \times m)$ matrix is a row vector. The convention used wherever possible is that matrices are denoted by capital letters, column vectors by lower case letters, and row vectors by lower case letters with a prime ($'$).

An $(n \times m)$ matrix A may be written out in terms of its elements as

$$
A =
\begin{bmatrix}
a_{11} & a_{12} & \cdots & a_{1j} & \cdots & a_{1m} \\
a_{21} & a_{22} & \cdots & a_{2j} & \cdots & a_{2m} \\
& & \vdots & & & \\
a_{i1} & a_{i2} & \cdots & a_{ij} & \cdots & a_{im} \\
& & \vdots & & & \\
a_{n1} & a_{n2} & \cdots & a_{nj} & \cdots & a_{nm}
\end{bmatrix}.
$$

The elements of A have two subscripts, with row index first and column index second. Thus a_{ij} is the element on row i and in column j of A. However, in some econometric applications, there is a choice to be made between the usual matrix convention, and a statistical convention which reverses the order of subscripts, on the grounds that partition by variable is more important than partition by observation number. Thus we may choose to write the elements of a data matrix X as X_{jt}, indicating variable j, observation t, located in *column j* and row t of X.

Matrix equality

Before moving to consider operations on matrices, note the meaning of the statement $A = B$, where the number of rows and columns in A is the same as the number of rows and columns in B (if A is $(n \times m)$, then B must also be $(n \times m)$). The statement $A = B$ implies that all elements are equal, that is, $a_{ij} = b_{ij}$ for all i, j. The statement $A \neq B$ implies that at least one element in A is different from the corresponding element in B.

386

Addition, subtraction, multiplication and transposition

Subject to certain conditions, it is possible to add, subtract and multiply matrices, and to perform various operations which have no parallel in ordinary (scalar) algebra. The conditions concern the number of rows and columns in the matrices used in each operation; the operation itself can be defined by showing how a typical element is formed. Thus we have

Matrix addition

$$C = A + B; \ c_{ij} = a_{ij} + b_{ij}.$$

If A is $(n \times m)$, B must be $(n \times m)$ and C will be $(n \times m)$.

Matrix subtraction

$$C = A - B; \ c_{ij} = a_{ij} - b_{ij}.$$

If A is $(n \times m)$, B must be $(n \times m)$ and C will be $(n \times m)$.

Multiplication by a scalar

$$C = \lambda A; \ c_{ij} = \lambda a_{ij}, \text{ where } \lambda \text{ is scalar.}$$

If A is $(n \times m)$, C will be $(n \times m)$.

Matrix multiplication

$$C = AB; \ c_{ij} = \sum_h a_{ih} b_{hj}.$$

If A is $(n \times k)$, B must be $(k \times m)$ and C will be $(n \times m)$. AB may exist when BA does not and, except under special conditions, $AB \neq BA$.

Transposition

$$C = A'; \ c_{ij} = a_{ji}.$$

If A is $(n \times m)$, C will be $(m \times n)$. Transposition is signified by a prime $(')$, and means that rows become columns and columns become rows.

In each case, it is understood that the scalar operation defining c_{ij} is repeated for all i and j.

It is possible to demonstrate various properties of the basic operations, and this provides rules which are useful for algebraic manipulation. In stating the rules, it is assumed that the matrices used satisfy any restrictions on the number of rows and columns, as appropriate to the basic operation involved. The reader may wish to construct proofs by showing the equivalence of a typical element on each side of the identity. Alternatively, one can devise simple numerical examples to check the validity of each of the following statements:

$$A + B = B + A$$

$AB \neq BA$, except in certain special cases

$$(A + B) + C = A + (B + C)$$

$(AB)C = A(BC)$

$A(B + C) = AB + AC$

$\lambda(A + B) = \lambda A + \lambda B$, where λ is scalar

$(A + B)' = A' + B'$

$(AB)' = B'A'.$

Vectors

Row and column vectors can be considered as special types of matrix, but it is also possible to treat vectors rather differently. In particular, an n element vector can be interpreted as a point in n dimensional space. For this purpose, all that matters is that a vector has n ordered elements, it being irrelevant whether it is written as a row or as a column.

There are some special vectors that we should mention. A zero or null vector has all elements equal to zero. A unit vector, written as e_i, has element i equal to 1 and all other elements equal to 0. A sum vector consists entirely of elements equal to 1.

Square matrices

If A is $(n \times n)$, it is said to be a square matrix, of order n. The elements $a_{11}, a_{22}, \ldots, a_{nn}$ are the diagonal elements of A (sometimes called *main* diagonal elements), and a_{ij}; $i \neq j$ are off-diagonal elements. The trace of A is the sum of diagonal elements:

$$\text{trace}(A) = \sum_i a_{ii}.$$

If $A + B$ exists, then

$$\text{trace}(A + B) = \text{trace}(A) + \text{trace}(B)$$

and if AB and BA both exist

$$\text{trace}(AB) = \text{trace}(BA).$$

A square matrix with off-diagonal elements equal to 0 is a diagonal matrix. A square matrix with zero elements above the main diagonal is described as lower triangular, and a square matrix with zero elements below the main diagonal is upper triangular. If a square matrix A is such that $A' = A$, that is, $a_{ij} = a_{ji}$, then A is said to be symmetric.

An important special case is a square matrix with diagonal elements equal to 1 and off-diagonal elements equal to 0. This is an identity matrix, written as I (or, to show order, as I_n). If any matrix is pre- or postmultiplied by an identity matrix, then that matrix is left unchanged. Thus if B is $(n \times m)$, $I_n B = B$ and $BI_m = B$.

Matrix inverse

If A is $(n \times n)$, it may or may not be possible to find an $(n \times n)$ matrix B such that $AB = I_n$. If such a matrix does exist, it is described as the inverse of A, and this is written as A^{-1}. When A^{-1} exists, $AA^{-1} = I_n$ and $A^{-1}A = I_n$. Often the order of I is implicit, and we simply write $AA^{-1} = I$, $A^{-1}A = I$.

To investigate properly the conditions under which the inverse exists, we need the concepts of linear dependence and independence of a set of vectors, and the concept of rank of a matrix.

Linear dependence and independence

If $a_1, a_2, \ldots, a_m$ are $(n \times 1)$ vectors, and $\lambda_1, \lambda_2, \ldots, \lambda_m$ are scalars, then $\sum \lambda_i a_i$ is described as a linear combination of $a_1, \ldots, a_m$. Clearly, a linear combination of $(n \times 1)$ vectors must define another $(n \times 1)$ vector and, in particular, we may consider conditions on the scalar weights $\lambda_1, \ldots, \lambda_m$, under which the linear combination is equal to the $(n \times 1)$ zero vector, that is,

$$\sum \lambda_i a_i = 0.$$

If the only way in which $\sum \lambda_i a_i$ can be made equal to the zero vector is by setting all the λ_i to zero, then $a_1, \ldots, a_m$ are said to be linearly independent. If $\sum \lambda_i a_i = 0$ with at least one λ_i nonzero, then $a_1, \ldots, a_m$ are linearly dependent. The essential fact about a linearly dependent set of vectors is that it must be possible to express at least one of the vectors as a linear combination of the other vectors in the set. To see this, suppose that $\sum \lambda_i a_i = 0$, with $\lambda_1 \neq 0$. Then

$$\lambda_1 a_1 + \lambda_2 a_2 + \ldots + \lambda_m a_m = 0$$

$$\Rightarrow \lambda_1 a_1 = -\lambda_2 a_2 - \ldots - \lambda_m a_m$$

$$\Rightarrow a_1 = -(\lambda_2/\lambda_1)a_2 - \ldots - (\lambda_m/\lambda_1)a_m.$$

If a set of vectors is linearly independent, then $\sum \lambda_i a_i = 0$ implies that all the λ_i are zero, and it is not possible to express any of the vectors as a linear combination of other vectors in the set.

The following rules can be deduced directly from the definitions of linear dependence and independence:

1. Any subset of a set of linearly independent vectors is also linearly independent.
2. Any set of vectors containing a linearly dependent subset is itself linearly dependent.
3. Any set of vectors which contains a zero vector is linearly dependent.
4. A set of m vectors, each having n elements, is linearly dependent if $m > n$.
5. A set of n linearly independent n element vectors forms a *basis* for the set of all possible n element vectors. This means that any n element vector can be expressed as a linear combination of the vectors forming the basis. One particularly simple

example of a basis is the set of unit vectors, $e_1, \ldots, e_n$; it is obvious that any other n element vector can be expressed as a linear combination of $e_1, \ldots, e_n$.

6. The choice of basis vectors is not unique, but the representation of any vector in terms of a given basis is unique.

Rank of a matrix

The column rank of a matrix A is the maximum number of linearly independent columns. The row rank is the maximum number of linearly independent rows. Since it can be shown that the row rank is always the same as the column rank, we may drop any distinction between the two measures, and refer simply to the rank of A, written as rank(A). This can be obtained either as row rank or column rank, whichever is more convenient.

It is sometimes possible to find the rank of a matrix by inspection. Otherwise, rank can be found by using what are known as elementary operations to reduce the matrix to a form from which the rank can be found by inspection. In what follows, we use elementary row operations; we could just as easily use elementary column operations instead.

Elementary row operations

There are three elementary operations that can be performed on the rows of a matrix. They are

(a) interchanging two rows;
(b) multiplication of a row by a scalar;
(c) replacing a row by the sum of that row and a scalar multiple of another row.

In symbols, we have

(a) a_{ij} exchanged with a_{hj}; $h \neq i$; $j = 1, \ldots, m$
(b) a_{ij} replaced by λa_{ij}, where λ is scalar; $j = 1, \ldots, m$
(c) a_{ij} replaced by $a_{ij} + \lambda a_{hj}$, where λ is scalar; $h \neq i$; $j = 1, \ldots, m$.

Each of the elementary row operations can be represented as a premultiplication by a square matrix. For example, to subtract twice the first row from the second row of

$$\begin{bmatrix} 2 & 3 \\ 4 & 6 \end{bmatrix}$$

we can premultiply by

$$\begin{bmatrix} 1 & 0 \\ -2 & 1 \end{bmatrix}$$

giving

$$\begin{bmatrix} 1 & 0 \\ -2 & 1 \end{bmatrix} \begin{bmatrix} 2 & 3 \\ 4 & 6 \end{bmatrix} = \begin{bmatrix} 2 & 3 \\ 0 & 0 \end{bmatrix}.$$

Other elementary row operations can be represented in a similar fashion; the matrices used for the premultiplication are known as elementary matrices.

None of the elementary row operations can change the rank of a matrix. To see that this is so, consider each type of operation in turn, and recognise that any set of rows which is linearly independent before an elementary row operation is still linearly independent after that operation, and any set of rows which is linearly dependent before an elementary row operation is still linearly dependent after that operation. If elementary row operations can be used to reduce a matrix to a form in which rank is easily obtained by inspection, we have a general method for calculating rank.

Echelon matrix

A (row) echelon matrix has the characteristic that the first nonzero element in each row is equal to 1, and this element is located at least one position to the right of the first nonzero element in the preceding row. It is also true of an echelon matrix that the rank is equal to the number of nonzero rows, by which we mean the number of rows containing at least one nonzero element. An example is

$$H = \begin{bmatrix} 1 & 1 & 2 & 3 \\ 0 & 1 & 0 & 1 \\ 0 & 0 & 0 & 1 \\ 0 & 0 & 0 & 0 \end{bmatrix}.$$

This can be thought of as consisting of four row vectors, each (1×4). The last row is a zero vector, and any set of vectors which includes a zero vector must be linearly dependent. To see this, let h'_1, h'_2, h'_3, h'_4 be the rows of H, and let $0'$ be the (1×4) zero vector. The statement

$$0h'_1 + 0h'_2 + 0h'_3 + \lambda_4 h'_4 = 0'$$

is true for any nonzero value of λ_4, so the rows of H are indeed linearly dependent. However, the first three rows of H are linearly independent. The key to this is that the first nonzero element in each row is at least one position to the right of the first nonzero element in the preceding row. This enables us to argue sequentially that for

$$\lambda_1 h'_1 + \lambda_2 h'_2 + \lambda_3 h'_3 = 0',$$

λ_1 must be zero to take out element $h_{11} = 1$, λ_2 must be zero to take out element $h_{22} = 1$, and λ_3 must be zero to take out element $h_{34} = 1$. So rows h'_1, h'_2 and h'_3 are linearly independent, rows h'_1, h'_2, h'_3 and h'_4 are linearly dependent, and rank $(H) = 3$.

Reduction to echelon form

Any matrix can be reduced to echelon form, by using elementary row operations, which cannot change the rank. The reader should check that elementary row operations can be used to reduce the matrix

$$A = \begin{bmatrix} 2 & 2 & 4 & 6 \\ 1 & 2 & 2 & 4 \\ 2 & 3 & 4 & 7 \\ 4 & 6 & 8 & 15 \end{bmatrix}$$

to the matrix H given above, so $\text{rank}(A) = 3$. This process can be represented as

$$H = EA$$

where E is the product of the elementary matrices used to achieve the reduction to echelon form. Since such operations cannot change the rank, we have

$$\text{rank}(A) = \text{rank}(EA) = \text{rank}(H).$$

Hence reduction to echelon form is a viable numerical method for evaluating the rank of any given matrix.

Nonsingular matrix

A square matrix A, of order n, is said to be nonsingular if $\text{rank}(A) = n$. It follows that if a nonsingular matrix is reduced to echelon form, the echelon matrix has main diagonal elements equal to 1, and elements below the main diagonal equal to zero. In fact it is possible to go further with a nonsingular matrix, to use elementary row operations to drive elements above the main diagonal to zero, so that we end up with an identity matrix. If E denotes the product of elementary matrices needed to produce an echelon matrix, and F denotes the product of a further set of elementary matrices needed to produce an identity matrix, we have

$$FEA = I.$$

Clearly, the product FE satisfies the definition of an inverse of A. It follows that for a nonsingular matrix, A^{-1} exists, and

$$A^{-1} = FE.$$

If A is $(n \times n)$ and $\text{rank}(A) < n$, A is said to be singular, and the inverse matrix does not exist.

Properties of the inverse matrix

If A and B are nonsingular $(n \times n)$ matrices, then

$$(AB)^{-1} = B^{-1}A^{-1}$$

$$(A^{-1})^{-1} = A$$

$$(A')^{-1} = (A^{-1})'.$$

Rules of rank

The following rules can be derived from the definition of rank as the maximum number of linearly independent rows (columns) in a matrix A. If A is $(n \times m)$, then

$\text{rank}(A) \le \min(n, m)$,

$\text{rank}(A) = \text{rank}(A')$.

If A is $(n \times n)$ and A^{-1} exists, then

$\text{rank}(A^{-1}) = \text{rank}(A)$.

If A is $(n \times k)$ and B is $(k \times m)$, then

$\text{rank}(AB) \le \min[\text{rank}(A), \text{rank}(B)]$.

If A is $(n \times n)$ nonsingular and B is $(n \times m)$, then

$\text{rank}(AB) = \text{rank}(B)$.

If A is $(m \times m)$ nonsingular and B is $(n \times m)$, then

$\text{rank}(BA) = \text{rank}(B)$.

Hence pre- or postmultiplication by a nonsingular matrix leaves the rank of the original matrix unchanged.

Linear equations

A set of n linear equations in the m variables $x_1, \ldots, x_m$ can be written as

$$a_{11}x_1 + a_{12}x_2 + \ldots + a_{1m}x_m = b_1$$
$$a_{21}x_1 + a_{22}x_2 + \ldots + a_{2m}x_m = b_2$$
$$\vdots$$
$$a_{n1}x_1 + a_{n2}x_2 + \ldots + a_{nm}x_m = b_n$$

where the elements a_{ij} and b_i; $i = 1, \ldots, n$; $j = 1, \ldots, m$ represent known values. Alternatively, we may write

$Ax = b$

where A is $(n \times m)$ with typical element a_{ij}, x is $(m \times 1)$ with typical element x_j, and b is $(n \times 1)$ with typical element b_i.

To decide whether any solution exists, and if so whether that solution is unique, the matrix A can be reduced to echelon form, and exactly the same row operations can be applied to b. This process is represented as

$EAx = Eb$

or

$Hx = h$

where E is the product of elementary matrices needed to reduce A to echelon form, H is the echelon matrix obtained as $H = EA$ and h is the vector obtained by applying the same row operations to b. To illustrate the process, consider the set of equations

$$x_1 + x_2 + 2x_3 = 3$$
$$x_1 + 2x_2 + 2x_3 = 4$$
$$2x_1 + 3x_2 + 4x_3 = 7$$
$$4x_1 + 6x_2 + 8x_3 = 15.$$

It is convenient to arrange the A matrix and the b vector together in a single matrix $[A \quad b]$, and to perform the reduction to echelon form on both parts together. This gives

$$[A \quad b] = \begin{bmatrix} 1 & 1 & 2 & | & 3 \\ 1 & 2 & 2 & | & 4 \\ 2 & 3 & 4 & | & 7 \\ 4 & 6 & 8 & | & 15 \end{bmatrix}$$

and

$$[H \quad h] = \begin{bmatrix} 1 & 1 & 2 & | & 3 \\ 0 & 1 & 0 & | & 1 \\ 0 & 0 & 0 & | & 1 \\ 0 & 0 & 0 & | & 0 \end{bmatrix}.$$

The third equation in the set $Hx = h$ reads as

$$0x_1 + 0x_2 + 0x_3 = 1$$

and it is clear that there is no way in which values can be chosen for x_1, x_2 and x_3 so as to satisfy this particular equation. In this case, reduction to echelon form shows that no solution exists.

If the exercise above is repeated with the last equation modified to

$$4x_1 + 6x_2 + 8x_3 = 14$$

a different answer emerges. In this case, $[H \quad h]$ has two zero rows, which imply redundant equations, and only the first two rows are relevant to the solution. These rows correspond to the equations

$$1x_1 + 1x_2 + 2x_3 = 3$$
$$0x_1 + 1x_2 + 0x_3 = 1.$$

One solution is $x_2 = 1$, $x_3 = 0$ and $x_1 = 2$, but this is not unique; another possibility is $x_2 = 1$, $x_3 = 1$ and $x_1 = 0$.

We can formalise the discussion above as follows. The echelon form shows a comparison between the rank of H and the rank of $[H \quad h]$. In the first case, the rank of $[H \quad h]$ is greater than the rank of H, and no solution exists. In the second case, $\text{rank}[H \quad h] = \text{rank}(H)$, and there are solutions, though these are not unique. Since H and $[H \quad h]$ are obtained from A and $[A \quad b]$ by elementary row operations, a comparison between the rank of H and the rank of $[H \quad h]$ is identical to a comparison between the rank of A and the rank of $[A \quad b]$. We have therefore shown an operational method of applying the following rule:

If $\text{rank}[A \quad b] = \text{rank}(A)$, the set of equations $Ax = b$ has at least one solution.
If $\text{rank}[A \quad b] > \text{rank}(A)$, no solution exists.

If there is at least one solution, that solution is unique if A has full column rank, that is, if $\text{rank}(A) = m$, where A is $(n \times m)$. A complete statement of the condition for a unique solution is thus given as

$\text{rank}[A \quad b] = \text{rank}(A) = m$, where A is $(n \times m)$.

There is a further implication of the reduction of a matrix to echelon form which can be stated here. If A is $n \times m$ with rank r, then there exists an $n \times r$ matrix B and an $m \times r$ matrix C, both with rank r, such that

$$A = BC'.$$

Determinants

The determinant of an $(n \times n)$ matrix A is written as $\det(A)$ and defined as

$$\det(A) = \sum (-1)^p a_{11} a_{22} \ldots a_{nn}$$

where the summation is taken over all possible permutations of the second subscript, and p is the number of pairwise interchanges of the second subscript needed to obtain a particular permutation. If A is (2×2), the above formula gives

$$\det(A) = a_{11} a_{22} - a_{12} a_{21}.$$

Higher-order determinants can be calculated recursively from the determinants of (2×2) submatrices. Calculations involving determinants are very tedious, and seldom represent the best approach to either theory or practical computation. However, for completeness, we list the following properties:

$\det(A)$ is defined only when A is square

$\det(A) = \det(A')$

If A is nonsingular, $\det(A^{-1}) = [\det(A)]^{-1}$

If A is singular, $\det(A) = 0$

If $\det(A) = 0$, then A is singular

If A and B are both $(n \times n)$, $\det(AB) = \det(A)\det(B)$.

Differentiation involving vectors and matrices

Calculus operations involving vectors and matrices use rules which follow directly from the scalar calculus. All that is required is that the results be arranged in an agreed form. Our basic convention is that if $y = f(x)$ is an $(m \times 1)$ vector-valued function of the $(n \times 1)$ vector x, $\partial y/\partial x'$ is defined as the $(m \times n)$ matrix with $\partial y_i/\partial x_j$ located on row i of column j, whilst $\partial y'/\partial x$ is the $(n \times m)$ matrix with $\partial y_j/\partial x_i$ located on row i of column j. Note that $\partial y'/\partial x$ is the same as $(\partial y/\partial x')'$.

With this basic convention in place, other cases can be treated in a consistent manner. If y is a scalar-valued function of the $(n \times 1)$ vector x, there are n first partial derivatives and n^2 second partial derivatives. Since y is scalar, $\partial y'/\partial x$ is equivalent to $\partial y/\partial x$, and $\partial y/\partial x$ is therefore a column vector, with typical element $\partial y/\partial x_i$. The second partial derivatives can be arranged into an $(n \times n)$ matrix, written as $\partial^2 y/\partial x \, \partial x'$. To ensure that dimensions are correctly maintained, the operator $\partial^2(\ )/\partial x \, \partial x'$ is considered to be equivalent to $\partial(\ )/\partial x'$ applied to the column vector of first derivatives. This suggests that $\partial^2 y/\partial x \, \partial x'$ has typical element $\partial^2 y/\partial x_i \, \partial x_j$. The vector $\partial y/\partial x$ is sometimes referred to as the gradient vector, written as $g(x)$, and $\partial^2 y/\partial x \, \partial x'$ is described as the Hessian matrix, written as $G(x)$. If the second derivatives are continuous, $\partial^2 y/\partial x_i \, \partial x_j = \partial^2 y/\partial x_j \, \partial x_i$, and the Hessian matrix is symmetric.

If y is a scalar-valued linear function of the $(n \times 1)$ vector x, then

$$y = a'x, \ \partial y/\partial x = a; \ \partial^2 y/\partial x \, \partial x' = 0, \text{ where } 0 \text{ is } (n \times n).$$

For a simple quadratic function defined with a symmetric matrix A, we have

$$y = x'Ax; \ \partial y/\partial x = 2Ax; \ \partial^2 y/\partial x \, \partial x' = 2A.$$

If A is not symmetric, the corresponding results are

$$\partial y/\partial x = (A + A')x; \ \partial^2 y/\partial x \, \partial x' = (A + A').$$

For a vector-valued linear function $y = Ax$, where A is $(m \times n)$ and x is $(n \times 1)$, our convention would give

$$\partial y/\partial x' = A \quad \text{and} \quad \partial y'/\partial x = A'.$$

In this case, all second derivatives are zero; in general, to display the second derivatives for a vector-valued function, we would need an array in three dimensions, or a set of two-dimensional arrays.

Quadratic forms

If A is an $(n \times n)$ symmetric matrix and x is an $(n \times 1)$ vector, the quadratic function $x'Ax$ is known as a quadratic form. Multiplying out in terms of individual elements, we obtain

$$x'Ax = \sum_i \sum_j a_{ij} x_i x_j, \quad \text{where } a_{ij} = a_{ji}.$$

The constraint of symmetry on A is not a problem. If $x'Bx$ is a quadratic form in a nonsymmetric square matrix B, we can define $a_{ij} = (b_{ij} + b_{ji})/2$, and note that

$$
\begin{aligned}
x'Bx &= \sum_i \sum_j b_{ij} x_i x_j \\
&= \sum_i \sum_j [(b_{ij} + b_{ji})/2] x_i x_j \\
&= \sum_i \sum_j a_{ij} x_i x_j \\
&= x'Ax.
\end{aligned}
$$

Since any quadratic form is equivalent to a quadratic form in a symmetric matrix, no loss of generality is involved in considering only those forms $x'Ax$ for which A is symmetric.

It is sometimes of interest to know whether $x'Ax$ is positive, nonnegative, negative or nonpositive, irrespective of the value of elements in x. If $x'Ax$ is positive for all $x \neq 0$, the matrix A is said to be positive definite. If $x'Ax$ is negative for all $x \neq 0$, A is said to be negative definite. If $x'Ax$ is nonnegative for all x (including $x = 0$), A is said to be positive semidefinite, and if $x'Ax$ is nonpositive for all x, A is said to be negative semidefinite.

In econometric theory, positive definite (pd) and positive semidefinite (psd) matrices are important, one reason being that a variance covariance matrix is at least psd, and is often pd. It is useful to note the following rules, which can help to determine whether a given symmetric matrix is pd, psd or of some other form:

1. If B is any $(n \times m)$ matrix, $B'B$ is at least psd and is pd if $\text{rank}(B) = m$, and BB' is psd and is pd if $\text{rank}(B) = n$.
2. If A is $(n \times n)$ pd, $\text{rank}(A) = n$, $\det(A) \neq 0$, A^{-1} exists and A^{-1} is pd.
3. If $A = B + C$, where B is pd and C is psd, then A is pd and $B^{-1} - A^{-1}$ exists and is psd.

There is a well-known identity which links quadratic forms and the trace operation. The trace of a scalar quantity is the scalar quantity itself, so that

$$\text{trace}(x'Ax) = x'Ax,$$

but applying the result that $\text{trace}(AB) = \text{trace}(BA)$, we find

$$\text{trace}(x'Ax) = \text{trace}(Axx').$$

Eigenvalues and eigenvectors

For some purposes, it is convenient to be able to summarise the characteristics of an $(n \times n)$ matrix A in terms of n numbers, known variously as eigenvalues, characteristic values, latent roots or just the roots of A. Associated with the n eigenvalues are n vectors, each $(n \times 1)$, which are known as eigenvectors (characteristic vectors, latent vectors). The eigenvalues and eigenvectors are defined as solutions to the equation system

$$Aq = \lambda q$$

where both the vector q and the scalar λ are unknown. We shall not consider the mechanics of obtaining the solutions for λ and q, beyond saying that for an $(n \times n)$ matrix A, there are n solutions for λ, which may or may not be distinct, and n eigenvectors that are orthogonal if A is symmetric. If A is nonsymmetric, the eigenvalues may include complex numbers and the eigenvectors are not necessarily orthogonal. Since all we want is a convenient decomposition for symmetric matrices, we shall confine our attention to the case in which A is symmetric.

Suppose now that we have obtained n values $\lambda_1, \ldots, \lambda_n$, with associated vectors $q_1, \ldots, q_n$, where each pair (λ_i, q_i) is one of the solutions to $Aq = \lambda q$. If the eigenvalues are arranged as the diagonal elements of the $(n \times n)$ matrix Λ, where $\Lambda_{ii} = \lambda_i$ and $\Lambda_{ij} = 0$; $i \neq j$, and the eigenvectors are arranged as the columns of the $(n \times n)$ matrix Q, then all the solutions to $Aq = \lambda q$ can be written together as

$$AQ = Q\Lambda.$$

When A is symmetric, the eigenvectors are orthogonal, so that $q_i'q_j = 0$; $i \neq j$. Moreover, eigenvectors are only determined up to an arbitrary scale factor, which can be chosen so that $q_i'q_i = 1$. It follows that $Q'Q = I_n$, and that Q' is in fact the inverse of Q. We can therefore write

$$A = Q\Lambda Q'$$

and argue that such a decomposition is possible for any symmetric matrix. This has several uses in econometric theory, though it is often the fact that the decomposition is possible, rather than the numerical calculation, that is of interest.

Eigenvalues do convey useful information about the properties of a matrix. A nonsingular matrix has nonzero eigenvalues, whilst a singular matrix has at least one zero eigenvalue. Positive definite matrices have positive eigenvalues, and negative definite matrices have negative eigenvalues. Similarly, positive semidefinite matrices have nonnegative eigenvalues, and negative semidefinite matrices have nonpositive eigenvalues. The determinant of a matrix is the product of eigenvalues, whilst the trace is the sum of eigenvalues. Finally, for a symmetric matrix, the rank is equal to the number of nonzero eigenvalues; this is not necessarily true for nonsymmetric matrices.

Symmetric idempotent matrices

In statistical theory, one often uses square symmetric matrices which have the property of idempotency, which means that the matrix reproduces itself under multiplication. Hence we have $A = A' = AA \Rightarrow A'A = A$. In general, such matrices are singular; the only symmetric idempotent (SI) matrix which is nonsingular is the identity matrix I.

Symmetric idempotent matrices have the following properties. First, the eigenvalues are 0 or 1. This means that an SI matrix is positive semidefinite (but not pd, unless $A = I$). Next, the rank is equal to the number of nonzero eigenvalues, which in this case means the number of eigenvalues which are equal to 1. Consequently the trace, which is the sum of eigenvalues, is also equal to the rank. Finally, if A is SI, then $I - A$ is also SI. These results all follow from the definition of an SI matrix, together with the equations defining eigenvalues and eigenvectors.

Partitioned vectors and matrices

It is often convenient to arrange the elements of an $(n \times 1)$ vector x or an $(n \times m)$ matrix A into blocks of elements that are themselves vectors or matrices of smaller dimension. For example, if

$$x' = [x_1 \quad x_2 \quad x_3 \quad x_4],$$

defining

$$z' = [x_1 \quad x_2], \qquad w' = [x_3 \quad x_4],$$

we can represent x as

$$x' = [z' \quad w'].$$

Similarly, the matrix

$$A = \begin{bmatrix} 2 & 2 & 4 & 6 \\ 1 & 2 & 2 & 4 \\ 2 & 3 & 4 & 7 \\ 4 & 6 & 8 & 15 \end{bmatrix}$$

could be represented as

$$A = \begin{bmatrix} A_{11} & A_{12} \\ A_{21} & A_{22} \end{bmatrix},$$

where

$$A_{11} = \begin{bmatrix} 2 & 2 \\ 1 & 2 \end{bmatrix}, \qquad A_{12} = \begin{bmatrix} 4 & 6 \\ 2 & 4 \end{bmatrix}, \qquad A_{21} = \begin{bmatrix} 2 & 3 \\ 4 & 6 \end{bmatrix}, \qquad A_{22} = \begin{bmatrix} 4 & 7 \\ 8 & 15 \end{bmatrix},$$

or as

$$A = \begin{bmatrix} B_{11} & v \\ y' & a_{44} \end{bmatrix},$$

where

$$B_{11} = \begin{bmatrix} 2 & 2 & 4 \\ 1 & 2 & 2 \\ 2 & 3 & 4 \end{bmatrix}, \qquad v = \begin{bmatrix} 6 \\ 4 \\ 7 \end{bmatrix}, \qquad y = \begin{bmatrix} 4 \\ 6 \\ 8 \end{bmatrix}, \qquad a_{44} = 15.$$

The rules of addition and multiplication of vectors and matrices generalise straight-forwardly to this framework, except that considerably more care is needed over the issue of conformability. If m is a 4×1 vector partitioned into two 2×1 subvectors n and p, then

$$x + m = \begin{bmatrix} z + n \\ w + p \end{bmatrix},$$

but, if the partitioning of m differed from that given, the sums in the right-hand-side vector would not be defined. The same principle applies to sums of partitioned matrices: even if the matrices being partitioned are of the same dimensions, they have to be partitioned in an identical way for the matrix sum to be represented in terms of sums of submatrices. In the example above, the product Ax clearly exists, given the dimensions involved, and it can be represented as

$$Ax = \begin{bmatrix} A_{11}z + A_{12}w \\ A_{21}z + A_{22}w \end{bmatrix}.$$

But, using the second partitioning of A into B_{11}, v, y and a_{44} would not permit a representation of this product as

$$Ax = \begin{bmatrix} B_{11}z + vw \\ y'z + a_{44}w \end{bmatrix}$$

simply because the indicated products do not exist due to lack of conformability. One can see from this a working rule for products of partitioned matrices or vectors: use the standard 'across and down rule', treating the submatrices or subvectors as if they were scalars, but being careful that any indicated product of these quantities does actually exist.

When A is a square matrix partitioned as

$$A = \begin{bmatrix} A_{11} & A_{12} \\ A_{21} & A_{22} \end{bmatrix},$$

in which A_{11} and A_{22} are square, there is a representation of the determinant of A in terms of the determinants of the component matrices. This is called the Laplace expansion of a determinant:

$$\det(A) = \det(A_{11}) \det(A_{22} - A_{21} A_{11}^{-1} A_{12})$$
$$= \det(A_{22}) \det(A_{11} - A_{12} A_{22}^{-1} A_{21}).$$

The indicated inverses must exist for the result to hold. There is also a rather complicated expression for the inverse of A, if it exists, in terms of the component matrices. This is known as the 'partitioned inverse' result (see, for example, Greene, 1995: 27; or Hendry, 1995: 635).

Kronecker product

If A is $(m \times n)$ and B is $(p \times q)$, the Kronecker product, written as $A \otimes B$, is defined as the $(mp \times nq)$ matrix

$$A \otimes B = \begin{bmatrix} a_{11} B & \cdots & a_{1n} B \\ & \vdots & \\ a_{m1} B & \cdots & a_{mn} B \end{bmatrix}.$$

Kronecker products satisfy fairly obvious rules, which include the following:

1. For conformable matrices, $(A \otimes B)(C \otimes D) = (AC \otimes BD)$.
2. $(A \otimes B)' = A' \otimes B'$.
3. For A, B square and nonsingular, $(A \otimes B)^{-1} = A^{-1} \otimes B^{-1}$.

Optimisation

As part of our brief survey of matrix methods, we consider the problem of finding maximum or minimum values of a scalar-valued function of a set of choice variables $x_1, \ldots, x_n$. If the function is written as $y = f(x)$, where x is $(n \times 1)$, the first-order conditions for a maximum or a minimum are

$$\partial y / \partial x = 0.$$

If x_0 is a point for which the first-order conditions are satisfied, then second-order (sufficient) conditions are as follows:

If $\partial^2 y / \partial x \, \partial x'$, evaluated at x_0, is negative definite, x_0 corresponds to a (local) maximum of $f(x)$.

If $\partial^2 y / \partial x \, \partial x'$, evaluated at x_0, is positive definite, x_0 corresponds to a (local) minimum of $f(x)$.

If the function $f(x)$ is to be optimised subject to a set of constraints on the values of x, and the constraints can be written as $h(x) = 0$, the optimisation proceeds by setting up the Lagrangian function

$$\phi(x, \lambda) = f(x) - \lambda' h(x),$$

where λ is a vector of Lagrange multipliers, and then differentiating with respect to both x and λ. In this case the first-order conditions are

$$\partial\phi/\partial x = 0 \quad \text{and} \quad \partial\phi/\partial\lambda = 0.$$

Second-order conditions for constrained optimisation can be represented in various ways, but in econometric applications, the conditions are usually straightforward. If dx is a vector of infinitesimal changes, which are not all zero, and the quadratic form $dx'(\partial^2\phi/\partial x\,\partial x')\,dx$, evaluated at the solution point, is positive for all dx which satisfy the condition

$$[\partial h(x)/\partial x']\,dx = 0,$$

then the solution obtained from the first-order conditions is a local constrained minimum. But in econometric applications, it is often the case that $\partial^2\phi/\partial x\,\partial x'$ is positive definite, so the required quadratic form is positive for all $dx \neq 0$, and not just for those dx which satisfy the constraint condition. Similar arguments hold for constrained maximisation, the difference being that if $dx'(\partial^2\phi/\partial x\,\partial x')\,dx$ is negative for all dx which satisfy the constraint condition, the solution found is a local constrained maximum.

Maxima and minima of quadratic forms

This discussion can be immediately applied to the problem of finding the maximum and minimum of the function

$$f(x) = x'Ax,$$

where x is an n vector and A an $n \times n$ positive (semi)definite symmetric matrix. Since the value of the function can be made arbitrarily large by multiplying x by a scalar, it is necessary to restrict x to prevent this. Normalise x by demanding that $x'x = 1$: then the Lagrangian function is

$$\phi(x, \lambda) = x'Ax - \lambda(x'x - 1)$$

with first-order conditions

$$\frac{\partial\phi}{\partial x} = 2Ax - 2\lambda x = 0, \qquad \frac{\partial\phi}{\partial\lambda} = x'x - 1 = 0,$$

showing that the solutions x and λ must be corresponding normalised eigenvectors and eigenvalues of A. Thus, for such an x,

$$x'Ax = \lambda.$$

The maximum (minimum) value of $x'Ax$ is therefore given by choosing x to be the eigenvector corresponding to the largest (smallest) eigenvalue of A.

Generalised eigenvalues and eigenvectors

Consider the problem of finding the maximum and minimum of the function

$$f(x) = \frac{x'Ax}{x'Bx},$$

where A is an $n \times n$ positive (semi)definite symmetric matrix, and B must be an $n \times n$ positive definite symmetric matrix. We can find a nonsingular matrix S such that $B = S'S$: putting $y = Sx$, we see that the function can be rewritten as

$$f(x) = \frac{y'S'^{-1}AS^{-1}y}{y'y}.$$

This has the same form as the previous example, and the same solution, providing that we set $y'y = 1$. This is equivalent to setting $x'Bx = 1$, and maximising or minimising $f(x)$ subject to this condition is equivalent to maximising or minimising $x'Ax$ subject to $x'Bx = 1$. Applying the Lagrangian conditions to this produces as first-order conditions

$$2Ax - 2\lambda Bx = 0, \qquad x'Bx - 1 = 0.$$

The solutions x and λ to the first-order conditions satisfy

$$Ax = \lambda Bx,$$

and are called generalised eigenvectors and generalised eigenvalues. An alternative terminology describes them as the eigenvectors and eigenvalues of A in the metric of B. Putting $B = S'S$ and rearranging using $y = Sx$ produces

$$S'^{-1}AS^{-1}y = \lambda y,$$

which shows that the generalised eigenvalues are the same as the eigenvalues of the matrix $S'^{-1}AS^{-1}$, and that the generalised eigenvectors x are related to the eigenvectors y of this matrix by $y = Sx$.

Conditional distributions and conditional expectations

If X and Y are two continuous random variables, with a joint probability density function $p(x, y)$ and marginal probability density $p_x(x)$ and $p_y(y)$, the *conditional density* of Y given that $X = x$ is defined to be

$$p(y|x) = \frac{p(x, y)}{p_x(x)}.$$

Then,

$$p(x, y) = p(y|x) \cdot p_x(x).$$

Expected values and variances can be defined using the conditional density in the usual way as

$$E(Y|X = x) = \int_{-\infty}^{\infty} yp(y|x) \, dy,$$

$$\text{var}(Y|X = x) = \int_{-\infty}^{\infty} [y - E(Y|X = x)]^2 p(y|x) \, dy.$$

However, these quantities are defined relative to a given value x of the random variable X, so that they can be considered as values of random variables. The conditional expectation random variable is usually denoted

$$E(Y|X),$$

with values $E(Y|X = x)$. The key result is that the expected value of $E(Y|X)$ is the expected value of Y:

$$E[E(Y|X)] = E(Y).$$

This is easy to prove using the definition of $E(Y|X = x)$ above. This result is often called the *law of iterated expectations*. Notice that in the result, there are three expected value signs, each relating to different distributions: from left to right, they are the marginal distribution of X, the conditional distribution of Y given that $X = x$, and the marginal distribution of Y. As usual, the marginal distributions could be replaced by the joint distribution of X and Y without changing the values of the expectations. A related result is that

$$E(XY|X) = XE(Y|X).$$

Conditional normal distributions

An important example of a conditional distribution is the normal distribution. Two random variables X and Y with a joint normal distribution have the distribution of the random vector

$$Z = \begin{bmatrix} Y \\ X \end{bmatrix} \sim N(m, \Omega),$$

where

$$m = \begin{bmatrix} \mu_y \\ \mu \end{bmatrix}, \qquad \Omega = \begin{bmatrix} \omega_y & \omega \\ \omega & \sigma_{11} \end{bmatrix}.$$

The (joint) density function of Z is given by

$$p(z) = [(2\pi)^2 \det(\Omega)]^{-1/2} \exp[-\tfrac{1}{2}(z - m)'\Omega^{-1}(z - m)],$$

and one can go through the arguments outlined above to show that the conditional distribution of Y given that $X = x$ is also a normal distribution. It is well known that the marginal distributions of a multivariate normal distribution are also normal. So, the new feature here is that a conditional distribution of a multivariate normal is normal: all that is required is to find out what the mean and variance of this distribution is.

The answer is

$$Y|X = x \sim N[\mu_y + \omega\sigma_{11}^{-1}(x - \mu_1), \omega_y - \omega\sigma_{11}^{-1}\omega].$$

The variance in this expression is deliberately left in an unsimplified form. It is easy to generalise to the case where X is actually a random vector,

$$X = \begin{bmatrix} X_1 \\ X_2 \end{bmatrix},$$

$$Y|X = x \sim N[\mu_y + \omega'\Sigma^{-1}(x - \mu), \omega_y - \omega'\Sigma^{-1}\omega].$$

Here, the vector ω contains the covariances between Y and X, and the matrix Σ is the covariance matrix of X:

$$\omega = \begin{bmatrix} \omega_1 \\ \omega_2 \end{bmatrix} = \begin{bmatrix} \operatorname{cov}(X_1, Y) \\ \operatorname{cov}(X_2, Y) \end{bmatrix} = \operatorname{cov}(X, Y),$$

$$\Sigma = \operatorname{var}(X) = \begin{bmatrix} \sigma_{11} & \sigma_{12} \\ \sigma_{21} & \sigma_{22} \end{bmatrix}.$$

In these distributions, the means and variances of the normal distributions are of course the *conditional* means and variances:

$$E(Y|X = x), \qquad \operatorname{var}(Y|X = x).$$

Define the random variable V to satisfy

$$Y = E(Y|X = x) + V$$

so that it too has a conditional normal distribution with conditional mean zero and conditional variance $\omega_y - \omega'\Sigma^{-1}\omega$. Then, one can show that X and V are independent of each other:

$$\operatorname{cov}(X, V) = 0.$$

Appendix B: Data sets

The data sets used in this text come from a variety of sources. Many of them are extracted from the United Kingdom Office of National Statistics data bank, once called the CSO Databank. One of the purposes of this appendix is to indicate the relationship between the variables employed in these data sets and the matching ONS data bank variable names. Another is to give some indication of how certain composite variables were constructed. The data sets themselves are available from the WWW site associated with this text:

http://les.man.ac.uk/~msrbslg/

Information on the data sets themselves is also available from this source, and is largely reproduced below.

In the ONS data bank, variables have a basic four-letter identifier – for example, *abcd* – to which is attached an indicator for the period, and whether or not the series is seasonally adjusted. So, *abcdqu* is quarterly unadjusted data for *abcd*, and *abcdqa* the corresponding adjusted series. All annual data are considered seasonally *unadjusted*, giving *abcdau* as the typical code.

Most data are transformed into the data set variables from the ONS variables, often just a conversion from £ million to £ billion: the transformations are indicated below.

Data set 1 Consumers' expenditure and income, UK, 1963–94

The variables in the data set are:

RCONS	Real consumers' expenditure (£ billion, 1990 prices)
PCONS	Implicit deflator, consumers' expenditure (1990 = 1.0)
RPDI	Real personal disposable income (£ billion, 1990 prices)
RLIQA	Real personal sector liquid asset holdings (£ billion, 1990 prices)

Source: ONS database

406

The mapping between the ONS variables and the data set variables is:

ONS variable name	Transformation	Data set variable name
CCBHAU	÷1000	RCONS
CAOXAU	÷1000	PCONS
CECOAU	÷100	RPDI

The variable RLIQA is obtained by deflation of nominal liquid assets by PCONS. The construction of this nominal liquid assets series was quite complicated, as a result of changes in the coverage of the ONS data bank. For completeness (and for updating the data set, given access to the ONS data bank), the details are given below. The following series are used:

ONS variable	Description	Period
AAPO	Personal sector bank lending, annual change	1963–94
AMFX	Sterling bank lending, excluding personal sector	1982–94
AAQI	Personal sector bank deposits, annual change	1963–94
RRGY	Total sterling bank deposits	1984–94
ACSB	Tax instruments	1963–94
ADHJ	Personal sector finance: local authority temporary deposits	1963–94
RMGR	Total building society deposits	1963–94
ACUV	Total outstanding national savings	1977–94
AAPD	Personal sector finance: net payments of national savings	1963–94

To 'recreate' the series *amfx*, *rrgy* and *acuv*, a backcasting technique was used. After verification that *aapo* and *aaqi* functioned as annual changes, a backwards recursion was used:

$$amfx(1981) = amfx(1982) + aapo(1982),$$

$$rrgy(1983) = rrgy(1984) + aaqi(1984),$$

$$acuv(1976) = acuv(1977) + aapd(1977).$$

Nominal liquid assets were then computed as:

$$amfx + rrgy + acsb + adhj + rmgr + acuv.$$

Despite the rather *ad hoc* approach to the construction of RLIQA described here, the values of the new series are broadly in line with those used in the first edition of this text.

Data set 2   Money, activity and interest rates, UK, 1963–94

The variables are:

RTDE	Real total domestic expenditure (£ billion, 1990 prices)
QTDE	Nominal total domestic expenditure (£ billion, 1990 prices)
INTL	Interest rate on long-dated UK Government securities, expressed as $(1 + \text{rate}/100)$
M4	Nominal money stock M4 (£ billion)

Source: ONS database

The mapping between the ONS variables and the data set variables is:

ONS variable name	Transformation	Dataset variable name
DIELAU	÷1000	RTDE
DIGSAU	÷1000	QTDE
AJLXAU	$1 + (\text{AJLXAU} \div 100)$	INTL
VQXVAU	÷1000	M4

Data set 3   Costs and prices, UK, 1959–94

The variables are:

ULC	Unit labour costs (1990 = 1.00)
UMC	Unit import costs (1990 = 1.00)
HUC	Implicit deflator for GDP at factor cost (1990 = 1.00)

Source: ONS database

The mapping between the ONS variables and the data set variables is:

ONS variable name	Transformation	Dataset variable name
DJAOAU, DJCWAU	DJAOAU/DJCWAU set to 1.0 in 1990	ULC
DJAGAU, DJCWAU	DJAGAU/DJCWAU set to 1.0 in 1990	UMC
DJCMAU	÷100	HUC

Data set 4   Absolute convergence hypothesis, selected countries, 1975–85

This is a version of a publicly available data set, accessible via:

http://www.nuff.ox.ac.uk/Economics/Growth/

The variables are:

AVGR	Average 1975–85 real GDP per capita growth rate
GDP575L	Logarithm of real GDP per capita in 1975, 1985 international prices
SYRM75	Average years of secondary schooling in male population over 25 in 1975
SYRF75	Average years of secondary schooling in female population over 25 in 1975
HYRM75	Average years of higher schooling in male population over 25 in 1975
HYRF75	Average years of higher schooling in female population over 25 in 1975
LIFEE03	Average 1970–74 life expectancy at age 0
GOVSH53	Average 1970–74 ratio of real government consumption to real GDP
AVPNST	Average 1975–85 measure of political instability
AVTOT	Average 1975–85 terms of trade shock
ASIAE	Dummy for East Asian countries
LAAM	Dummy for Latin American countries
OECD	Dummy for OECD countries
SAFRICA	Dummy for sub-Saharan African countries

Source: NBER

Data set 5   Consumers' expenditure and income, UK, 1963(Q1)–1995(Q2)

This is a quarterly version of data set 1, using exactly the same ONS variables and the same technique for computing RLIQ. Note that the ONS variables have the suffix *qu* for 'quarterly unadjusted'.

Data set 6   Consumers' expenditure and income, with instrumental variables, UK, 1963(Q1)–1995(Q2)

This contains the same variables as data set 5, but augmented by the following variables:

RGOV	Real general government consumption (£ billion, 1990 prices)
RXPR	Real exports of goods and services (£ billion, 1990 prices)
DTR	Direct tax rate
PRODY	Productivity per employed person (1990 = 1.0)

Source: ONS database

The mapping of the additional variables to the ONS database is:

ONS variable name	Transformation	Dataset variable name
DJCZQU	÷1000	RGOV
DJCVQU	÷1000	RXPR
CECOQU, CAOVQU, AIIAQU	$1 - (\text{CECOQU} \times \text{CAOVQU} \div \text{AIIAQU})$	DTR
DJCWQU, BCADQU	constant $\times$ (DJCWQU/BCADQU)	PRODY

The constant in PRODY is the ratio of the average values of DJCWQU and BCADQU in 1990 to give a 1990 = 1.0 base for this variable.

Data set 7 Computer-generated series

A computer-generated data set containing:

u	An N(0, 1) random variable
z	An AR(1) process with intercept 0.5 and slope 0.7
x	A random walk
w	A random walk with drift 0.05

Data set 8 Nelson–Plosser data set

This is the Nelson–Plosser (1982) data set of annual observations for the United States, 1860–1988, on the variables:

rgnp	Real GNP
gnp	Nominal GNP
prgnp	Per capita real GNP
ip	Industrial production
emp	Employment
unemp	Unemployment
prgnp	GNP deflator
cpi	Consumer price index
wg	Nominal wages
rwg	Real wages
m	Money
vel	Velocity
sp500	Nominal Standard and Poor's stock price index
bnd	Bond yields
Dcpi	First difference of cpi

Source: Nelson and Plosser (1982); Schotman and van Dijk (1991)

All series are in logs except bnd.

Data set 9 Computer-generated series for spurious regression and cointegration graph

This data set contains:

u1	N(0, 1) random variable
u2	N(0, 1) random variable
y1	Random walk using u1
x1	Random walk using u2
y3	$2 + 0.5 * x1 + u1$

Data set 10   Hendry–Ericcson data set

This is the Hendry and Ericcson (1991) data set, available also from:

ftp://hicks.nuff.ox.ac.uk/pub/dynects/

The reader should examine the file *readme.ukm* at this site for more details. The variables are:

M	Nominal money supply, M1 (£ million, seasonally adjusted)
P	Deflator of total final expenditure (seasonally adjusted, 1985 = 1.00)
Y	Real total final expenditure (£ million, 1985 prices, seasonally adjusted)
R	Differential between 3-month local authority bill rate and learning adjusted retail sight deposit interest rate

Source: Hendry and Ericcson (1991)

Data set 11   IS/LM model data, after Johansen and Juselius (1994), UK, 1962(Q4)–1995(Q4)

The variables are:

B20	Par yield (per annum) on 20-year British Government stocks
TBILL	Yield on 3-month Treasury bills
LNRGDP	Log of real GDP at factor cost (1990 prices, seasonally adjusted)
LNPGDP	Log of implied deflator of GDP at factor cost (1990 = 1.00, seasonally adjusted)
LNM4	Log of nominal money stock, M4 (seasonally adjusted)

Source: ONS database

The mapping between the ONS variables and the data set variables is:

ONS variable name	Transformation	Dataset variable name
AJLXQU		B20
AJNCQU		TBILL
DJBAQA, DJCMQA	ln(DJBAQA/DJCMQA)	LNRGDP
DJCMQA	ln(DJCMQA)	LNPGDP
AUYNQA	ln(AUYNQA)	LNM4

Data set 12   Grunfeld–Griliches data set, US, 1935–54

This is the Grunfeld–Griliches (1960) data set, available in Greene (1993: 445–6). The variables are:

I	Gross investment
F	Market value of firm at the end of the preceding year
C	Value of stock of plant and equipment at end of preceding year

and the corporations involved are General Motors, Chrysler, General Electric, Westinghouse and US Steel.

Data set 13   Klein model 1 data set, US, 1920–41

This is also available in Greene (1993: 629) and Theil (1971: 456). The variables are:

CONSUM	Consumers' expenditure
PROFIT	Profit
WAGEPR	Private wage bill
INVEST	Net investment
PRODUCT	Total private product
WAGEGOV	Government wage bill
CAPITAL(-1)	End period capital stock, lagged
GOVEXP	Government expenditure
TAXES	Taxes

Appendix C: Statistical tables

These tables were produced by members of the Department of Econometrics and the Research Support Unit, University of Manchester. Table C4 is extracted from tables prepared by R. W. Farebrother.

Table C1 Critical values for the t distribution. The table shows critical values $t_{df}^{\alpha/2}$ such that $\Pr(t > t_{df}^{\alpha/2}) = \alpha/2$ and $\Pr(-t_{df}^{\alpha/2} \le t \le t_{df}^{\alpha/2}) = 1 - \alpha$

df	$t_{df}^{0.05}$	$t_{df}^{0.025}$	$t_{df}^{0.01}$	$t_{df}^{0.005}$
3	2.35	3.18	4.54	5.84
5	2.01	2.57	3.36	4.03
6	1.94	2.45	3.14	3.71
7	1.89	2.36	3.00	3.50
8	1.86	2.31	2.90	3.35
9	1.83	2.26	2.82	3.25
10	1.81	2.23	2.76	3.16
12	1.78	2.18	2.68	3.05
14	1.76	2.14	2.62	2.98
16	1.75	2.12	2.58	2.92
18	1.73	2.10	2.55	2.88
20	1.72	2.09	2.53	2.84
22	1.72	2.07	2.51	2.82
24	1.71	2.06	2.49	2.80
26	1.71	2.06	2.48	2.78
28	1.70	2.05	2.47	2.76
30	1.70	2.04	2.46	2.75
40	1.68	2.02	2.42	2.70
60	1.67	2.00	2.39	2.66
∞	1.64	1.96	2.33	2.58

Table C2 Critical values for the χ^2 distribution. The table shows critical values $\chi_{df}^{2(\alpha)}$ such that $\Pr[\chi^2 > \chi_{df}^{2(\alpha)}] = \alpha$

df	$\chi_{df}^{2(0.10)}$	$\chi_{df}^{2(0.05)}$	$\chi_{df}^{2(0.01)}$
1	2.71	3.84	6.64
2	4.61	5.99	9.21
3	6.25	7.81	11.34
4	7.78	9.49	13.28
5	9.24	11.07	15.09
6	10.64	12.59	16.81
7	12.02	14.07	18.47
8	13.36	15.51	20.09
9	14.68	16.92	21.67
10	15.99	18.31	23.21
11	17.27	19.68	24.72
12	18.55	21.03	26.22
13	19.81	22.36	27.69
14	21.06	23.68	29.14
15	22.31	25.00	30.58
16	23.54	26.30	32.00
17	24.77	27.59	33.41
18	25.99	28.87	34.81
19	27.20	.30.14	36.19
20	28.41	31.41	37.57
22	30.81	33.92	40.29
24	33.20	36.42	42.98
26	35.56	38.89	45.64
28	37.92	41.34	48.28
30	40.26	43.77	50.89
40	51.80	55.76	63.69
50	63.17	67.50	76.15
60	74.40	79.08	88.38
80	96.58	101.98	112.33
100	118.50	124.34	135.81

Table C3 5% critical values for the *F* distribution. The table gives critical values $F_{df_1,df_2}^{0.05}$ such that $Pr(F > F_{df_1,df_2}^{0.05}) = 0.05$

df_1	1	2	3	4	6	8	10	24
df_2				$F_{df_1,df_2}^{0.05}$				
3	10.13	9.55	9.28	9.12	8.94	8.84	8.79	8.64
5	6.61	5.79	5.41	5.19	4.95	4.82	4.73	4.53
6	5.99	5.14	4.76	4.53	4.28	4.15	4.06	3.84
7	5.59	4.74	4.35	4.12	3.87	3.73	3.64	3.41
8	5.32	4.46	4.07	3.84	3.58	3.44	3.35	3.11
9	5.12	4.26	3.86	3.63	3.37	3.23	3.14	2.90
10	4.96	4.10	3.71	3.48	3.22	3.07	2.98	2.74
12	4.75	3.88	3.49	3.26	3.00	2.85	2.75	2.51
14	4.60	3.74	3.34	3.11	2.85	2.70	2.60	2.35
16	4.49	3.63	3.24	3.01	2.74	2.59	2.49	2.23
18	4.41	3.55	3.16	2.93	2.66	2.51	2.41	2.15
20	4.35	3.49	3.10	2.87	2.60	2.45	2.35	2.08
22	4.30	3.44	3.05	2.82	2.55	2.40	2.30	2.03
24	4.26	3.40	3.01	2.78	2.51	2.35	2.25	1.98
26	4.22	3.37	2.97	2.74	2.47	2.32	2.22	1.95
28	4.20	3.34	2.95	2.71	2.44	2.29	2.19	1.91
30	4.17	3.32	2.92	2.69	2.42	2.27	2.16	1.89
40	4.08	3.23	2.84	2.61	2.34	2.18	2.07	1.79
60	4.00	3.15	2.76	2.52	2.25	2.10	1.99	1.70
100	3.94	3.09	2.70	2.46	2.19	2.03	1.92	1.63
∞	3.84	3.00	2.60	2.37	2.10	1.94	1.83	1.52

Table C4 Lower and upper bounds for critical values in the Durbin–Watson test (the table gives lower d_L and upper d_U bounds for critical values c, such that $\Pr(d < c) = 0.05$, under the null hypothesis of no serial correlation)

	k = 2		k = 3		k = 4		k = 6		k = 10	
n	d_L	d_U	d_L	d_U	d_L	d_U	d_L	d_U	d_L	d_U
15	1.08	1.36	0.95	1.54	0.81	1.75	0.56	2.22	0.17	3.22
16	1.11	1.37	0.98	1.54	0.86	1.73	0.61	2.16	0.22	3.09
17	1.13	1.38	1.01	1.54	0.90	1.71	0.66	2.10	0.27	2.97
18	1.16	1.39	1.05	1.53	0.93	1.70	0.71	2.06	0.32	2.87
19	1.18	1.40	1.07	1.54	0.97	1.68	0.75	2.02	0.37	2.78
20	1.20	1.41	1.10	1.54	1.00	1.68	0.79	1.99	0.42	2.70
22	1.24	1.43	1.15	1.54	1.05	1.66	0.86	1.94	0.50	2.57
24	1.27	1.45	1.19	1.55	1.10	1.66	0.92	1.90	0.58	2.46
26	1.30	1.46	1.22	1.55	1.14	1.65	0.98	1.87	0.66	2.38
28	1.33	1.48	1.25	1.56	1.18	1.65	1.03	1.85	0.72	2.31
30	1.35	1.49	1.28	1.57	1.21	1.65	1.07	1.83	0.78	2.25
35	1.40	1.52	1.34	1.58	1.28	1.65	1.16	1.80	0.91	2.14
40	1.44	1.54	1.39	1.60	1.34	1.66	1.23	1.79	1.01	2.07
50	1.50	1.58	1.46	1.63	1.42	1.67	1.33	1.77	1.16	1.99
75	1.58	1.65	1.57	1.68	1.54	1.71	1.45	1.77	1.37	1.90
100	1.65	1.69	1.63	1.71	1.61	1.74	1.57	1.78	1.48	1.87
200	1.76	1.78	1.75	1.79	1.74	1.80	1.72	1.82	1.67	1.86

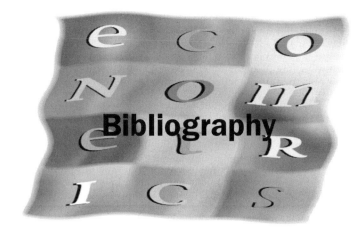

Bibliography

Banerjee, A., Dolado, J., Galbraith, J. W. and Hendry, D. F. (1993), *Cointegration, Error Correction and the Econometric Analysis of Non-Stationary Data*, Oxford: Oxford University Press.

Barro, R. J. and Sala-i-Martin, X. (1995), *Economic Growth*, New York: McGraw-Hill.

Bollerslev, T., Engle, R. F. and Nelson, D. B. (1994), 'ARCH models', in R. F. Engle and D. L. McFadden (eds) (1994), *Handbook of Econometrics*, vol. 4, Amsterdam: Elsevier.

Breusch, T. S. and Pagan, A. R. (1980), 'The Lagrange Multiplier test and its applications to model specification tests in econometrics', *Review of Economic Studies*, **47**, 239–53.

Chow, G. C. (1983), *Econometrics*, New York: McGraw-Hill.

Davidson, R. and MacKinnon, J. G. (1993), *Estimation and Inference in Econometrics*, Oxford: Oxford University Press.

Doornik, J. A. and Hendry, D. F. (1994), *PcGive 8: An interactive econometric modelling system*, London: International Thomson.

Engle, R. F. (ed.) (1995), *ARCH: Selected readings*, Oxford: Oxford University Press.

Engle, R. F., Hendry, D. F. and Richard, J.-F. (1983), 'Exogeneity', *Econometrica*, **51**, 277–304.

Fuller, W. A. (1976), *Introduction to Statistical Time Series*, New York: Wiley.

Gilbert, C. L. (1986), 'Professor Hendry's econometric methodology', *Oxford Bulletin of Economics and Statistics*, **48**, 283–307.

Godfrey, L. G. (1984), 'On the uses of misspecification checks and tests of non-nested hypotheses in empirical econometrics', *Economic Journal*, **94**, suppl., 69–81.

Godfrey, L. G. (1988), *Misspecification Tests in Econometrics*, Econometric Society Monographs No. 16, Cambridge: Cambridge University Press.

Goldberger, A. (1991), *A Course in Econometrics*, Cambridge, Mass.: Harvard University Press.

Gourieroux, C. and Monfort, A. (1995), *Statistics and Econometric Models*, Cambridge: Cambridge University Press.

Greene, W. H. (1993), *Econometric Analysis*, 2nd edn, New York: Macmillan.

Hamilton, J. D. (1994), *Time Series Analysis*, Princeton: Princeton University Press.

Hansen, B. E. (1995), 'Rethinking the univariate approach to unit root testing: using covariates to increase power', *Econometric Theory*, **11**, 1148–71.

Harris, R. I. D. (1995), *Using Cointegration Analysis in Econometric Modelling*, London: Prentice Hall.

417

Hartley, B. and Hawkes, T. O. (1970), *Rings, Modules and Linear Algebra*, London: Chapman & Hall.

Harvey, A. C. (1990), *The Econometric Analysis of Time Series*, 2nd edn, Oxford: Philip Allan.

Hatanaka, M. (1974), 'An efficient two-step estimator for the dynamic adjustment model with autoregressive errors', *Journal of Econometrics*, **2**, 199–220.

Hausman, J. A. (1978), 'Specification tests in econometrics', *Econometrica*, **46**, 1251–71.

Hendry, D. F. (1995), *Dynamic Econometrics*, Oxford: Oxford University Press.

Hendry, D. F. and Ericcson, N. R. (1991), 'Modelling the demand for narrow money in the United Kingdom and the United States', *European Economic Review*, **35**, 833–81.

Hendry, D. F., Leamer, E. E. and Poirier, D. J. (1990), 'The ET dialogue: a conversation on econometric methodology', *Econometric Theory*, **6**, 171–261.

Hendry, D. F. and Richard, J.-F. (1982), 'On the formulation of empirical models in dynamic econometrics', *Journal of Econometrics*, **20**, 3–33.

Hendry, D. F. and Richard, J.-F. (1983), 'The econometric analysis of economic time series', *International Statistical Review*, **51**, 111–63.

Johansen, S. (1991), 'Estimation and hypothesis testing of cointegration vectors in Gaussian vector autoregressive models', *Econometrica*, **59**, 1551–80.

Johansen, S. (1995), *Likelihood-Based Inference in Cointegrated Vector Autoregressive Models*, Oxford: Oxford University Press.

Johansen, S. and Juselius, K. (1994), 'Identification of the long-run and the short-run structure: an application to the ISLM model', *Journal of Econometrics*, **63**, 7–36.

Lafontaine, F. and White, K. J. (1986), 'Obtaining any Wald statistic you want', *Economics Letters*, **21**, 35–40.

Leamer, E. E. (1978), *Specification Searches*, New York: Wiley.

Leamer, E. E. (1983), 'Let's take the con out of econometrics', *American Economic Review*, **73**, 31–44.

McAleer, M. and Pesaran, M. H. (1986), 'Statistical inference in non-nested econometric models', *Applied Mathematics and Computation*, **20**, 271–311.

MacKinnon, J. G. (1991), 'Critical values for cointegration tests', in R. F. Engle and C. W. J. Granger (eds), *Long Run Economic Relationships: Readings in cointegration*, Oxford: Oxford University Press.

MacKinnon, J. G. (1994), 'Approximate asymptotic distribution functions for unit root and cointegration tests', *Journal of Business and Economic Statistics*, **12**, 167–76.

MacKinnon, J. G. (1996), 'Numerical distribution functions for unit root and cointegration tests', *Journal of Applied Econometrics*, **11**, 601–18.

Maddala, G. S. (1983), *Limited-Dependent and Qualitative Variables in Econometrics*, Cambridge: Cambridge University Press.

Nelson, C. R. and Plosser, C. I. (1982), 'Trends and random walks in macroeconomic time series: some evidence and implications', *Journal of Monetary Economics*, **10**, 139–62.

Osterwald-Lenum, M. (1992), 'A note with quantiles of the asymptotic distribution of the maximum likelihood cointegration rank test statistics: four cases', *Oxford Bulletin of Economics and Statistics*, **54**, 461–72.

Pagan, A. R. (1987), 'Three econometric methodologies: a critical appraisal', *Journal of Economic Surveys*, **1**, 3–24.

Phillips, P. C. B. (1986), 'Understanding spurious regressions in econometrics', *Journal of Econometrics*, **33**, 311–40.

Rao, C. R. (1973), *Linear Statistical Inference and its Applications*, 2nd edn, New York: Wiley.

Schotman, P. C. and van Dijk, H. K. (1991), 'On Bayesian routes to unit roots', *Econometric Theory*, **6**, 403–11.

Silvey, S. D. (1970), *Statistical Inference*, Harmondsworth: Penguin.

Sims, C. A. (1980), 'Macroeconomics and reality', *Econometrica*, **48**, 1–48.

Stewart, J. (1984), *Understanding Econometrics*, 2nd edn, London: Hutchinson.

Stock, J. H. (1994), 'Unit roots, structural breaks and trends', in R. F. Engle and D. L. McFadden (eds) (1994), *Handbook of Econometrics*, vol. 4, Amsterdam: Elsevier.

Stoll, R. R. (1952), *Linear Algebra and Matrix Theory*, New York: Dover.

Theil, H. (1971), *Principles of Econometrics*, New York: Wiley.

White, H. (1980), 'A heteroscedasticity consistent covariance matrix estimator and a direct test of heteroscedasticity', *Econometrica*, **48**, 817–38.

White, H. (1984), *Asymptotic Theory for Econometricians*, Orlando, Fla.: Academic Press.

Wu, D. M. (1973), 'Alternative tests of independence between stochastic regressors and disturbances', *Econometrica*, **41**, 733–50.

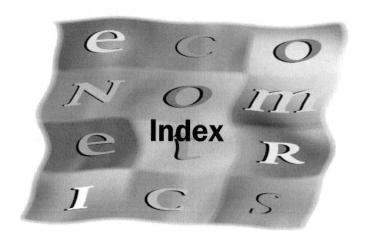

Index